Time and Tide

Thomas Fleming is a Fellow of the Society of American Historians. From 1970–81 he was chairman of the American Revolution Round Table. He has also served as president of the American Centre of P.E.N. He lives in New York with his wife, Alice, a distinguished writer of books for young readers.

He is the author of the bestseller *The Officers' Wives*, among many others.

Thomas Fleming

TIME AND TIDE

PAN BOOKS
in association with Macmillan London

First published in the USA 1987 by Simon and Schuster, Inc.
First published in Great Britain 1988 by Macmillan London Ltd.
This edition published 1989 by Pan Books Ltd,
Cavaye Place, London SW10 9PG
in association with Macmillan London

9 8 7 6 5 4 3 2 1

© Thomas Fleming 1987

ISBN 0 330 30197 7

Photoset by Parker Typesetting Service, Leicester

Printed and bound in Great Britain by
Richard Clay Ltd, Bungay, Suffolk

To Alice, for so many things

There is no steady unretracing progress in this life; we do not advance through fixed gradations, and at the last one pause: through infancy's unconscious spell, boyhood's thoughtless faith, adolescence's doubt (the common doom) then skepticism, then disbelief, resting at last in manhood's pondering repose of If. But once gone through, we trace the round again: and are infants, boys and man and Ifs eternally.

Herman Melville

Yet Melville was never without hope. . . . There remained the 'saving remnant,' a 'band of brothers' whose 'lavish hearts' might enable them to see the truth and set the example that would restore the promise of an America in which fraternity would open the gates to man's pilgrim quest.

Wilson Carey McWilliams

Sea Change

The historian stared into the July sun glinting on the whitecapped Pacific. He saw forgotten islands sweltering in this merciless glare, burning planes plummeting out of the empty sky, a continent at the bottom of the world where smiling women taught men to forget their loneliness. He saw murderous machines and ravenous fish moving silently through the blue-black depths. He saw ships in the dimness of a thousand fathoms, their hulls gashed by awful wounds, their guns jutting aimlessly.

Pain throbbed in the historian's eyes. Forty years ago they had been seared by that cruel sun. Lately there were whole days when he could see nothing but shadows. He drew the venetian blinds, obliterating sun, sky, ocean.

The pain corkscrewed down the historian's temple into his jaw. He was seized by a violent wish to escape this view of the Pacific. The wish conflicted with the facts of the historian's life. The gleaming white and black yawl he kept in a harbour a few miles away. His biographies of admirals George Dewey, Raymond Spruance, Ernest King on the shelf behind his desk, beside his prize-winning history of the Union Navy in the Civil War. But the historian had stopped trying to explain everything.

His books had won him plaudits from critics and readers. *Time* magazine had dubbed him the greatest living naval historian, a backhanded compliment that implied the deceased Samuel Eliot Morison was better. But they conceded (grudgingly, of course – the historian had not gone to Yale or Harvard) that no one could match his grasp of the inner pathos of high command, his depiction of the intimate side of his heroes' lives.

Still lunchless in the middle of the afternoon – he often skipped meals when he was in what his wife called his anchorite mood – the historian put on dark sunglasses and descended the spidery wooden steps that led down the face of the cliff to the narrow beach. He walked and walked, while huge combers rumbled towards him. When the cold water began swirling around his feet, the historian knew he should turn back. The moon would be full tonight and the high tide would wash out the beach. He would have to swim to his ladder.

The hell with it. The historian kept on walking.

Should he, could he, finally write the whole story? It was all up there in the filing cabinets. Drawers full of notes, interviews, biographical data. He knew the individual stories, with their illogical blend of laughter and tears. He had talked to parents, brothers, friends, above all to the women who had shared the voyage. He had interviewed admirals and captains, he had consumed hundreds of pages of after-action reports, diaries, testimony at courts of inquiry. Still he had been unable to write a word.

The combers rumbled towards him, ghostly now in the descending darkness. Suddenly the surging walls of water were no longer white. They had turned bloodred. They rose up with the grinning gums of memory to swallow him. The historian trembled The pain throbbed behind his eyes. It was impossible. Yet it had to be done. Tears poured down his face. It had to be done, but how?

A hand touched his hunched shoulder. He looked up at his anxious wife, her black hair streaming in the windblown spray.

'The tide –'

'I know –'

She wrapped her long arms around him. 'I saw it coming yesterday.'

As usual, she knew what he was thinking. She always knew. She had helped him heal his memories, defeat his dread of the depths. They had swum down into the sunless shadows together, fishy fins on their feet, oxygen on their backs, and listened to the whispering voices of the dead.

'I think it's time you wrote it,' she said.

The historian looked into her sombre green eyes, her mournful mouth. After forty years he could read her

thoughts too. She also feared the ghosts, the memories.
  They would face them together.
  'Yes,' the historian said. 'It's time.'

BOOK ONE

Voyage

Out of the night into the dawn the big grey ship steams boldly, unaware that she is a ghost. Behind her trails a mile of phosphorescence churned out of the living sea. More of this spectral whiteness flecks the foam around the proud bow, the water leaping from her strakes.

She is not a ghost! She is real. Oil blazes beneath her boilers, superheated steam surges in her turbines. Living men walk her decks. She is heading towards green fields, soaring mountains, shining cities. Towards women's welcoming arms, children's laughter, a California of mythic contentment.

Out of the night of memory, which will endure as long as a single man or woman survives the voyage, the ship sails into the present. Not yet history, even though decades of darkness have rolled over her, because no one has rescued her from the blankness of the past. History does not live in memory, it lives in words.

As the USS *Jefferson City* churns towards us, the first word leaps in the historian's mind: *cruiser*.

The word, the name, combines two things that have always fascinated Americans – speed and power. A salvo from the nine eight-inch guns in her main battery can hurl a ton of murderous metal over the horizon. Her turbines can send the strength of 95,000 horses pounding into her four propellers. She is 608 feet, four inches long – the equivalent of two football fields – and only sixty-one feet, seven inches wide. She has none of the squat ugliness of those floating gun platforms called battleships. Never did you see her perform a battleship's pachydermatous wallow. Her bow has a racing curve, a harp's bend, that bespeaks grace as well as power, beauty as well as brutality. She was born to battle a rising sea as fiercely as an enemy fleet.

At first glance the USS *Jefferson City* was alone on the vast western ocean. But no ship is ever really alone, even on a sea as immense as the Pacific. At the very least, the sailor believes – or at least hopes – his ship is a dot in the eye of God. That is a comforting thought, even if the nature of that God is in doubt in every honest sailor's heart and mind. If the Divinity is mirrored by the ocean over which He presides, then He is both cruel and kind, both capricious and exact. He takes infinite pains to fashion the anemone's petals – and the shark's jaw. For reasons a sailor cannot understand but has learned to accept, God sometimes turns His face away from a ship. Above others He extends a sheltering hand.

For a US Navy ship at sea in 1942, there were other gods besides the Supreme Being who presided over the stupendous dome of the world. They spoke an equally incomprehensible language, their scrambled words hurtling across night and day from Hawaii, where a god named CINCPAC reigned, and from Washington, DC, where the most awesome god of all, COMINCH, held in his stupendous mind all the warships flying the American flag on all the oceans.

NERK NERK NERK

The powergods spoke in Radio Central on the second deck. Red bulbs glowed on the big transmitters. Radiomen, with the lightning flash of divinity on their sleeves, leaned back in their chairs while the codes swirled through the headphones on their weary ears. The morning watch, from 0400 to 0800 hours (4 a.m. to 8 a.m. landlubbers' time), was the worst of their many ordeals. Slurping gallons of stale coffee, they tuned their frequencies and listened to the bizarre alphabetical tangle designed to baffle other listeners in Berlin and Tokyo.

From the cleaving bow of the *Jefferson City* to the drumming stern other sailors struggled to keep their eyes open as night dwindled into day. These surface lookouts ceaselessly scanned specific sections of the sea out to the horizon, 2.8 miles away. Other lookouts in the superstructure scrutinized the placid surface with binoculars, five degrees of a 360-degree circle at a time, out to another horizon, 12.3 miles away. For the men of the *Jefferson City*, the peaceful sea was rife with menace. In the depths swam yellow men in submarines hoping to fire a torpedo into the cruiser's guts. It was the lookouts' job to spot the white wake of this engine of death before it struck home.

On the bridge, a broad platform encased in steel and glass overlooking the two forward turrets, a lesser god, the officer of the deck, presided over the ship. The OOD was surrounded by men sworn to obey him and by scientific instruments designed to perfect his commands. A quartermaster supplied him with charts that informed him of the currents, the prevailing winds, the contour of the ocean bottom, the depth of the sea and the hazards of the coast the ship was approaching. A boatswain's mate stood ready to relay his commands over the public address system, first seizing everyone's attention with a shrill blast on his ancient pipe, which had been piercing the skulls of sailors since the Crusades. A helmsman kept the ship on course, constantly checking the gyrocompass, a guide whose needle, thanks to an inner wheel whirring at eight thousand revolutions a minute, pointed to true north.

To the left of the helmsman stood the engine telegrapher, ready to signal with a shove of the handle on his annunciator any change in speed ordered by the OOD. An identical machine stood on the deckplates far below them in the forward engine room. Facing it was a burly throttleman who instantly obeyed its commands. A telephone talker gave the OOD verbal communication with the engine room and the lookouts. A messenger, a seaman second class in the uniform of the day, stood a few feet behind him, ready to rush to any section of the ship not reachable by telephone. At arm's length was a panel of switches for operating lights and alarms.

Everything that the great gods of COMINCH and CINC-PAC could devise to ward off disaster at sea was at the service of the OOD. But these gods, awesome as they were, had only haphazard control over the courage and intelligence of the men who wore the insignia of rank and possessed the power of command, which was the power of life and death, over the crew of the *Jefferson City*. That was why a sailor trusted in God or destiny or luck, depending on whether the man was a believer, a fatalist or a gambler.

NERK NERK NERK

Every message that chattered through Radio Central was repeated twice. The powergods obviously had less than total confidence in the alertness of their listeners. Only when a message was preceded by the call letters of the *Jefferson City* did it have to be transcribed.

Suddenly the warning letters were sputtering in the earphones, *dit-dit-dah-dah*, coming over NPG from San Francisco on 386 kc, a frequency that meant *important* even before the message was decoded. Paper was hastily rolled into a typewriter and the scrambled words were copied by a radioman first class at amazing speed. The gobbledygook was rushed to a nearby compartment with TOP SECRET AUTHORIZED PERSONNEL ONLY on the door. There, an officer translated it and another officer rushed it to the OOD, who read it and immediately ordered his messenger to deliver it to the greatest god aboard the USS *Jefferson City*, the captain.

At 0510, the OOD sent his messenger to awaken the boatswain's mates and other petty officers of the divisions into which the 1,300 men aboard the USS *Jefferson City* were separated. Precisely at 0530, as the first red streaks of sunrise began to brighten the eastern horizon, the boatswain's mate of the watch stepped to the PA system and blew All Hands. He took three long deep breaths and held each for ten seconds at the top of the shrill, then clinched the pipe to produce a soft falloff. He repeated the call a second time and translated it into words: 'All hands turn to. Execute morning orders.'

Struggling up from sleep, from the private world of dreams and hope and wish, the crew of the *Jefferson City* assumed the selves assigned to them by the gods who presided over their destinies. As far as they could see, none of these beings was particularly interested in their happiness. Efficiency, duty, obedience, cleanliness, safety, these were the watch-words of all of them, from Cominch to the division officers to the petty officers who made grimly certain that their clothes were clean, their sleeping compartments and work stations were scrubbed daily.

Not all of them viewed their fates as cynically as the deck

apes, the men who manned the great guns and were responsible for holystoning the teakwood main deck of the *Jefferson City* until the captain could, if he chose, use it as a mirror in which to shave his aristocratic jaw. In other divisions, where expertise was more important than muscle, many refused to let this steel world, this regime of commands and routines repeated endlessly until hands performed no matter what the mind was thinking, extinguish their individual selves. There was pride as well as resentment on the lower decks of the *Jefferson City*.

On the second deck lived some sixty-five lesser gods in a place called Officers' Country. They gathered in the wardroom to dine three times a day on good china. Their food was served by smiling black steward's mates, who also made their beds and shined their shoes and pressed their uniforms. Their privileges were justified by that awesome word command. Each of these gods was responsible for seeing that the 1,300 sailors of the crew carried out the various tasks assigned to them in the Plan of the Day, promulgated each morning by the ship's executive officer.

Yet all of them, officers and petty officers and seamen and firemen first and second class, shared a common bond, summed up in another word: shipmate. They were married to this floating steel creature and to each other. The ship was their home, with everything aboard her that was needed to survive the sea and the enemy who sought to destroy them from the sky above, from the surface beyond the horizon and from the depths beneath them. Her kitchens fed them, her desalting boilers extracted fresh water for them to drink, to wash, her sick bay healed them when they fell ill. Her chaplain besought God's blessing on them.

At the risk of his reputation, the historian will talk of women sharing, surviving, the voyage of the USS *Jefferson City*. It is simply the truth. Although only a handful of them ever actually walked her decks, they were there in the minds and hearts of officers and crew, whispering words only women can speak, promising a future that made life in the steel shell of the ship worth the boredom, the drudgery, the risk.

There was another dimension in which the *Jefferson City* sailed. A dimension in which risk blended into courage and courage ventured into the uncharted darkness of death. The men of the *Jefferson City* shared this bond too. Their ship's fate was their fate.

This is the story that the historian wants to tell you about his ship. This struggle to find the meaning of certain words in the heart and mind and to keep alive in these private places a second self that still believed in that most perplexing of all English words, happiness. A private struggle that counterpointed the public struggle, the steel necessities of survival in a world at war.

NERK NERK NERK

The powergods continued to squawk and splutter in Radio Central. In the crew's mess and in the wardroom, the information in the top-secret telegram was travelling from mouth to mouth.

'They're yankin' him. We're gettin' a new skipper.'

'Praise the Lord.'

'Let's hope we get one with some guts.'

'Whatya want to be, a hero?'

'Now for the bad news. We're not going to Long Beach. We're heading for Portland.'

'What the hell can you do on liberty in Portland? There isn't even an officers' club.'

'Chop trees.'

'Chop them hell. I'll pull them up by their roots.'

'Maybe they plan to smuggle our cowardly leader off the ship.'

In a spacious cabin below the bridge, the captain stared at the crumpled message on his bunk. Silently, bitterly, a broken god began to weep.

Able Seamen

The USS *Jefferson City* loomed above them, her grey super-structure gleaming dully in the rainy Oregon night. She was so big they could not see the bow or the stern. Cannon jutted from shadowy turrets, smaller guns poked snouts from open mounts. But there was not a sign of life on the long wet deck. Only one small bulb glowed above the gangway. Behind the 150 seamen second class who mustered on the dock, the city of Portland seemed almost as dark and deserted. It was 7 September 1942, exactly nine months after Pearl Harbor, and blackout regulations were strictly enforced.

The fine rain drooled down eighteen-year-old Frank Flanagan's neck as a heavy-jowled chief boatswain's mate focused a flashlight on a clipboard and droned the list of names. Kelly, Lombardi, Brodsky, King, Semple. For five days they had ridden across the continent from the Sampson Naval Training Station in New York, gazing open-mouthed at their country. Like most Easterners, they had only the dimmest idea of the reality behind those verses in 'America the Beautiful' about verdant plains and shining mountains.

Beside Flanagan, diminutive Marty Roth stood on tiptoes to get a look at the USS *Jefferson City*. 'Is it a battleship?' he asked.

'A cruiser. They name cruisers after state capitals,' Flanagan said.

'What the hell state is *Jefferson City* the capital of?'

'Missouri.'

'Jesus, is there anything you don't know?'

In their first week in boot camp, Roth had christened Flanagan the Brain for his seemingly encyclopaedic knowledge of historical, geographical, religious and political facts. He could recite lists of the popes, the presidents, the kings of England. He also remembered a good chunk of the Declaration of Independence and the whole Gettysburg Address, huge passages of Longfellow's 'Hiawatha' and all of 'Casey at the Bat'. To Flanagan, none of these recitations was proof of

17

intelligence. He simply happened to have a very good memory, which twelve years of Catholic education had strengthened, like a muscle that was constantly exercised. He stopped Roth from demanding more recitations by threatening to inflict the entire Baltimore Catechism on him.

Roth had wanted to know why Flanagan was not in a V-12 programme at Columbia or Harvard, on his way to getting a commission. Flanagan told him he did not like officers. He wanted to fight the war in the ranks with the people. Roth was impressed. He told Flanagan he was an idealist like his cousin Harry Feder, who had joined the Abraham Lincoln Brigade to fight the fascists in Spain. 'The only trouble is, he got himself killed,' Roth said.

Flanagan did not try to explain to Roth the real reason why he wanted to fight in the ranks. He was a man on the run from Father Francis Callow, S.J., student counsellor of Fordham Preparatory School in the Bronx. With the enthusiastic support of Flanagan's mother, Father Callow had spent much of the previous two years trying to talk Flanagan into the priesthood. Hour after hour in the small office, almost knee to knee with Callow's hulking black-robed presence, Flanagan discussed the sins of the flesh and the difficulty of saving his soul. With impeccable logic Father Callow demonstrated that it was ridiculous to gamble eternal happiness for a few years of earthly pleasure.

The war had rescued Flanagan. He had told Callow that for the time being he felt his country's fight against fascist tyranny was a higher, even a nobler calling than a lifetime of service in the Society of Jesus. After the war – if he survived – he would decide what to do with the rest of his life. Flanagan sometimes wondered if he was the only American who was glad the Japanese had bombed Pearl Harbor.

Unfortunately, this escape left him with a large residue of guilt, which his mother and Father Callow did their best to augment. To prove he was not seeking aggrandizement in any form, Flanagan had spurned the V-12 programme and chosen the enlisted ranks. He liked the pathos of his humility, his self-sacrifice. He regarded his fellow enlisted men with mild condescension, never dreaming that they too had spiritual dramas inside their heads.

The chief boatswain's mate finished reciting the names and handed the list to a tall swarthy sailor in dungarees, with a white hat slung on the back of his head. 'Draft 587 present and accounted for,' the chief said in a bored voice. According to rumour, he had been drunk for the entire five days on the troop train.

The tall swarthy sailor had an oddly shaped head. His forehead was broad but his face tapered to an almost pointed chin. There was something crafty – and mean – about his thin-lipped mouth. 'OK,' he said, in a deep voice with a Midwest twang in it. 'You're goin' aboard your first ship. When you go up that gangplank, you stop at the top and salute the flag on the fantail. That's her ass end – that way.' He pointed to the stern of the ship, invisible in the rainy darkness. 'Then you salute the officer of the deck and follow me below.'

As they hoisted their seabags to their shoulders, a half dozen sailors reeled out of the drizzly darkness. Sticking their hands in their peacoat pockets, they leaned drunkenly against each other and smirked at the new recruits. 'Hey, gobs,' one of them called. 'They issue you a yellow stripe down your backs? That's what everybody on the Shitty City wears.'

'Yeah,' chortled another smirker. 'I hear they're gonna paint a big one down the forward stack.'

The swarthy sailor whirled. 'One more word out of you tin-can heroes and you'll be swimmin' for your fuckin' lives.'

'Ain't that what everybody who depends on the Shitty City winds up doin'?' asked a short bucktoothed sailor.

Flanagan did not see the swarthy sailor's hand move – the punch travelled so fast. Suddenly the bucktoothed sailor was lying on his back, clutching his mouth. His buddies snarled curses at his assailant. 'Get him out of here,' he growled. 'One blast on this pipe and I'll have enough men on this dock to put you all in the hospital.'

Flanagan noticed a small silver instrument with a slight bend in the reed dangling from a cord around the swarthy sailor's neck. It was his first glimpse of a boatswain's pipe. He had no idea it would soon be shrilling through his dreams.

The tin-can heroes looked over their shoulders at the cruiser, picked up their semi-conscious buddy and dragged him down the dock.

'Let's go, swabbies, let's go,' barked the swarthy boatswain's mate.

Flanagan followed him up the gangplank and performed the two salutes with, he hoped, military precision. An officer who did not look much older than the new seamen second class returned a very perfunctory salute and said to the boatswain's mate, 'What the hell happened down there?'

'Don't worry about it,' the boatswain's mate said.

Flanagan thought the officer's soft, thick-lipped mouth betrayed anger. But he did not answer this peculiar boatswain's mate, who seemed to treat him as an inferior. Maybe the officer was too busy returning all the salutes as the new recruits streamed aboard. Flanagan did not have time to think about it. 'Come on, sailor,' the boatswain's mate said, grabbing him by the shoulder and shoving him toward a hatch.

Flanagan had trouble descending the steep ladder with his seabag on his shoulder. He missed the last step and lurched into the steel bulkhead on the other side of the passageway. His head thudded against the unyielding metal. 'Jesus Christ,' the boatswain's mate said, hoisting him to his feet. 'How are you yo-yos gonna keep your feet when this old girl does one of her thirty-degree rolls?'

Flanagan got a strong odour of cheap cologne as the boatswain's mate pulled him erect. His head ringing, Flanagan followed him into the interior of the USS *Jefferson City*. There was nothing but steel and more steel and a bewildering array of pipes and wires snaking along the bulkheads and overheads. Fire hoses were coiled on polished metal wheels every ten feet, so it seemed to Flanagan, who saw nothing that looked even slightly inflammable.

They struggled through numerous narrow hatches with foot-high bases. Several of the newcomers tried to walk through them as if they were ordinary doors and fell on their faces, further enraging the boatswain's mate. In some compartments, these blunders provided entertainment for sailors lying in tiers of bunks, four deep, suspended by steel chains from the overheads.

'Hey, we got some boots,' someone yelled.

'How are you, girls? Have a nice trip?' someone else shouted.

Finally they reached a big compartment full of tables and benches with a stainless steel cafeteria setup along one side: the crew's mess. A half dozen older men were waiting there, some in dungarees, one in the blue uniform and visored hat of a chief petty officer. The swarthy boatswain's mate threw the list of names and the bulky manila envelopes containing their service records on one of the tables.

'OK, you birds,' he said, when the recruits had crowded into the compartment. 'Here's the most important guy you're gonna meet on this ship. Chief Boatswain's Mate Biff Nolan. He's the master at arms. That means he's in charge of makin' sure you behave. He used to be light heavyweight champ of the Navy. When he says shit, you squat and strain, get me?'

Flanagan's father was captain of the 113th Precinct in the Bronx. That added special interest to his study of the *Jefferson City*'s top cop. He saw an Irish face that he had encountered a hundred times at picnics and parties thrown by his uncle, Barney Flanagan, one of the chieftains in Boss Flynn's Bronx political machine. The brow was low, the nose pug, the mouth hard. Venality and stupidity mingled in the sneering smile. Nolan was the sort of lug his father would transfer out of his precinct in five minutes if he could get away with it. But that was not always possible. Lugs often had powerful friends.

Only one man seemed interested in the records. Built like a barrel, with ruddy cheeks and hair so blond it was almost white, he wore a boatswain's pipe around his neck. He began reading the manila-bound files, one by one.

'For Chrissake, Homewood,' snapped the swarthy boatswain's mate. 'We ain't got time to go through that paper. Let's just divide them up.'

'It don't matter what kind of trash you get in your division, Wilkinson. I need guys with brains,' Homewood said. He had a thick Southern accent.

'You fuckin' fire controllers,' Wilkinson said. 'All your fuckin' brains couldn't hit Australia if we was moored in Sydney Harbour.'

'With you and your asshole buddy on the bridge, Australia's the only thing we'll ever shoot at,' Homewood said.

'You watch your fuckin' mouth, Homewood. A man could be up to his ears in shit for talkin' that way,' Wilkinson roared.

'Go fuck yourself,' Homewood said, continuing to look through the service records. 'Jesus. Here's one I want. Flanagan. Look at that IQ ratin'.'

'Look at that mechanical aptitude,' Wilkinson said. 'The guy mustn't know a wrench from a screwdriver.'

'We'll teach him if he's got brains,' Homewood said. 'Flanagan, where the hell are you?'

Flanagan raised his hand. Homewood looked him over. 'You're in F Division.'

'God damn it, Homewood,' Wilkinson said. 'Look at the size of him. He's the kind of muscle I need in a handlin' room or on a workin' party.'

'You got plenty of muscle already,' Homewood said. 'We got fifteen empty racks to fill. I want a good man in each one of them to replace the good men we lost.'

Something about the hard, deliberate way Homewood said this reduced Wilkinson to surly silence. Homewood selected another fourteen recruits and led them out of the mess compartment. His Bronx buddy Roth gave Flanagan a glum wave as they departed. So did Harold Semple, a shy red-cheeked kid from Michigan who had been Flanagan's boot-camp bunkmate.

The new members of F Division followed Homewood up a ladder and found themselves in a compartment that the boatswain's mate told them was amidships. 'That's the centre of the ship.' He gave them a quick rundown of other nautical lingo. 'You never go upstairs. You go above. Or downstairs. You go below. This is not a boat. It's a ship. A she, not an it. You don't go to the back – you go aft. Or to the front – you go forward. It's all in your *Bluejacket's Manual*, but I'm presumin' that you all are like every other sailor who's ever been issued that goddamn thing. You put it in the bottom of your seabag and never looked at it. I want you to remember these things, 'cause you're an F Division sailor. You're supposed to be the best we got aboard. We aim them guns, see. We score the hits. The rest of the crew's black gang and deck apes – they keep the engines oiled and the guns loaded. But we make this old lady a warship.'

He paused and paced up and down the compartment. 'Get one thing straight. You never talk down your ship to out-siders. You don't let anyone else talk her down either. That includes everyone from flyboys to Marines. When we hit Long Beach the day after tomorrow and you get liberty, you may hear some shitty things said about the old J.C. Don't take 'em lyin' down.'

'What if they're true?' asked a voice that floated from the shadows in the far corner of the compartment.

'Shut your mouth,' Homewood roared.

'Hey, Boats,' said the voice, 'why don't you stop shovelin' it against the tide and admit the truth? We fucked up. We fucked up royally. They probably got twelve admirals and thirty-six captains in Washington right now tryin' to explain it away.'

A sailor emerged from the row of bunks. He was only about five feet eight, but he walked with a rolling swagger that matched the cocky smile on his handsome face. Except for the way he wore his white hat parked on the back of his head, instead of the regulation two inches above the eye-brows, he might have stepped off a recruiting poster. His black shoes gleamed. His white blouse and pants were so tight they seemed glued to his burly body. On his sleeve was sewn a small horizontal pipe on a tripod with a single V-shaped stripe beneath it. He was a fire controlman third class. Lower on his sleeve were four slanted white stripes called hash marks, which meant he had been in the Navy twelve years.

'Peterson's the name, guys,' he said. 'Anything you want,

gedunk at bedtime, a little action with the bones or a hot deck, the best nooky on the beach, speak to Poppa Jack. But remember, his services don't come cheap.'

'You son of a bitch, how'd you get liberty here?' Homewood said.

'I got a sick sister in Portland, Boats,' Peterson said. 'She called the chaplain, who called our new division officer, who broke down and cried at the thought of me goin' back to war without seein' her.'

'Jesus Christ,' Homewood fumed. 'Can't you shut that trap of yours long enough to let me give these kids some esprit de corpse?'

'The corpses are down in main plot, Boats,' Peterson said. 'Maybe they ought to hear about them before you hand out the assignments.'

'They'll find out about them soon enough,' Homewood said. 'The thing I want them to understand is – We wanted to fight. We're still a fightin' ship . . .'

The boatswain's mate's face was flushed, his broad brow was furrowed. He was struggling with an emotion he did not want to admit. An emotion that was almost incomprehensible to this brawny sailor whose huge hands and massive arms looked as if they were capable of bending steel.

Peterson's abrasive style softened surprisingly. 'I know, Boats. We'll be one again – if they give us a chance.'

Flanagan and his fellow recruits could only exchange bewildered stares. Yellow stripes down backbones and smokestacks, corpses in main plot, whatever that was. What had happened aboard the USS *Jefferson City*?

Black Gang

'What do you do on the ship?' Marty Roth asked as he followed the man who had chosen him and ten others for something called B Division down an endless series of ladders into the bowels of the *Jefferson City*.

The man had a flat sullen face and pale blond hair slicked down on his head. Without looking back, he replied, 'The same thing you're gonna be doin'. Sweatin' your fuckin' balls off.'

Down one more ladder they struggled with their seabags on their shoulders into a compartment half full of men lying in racks. It had a different odour from the rest of the ship, which smelled of metal and electricity. A lot of talcum powder was used in this compartment.

Some of the faces on the racks looked as old as his father's. But Roth's attention quickly focused on a stumpy man with a dead cigar in the corner of his mouth, standing in the centre of the compartment. He wore the khaki uniform of an officer, without a tie or coat.

'OK, swabbies,' he said. 'My name's Oz Bradley. I'm the engineering officer on this tub. That means I'm your boss. It also means you aren't swabbies any more. You're firemen. You're in the engineers, the black gang. For your information, that's the most important part of this ship. Those assholes up on deck can't get this thing away from the dock without us. They hate to admit that. They'll try to prove their fucking superiority by shitting all over you. Anytime they try it, let me know. They won't try it again.

'One more thing. You'll hear some lousy stories about this ship. Pay no attention to them. We did our jobs. It was those heroes on the bridge who screwed up.'

Bradley mounted the ladder to the upper decks and vanished. The flat-faced man resumed charge of their destinies. He read off their names and assigned them lockers and racks. 'Roth,' he said, 'take the top rack back there in the corner.'

In the corner, Roth found two Slavic faces confronting him. They shared narrow creased foreheads and small pointed noses. One was beefy, the other bony. 'Roth,' the bony one said, 'are you a fuckin' Hebe?'

'Yeah, I'm Jewish,' Roth said, trying to push past them.

'We don't want no fuckin' Hebes back here,' the beefy one said, blocking his path. 'It stinks bad enough back here already.'

In one of the middle racks, a man was lying with his face to the bulkhead, apparently asleep. He rolled over and simultaneously uncoiled on to the deck. Between Roth and his persecutors stood a Negro who was at least six feet four. He looked as if he could play fullback for the Chicago Bears on five minutes' notice. 'Did that last remark by any chance refer to me?' he asked.

'What if it did?' said the beefy bully, a sneer flitting across his face.

The Negro gathered about half of the bully's blue shirt in his fist. 'Why, I just might be required to rearrange your face, Throttleman. I'd hate to do that to a shipmate.'

'Hey, Amos, we was only kiddin',' the bony one said.

'Neither of you is very good at kiddin',' the Negro said. 'Maybe it's because your fuckin' brains are pickled in that torpedo juice you're always cookin' in the engine room.'

He slapped the top rack. 'Spread yourself up here, Jewboy. Don't pay no attention to these two asshole machinists. You're gonna be in the fire room with me, where the stuff really happens. I'm lookin' for a striker with brains.'

All Roth could do was gape. 'Hey, don't look so surprised,' the Negro said. 'I'm Amos Cartwright. They keep me around to remind everybody they're in the black gang.'

Officers and Gentlemen

'I want to see it,' Rita McKay said, 'I want to see him squirm.'

Captain Arthur McKay gazed at his wife with undisguised dismay. There were times when she became almost a stranger to him. The sense of alienation was not helped by the contrast between her lovely face, with its marvellous skin and perfect bone structure, and her bulky body.

'It just isn't done,' Captain McKay said as the American Airlines DC-3 began descending to land at Los Angeles. 'Women aren't invited to a transfer of command. It's not a goddamn party.'

Muscles bunched above his solid jaw. His grey eyes darkened. He shoved his hand through his thinning sandy hair.

Rita ignored the storm signals. 'It'll be the party of the century as far as I'm concerned,' she said.

'It's out of the question! Even if it could be done, I wouldn't go along with it. I don't like this whole deal.'

Rita checked her lipstick in her compact mirror. She ran a comb through her thick blonde hair, still in the same no-nonsense bob she had worn at their wedding. 'You've been spooked by every assignment I've got you. Each one was going to finish you.'

'That isn't what I'm talking about. I mean relieving Win this way.'

'He'd relieve you in ten seconds if the situation was reversed.'

'I don't believe that.'

'Arthur McKay, may I remind you, not for the first time, that you are a sentimental slob?'

The slipstream whined, the engines strained. The DC-3 was in its final glide, bucking a strong headwind. Los Angeles was a sea of gloom below them in the twilight. Only an occasional light defied the blackout. Beyond the land, the Pacific was a darker, gloomier sea.

'Maybe it will be more fun to see Winfield the Great squirm in private,' Rita said. 'He's such an actor, he probably won't twitch a muscle in that handsome face aboard ship.'

Thump thump thump, they were on the ground and the stewardess was telling them what they already knew, they were in Los Angeles. Palm trees and oil derricks wavered in the fading light. On the tarmac the temperature was at least a hundred. Rita hurried to keep up with her long-legged husband. 'How many times do I have to tell you not to walk so damn fast?' she gasped.

'Yeah, yeah,' McKay said, slowing down, but not enough to satisfy her. 'If you'd lose some weight, a fast walk wouldn't bother you.'

'I'm going on a diet the minute you sail,' she said.

She would too, Arthur McKay thought glumly. She would

lose forty or fifty pounds, and when he came back – if he came back – he would find Rita the lean tigress waiting for him. Being married to Rita was like living with two or three different women. For the first year of shore duty, she was the tigress. She could not get enough of him in the bedroom. Sometimes, lately, he did not have enough to give. The second year, she got fat and their sex life dwindled to zero. The bickering and the drinking began – and the scheming for a new sea duty assignment.

In that department, Rita was a nonpareil. No other Navy wife could come close to her shrewdness. She was a genius at spotting assignments that put her husband in daily contact with higher ranks whose fondness for him – or Rita's father, Vice Admiral Robley Semmes – had accelerated his career. Arthur McKay had to admit that Rita had had a lot to do with the four gold stripes he wore on his sleeve. He had been the second man in the class of 1917 to become a captain. The first had been the man he was about to relieve from command of the USS *Jefferson City*, Captain Winfield Scott Schley Kemble.

They collected their luggage and found a taxi. The driver was an Okie, one of those people John Steinbeck wrote about so movingly in *The Grapes of Wrath*. He complained about how many niggers were coming to Los Angeles to get jobs in the shipyards at Long Beach or the aircraft plants out in the valley. Ignoring this civilian chatter, Arthur McKay tried to imagine how the ceremony would go tomorrow when he relieved the man who had been his roommate at Annapolis, his mentor, his closest friend for the past twenty-five years in the Navy.

'Remember the first time we visited your house?' he said.

'No,' Rita said.

Arthur McKay was not surprised. Rita had made a fool of herself that afternoon, throwing seductive glances and sexy innuendos at Win Kemble. 'You must remember it,' he said. 'You jumped into the pond with your best white dress on to get Win to notice you.'

'That is a goddamned lie,' Rita said. 'I slipped on some dried pine needles and fell in. I was horribly embarrassed by the whole thing. That dress was just glued to me.'

'So I noticed,' McKay said. 'I damn near proposed on the spot.'

A lot of people thought Arthur McKay was stupid, when he was simply quiet. Several generations of farm life on the vast silent plains of Kansas had deepened the reflective habits the McKays had brought from New Hampshire. They watched and thought and watched some more and thought some more. Then they spoke, often with devastating effect.

'It's too far back to think about,' Rita said as the taxi climbed into the hills above Los Angeles.

She was telling him that she did not want to think about it – or talk about it. But Arthur McKay was not always an obedient husband. He had turned down more than one assignment because it consisted mostly of ass-kissing the hot admiral of the moment. He had tried to turn down this assignment, even though he risked losing the favour of the hottest admiral of the century, Ernest J. King, Cominch himself, Commander in Chief, US Fleet, and Chief of Naval Operations, the most powerful naval officer in the history of the United States.

'Twenty-seven years?' McKay said. 'That's only a pimple on the ass of time, Rita.' Loosening his tie, he sprawled in the corner of the rear seat so he could stretch out his legs. 'When I think of how green I was in 1915. I still had corn sprouting out of my ears.'

Rita scowled. 'I wonder how Lucy is taking it,' she said. 'She probably doesn't have any idea what it really means.'

They had been youngsters, as they called sophomores at Annapolis. It was a heady year. They had got through plebe year, a nightmare of abuse and insults from upper classmen, designed to break individuality into fragments and reconstruct it according to Rocks and Shoals, the Navy code of discipline. Arthur McKay would have walked out at the end of the first month, except for Win Kemble. When you have a grandfather who was an admiral, you can take a long view of such idiocy.

Arthur McKay still marvelled at the good fortune that had given him, the quintessential Kansas hayseed, a roommate with the sophistication Win Kemble possessed from birth. Although his family's finances were modest (his father had died in a polo accident the year he was born), Win had grown up in a Philadelphia world of old money and blue blood. Relatives powerful in business and politics flowed through his house. He vacationed with them in Europe and Maine. Very early in his life, Win acquired the conviction that some people were born to command and others to obey – an idea Arthur McKay's Midwest populist instincts found hard to accept – even when Annapolis told him he was being endowed with the mystic authority of the naval officer.

Win had shared his knowledge of this world of inherited wealth and cool indifference to conventional morals with Arthur McKay. He mocked and to some extent overcame his country boy's suspicions and hostilities and, most important, eliminated his awe. It was delightful to discover that the Eastern powergods had as many warts and inconsistencies, yes, as much personal unhappiness, as ordinary folk. Those revelations, which Win shared with no one else, had become part of a bond of gratitude and affection that nothing in the fortunes of war or the vagaries of peace could ever break.

Winfield Scott Schley Kemble had a long view of a lot of things. After lights out he lay in the darkness and lectured Arthur McKay on the art and science of becoming Chief of Naval Operations. CNO. That was what he was shooting for, the Navy's top job, from the moment he walked into Bancroft Hall. He was not secretive about it. Before they graduated, the whole class mocked his ambition, as only classmates can. In the *Lucky Bag*, their Annapolis yearbook, he was accused of creating a 'noxious gas, C/2N/20/2', which stupefied everyone from professor to plebes into a state of 'hysterical admiration'.

Only his roommate knew the real reason for the hauteur Win Kemble flaunted in public. Winfield Scott Schley Kemble had come to Annapolis to avenge the insults and obloquy heaped on his grandfather, Commodore Winfield Scott Schley, hero of the great naval clash of the Spanish-American War, the battle of Santiago.

Off the Cuban coast on 3 July 1898, the squadron under

Commodore Schley's command sank or captured the entire Spanish Fleet, ending the war in a half hour. But Schley's commander, Admiral William T. Sampson, who had been absent when the battle was fought, refused even to mention Schley's name in his victory report. For the next decade a virtual civil war raged inside the Navy between Schley and Sampson factions. By and large, Schley got the worst of it. He was accused of sailing his flagship, the cruiser *Brooklyn*, in the wrong direction until he saw it was safe to return to the fray. Win Kemble had come to Annapolis to expunge this lie from the Navy's annals by performing deeds at sea that would win him a place beside Farragut and Dewey in the history books.

It was a large burden to lay on a young man's shoulders. But Win seemed to bear it gladly, even with a swagger. From the day he walked through the main gate, the slim, crisp Philadelphian with the icewater-blue eyes seemed older, wiser than the rest of them. There was not a trace of adolescent rawness in his aristocratic features. Win's clearly defined ambition was an even greater advantage over his classmates, most of whom spent the first four years wondering why they ever went to Annapolis and the next ten trying to decide whether to risk a career in an organization as encrusted with meaningless traditions and regulations as the peacetime US Navy.

'God, I'm sticky,' Rita said. 'I can't wait to take a shower.'

Arthur McKay was back twenty-eight years in the shower room in Bancroft Hall at Annapolis. He was soaping up, and Win Kemble was beside him, his slim, sinewy, runner's body wet and gleaming. 'This,' Win said, holding his penis in his hand, 'is a very important weapon. You have to know exactly how and when to use it.'

Later, in their darkened room, he expanded on this thought. 'Anyone in this man's Navy who marries for love needs his brain analysed for airholes.'

This did not strike Arthur McKay as a particularly outrageous thought. Thanks to that McKay habit of watching and thinking and watching some more, he had already concluded that love was a rarity in marriage. His mother had married his father before she decided she hated farm life. His father worshipped it. This fundamental disagreement had cooled things to January temperatures by the time Willa McKay's fourth child and only son, Arthur, was born in 1896.

Win Kemble's opinions about love and marriage had led them to Patapsco. Maryland, in 1915 to call on Vice Admiral Robley Semmes and his two daughters. The introductions had been arranged by Win's mother. Few families had more salt water in their veins. A great-great-grandfather had captained a privateer in the Revolution. A great-grandfather had fought beside Hull aboard the *Constitution*, and a grandfather had sailed with Perry to Japan.

One of the crustiest characters who ever stalked a bridge, Admiral Semmes had been a Schley man in the great feud, probably because that guaranteed him a larger number of enemies. He was the author of reports such as 'The Crushing Superiority of British Naval Marksmanship', which had won him the admiration of President Theodore Roosevelt and the enmity of his superiors. After a drink or two, he was fond of pointing out that the Navy had fired eight thousand rounds in the battle of Santiago and scored only a hundred and twenty hits.

The admiral's wife never disagreed with him in public. 'Of course, dear' was her usual reply to everything he said. His younger daughter, Rita, disagreed with him about everything. His older daughter, Lucy – the sisters were only a year apart – took her mother's approach. Arthur McKay had seldom seen two more dissimilar sisters. Rita was all battle smoke and flame. Lucy spindrift and mist. Whenever Lucy came into the room, the admiral glowed. When Rita appeared, his temper instantly went to General Quarters.

What surprised McKay was Win Kemble's choice of Lucy Semmes as his ideal Navy wife. Why didn't an ambitious midshipman choose Rita, who was fascinated with the Navy and never stopped talking about it? Win had made his preference clear on their first call. 'Ram that dreadnought if necessary, McKay,' he had whispered as Rita bore down on them. 'Get her out of my way.'

On that first visit, they sat on the porch, which jutted into a pond, not unlike the prow of a ship. The admiral served them gin slings, a clear violation of Annapolis regulations, which forbade midshipmen to drink. When Rita pointed out this infraction the admiral's jaw jutted.

'It's a goddamned crime the way the civilians have stuck their noses into the Navy's business. We should still be serving grog to the fighting men in the fleet and drinking whisky in our wardrooms and letting midshipmen get drunk when they feel like it, as long as they don't disturb the peace or damage Navy property.'

The daily ration of liquor to enlisted men had been banned in 1862, ten years before the admiral entered Annapolis. But officers had drunk freely in the wardroom until the previous year, 1914, when Secretary of the Navy Josephus Daniels, a pious populist from North Carolina, stopped it, supposedly because it discriminated against enlisted men. The admiral had been commander of the US Atlantic Squadron at the time. He had sent a bristling statement to the newspapers, which more or less declared that if officers were not treated as gentlemen and enlisted men as something else, Congress might as well beach every ship in the fleet. A week later he retired.

At the moment, Arthur McKay was not remembering the point at issue. He meditated on the sentiment that the civilians should have nothing to do or say about the way the Navy was run. It was the first but by no means the last time McKay would hear it.

The opinion was alive and well in the person of Fleet Admiral Ernest J. King, on whose staff Arthur McKay had been serving when the battle of Savo Island was fought on 9 August 1942. As duty officer aboard King's flagship, USS *Dauntless*, moored at the Washington Navy Yard, McKay had brought the bad news of that ruinous night to the admiral early on the morning of 12 August.

Once, twice, three times King had read the appalling report from Rear Admiral Richmond Kelly Turner, his commander in the Solomon Islands. By the third time, Cominch was out of bed, glaring at Captain McKay. 'They must have decoded it wrong. This couldn't have happened!'

Facing those baleful eyes in that lined, weary face, McKay suddenly understood the story of the ruler who killed messengers who brought him bad news. 'I'll have them decode it again, Admiral,' he had said.

The decoding was perfectly accurate, of course. The message informed Admiral King that his brainchild, Operation Watchtower, whereby the US Navy and Marines were going to seize the initiative from the Japanese, was in peril. Off Savo Island, a volcanic dot near the tip of Guadalcanal, where the Marines were slugging it out with an enemy garrison, the Japanese had sunk one Australian and three American cruisers and a destroyer, killing 1,700 officers and men and wounding 709, without losing a ship or, as far as the Americans knew, even a man.

Pearl Harbor had been a disaster, not a defeat. The Navy, the Army, everyone up to and including the President had been caught by surprise, and the damage had been inflicted from the air. Savo Island had been fought ship to ship in a war zone where there was more than reasonable expectation of an enemy attack. There were no excuses available. It was simply the worst defeat in the history of the US Navy.

So far, not a word about this humiliation had been released to the American people. In fact, Arthur McKay strongly suspected that not even the President knew about it. When something went seriously wrong, Admiral King believed that someone had to be accountable. At Savo Island, everything had gone seriously wrong, and the admiral was determined to find the man at fault and make him pay the penalty. When Cominch in his wisdom decided to tell the President and the American people the dolorous truth, he wanted to be able to report that the perpetrator of the débâcle had been punished.

That was one of the reasons why Arthur McKay had been selected to relieve Win Kemble. He could find out from him, the only senior officer in the battle who had not lost his ship, what had happened. Rita had pointed this out with almost fiendish delight when Arthur King paid her one of his unannounced visits the day after the bad news arrived. King had served under Rita's father in the Asiatic Fleet and had been a frequent visitor to the Semmes' house in Shanghai. Mrs Semmes had been the first human being to persuade King to take advice on anything. She had got him to moderate his fondness for fast women and alcohol. Now, with the weight of a losing war on his shoulders, he found nostalgic consolation in telling his troubles to another Semmes woman.

In fact, King spent so much time at the McKay home, while Captain McKay was working double shifts like the rest of the admiral's staff, that McKay found himself wondering if Cominch was doing more than talking. His fondness for the ladies, young, old, and middle-aged, was notorious throughout the Navy.

But that worry was not what made Arthur McKay writhe now as the taxi roared along the crest of a hill overlooking blacked-out Los Angeles. McKay had heard – and ignored – a dozen rumours of Rita's unfaithfulness. What tormented him was the suspicion, growing larger every time he read the by now voluminous after-action reports of Savo Island, that Captain Winfield Scott Schley Kemble might become Ernest King's scapegoat. Relieving Win of command of the USS *Jefferson City* was difficult enough. But to play the secret investigator-cum-prosecutor was intolerable. Win was still his best friend.

The taxi swung off the boulevard on to a white gravel drive that formed a small oval in front of a stucco house in vaguely Spanish style. A Mexican maid greeted them with a broad smile. Arther McKay set their bags down in the centre hall and looked up to find his sister-in-law, Lucy Semmes Kemble, descending the stairs. She was wearing a black dinner dress, with a rope of pearls on her slim neck. Her oval face was aglow with a smile so rich in affection, McKay almost winced. 'Oh, Rita, Art, it's so good to see you,' she said in that sibilant breathy voice that was the opposite of Rita's harsh clang.

She kissed him and he inhaled a perfume Rita only wore when they went to formal dinners. Lucy's waist size had not changed since 1915. Her black hair still had the sheen of youth. 'She's pure woman, the purest I've ever seen, except for my mother,' Win Kemble had said. Was it this purity that enabled Lucy to ignore the passage of time?

They dutifully admired the house. It did not belong to Win Kemble. It was owned by their ex-classmate Greg 'Clinch' Meade, who had resigned his commission in the early 1920s and headed for Wall Street. Clinch had made millions by using his wife's money to buy into steel companies and shipyards which did business with the government, and then deploying his insider's knowledge of Washington – his father had been a congressman – to land lucrative contracts.

Although several congressional investigations had connected Clinch to operations that reeked of payoffs and padded costs, Win continued to nurture the friendship. In return, Clinch made available to Win his houses in various parts of the country, his private railroad car, his racing sloop. To Arthur McKay, Win made no secret of his loathing for Clinch and the kind of businessmen with whom he associated. Their methods, their ethics, had to be tolerated for the Navy's sake. 'Make friends with the mammon of iniquity' was one of Win's favourite maxims.

The maid served cocktails. Rita ordered her usual double martini. That could be the beginning of trouble, Arthur McKay thought. But Rita allowed the conversation to cruise in family channels. They discussed the McKay children. Lucy's delicate health had made childbearing out of the question, but she functioned as a kind of alternate mother for Semmes, known as Sammy, and his sister Barbara. Rita reported that Sammy had just become a four-striper – a battalion commander – at Annapolis. Barbara was in her freshman year at Wellesley and, for the twenty-fifth time, no longer speaking or writing to her mother. But she wrote regularly to Lucy, and Rita had to sit there, barely controlling her temper, as Lucy told her Barbara was thinking of joining the WACS.

Rita squawked as if Lucy had stuck a pin in her. 'What's wrong with the WAVES?'

'You know what she thinks of the Navy, Rita.'

'I don't call that thinking,' Rita said.

Lucy smiled tolerantly at her younger sister. No one, not

even Rita, could alter the depth of Lucy's affection for those she called family. 'How are *you*, Art? Has the uncrowned king been working you to death, in his usual cold-blooded way?'

'Not at all. I've got at least three hours' sleep a night. That's two more than he gets, I think.'

'Art – I've said it before. You're simply too good-natured to be in the Navy. You let people like Ernie King take advantage of you.'

Gratitude swelled in Arthur McKay's chest. Every time he saw her, Lucy Semmes Kemble awakened in his soul a yearning Rita could never satisfy. It was not lust. It was a hope, a wish for a love beyond words, beyond touch. A love that satisfied the soul.

'Jesus Christ,' Rita said. 'I've never heard such horseshit in my life. What's the latest on Mother Kemble?'

'She'll be here tomorrow.'

'Oh God,' Rita said.

Katherine Schley Kemble had been her lifelong antagonist. For twenty-five years, Rita had tried to match her influence and guile to advance the career of Arthur McKay on a par with the rise of Win Kemble. Not that Katherine Schley, a lady in the grande dame tradition of Douglas MacArthur's mother, ever betrayed the slightest consciousness of a rivalry. For her, Arthur McKay was Win's friend, which qualified him for her assistance, as an afterthought. During their final Annapolis year, she lived only six blocks from the Academy and had Win and his roommate to tea every Sunday. A regular feature of the visit would be a report on lunch or dinner with some admiral or a congressman on the Naval Affairs Committee who had promised to 'keep an eye' on Win when he graduated. Invariably she added, 'I put in a good word for you too, Arthur.'

'She's terribly upset by this battle off Guadalcanal,' Lucy said. 'What do you make of it, Art?'

'Not much,' he said. 'It's too early to get a clear picture of what happened. I'm hoping Win will fill us in.'

'Yes,' Rita said, with a sarcasm only Arthur McKay heard.

'We can't wait to hear from him. Has the *Jefferson City* made port?'

'She's due the day after tomorrow,' Lucy said. 'She's stopping in Portland to pick up a draft of new recruits.'

Lucy sipped her drink. 'There can't be anything to worry about, as far I can see. Win brought his ship back in one piece. That's more than anyone else did.'

'Yes,' Arthur McKay said.

'The fact that Admiral King chose you to relieve him – that proves there's nothing negative in the reassignment.'

Arthur McKay was wordless. Gazing into Lucy Semmes Kemble's lovely face, he found himself incapable of telling her another lie. He had told her so many over the years. She was woman as God or nature intended her to be in another time. Woman unstained by the modern world's ugliness.

'There isn't – is there, Art?'

'No, of course not,' he said. 'As a matter of fact, the admiral sent you his regards.'

Lucy's eyes darkened. 'I wish I could return them with sincerity. But he seems to me the absolutely worst choice Roosevelt could have made.'

'Good God. You sound like Drew Pearson!' Rita cried.

The two sisters were nothing if not consistent in their differences. Lucy always admired admirals who were gentlemen and scholars, such as genial dignified Harold R. 'Molly' Stark, the Navy's top commander when the Japs struck Pearl Harbor. Rita preferred the SOB's like Ernie King, who clawed their way to the top with minimum attention to the niceties.

Rita launched a diatribe against columinist Drew Pearson, who had attacked King for living on a flagship which was really the former Dodge family yacht, *Delphine*. McKay thought Pearson had a point, but he nodded and pretended to agree with Rita. Anything was better than discussing the battle of Savo Island.

They got through dinner on reminiscence. Those marvellous days from 1925 to 1928 on the China Station. Trips to Peking and the Great Wall and dinners with Dutch, British, French officers and their wives at the Jockey Club on

Shanghai's Bund. They avoided the less lovely memories of a China in revolutionary upheaval, of menacing mobs confronting Marines and gunboats, the denunciations of foreign devils. From China they segued to Win's tour as naval attaché in London, where he and Lucy discovered the moral superiority of the British Empire. Next came the McKays' less hospitable but more intellectually stimulating year among the Japanese in Tokyo. It was the second or third time around for all the stories, but Lucy seemed to enjoy them and Rita drank another martini and chimed in on the same frequency.

After dinner, Rita announced she was exhausted from the trip and retreated to their bedroom. Lucy poured Arthur McKay another cup of coffee and sat down on the couch with him in the living room. She began talking about the war, not as a series of campaigns to be fought but as an experience that was corrupting America's spirit. 'When I think of what the last war did to us,' she said, 'I can't help but wonder what this one will do. I work at the USO and the YMCA. The enlisted men all look so young, so innocent. You think of what they're being exposed to down on the Long Beach Pike.'

It was not the sort of thing anyone worried about on the third deck of the Navy Building in Washington, DC, where Cominch King reigned.

'We can't change human nature, Lucy.'

'How well I know that,' Lucy said, staring into the cup of black coffee in her hands.

Was she referring to her father? He had had a White Russian mistress in Shanghai and favourites in a half dozen other ports where he had two-blocked his admiral's flag. For a moment, Arthur McKay was certain Lucy was not talking about that irascible old sea wolf. She was talking about her husband. But it was impossible. If there was one thing Win Kemble had succeeded in doing, it was convincing his wife that he was the Navy's Lancelot, and she was the lily maid whom no Guinevere could ever tempt him to betray. He had kept her as innocent of what a sailor was really like as she had been on the day they walked on to Admiral Semmes's porch in Patapsco twenty-seven years ago.

If he was wrong, if Lucy was about to tell him how much she knew about Win Kemble's other women, Arthur McKay did not want to hear it. There was only so much anguish a man could handle at one time. Then he had to reach for the booze. Rita had made him do that more than once. Liquor allowed him to unleash his rage for a little while without feeling guilty, without hearing his father snarling sarcastically at his mother.

This was a different kind of anguish, this pain in Lucy's innocent eyes, this dismay staining her exquisite face. He was afraid of what liquor might do, what it might release in his soul, if he tried to face it. Arthur McKay set down his coffee cup and said something about seizing the opportunity of getting a decent night's sleep.

Lucy nodded sympathetically. 'I hope Win doesn't go on King's staff. I'd hate to see him worked to a frazzle for that awful man's greater glory.'

'I doubt if he will. But there are plenty of other staffs where I'm sure people will fight to get him.'

McKay kissed Lucy on the cheek and trudged upstairs, full of self-reproach for deserting this woman when she obviously needed to talk to someone about the anxiety she was feeling.

'Welcome to Shanghai.'

Rita was lying on one of the twin beds without a stitch on. Her belly was a shining globe. Below it the mound of dark hair glistened with drops of water. Her breasts were as massive as the mythic equipment on statues of earth goddesses he had seen on Cyprus on his first midshipman's cruise. He remembered Win Kemble leading them to a bordello in Casablanca where there were real teats almost as big. He also remembered reading about the way worshippers of these ancient earth goddesses, variously named Astarte, Cybele, Demeter, used to castrate themselves as an act of supreme adoration.

Rita fat was sexier than Rita thin. At least she was more ingenious, more outrageous. Maybe she felt she had to compensate for the visual inadequacy. 'Come on,' Rita said. 'It's your last chance for a trip up Bubbling Well Road.'

Shanghai and its street names were a private code for sex games from a fuck book Rita had bought in China when she was fourteen. It described everything from cunnilingus to blow jobs in steamy detail.

Arthur McKay wanted her. He wanted her from behind and in the mouth and every other way that Rita let him have her when she was in her Shanghai mood. But he knew what it meant this time around. He was going to help her make Win Kemble writhe. He was going to be Admiral King's investigator-prosecutor.

The admiral's fucker. That was what Rita wanted him to be.

'I think I'll take a hot bath instead,' Arthur McKay said. 'Maybe I'll get to see Shanghai aboard the *Jefferson City*.'

Heavy Weather

The USS *Jefferson City* rolled and pitched in a rising sea. In his cabin, Lieutenant Junior Grade Montgomery West was reading a letter.

Dear Joey,

By the time you get this I'll be in Dubuque or Paducah helping the stars sell war bonds. It's worse than hand-to-hand combat on Guadalcanal. People tear the earrings out of their ears, the bracelets off their wrists. Rita Hayworth collapsed in the middle of the last tour. Anybody who buys a $25,000 bond gets a big wet kiss. That was Hedy Lamarr's bright idea. Or her agent's, to put it more exactly.

Nobody would do it twice or even once if I hadn't persuaded Louis B. to pass the word that it's sell or else you'll never work for any major studio again.

You won't recognize Tinsel Town when you get back. At midnight Hollywood and Vine is as dark as Main Street in Wappinger Falls. Everybody says glamour is out for the duration. You're not supposed to have servants or give parties. Agents spend more time trying to get their people on to the Hollywood Canteen night shift than they do getting them parts, Patriotism it's wonderful!

I still say you were nuts to join up, *after* Roosevelt declared the movies an essential industry. The studios are desperate for guys your age with your kind of handsome puss. You could be making five pictures a year and be a hero in every one of them. You could kill more Japs on celluloid in thirty days than you'll see if the war lasts ten years. You've probably heard that they froze the salaries, but between you and me and Louis B. we're promising everyone that we'll squirrel away some of the loot and pay up after the bullets stop flying. Maybe you could get a 30-day leave and make a picture. How would you like to have 100 grand to come home to?

What the hell is the Navy doing out there? The Marines on Guadalcanal get all the publicity, as far as I can see. I wish you could tell me something we could stick in a press release. Like maybe doing the tango on a turret with some native beauty? Give it some thought. If you don't get your name in the papers around here at least once a month, you don't exist. How many times do I have to tell you that?

Your favourite uncle,
Mort

Montgomery West sighed and crumpled the letter in his hand. Good old Uncle Mort, still running his life. West found it hard to make up his mind what he thought and felt about his mother's favourite brother. On the one hand, if it wasn't for Mort and his boyhood friendship with Louis B. Mayer, Montgomery West might still be one of the faceless thousands on the studios' extra lists. On the other hand, he might be a star in his own right. He might be playing opposite Norma Shearer instead of her B-picture imitation, Ina Severn. He might be Franchot Tone instead of *his* B-picture imitation. Uncle Morty got nephew Joey ahead all right – but only so far.

Maybe with this Navy service under his belt he could finally shake off Uncle Mort's controlling hand. Maybe he would no longer feel compelled to do everything Mort and his fellow publicity geniuses at Metro-Goldwyn-Mayer suggested. He could stop sleeping with ageing silent queens and cease straining his brain trying to make conversation with starlets like Marilyn what's-her-name.

Mort was the closest thing to a father West had ever

known. His real father had died in an automobile accident in 1920, when West was seven years old. He had only a vague memory of a big deep-voiced man who owned a magnificent speedboat in which he took West for exciting rides on Long Island Sound. Not until he was in his late teens did he discover (from Uncle Mort) that his father had been a bootlegger and had died in a police chase on a rain-slick Connecticut highway.

Punching up his pillow, West began kissing Ina Severn's cool unyielding English mouth. His hands roved up and down and around her slim supple body. He had been kissing Ina Severn in his head this way for the last four months.

'Cut, cut,' the Hungarian director yelled. 'Ina for d' loaf of God, can't you show entoosiasm?'

'Mr West isn't kissing me, he's raping me.' Ina sniffed.

Maybe she would change her mind now, when he strolled on to the Metro lot with one and a half gold stripes on his sleeves. Hail the conquering hero.

Unfortunately, the USS *Jefferson City* had not conquered anything. He could not even give an interview about his thoughts and feelings during the battle of Savo Island. The story of that ruinous encounter was top secret. Anyway, if he told the truth about the *Jefferson City*'s performance, Uncle Mort would rend his press releases in despair.

A hand yanked aside the curtain that served for a door on his stateroom. Ensign Richard B. Meade, Annapolis 1940, stuck his head into West's cabin. He had a glass of whisky in his hand. Meade was trying very hard to overcome his Annapolis nickname, 'Babyface'. But it was not easy. Although his build was burly, his cherubic dimpled face still looked no more than sixteen.

'Hey, Monty, old chap,' he said in a fake British accent that recalled parts West had played in several recent movies. 'Care to join us for a swallow?'

Captain Kemble's toleration of liquor was one of the few things that had made life bearable aboard the *Jefferson City*. West thought for a moment about the bite of a Scotch and soda at the base of his tongue.

'Sorry. I've got the watch.'

'Then you better get the hell up there. The captain's on the bridge.'

'Christ!'

West began struggling into his foul-weather gear. Meade swigged his drink and recited from the *Watch Officer's Guide*. '"When the commanding officer is on the navigating bridge, the officer of the deck shall not, unless to avoid immediate danger, change the course, alter the speed or perform any important evolutions without consulting him." Remember that one, West. It's a fetish with Captain Crumpleplate.'

'Aye, aye, sir.'

Meade was the son of Clinch Meade, one of Captain Kemble's Annapolis classmates. Before Savo Island, he had practically levitated every time he talked about the Great Man. Now he sneered at him at every opportunity.

'Listen. What do I get for tutoring you in basic seamanship? Maybe a date with Rita Hayworth?'

'She's worn out from selling war bonds.'

Meade guffawed. 'Hey, that's a new way of describing it. I like it.'

Every bachelor in the wardroom – and a few husbands – expected West to lead them straight to the nearest Hollywood orgy. He had tried to tell them that sex in Hollywood was usually a business arrangement. He might as well have spoken Chinese.

Feeling as bulky as a bear in the fur-lined foul-weather jacket, West hustled down the dim passageway and almost collided with Ensign Herman Kruger. As usual, Kruger had a scowl on his Germanic face. The jutting jaw, the glaring thyroid eyes reminded West of several character actors who specialized in playing Junker generals or *Unterseeboot* captains. Unfortunately, Ensign Kruger was real. A chief fire controlman who had got a commission when the war began, he was at least forty and had been in the Navy twenty-three years. He found it hard to accept ninety-day-wonder West as his superior officer in charge of F Division.

'The exec says the captain wants those bodies out of Main Plot before reveille the morning we arrive in long Beach. We'll need a forty-man working party.'

The *Jefferson City* rolled at least thirty degrees to star-board. West lost his balance and crashed into the bulkhead. Kruger never even swayed. He smirked and shook his head as West struggled to keep his feet. 'Shall I order up the working party?'

'Yes – would you?'

'I think you should be there when we take them out.'

'Of course I'll be there,' West said.

They were talking about the fifteen drowned men floating in the water-filled coffin that the main battery plotting room – main plot – had become. One of them was the former commanding officer of F Division. If West stayed aboard the *Jefferson City* after she was repaired and returned to sea, he would have to go down into that compartment when they went to General Quarters. The thought made it difficult for him to get his breath. Did Kruger know that? Was that why the smirk was on his face?

'I don't know why the hell we didn't bury them at sea,' West said.

'The captain nixed it,' Kruger said.

'Was he afraid it would hurt morale?'

'I think he couldn't face them with the whole crew watching.'

Kruger too had turned against Captain Kemble. Before Savo Island, Kruger had admired his ferocious discipline, the harsh sentences he handed down for minor infractions of the regulations. Kruger's vision of the perfect ship was a crew of terrified robots who never broke a rule or loafed on the job.

On deck, West was greeted by a cascade of icy saltwater. Beyond the rail, white-crested swells loomed against the black sky. The rain squall was building to a gale. They had lifelines up. He hung on to one as he made his way forward to the bridge. His watch read four minutes before the hour when he stepped into the pilothouse. The junior officer of the deck had already relieved his opposite number. So had all the other men, the telephone talker, the helmsman, the engine telegrapher, the quartermaster, the boatswain's mate of the watch. The officer of the deck stood in the usual place, on the starboard side. 'Hello West,' he said.

It was the air defence officer, Lieutenant Robert R. Mullenoe, Annapolis 1931. He was six feet two, with a jaw like the prow of a battleship and the thick neck, the tree-trunk legs of a heavyweight boxer. He had in fact won several amateur championships at the Naval Academy. His red hair and hard green eyes emanated a cool, controlled pugnacity. Unlike his rowdy friend Meade, who specialized in needling West, Mullenoe ignored him. The son and grandson of admirals, he would sit beside West at the wardroom table and discuss with Meade and other graduates the Academy football team, the antics of his class's 100th Night show, the idiosyncrasies of various Annapolis town characters. After a while, West – and other reserve officers – would begin to feel invisible.

'Lieutenant West,' said a voice from the darkness on the port side of the bridge. 'You must have read in your *Watch Officer's Guide* that a good officer relieves at least five minutes early. At sea, as I think I've made it clear, ten minutes is a better time allotment. Especially at night.'

'Yes, Captain. I'm sorry. I was reading and lost track of time.'

'I'm not interested in your excuse, Mr West.'

'It won't happen again, Captain.'

'We're at Condition Three,' Mullenoe said, meaning a third of the crew was on watch. It was the standard condition for wartime cruising when an attack was unlikely. 'There's a merchant marine report of hostile submarines in the area.' He gave West the course and bearing and the location of their escorting destroyer, the USS *Reuben Davis*. Mullenoe noted that the barometer had fallen ten points and was expected to go down another five. The rest was the usual routine: what boilers were in use, initialling the night order book.

'I relieve you, sir,' West said.

Lieutenant Junior Grade Montgomery West was now responsible for the 1,300 men and ten thousand tons of steel and oil and explosives beneath his feet. That was unnerving enough for a man whose chief worry, until nine months ago, had been memorizing two hundred lines of dialogue a week. The presence of Captain Winfield Scott Schley Kemble gave him an acute case of butterflies. West had never expected to have this kind of responsibility thrust on him when he let Uncle Mort pull a string or two and get him made a lieutenant junior grade (the equivalent of an Army first lieutenant) a month after he had been commissioned an ensign. Captain Kemble had promptly announced that a lieutenant junior grade had to stand watch as OOD and proceeded to tutor West in ship-handling in his coldest, most sarcastic style.

'Steer course three one,' West said, confirming the course they were on, as regulations required.

'Do you mean oh three one, sir?' the helmsman asked.

'Yes. I was just checking,' West muttered. He could not understand why, when he made a mistake, the enlisted men showed him so little mercy. They seemed to have it in for him as much as the Annapolis types did.

'Why did you join the Navy, Mr West?' Captain Kemble asked.

'I wanted to do something – after Pearl Harbor.'

'I mean – the Navy. Why not the Army? I thought you performed beautifully as the cavalry colonel in that western about the Oregon Trail. Just the right amount of stiff-jawed brainlessness.'

'I thought the Navy had more class.'

West was not about to confess that he had also thought the Navy was safer. Nor was he going to tell Captain Kemble that if it were not for Ina Severn he would probably be in bed in his house in the Hollywood hills instead of on this damp cold bridge, surrounded by the heaving Pacific Ocean.

'No doubt you'll be joining up?' she had said on the day after Pearl Harbor. When he shrugged, she had flung herself back in her commissary chair in appalled exasperation. 'How can any real man ignore this war?' she cried.

All the British in Hollywood were the same way, ready to work for nothing in the movies that urged the Americans to get into the battle to save dear old England's ass. Why had he let this icy English bitch get to him? He had stayed out of Hollywood's perfervid politics and felt no burning need to beat Hitler to save the world from fascism. Nor had the Nazis' persecution of the Jews disturbed him. He never thought of himself as half Jewish. Like his grandfather, who had changed Hyman to Lyman, most of his mother's Connecticut relatives had anglicized their names and lost touch with Judaism.

West was not especially patriotic, either. If anything, he had something of a grudge against his country. He would have grown up in comparative luxury if the idiotic Protestants had not rammed Prohibition down the nation's throat and forced his father to close down one of the oldest, most prosperous saloons in New Haven. There were times when he saw his father and to some extent himself as victims of American narrowness and instability.

Nevertheless, West had enlisted – without bothering to tell Uncle Mort, who almost had a seizure when he heard about it. West intended to fight the goddamn war and prove to Ina Severn – and himself – that behind his spoiled-scion façade lurked a genuine male.

Captain Kemble's unnerving voice floated from the darkness again. 'Well, you've given a pretty good performance so far. Most of the time the average observer would think you're a genuine Navy officer.'

'Thank you, Captain,' West said.

West could see smiles playing across the faces of the helmsman and the boatswain's mate. They had watched the captain eviscerate this ninety-day wonder before.

'Fame,' Captain Kemble said. 'Is that what you're after, West?'

'Not really. I like acting.'

'Why? Always pretending to be someone else – someone unreal. Isn't that a strain after a while? Don't you start to lose sight of who you really are? You've even changed your name – not that I blame you for wanting to get rid of Joseph Lyman Shuck.'

The helmsman's grin widened. Captain Kemble had dug West's real name out of his personnel file within a week of his coming aboard. It had been a running joke in the wardroom for the next six weeks. The gunnery officer, Lieutenant Commander Edwin Moss, six feet four inches of towering Annapolis snobbery, had professed bewilderment that a man

48

could change his name and his identity. He seemed to think there was something immoral about it. Meade and several other Annapolis types called him 'Shuckie' for a while.

'Acting's an art, Captain. As long as you think of yourself as an artist, you're in control. As a matter of fact, I think everyone does a lot of acting. There's a lot of it in the Navy.'

'Oh?'

'The men know it. They know the officers don't believe fifty percent of the stuff they hand out about God and country.'

'I don't think that's a healthy attitude for a Navy officer to have, West.'

Kemble's voice had shot up several decibels. West had struck a nerve. 'Sorry, Captain. I thought this was a personal conversation.'

'I don't have personal conversations with anyone on this bridge, West.'

'I understand, Captain.'

He could not see Winfield Scott Schley Kemble's handsome face in his dark corner of the bridge. But West could visualize it easily enough – the arrogant, disdainful mouth, the cold blue eyes, the beaked nose. He was named after some Spanish-American War admiral, and he looked it. He looked like a man who was born to command lesser men. Yet, according to his more vociferous critics in the wardroom, in a moment of terrific crisis thirty days ago, he had failed catastrophically. Why?

West wanted to ask him, because he was more than a little angry at losing his thousand-dollar-a-week salary for the past nine months and getting nothing for his trouble but a sour taste in his mouth. Who the hell was writing this script, anyway? If Louis B. Mayer were running the show, he would have fired him long ago. Come to think of it, if the rumour of the captain's being relieved was true, maybe he had been fired.

They would probably bring him back to Washington and make him an admiral. These goddamn Annapolis graduates stuck together no matter what happened. Only schnooks without that ring on their fingers got crucified for making mistakes.

'Man overboard!'

The telephone talker's shout clanged around the bridge like a pistol shot.

'Where away?' Lieutenant West gasped.

'Off the fantail to starboard.'

'Right full rudder,' West said.

Too late, he heard Ensign Meade's mocking voice. *When the commanding officer is on the navigating bridge, the officer of the deck shall not, unless to avoid immediate danger, change the course . . . without consulting him.*

'Steady as you go,' snapped Captain Kemble. 'What the hell are you doing, West?'

'I was going to execute the Williamson turn, Captain.'

'We have a half dozen flooded compartments amidships, West. You try to turn thirty degrees in this sea and you could find yourself broaching to. In the second place, we've received a warning of enemy submarines operating off this coast. Only a fool would risk thirteen hundred lives and a capital ship to save one man.'

'Yes, Captain.'

'Order life buoys overboard and send the *Davis* back to look for him.'

West obeyed both commands. Pounding ahead at twenty-five knots, they were already a half mile from where the man had gone over the side. The buoys were a pathetic gesture, no more. The *Reuben Davis*, their escorting destroyer, had no more chance of finding him than West had of persuading Captain Kemble to let him try the Williamson turn, a manoeuvre that enabled a ship to regain the same course in the opposite direction without reducing speed.

'Muster the ship. Let's find out who he is, at least,' Captain Kemble ordered.

'All hands, all hands except the watch report to your division compartments for muster,' West said over the PA.

For the next half hour there was silence on the bridge as they ploughed into the storm. Then Radio Central reported a message from the *Davis*. No sign of the overboard. About five minutes later, the Executive Officer, Commander Daniel Boone Parker, came puffing on to the bridge. His big belly made it difficult for him to climb ladders.

'It seems to be Quartermaster First Class George Massie, Captain.'

'What do you mean, it seems to be?'

Between Captain Kemble and Commander Parker there was a gulf filled with barely disguised loathing. West usually sympathized with the Executive Officer. Parker, too, was not an Annapolis man. He had joined the Navy in 1917, when World War I began, and stayed in. He made no secret of how much he resented Annapolis favouritism. He frequently pointed out at the wardroom table that he had been commissioned three months before Captain Kemble.

'He didn't answer muster call. Someone said they saw him going topside.'

'Why in God's name would he go up on deck on a night like this?'

'I have no idea, Captain. Maybe he liked wet weather.'

'Make out a report.'

'Aye, Captain.'

West stared into the rain and wind. Kemble did not give a damn. A man had just drowned and this Annapolis bastard did not give a damn. West had stood several watches with Massie, a slight fussy man, as quartermasters tended to be. They were the keepers of the ship's log, the guardians of the navigation charts. Massie had told West one night that his ambition was to retire from the Navy and breed Irish setters.

Captain Kemble went below with a farewell thrust. 'Don't change your course without consulting me, West.'

'Aye, aye, Captain,' West said.

For another minute the bridge was silent. Then West heard the quartermaster cursing.

'What's the matter with you?' he asked.

'He was my buddy, George Massie. One of the straightest, best buddies I ever had in this fucking Navy.'

'I'm sorry.'

'Yeah. Sure you're sorry. You know as well as I do what happened to him – and why.'

'What the hell are you talking about?'

'He was on the bridge that night. Off Savo Island. He knew too much.'

West stared into the storm. The wind seemed to be rising. A huge wave crashed on to the bow of the USS *Jefferson City*, burying everything up to and including turret one. The ship staggered under the impact of the tons of water. For a moment she seemed to be angling down into the depths. All West could think about were the fifteen dead men from F Division in main plot. They were not a fighting ship, they were a floating coffin, about to meet their doom. This script was neither a mystery nor an adventure story, it was a horror show.

Like a tired but still game athlete, the *Jefferson City* refuted these bizarre products of West's Hollywood imagination. Her forty-foot-high prow rose from the churning sea. White water poured from her decks. Bolts creaked, steel plates groaned. She was up, proud, free, thrusting her bow into the next wave.

Officer of the Deck Montgomery West stood there on the bridge, trying to make sense of what the quartermaster had just told him. What was happening aboard the *Jefferson City* was a mystery, all right. But it was not made in Hollywood.

I Relieve You, Sir

A totally unhappy marriage is as rare as a totally happy one.

Captain Arthur McKay jotted this epigram in the small notebook he kept at his bedside. On his first summer cruise as a midshipman at Annapolis, he had wandered into a bookstore in Marseilles and picked up a copy of La Rochefoucauld's *Maxims*. Their pithy wisdom had delighted him. Ever since, he had used the form to condense his thinking and feeling about life as he encountered it.

In the twin bed on the other side of the room, Rita slept face down, her hands clutched into fists, like a five-year-old. Her tousled hair, the squeezed mouth added to the little-girlish impression. He could see his wife in the big house at Patapsco, dreaming of commanding a battleship. She was a hard woman to love, but he managed it most of the time.

Arthur McKay was a strong believer in learning from

experience. He did not take many ideas on faith. In marriage, for instance, he had decided that a certain amount of unhappiness was not necessarily a disaster. Unhappiness stirred up the status quo. It made the children want to improve on their parents' performance. Growing up, McKay had been bombarded by his mother's exhortations to 'get off this damn farm, out of this damn country, this flat boring state, and see the world'. That sort of propaganda, plus enlistment posters guaranteeing that opportunity to those who joined the US Navy, had prompted him to take the examinations for Annapolis in 1912. He found them surprisingly easy, and their local congressman happened to be his mother's second cousin. That was how Arthur McKay showed up with his cardboard suitcase at the US Naval Academy in 1913.

His unorthodox opinions about love and marriage had had a lot to do with Arthur McKay's proposal to Rita Semmes as he took her home from her sister Lucy's wedding. He knew Rita had been bitterly disappointed by her failure to attract Win Kemble. That knowledge stirred in Arthur McKay a wish to comfort her, a feeling he had often had when he saw his mother on the porch or at the window of their farmhouse, gazing wistfully across the brown wheat fields at the unreachable horizon. There was also Win Kemble's strenuous advice to make the offer. 'That girl can do you a hell of a lot of good in the Navy, Mac.'

There was a clear implication, of course, that Win Kemble did not need that kind of help and Arthur McKay did. That was all right, because in 1922 it certainly looked that way. Everything about McKay still said hayseed, from the way he parted his hair straight down the middle to the awkward way he sat in company, both hands on his knees.

So he had put his arm around Rita in the back of the taxi and said, 'I'm not sure if you're in love with me, but I'm in love with you and I know you're in love with the Navy, so that's a pretty good start. What do you say we repeat that performance?'

She had kissed him with wild, tearful enthusiasm. 'I – do love you,' she said, admitting with the hesitation that the words were manufactured for the moment. 'I'll be the best damn wife to you that the Navy's ever seen, Arthur.'

Most of the time, Rita was still trying to keep that promise.

McKay got up and shaved. When he emerged from the bathroom, Rita was awake, sitting up in bed, her hair combed. She gave him a look straight out of her father's repertoire of glares. But she did not take the offensive. She had found out a long time ago that tantrums and harsh words had no impact on Arthur McKay.

'Did you sleep well?' she said.

'No,' he said.

'I did.'

'Good. Sorry about not being in the mood last night.'

'That's all right. You know where I'd really like to do it.'

One of Rita's favourite thrills was making love aboard the ships on which he had served. It had not been difficult in the peacetime Navy, when wives were frequently invited aboard for parties. It was easy to slip away for a half hour. But McKay had never enjoyed it. There were no locks on the doors of junior officers' staterooms. Even when he was captain of the destroyer *Stacy Wright* and had a lock on his door, he had objected to the idea on some deep level of his self.

He decided to try diplomacy. 'I wish we could,' he said. 'But the crew watches every move a new captain makes. It could lead to all sorts of smutty jokes.'

'Who cares what a bunch of raunchy swabbies think?'

I do, Arthur McKay thought. He wondered if Rita secretly liked the idea of 1,300 sailors imagining themselves in bed with her.

No. That was too crude. It was all part of her passion to share his career, which she had done so much to shape, to be with him in heart and mind as he commanded this capital ship. He let silence be his final answer, and Rita accepted it.

They breakfasted alone. They knew from previous visits to the Kemble household that Lucy never emerged from her room before ten. It was a habit she acquired from her mother. Rita, on the other hand, was like her father. Up and ready to go even if reveille was 5.30 a.m.

Rita seized the morning's copy of the Los Angeles *Times*

and gave him a rapid summary of the war news. The Germans were still devouring the Russians, but at a slower pace. MacArthur was still sitting on his hands in Australia. The situation on Guadalcanal and in the sea round the Solomon Islands remained critical. 'If Guadalcanal goes down the tube, Ernie King will go with it,' she said. 'If the landings in North Africa fizzle, George Marshall will go too. They'll bring MacArthur home and make him commander-in-chief of everything in sight, including Roosevelt.'

'Too much grand strategy for me.'

'It pays to think ahead. MacArthur would favour people with Asiatic Fleet duty. He's big on the Oriental mind. You can bet Win is thinking ahead. He's praying for Guadalcanal to collapse. Getting rid of King is his only hope.'

'I'm sure he's got a few other hopes. Don't we all?'

'I want a blow-by-blow of the ceremony.'

'Agreed. If you promise not to give Win a going-over tonight at dinner.'

'He'd give you one – in his hypocritical condescending way.'

'Let's not start that again. Keep your mouth shut for Lucy's sake. She's not stupid. She suspects something's gone wrong.'

'Why not tell her the truth? She's forty-seven years old. She ought to find out a lot of truths about her hero.'

'Maybe. But I don't think you ought to tell her. In fact, I'm giving you an order not to.'

Rita's jaw jutted. She did not get many orders from her husband. But she had learned it was a mistake to disobey them. 'You take half the fun out of life with your goddamn conscience,' she said.

The maid appeared in the doorway. 'Your car is here, Captain.'

The Marine driver sat behind the wheel of a battered-looking 1936 Ford. It had to be the worst car in the motor pool. George Tomlinson, the admiral in command of the Terminal Island Naval Base, was not a devotee of Ernest J. King. Tomlinson had been plans deputy on the staff of Admiral Husband E. Kimmel, commander of the Pacific

Fleet on the day the Japanese attacked Pearl Harbor. His career was in shreds, along with Kimmel's.

'Think this thing will make it to Terminal Island?'

'Don't know, Captain,' the Marine said.

'How do you like shore duty?' McKay said.

'Better than the fleet. But I'd rather fight Japs than the chippies on the Long Beach Pike.'

'That's the spirit.'

'How come the Navy left the Marines on the beach out there in Guadalcanal and just sailed away, Captain?'

'Where'd you hear that?'

'It's basic scuttlebutt all through the Corps, Captain.'

'It isn't true. I'm taking a ship out there in two weeks, if the yardbirds do their jobs on schedule. We're going to give it everything we've got.'

'Good to hear, Captain.'

At the Terminal Island headquarters building, McKay spent a half hour reading magazines before an ass-wiggling yeoman led him into Tomlinson's office. Still built like the All American guard he had been in 1908, the admiral mashed his hand and waved him to a seat. McKay had been a lieutenant under him aboard the heavy cruiser USS *Pensacola* in 1930. But Tomlinson did not even mention it; he was not the nostalgic type.

'What the hell are you hotshots in COMINCH going to do to save your skins after Savo Island?' Tomlinson sneered.

'I have no idea, Admiral.'

'Do you know what the fuck happened? Can you at least tell me that?'

'We got our asses kicked.'

'Why did you put a fucking Limey in command? They haven't won a sea battle since Trafalgar, for Christ's sake.'

He was talking about Admiral Victor Alexander Charles Crutchley, commander of His Majesty's Royal Australian Squadron. He had issued the orders that resulted in the slaughter of Savo Island.

'He did everything wrong that a fucking admiral can do, in one place at one time,' Tomlinson said.

'Hard to contest that one, Admiral.'

'I'm not supposed to know what happened. I'm only a shipyard foreman. But this is what I hear.'

Tomlinson whipped out a piece of paper and swiftly drew a round circle several inches from a wavy hump. 'Here's Savo Island and Guadalcanal,' he said, pointing to the circle and the hump. 'Here's our cruisers.' He drew two lines to the north of Savo Island and three more on the south. He scratched in a few more lines on the edge of the page. 'Picket destroyers.'

Obviously, Admiral King's silence on the disaster at Savo Island had not prevented the news from travelling through the Navy at close to the speed of sound.

'Crutchley divides his force in half instead of concentrating it. He doesn't give anybody a battle plan. Then he sails away and leaves the boy wonder Kemble in command.'

The admiral drew a line around the lead cruiser in the southern division.

McKay winced at the term boy wonder. Win Kemble had made a lot of enemies by always being the first man in his class to be promoted.

'He had no business commanding a cruiser, much less a fucking cruiser division at the age of forty-seven.' Tomlinson said. 'Personally I don't think he's fit to command a destroyer. A goddamn glory hog, like his grandfather.'

'He was my roommate at the Academy, Admiral.'

'You've got my deepest sympathy.'

The admiral glowered at his drawing. 'So what happens? The Jap comes up from Rabaul. He hits the southern division first. He blows HMAS *Canberra* out of the water and comes around Savo and does the same thing to the *Quincy*, the *Vincennes* and the *Astoria*. Meanwhile, where the fuck is the *Jefferson City*? From what I hear, after taking a shell that flooded a couple of compartments, the boy wonder sailed west, away from the Jap battle force as fast as his fucking engines could take him. He never even broke radio silence to let the other three cruisers know the Japs were in range. That's why you're here with orders to relieve him, right?'

Arthur McKay took a deep slow breath. Keep your temper, he told himself. They are all watching you to see how you are reacting to this situation. 'That's not a bad description of the débâcle, Admiral,' McKay said. 'But it leaves out one or two things. Such as the fact that Kelly Turner, who was in overall command, didn't seem to know what the hell he was doing either. He approved Crutchley's dispositions. Then in the middle of the night he orders him and his ship to withdraw from the danger zone and steam twenty miles to confer with him on what they should do the next day. Turner seems to have made the fundamental boner we were warned against in our first week at the Naval War College – basing your actions on what you assume the enemy is going to do.'

A deep magenta crept up Admiral Tomlinson's thick neck. Admiral Richmond Kelly Turner had been his classmate at Annapolis and was a close friend. He was also Tomlinson's best hope of getting sea duty again.

'McKay,' he growled, 'there's such a thing as being too smart for your own good.'

'Do you think you can get the *Jefferson City* ready in two weeks, Admiral? They need her out there in the Solomons mighty bad.'

'Two weeks? Two *months* is more like it. We've got to replace a lot of her fire control equipment, add four of those new forty-millimetre Bofors mounts and this new SC radar. Do you think we're fucking magicians?'

'Admiral King said he wanted it done in two weeks. Shall I call him and tell him it's impossible?'

'No!' snapped Tomlinson. 'If he wants it in two weeks, he'll get it in two weeks. But it's going to bring everything else in the yard to a fucking dead stop.'

'I'll tell him that.'

'No you won't. I will, Captain McKay.'

Arthur McKay let the muzzle heat from that blast subside and asked, 'Are you coming out to the *Jefferson City* for the change of command, Admiral?'

'Yes. I don't get many chances to go aboard ships that aren't in a fucking dry dock these days.'

Admiral Tomlinson's five-passenger 1940 Cadillac beeped its way through swarms of workmen arriving for the 8 a.m. shift. In the dry docks, welding torches glowed around the hulls of a half dozen ships, one of them a carrier. 'A couple of near misses at Midway played hell with the *Enterprise*'s steering gear,' the Admiral said. 'I still think we're betting too much on those floating eggshells. What we need is more battleships. If we'd had some at Midway, we could have ended the war then and there. Instead, Spruance had to run for his life after he knocked out their carriers.'

The Admiral was a battleship man. He had bet his naval career on the pre-eminence of those floating gun platforms, capable of hurling 2,300-pound shells over twenty miles. He and his friends had spent the previous decade sneering at carriers as 'the hooligan navy'. Pearl Harbor had sunk his career along with the battleship's reign as monarch of the ocean. But Tomlinson could not bring himself to admit it. That was understandable. A man does not like to admit a mistake that big.

As Tomlinson and McKay boarded the Admiral's black-hulled barge, Tomlinson pointed to a Higgins boat tied up at the dock, its flat bottom slapping in the slight swell from a passing harbour tug. 'Do you know what that is?'

'No idea.'

'A fucking morgue. They took fifteen bodies out of the *Jefferson City*'s main plot before dawn. Captain Kemble said he was afraid if they were taken out while the ship was in dry dock it would make the newspapers. Wouldn't that be terrible?'

'He's just obeying orders, Admiral. Cominch wants a lid on Savo Island.'

Tomlinson grunted contemptuously. But he would keep his mouth shut. He was a Navy man.

'What's the biggest ship you've commanded, McKay?'

'A destroyer, the *Stacy Wright*, in 1937.'

'You're going to find a cruiser a lot different. It's closer to a battleship. You've got to have a good exec and a tough master at arms. You can't run a capital ship on personality, the way a lot of destroyer captains get by.'

'Thanks for the advice, Admiral.'

In his own crusty way, Tomlinson was wishing him well.

They rounded a tanker's stern, and suddenly there was the

USS *Jefferson City*, silhouetted between the open breakwater and the sea. Arthur McKay felt his chest tighten, his throat fill. Not from anticipation of the imminent encounter with Win Kemble. It was the beauty of that long slim hull, the haughty curve of her cruiser's bow, that moved him. The superstructure was a clutter of housing and equipment necessary for survival in battle: fire control towers, radar gear, gun directors. But it did not detract from the spirit of speed and power the unknown naval architect had infused into her basic design.

The crew was mustered on deck in dress whites, row on row of men in compact divisions, facing their officers. Their presence added to the tightness in Arthur McKay's chest. Within the hour, these 1,300 sailors would become his men. This great steel creature would become his ship, his to command, to lead, to conn. His responsibility. Whatever had happened under Win Kemble's command would make no difference in the assessment the Navy made of Arthur McKay's performance as captain of the USS *Jefferson City*.

As Admiral Tomlinson's black-hulled barge came alongside, a bugle rang across the still harbour. Tomlinson's two-star flag soared up the mainmast. When the Admiral reached the top of the accommodation ladder, a boatswain's pipe shrilled and six sailors – the prescribed number of sideboys for a rear admiral – snapped to attention. The ship's band gave him two ruffles and flourishes.

'Request permission to come aboard, Captain,' the Admiral growled, throwing a salute to Winfield Scott Schley Kemble.

'Permission granted, Admiral.'

They shook hands. Captain Arthur McKay also saluted the American flag on the stern and asked his best friend for permission to come aboard. Until he was relieved, Win Kemble was absolute ruler of the USS *Jefferson City*. If he decided for some insane reason to order Captain McKay and Admiral Tomlinson back into their barge, they would have had no choice but to obey.

'Hello, Win,' Art said as they shook hands.

'Hello, Art.'

McKay was shocked by the haggard face that confronted him. There were dark ovals of sleeplessness beneath Win's blue eyes, lines of weariness – or grief? – around his mouth. His skin looked papery, drained of the vital force he had always exuded. Was this what combat did to a man?

Win was looking him over too and did not seem to like what he saw. Was it the standard reaction of the fighting sailor to the rear area desk jockey? If Win gave him a chance, McKay was sure he could convince him that working for Ernie King was almost as harrowing as combat.

'The crew would welcome an inspection, Admiral, if you have time,' Win said.

A nod from Tomlinson signified agreement. They walked swiftly past the assembled ranks until they reached the fire control division. The Admiral stopped and peered at a third class petty officer. 'Peterson,' he said, 'did you get busted again?'

'I'm afraid so, Admiral.'

'You should be a warrant officer by now, Peterson.'

'Thanks, Admiral.'

'Best damn fire controlman I've ever seen,' the Admiral said to Arthur McKay. 'Also the worst goddamn fuckup.'

Peterson almost smiled but wisely changed his mind at the last moment.

'What did you do at Savo Island?' Tomlinson asked.

'Not a damn thing, Admiral,' said Peterson.'

'So I heard,' Tomlinson said.

You son of a bitch, Arthur McKay thought. Win Kemble's face remained expressionless.

The inspection completed, the two captains and the admiral walked to a row of leather wardroom chairs set up in front of turret one. The grey eight-inch guns lifted their snouts toward them like submissive animals. Captain Kemble introduced his Executive Officer, Commander Daniel Boone Parker. Was Win's use of the full name sarcastic? McKay did not like the fat that hung from Parker's jowls, but he had a man's handshake. Next came the chaplain, a short, doleful lieutenant named Emerson Bushnell. McKay did not like his looks either. He preferred cheerful chaplains.

A microphone and a lectern had been set up facing aft. Win Kemble turned to Admiral Tomlinson. 'Would you like to say a few words, Admiral?'

'No.'

Win asked the chaplain to give an invocation. Bushnell walked to the microphone and uttered a series of lugubrious platitudes about the need for God's blessing on the ship and the man who was about to take command of it.

Win stepped to the lectern. 'Men of the *Jefferson City*,' he said, in that crisp voice which made many people urge him to run for political office, 'I am leaving you, after seven months as your captain. I've tried to make you into a crew that is second to none in the US Navy. Fighting men. Men ready to do their duty for their country and their God, no matter what price the fortunes of war may exact. You have performed well. I take pride in handing you over to your new captain. He is my closest friend, and I am sure he will find you as willing to obey his commands as you were to obey mine. Godspeed to you all.'

He turned to Arthur McKay. 'Sir, I am ready to be relieved.'

McKay advanced to the microphone. 'Captain Kemble,' he said, 'I have received the following orders from the Bureau of Navigation.' As he read the officialese of his document, Arthur McKay felt the eyes of the crew studying him with an intensity few human beings ever encounter. He understood they were all trying to decide whether he was soft or hard, mean or generous. Would he give them a happy ship or a miserable one? This was the standard question every crew asked when a new captain came aboard. But today, there was something more ferocious in their scrutiny. Looking at the impassive faces beneath the white hats, he sensed a different question – but he did not know what it was.

When McKay finished reading his orders, he turned to Win, saluted and said, 'I relieve you, sir.' Win returned the salute. McKay then turned to Admiral Tomlinson, saluted and said, 'Sir, I report for duty.' The admiral returned his salute.

Arthur McKay faced the microphone again. 'I'm not much

good at making speeches, so I won't try. I only want to wish Captain Kemble the best of luck in Washington, where his brains are badly needed. I'm proud to take command of this ship. I hope to be even prouder of its performance – your performance – in the months ahead.'

The officer of the deck dismissed the crew. 'You've got your own gig now, McKay,' Admiral Tomlinson said. 'You don't need my boat.' He departed with another series of ruffles and flourishes and the whine of a boatswain's pipe.'

'Let me show you your cabin, Captain,' Win said, in a light tone of voice that McKay found encouraging.

McKay nodded to the chaplain and the Executive Officer. 'We'll have lots of time to talk in the next two weeks,' he said. 'I haven't seen this fellow for a good year and it'll probably be longer than that before I see him again. I want to get the word on everything from the war to who's going to win the pennant races.'

'Of course, Captain,' the chaplain said. 'We understand.'

The expression on the Executive Officer's face made McKay wonder what he undestood. It seemed to be something unpleasant. Win turned his back on them without a word and led McKay below to the Captain's cabin. A large compartment served as a combination office and sitting and dining room; behind it was a smaller sleeping compartment. Here was where he was going to spend a lot of lonely hours, McKay thought. On a cruiser, as on a battleship, the captain ate alone and slept alone, except when he invited someone to join him for dinner or supper. It was a tradition inherited from hundreds of years of seafaring wisdom. The greater a captain's power, the more remote he must become from the men over whom he exercised it.

'I'm all packed,' Win said. 'I trust I can borrow the gig. It may take two or three trips. I had a lot of my China stuff with me.'

He gestured toward a half dozen paintings lying on their sides against the bulkhead. Arthur McKay instantly recognized one of a bearded Chinese sage coming down a mountain road in the mist, while peasants toiled in the fields below him. He had one just like it. They had purchased them together on

Bubbling Well Road in Shanghai when they were lieutenants, mutually fascinated with China. The paintings were also part of their half serious, half joking plan to furnish their offices exactly alike, when Win became Chief of Naval Operations and Arthur McKay was his chief of staff.

'Consider the gig yours for the day. But what's the hurry?' McKay said. He picked up the painting and stood it against the wall, right side up. 'I've been hoping for a letter from Po Chu-i for a good three months now. A couple of hours of conversation would be even better.'

After their tour in China, Win had begun writing elaborate letters to Arthur McKay, in imitation of the epistles that the great Chinese poet Po Chu-i sent to his friend Yuan Chen. Like those two state servants from the eighth century, they were fated to live apart most of the time. So they sent letters 'from one side of the civilized world to the other side' with news of their inner and outer lives, their hopes, their disappointments with wives, mistresses, children, careers. The letters always began with a salutation from the Chinese, 'Friend of all my life.' Often they were full of mocking sarcasm about 'our noble Navy' and wry comments on the 'lamentable civilians'.

'I'm afraid what Po Chu-i has been thinking could get us both courtmartialled,' Win said. 'He decided it might be better to keep it to himself.'

'Come on,' Arthur McKay said. 'You're just afraid you might lose an argument or two.'

Win stared at a silk scroll of a husband rebuking his wife, by the fifth-century painter Ku K'Ai-chih. McKay had given it to him and Lucy for their tenth wedding anniversary.

It was odd, McKay mused, the role China played in their friendship. It was the place where Win's sense of destiny, his life-drama of himself as a man who would lead Americans into an imperial future, had been confirmed. Arthur McKay and everyone else had been awed by the masterful way Win had dealt with the Chinese – and the Japanese and the British – when he was captain of the gunboat *Monocacy* on the Yangtze. They had called him the 'Mandarin'.

But the following year, when Arthur McKay became

captain of the *Monocacy*, China became the place where they discovered fundamental disagreements in their views of America's role in the world. They had argued about it – and other things, such as differing views of careers, women, politicians – ever since. Cheerful arguments, of course, full of the kinds of insults best friends fling at each other, knowing there is no possibility of offence.

Arthur McKay was not trying to revive any of those arguments now. He was reaching back into a deeper part of the past. He was trying to regain those magical days when he and Win had sat in their battered easy chairs in Bancroft Hall and Win had held forth about Annapolis, the Navy, women, politics, war, heroism, leadership. He wanted to recall the exhilaration of those days, when Win Kemble had been part older brother, part father, but above all, his friend.

'Anyone from our class aboard?' he asked.

Win shook his head.

McKay began filling him in on what various members of the class were doing. Win had always enjoyed hearing this kind of information in the past. He invariably had a pungent comment on the foibles of some, the ambitions of others. Today he barely listened. McKay could not resist noting how many men who had gone into aviation were rising rapidly on staffs and on ships at sea. Win had never favoured the 'aviators', as the battleship men contemptuously called them, when they were not sneering at the hooligan navy.

'Sammy's trying to decide whether to apply for flight training,' McKay said. 'Rita's all for it. What do you think?'

'I don't know,' Win said, his voice toneless. A few years ago they had devoted entire letters to planning Sammy's career for him. Win was his godfather – and almost a second father.

'I'm inclined to agree,' McKay said. 'Although Cominch doesn't let the wings on his chest prejudice him too much. He didn't start flying until he was forty-five. He's still got a lot of battleship in his blood.'

Suddenly there was an expression on Win's face that Arthur McKay had never seen before. It mingled anger and dislike and something worse – something close to contempt.

'Let's cut the bullshit,' he said. 'Why am I being relieved?'

Arthur McKay felt his face flushing, his palms sweating. Suddenly he was back in plebe year at Annapolis, struggling with the morbid shyness that had made him duck his head and avoid the instructor's eyes when he recited in class. Win had bullied and bellowed and mocked him out of that ruinous habit in hours of rehearsals in their rooms. He could hear him roaring, *Look me in the eye, McKay. Think of yourself as Jesse James. Imagine yourself pointing a gun at those fucking instructors.*

'King says he wants to rotate people back and forth from sea duty –'

'I said cut the bullshit, Art. Look me in the eye and tell me the truth.'

They were back in plebe year, but Arthur McKay did not like it. His temper rose. 'I can't read the bastard's mind, Win. But I know he's going to ask you what the hell happened off Savo Island. You were the OTC –'

Win Kemble laughed. But it was not a pleasant sound. His haggard face changed into a stranger's in front of McKay's eyes. Dark hollows appeared in the smooth cheeks that had won him comparison to Richard Harding Davis and other beau ideals of their youth. The mouth on which Arthur McKay had never seen anything but a smile of friendship became a sneer.

'I knew it. I saw this or something like it coming the minute I heard our bubblehead President had made that bastard Ernie King Commander-in-Chief of all the ships at sea. I saw Rita turning you into a ball-wiping slob, with me as target number one. This is her idea, isn't it? Her way of winning the game we've been playing for the past twenty years? You're not here just to relieve me. You're here to get a confession of guilt, right? I'm supposed to spill my guts to you now – or sometime tonight, after three or four drinks, up in the Hollywood hills.'

'Jesus Christ, Win! Don't you know me better than that?'

'Maybe I know you better than you know yourself, Art.'

'Bullshit! That might have been true in 1913, but it isn't true in 1942.'

Win's smile was crafty now, almost cruel. 'Are you absolutely sure of that?'

Arthur McKay looked the friend of his life in the eyes. What he saw there was not pretty. A bitter icy blankness that suggested their friendship was a sham. Was it possible? Was he seeing his own soul, corrupted by Rita's tireless denigration of Win?

For a moment Arthur McKay almost capitulated to Win's old dominance. It took a terrific effort to deny the redoubled accusation that whirled in his brain.

'Absolutely sure. I didn't want this job, Win. I told King to his face I didn't want it. He gave me a goddamn order.'

'And you had to obey it. You had to come out here to shaft your best friend.'

'I'm not here to do anything of the sort!' It was incredible the way Win could throw him on the defensive. For a moment Arthur McKay almost hated him.

'OK. I can play the game too. I'm not going to tell you anything. I'm going to let you take this ship to the South Pacific and find out for yourself the travesty of a war we're fighting out there.'

'What the hell are you talking about?'

'I'm not answering any questions on the subject. Do you understand? I will only answer questions at a formal court of inquiry. Or before a congressional committee. Send that message to Fleet Admiral Ernest J. King.'

'You tell him,' McKay said. 'You'll be seeing him before I will. I've got a ship to get ready for sea.'

There was the ultimate answer, as brutal as the accusation Win had shoved in his face. Whatever his motives, whatever his fate, Arthur McKay was now the captain of the USS *Jefferson City*.

Dear Liberty

'It's the most beautiful word in the English language, kid,' Jack Peterson said as he spitshined his shoes.

'It's what we're fighting for,' bellowed George Jablonsky. 'For liberty, God, country and Poland.'

'Why didn't you join the fucking Polish Navy?' someone yelled from the other side of the compartment.

'Because I'm a fucking American,' Jablonsky said, 'and today, with the help of a certain brunette named Hildegarde, I'm gonna prove it.'

'What can you do on liberty when you don't know a soul in California?' Frank Flanagan asked.

'What can you do?' Peterson said. 'You can find a dame and some Jack Daniel's and for a little while you can forget you're livin' like a goddamn slice of baloney in a sandwich while those assholes in Officers' Country are lyin' around like millionaires. You can buy yourself a steak instead of having some yo-yo of a Navy cook feed you shit on a shingle.'

The savagery with which Jack Peterson denounced the enlisted man's life bewildered Flanagan. He had to admit that being a sailor aboard the *Jefferson City* had its disadvantages. Sixty men slept in a compartment about the size of his parents' bedroom. The only space a sailor could call his own, besides the twenty-four inches between his rack and the one above it, was his locker, which was two feet high, two feet wide and two feet deep. In this six cubic feet he had to keep his white and blue dress uniforms, his spare dungarees and underwear, his extra hats and pair of shoes, his socks and his neckerchiefs and his toiletries – all squared away in perfect order.

Everywhere aboard the *Jefferson City*, a sailor was part of a crowd. He had to stand in line to shower, to shave, to urinate, to move his bowels and to get dubious substances slung on his tray in the chow line. Yet Flanagan refused to complain. For him, the experiece was a test, a chance to find out whether he was a man among men or some special creature, set apart by his mother's solicitude and Father Callow's rhetoric.

'Listen to me, you guys, especially the boots,' Boats Homewood shouted from the centre of the compartment. 'There's one place I want you to stay out of – Shanghai Red's over in San Pedro. The only thing you'll lose there is your wallet. If you get anywhere with Red's broads, the clap comes with it and maybe the syph in the bargain. I knew the bastard in Shanghai and he was no good then. He's not a sailor, he's a fuckin' thief.

'One more thing. If by some miracle any of you assholes get to the point of makin' out with any broad, put a boot on it, do you hear me? I don't care if she's Agatha Vanderbilt Rockefeller the Fourth or Admiral Tomlinson's wife, any dame who fools around with a sailor is liable to have something that will make you flunk short-arm inspection. If you do, you're on my shitlist. Because it's just stupidity get me? Stupidity.'

'Jesus Christ, Boats,' Jablonsky said. 'You'd kill a romance with Shirley Temple.'

'I'm just givin' you some good advice,' Homewood said. 'If you can't manage to fit a condom in your fuckin' tailor-mades, hit the pro station on the way back. Do you read me?'

'Yeah, yeah.'

Obviously, the veterans of F Division had heard this lecture before.

Flanagan was able to translate most of Homewood's harangue. He had already gone through several short-arm inspections at boot camp. You filed past a doctor and dropped your pants and squeezed back the head of your penis. If a telltale drop of fluid oozed out, that meant gonorrhea. A chancre sore on the head could mean syphilis.

Flanagan also understood the reference to tailor-mades so tight a condom would not fit in the pocket. These were bought on shore by liberty hounds such as Jack Peterson. The tighter the fit the more expensive the tailor – and the more attractive the wearer theoretically was to the opposite sex.

The pro station reference left Flanagan confused. He did not have the slightest intention of losing his virginity. He had given Father Callow a solemn promise that he would not touch a woman. But he wanted to know how everything in the Navy worked. 'What the hell's a pro station?' he asked.

'Prophylactic station. They got one right on the pier next to the Shore Patrol shack,' Peterson said. 'They make goddamn sure you won't get the clap. They pump you full of iodine and swab your dick with hydrochloric acid.'

'It ain't that bad, but Boats is right. Putting a boot on it is a lot easier,' Jablonsky said.

'Romance, Navy style,' Peterson said, spitting on his already gleaming left shoe.

In the sleeping compartment of Deck Division One, deep in the bow of the USS *Jefferson City*, First Class Boatswain's Mate Jerome Wilkinson was also preparing for liberty. He watched Seaman Second Class Harold Semple shine his shoes. 'Prettyboy,' he said. 'Pretty goddamn stupid. I told you to have them shoes ready last night so I could see your ass shine in them. I wanted them in my fuckin' locker this mornin'.'

Semple pushed aside the red curls that fell down his forehead. The red spots on his cheeks gleamed.

'Why the fuck didn't you get'm done, Prettyboy?' Wilkinson demanded.

'I was seasick. I was afraid if I came below I'd throw up in the compartment.'

'If you did that, we really would have beat the shit out of you,' Wilkinson said. 'Right, men?'

Four of his followers sat on racks or lounged against stanchions, watching Semple work. 'You bet your ass we would have,' one said.

Semple and the half dozen other second class seamen who had landed in Wilkinson's division were beginning to discern the purgatory in store for them. They were immediately converted into house servants. The men assigned to clean the compartment handed them their brooms and mops. They were sent scurrying to the galley for coffee, pie, cake – the bonuses that Wilkinson obtained for those who catered to his whims and moods. They learned to grovel in front of their division's ruler or get kicked and punched across the compartment. If they thought about complaining to someone, they were told stories of men who disappeared over the side during the night.

Semple swiftly became Wilkinson's favourite victim. His red hair, his shyness, which brought on terrific blushes, had prompted some high school classmates to call him Harriet. His father, a skilled worker at the Ford Motor Company in Dearborn until he got laid off in 1933, never paid much attention to his youngest child. Within a year the Semples had used up their savings and gone on relief. His father drank too much beer and quarrelled with his mother. Often there was not enough food or clothes in the house for Semple and his six brothers and sisters. Sometimes he had gone to school with his pyjamas pulled down into his shoes as socks.

'What you gonna do on liberty, Prettyboy?' Wilkinson asked.

'I have an uncle in Los Angeles,' Semple said. 'He's the minister of a Methodist-Episcopal church. I'm going to see him.'

'Jesus Christ.' Wilkinson sneered. 'I shoulda known you was one of them chaplain's assistant types. Why'nt you come with us? We're headed for Shanghai Red's in San Pedro. He's an old pal of mine from Asiatic days. He's gonna fix us up with the best broads in the house.'

'My uncle's expecting me,' Semple said.

A punch sent him crashing into the chains of a tier of racks halfway down the aisle. 'You're comin' with us,' Wilkinson said. 'We're gonna make a sailor outa you.'

Down in the compartment shared by engineering divisions B and E, Marty Roth was having trouble tying his thick, shiny black neckerchief in the regulation knot. Ties were not a big item in his family. His Uncle Izzy, father of the cousin who had died in Spain, had never worn one, not even to his wedding. Ties were appendages of the upper classes, the oppressors. Marty did not buy Izzy's socialist bullshit, but if he did not get this goddamn tie knotted in five minutes, he might become a revolutionary.

Maybe his fingers were all thumbs because he did not know exactly why he was going on liberty. Unlike the rest of the sailors in Division B, he did not intend to get laid as often as possible until his money ran out. Marty was in love. He had told only one sailor on the ship about it – Flanagan, on the train ride out to Portland. He was sorry he had told him, because it sounded like he was bragging. It was impossible to explain what Sylvia Morison meant to him.

She had come to his bar mitzvah when he was fourteen, in a Cadillac long enough to show a movie in. Her mother was his mother's first cousin, but as far as they both were concerned, they were sisters. They had grown up on Hester Street on the Lower East Side in adjoining coldwater flats, the only girls in two families full of loud-mouthed brothers. Sophie Katz had married luck, as his mother used to put it. Sam Morison was an ugly schmuck, but he knew how to make money at everything from hotels to nightclubs to restaurants. He even made money in the Depression, when everyone else was losing his life savings.

Marty had danced with Sylvia at the bar mitzvah, in the upstairs room of Chasen's Restaurant on Fordham Road and the Grand Concourse. She smelled of flowers and had long eyelashes that seemed to cover half her cheeks when she lowered them and smiled shyly. He had frantically tried to think of jokes the comedians had told when they vacationed in the Catskills the previous summer. But his mind had been a blank.

He did not see her again for the next four years, although he heard a lot about her. He had always heard a lot about Sylvia – how smart she was in school, how she was always getting promoted two years instead of one while he was barely passing. That was why she was in college – some swank place called Radcliffe – while Marty was just getting out of high school.

When he decided to join the Navy, his mother had taken fifty dollars out of a drawer in her bedroom and said she wanted him to have a good time with it. 'Take one of your girlfriends to a show, dinner, the works,' she said.

Roth turned down the idea. He knew she was saving the

money for a new winter coat. She had to hide it, because if his father got his hands on it, he invariably lost it in the Thursday night card game at the Harry Kleindienst Political Club. He told her he did not have a girl who was worth spending that kind of money on. His mother had picked up the phone and called her cousin Sophie. Before he knew what was happening, he had a date with Sylvia Morison.

They went to the Rainbow Room for dinner and danced to Tommy Dorsey. This time Marty's mind was not a blank. Sylvia was tremendously impressed that he had joined the Navy. Pearl Harbor had made the Navy sound dangerous. He gave her a line about wanting to kill Japs and Germans because they were racists as well as no-good fascists. She moved closer to him and told him how much she admired his courage.

Much later, on Central Park West, she invited him into her apartment. Her parents were away. They were always away, it seemed, checking out new hotels Sam Morison had bought or was about to sell. Sylvia put on some Fred Astaire records and began telling him how *meaningful* she thought his decision was, how *purposeful*, as well as how brave. She had never thought of him, she had never thought of anyone in the Bronx, as having this sort of dedication, this sort of 'moral clarity'.

After that, Marty stopped listening closely. He had been trying to get up the nerve to kiss her, and maybe to let his hands stray up under and over those full breasts beneath her white silk blouse. Instead she kissed him, and then his hands were everywhere and so were hers. Soon they were in a pink and white bedroom, and in the living room Marty could hear Fred Astaire singing some love song in which he repeatedly declared he was in heaven.

Marty stayed in heaven until about 4 a.m. He was a little shocked to find out how much Sylvia liked to screw. It did not seem to fit her delicacy, her intelligence. He could only conclude it was a compliment to his courage, his moral clarity, as well as his equipment, which had heretofore only been tested hastily, furtively, on a few couches in the Bronx.

Jesus! Once more the goddamn knot had come apart. Maybe he ought to stay on board.

'Hey, Jewboy,' said a big dark voice. 'Lemmy help you out.'

Amos Cartwright towered over him. In his dress whites, he seemed to emanate darkness. Cartwright and everything else about his life on the *Jefferson City* were still unreal to Roth. He still did not like the idea of working in the bowels of the ship. He read the papers and knew that ships had a habit of sinking. He was not a coward. He was willing to take his chances on deck, manning guns, whatever. But he did not want to drown like an accident victim.

He had been even more dubious when he descended to the forward fire room on the voyage from Portland and found Watertender First Class Amos Cartwright in charge. What could a nigger possibly know about all this machinery? Roth looked up at miles of pipe and steel overhead and thought of the four decks between him and the sky. Water sloshed menacingly against the hull. There were no portholes. The only way out was the narrow hatch through which he had entered. He stood there, frantically trying to figure out how he could get a transfer.

'I know what you guys are thinkin',' Amos Cartwright said. 'How the fuck am I gonna get outa here when they abandon ship? Hell, it ain't that hard. Let's have a demonstration. You, Jewboy, you look about as scared shitless as any of them. Here's a stopwatch. When I yell abandon ship, you head for that door and keep goin' like electricity until you hit topside.'

Roth scrambled up ladders, darted down passageways, bounded through hatches, rocketed across compartments and up a final ladder to stagger gasping on to the rainswept main deck. He looked at the stopwatch and could not believe it. He had made it in thirty-two seconds.

Back in the fire room, Cartwright had given them a lecture on the importance of their jobs. He pointed to the looming twenty-foot-high boilers and explained that this was where they produced the superheated steam that travelled at six hundred pounds to the square inch through the maze of pipes to the forward engine room in the next compartment, where it powered the turbines that turned the *Jefferson City*'s four propellers.

'What you gonna do on liberty, Jewboy?' Cartwright asked as he knotted Roth's neckerchief. 'Goin' to make yourself a Hollywood starlet? Got an uncle at Metro-Golden-Mayer who'll fix you up?'

'The only uncle I got cuts suits on Seventh Avenue,' Roth said. 'When are you going to stop calling me Jewboy?'

'Don't you call me a nigger behind my back, like the rest of them?'

'No.'

He might think of Cartwright as a nigger, but he had not called him that. One thing, maybe the only thing, Marty Roth bought from his socialist Uncle Izzy was his talk about human rights and all men being equal in the United States of America. He agreed with him that Negroes were getting a lousy deal in the United States, almost as bad as the Jews got in Tzarist Russia.

Cartwright stared sceptically at him. 'You know you're the first Jewboy I ever met?' he said.

'You're the first Negro I ever talked to. If you call me Jewboy once more you'll be the last one.'

Cartwright chuckled. 'OK, sailor. You come on liberty with me. I'll show you what a good time in LA's really like.'

'Now remember,' Boats Homewood shouted as the Higgins boat approached the Pico Avenue landing. 'Liberty ends on the dock at 0400 hours. That's four a.m. to you greenhorns.'

Nobody seemed to pay much attention to him as the sailors of F Division scrambled up on the dock and headed inland. Flanagan found himself strolling beside Leo Daley. It was not the first time Daley had displayed a penchant for his company. Maybe it was because they were fellow Catholics. Unfortunately, Flanagan did not like him very much. Daley complained about everything in a bitter whiny way that got on Flanagan's nerves.

'Got any plans?' Daley said.

Flanagan shook his head. They headed across a long

pedestrian bridge that spanned the Los Angeles River and got them to the Long Beach Pike, the West Coast's biggest amusement park. They strolled along the midway past barkers urging them to see some beautiful ladies take it all off, swamis begging to read their palms and predict their fates, wheel-of-fortune spinners offering them a chance to double their money. The Hippodrome merry-go-round blared a military march. A roller coaster called the Cyclone Racer rumbled overhead. The smell of roasting popcorn, cooking hot dogs mingled in the air. It was like the boardwalk at Asbury Park, New Jersey, where Flanagan's father rented a house for a month each year.

Except for the women. There were no women like these on the Asbury Park boardwalk. All wore atrocious amounts of rouge and the cheapest imaginable skirts and blouses. There was not a decent looker in sight. Bowed legs, lantern jaws, flat noses assailed Flanagan's eyes. Several asked them if they would like to have a good time. If these were the sort of women who tempted sailors, Flanagan thought, Father Callow had nothing to fear. Frank Flanagan was guaranteed for the Jesuits, if the Japs did not get him first.

'Hey, let's try the Cyclone Racer,' Flanagan said.

Daley demurred. 'My stomach still hasn't settled from that ride from Portland.'

Ride. The word grated on Flanagan's ear. Daley did not even talk like a sailor. They settled for a spin on the whip. Ahead of them, a gunner's mate had a redheaded girl who screamed and threw herself against him with every whirl of the car. She was obviously a lady of the Pike but she was not quite as ugly as the ones still soliciting on the midway.

Daley pronounced the Pike a waste of time and suggested they head for Los Angeles. They boarded one of the Pacific Electric's big red cars and for forty-five cents were whizzed out of Long Beach's tawdry pleasures to the opulence of the city of the angels. The broad boulevards, the handsome mansions, the expensive restaurants were something to see. But all the doors were locked to sailors. The restaurant prices were breathtaking – $3.95 for a steak! One fifth of the twenty-one dollars they got paid each month.

They found themselves wandering, hot and hungry, along a seemingly endless boulevard. Ahead of them loomed a gleaming white church, with a wealth of exterior carvings and statuary of angels and saints. From one corner soared a tower at least a hundred feet high, with an inlaid tile dome. It was obviously Catholic, and the name on the sign out front, CHURCH OF ST SEBASTIAN, confirmed it. 'Listen,' Daley said, 'I got a cousin out here who's a nun.'

'A nun?' Flanagan said. He wondered if the California sun had cooked Daley's brain.

'I don't know what parish she's in. But if I could find her, I bet we could get a free meal. She'd introduce us to the pastor.'

'Let's try the Hollywood Canteen.'

Daley was adamant. He seemed to think the Canteen was full of starlets dying to seduce him. Maybe his cousin's mother superior would introduce them to some nice Catholic girls. 'Why don't you make a visit while I try to find someone in the rectory who can help us,' Daley said.

Flanagan strolled into the church and sat down in a rear pew, hoping the pastor would tell Daley to get lost. The interior of St Sebastian's was even more spectacular than the exterior. Polychrome murals of the Stations of the Cross glowed on the walls. Above the altar was a tabernacle of gilded bronze and behind it a great screen of carved and gilded wood. A pamphlet in the pew informed Flanagan that the church had been built by an oil magnate and his wife at a cost of ten million.

An immense statue of Jesus writhing on the cross dominated the right side of the nave. Several people were kneeling before it. Intimidated, Flanagan knelt too. He stared at the statue and began thinking of what Father Callow had told him about the gratitude he should feel for Jesus's sacrifice. The Saviour had died for him, to save his soul from damnation.

Jesus was also God, who had come to earth and taken a man's body to suffer and die on behalf of the sinful human race. Why? If God created the world and was omnipotent, why did he allow evil to rampage through His creation? Why did He have to go to the trouble of becoming a Jew in Roman Palestine and get himself crucified to redeem mankind? Father Callow said that was a mystery. More important was faith in Jesus's claim to be the Son of God, the redeemer, the fount of love.

Exaltation swirled in Flanagan's chest. He remembered a moment when he had stood on the Fordham campus looking across the flat roofs of the Bronx at twilight and thought about the sorrow, the pain, the disappointment in those modest apartments and houses. He wanted to comfort, to console, to encourage all those whose lives were pinched and battered and broken by the misery of the Great Depression that had filled the newspapers with tragedy and lamentation since he was six years old. How could he hope to do any of these things without the help of Jesus? He was only one individual. Through Jesus he could achieve power to help, heal, comfort millions.

'Excuse me. Do you know you're in Satan's clutches, sittin' here?'

There was a woman next to him in the pew. She was about his age, maybe a little older, with straight, shiny brown hair worn shoulder length and an oval face that reminded him of the movie star Jean Arthur. She had a sensitive, delicately curved mouth, a small fine nose, and bold blue eyes. Although her green sport coat and grey skirt were showing signs of wear, the net effect was spectacular. She looked about a thousand percent better than any woman Flanagan had seen on the Long Beach Pike.

'My name is Teresa Brownlow. I'm from the Adventist Church of the Second Coming. My father's the pastor. Each day I visit here to try to save at least one person – preferably a sailor like yourself.'

'Save?' Flanagan said.

'This is the headquarters of the devil beast. It's right in the Bible, if you want to read it. Revelations Thirteen. The Roman Church is the Antichrist we're expectin' in these last days. Why don't you come with me to my daddy's church? I guarantee you that you'll never be the same man again, if you find Jesus with his help.'

'You personally guarantee that?'

'I do,' she said, ignoring the mockery in his voice.

Daley hustled up to the pew. 'I got the address,' he whispered. 'She's in West Los Angeles. I called her and she said come on out. She can only see us for fifteen minutes in the parlour, and another nun has to be present. But she's going to ask the pastor to meet us.'

Flanagan thought about trekking across Los Angeles to spend fifteen minutes with a couple of nuns on the dubious chance they might persuade the pastor to give them a free meal. He compared this to finding Jesus with the help of blue-eyed Teresa Brownlow. She was the first Protestant he had ever talked to in his life. Maybe he would turn the tables on her, convert her and save her soul. At the very least, it would be interesting.

Daley was horrified when Flanagan informed him he was accepting Teresa's challenge. He refused to come along. In five minutes, Flanagan was riding back toward Long Beach with Teresa. About halfway there, they changed cars and headed for San Pedro. 'Ever save anyone from Shanghai Red's?' Flanagan asked.

'Oh, yes. Daddy and I have gone in there and saved I don't know how many,' she said.

'Where are you from?'

'Oklahoma. We came out here in 1935, when the dust storms blew all the farms away. My daddy likes to say the Lord dried up his church but He didn't dry up his faith. He brought most of his congregation out here with him.'

'I saw the movie *The Grapes of Wrath*. With Henry Fonda.'

'Yes. I saw it too.'

'Was it really that bad?'

The boldness faded from Teresa's blue eyes. She breathed a long trembling sigh. 'The Lord turned His face away from so many good people. I never have been able to understand it.'

Flanagan glimpsed in her pinched cheeks, her tight mouth, a misery beyond his comprehension. He was blundering into a part of America about which he knew nothing. 'We had a lot of people on relief in New York,' he said.

'We were too proud for that. We wouldn't ask for help. Awful things happened to some people.'

They got off the streetcar and walked through San Pedro. It was a cross between New York's Bowery and Greenwich Village, a warren of tottering flophouses, shabby cafés and thinly concealed bordellos, before which women lounged in the late afternoon sun. Sailors outnumbered civilians on every block. In a storefront in the middle of one of the grimier blocks, only about a dozen doors from the gaudy corner entrance of Shanghai Red's, was the Advent Church of the Second Coming.

On the second floor of Shanghai Red's Cafe, Harold Semple sat at the end of the bed, staring at the naked body of a prostitute named Helen. She looked older than his mother. Her narrow breasts flopped on her chest like empty sacks. Ugly varicose veins bulged on her calves. In the cavern between her thighs he thought he saw scabs. A foul smell had filled the room the moment she took off her dress.

'I'm sorry,' he said. 'I don't want to do it.'

'Hey, that's all right, sailor. Lot of guys don' wanna,' Helen said. 'Be surprised how many guys put on big act, come up here and just sit and look.'

Helen staggered to her feet, finished the drink Harold had bought her downstairs and put on her purple dress. She cinched the belt, fluffed her hennaed hair and held out her hand. 'Just gimmy ten bucks and I won't say a thing.'

'Ten? You said it was five.'

'It's ten now, sonny. Or do you wan' me to go downstairs and tell your pals you couldn't get it up?'

Tears in his eyes, Harold gave her the ten dollars. Downstairs, several hundred sailors and considerably fewer women sat at tables or reeled around the smoke-filled room, which reeked of spilled liquor and the chow mein the proprietor claimed he had learned to cook in Shanghai.

Helen hauled him back to the table where Jerome Wilkinson and his servitors were drinking boilermakers, shots of bourbon and glasses of beer. 'Wow,' Helen croaked, wang-wanging her hands as if Semple had the best equipment she had seen since the flood. 'You got a stud here, boys. Put him in the main battery turret. He knows how to fire a big one.'

'How much'd he pay you to say that?' asked a tall needle-nosed seaman first class.

'Ten bucks,' Helen said.

Everyone guffawed, and Boatswain's Mate Wilkinson bought Helen another drink. He pulled out his wallet to pay for it and cursed. 'Who's got some dough?'

No one volunteered a cent. 'Pay for that, Prettyboy,' Wilkinson said.

'That's all the money I've got,' Semple said, handing the waiter a dollar. 'I'm going back to the ship.'

'The hell you are,' Wilkinson said. 'This liberty's just warmin' up. We're gonna fill this wallet before midnight, and you're gonna help us. We'll have a good time in the bargain.'

He winked to his followers. Exultation glowed on their ugly faces. 'A little fag bashing, boss?' asked Kraus, a squat thick-necked brute who served as Wilkinson's lieutenant.

'You ready for it?'

'Let's go!'

Wilkinson borrowed five dollars from a boatswain's mate at a nearby table and they boarded a trolley that took them to downtown Los Angeles. Soon they were strolling through a mostly deserted park. It was about eight o'clock, and Semple was feeling queasy from the boilermakers he had been forced to drink on top of the foul chow mein at Shanghai Red's.

'Sit on that bench,' Wilkinson told him. 'You won't have to wait ten minutes for one to come along. We'll be in the bushes right over there.' He pointed to some shrubbery about ten feet away.

'What am I supposed to do?' Semple asked.

'You won't have to do a fuckin' thing. You're the bait, Prettyboy.'

In less than five minutes a man wearing a white suit and a yellow Panama hat strolled toward him on the darkened path. He had black and white shoes like Semple's father had worn to church on summer Sundays, before he lost his job at Ford. The man sat down on the bench, about three feet away. 'Hello,' he said. 'Are you waiting for a friend?'

'No,' Semple said.

'What brings you here?'

'I ran out of money. I didn't know what else to do.'

'I've got lots of money,' the man said. 'I've got a car right outside the park. What time do you have to go back to your ship?'

'Four a.m.'

'Lots of time. We could have a lot of fun together.'

The man had a deep, liquid voice. Semple wondered if he was an actor.

'What's your name?'

'Harold.'

'Mine's Peter.'

Suddenly Jerome Wilkinson and his four hulking followers surrounded them. 'What the fuck are you tryin' to pull with our shipmate?' the boatswain's mate snarled.

'Not a thing,' Peter said, trying to stand up. 'We were just talking.'

'The hell you say. You're a fuckin' queer. Sailors don't like queers. Don't you know that?'

'That's news to me,' the man said.

Wilkinson punched Peter in the face so hard he went backwards over the bench on to the grass. 'Grab him,' Wilkinson ordered.

The four dragged the groaning man across the grass into the shrubbery. Behind it was a secluded flower garden, with statuary and stone benches. Semple followed them dazedly, afraid to protest, terrified they would all end up in jail. One of the four extracted the man's wallet. 'How much?' Wilkinson asked.

'Plenty, boss.'

'You know what you're gonna do now? You're gonna taste some Navy cock,' Wilkinson said, standing over the man. 'You're gonna suck off each one of us.'

Someone dragged the man to his knees. 'No,' he sobbed. 'Please –'

It was all being done in darkness shot through with streaks of light from a park lamp on the walk, just beyond the bench. Semple only had glimpses of Wilkinson and the others unbuttoning their pants. he listened to their gurgles of laughter, Peter's strangled protests. Semple stumbled into the shrubbery and threw up. Oh God, he prayed, save me. Why did you condemn me to this hell on earth?

'Prettyboy,' Wilkinson barked. 'Where the hell are you? It's your turn.'

'No,' he sobbed. 'I don't want to.'

'What the fuck are you talkin' about?' Wilkinson dragged him over to the man. 'Unbutton his fuckin' pants, boys.'

The laughing foursome swiftly obeyed. One of them grabbed Semple's penis and thrust it into Peter's mouth. He felt more than his penis – he felt his whole self sliding down a tunnel of soft slithery flesh. Sempleness was being obliterated, Haroldness was vanishing. His penis swelled as it had in midnight moments in his bed when he let his hand caress it. That was supposed to be a sin, yet everybody including his older brothers laughed about jerking off, but this was unquestionably sin beyond laughter into terror, mystery and pleasure, incredible shivers of these three words in one enormous *rush* down Peter's gurgling throat.

Oh, God, not my fault. Why didn't you stop it?

And what came next. Why didn't He stop that? Wilkinson and the four apes began punching and kicking Peter until he lay on the grass moaning and sobbing, begging them to stop. That only brought more laughter for the fucking fag crybaby, another round of punches and kicks. Semple could only conclude God was not listening. He seemed to have taken the night off.

'Niggers and Jews. We got a lot in common,' Amos Cartwright said. 'I been thinkin' about it. Solomon, your old Bible king, he married the Queen of Sheba, right? She was as black as I am.'

'Hey, I haven't thought about the Bible since my bar mitzvah,' Marty Roth said.

'You oughta think about it. I read that book three times before I was your age.'

'The hell you say.'

'Truth.'

Roth burped spectacularly. He had just downed one of the most fantastic dinners he had ever eaten, pork fried in a fatty gravy that tasted of strange vegetables. He did not eat pork regularly, because his maternal grandfather, who lived with them in their Bronx apartment, refused to touch it. But he had no objection to it. He was an American. This was American food he had never tasted before. It was cooked in a little hole in the wall in South Los Angeles, in a section of the city that was almost entirely black.

But the food was only a small part of his exhilaration. Throughout dinner, Cartwright had talked to Roth about what a watertender did, why it was the most important rating on the ship. Watertenders had to know exactly how to mingle oil, air and water inside the boiler to create the superheated steam that was the lifeblood of the *Jefferson City*'s power system. Too much air and not enough water, and the boiler's pipes could melt. Too much water and not enough air, and water could get into the turbines, wrecking them. They had to be constantly alert for signs a boiler was faltering under the wear and tear of this terrific demand.

Brains, that was what Cartwright insisted a watertender and any sailor who worked in the fire room had to have. He assumed Roth had them because he was Jewish. Roth was tempted to tell him flatly that he was wrong. He had never seen much point in studying. His father had got an engineering degree from City College after World War I, and what good had it done him? The textile plant that he had managed in Port Chester had gone bankrupt in 1933 and he had been glad to get a boring job in the US Customs Department, inspecting imported cloth. But something about Cartwright's presumption, his pride in the importance of the forward fire room and his delight in explaining how it worked stirred curiosity in Roth. Maybe he could learn a few things about those bewildering pipes and gauges and boilers. He would give it a try.

Outside the restaurant, four young blacks strutted past them wearing the wildest zoot suits Roth had ever seen. The trousers were bright blue and ballooned out at least six inches on each side of their legs. Their yellow coats almost reached their knees. Gold chains clanked beneath them.

'Whyn't you take the fuckin' money you spend on them duds and buy yourself some books?' Amos Cartwright said. 'Put somethin' in your head instead of on your ass.'

'Go tell it to the admiral, old man,' one of them said.

'I did tell it to him. That's why I'm wearin' this rate,' Cartwright said.

He pointed to the three-bladed propeller on his upper sleeve, with WT and three inverted stripes beneath it.

The young blacks just stared and shrugged. 'What's it say?' one asked.

'Watertender first class.'

That broke them up. 'Shee-it,' another one said. 'What kinda brains it take to tend *water*? My momma can do that.'

'Your momma probably too busy tendin' your uncles and cousins to tend anything else,' Cartwright said.

'Your momma look like she tended a gorilla.'

'Hey, you're pretty good at the dozens,' Cartwright said. 'Let's go down to Jubilee's and I'll buy you boys a drink. I ain't as mean as I look.'

'Is that a fact?' one of them asked Roth.

'Absolutely,' Roth said, amazed that a riot had not started over the exchange of insults about their mothers. In the Bronx, where he and his friends had had a few brushes with Irish gangs, those accusations would have started a neighbourhood war. He knew nothing about the Negro insult game called the dozens.

'How come you got to go to an ofay for a buddy?'

'He ain't an ofay. He's a Jew,' Cartwright said. 'Us and them, we're on the short end of the stick and always has been. Don't you read what Hitler's doin'?'

'Hey, what the fuck we care about Hitler? It's the Japs that want to chew our asses off. This is California, old man.'

'We're goin' out there to stop them in just about two weeks. Come on and have a drink with us and wish us luck.'

'Two weeks we'll be in the Army. We're goin' to have our own good time tonight. Coupla lamb daps waitin' to fuss over these duds. But here's one for luck, old man.' The two of them tapped Cartwright's outstretched hand.

'The minute you get in that Army, start buckin' for sergeant,' he said. 'Watch what a sergeant does. Write it all down and read it over and over.'

'Yeah. Yeah.'

Cartwright sighed and led Roth down the street to Jubilee's, another storefront with a bar full of drinkers and a jazz combo playing blues in the back. 'I been to Harlem and North Philadelphia and West Baltimore spreadin' that message,' he said. 'Rise up, You got to bide your time and rise up!'

'How'd you get your rate?'

'I asked Captain McKay if I could study for it, and he said it was fine with him.'

'Captain McKay? The same guy we just got?'

'Yeah. He was captain of a destroyer I was on. Course I always had it in mind. My granddaddy was a rated man, a boiler tender, before World War I. The Navy had seven or eight hundred rated niggers back then. After the war they only enlisted us as mess stewards, and you had to be from the South. They figured Southern niggers knew their place. I had to move to Charleston to get in the fuckin' Navy!'

For a moment the expression on Amos Cartwright's face made Roth wonder if he was going to throw his drink through the mirror on the other side of the bar. But he continued in the same calm voice. 'Captain McKay knew all about it. He's a historian, you know. He remembers things. His people went out to Kansas before the Civil War to fight the slavers, and that made him inclined to help me out. Keep your mouth shut about it. He's goin' to have enough probelms on the Jeff City without everyone knowin' he gave Nigger Cartwright a chance to get his rate.'

On the tiny stage at the rear, a big black woman began singing,

'If you want the thrill of love,
I've been through the mill of love.
Old love, new love, every love but true love.
Love for sale. Appetizin' young love for sale.'

'That's Big Bertha,' Cartwright said. 'You and me, we're gonna buy some of that love before the night's over.'

Cartwright saw the alarm on Roth's face and started to laugh. 'Don't worry. She'll find a filly your age. Drink up.'

'No – listen. I'm sorry.'

He wanted to be this man's kind of sailor. But he had to remain faithful to Sylvia Morison and those hours in that pink and white bedroom on Central Park West. He had that memory at the centre of his body and he did not want to let it go. He started to explain it to Cartwright, sure he would never understand. To his amazement the watertender nodded. 'I shipped out that way once. It's OK. I just wish you luck. When I got back to Philadelphia, I found another guy, bigger 'n' blacker than me in her bedroom.'

Marty Roth gulped his drink. The liquor swirled in his brain. He had never drunk anything stronger than beer before in his life. Cartwright had had at least six bourbons during dinner, with no visible effect. What was happening here? Roth felt as if he were voyaging down a midnight river into a dark sea. The dim bar, the Negros faces all around him, Cartwright hulking over him – was he being summoned like his first cousin, the family hero, whose picture stood bordered in black on his grandfather's dresser?

Roth thought of the fire room fifty feet below the main deck, the looming boilers, the gauges, the challenge of learning how the *Jefferson City* worked. Was life, opportunity, standing at this bar, drinking with him and Amos Cartwright? Or death in an explosion of steam and flame in the Pacific's depths?

'Ah tell you, Jesus is waiting' for your hand. He has His hand out to you, just as my hand is out here. Ah'm speakin' for Him. Ah'm reachin' for Him. Is anybody ready to reach back? Is anyone *anxious* enough about the whirlpool of sin and sorrow and war in which we are plunged in these last days? Is anyone *anxious*, is anyone *courageous* enough to seize this lovin' hand?'

The Reverend James Brownlow prowled the aisle of his church, his hand out, madness or divinity – take your pick – dancing in his blue eyes. He was a big man, as broad as Boats Homewood and a good three inches taller. He was at least

87

sixty, possibly seventy. His skin was as brown and corrugated as the bark of an ancient oak.

'Someone in this church is ready for Jesus. I can feel it in my gut. Who is it? Who's ready?'

'I am.' Frank Flanagan yelled and leaped to his feet.

Was it a gag? he wondered as he lunged toward the leathery hand and saw the joy spilling across James Brownlow's haggard face. He was one of those men who the last ten years in America had battered. Flanagan knew his story. Teresa had triumphantly introduced him to her father and he had eaten supper with them. He had heard about the prosperous church in the wheatlands of Oklahoma that the drought and dust had swept away. As he listened to Brownlow talk, Flanagan had grasped the inner drama of this storefront church, this congregation which had to be scoured from the flophouses and bars for each service. This man was daring God to fail him again. Each time he held a service, he was throwing down a gauntlet on high. He was saying, I dare you not to send me some souls to save.

Flanagan had joined Teresa in prowling the alleys and back streets of San Pedro for recruits for the evening service. They sat on the metal chairs now, a collection of derelicts lured by the promise of doughnuts and coffee, sailors out of money and looking for someplace to sober up before going back to their ships, a half dozen regulars, remnants of those who had followed Brownlow from Oklahoma.

The glow of pleasure on Teresa's face doubled Flanagan's sense of reward, even if it did not add an iota of genuine faith to the burlesque he was performing. But it broke the fog of lethargy and alcohol into which the congregation had been sinking. Another sailor, two derelicts, a withered woman from the Oklahoma remnant also seized the Reverend Brownlow's hand and allowed him to lead them to the front of the church, where they all knelt before the pulpit.

'Lord,' he roared in that voice that mingled awe and anger, 'Lord God Jesus Christ, Son of Revelation, Bless these souls as they begin the perilous voyage of faith. Keep them safe from the whirlpools of doubt, the typhoons of despair, the shipwrecks of damnation. Protect them from the noonday devil and the midnight demon. Keep them strong in their faith unto a blessed eternity.'

Teresa rippled the keys of a small organ and began to sing.

> *'Every day with Jesus*
> *Is sweeter than the day before.*
> *Every day with Jesus*
> *I love him more and more.'*

Beside Flanagan one of the derelicts was singing the words in a croaking voice that might have come from the grave. A tremendous crash interrupted this dubious harmony. A sailor had come flying through the front window of the church to flatten the gold-lettered cardboard sign that hung there and landed on his back in the aisle.

It was Jack Peterson. He stood up, shook broken glass out of his hat and yelled, 'Anybody here from the *Jefferson City?*'

'Excuse me,' Flanagan said and headed for the street.

Peterson was fighting three sailors, who outweighed him by a grand total of at least two hundred pounds. One was a gunner's mate with red, white and blue anchors tattooed on the backs of his huge fists. The second was a boatswain's mate with a red moon of a face and a fifty-four-inch chest. The third was a smaller gunner's mate who looked as if he was one quarter shark. His mouth was a mean slash above an almost nonexistent jaw. Each looked capable of murdering his mother. Jack was too drunk to register this fact. 'I'll show you crumbs who's got a yellow belly,' he yelled.

He took a swing that would have annihilated all of them if it had landed. Fortunately, his opponents were not in much better shape. They weaved around him, getting ready for a united rush. Flanagan grabbed the big gunner's mate and belted him half way across the street. Whirling, he caught the smaller gunner's mate with a terrific punch in the stomach. He staggered away, puking whisky.

'You fuckin' –'

The boatswain's mate charged Flanagan, fist high. 'Watch out, kid, he's got brass knucks,' Peterson yelled.

Jack tripped the behemoth as he lumbered past and he went sprawling on his belly. Peterson kicked him in the face and he rolled away howling, abandoning his weapon.

'Goddamn,' Peterson said, 'I always meant to buy one of these.'

He picked up the wicked-looking piece of moulded metal and clamped his fist inside it.

'Destroyers,' roared one of the gunner's mates. 'Get the fuckin' yellow cruiser bastards.'

Sailors poured out of Shanghai Red's at the end of the block. About ten of them came at Peterson and Flanagan on the dead run, several wielding whisky bottles and the legs of chairs. Flanagan thought they were finished.

Out of an alley charged a massive sailor who hit this wave of destruction head down from the starboard side and demolished them. He waded among them throwing bodies in all directions.

'Thank Christ, it's Homewood,' Peterson yelled. 'If he's drunk enough, he'll take on the whole goddamn fleet.'

'*Jefferson City*,' bellowed Homewood. '*Rally round the fuckin' flag.*'

He charged another ten-man wave single-handed, as Flanagan and Peterson turned to face an assault from the rear. Jablonsky and several other familiar faces from F Division waded into the fray along with dozens of sailors Flanagan had never seen before. He took on a runty machinist's mate who tried to kick him in the stomach. He stiffened him with a right jab and finished him with a left hook, thanking God he had paid attention to the boxing lessons the Navy had given them in boot camp. A moment later someone spun him around and gave him a terrific shot in the eye. He reeled away and got an equally bad clip in the lip. It was a mêlée now, with no way to protect yourself. There were at least a hundred sailors pounding each other all over the street.

Someone hit Flanagan from behind with what felt like a full bottle of whisky. He went down on all fours. Whistles began shrilling. 'Shore Patrol,' someone shouted. But the announcement did not diminish the ferocity of the battle. Through a break in the writhing bodies Flanagan saw Teresa

Brownlow and her father standing in the doorway of their church, dismay on their faces. He felt an enormous rush of sympathy for them.

Peterson got knocked down and crawled over to him. He looked deliriously happy. 'We may not be any good at fightin' the fuckin' Japs, but we do a hell of a job on each other,' he yelled. Someone kicked Flanagan in the side of the head and that was the last thing he remembered for a while.

Can This Be Love?

'Ensign Schnable, you're shitfaced.'

'Lieutenant Jackson, you're blotto.'

'What else is there to do when you're stuck on a fucking cruiser?'

'Absolutely agree. Flattop at Savo Island would have sunk whole goddamn Jap fleet. Admirals don't know what the fuck they're doing.'

'Need us. Strategic geniuses.'

'Absolutely.'

'Some Navy.'

'Some war.'

'Hey, listen. Could be worse. We're still alive for Chrissake.'

'Just barely.'

Lieutenant Junior Grade Andrew Jackson was the senior flier aboard the USS *Jefferson City*. Ensign Donald Schnable was the junior pilot. They regularly commiserated with each other about their sad fates, to be assigned to fly the slow-moving fabric biplanes that the *Jefferson City* carried in her hangar when they should be on an aircraft carrier flying Skyhawks or Douglas dive bombers, sinking Jap ships and becoming famous.

Jackson was from the mountains of Tennessee. He had a hefty slope-shouldered build and a wide reckless mouth. At flight school he had been Schnable's instructor. Irked by the assignment, Jackson had added to the course the art of zooming under bridges and around smokestacks, daring his students to imitate him. Schnable, a compact pink-cheeked German-American from Long Island, was the only one who followed Jackson everywhere. Unfortunately, an admiral happened to be sunbathing when they made a pass over a Key West beach at an altitude of ten feet. Instructor and student were assigned to the *Jefferson City* when Schnable graduated.

The fliers were exchanging their profound thoughts in their stateroom aboard the dry-docked *Jefferson City*. 'Holy shit,' Jackson said, peering at his watch. 'We're gonna miss West's party.'

'Not *his* party. Some guy named Mayer. Got the address right here,' Schnable said.

Montgomery West had invited all the officers on the *Jefferson City* to a party being given for him and Mickey Rooney by Louis B. Mayer, a name which meant nothing to Jackson, Schnable or anyone else on the ship. They had no idea Mayer was the head of Metro-Goldwyn-Mayer, the Cominch of Hollywood.

'Transportation,' Schnable said. 'Where do we get some transportation?'

'Motor pool,' Lieutenant Jackson said.

They made their way to the motor pool and strode into the compound looking as authoritative as possible. 'Let's take the Cadillac,' Jackson said.

In a few minutes, using the knowledge of engine technology they had acquired at flight school, they had the motor purring. At the Navy yard gate, the Marine sentry came to attention but his eyes bulged with alarm. 'You got permission to take the admiral's car, Lieutenant?' he said.

'Of course, I've got permission. The admiral happens to be my goddamn father,' Jackson said.

They headed for Los Angeles at suicidal speed, convinced, like most fliers, that they were immortal.

In a bedroom at the Coronado Hotel, thirty-seven-year-old Lieutenant Commander Edwin Moss, the gunnery officer of the USS *Jefferson City*, was making love to his wife. It was not very good. Eleanor just lay there, letting him do it. They had had a nasty argument over lunch about whether he should try to get transferred off the *Jefferson City*. He felt the new captain was going to need all the help he could get from his senior officers. Eleanor was convinced Moss was going to ruin his career if he stayed on board.

When they married in 1932, Eleanor knew absolutely nothing about the Navy. Her father was a New York banker. She had gone to college in Emmitsburg, Maryland, at Mount St Mary's. Moss, the son of a Presbyterian minister from Morristown, New Jersey, had been amazed to find himself in love with a Catholic. Now, three children and ten years later, he was wondering if he had made a mistake – and what he could do about it.

He had never been one of the wild men of the class of 1927. On their midshipman cruises, he had visited famous cathedrals, mosques, temples, instead of famous whorehouses. He had liked the idea of marrying someone with a strong sense of morality, with a spiritual life. But trying to raise three children on a Navy salary had severely diminished Eleanor's interest in sex. Simultaneously, she had begun taking a dislike to the Navy. She found fault with the promotion system, particularly at the top, where according to rumour so many men became admirals thanks to political pull or family connections. This seemed to be the main topic of conversation among the Navy wives in Norfolk.

Moss was inclined to dismiss most of these tales of influence and favouritism. He had moved up to his present rank with no difficulty by doing a good job, no matter where he was assigned. He was not stupid about trying to get good assignments, of course. Everyone with brains and ambition did that. He had gone for gunnery because that was a fast promotion track. Captains, admirals, paid attention to the performance of a gunnery officer. Gunnery was what the Navy was all about, when you got down to essentials.

Moss was not sure whether he was disenchanted with Eleanor or with marriage or with the Catholic Church running his sex life. He only knew he was very tired of having to wait until his wife took her temperature and consulted her menstrual calendar before he found out whether they could have intercourse. They were practising rhythm to avoid having another child. Eleanor would not even consider the possibility of getting a diaphragm or letting him use a condom. Birth control was immoral. It was a belief she held far more fervently than almost anything else on her theological-moral spectrum. It made absolutely no sense to Moss, and this conflict made it difficult for him to accept Eleanor's advice on his naval career or anything else.

Tall and stoop-shouldered, with a big bony nose, Moss knew he was no Adonis. But Eleanor was not exactly Betty Grable either. Her body was built on his own elongated lines, without much on top – or on the bottom, for that matter. Moss was frequently struck by the way the bachelors on the ship, retailing their conquests, smacked their lips over a woman's rump. 'She had the greatest ass I've ever seen,' Lieutenant Robert Mullenoe said about a triumph he had scored on their one-night layover (an apt term for Mullenoe) in Portland. Eleanor had no ass worth mentioning. It was practically flat.

Finished, Commander Moss lay beside his wife. He did not smoke, so he could not light a cigarette, à la lovers on the stage and screen. 'I wish I never wrote you those letters,' he said. 'It'd be better if you didn't know what's happened on the ship.'

'I thought sharing that sort of thing with your wife was what marriage was all about,' Eleanor said.

Lately Eleanor had been overusing that phrase. She was too quick to tell him what marriage was all about. Yet she was right. He had believed in total frankness, total honesty, total sharing between man and woman. They had discussed the subject in infinite detail during his last year at Annapolis, when they had been engaged and he had endured torments of desire whenever he kissed Eleanor or even held her hand.

'It is,' he admitted. 'But what to do about it is something only I can decide.'

'Why? I graduated summa cum laude, you may recall. I've been in the Navy almost as long as you have. I have a brain, Commander Moss, and I've got a right to a few opinions about this wonderful organization. I was talking it over with Anne Marie Condon only a few days ago. She said there are certain ships that become pariahs. Everyone gets blamed for being aboard them when they mess up. As one of the senior officers, you're more likely than most to get tarred.'

'We didn't mess up! It's all very confused. Captain Kemble may have done the right thing. Only a board of inquiry can decide that. I only know Kemble is one of the finest officers I've ever served under. He has the highest standards and he tried to enforce them. But that fellow Parker, the Executive Officer, constantly frustrated him. That's why I think the new captain needs me. He needs support.'

'What thanks will you get for this noble gesture?'

'Eleanor, this isn't the peacetime Navy. We're fighting a war. What do you think the people at the Bureau of Navigation will say if I ask for a transfer from a ship that's about to return to the South Pacific?'

'Ask for a transfer to another ship that's going there. Ye gods, do I have to draw a diagram for you?'

'No. I'm very good at drawing diagrams, thank you. Let's get dressed and go to this Hollywood party.'

As if the movement was created by a director's guiding hand, the crowd on the terrace parted, and there, wearing a silver mink over a gold lamé evening dress, stood Ina Severn. 'Ina,' Montgomery West said. 'I was hoping you'd come.'

'How could I say no? I was so glad to hear you're safely home again.'

'Only for two weeks.'

'Really? Hardly worth the trip, I should say.'

'That depends to some extent on you.'

She smiled. Montgomery West could not tell if she was bored, amused or pleased. West found himself writhing with the same mixture of confusion and desire that had disoriented him since the first day he saw Ina Severn. Why did everything he said to this woman sound like lines from a third-rate script? She had him completely intimidated. A year ago, he had been getting twice her salary, he had been ready to move up to A pictures. For a moment West hated this cool remote bitch. But a touch of his hand on her arm as he led her into the party was enough to change his mind. He wanted this woman. He did not understand why, and that infuriated him all over again.

There was some truth to Captain Kemble's suggestion that Montgomery West did not really know who he was. Like many handsome men, he had used women to define himself thus far in his life. In the beginning, Ina Severn had been a definition that revolved around the word class. Now she had become something else, something connected with this war and a new idea of himself.

Maybe there was nothing to it. Maybe he just wanted to make a difficult score. After eight years in Hollywood with starlets throwing themselves into bed with him in the hope that he would mention their names to his big-shot uncle, Montgomery West was ready for a challenge. He had heard Ina Severn had refused to sleep with Louis B. Mayer and that was why, after arriving with a hit comedy from London in her credits, she had been banished to the B's. Around the studio's executive offices, according to Uncle Mort, she was known as the English icicle.

'My goodness, Monty,' Ina said, gazing at the crowd spilling off the terrace and down the lawn to the swimming pool. 'I thought Mr Mayer abolished this sort of thing.'

'What God disposes, he can also undispose,' West said.

Among the two-tone suits and glittering dresses were the white uniforms of his fellow officers of the USS *Jefferson City*. Down by the pool, Ensign Richard Babyface Meade was demonstrating to a blonde starlet named Maggie MacGuire a dance called the Solomon Islands shimmy. Other ensigns and lieutenants were manoeuvring around similar targets of opportunity.

Most of the big shots and reporters were clustered around Mayer and Mickey Rooney on the terrace. No doubt Uncle Mort would tell his nephew he had been included in this Toast to the Heroes party only through his good offices. But it was still pretty galling to be invited and then ignored by everyone above the associate producer level. He remarked this wryly to Ina

Severn as he led her to the bar and ordered a Pimm's Cup for her. Again, all he got was that cool enigmatic smile.

One of his old girlfriends, red-haired Helena Hopkins, rushed up to him. 'Oh, Monty,' she said in her breathy way, 'is it true what I hear? You're coming back as a star?'

'I thought he *was* a star,' Ina Severn said.

Helena gave her a baffled glare and returned to the arm of Lieutenant Robert Mullenoe, who no longer seemed to regard West as the carrier of an obscure Asiatic disease. 'Great party, West,' he said.

'Well,' Ina Severn said, after a sip of her Pimm's Cup. 'Tell me all about your heroic deeds on the high seas.'

'There's not much to tell,' he said. 'We have met the enemy, but they are definitely not ours. They put a shell into our midsection and we reeled back here for repairs.'

'That script will never make it through the front office,' Ina said in her wry English comedienne manner. Without any warning her tone changed. 'How terribly discouraging. Did you lose any men?'

'Fifteen in my division,' West said. 'About fifty all told.'

'Oh.'

Montgomery West was amazed. She seemed genuinely distressed. Did Ina Severn have emotions, after all?

'Hey, Lieutenant,' said a deep hearty voice. 'How about passing some of that glamour around?'

Daniel Boone Parker, the executive officer of the USS *Jefferson City*, beamed at Ina. He patted his big belly like a benevolent paterfamilias.

'Commander, I'd like you to meet Ina Severn, one of the best actresses in Hollywood.'

'I saw you in *Two's a Crowd* in London when I was with the embassy as a naval aide,' Parker said. 'Why don't they give you that kind of comedy part here?'

'One of the many mysteries of Hollywood,' Ina said.

Across the lawn strolled Louella Parsons, gossip columnist supreme, and one of her favourite sources, a sour-mouthed character actor named Jack O'Rourke. He had played the villain in a hundred B movies. He was one of Uncle Mort's closest friends.

'Monty darling,' Lolly said, with a smile that belonged on the face of a werewolf, 'I've been looking in every nook and cranny for you. I want to be the first to break the story.'

'What story?'

'It's all over town. How you were the officer of the deck when a man fell overboard and you personally jumped in to rescue him.'

'Not really. I . . . wanted to rescue him, but the Captain thought otherwise. There were submarines reported in the area. So . . . we kept going.'

'Oh?' Lolly said. 'That's not very heroic, is it?'

'You started the story at the wrong end, Lolly,' Jack O'Rourke said. 'What you really want to know is how many ships Monty sank off Guadalcanal. I understand it was four Jap cruisers.'

Was someone trying to make him look like a fool by spreading these stories around? West wondered. He ransacked his list of enemies and could not imagine how any of them knew enough to ask these nasty questions. It has to be someone aboard the *Jefferson City*.

'I'm afraid that's another rumour,' he said. 'I wasn't even on the bridge when we –'

'What?' Lolly said. 'If it's top secret darling, I swear I won't print it. But I'm dying to know.'

She looked giddily around the circle of sycophants who had gravitated toward her like moths to a destructive flame. Everyone was cringingly nice to Lolly; a single puff of her angry breath could wither a career.

'It would be so thrilling to hear the story of an action at sea from your lips. We poor ignorant civilians on the home front need to know more about your heroism. We need hope, faith. The enemy seem to be winning everywhere.'

Montgomery West glanced uneasily at Commander Parker. 'I think you ought to answer that, Commander. I don't want to give away any secrets.'

Daniel Parker took a long swallow of his drink. 'Do you know where Savo Island is, Miss Parsons?'

'Savo Island?' Lolly said. He might as well have asked

her if she knew the location of the after engine room on the *Jefferson City*.

'It's a volcano. An extinct volcano off Guadalcanal,' Commander Parker said. 'At a recent battle around Savo, we took on a Japanese fleet three times our size. When it was over, a half-dozen of their destroyers were on the bottom and the rest were running for their lives. Right, West?'

Monty suddenly remembered the way he had felt the day Uncle Mort had called him to his office and read him his 'biography'. It told him and the public about his troubled boyhood as the son of a wealthy mother with several divorces, his career as a merchant seaman, gun runner in South American revolutions, and oil prospector in Mexico. West had felt as if someone was turning him inside out and shaking his guts onto the floor. He felt the same way now.

'Yeah,' he said. He was looking away from Parker at Ensign Meade and Lieutenant Mullenoe. There was only one word to describe the expression on their faces: loathing.

'And what did you have to do with it, Monty?'

'Nothing,' West said. 'Commander Parker and the captain were on the bridge. I was in main forward – the main battery control station – dialling in ranges. I mean . . . the machines do all the work.'

'As the daughter of a British naval officer, Ina, what do you think of all this?' Jack O'Rourke asked.

West was astounded by this revelation about Ina's parentage. He was even more astonished by her next words. 'I'm awed by the courage of any man who fights on the sea, Jack. It's much more harrowing than being a soldier, in my opinion. On land, if you lose, you can run away. On a ship, the sea is another enemy, waiting to devour you.'

'Are you suggesting Mickey Rooney is not a hero because he joined the Army?' Lolly bristled. 'Really, Miss Severn, I think you're letting your British prejudices run away with you. In America we regard the Army and the Navy as equals in heroism!'

'I agree, of course,' Ina said, wide-eyed at such brainlessness on the loose.

'Now, Monty, there's one more rumour I want to check

99

out, as a good reporter,' Louella said. 'Is it true that you're leaving the USS *Jefferson City* to serve as the naval adviser for a series of pictures being planned at M-G-M?'

'That's more than a rumour,' Jack O'Rourke said. 'I was talking to one of the top executives yesterday. He said the contract was all drawn up. All they need is the OK from the Navy Department.'

'I can't think of a better man for the job – except myself,' Commander Parker said.

It was Uncle Mort. This was his cute-vicious way of rescuing him from death and simultaneously re-launching his career. Montgomery West looked around him at his fellow officers. On the faces of those near enough to hear the conversation with Louella Parsons, West saw a range of expressions, from glum envy to wry cynicism. They all assumed Montgomery West was going to take this offer. At Savo Island he had discovered that anyone, even a Hollywood star, could get killed in the South Pacific. He was jumping ship, like the phoney he was, having acquired an ersatz battle star.

'Is *that* rumour true, Monty?' Ina Severn said.

Incredible, the sadness in her voice, her eyes. Did only he hear it? On her face was a wisp of that enigmatic smile.

Montgomery West shook his head. 'When the *Jefferson City* sails in two weeks, I'm going to be aboard,' he said.

For a moment he could not decide which he liked more, the admiration in Ina's eyes or the amazement on the faces of his fellow officers. Mullenoe looked particularly astonished. On Jack O'Rourke's face was something almost as satisfying, dismay at the thought of what Mort was going to say to him when he failed to return with West's name on that contract.

'I've heard of headstrong actors, but this tops them all,' O'Rourke said.

Those glum words jerked Montgomery West back to reality. He stood there dazed, appalled at what he had just done. Ina Severn had extracted that answer from him. She and those arrogant Annapolis bastards like Mullenoe. For a moment he felt nothing but rage. What did this English bitch in her gold lamé dress know about staying at General

Quarters for thirty-six-hours, staring into the sun and the darkness until your eyelids felt like they were peeling off? Why did he give a damn about the opinion of these professional sailors with their ridiculous rules and regulations, which did nothing to prevent a man from getting incinerated or drowned?

A big arm circled his shoulder. It belonged to Lieutenant Robert Mullenoe, Annapolis 1931. 'West,' he said, 'I can't believe it. You're turning into a goddamn Navy man.'

'Don't pay any attention to these birds,' Lieutenant Andrew Jackson said, casually peeling a redheaded starlet off the arm of a *Jefferson City* turret officer. 'They can't see beyond the horizon. We're the guys who tell'm what they're shooting at.'

'Exactly,' Ensign Donald Schnable said, performing the same operation on an engineering officer's sloe-eyed brunette.

'You're fliers,' the brunette said, woozily running a finger over the wings on Schnable's chest. 'Were you at the battle of Midway?'

'Were we at the battle of Midway? What a question,' Lieutenant Jackson said.

'Let us answer that question,' said the turret officer, regaining his redhead. The brunette was similarly reclaimed.

'No respect, that's the problem of the Navy Air Corps when you're stuck on a goddamn cruiser,' Andrew Jackson said.

'Good thing we found the bar,' Schnable said. They were drinking straight Scotch in water glasses. 'This stuff isn't bad.'

'It's older'n you are,' the bartender said.

A stentorian voice reached them across the lawn. Admiral Tomlinson, the commander of the Navy Yard, was talking to the *Jefferson City*'s Executive Officer. 'The Marine sentry gave me a very good description of them,' he roared. 'I'm certain they're here. He said they wore wings. I'll put angels' wings on them before I'm through with them.'

'Jesus,' Ensign Schnable said. They retreated into the depths of the mansion, where they found a magnificent buffet and several dozen people sitting at tables feasting on roast beef, turkey and innumerable side dishes. 'Need some food if we got to retreat,' Lieutenant Jackson said. 'My granddaddy fought with Stonewall, you know. That was one thing he learned. Always raid the hen coop.'

He tucked the entire turkey under his arm. Ensign Schnable seized two drumsticks, which had already been detached. They wandered through the dining room, smiling and nodding to all sorts of familiar faces. 'He hasn't got a leg to stand on,' Schnable said, gesturing with the drumsticks.

Lieutenant Jackson paused to examine the food on the plate of a woman who had an incredible resemblance to Bette Davis. 'Is that caviar?' he said, dipping his finger in a black sauce.

'Really!' she cried and stormed out of the room.

Sitting at the table was a guy who was a dead ringer for William Powell. 'Hey, buddy,' Schnable said. 'Where did you ditch Myrna Loy?'

Both fliers thought this was hysterical until the guy replied, 'She's home with the flu.'

'You mean that really *was* Bette Davis?' Jackson said.

'Here she comes with Mr Mayer,' Powell said. 'I suggest you go that way. Mingle in the crowd around the pool.'

He pointed to a side door. As they exited at top speed they caught a glimpse of a short man with a politician's paunch and a wide unpleasant mouth shouting, 'You! You two schlemiels! Stop!'

'Schlemiels,' Jackson said as they paused in a drawing room to wipe their hands on the furniture and down a few chunks of turkey. 'What the hell does that mean?'

'Trouble,' Schnable said, glancing nervously over his shoulder as Mayer kicked the door they had locked.

'I'm going to report you to the Admiral for insulting my guests,' yelled their host.

Andrew Jackson chomped a final hunk of turkey and gulped his drink. 'Let's find us a nice little cloud of fluff and hide in it for a while, Ensign.'

'Roger, Lieutenant.'

They climbed out a window and rejoined the crowd

around the pool. This time they gathered an appreciative audience of starlets, who listened raptly to their dive-bombing exploits at Midway. Without warning, Mayer burst into their coterie. 'You two have to leave,' he said. 'You may be heroes, but drunk and disorderly heroes I won't stand for in my own house.'

'Sir,' Jackson said. 'Do you know you have an uncanny resemblance to Admiral Yamamoto? When my buddy and I see a picture of him we go beserk. Right, Ensign Schnable?'

'Right.'

Jackson seized Mayer under the right arm, Schnable under the left. Before the Cominch of Hollywood could do more than squawk, he was lifted off his feet and landed on his back in the swimming pool.

'Man overboard!' howled Jackson.

'Away the motor whaleboat,' whooped Schnable.

Floundering in his water-soaked silk suit, Mayer started to gurgle. A half dozen producers, vice presidents, directors leaped into the pool to rescue their leader.

'Good Christ!'

The *Jefferson City*'s air corps turned to confront an aghast Montgomery West. 'You crazy bastards have just sunk my career,' he said.

'Best thing that ever happened to you, West,' Jackson said. 'You're a lousy fucking actor anyway.'

Commander Edwin Moss was tiddly. He walked very carefully through the lobby of the Coronado Hotel, determined to conceal his condition from the public. How had it happened? He suspected Robert Mullenoe, his air defence officer. He had offered to get Eleanor a refill of her Coke, and Moss had asked him to refill his as well. He must have spiked it with rum. Mullenoe was capable of such a thing. He was one of the wild men who had resisted every attempt to discipline them at Annapolis. Moss had been his company commander when he was a first classman and Mullenoe a plebe. He saw at a glance that he was going to be a demerit collector, a rule breaker.

'I'm so dizzy,' Eleanor said, beside him. 'I'd almost swear I had something serious to drink.'

That was a dig. She did not approve of his Presbyterian refusal to drink liquor. Her mother was Irish-American. They always had liquor in the house.

'I hope they court-martial those flyboys,' he said as they went up in the elevator. 'Their conduct was outrageous.'

'I agree,' Eleanor said. 'But it was pretty funny, the way those other people practically drowned Mr Mayer trying to be the first to rescue him.'

'It's the Navy's reputation I'm thinking of. M-G-M's never going to make any pictures that give the Navy a fair shake unless we make an example of those two roughnecks. Thank God neither of them are Academy graduates.'

'Oh, heaven forbid,' Eleanor said.

In the bedroom, Eleanor sat down in a chair with a funny plop. 'You know what's wrong with you, Edwin?' she said.

'What?'

'You're too good for your own good. But I love you.'

He did not know what to make of this outburst. 'You sound as if you were thinking of changing your mind.'

'You have. I can tell. I don't know what to do about it.'

'I don't either,' he said.

'Let's do something daring.'

'What?'

'Order drinks from the bar.'

'Then what?'

'Maybe you'll find a girl who's willing to take a chance with a sailor without consulting that goddamn thermometer.'

Ina Severn drove a soused Montgomery West home to his deserted house in the Hollywood hills, where the B-picture stars lived. She had a house of her own on the next block. 'I'll never come down off the hill now,' he said, using the standard Hollywood expression for making it into the big time.

'You can never tell. That awful old man may not be running everything after the war,' Ina said.

'Would you be willing to have a nightcap with a pariah?' he said.

'Why not?' Ina said.

His romantic hopes were as awash as his career. Ina would not dare to begin a public attachment with a man whose friends had just thrown Louis B. Mayer into his own swimming pool.

Ina stretched herself on the couch, her gold lamé evening dress draped around her so that the outline of her slim body was visible under its folds. 'Your Commander Parker is a baddy,' she said as West handed her a Scotch and soda. 'There's one in every Navy. Pa used to say, Watch out for the ones with too much black in their eyes. There's black in their hearts too.'

'What's your father's rank?'

'Gunner's mate first class.'

'I thought he was an officer.'

'That's just some of your Uncle Mort's bull.'

'Is he still in the Navy?'

'He went down with the *Prince of Wales*.'

She said it in a perfectly matter-of-fact voice. For a moment Montgomery West thought she meant the son of the King of England and wondered if she was talking about kinky sex. Then he remembered that the *Prince of Wales* was a British battleship that Japanese torpedo planes had sunk in the China Sea a few days after Pearl Harbor.

Ina swung her feet off the couch and sat up. 'If you tell that to your goddamned uncle so he can use it in a press release, I'll never speak to you again.'

'Don't worry,' Montgomery West said.

It was amazing. He was completely sober. He no longer felt sorry for himself.

'I wanted to go to bed with you the first time I saw you,' Ina Severn said. 'But I was damned if I was going to let you know about it. You would have put me on that list of poor little tail waggers who think your uncle can make them stars with a press release.'

'No I wouldn't,' West said. The words were automatic. He realized he did not know what he might have done.

Suddenly Ina was looking away from him, and he realized she was fighting tears. 'I know I taunted you into joining the Navy. I wanted to get rid of you. You were mixing me up. All my life I've been determined not to act like a sailor's daughter. That was the one thing Pa asked of me.

'I thought – I know this sounds stupid – but I thought it was a fairly harmless thing to do. I always thought of the Navy as fairly safe, compared to the Army. I even told myself I was doing you a favour. Your uncle was running you. You were never going to find a director who might make you act up to your potential, because no one respected you. I didn't blame you for it. This town would corrupt an angel.

'Then, a week or two after you'd joined up, I got the news about Pa. That made me feel awful enough. But when I thought about you, I almost couldn't bear it. I still can't in a way. That's why I'm telling you this. So you can throw me out of here and –'

Montgomery West seized her arms and kissed her. 'I've heard that's the best way to stop a woman from talking too much.'

She still refused to look at him. 'No,' she said. 'It won't work. You'll remember what I just told you when you're out there dodging torpedoes.'

'Listen to me,' he said, turning her face to him. 'I thought the Navy was safe too. And I was so goddamn glad to get away from Uncle Mort, I would have paid you a fee if I knew you were in on the scheme. All that's irrelevant. I've spent the last nine months thinking about you four or five hours a night. I . . . I love you, Ina.'

Amazement, no doubt, caused his hesitation. He had said those magical words in rehearsals and before cameras a thousand times. He had said them almost as often in back seats of cars in Connecticut and in boudoirs in Beverly Hills. This was the first time in Montgomery West's life that he meant them.

After a kiss that lasted at least five minutes, she whispered, 'Don't call me Ina. My real name's Gwen. Gwendolyn Pugh. Isn't that God-awful?'

Gwendolyn Pugh, daughter of a gunner's mate? She had not grown up in one of England's more stately mansions surrounded by 'every imaginable luxury', as Uncle Mort put it in one of his press releases. To Montgomery West's delight, he did not give a damn.

'Meet Joseph Lyman Shuck,' he said. 'My mother's Jewish.'

'Mine's Irish.'

They started kissing again. After a while they went upstairs and spent most of the next two days there.

Dry-Dock Sailors

> *'Wakey wakey, rise and shine; you've had yours and*
>   *I've had mine.*
> *Show a leg, show a leg; let's go, let's go*
> *The cook's in the galley, the fire's below.*
> *Show a leg, show a leg; let's go, let's go.'*

The metallic notes of the reveille bugle had barely stopped hurtling through the ship when Boatswain's Mate First Class Ernest Homewood began bellowing this refrain in a basso that shook the racks of F Division's compartment. Frank Flanagan opened one eye and discovered he could not see much out of it. He let his tongue curl cautiously over his upper lip and found that it was swollen to twice its ordinary size.

'Hey, how's the Bronx Bomber?' Jack Peterson asked from his middle rack across the aisle. He lit a cigarette and smiled up at Flanagan. 'You're OK, kid. Not many guys would have waded into those bastards to help a shipmate.'

'I thought that was the general idea,' Flanagan said.

'Like a lot of general ideas, it only gets lip service if the odds don't look good.'

Flanagan dropped to the deck and seized his toilet kit and towel from his locker. Boats Homewood grabbed him by the shoulder and spun him around. 'I hope the other guys look a lot worse,' he said.

'You ought to know. You inflicted most of the damage on them,' Flanagan said.

'I don't remember a goddamn thing. I was drunk.'

'You can't believe the message they've put out on us,' Jack Peterson said. 'Half the numbers in my little black book wouldn't even talk to me because I'm on the *Jefferson City*. I wound up gettin' loaded in Shanghai Red's. On the way back to the Navy yard I see some of my old shipmates from the *California*. They're on that tin can the *Reuben Davis*. They give me that yellow strip stuff and I went after them. It was three against one and they were kickin' the shit out of me until Flanagan here waded in.'

'It was easy,' Flanagan said. 'I was the only sober guy in sight.'

Boats Homewood beamed at him. 'I figured someone with an Irish name could fight as good as he thinks.'

Unfortunately Flanagan and Peterson had got nailed by the Shore Patrol and denounced by a somewhat frantic officer of the deck, who told them they were the seventy-fourth and seventy-fifth members of the crew to be returned to the ship under arrest that night.

'What happens now?' Flanagan asked Jack Peterson as they stood in the chow line.

'You got put on report. That means Captain's Mast if you're a first offender. I'm liable to get a summary court-martial. That's what old God and Country Kemble told me the last time I was up. I don't imagine his pal McKay will be any different.'

Boats Homewood disagreed. 'The scuttlebutt on McKay is pretty good. I talked to a couple of guys who was with him on the *Augusta*. They said not to underestimate him – or try to pull any clever shit on him. He's a lot smarter than he looks or acts.'

Flanagan was fascinated by the way everyone in the Old Navy – the one that existed before the world crisis began expanding the ranks at exponential rates – seemed to know everyone else from admirals to enlisted men.

'Why did you join the Navy, Boats?' he asked Homewood.

'You wouldn't ask that question if you saw the house I grew up in. It was one room and we had twelve people sleepin' in it. That was luxury for a sharecropper in Alabama in 1913. The Navy was three square meals a day, son. That's why I joined.'

'How about you?' he asked Peterson.

'I grew up in a Navy town – Bremerton, right across the sound from Seattle. My father was a Navy man, so my mother told me. I never saw him. I had a stepfather who used to call me the little bastard when he came home drunk. One day he called me that, but I wasn't little any more. I decked him and headed for the nearest recruitin' station.'

After breakfast, they mustered on deck in the California sunshine. The formations were sloppy and there was a lot of chatter in the ranks. They were all feeling strange, with the ship in the middle of a Terminal Island dry dock. Around them civilian workers were swarming over the *Jefferson City*. Thick electric cables snaked in all directions. The acrid smell of acetylene torches drifted in the humid air. 'Goddamn yardbirds,' Homewood groused. 'It'll take us two weeks to clean up this ship.'

Captain McKay was nowhere to be seen. Instead they got a lecture from him via the executive officer. 'The Captain has directed me to say that he is extremely perturbed by the number of men in the crew who are being returned to the ship by the Shore Patrol. If the numbers continue to be as large as they were last night, all liberty will be cancelled. Do I make myself clear? All liberty will be cancelled.'

'Not for Daredevil Dan Parker,' Peterson said. 'I hear he's got Monty West to line up his Aunt Mae for him.'

'Silence in the ranks,' barked Ensign Kruger.

'Up yours, Herman,' muttered Peterson.

Jack Peterson – and Boats Homewood – despised Kruger for becoming an officer. They considered his switch on a par with treason. For them, there was a gulf between officers and the enlisted ranks that a man could only cross at the risk of losing his soul. Kruger, who had a scowl on his face eighty percent of the time, seemed more in danger of losing his mind. He flew into tantrums over a man wearing his hat at the wrong angle and similar trifles.

Dismissed, Flanagan followed Jack Peterson up the

ladders to their duty station, main forward, high in the ship's superstructure. In this compartment, which resembled the conning tower of a submarine, were auxiliary computers and radar screens to back up the machines in main plot. On the deck outside was the main battery gun director, a huge tin can crammed with more computers and a telescopic range finder. Jack Peterson operated the range finder, one of the most important jobs in the division.

The other three sailors assigned to main forward straggled in. First to arrive was Leo Daley, who gave Flanagan a look of shocked reproach for flirting with Protestantism. Next came Jim Booth, a smaller silent Midwesterner of about twenty-five, with the face of a disappointed weasel. Booth was known as the Radical. When the war began, he had joined the Navy to start a revolution.

According to him, the Russian Revolution had started in the Russian Navy aboard the cruiser *Potemkin*. The Germans had had a revolution in 1919 that started in their Navy. Booth was convinced that when average Americans saw the way the capitalist officers lived in the Navy, they were certain to revolt when the war ended. He wanted to be on hand to lead the uprising aboard the *Jefferson City*.

So far, the Radical had made very few converts. Peterson laughed at him. Homewood had threatened to break him into several pieces. Daley had written to Father Coughlin, the famed radio priest and foe of Communism, hoping he would tell his friend J. Edgar Hoover, the head of the FBI, about Booth.

Last to arrive was Louis 'the Mutt' Camutti, a huge incredibly ugly Philadelphian who claimed his father ran the best Italian restaurant in the country. Camutti had a massive head, shaped remarkably like Frankenstein's monster's, a mouth full of yellow teeth and a face pockmarked by a childhood bout with smallpox. The Mutt did not let these defects prevent him from being one of the Navy's great lovers. He had an infallible technique, which he demonstrated to Flanagan on his first day in main forward. He pulled up his undershirt and revealed a chest that was a mass of scars. 'I got that manning a twenty-millimeter aboard the

Arizona at Pearl,' he said. 'I give a chick one look and it's all over. I get her in bed within the next five minutes.'

Impressed, Flanagan had mentioned Camutti's heroism to Peterson. 'That fuckin' eightball was washin' dishes in his old man's restaurant last December seventh,' Peterson said. 'He's only been in the Navy six months longer than you.'

'Where'd he get the scars?'

'I think his father tried to drown him in scalding dishwater when he saw how ugly he was.'

While Flanagan swabbed the eight-by-ten compartment, Camutti regaled them with details of his latest conquest. As usual, she was a blonde, a waitress at the Brown Derby in Hollywood, where one of his father's cousins was a chef. 'Gloria, I said. In two weeks, I'm gonna be sailing back into Hell. That's what it is out there in the Solomons. Hell, Gloria. Can you give me something to take with me? The scars keep me awake at night, Gloria. I want to have something, someone, to think about.'

'If you're telling even ten percent of the truth, Camutti,' Leo Daley said, 'you should be locked up as a menace to public morals.'

'Say a rosary for me,' Camutti chortled.

Flanagan dry-mopped the compartment and retreated outside, where Peterson was checking out the director with one of the shipyard engineers. 'Camutti scored again,' he said.

'I'll believe that when this fuckin' director sprouts wings and can take off to correct the ranges from five thousand feet,' Peterson said. 'What did you do on liberty, kid?'

'Not much.'

'You must have met Teresa. That's how you wound up in that church.'

'Do you know her?'

Peterson grinned. 'All the sailors know Teresa. She's quite a girl. You can't push it with her. You've got to let her make the first move.'

Flanagan was baffled by this remark. What sort of move could you expect from a girl who sang 'Every Day With Jesus'?

Jack Peterson was in a nostalgic mood. 'In the Old Navy, you couldn't stay cherry and get any respect. I went to a whorehouse in Frisco, right out of boot camp. I thought it was strictly from hunger. It's all over in ten seconds and you're out five bucks. I realized you got to find your own women. Sailors' women. I've found a few. One of them's comin' down from Seattle. The next liberty, you call Teresa for a date and we'll hit the beach together.'

Flanagan almost told him to forget it. He could not imagine him and Teresa hanging around with Jack and his sailor's woman. How could someone who grew up next door to the Navy yard in Bremerton understand Irish Catholicism's fanatic insistence on sexual purity? Not that Flanagan was indifferent to women. He thought about them constantly. He could not go through the cheesecake section of *Life* or *Look* without getting an erection. But yielding to the desire was unthinkable.

'Do you like women, kid?' Peterson said.

Flanagan thought that was a peculiar question. 'Sure,' he said. His two sisters were brats, but he liked them. He liked his mother when she wasn't driving him crazy with silly worries and demands to know about every move he made.

'I mean really like them. Most sailors don't. Half the guys in the Old Navy were running away from some dame – or from all dames. Not that you can blame them. Most women specialize in drivin' guys nuts. You got to take that into account. You got to understand that most of them get an even shittier deal than sailors.'

Flanagan did not know that most women got a shitty deal. His father devoted most of his off-duty hours to trying to keep his wife happy. Kitty Flanagan always wanted some part of the house painted or repapered. There was always a new coat or a new hat or a new car she wanted to buy. Flanagan suddenly remembered the last thing his father said as they drove downtown to the recruiting station. 'If you get mixed up with a woman, just remember one thing. Don't get married. You marry someone, that's the ball game.'

At breakfast the following day, Jack Peterson reported that his Seattle girlfriend had arrived. At 1300 hours, they hit the quarterdeck in dress whites, shoes spitshined, hats at regulation two inches above the eyebrow. Ensign Kruger was the officer of the deck. 'If you get arrested again, Peterson, I swear to Christ I'll take that rate away from you. You'll be a goddamn second class seaman.'

'Message received, Herman,' Peterson said.

'What did you call me?'

'Message received, *sir*.'

The minute they stepped off the ship, Peterson shoved his hat to the back of his head and thumbed his nose in Kruger's direction. 'He and I were fire controlmen aboard the *California*,' he said. 'He was a no-good Prussian prick then too.'

Outside the Terminal Island gate, a woman in tan slacks and a white blouse waved to Jack Peterson. Her face was narrow, with intense green eyes, a haughty, almost pointed nose. Her dark hair was shoulder length, parted to the left and held in place by a silver barrette. She was tall and slender, with no more than an average figure. But there was something unusual about the way she stood – very straight, her head up, her shoulders almost braced. She looked sure of herself and surprisingly intelligent. Flanagan had expected a languid, luscious Hedy Lamarre type with a brain the size of a pea. Or a bubbly ingenue.

Jack strolled toward her with his best sailor's swagger. She did not wait for him to kiss her. She threw her arms around him and kissed him boldly, firmly on the mouth. It lasted a full minute, then Jack held her at arm's length. 'Jesus, you look like Christmas and my birthday rolled into one,' he said.

He waved Flanagan over and introduced him. 'Flan, this is Martha. I think her last name's Johnson. You got a friend for my buddy if he can't get a girl? He's new on this beach. But he's got one possible call.'

'Let's call her instead of just talking about it. Tell her we can pick her up wherever she's hanging out.'

Peterson stopped astonished. 'Where the hell'd you get a car?

'It's my father's.'

'You're speaking to him again? Where'd you get the petrol?'

'The black market. Are you going to report me to the FBI?'

'You bet I am. Don't you know there's a war on? How do you think our brave boys in the fleet are gonna win the fight against the yellow peril if they don't have enough fuel?'

'The only kind of fuel you lugs care about doesn't run engines.'

'Flanagan's old man's a cop. He'll turn us in for sure.'

'My father's LAPD,' Martha said. 'I moved to Seattle to get away from him. Are New York cops ballbreakers too?'

'More or less,' Flanagan said, shocked at her language.

They headed down the street to a telephone booth. Flanagan called the Advent Church in San Pedro and got Teresa, who said she would be delighted to go out with him and his friend Peterson. He did not mention that Jack was the sailor who demolished her father's window. They walked another block to a blue 1938 or '39 Chevrolet, with no treads on the running boards and big rust spots on the doors and fenders. 'Are you sure this thing hasn't been condemned for scrap?' Jack Peterson asked.

'It runs,' Martha Johnson said, getting behind the wheel. She gestured Frank Flanagan into the back seat and pulled away from the curb in a racing start that inspired a lot of beeping from a Cadillac that almost ran into them. 'Good Christ, I think that's the admiral,' Jack Peterson said.

'What are my chances of getting a job in his shipyard?' Martha said.

'Zero if you drive like that. Anyway, we're pullin' out in two weeks. It won't be worth it, babe.'

'Two weeks?' Martha glared at Jack, her face full of pain. 'Shit,' she said, and looked back at the road just in time to stop for a red light. 'You told me it would be two months.'

'That's what I figured from the damage they had to repair. But the yardbirds're workin' triple overtime. They're crawlin' all over us like a goddamn ant colony.'

Martha sighed and accepted the bad news. 'I heard Bernie Mapes got killed at Pearl,' she said.

Peterson nodded. 'He tried to get a wounded buddy

down from a twenty-millimetre mount, and a strafer riddled him with a burst.'

'I liked Bernie a lot,' Martha said. Her voice darkened. Flanagan sensed a meaning in 'a lot' that went beyond admiration. Jack Peterson said nothing for a moment. Was he glad Bernie Mapes was dead?

'We lost a lot of friends at Pearl,' he said. 'And a lot more at Savo Island.'

'What's Savo Island?' Martha asked.

Peterson told her in his most vivid Navy language what had happened at Savo Island. 'Joe Hanrahan went down with the *Astoria*, Bill Boyd on the *Quincy*. What it's done to us is almost as bad. We're goddamn pariahs. The ship that ran way,' he said.

'How come Savo hasn't been in the newspapers?' Martha asked.

'Because most of the guys who know about it are feedin' the fishes.'

Driving as if she were in the Indianapolis 500, Martha got to the Advent Church of the Second Coming in San Pedro in twenty minutes. Teresa was waiting for them in the doorway. The window had been replaced, the sign restored. She was wearing a pretty yellow dress and a big white sunhat. 'You look ready for the beach,' Martha said. 'A good thing, because that's where we're going.'

Jack asked Teresa how the church was doing.

'Flourishin',' she said. 'Pretty soon we'll have every sailor in the fleet converted.'

'When you convert Shanghai Red, let me know,' Jack said. 'I'll join right after him.'

Soon they were out of Los Angeles, rolling south along a highway that ran parallel to the ocean. The weather was summery. The air flowing in the car windows felt more like July than mid-September to Flanagan. After about a half hour they pulled off the road and headed for a collection of bungalows. 'What's this place?' Peterson asked.

'Laguna Beach Junior,' Martha said. 'A couple of LAPD went in on it together.'

'Your father knows you're with me and he's lettin' you use it? Ten to one it's booby-trapped.'

'The old enforcer's changed his mind about sailors since Pearl Harbor. He's got patriotic.'

'Three cheers for Admiral Yamamoto,' Jack said.

Martha unlocked the front door of the bungalow and led them into a plasterboard interior. There were two bedrooms, a kitchen and a living room. Everything was scrupulously clean. Jack opened the icebox and handed them two beers. 'Why don't you two kids take a walk on the beach?' he said. 'The old lady and I want to do a little reminiscin'.'

'What's that? Something you learned in the Solomons?' Martha said.

'The only thing I learned in the Solomons was how to feel like a crumb. I'm bettin' on you to change that around.'

Jack put his arm around her waist. Martha ran her hand up the back of his neck and tipped his hat over his eyes. 'This could be your lucky day, sailor.'

Flanagan's face, his hands, his whole body flushed. On the beach, he started to apologize for his friend Jack's morals. Teresa smiled. 'It's all right. Martha's in love with him. I could see that the minute we got to the house. It just shines out of her.'

Being in love did not make sex all right as far as Flanagan was concerned. He was amazed by Teresa's tolerance – and her lack of embarrassment. He could not imagine any of the Irish-Catholic girls he knew in the Bronx so serenely approving Martha and Jack's reminiscing.

They strolled along the sand for a good mile, passing houses on low grassy bluffs. Teresa said she was glad Flanagan had not got hurt in the fight outside the church. 'That's the fourth one this month,' she said. 'In the first a sailor got killed. Men are really stupid, the way they like to fight.'

Flanagan agreed with her. They discussed her father's church. It was failing, day by day. She knew it, but she could not bear to tell him to quit. 'I could get a job in a factory and support both of us.'

'Where's your mother?'

'Momma's in the state hospital.'

'What's wrong with her?'

'Daddy says her faith has failed her. Or she failed her faith. I don't know which. Anyway she sees things that aren't there and cries a lot. She cries all day, sometimes. Other times, she thinks she's back in Oklahoma. That's where she was happiest.'

Flanagan shook his head. Compared to this girl's spiritual problems, his own were ludicrously insignificant. He started telling her about Father Callow. He left his mother out of it. Somehow he could not badmouth her. But he had no trouble whatsoever badmouthing Father Callow. He lit a cigarette and started imitating his hoarse, anguished voice. 'Dear Frank,' he said. 'Don't you know that the Blessed Mother — and your own wonderful mother — are silently weeping over your refusal to heed God's call? I honestly suspect, dear Frank, that you are hoping to be lured into temptation. You are secretly hoping to succumb to the sins of the flesh so you can then say you are unworthy of a vocation.'

Ripples of silken laughter shook Teresa's fragile body. Flanagan found himself wishing he could touch the trembling breasts beneath her yellow dress. He doubled his burlesque of Father Callow. He threw in imitations of other Jesuits and went on to some of his father's better stories from the precinct.

Teresa enjoyed the comedy so much, she insisted Flanagan repeat some of it for Jack and Martha, when they eventually joined them on the beach. They were in bathing suits. Jack said there were plenty more in the house. Flanagan quickly found a pair of trunks that fit him. Teresa had a little more trouble with the women's suits. She settled for a blue tank suit that was too big for her and gave Flanagan a look at her surprisingly full breasts.

Back on the beach they found Jack Peterson in the water, pretending he was drowning. Martha lounged on the sand with a beer in her hand, paying no attention to him. 'Rescue the lug, Frank,' she said.

Flanagan had been a lifeguard at Jones Beach on Long Island the previous summer. He knew all the holds. He swam underwater and surfaced behind Peterson and threw him into a chest carry. 'Keep his head under,' Martha called.

'Like this?' Flanagan said.

A half-drowned Peterson staggered up on the beach. '*This* is my buddy?' he said. 'It's a good thing I just got laid, Flanagan. Otherwise they'd find you floatin' off Catalina Island.'

Flanagan thought sure Martha would blush or avoid his eyes. But she did not even blink. 'Isn't he charming?' she said. 'Gentleman Jack, they call him in Seattle. In the drunk tank.'

Flanagan was baffled. Martha did not fit into any of the female categories in his Irish-American mind. She slept with sailors like Jack, but she did not seem in the least ashamed of it. Moreover, she seemed to have no illusions about Jack's less admirable traits.

Everyone except Teresa drank a lot more beer and they went to dinner at a restaurant down the beach, where they gorged on Puget Sound oysters and Alaska king crab. Jack told marvellous stories about liberties in Pearl Harbor with no money and in Shanghai with too much money. He described life in the brig aboard the USS *California*. He gave a hilarious description of the time he went to a Baptist revival and found Jesus when he was home on boot leave. Everyone stuffed money in his pocket and the next night he was arrested for starting a riot in a waterfront bar. Although Teresa Brownlow laughed, Frank noticed that her eyes remained sad.

'Speaking of money, who's going to pay for this dinner?' Martha said.

'Your rich Uncle Jack,' Peterson said. 'I had a great night with the bones down in the after engine room.'

'You promised me you were going to start saving your money.'

'I'll promise you anything, honey. You know that,' Peterson said.

'That's what I'm afraid of,' Martha said.

They drove back to the cottage and drank some more beer. Martha got out a phonograph and played some records of Harry James, Benny Goodman and other name bands. She and Jack danced to a couple of songs. Flanagan was fascinated by the bold way Martha moved her body against Jack. Flanagan asked Teresa to dance and she told him her father said it was a sin. Flanagan promised her absolution and they joined the action. She was a very good dancer, which suggested she had been committing a lot of sins.

Finally, Martha asked Jack if he wanted to reminisce some more. They disappeared into one of the bedrooms. Teresa and Frank continued dancing, although Flanagan was pretty drunk. Teresa seemed drunk too, although Flanagan did not remember her drinking anything. They did a dopey lindy to Glen Miller's 'Chattanooga Choo Choo', laughing at the way they were goofing it up. 'Let's go for a swim,' Teresa said.

This time Teresa found a two piece bathing suit that revealed even more of her small firm body. They splashed around in the dark ocean for five or ten minutes and returned to the beach. There was no moon. They sat on the sand and watched the waves rumble toward them. 'I like you, Frank. I like you a lot,' Teresa said. 'You remember that song I sang at the service, about how sweet it was to be with Jesus?'

'Sure.'

Teresa took Frank Flanagan's hand and slipped it under the top of her bathing suit. 'Jesus is here. Frank. And here. And here.'

His hand descended to a place he barely knew existed. 'Take off your bathin' suit,' Teresa whispered.

He obeyed, while she slipped off her suit. She rolled on top of him and placed her mouth on his lips. In an instant he had the most tremendous erection since Adam encountered Eve in the Garden of Eden. Slowly, carefully, with a skill that amazed him, she lowered herself upon this pulsing rod of flesh, this forbidden part of himself and took it into her body. Into a soft supple darkness where every movement sent astonishing cascades of pleasure into his thighs, his belly, his chest, his soul. The world began to explode. Stars shifted orbits, the night sky was swept by splendour. When her hair fell against his face he was sure it was tipped with fire, like an angel's wing. In that moment of freedom and wonder and ecstatic discovery, Teresa whispered, 'Isn't this Jesus, Frank? Isn't this the sweetest love you've ever known?'

'Yes, yes,' he said his hands finding her breasts. He drew her down for a kiss that blended them into one being. He crushed her against his chest with his muscular arms, wondering if she would cry out, if he was hurting her. But she only locked her arms around him and returned the kiss, sliding her tongue deep into his mouth. Soul kissing, they called it in New York in 1942. Flanagan had managed it with a few girls. How trivial the phrase seemed now, compared to this reality.

He began to come – great spurts of pleasure that sent shudders through her body. 'I love you,' he said. 'I love you.' He was in love with love, with Jesus, with this woman who had suffered America's woes and still responded with tenderness and hope and faith, who somehow abolished sin.

Teresa gave a final shuddering sigh. For a long time she lay still, her lips on Flanagan's mouth. Then she said, 'I think I'd like to love you too, for a while.'

'Not for a while. For as long as we live. I want to marry you.'

'We'd better get dressed. You've got to get back to your ship.'

'The hell with the ship. Let's stay here – for our honeymoon.'

Jack Peterson's voice came out of the darkness. 'What the hell's he talkin' about?'

Flanagan pulled on his trunks and stumbled up the beach. 'Jack, I love her. I'm not going back to that goddamn ship. I'm going to stay here until we find a priest so I can marry her.'

'Like hell you're stayin' here,' Peterson said. 'You're already on report for drunk and disorderly. You'll get brig time.'

'So what?' Flanagan said. He was drunk on love and liquor. He wanted to fondle those lovely breasts for the rest of his life. He was appalled at the thought of returning to the USS *Jefferson City*'s world of metal and regimentation.

'I'll see you again, Frank,' Teresa said.

In the car she turned his head toward her and kissed him gently on the lips. Flanagan fumbled for her breasts. She pushed his hand away. 'Not now,' she said. He realized he was making a fool of himself, but she did not seem to mind. 'I love you, I really do,' he said.

At the Terminal Island gate, Martha kissed Jack Peterson passionately. 'I'll see you in two days,' he said.

Peterson dragged Flanagan out of the back of the car. With an iron grip on his upper arm, he steered him to the *Jefferson*

City's dry dock. 'Now take two deep breaths,' he said. 'And listen to what you're gonna do. You're goin' up that gangplank without missin' a step. You're gonna salute the flag and salute the OOD perfectly.'

'Aye, aye, sir.'

Below decks, Peterson leaned Flanagan against a bulkhead. 'Did you put a boot on it, kid?'

'What the fuck are you talking about? I'm a Catholic. I want to marry her.'

'Shhh.' Peterson put his hand over his mouth. 'You're not exactly the first guy Teresa led to Jesus. She's kinda famous, kid. I don't know whether she's got anything but you can't afford to take a chance. Let's go down to sick bay now. There's probably a pharmicist's mate on duty handin' out pro kits.'

'Go fuck yourself,' Flanagan said. 'if I wasn't so drunk I'd punch your goddamn head off for saying that about her.'

'Jesus. You *are* Irish.'

He boosted Flanagan into his top bunk. 'Go on sick call and get a pro tomorrow. If you get one inside twelve hours they usually work.'

'Fuck you,' Flanagan said. He refused to believe it. He refused to believe Teresa Brownlow had ever performed that beautiful exalting act with another man.

Peterson gave his shoulder an affectionate shake. 'You're half way to being a sailor, kid.'

What do Women Really Want?

'To the men of the Asiatic Fleet, above all, Al Rooks.'

Win Kemble raised his wineglass. Arthur McKay picked up his glass of California cabernet and studied the expression on his wife's face. He could see what Rita was thinking: What's the point in drinking to a corpse? That was Rita, full of warmth and compassion, as usual.

For the previous two weeks, Arthur McKay had stayed aboard the *Jefferson City*, claiming a need to supervise the day and night overhaul of the ship. Rita had been less than happy about this celibate existence. He could not explain to her that he was avoiding another encounter with Win. McKay had expected Win and Lucy to depart for Washington, DC, early in the first week. But Win had asked for – and received – a thirty day leave. It was a strange thing to do in the middle of a war.

Yesterday the *Jefferson City* had floated out of her dry dock, and chuffing Navy tugs had pushed and prodded her to a buoy in the harbour. Captain McKay already had orders to report without delay to CINCPAC in Hawaii, where, he had no doubt, another set of orders would dispatch the ship to the Solomon Islands within twenty-four hours. He had been tempted to use the rush to battle as an excuse to avoid this dinner. But he found it hard to resist the wish, yes even the need, to see if the breach between him and Win was as serious as it seemed to be the day McKay relieved him.

The arrival of Win's mother made it impossible to resist Lucy's invitation. The formalities of friendship had to be maintained at this farewell dinner for Mrs Kemble's sake. And for Lucy's sake. Her final plea had demolished all thoughts of evasion. 'Oh, Art,' she had sighed. 'Now if ever Win and I need true friends around us.'

As they put down their glasses, McKay glanced across the table at Lucy. Ater two weeks with Win, there were shadows of grief in her eyes, a tremor of sadness on her delicate mouth. Every time Arthur McKay looked at her, he felt the same tremor deep in his body. He yearned to comfort her, to tell her that all was well. But it was impossible. What he had seen in his two weeks as captain of the *Jefferson City* only redoubled his concern for Win Kemble.

To McKay's immense relief, Win showed every sign of wanting to put aside that ugly scene in the Captain's cabin. He had greeted him with a smile and a joke about being surprised they let the 'fighting Navy' mingle with civilians. He had tried to laugh at Rita's stories of high life and low intrigue in wartime Washington.

When they sat down to dinner, Win found it harder to conceal his bitterness. He began talking, not about Savo

Island, but another débâcle that had preceded it – the destruction of the US Asiatic Fleet. It was a sad story. As a COMINCH staff officer, McKay knew most of it, of course. But the details still made him wince. When the bombs fell on Pearl Harbor, the surface ships of the Asiatic Fleet had consisted of the heavy cruiser *Houston*, the light cruiser *Marblehead*, which was 'old enough to vote', and thirteen equally ancient destroyers. Against them the Japanese had sent ten battleships, ten aircraft carriers, eighteen heavy cruisers, eighteen light cruisers, and a hundred and thirteen destroyers.

The *Jefferson City* had just escorted an Army convoy to Manila and was told to join the Asiatic Fleet's pathetic ranks. The orders they received from COMINCH were as simple as they were brutal: stand and die. There is not much doubt that the *Jefferson City* would have followed the rest of the fleet to the bottom of the Java Sea, but for a quirk of fate. She had hit an uncharted reef off Balikpapan, Borneo, and had been forced to limp to Bombay for repairs. Within weeks, the rest of the Asiatic Fleet was annihilated. The last to go down was the flagship *Houston*, captained by one of the stars of the class of 1910, handsome, brilliant Albert Rooks.

In a voice clotted with rage, Win annotated the débâcle. Only one in ten of the five-inch anti-aircraft shells in the *Houston*'s magazines exploded when fired at enemy planes. Only one in five of the torpedoes carried by the destroyers functioned when they were launched. It was a paradigm of the Navy's unreadiness to fight a fleet as formidable as Japan's.

Win read them selective passages from a 103-page report sent to Washington by Captain Rooks on 18 November, 1941, less than a month before Pearl Harbor. It was entitled 'Estimate of the Situation, Far East Area'. McKay had glanced at a copy when he reported to COMINCH from his teaching job at the Naval War College. It was an assessment of the relative strength of the Japanese, Dutch, British and American navies in the Far East, which predicted precisely what had happened when the war started. A total disaster for the Allies.

'That report alone should have made Roosevelt think twice about the way he was baiting the Japanese to attack us,' Win said.

'He used the Navy – he risked it – to get us into the war with Germany. There was no need whatsoever for us to provoke Japan,' Mrs Kemble said.

She was voicing an opinion that Arthur McKay had heard at the Naval War College in Newport and on the third deck of the Navy Building in Washington, DC. Arthur McKay was inclined to dismiss it as irrelevant. The war was a fact. But he found it hard to resist the jeremiad Win preached on the final days of the *Houston*.

The Dutch admiral in command of the squadron had been an idiot who sent his little fleet into battle violating every rule in the book of naval strategy. 'He put his destroyers *behind* the cruisers,' Win said. 'He didn't even try to find out from the Dutch Army, which knew exactly what was happening, that the Japanese were landing a huge army on Java's south coast, with a major fleet protecting it. They sailed right into it and were blown out of the water.'

What agony it must have been for a man like Albert Rooks, the captain of the *Houston*. If there was anyone on whom Win Kemble had modelled his career, it was Rooks. Like him he had won the annual essay prize in the *Proceedings of the US Naval Institute*, he had studied at the Naval War College, he had blended staff work for potent admirals with commands at sea. To see such a man trapped in the doom that engulfed the Asiatic Fleet must have been agony for Win.

More disturbing to Arthur McKay was what he heard behind and beneath Win's monologue. One ugly word summed it up: defeat. Win's soul was drenched in it. The same malaise had infected the soul of the USS *Jefferson City*. Captain McKay had sensed it within a day of his arrival. Demoralization was visible in the eyes of the officers and crew. In their atrocious conduct ashore. In the dirty sleeping compartments of the deck divisions. In the repulsive food being served in the crew's mess. Nobody wanted to serve on the *Jefferson City*. In the past two weeks over two hundred enlisted men had transferred off her. Most of them were Old

Navy veterans, chiefs and first class petty officers. They had been replaced, McKay feared, by men whom nobody wanted – troublemakers, screwups. The turnover had been almost as heavy among the officers.

'Win's written a letter to Frank Knox,' Mrs Kemble said.

Arthur McKay was getting drunk. They had killed three bottles of this excellent California wine. He gazed into Mrs George Stapleton Kemble's wide brown eyes and marvelled at her serenity. It was a trait shared by her daughter-in-law, most of the time. Was this serenity created by an act of the will? he wondered. Did such women carefully cultivate their refusal to face facts, their ability to ignore realities? It was an immensely touching trait; it stirred a wish in the male soul to preserve, protect, such innocence.

Then the meaning of her words penetrated the cabernet haze. 'The Secretary of the Navy?' he said.

'I believe that's his title,' Rita said wryly.

'It's like Daddy's letter to TR,' Lucy said. 'Look what that accomplished.'

In 1903, Commander Robley Semmes had written a letter to President Theodore Roosevelt, informing him that the US Navy was building battleships manned by sailors who were lucky to score one hit out of a hundred shots fired, thanks to their antiquated gunnery systems. The President had appointed Semmes his naval aide and launched an overhaul of the Navy that eventually produced a modern fleet – and an admiral's rank for the daring commander.

'Mother, that letter's a confidential matter. I wish you hadn't mentioned it to a member of Fleet Admiral King's staff,' Win said.

'A former member,' Arthur McKay said.

'From what I hear, your wife remains – what shall we say – a distaff member?' Win said.

'What the hell do you mean by that?' Rita said.

'Calm down, you two,' Arthur McKay said. 'What did you say in the letter, Win?

'After some preliminary remarks about the madness of starting a war with the world's second largest Navy two years before we were ready to fight it, I told Knox exactly what I thought of putting nineteen thousand marines armed with 1903 Springfield rifles and machine guns that have been in cosmoline since the battle of Bellau Wood ashore on Gaudalcanal, within a few hours of a hundred and fifty thousand Japs on New Guinea and a fleet that outguns us four to one. I wrote it before Savo Island, I might add.'

The Secretary of the Navy was a Republican whom FDR had brought into his war cabinet. He was also a former Rough Rider who had charged up San Juan Hill behind Theodore Roosevelt in 1898. Knox had been a close friend of another Rough Rider and TR intimate, George Stapleton, the man after whom Mrs Kemble's late husband had been named. Between them, the Kembles and the Stapletons were a formidable Republican phalanx in the states of New Jersey and Pennsylvania. They shared ancestors who had signed the Declaration of Independence, fought in the American Revolution. They personified the old money, the old blood, that gave Win Kemble his conviction that he was born to command.

'At my suggestion, Win sent a copy to Senator Wheeler,' Mrs Kemble said.

Senator Burton K. Wheeler of Montana was a Democrat who also was the leader of the anti-Roosevelt isolationist block in Congress. A year before Pearl Harbor, he had predicted that Roosevelt's policies would 'plough under every fourth American boy.' He was widely suspected of leaking to the Chicago *Tribune* the top-secret 'Victory Plan', calling for the drafting of ten million men, which Roosevelt had ordered the Navy and Army to prepare six months before the Japanese struck. Published on 4 December 1941, the document had rocked the Roosevelt administration. Only the Japanese attack three days later had rescued the President from political humiliation.

'What do you expect to accomplish?' Arthur McKay asked.

'I don't know,' Win said. 'Maybe a change of command.'

Arthur McKay shrugged. 'It might work.'

'You're out of your skull,' Rita said. She glared at Win. 'Cominch is going to cook you over a slow fire.'

126

Arthur McKay was amused by Rita's indignation. Only two weeks ago, on the morning they arrived, she had been coldly considering the possibility that if Operation Watchtower failed and Guadalcanal had to be abandoned, Admiral King might soon be on the retired list. Now her old rancour at Win made her the Admiral's disciple. She was right about one thing. Cominch would not surrender without a savage struggle.

But startling things could happen in a democracy at war. Congress was still fulminating over the disaster at Pearl Harbor. Waiting in the wings were men like Admiral James O. Richardson, who had been relieved as commander of the Pacific Fleet for telling Franklin D. Roosevelt it was a mistake to base the battleship force in Hawaii, where it was vulnerable to a surprise attack. Win Kemble had been on Richardson's staff and had written a brilliant analysis of what could happen at Pearl Harbor, based on the way the British had smashed up the Italian Navy while it was at anchor in the harbour of its main base at Taranto in 1940. It had proved to be as close to prophecy as a Navy officer could come. Richardson – and the men around beloved 'J.O' the most popular admiral in the US Navy in memory – could suddenly become a very appealing alternative to scowling, snarling Ernest King, the personification of the admiral as son of a bitch.

It would not be difficult to obtain Frank Knox's backing for such an idea. Knox loathed King's imperial style, his habit of going over his head to the President, of issuing orders, announcing policies, as if the Secretary of the Navy did not exist. So far, King's admirals had won victories at Midway and Coral Sea. But they had been defensive battles, desperate parryings of massive enemy assaults. If Watchtower collapsed and the American Navy lost the offensive momentum they were trying to build with it, more Japanese thrusts toward Hawaii and Australia could be expected. A new strategy, a new Cominch might be summoned to repel them.

In her present mood, Rita was not prepared even to consider such a possibility. 'You're dealing with a very different President, even though they have the same last name,' she said. 'Daddy was the luckiest man in the history of the Navy, to get away with that letter. I think you may have finished yourself, Win. If Savo Island hasn't done it already.'

Pain – and something close to hatred – flickered in Win's eyes.

'Really, Rita,' Lucy said.

There were tears in Mrs Kemble's eyes. Her veined hands trembled as she raised her wineglass to her lips. For Arthur McKay it was an intolerable sight. He was aware of Mrs Kemble's limitations. But he remained her defender, her devotee, because of the generosity with which she had received his mother during the painful week she had spent in Annapolis visiting him in McKay's first class year. She had been awed, overwhelmed by the great cities, the wealth and elaborate snobbery of the East. She had seen it was too late to fulfil her dream of moving there. She was a farmer's wife, a country bumpkin, forever. Nevertheless Mrs Kemble had welcomed Willa McKay to her Annapoplis parlour, she had invited her to dinner with admirals and congressmen. She had given her a glimpse, at least, of the world of sophistication and privilege for which she had yearned in Kansas.

'Rita,' Arthur McKay said. 'This is our family. We don't discuss naval tactics, we don't discuss careers.'

'Aye, aye, sir,' Rita said. She was ready to quit now, having scored a direct hit on Win's ego.

Rita would go back to Washington and tell Cominch everything. Arthur McKay could not stop her. Perhaps it would be disloyal to a man who had just given him command of a capital ship even to try.

Lucy said that her mother, now in her eightieth year, had invited them to live with her in the Patapsco house if Win was stationed in Washington.

'I can't go near the place,' Rita said. 'I'm afraid I'll see Daddy's ghost in every corner.'

'What's wrong with that? You loved him, didn't you?' Mrs Kemble said.

'I'm afraid I'll start arguing with him. And he'll start arguing back.'

'He was a brave man,' Mrs Kemble said. 'I remember Father saying that even if he had no one else among the younger men to defend him against the slanderers, he would have had nothing to fear as long as Robley Semmes was on his side.'

For a moment Arthur McKay wanted to tell Mrs Kemble she was dredging up ancient history, defunct quarrels. But he said nothing. These women were inseparable parts of his life, of Win's life. They embodied the past in its maddening mixture of hope and disappointment and happiness. They presided over the sacred altars of home, where the only gods worth worshipping – love and loyalty and friendship – hovered.

'I want to drink to something important to all of us,' Lucy said. 'The success – the victories – of the USS *Jefferson City*.'

The words connected to what Arthur McKay was thinking in an amazingly immediate way. He struggled with a rush of emotion. 'Thank you, Lucy,' he said.

Rita looked overwhelmed by remorse. It was not the first time Lucy had intimidated her with the purity, the inviolability, of her affection.

'They're overdue,' Win said, gamely raising his glass.

'Amen to that,' Rita said.

'And now,' Lucy said, pushing her chair away from the table, 'I'm sure these two old salts want some time alone to work out a comprehensive plan for winning the war by Christmas. I, for one, am going to demonstrate my unbounded faith in them by going to bed.'

Mrs Kemble smiled somewhat forlornly. 'I think I'll imitate your example,' she said.

The expression on Rita's face made it clear she did not want Arthur McKay to spend any time alone with Win Kemble. But she could not think of a plausible objection. She was towed out of the room in the wake of Lucy and Mrs Kemble, grumpily warning her husband she would not stay awake indefinitely.

Captains McKay and Kemble regarded each other warily

for a moment. Then Win seemed to relax. Physically he looked fifty percent better than the man who had greeted McKay on the quarterdeck of the *Jefferson City*. Maybe it was his turn to look haggard, McKay thought wryly. Rita with her inimitable talent for compliments, told him he had aged two years in the past two weeks. It was her sweet way of expressing her fear that he could not handle the job.

Win strolled to the bar and flung ice into two glasses. 'I suppose you're still drinking that swill known as bourbon,' he said.

'Still a man of the people,' McKay said.

'Sometimes I think all my labours to make you an officer and a gentleman have been in vain.'

'Remember what I used to tell you. The real trick is to make a sow's ear out of a silk purse. That's how to get someplace in the American Navy.'

Win poured him a double shot of bourbon and himself an equal amount of Scotch. He sat down in the easy chair facing Arthur McKay and took a long defiant swallow. 'You don't approve of my letter?'

McKay sighed. 'Why didn't you talk it over with me first? Didn't it occur to you that after nine months in Washington, I might have had some suggestions?'

Over the years, in their letters and in meetings such as this one, Arthur McKay had spent almost too many hours trying to temper Win Kemble's violent opinions, to moderate his headstrong ways. Win had always been too fond of challenging the policies of officers who outranked him. Even as a lieutenant he had not hesitated to present admirals with a plan of operation, complete with chapters on strategy tactics and politics. Worse, he became outraged and depressed when his recommendations were rejected.

Win took another large swallow of his Scotch. 'The last time we met, you didn't seem that interested in my opinions. All of which turned out to be correct, I might add.'

They had gone to their class's twenty-fourth reunion in June of 1941. Win had spent hours condemning Roosevelt and predicting disaster at Pearl Harbor.

'I never argue with a man who relies for evidence on a crystal ball,' McKay said.

'Why not?' Win snapped. 'Isn't that what the world professional means? We're supposed to know more than the fucking civilians. We're supposed to be able to foresee trouble – and prevent it.'

'True enough.'

'I know what you're going to say. About the other truth. I've never been able to swallow your philosophy of RHIP.'

For a moment, they were back in Shanghai and Arthur McKay heard himself saying, *Win, Rank hath its privileges, and one of them is to be wrong.*

'It isn't a philosophy. It's fact.'

'You've always been too impressed with facts, Arthur. Too quick to accept the status quo as an eternal verity.'

'Is that a new way of telling me I don't know my ass from my elbow?'

'You know a lot, Art. We all know a lot. The question is – What to do, how to act on that knowledge.'

'Now there's an eternal verity.'

'It's not funny, Art. Look where our inaction, our supine obeisance to the civilians has left us. With second-rate ships in a second-rate Navy.'

Again McKay heard echoes of old anger in those words. Throughout the 1920s and '30s, as the politicians postured and negotiated on behalf of peace through disarmament, Win had been infuriated by the concessions America's diplomats had made, limiting the weight and armament of destroyers and cruisers, actually forcing the United States to sink some of its ships. More and more he had become the vociferous proponent of the idea that the Army and Navy should take the offensive against civilian timidity and ineptitude. He had had not a little to do with persuading Admiral James Richardson to go to Washington to tell Franklin D. Roosevelt he was wrong to base the fleet at Pearl Harbor.

'That's changing fast, Win. The pols are scared out of their shoes. They're doubling and tripling everything we ask for.'

There were intimations of multiplying battle fleets in those words, of dozens of task forces for ambitious young admirals to command. Win splashed some more Scotch in his glass. 'You think I should withdraw the letter? Wire Knox and tell him I was drunk when I sent it? Something like that?'

'Something like that. Maybe your mother could call him.'

'Jesus Christ.' Win stared at Arthur McKay across his upraised glass. 'Do you know how old I am?'

'Forty-seven.'

'Do you think, in all honesty, Friend of My Life, that a man of forty-seven should let his mother make phone calls for him?'

McKay was tempted to point out Win had never objected to his mother making calls for him during their first decade as officers, when the Republican Party had ruled in Washington. But that remark might lead to revealing that McKay never thought Mrs Kemble's calls were a good idea.

'I suppose not.'

'The letter is a fact. Maybe we should consider it part of that vast nauseating fact you call RHIP. I do have some rank in this excuse for a Navy. Maybe I'm entitled to a mistake. What do you think?'

'We're all entitled to a lot of mistakes, Win.'

Face to face, shorn of their women, now if ever was the time to speak the truth. For a moment McKay could almost tangibly feel Win's impulse to tell him what had happened at Savo Island. McKay sensed his spirit depart from them – perhaps to ascend the stairs and pause outside his mother's door, then Lucy's door. Or was he visiting a more mysterious shrine? Wherever it was, he made the journey and McKay heard his answer. No. The unspoken word thudded between them like the slam of a watertight door.

'I don't know about the Navy you serve in. But in mine, a single mistake and there'd be a laughing chorus dancing on my entrails in the scuppers.'

'It's not that bad, Win. I've told you a hundred times it's never been that bad. You've got a lot of friends.'

'Optimistic Arthur. The man who still believes we can save the world for democracy. When all that's ever saved the world is steel and iron, applied by men with the same metal in their blood.'

McKay drained his glass. 'Now I know it's time to go to bed.'

'I hope Rita is still waiting.'

McKay stood up. He looked calmly, steadily at Win Kemble, trying to tell him once and for all that Arthur McKay was no longer the scared stammering plebe of 1913. 'I hope so too,' he said.

He turned his back on the friend of his life. Turned his back on Win's rage, his pain, his bitterness. In Long Beach Harbor a troubled ship awaited his command. Off Guadalcanal, on the edge of the Coral Sea, the war insisted on its absolute pre-eminence, its guttural demand to set the cruelest limits on love and loyalty and friendship.

Win's voice, harsh, choked, caught him at the door. 'Art!'

McKay looked over his shoulder, wondering what else there was to say.

'Good shooting out there.'

Hot incomprehensible regret surged in McKay's throat. Win Kemble vanished in a blur of tears. Somehow the new captain of the *Jefferson City* found the strength to stifle them.

'Thanks.'

BOOK TWO

Steaming

After a day and night of loading ammunition and stores, the *Jefferson City* was ready for sea. The officer of the deck had tested the steering engine, ordered the accommodation ladders rigged in, checked the fathometer, the whistle and siren. The sea details were on station.

'Why don't you take her out, Commander?' Captain McKay said to Daniel Boone Parker, his executive officer.

'Glad to, Captain.'

Parker turned to the boatswain's mate of the watch, massive Ernest Homewood. 'Pass the word for Wilkinson to report to the bridge.'

Both Homewood and the officer of the deck, Lieutenant Robert Mullenoe, glowered and glanced at Captain McKay, as if they longed to tell him something. Homewood blew a call to attention on his pipe and passed the order: 'Now Bosun's Mate First Class Wilkinson, lay up to the bridge.'

Nothing happened for several minutes. A party of sailors gathered on the bow; a petty officer checked the capstan, the big metal drum with which the anchor chair was hauled in. But nothing else was done until Wilkinson, tall, swarthy and, McKay thought, shifty-looking, appeared on the bridge. He glanced uneasily at Captain McKay, saluted and said to Parker, 'Ship is ready for sea, sir.'

'I like to keep Wilkinson around when I take a ship into or out of port, Captain,' Parker said. 'He's forgotten more seamanship and ship-handling than the average deck officer has ever learned.'

Speak for yourself, Commander, Arthur McKay thought. But he simply nodded. He had had several conversations with Parker since he took command. All had been sparring matches. Parker seemed to resent even the most casual inquiry into the morale and competence of the ship's personnel. He assured Captain McKay there were no problems

'Uncle Dan' (he liked to refer to himself in the third person) could not handle. He had followed up this straight-arm with a lecture on how the captain and executive officer should function. The exec was the nuts and bolts man – he ran the ship and freed the captain to worry about their relationship to the fleet.

McKay had seen this kind of executive officer before. He wanted to convert the captain to a passenger on his own ship. That way, there was nothing for the exec to worry about when the captain evaluated his performance in his fitness report. The captain did not know enough to decide whether the exec was doing a good, bad or mediocre job. There were more than a few captains who preferred this arrangement. They were not comfortable dealing with the crew. They preferred a lofty isolation. They were more interested in their relationship with the admiral in immediate command.

McKay, with his inclination to take nothing for granted, wanted to find out a lot more about Commander Parker before he trusted his judgement and ability to deal with the crew. He had read his personnel file and was impressed by the invariably high praise Parker's superiors had bestowed on him. Parker's tour as a naval attaché in London suggested he had some political pull too.

None of this had prepared McKay for Boatswain's Mate First Class Wilkinson's appearance on the bridge. He put his pipe to his lips and sounded Boat Call. 'Away the motor whaleboat,' he barked into the PA system.

The motor whaleboat putted along the starboard side of the ship with the buoy man, a life-jacketed sailor who had the ticklish job of freeing the anchor chain from the buoy. Beyond the breakwater, the two destroyers that were going to escort them to Pearl Harbor, the *Hamilton Bruce* and *Quentin Calhoun*, were sweeping the turbulent sea with their sonars to make sure there were no submarines out there waiting to greet the *Jefferson City* with a spread of torpedoes.

McKay waited for Parker to begin the standard routine for getting under way, first testing the engine order telegraph (also called the annunciator), then the main engines. Apparently in a hurry, Parker skipped the first test and barked, 'Test the main engines.'

From the belly of the ship came the rumble of the turbines turning over. The engine telegrapher said, 'Ready to answer all bells.'

Wilkinson murmured something in Parker's ear. It was obviously a reminder to test the engine order telegraph. 'OK, OK,' he growled. 'Let's test the telegraph. All ahead one third, all back one third –'

The engine telegrapher shoved the annunciator to ahead one third. Before he could slick to back one third, the engines rumbled again and the ship lurched forward. The engine room, confused by the departure from the standard routine, thought they had received an order to go ahead.

There was a cry of alarm from the telephone talker on the bow. 'Back off! Back off!

'What happened?' Wilkinson shouted into the PA system.

'The buoy man's in the water! He got hit by the bow!

Parker looked wildly around the bridge. Everyone was waiting for him to give an order. His eyes finally settled on Wilkinson. 'All back one third,' muttered the boatswain's mate.

'All back one third,' Parker cried.

'All back one third', the engine telegrapher said, shoving the annunciator into position.

'Goddamn those fucking black-gang assholes. Don't they know an engine telegraph test when they see one?' Parker cried. 'I think you ought to ream their asses for this, Captain.'

'Why?' McKay said.

'If it isn't obvious, I won't try to explain it.'

Commander Parker, I will give you exactly ten seconds to retract that remark. If you don't, you're relieved from command of this bridge.

These furious words hurtled through McKay's mind, but he did not speak them. It had never been his style to issue reprimands or corrections to subordinates in front of other men. The last thing he wanted was a brawl with his executive officer. The moment the crew scented that kind of acrimony at the top, a ship became a madhouse.

Parker saw the glare in McKay's eyes and switched from truculence to contrition. 'What do you want me to do, Captain?'

'Shut down the engines. Signal those destroyers we've had an accident. No point in putting it on the radio and telling the whole goddamn port,' McKay said. 'Find out if the buoy man's hurt.'

Within seconds, signalmen began using blinkers to send this message to the destroyers. The sea detail on the bow reported the buoy man was unconscious. One of the men in the motor whaleboat had jumped into the oily waters of the harbour to rescue him.

'Get him aboard,' McKay said. 'Tell the doctor to lay up to the fo'c'sle on the double.'

McKay got to the forecastle as a half dozen sailors hoisted the dripping buoy man aboard. He was a tall thin kid with a narrow face and an odd Pinocchio nose. A trickle of blood drooled from a corner of his mouth. He groaned and coughed up water and blood when they laid him on the deck. 'I'm sorry, sir,' he mumbled. 'It happened so fast. I couldn't see the ship movin'.'

'It was our fault, son,' McKay said.

Lieutenant Commander Wyatt Cadwallader, the ship's doctor, appeared, accompanied by a pharmacist's mate. McKay had served on several ships with Cadwallader, a heavy-set handsome man who moved and spoke with the solemnity of an undertaker. The captain had never had to seek his medical advice, but he suspected from his wardroom conversation that he was not very bright.

'Is he badly hurt?' McKay asked.

'I don't think so,' Cadwallader said, peeling back one of the boy's eyes. 'His vital signs are good.'

'What about that blood?'

'Probably just a few teeth shaken loose.'

It would take at least an hour to transfer the kid to a hospital on shore. Provisioning and arming the ship had taken thirty-six hours instead of the twenty-four McKay had allotted to it. He would have to report the accident to Admiral Tomlinson and put up with his sarcastic remarks. 'Take him down to sick bay,' McKay said, feeling vaguely uneasy about the decision. The kid was about the same age as his own son, sitting safe and sound in an Annapolis classroom.

They sent out another buoy man, and McKay ordered Boatswain's Mate Wilkinson up the bow to make sure things went smoothly. Without Wilkinson on the bridge, Parker was as jittery as a green ensign. 'Meet her, meet her, you stupid bastard,' he snapped at the helmsman, when the *Jefferson City*'s head swung slightly off course as they got under way.

They made it out of the harbour without further mishap and set a course for Hawaii at twenty-five knots. The destroyers steamed ahead of them to port and starboard on a standard zig-zag plan. Captain McKay went below to his cabin. Thinking over the incident on the bridge, McKay decided to invite Commander Parker to dinner. He sent the invitation via one of the Marine orderlies who sat outside his cabin twenty-four hours a day. A few minutes later, Horace Aquino, his stocky, solemn Filipino steward, appeared at the door to ask the captain what he would like to have for dinner.

'What's the crew eating today?'

Aquino looked blank. 'I don't know, Captain.'

'Whatever it is, we'll have it. Commander Parker's joining me.'

'Yes, Captain.'

'Don't do anything fancy to what you get from the crew's mess. Just load two trays and bring them up here.'

'Aye, aye, Captain.'

McKay glanced at his watch. They had two hours to dinner, which was served at 1200 hours. Plenty of time for some drills. Ordinarily, a captain notified the executive officer well before he staged a drill. Commander Parker's performance on the bridge inclined Captain McKay to alter this routine. It was peacetime Navy nonsense, anyway. Everything – inspections, drills – was announced in advance to guarantee a perfect performance. The Japs were not going to announce anything in advance. Captain McKay picked up the phone and called Lieutenant Mullenoe on the bridge. 'McKay here. Sound Abandon Ship Drill.'

Frank Flanagan sprawled on the deck outside the main battery fire control director listening to Jack Peterson torment the ship's weatherman. Every day while they were at sea, he sent up a bright grey balloon and wrote a forecast for the benefit of the Captain and the navigator. According to Jack, he had yet to be right. The aerographer, an intense, skinny little redhead from Minnesota, spluttered and swore he would back his latest prediction with ten dollars, if Jack gave him decent odds. Jack gave him four to one, and the seer departed, leaving his striker to wind up the mile and a half of twine attached to the balloon.

Flanagan found it hard to muster a smile for this entertainment. He could not decide which ached more acutely, his muscles or his conscience. He had spent most of the previous night lugging fifty-five pound five-inch shells half the length of the ship on his shoulder. In his head, Flanagan caressed Teresa Brownlow. Over the past two weeks he had seen her a half dozen times. The first three times, they made love. The next three times, they argued. Flanagan wanted her to promise him she would not let any other sailor find Jesus in that special place. She absolutely refused and amply confirmed what Jack Peterson had told Flanagan on their first liberty together. When the spirit of the Lord moved her, Teresa had been inviting sailors to discover divine love there for some years now. When Flanagan told her it was a sin, Teresa serenely informed him Jesus had abolished sin, and quoted St Paul to prove it. In his twelve years of Catholic education, Flanagan had never read a line of the Bible. He found himself baffled and enraged.

Jack Peterson grinned at him. 'You look like a lovesick porpoise,' he said. 'I knew you'd kick yourself for makin' Teresa so sore she wouldn't let you touch her. Take it when you can get it kid, that's the only philosophy for a sailor.'

'What does Martha think about that?'

'Not much. But I don't think much of the way she plays around and talks about it to my face.'

'That's what you do,' Flanagan said.

'That's my privilege.'

'You're nuts about her and you won't admit it. You're afraid you might have to turn something down if you did.'

'Jesus Christ. Maybe you ought to become a Jesuit preacher. You're great at mindin' other people's love lives and you mess up your own.'

The ship's alarm bell clanged through this acrimonious profundity. It was followed by the blast of a bugle and a shrill whine of a boatswain's pipe. 'Now hear this. All hands stand by for a drill. Abandon ship.' boomed the PA system.

'Holy shit,' Peterson said. 'I hope you know your station. I'm not sure if I remember mine.'

Flanagan could hear Boats Homewood urging him and all the other new men to study the Watch Quarter and Station Bill on the bulletin board in their compartment. Beside each man's name was the place where he was supposed to go for General Quarters, Fire, Collision, Abandon Ship and a half dozen other emergencies. Like most sailors, Flanagan only paid serious attention to his General Quarters station. Two weeks in port had obliterated the other assignments.

He fought his way down ladders and along passageways full of snarling, cursing sailors in the same state of ignorance. In the F Division compartment, a furious Homewood stood by the bulletin board bellowing out names and assignments. 'I knew you'd forget it, Romeo,' he roared at Flanagan. 'The Captain won't be the last man off this ship. The fucking F Division will.'

Flanagan was supposed to muster by the number-two boat. Unfortunately he forgot to ask Homewood where that was. Losing his head completely, he rushed up to Ensign Kruger and asked him for directions. 'Forget it. You're on report,' Kruger snarled.

'Gangway, gangway,' roared a voice behind them. It was the Marine orderly preceding Captain McKay. For a moment all Flanagan could see was the gold braid on his hat. He had never seen such thick crusts of it, surrounding a menacing-looking eagle.

'Where's your station, sailor?' the Captain asked in an amazingly mild voice.

'Boat two, Captain. But I don't know where it is.'

'How long have you been aboard this ship?'

'Two and a half weeks, Captain.'

'That's a pretty good excuse. But I don't think the sharks would be interested in it. Ensign Kruger, take this man over to number-two boat.'

'Aye, aye, Captain.'

He grabbed Flanagan by the arm and led him to the starboard side of the ship, aft the number-two turret. There was no boat in sight, just a life raft lashed against the side of the turret. 'You're a lucky son of a bitch.' Kruger said. 'If that was Captain Kemble, you'd be up for another mast.'

'Where's the lifeboat?'

'We don't put lifeboats on a ship in wartime.'

'Wouldn't it help to change that on the Station Bill?'

Kruger's eyes bulged. 'Stand at attention when you speak to me! Say sir!'

Flanagan came to attention. 'Wouldn't it help to change that on the Station Bill, sir?' he said.

'You've been spending too much time with Peterson,' Kruger said. 'Wise guys get taught hard lessons in this man's Navy. You better start changing your attitude now, sailor.'

'Yes, sir.'

'Jesus Christ, Kruger,' hissed Lieutenant Montgomery West, dismay all over his handsome face. 'We turned in the worst performance on the ship. Half our yo-yos couldn't find their stations.'

'I've been telling you to stop treating them as if they were in a college fraternity. They're just a bunch of deck apes who happen to be aiming the guns instead of loading them.'

The bugle sounded secure from Abandon Ship. Lieutenant West mustered F Division beside turret one and ordered Boats Homewood to read off everyone's station for every drill on the list. He was about halfway through the ninety names when the bugle sounded again, followed by another whine of the boatswain's pipe.

'Now hear this. General Quarters. All hands man your battle stations,' boomed the PA system.

There was another wild scramble up and down ladders. Flanagan's battle station was inside the main battery gun director. Six men squeezed into this barrel on top of the ship, containing the range finder and a backup computer that would enable the guns to keep firing even if main forward and main plot were knocked out. Jack Peterson manned the range finder. The others dialled information into the computer as he gave it to them. A chubby ensign was in theoretical command. But Peterson really ran the show.

It was not the most exciting battle station on the ship or the most comfortable. Flanagan's six-feet-two-inch frame was jammed into a space designed for a man half his size. He could see nothing except the glowing dials of the computer and the handle on which he cranked in the range. The ventilation was poor. Next to him sat Leo Daley, who did not shower more than once a week. On the other side of the computer sat Louis Camutti, who used a bottle of cologne a day. The mixture of odours was peculiarly unpleasant.

'OK, guys,' Peterson said. 'We're gonna blow one of those fuckin' tin cans out of the water.'

Using pedals that turned the director from left to right with electric power, he whirled them around the horizon, barking out ranges and bearings. 'Fire!' he howled. 'There goes the goddamn *Calhoun*.' Peterson loved this part of his job. He had already given Flanagan a lecture on the range finder. It contained 1,500 mechanical parts and 160 different lenses and prisms. It took a year and a half to build one.

'Hey, I'm getting seasick,' Leo Daley said as Peterson swivelled them in the opposite direction to sink the other destroyer.

'Me too,' said the ensign, who was a ninety-day wonder on his first cruise.

The bugle sounded secure from General Quarters. They

crawled out of the director, and Peterson said, 'Daley, from now on you take a shower every day or we'll all throw up in there.'

'You're not supposed to spin that thing around that way,' Daley said.

'The hell I'm not,' Peterson said. 'In a couple of weeks I'll be spinnin' it like a goddamn top. Our asses depend on what I see through that range finder. The Japs are gonna be out there lookin' for us the same way.'

'Japanese equipment can't match ours,' Daley said. 'We beat the hell out of them at Midway and in the Coral Sea.'

'You don't know what you're talkin' about, sailor,' Peterson said. 'I saw their gunnery at Savo Island. Every fuckin' shell was on target.'

'How come they didn't sink this ship?'

'We ran away.'

The ensign frowned. He wanted to tell Peterson to shut up, but he didn't know how. He wanted to be one of the boys and an officer at the same time.

Another bugle call blasted their ears, followed by another boatswain mate's pipe. 'Fire. Fire on the hangar deck,' boomed the PA. 'All hands man their fire stations.'

'Christ,' Flanagan said. 'I've forgotten that one already.'

'Now this gauge is the most important one on the ship. It tells us how much water's in the boiler. If there ain't enough, you get a low-water casualty. That's the word we use in the Navy for a breakdown. It ain't chosen by accident. Down here a casualty can cause casualties, get it? In a low-water, the pipes inside the boiler melt and superheated steam comes blastin' out into your face. In about ten seconds you ain't got no face. If there's too much water, it goes through the pipes and into the turbines in the engine room next door. It'll bend the blades and tear them fuckin' turbines apart.'

Marty Roth and a half dozen other new firemen stood in the well of the after fireroom listening to Amos Cartwright explaining the various emergencies that could turn life in the fireroom from boredom to terror in the blink of an eye.

'You see them pipes up there?' Cartwright pointed to the

confusion of pipes on the overhead. 'They're carryin' oil from the fuel tanks and six hundred pounds of live steam to the inch. They all got flanged connections. There's a gasket in the flange, and if that blows out, you got steam or oil comin' down on you. That oil hits a hot pipe and you got a fire. So you got to know – I mean *know* – exactly what valve to turn to cut off that pipe and what one cuts in a backup so we don't come to a fuckin' dead stop with Jap shells fallin' all around us.'

Six hundred pounds of superheated steam to the square inch, Roth thought, eyeing the pipes. Apply for a transfer now, urged the survival voice, the one that had whispered to him about death in the Negro bar in Los Angeles.

'Attention. Attention,' roared a voice from the ladder to the main deck. It was Commander Oswald Bradley, the engineering officer. With him was none other than the Captain. Everyone stiffened his spine.

'At ease, at ease,' the Captain said. 'This isn't an inspection. I just found out an old friend is aboard.' He strolled over to Amos Cartwright. 'How are you, Amos?'

'Just fine, Captain,' Amos said.

He turned to Marty Roth. 'What's your name, sailor?'

'Roth, sir.'

'He's just come aboard, Captain,' Cartwright said. 'From Bronx, New York. He's strikin' for watertender. I'm teachin' him.'

'You couldn't have a better professor.'

The Captain asked the names and hometowns of everyone else on watch in the fireroom. Then he made a little speech. 'I hope you fellows understand how much we topside sailors depend on you when the going gets tough and we need all the speed we can get out of this big lady. Don't let the deck apes put you down. This is the really important part of the ship.'

Commander Bradley looked amazed. Later Roth found out why. It was the first time in Bradley's twenty-three years in the Navy that he had ever heard such words from a deck officer.

The Captain and the Engineering Officer climbed the ladder to the main deck and vanished. 'He's a great man,'

Amos Cartwright said. 'He don't look it or act it, but he's a great man.'

Marty Roth stared up at the two twenty-foot-tall boilers where blazing oil was creating superheated steam. Death, he thought. Out of the maws of these monsters could spew death. Only his brain could prevent it. He had to learn how this lethal machinery worked to challenge death. He summoned the memory of Sylvia Morison whispering praise of his courage, his moral clarity. Besides, how could he walk out on Amos Cartwright now?

A knock on the door.

'Captain,' said the orderly on duty, 'Commander Parker is here.'

'Come in,' Captain McKay said.

Commander Daniel Boone Parker eased his bulk through the door. He glanced with approval at the table set with the heavy silver, the gleaming water goblets and gold-rimmed china with the seal of the state of Missouri emblazoned on them. In his right hand was a briefcase with an odd bulge in the centre.

'I thought perhaps you'd accept this little addition to your private stock on behalf of the wardroom, Captain,' he said. From the briefcase he extracted a bottle of twelve-year-old Ballantine Scotch.

'Why . . . thank you,' McKay said, taken by surprise.

Without missing a beat, Parker continued. 'Since you haven't said anything about it, I assume you're going to let the old J.C. stay a wet ship. I keep a very close eye on the drinkers. No one's abusing it. I think it does wonders for a man's morale to be able to invite a friend to his cabin for cocktails before dinner or relax with a snort when he comes off a late watch.'

Arthur McKay sat there, a polite smile on his face, silently cursing his friend Win Kemble. Or should he curse Rita and Fleet Admiral Ernest J. King? Normally, Win would have told him the *Jefferson City* was flouting Order 99 banning liquor in the wardrooms when they talked things over after the transfer of command.

Parker was on perfectly safe ground assuming Captain Kemble had done so. The Executive Officer was repeating, probably word for word, sentiments Arthur McKay had heard from Win Kemble more than once. Win agreed with his father-in-law and a lot of other admirals, such as Bill Halsey, that Order 99 was the dumbest, most vicious thing the civilians had done to the Navy since they stranded John Paul Jones in Paris.

For several reasons, McKay did not agree with this aristocratic stance. But he was confronted with a totally unexpected decision here. Should he tolerate this already established custom among his officers? Intersecting and confusing his reaction was his friendship with Win.

'I'll go along with breaking the reg for the time being,' he said. 'But I reserve the right to change my mind when the shooting starts. It's hard to predict how people react to danger.'

'I'd say that's when a man will need a drink more than ever,' Parker said.

'Maybe,' McKay said.

He put the bottle in a drawer of his desk without opening it. An amazingly intense glare of dislike flashed across Parker's face. At this unpropitious moment. Horace Aquino arrived with the trays from the crew's mess. With the flourish of a headwaiter in a posh LA restaurant, the steward transferred rubbery-looking hot dogs and soggy french fries to the gold-rimmed plates.

'Is this your idea of a joke?' Commander Parker said.

'Did you ever work for Admiral T.T. Craven?' Arthur McKay said.

'Tireless Tom, the sailor's friend? No. He was a nut, from everything I've heard.'

'The battleship boys hung that one on him because he fought for carriers. He had a lot of ideas about how to change the Navy. He thought the food served to enlisted men would improve about a hundred percent if the officers ate the same thing. He could never convince anyone it was a good idea.'

'You're convincing me he really was a nut.'

'He was a little crazy. You get that way when you buck the

system. My father-in-law, Rob Semmes, had a couple of screws loose by the time he died. Anyway, I was on Craven's staff in the late twenties. I've always thought his idea about eating the crew's food was worth trying. But it would take a revolution to put it over. So I'm doing it my way. I'm going to sample one meal a week, at random.'

'The officer of the deck eats every meal that's served while he's on duty. That's regulations.'

'Has any OOD ever complained to you about the food?'

'No.'

'If you were the OOD and you got this for a meal, what would you think of it?'

'It's edible,' Parker said.

McKay chewed on a piece of hot dog. 'Just barely,' he said. 'Why isn't the food better?'

'We've got to feed these men on sixty-nine cents a day, Captain,' Parker said. 'Let's start with that.'

'I know. But we're buying wholesale from the Navy. I think we can do a lot better than this. Talk to the supply officer about it. If you don't, I will.'

'Yes, Captain.'

Parker sat there waiting for Steward Aquino to take away the tray and replace it with some decent food. McKay started eating the hot dogs and french fries. Parker had no choice but to follow suit.

'I didn't think much of our performance at those drills today,' McKay said.

'We've got 350 new men aboard. The petty officers haven't had a chance to shape them up.'

'We had a lot more than 350 men who didn't know where the hell they were supposed to go if we had to abandon ship.'

'I didn't see the point of that drill, Captain. I think it's bad for morale. If we ever have to abandon ship, no one's going to have time to go to his station. We'll all go over the side wherever we happen to be.'

'That's a panic situation, Commander. The point is, if the principle of going to his station is drilled into every man, someone will show up at the stations and cut loose the life rafts. That could save a couple of hundred lives.'

Parker shrugged. 'OK. We'll drill them until all they think about is abandoning ship. But we'll have a lot of guys shitting in their pants when we sound General Quarters.'

McKay was starting to enjoy Commander Parker. It was fascinating the way he walked right up to the edge of insubordination, then veered away.

'Who was the officer of the deck when the Japs hit us at Savo Island?' McKay said.

'I was.'

'Weren't you at General Quarters?'

When the ship went to General Quarters, the executive officer was normally in Battle II, an after steering house where he could take command if the bridge was hit and the captain was killed.

'We'd secured from General Quarters.'

'Where was Captain Kemble?'

'He was asleep.'

'Asleep?'

Was it possible? Would Win Kemble go to sleep when his ship was on patrol, expecting an imminent Japanese attack?

'We'd been at General Quarters for thirty-six hours,' Commander Parker said. 'The men were coming apart. I told Kemble we had to secure and let some of them sleep. He didn't want to do it. I had to get the chaplain and the doctor up on the bridge to talk him into it.'

Commander Parker chewed his last piece of rubber hot dog. 'He needed a rest more than anyone on the ship. But he wouldn't admit it.'

'What happened when the Japs attacked?'

'Haven't you read Kemble's after-action report?'

'Yes. But it didn't explain very much.'

'Don't expect me to explain any more, Captain. I know how the Annapolis system works. You're here to hang the blame for that disaster around my neck. You're here to tie the noose on Uncle Dan Parker – the noose you ring knockers have been trying to tie for twenty-five years. Let me tell you something, Captain. No one's going to hang Uncle Dan. He's got friends in Congress, friends on the Naval Affairs Committee who can blow your career out of the water if you try to rough him up.'

'You've got me all wrong, Commander. I'm not the hangman type. I want to find out what happened to make sure it doesn't happen again.'

'The hell you're not the hangman type. Why are you serving me garbage for dinner? Why are you pulling all these drills without telling me in advance so I could pass the word to the division officers and get the men ready for them? I give you a bottle of my best Scotch and you don't even offer me a drink. You're not treating me with respect, Captain.'

Now Arthur McKay understood how Commander Parker had received all those glowing fitness reports in his file. He had perfected the art and science of intimidating his superiors. McKay also knew how the Captain of the *Jefferson City* should respond to this outburst of defiance. He should inform Commander Parker that he was in hack – confined to his cabin – until they reached Pearl Harbor, where he would be replaced by a new executive officer. At the same time, McKay realized that this extraordinary behaviour could only be motivated by extreme desperation. Was Daniel Boone Parker risking the disgrace of being relieved for insubordination to conceal something far worse – something to do with his conduct at Savo Island?

'As for what happened at Savo Island,' Parker said, 'the only way to prevent it from happening again would be to get rid of a few dozen admirals who got their stripes because they started kissing the right asses the day they graduated from Annapolis. That's all you'll find out if you keep on investigating Savo Island.'

'I wonder if that's all I'll find out,' Captain McKay said.

Warning Signals

'What do you think of President Roosevelt, Dr Levy?' asked Lieutenant Wilson Selvage MacComber in his languid Georgia way.

'A great man,' Dr Levy said, spooning down his chocolate

sundae. He was the ship's junior physician, in the Navy less than six months. Short and swarthy, he had an irritated look on his face most of the time, as if he had weighed the world and found it wanting in some fundamental way. He spent most of his time in his cabin reading medical books.

'That seems to be a virtually universal opinion among your race,' MacComber said.

'My race? I think opinion about him varies widely among white Americans.'

'There's a perfect example of why I dislike Roosevelt so much. Jews now consider themselves part of the white race, thanks to him. He's given you delusions of grandeur, Dr Levy.'

'I think it was Thomas Jefferson who did that, Mr Mac-Comber. When he wrote that stuff about all men being created equal.'

'You don't consider Jews a special race. A chosen people?'

'No more chosen than anyone else. I'm not religious, Mr MacComber.'

'Really? I find it hard to respect someone who allows his traditions to lapse.'

'If they become meaningless, what's the point? Do you still salute the Confederate flag?'

'In my heart I do, Dr Levy. Are you by any chance related to Commodore Uriah P. Levy, who was in the Navy during and after the Civil War?'

'No. My family was still in Russia in 1860.'

'He was a very difficult man, Uriah Levy. He went from one court-martial to another, always blamin' his altercations on anti-Semitism. I've investigated some of his allegations rather thoroughly. I concluded he was a Jewish version of an uppity nigger.'

'MacComber,' said Lieutenant Mullenoe, who was sitting beside him, 'you're the most prejudiced human being I know.'

'*Au contraire*, Mr Mullenoe,' MacComber said. 'I simply see things as they are. Where have I exhibited the slightest prejudice to Dr Levy?'

'Didn't you just compare him to an uppity nigger?'

'I compared Uriah Levy, who may or may not be related to him, to an uppity nigger. But that only suggests the spirit of utter equality that breathes in my veins and, if I may say so, the veins of the entire South. We hold no prejudice against Jews. We consider them every bit as good as niggers.'

MacComber smiled beatifically at Levy. 'I need hardly add, Dr Levy, that I'm an admirer of the Negro race – as long as they keep their place.'

Montgomery West found himself grinding his teeth. He surveyed the table, looking for someone to support Levy if he decided to fight back.

At the head of the table, Dr Cadwallader discussed Missouri politics with the Executive Officer. They were both from the Show Me state. Nearby, Commander George Washington Tombs, the new damage control officer, was discussing the 1941 World Series between the Dodgers and the Yankees with the Engineering Officer, Oz Bradley. Lieutenant Commander Moss, on the borderline between the commanders and the lieutenants, was listening to MacComber with what seemed to be complete approval on his prissy Presbyterian face. On the borderline between the lieutenants and the ensigns, the dentist, a Boston Irishman who roomed with Levy, was frowning. Beside him, Ensign Meade and another ensign were shaking their heads and smiling.

Unfortunately, Levy was too new to the wardroom wars to understand there was only one way to deal with someone like MacComber, you had to give it right back to him. By dropping the argument, he was figuratively striking his colours, giving the younger macho types the privilege of enjoying MacComber's outrageousness.

Montgomery West was fairly sure the dentist and possibly Mullenoe would cheer if Levy threw his chocolate sundae in MacComber's sneering face. Meade and the other ensign would probably applaud. But Levy kept his head down. Briskly, he finished his sundae, downed his coffee and left the table. West followed him into the passageway. Although he was not about to reveal that his mother was Jewish, he wanted to say something affirmative. 'Doctor,' he said, 'I just thought you'd like to know not everybody agrees with that asshole.'

Levy shrugged. 'If you have a scientific view of things, it doesn't bother you. A few more centuries of evolution will eliminate that kind of stupidity.'

After dinner, Harold Semple felt sick. The repulsive hot dogs and french fries floated in a pool of rancid coffee in his churning stomach. He stumbled into a head and vomited.

Semple's body ached from thirty-six hours of loading provisions and ammunition. They had worked last night until 4 a.m. and had been blasted out of an exhausted sleep by reveille at 5.30. In between the captain's idiotic drills, he had spent the morning swabbing the main deck. He reeled down to the First Division's compartment and crawled into his bottom rack. Maybe they would let him sleep for a half hour, at least.

A few feet away, a voice said, 'You looked bushed, Prettyboy.' It was Boatswain's Mate First Class Jerome Wilkinson.

'I'm sick,' he said.

'Yeah. I heard what you had for dinner,' Wilkinson said. 'At the Muscle Inn we had veal chops. Apple pie for desert. Same as the wardroom.'

The Muscle Inn was a separate mess somewhere in the forward part of the ship that Wilkinson and some of his friends had set up with the help of the Chief Steward's mate. Wilkinson occasionally invited his favourites to join him for a meal there.

Semple had been lying with his face to the bulkhead. He turned over and realized Wilkinson was sitting on the rack opposite him. The compartment was empty, except for a dozen or so sailors dozing in their racks. 'How'd you like to take it easy?' Wilkinson said. 'Maybe get assigned to one of the shell-handlin' rooms, where you only got about a dozen square feet to keep clean each day? Skip a workin' party now and then. Get friendly with a couple of steward's mates who'll slip you some real chow.'

'I'd like it.'

'So would a lot of other guys. If I did all that for you, I'd expect you to sort of return the favour.'

'How could I?'

'There was a boatswain's mate I knew in China. He broke me into the Navy. He used to say, "On the beach I got the pretty girls, at sea I got the pretty boys." You get the idea?'

Suddenly the hot airless compartment was cold. Semple shivered from head to foot.

'It don't hurt if you relax. You get to like it,' Wilkinson said. 'A lot of guys who spent time in China do it. Even officers.'

Semple lay there shivering, the cold clutching him.

'We're gonna be at sea a long time, Prettyboy.'

'If you touch me I'll tell the Chaplain,' Semple whispered. 'I'll tell the Chaplain and the Captain. I'll tell them what you did to that man in Los Angeles.'

'You miserable little cunt!'

Wilkinson dragged Semple from his rack. A shower of punches and kicks drove him whimpering into a corner. 'Get up on deck. I want to see every fuckin' piece of brass forward of turret one so bright by sundown we'll have to put black tape on them so they won't give us away to a fuckin' submarine.'

He dragged Semple to his feet by the back of his collar. 'Let me tell you somethin' else. If you ever say a word about what happened in LA to anybody, you'll be over the side that night. You won't be the first guy I put over. And you won't be able to make a fuckin' sound, because before you go your fuckin' throat will be a lot wider than your mouth.'

A knife with a curving blade was in Wilkinson's hand. Semple felt the steel edge against his throat. He fled to the main deck and began polishing the brightwork. Toward sundown, as he laboured over the brass knobs on the stanchions on the bow, Wilkinson seemed to materialize behind him.

'Take a good look at that ocean, Prettyboy,' he said. 'It's awful deep.'

'OK, gobs,' Jack Peterson announced in the compartment after dinner. 'The word's out. We hit Pearl on September thirtieth. It's time to get in the anchor pool.'

Having grown up in the Bronx where betting was a way of

life, Flanagan was instantly ready to bite. 'First, what is it?' he said. 'Second, how much?'

'You select the hour and minute when we anchor, moor or dock at Pearl. The price is two bucks.'

'Who's running it?'

'Who runs everything on this tub? Wilkinson and his pal the master at arms, Boffo the Great Nolan.'

'Two crooks,' Boats Homewood said. 'I once lost a hundred bucks on Nolan when we was on the *Pennsylvania* and he was fightin' some boon from the *California*. He took a dive on his own shipmates.'

'Jesus Christ, Boats. How can you rig an anchor pool? Anyone who owns a wristwatch knows if they win it,' Peterson said.'

'There's lots of ways. If you're an asshole buddy of the exec like Wilkinson, you got a very good idea of what time we're goin' to make Pearl. You buy up all the times around that.'

'What do you think, Boats?' Flanagan said.

'I think we ought to run our own pool.'

'Boats, the winner of this thing will walk away with a thousand bucks,' Peterson said.

'I'll take 0805,' Flanagan said. It added up to thirteen which he considered his lucky number.

Flanagan rushed to his locker to get his wallet. He shoved his hand through his skivvies to the back corner where he had tucked it after his last liberty. No wallet. He frantically pulled everything out of the locker and piled it on his rack. No wallet. 'Someone stole my wallet,' he said.

A half dozen other sailors dashed to their lockers. 'Christ, my watch is gone,' one yelled. Another one had a wallet missing. A fourth had lost a silver bracelet that he had bought in Long Beach. All of the losers were new men.

Boats Homewood paced up and down between the racks. 'The thief's back. I shoulda warned you. He laid low homeward bound from the Solomons. He's hit us before. I thought I scared him off.'

It was amazing how the lost wallet changed Flanagan's feelings for his shipmates. Suddenly they were no longer friends or potential friends. They were like people in a subway car in New York. Except on this subway, you had to sleep, eat, bathe and work with the passengers.

'We'll catch the bastard. I got some tricks up my sleeve I learned before you guys were out of diapers,' Homewood said. 'When I do –' He balled one enormous fist.

Flanagan almost felt sorry for the thief.

Another bugle call blasted over the PA system followed by the inevitable boatswain's pipe. 'Now hear this,' rasped the PA. 'Stand by to abandon ship.'

'Jesus Christ. I hope this time it's for real,' Jablonsky yelled as they dashed for the ladders. 'Anything to get off this tub.'

'As I see it, Captain, the fundamental question for religion today is this: Is Christ King of the Earth City or only of the Heavenly City?'

Captain McKay glanced at the clock above his desk. Unbelievable. It was 2100 hours and Chaplain Emerson Bushnell was still talking. They had finished supper two hours ago. By now he had acquired a comprehensive knowledge of the chaplain's ancestry. He was the fifteenth in an unbroken line of Bushnell preachers who went back to the day the Puritans landed in Massachusetts in 1630. His most famous forebear was his grandfather, Horace Bushnell, who flourished after the Civil War. Horace had written a bestselling book, *The Moral Uses of Dark Things*, which his grandson reread once a year. Unfortunately, he no longer agreed with it.

While Bushnell was in Yale Divinity School, his older brother Alcott had volunteered for the infantry in World War I. He had been killed in the battle of the Argonne. A dark anguish had crept into Bushnell's voice as he talked about the impact of his death on his thinking about religion. It had prompted him to begin reading books written by people with long German names and some by a Dane named Kierkegaard, all of whom cast doubt on his grandfather's optimistic thesis that God's love could be understood and even experienced by human beings. Just what Chaplain Bushnell now believed, McKay was not sure. After listening to him for three hours, he suspected Bushnell was not sure either.

'I'm afraid I've got quite a bit of reading to do before I turn in, Chaplain. I've enjoyed our conversation. I haven't talked this much religion since I got baptized at fourteen back in Kansas.'

'What exactly is your belief, Captain?'

'I was raised a Baptist. Lately I've been inclined to agree with Disraeli, who said all sensible men belong to the same religion.'

'What religion is that?' the chaplain asked.

'Sensible men never say.'

Chaplain Bushnell looked blank. Then he forced a laugh. 'Oh, I get it,' he said. 'Very clever. Essentially, you're an agnostic.'

'What's your impression of the ship, Chaplain?

'I haven't seen the poor fellows so worn out since Savo Island,' the chaplain said. 'They got very little sleep last night while we loaded that ammunition. Then all these drills. I wish you'd given them a day or two of pleasant cruising.'

'They've got to get used to living under pressure. What do you think of the ship's morale, the feeling the men have about her?'

'For a while I had a church in Jersey City. As you can imagine, there aren't many Congregationalists in a town like that – mostly Irish and Italian and Polish Catholics. I decided I needed to find out more about the city as a whole, the community of believers in which we lived. It wasn't enough merely to minister to my own small flock. I wanted us to be a living cell in the earthly city we are supposed to be perfecting. I sent out a questionnaire asking people to describe the city as they experienced it. Nobody answered.'

'Why not?'

'They were afraid, Captain. Jersey City is run by one of the most ruthless political bosses in the nation. They were afraid to say anything against him. Jersey City remained opaque to me. I had to fall back on formulas, rote religion.'

'I don't get your point.'

'The ship is opaque to me, Captain. As opaque as Jersey City.'

'Is that because the men are afraid to talk to you?'

The chaplain's smile was enigmatic. Or was it wary? 'Perhaps. I sometimes get the feeling everyone in the Navy is afraid. The system is based on fear, wouldn't you say, Captain? It presumes men are fallen creatures who can only be coerced into doing their duty. John Calvin would have approved it completely.'

'If you and John Calvin made that judgement, Chaplain, you'd have to be looking at the Navy – and this ship – from the outside. It may look like the setup's based on fear, on regulations, discipline. But from the inside, there's a lot more to it. If you want a non-theologian's opinion, it's really based on faith.'

'Faith? You mean in the American way, the four freedoms?'

McKay shook his head. 'That's belief, Chaplain. I've always made a distinction between faith and belief. I think Jesus did too, if you read him from a certain perspective. Didn't he describe faith as a rock? Faith is indefinable, Chaplain. When you've got it, you're steady as that rock in the New Testament. When you haven't got it, you can come apart at the most inconvenient moments.'

'But faith resides in something.'

'It's not in a set of ideas. It's in an entity. In a man, a church, a country, a ship – a god. Faith is what leadership is all about. FDR's spent the last eight years trying to create or preserve faith in the country in spite of the Depression. Admiral King sweats about faith in the Navy, in spite of Pearl Harbor and Savo Island. My job is to create faith in this ship. You've got the hardest job – sustaining faith in God. I don't envy you, Chaplain.'

Emerson Bushnell seemed to find that remark very upsetting. He put his coffee cup down on his plate with a clink. 'Are you sure you're not a theologian, Captain?' he murmured.

'Quite sure.'

'I have a different definition of faith. I think it exists only when souls intersect, spiritually, morally, when the opacity that dooms us to our lonely individualism is overcome for a

160

little while. I had that experience with Captain Kemble. It's why I stayed on this ship. To protect his reputation, if I can.'

'Did you advise Captain Kemble to relieve the men from General Quarters just before the shooting started at Savo Island?'

Suddenly there was a mocking, almost hostile smile on the chaplain's face. 'Is that a court-martial offence, Captain?'

'I doubt it. Did you think it might be when you gave him the advice?'

'It so happens I did not say a word to him that night. But if he had asked me, I would have given him that advice. The men were in a state of physical and spiritual collapse. I would have approved the course he and Commander Parker chose for this ship.'

'Are you speaking as the navigator or the chaplain now?'

'The chaplain. On that terrible night, Captain Kemble and Commander Parker made more than a military decision. They made a moral decision. A moral decision that I will never cease to defend, whatever the Navy does to them. Beyond this statement, Captain, my lips are sealed. I will refuse to discuss the subject at any court-martial proceeding you and your superiors convene at Pearl Harbor.'

'Who told you we were going to do that?'

'It's more or less assumed by everyone, officers and men. In Long Beach, the Navy doesn't control the news. In Pearl Harbor it does.'

The telephone rang. It was Lieutenant Commander Cadwallader. 'Captain, I hate to bother you at this hour. But I'm afraid that sailor who was hit by the bow has taken a turn for the worse. If we don't get him to a hospital I doubt he'll last the night.'

'We're almost three hundred miles at sea. How the hell are we going to get him to a hospital?'

'Can't you radio for a seaplane?'

'We can't break radio silence. A Japanese submarine could pick up the message.'

'Send him back aboard one of the destroyers?'

'Those ships are needed in the South Pacific.'

It was infuriating the way Cadwallader dumped the

responsibility in his lap when it was his misdiagnosis that was killing the boy.

McKay led the chaplain down to sick bay. Everything modern medicine could cram on to a ship was here. Surgical instruments gleamed on trays, big sterilizers with roll tops guaranteed antisepsis. Cadwallader motioned them to the rear of the compartment, where the sailor lay on a bottom bunk, a bottle of plasma rigged above him. A pharmacist's mate was giving him a transfusion.

'His vital signs are not good. There's some sort of internal derangement,' Cadwallader said. 'For a while I thought there might be a locus of infection somewhere.'

'What do you think?' McKay said, turning to the ship's second physician, the scowling hook-nosed young reservist named Levy.

'The locus of infection is a medical theory that expired around 1929,' Levy said. 'He's got a ruptured spleen. There's not much anyone can do about it.'

The sailor was delirious. 'Momma,' he mumbled. 'I'm sorry I've been bad. I won't be bad any more, I promise you. It's the bosun. He makes us do things to people, Momma. I knew they were wrong.'

'What's he talking about?' McKay asked the chaplain.

'I have no idea,' Emerson Bushnell said. He seized the boy's hand. 'Son,' he said, 'can you hear me? Can you pray with me? Jesus loves you, son. He wants to help you.'

Listening with an ear attuned to the nuances of sincerity, Captain McKay concluded Chaplain Bushnell did not believe a word he was saying. He was not achieving that intersection of souls that had lifted him and Win Kemble to an encounter with faith. Bushnell sincerely wanted to help the boy. He was trying to console and comfort him as he drifted into the darkness. But all he could offer him was rote religion.

In the Navy they called that doing things by the book. Had he allowed that mentality to kill this boy? Over the years he had heard Win Kemble condemn this habit of the military mind a hundred times. What had Win done at Savo Island that lifted his soul into precarious contact with the unmilitary, even anti-military soul of Emerson Bushnell?

Captain McKay went back to his cabin and lay in his bunk staring into the darkness for a long time, while the *Jefferson City* steamed toward the war at twenty-five knots.

Chief Steward's Mate Walter Davis was a large, formidable black man. When he appeared in the compartment where the *Jefferson City*'s thirty-eight black stewards slept, people stood up or at least got out of their racks and came to semi-attention as if the Captain himself had come down the ladder.

'Otis. Where the fuck is Otis?' he demanded.

Willard Otis emerged from a bunk in the rear of the compartment. He was short and very black, with a wide cheerful mouth and loving-cup ears.

'What the fuck is this?' Davis said.

He shoved a slip of paper in Otis's face.

It's a request, Chief,' Otis said. 'A request for a transfer to B Division.'

'What the fuck kinda game you playin'?' Davis said, lifting Otis off the deck by the front of his workshirt.

Buttons popped as Otis struggled to explain. 'I'd like to strike for watertender, Chief. Amos Cartwright says he thinks the Captain would OK it.'

'What'd I tell you about talkin' to that Philadelphia nigger?' Davis said, banging Otis against the bulkhead for emphasis.

'I didn't do it, Chief. He talked to me,' Otis said. 'Heard me gassin' at the movies about the work I done on my car and said if I was interested in engines maybe I oughta try for a transfer.'

'How much you weigh, you stupid little fucker?'

'Hundred and thirty pounds.'

'Christ almighty. You think it'd be any trouble for one of them Polacks in that division to put you over the side some dark night? They'd do it to that other fucker from Philadelphia in five seconds if he wasn't as big as he is. If they didn't, what do you think would happen to you in Georgia if you came struttin' down the street with that rate on your arm, talkin' and actin' like that big-mouthed nigger? They'd find you drippin' off a tree next mornin' sure as your name's Otis. They'd be nothin' left of you but a tear in your momma's eye.'

'Chief,' Willard Otis said in a barely audible voice as Davis, his hand now around his throat, banged him against the bulkhead again, 'my momma's dead. Maybe I don't have t'go home t'Georgia no more.'

'Your momma'll be glad she's dead if she could see what'll happen to you if you send me up another chit like this one,' Davis said. 'We got the best deal on this ship, and I don't want nobody messin' it up, get me? We're eatin' better, we got better hours, we got better everythin' than these white assholes standin' four-on, four-off and gettin' fed shit for their trouble. So just cool it, you get me, boy?'

Various parts of Otis's body including his head banged against the bulkhead again.

'I got you, Chief,' he said.

Davis threw him against the bulkhead one more time for good measure and departed. Otis's rackmates picked him up and applied first aid to a cut on the back of his head. 'I *tole* you that was goin' to happen,' said Cash Johnson, a lanky Floridian.

'Chief's right about the deal we got though,' said Casey Quinn, who was from Charleston. 'I don't want no four-on, four-off shit.'

'Only deal the chief's tryin' to protect is the one he's got,' Otis said. 'You saw how much new furniture we lugged into that house of his in Los Angeles. Musta cost two thousand dollars. 'Only one place he'd get that kind of money, and it ain't playin' craps.'

'Boy, you keep talkin' out loud like that and you *will* be over the side,' Casey Quinn said.

'So we commend our shipmate Donald's body to the deep and his soul to God,' Chaplain Emerson Bushnell said.

All hands were in ranks on the stern for the burial of the sailor who had been hit by the bow as the *Jefferson City* got under way from Long Beach. No one in F Division knew him, but everyone agreed with Boats Homewood that it was a bad omen. It suggested that the new captain could not break the jinx which seemed to be permanently attached to the *Jefferson City*.

A Marine bugler played taps. A Marine honour guard in dress blues fired a volley over the corpse. At a gesture from the chaplain two deck apes lifted the stretcher on which the body lay, and it slid over the side and vanished beneath the surface.

In Flanagan's imagination he saw the sailor spinning down, down in his shroud, refusing to believe in his own death. That was what he would do. He would demand proof that he was dead. He would ask how come. What had he done to deserve death at eighteen?

That thought reminded him he had a mortal sin on his soul. According to Father Callow and the Catholic Church, he was spiritually dead. Sanctifying grace was absent from his soul and body. But he did not feel dead. Every time he thought of Teresa Brownlow, life leaped in his belly, his heart pounded, his tongue grew thick with desire. Woman, she was woman, with her sweetness, her wildness, her body that made his body as insubstantial as fire.

It was impossible to believe in sin or death this morning. Life was filling his lungs, cascading in his veins. The immense Pacific sea and sky were so incredibly beautiful. A procession of fat white clouds, like a line of galleons, sat on the horizon. The sun burned in a sky so intensely blue it seemed to radiate its own light.

In front of the division, Ensign Herman Kruger was reminding them of various things from the Plan of the Day. There was a gunnery drill scheduled for 1000 hours. He urged everyone to do his best to impress the new captain. 'First, however, two of you have some business with the captain. Flanagan and Peterson, report to the master at arms office for captain's mast.'

Chief Boatswain's Mate Biff Nolan, the master at arms, greeted them with a hostile leer. 'F Division fuckups,' he said. 'They gave you guys the right initial all right. Especially you, Peterson.'

'How come we're the only guys who got charged? What

happened to the other seventy-five who got grabbed by the SP's while we were in Long Beach?' Peterson asked.

'The exec dismissed all the other cases at his mast. But when he saw your name, he said he wished he could triple the charges. I told you to get off this tub before he fixed your ass permanently.'

'Can you give us a look at the charges?' Peterson said ignoring Nolan's remarks.

Nolan showed Peterson the report on him and Flanagan. They were lumped together as drunk and disorderly, and accused of causing a riot and resisting arrest.

'Let me do the talkin',' Peterson whispered to Flanagan as they made their way forward to the Captain's cabin. The maroon rug on the deck, the red leather couch and chairs against one bulkhead, the gleaming walnut table and drop-lid desk opposite them, looked like luxury to Flanagan. The executive officer, Commander Parker, and Ensign Kruger arrived just ahead of them. Kruger explained to the Captain that he was acting as F Division officer because Lieutenant West had the watch on the bridge. The Captain stood in the centre of the cabin and listened gravely while the Executive Officer read him the charges.

'Those are pretty serious. Do you have anything to say on behalf of these men?' the Captain asked Kruger.

'Only that I feel Third Class Petty Officer Peterson should be disciplined severely, Captain,' Kruger said. 'He constantly sets a bad example to the younger men.'

The Captain gave Kruger a puzzled look. 'I thought a division officer defended his men at Captain's Mast, Mr Kruger.'

'I'm here to speak for Flanagan. It's his first offence. But take a look at Peterson's record, Captain. He seldom goes ashore without getting into trouble.'

'What have you got to say for yourself, Peterson?' the Captain asked.

'It's definitely my fault, Captain,' Peterson said. 'Seaman Flanagan came to my support after the fight started. He left his girlfriend at a very crucial moment and rushed to my defence. A lot of other guys whose charges have been

166

dismissed by Commander Parker did the same thing. They all saw I was fightin' for the honour of the ship. Those tin-can guys were callin' us yellow. I couldn't let them get away with that.'

'Why were they calling us yellow?'

'They say we ran out on the other ships at Savo Island. And in the Java Sea.'

The Captain flushed. A tinge of red ran up his neck into the smooth olive skin of his cheeks. Flanagan wondered if Peterson had just talked them into a life sentence. 'Do you believe that?'

'No, sir,' Peterson said. 'I wish we could have gotten in a few licks at the other guys at Savo. I had ranges on at least two Jap ships, but we never got the order to fire. I guess it was because that shell knocked out main plot.'

Even Flanagan knew enough about fire control to realize Peterson was ignoring the auxiliary computers in main forward and in the range finder itself that could have taken over main plot's job. Even if these were not functioning, the turrets could fire independently on local control. Jack was going out of his way to tell the Captain something he wanted him to know.

'What the hell are you talking about, Peterson?' Commander Parker snarled. 'It was pitch black that night. You couldn't get a range on anything.'

'Sir, on the *California*, they used to call me Jack the Cat. I've got very good night vision,' Peterson said. 'I called down ranges on two ships. One was a destroyer, the other a cruiser.'

'What's your explanation for why we didn't fire on those ships?' Captain McKay said.

'I have no idea, Captain. Some people believe there's been a jinx on the *Jefferson City* ever since we took two chaplains out to Manila, just before Pearl Harbor. Two chaplains on a ship is bad luck.'

'I've never heard that one before. That's as dumb as the flying fish jumping through a porthole.'

'I guess it depends on whether you're superstitious or not, Captain.'

'We're going to get plenty of chances to change our luck – and prove we aren't yellow – very soon. In the meantime, I'll dismiss these charges.'

'Thank you, Captain,' Peterson said.

'But in deference to Ensign Kruger's opinion, you're confined to the ship at Pearl Harbor, Peterson. Does that satisfy you, Mr Kruger?'

'Not entirely, Captain. I just hope that Peterson realizes it's a serious warning.'

'Consider yourself warned, Peterson,' the captain said.

'Seriously warned,' Commander Parker said.

Parker and Master at Arms Nolan were glaring at Peterson. Flanagan was baffled. He could understand why Kruger was perpetually furious at Jack. Why did the other two dislike him so much?

Gunnery

In the sea outside the *Jefferson City*'s hull, depth charges thudded. One of the escorting destroyers had picked up a submarine contact. Captain McKay had ordered the gunnery exercise to continue. He probably considered it a good chance to simulate battle conditions. For the fire controlmen in main plot, it was almost too realistic.

Lieutenant Junior Grade Montgomery West watched Fire Controlman First Class Ralph Bourne dial into the Mark VII computer the range he was receiving from Jack Peterson in the main battery director high in the ship. West noticed that Bourne's hand was shaking. He looked at the range and saw 5,000 yards when he could have sworn the talker had just reported 4,000. Elsewhere around the big computer, other fire controlmen were dialling in wind velocity, the speed of the ship and the target. Their faces were expressionless. Two of them, Bob Edison and Bob Finch, had already requested transfers to another battle station. No one wanted to work where so many shipmates had died.

'Christ,' Edison gasped when the depth charges came closer. 'I wouldn't put it past those destroyer jerks to blow a hole in us.'

'Yeah,' muttered Finch. Both blond giants from Minnesota, they were known as the Bobbsey Twins because they perpetually echoed each other's opinions.

West kept asking himself how an officer dealt with this incipient panic. Should he meet it head-on, pour scorn and sarcasm on it? The trouble was, he understood its source. He could not stop remembering the grotesque shapes and postures of the dead when he led the working party into this compartment on that first morning in Long Beach Harbor.

'Is that range right, Bourne?' he asked.

Bourne twitched. 'Sure it's right,' he said. He was a slim balding man with a tattooed heart on the back of his hand. From Connecticut, he had a Yankee's instinct for machinery. He liked to boast there was nothing on the ship that he could not fix. He could take a computer or a gun director apart and put it back together again in a day. But this gift did not make him a warrior. He had been planning to get out of the Navy when Pearl Harbor froze all enlistments for the duration.

'What was the range you just gave us?' West asked the talker, a pudgy kid from New Jersey, with a projecting underlip that made him look perpetually worried.

'I don't remember,' he said.

'Ask it again.'

'Plot to main forward. Could you repeat the range?'

A torrent of sound poured into the talker's ears. 'Sir, it's the Gunnery Officer,' he said, looking as if he was about to burst into tears. 'He wants to talk to you.'

'What in God's name are you doing down there, West?' screamed Lieutenant Commander Edwin Moss. 'If you don't get the range into your computer the second you hear it, we'll all be at the bottom of the ocean.'

'Sorry sir. What is the range?'

'Four thousand yards.'

His face burning, West handed the earphones back to the talker. 'It's four thousand yards,' he said to Bourne.

'That fucking kid told me five thousand,' Bourne shouted.

'Forget it. Just get it right,' West said.

'I want that fucking kid out of here. I don't like the fucking expression on his face,' Bourne raged.

'Dial it in, for Christ's sake!'

'What do you know about Christ, you fucking phoney? You're just here for the publicity.'

For a moment those vicious words reduced everything in West's soul to junk. The memory of Ina Severn's love, his defiant commitment to Navy, country, manhood, at the risk of his movie career, collapsed. So this is what the enlisted men thought of him? In the ruins, he heard his answer as if it were a stranger's voice.

'I'm going to forget what you just said, Bourne. Let's get the goddamn guns on target.'

Bourne glared at him with wild hatred in his eyes. Montgomery West realized the man was hoping he would return hatred for hatred and banish him from main plot. Bourne was that scared. Somehow, seeing and understanding the petty officer's frenzy ignited fresh terror in West's mind and body. It was not only the threat of death, it was revulsion at the thought of dying in such a muddle of rage and frustration. He was an officer. He was supposed to know something about leadership. But how did you lead men when the enemy was invisible, when all you could see were numbers and machines and a sealed hatch and a three quarters of an inch steel bulkhead holding back the sea? When so much of your strength went into concealing your own fear?

On their second day of gunnery exercise, Frank Flanagan ascended to his station in main forward to find Boats Homewood and Jack Peterson having a violent argument.

'It's a shitty assignment, Boats. Whatya tryin' to do, get rid of the kid?' Peterson said.

'That's not the goddamn point. I think he'd be good at it. We need some good men on them guns.'

'Who'd be good at what?' Flanagan said.

'Nothin'. Forget it,' Peterson said.

'I want to give you a shot at the forty-millimetre gun directors,' Homewood said. 'Jack says it's too dangerous.

170

You don't look the kind of guy who worries about that sort of thing.'

'Tell him how many other guys have volunteered,' Peterson said.

'So far I only got six and I don't like any of them. They're just tryn'a get out'n main plot,' Homewood said.

'How about giving me a look at the deal,' Flanagan said. He had been wondering how he could escape the main battery director without hurting Jack Peterson's feelings. He hated the foul air, the impossibility of seeing what was happening inside that overgrown tin can. He had complained about it to Homewood.

Peterson took him down a short ladder to the Mark 51 director that aimed one of the forty-millimetre mounts they had added to the *Jefferson City* in the dry dock at Long Beach. Four Swedish-made Bofors guns were in each mount; they had long menacing barrels and flaring muzzles.

The director was on a small platform beside the mainmast, about twenty feet above the mount. It looked like a half-finished robot. The squarish head was the sight. You stepped inside two bicycle-handle arms that protruded backward. The thing practically embraced him when Flanagan pressed his body against it and looked through the glass head.

'Stop and think about it for a second, kiddo,' Jack Peterson said. 'This is a hell of a dangerous battle station.'

'What difference does that make? If the ship goes down we all go together, right?'

'An awful lot of guys can get killed without the ship goin' down. You'd be surprised how much thought most guys give to where they want to be stationed at General Quarters. You got about as much protection up here from strafin' planes and shrapnel from near misses as the Christians had against the lions in the Collasalum. The director's pretty safe, believe it or not. It's armoured against strafers, and most main battery hits on a ship are in the hull.'

'I still want to go for it,' Flanagan said, deciding not to correct Jack's pronunciation of Colosseum. 'I like the idea of being able to shoot back.'

'You barely hear the big guns inside the range finder. Out

here they're gonna blow your fuckin' ears off.'

'Stop tryin' to scare him, and give him a lesson, Jack,' Homewood said. 'I don't want any of Kruger's asskissers to get this job. They'll be so busy wipin' the shit off their legs they won't have time to fire a shot. These guns could save our hides against them Jap torpedo planes.'

Peterson shrugged and showed Flanagan how to sight and aim the director. 'It's got a gyroscope inside it that measures the rate of turn and elevation of the target so you get the guns at the right angle and with the right lead,' he said. 'Those Bofors fire a hundred and twenty shells a minute. You don't need to hold the trigger down too long. Steady, that's the key to good gunnery. Steady aim, steady shootin'.'

Flanagan did a half dozen dry runs, getting a gull or flying fish in the small oval circle inside the larger sight, holding the target there and pressing the trigger on the handle. 'I definitely want to go for it,' he said.

Homewood watched, beaming. 'You got an Irishman on your hands, Peterson.'

'I don't mind him on my hands,' Peterson said. 'I just hope he don't get splashed all over the deck.'

Jack went off to work on the main battery director. Homewood waited until he was well out of earshot and grabbed Flanagan's arm. 'OK, I done you a favour and talked Jack into doin' one too. Now I want you to do me one. And him too, but he won't know about it.'

'Sure,' Flanagan said.

'Stick close to Jack till we get to Pearl. That's where we'll find out just what sort of shit's likely to come down for our fuckup at Savo. They told Jack to get the hell off like the rest of the guys who could testify, but he don't take orders from anybody if he can help it. I backed him in this case because I think somebody ought to get his pecker hung out to dry for what happened that night. But these guys are playin' a rough game. They put one man over the side already to show they mean it. You got a knife?'

Flanagan shook his head. He was too astonished by what he was hearing to do anything else.

'Take this one,' Homewood said, unbuttoning a bone-handled knife in a leather sheath from his belt. 'You musta used one grown' up in the Bronx. Pretty rough place from all I hear.'

Flanagan decided not to try to explain to Homewood that there were no gang wars in the sedate middle-class neighbourhood off Fordham Road where he had grown up.

'I mean really stick with him. If he heads for the big crap game in one of the handlin' rooms after lights out, or to the card game in the chief's quarters, you got to go with him. I'll cover whatever you lose. Especially don't let him go up on deck alone after dark. That's when you want to keep this thing real loose.'

Homewood worked the blade out of the sheath. Flanagan wondered if he was having a bad dream.

Whistling determinedly, Ensign Richard Meade led his men up the ladder into mount one. The hatch was barely big enough to admit his strapping body. He squeezed through the opening and stood to one side while the rest of the gun crew grunted past him. Meade inhaled the odour of burnt gunpowder inside the box-shaped capsule. He studied the gleaming brass and silver breeches and rammers of the two five-inch guns. It was his third day on the job, and Dick Meade stubbornly told himself that in spite of what had happened yesterday, he loved it.

On their previous voyage, he had been in damage control. He had begged Captain Kemble to let him become a gunnery officer, but he had insisted on keeping him in damage control. Captain McKay had been more amenable.

When Dick Meade was six, he had listened in rapture to his father describe his experience as a turret officer on the cruiser *Marblehead*. His father had decided to make money instead of war, as he liked to put it; Meade sensed – no, he knew – that his mother regretted this decision . She was part of the reason he had decided to make the Navy his career, in spite of his father's disapproval.

Meade watched while his mount captain, Johnny Chase, a lean aloof man with a livid scar down one side of his face, positioned himself between the guns. Under Chase's cold eye, the shell men and powder men took their positions on opposite sides of the two guns. Meade stuck his head out the slot at the top of the mount, jamming his helmet with its combination headphone and earmuffs on to his head to protect himself against the muzzle blast. Five-inch were the loudest guns in the Navy.

'No snafus today, boys. Everything's going to be on target,' Meade said.

'We'll see what the old rabbit's foot can do sir,' Chase said, his hand moving along the edge of his scar. He had got his face blown apart in a turret explosion aboard the *Minneapolis* six years ago. The younger members of the gun crew were in awe of him. There was something spooky about him. Not many people survived explosions in a turret.

Meade thought he heard an edge of contempt in Chase's voice. Yesterday, after an hour of firing, a dented powder case had jammed in number-one gun. The powder can's corked tip became stuck to the bottom of the shell in the white-hot chamber, making it impossible to yank out. There was imminent danger of the shell 'cooking off', blowing the gun and the mount apart. Gunnery Officer Moss began asking in his usual strident tones what was wrong in mount one. Panicky, Meade had asked Chase if he should hit the emergency alarm and evacuate the mount and the handling room below it.

'We'll get it out,' Chase said. Calmly, he had cut six inches off another powder case and rammed it into the breech. They got rid of the hot shell and completed the firing exercise. But Mead wondered what Chase and the gun crew thought of his moment of panic. He knew some of the sailors called him Babyface behind his back. Was it his fault he looked too young to be an officer?

Down in the handling room under mount one, Harold Semple's arms trembled as he placed another fifty-five-pound five-inch shell in the hoist. In other hoists, cans of gunpowder were waiting for the order to rise to the hungry guns. With a shrill whine, the shell vanished. Instantly the man behind Semple thrust another shell into his arms.

Semple's stomach churned. What was he doing here caressing these snub-nosed metal monsters?

In the mount, the gun captains opened the breeches and the rammer men shoved the shells home with their electrically powered rammers. Next came the powder cans. The gun captains slammed the breeches and reported to Mount Captain Frank Chase.

'Ready one.'

'Ready two.'

Ensign Meade pressed the ready button, informing Air Defence Officer Mullenoe and Gunnery Officer Moss that mount one was prepared to fire. As the other five-inch mounts and eight-inch turrets began to report, a shout ripped into Meade's ears on the telephone circuit. 'Loose shell in mount one handling room!'

Harold Semple had lost the shell as he tried to place it in the hoist. It rolled across the deck. Hulking Fred Kraus, the captain of the handling room, dove on top of it like a football player going after a fumble. If that snout smashed against the bulkhead as the ship rolled, a large chunk of *Jefferson City* might go skyward in a million fragments.

'Jesus fucking Christ,' snarled Kraus. 'I told Boats not to put that green little kid on the shell line.'

'I'm sorry,' Semple sobbed. 'They're too heavy. I can't lift them.'

Ensign Meade dropped into the handling room, his face livid. Commander Moss's denunciations were still ringing in his ears. 'Everyone report here at 1900 hours. We're going to rehearse loading until your goddamn arms fall off,' Meade snapped. He was not going to let these idiots ruin his Navy career.

'Hey, Monsignor, take off your shoes. I want to make sure you ain't part rabbit,' Jack Peterson said.

'Nah, I've got a cloven hoof,' Flanagan said.

There were no smiles on the other nine or ten faces in the handling room beneath turret three at the stern of the ship. For an hour they had cursed and scowled and slammed big fists against the steel bulkheads as Jack made pass after pass with the dancing dice. In front of him now rose a veritable pile of five- and ten-dollar bills.

Flanagan was feeling almost as cocky as Jack. In spite of the blasts of the big guns, which were as bad as Peterson had predicted they would be, he had run up the best score of any of the fire controlmen on the forty-millimetre directors.

'Start countin' them, Monsignor,' Jack said as he blew on the cubes. 'This'll be my last round.'

'What the fuck are you talkin' about?' growled Jerome Wilkinson. 'You gotta give us a chance to win some of that back.'

'Relax, Jerry,' said Master at Arms Biff Nolan. 'He'll be back tomorrow night. He can't have this kind of luck two nights runnin'.'

'Tomorrow night we'll be in Pearl, you asshole,' Wilkinson said. 'We may have a lot of other things on our minds.'

'You might, Wilkie,' Jack said. 'I don't know about the rest of us. I hear a lot of guys in your division are dyin' for a chance to talk to somebody about you. All we gotta do is get rid of our fuckin' executive officer. It'll be like pulling the lid off a can of goddamn worms.'

'What the fuck are you doin' here if you ain't one of the worms, wise guy?' Biff Nolan said.

'I happen to be a sailor. That automatically makes me a worm that the pricks in the wardroom like to step on. But even a worm can turn, Biff. It depends on what's at stake.'

Wilkinson pointed a finger at Jack as he rolled the dice. 'I told you once, your ass is at stake. Literally.'

'Eight. Anyone wanta bet I make it on the first pass? How about makin' it with two fours? I'll give you fifty bucks on both of them.'

'You got it,' Wilkinson said, throwing down a hundred dollars in tens. Biff Nolan threw in fifty against the two fours. Everyone else was either broke or too intimidated by Jack's streak to buck him again. Flanagan, who had won nothing on his own rolls, threw down ten dollars behind Jack and Wilkinson covered him.

Exactly where these sailors, no one of whom had a base pay

of more than $138 a month, got this kind of money was a question Flanagan was unable to answer. But listening to them talk for the past two hours had been an education in the *Jefferson City*'s underworld. There were several crap or card games like this one going on almost every night. One of the men in the game, a bald, wizened storekeeper named Conti, whom everyone called Tony Bucks, was kidded about losing or winning five for four. As the son of a cop, Flanagan knew the terminology. That was shorthand for a loan shark's standard rate of interest, twenty percent. The ship's baker was one of the big losers, which inspired a lot of jokes about him being forced to raise his prices. Another heavy loser was the wiry yeoman who kept the books for the ship's gedunk stand, where sailors bought ice cream. There were a lot of jokes about green and red ink in that department.

'Give us your blessing, Monsignor,' Peterson said. He had introduced Flanagan as an escaped seminarian who was eager to be corrupted by the sinners of the *Jefferson City*.

'*Veni, vidi, vici,*' Flanagan said, making a sign of the cross over the cubes.

The dice scampered across the brown blanket on the handling-room deck. Everyone stared in disbelief at two fours.

'OK, Biff, the drinks are on me,' Jack Peterson said.

He threw a twenty-dollar bill to the master at arms, and Nolan handed out flasks of bourbon to all hands. A single flask, courtesy of their host, had been passed around during the game. Flanagan did not need any more to drink. He was aghast when everyone chugalugged half of his bottle. Flanagan's eyes rolled, but he managed to get the whiskey down.

Flanagan counted $420 in Jack's pile. They handed fifteen percent to the master at arms; it was part of the deal. Flanagan wondered whom Nolan paid off up the line.

'Let's get some sea air,' Jack said.

'Let's hit the sack instead,' Flanagan said as they left the handling room.

'I'm too jazzed up to sleep,' Jack said as they climbed the ladders to the main deck. Before they opened the hatch, Jack counted out a hundred dollars and offered it to Flanagan.

'No,' he said.

'Bullshit, I never had luck like that before. Except the night after I met Martha Johnson. I told her about it and she gave me a lecture on why I shouldn't gamble. The next night I lost every dollar I had. That dame's brought me nothin' but grief.'

'I didn't see or hear any grief when we went down to that beach house.'

'Yeah, she's great in the sack. I never met anyone like her in that department. But she wants to reform me, for Christ's sake. If a dame ain't tryin' to ruin you, she's tryin' to reform you. Either way they spoil things. Don't you do the same thing by pullin' a straight-assed Catholic act on me.'

Flanagan let Jack cram the hundred dollars in the pocket of his shirt. On deck, they strolled toward the bow. 'Jesus, look at them stars,' Peterson said. 'That's why I stayed a sailor, Flan. I love to look up at those goddamn things at sea. They don't look the same on the fuckin' beach. There's always a house or a telephone pole in the way. You can look up there and forget you're a shitbird who's gotta salute and say yes sir to a lot of asshole officers who ain't any better than you are and some are a lot worse.'

'You think they're going to ask you to testify about what happened at Savo Island?'

'I don't know. This captain's playin' a cool game. No one can figure out his moves so far. The Marine orderly said the Exec came out of dinner in the old man's cabin the other day lookin' like he'd just swallowed a pound of shit. Which is more or less what he did, because the Captain fed him the crew's menu.'

'Get them,' rasped a voice, as they passed turret two.

There was a rush of shadowy figures. Flanagan reached for his knife, but he had forgotten to keep it loose in the sheath. Before he could get it out, someone hit him hard on the back of the head and he fell to his knees. Jack was down on the deck too, held by at least two sailors. A tall figure stood over them with something in his hand. It gleamed faintly in the starlight. A knife?

'The money – get the goddamn money,' Jerome Wilkinson said.

'I can't find it.'

With a terrific effort, Flanagan cleared his swimming brain. He dove on top of one of the sailors holding Jack down and pressed the blade of Homewood's knife against the side of his neck.

'Let him go or I'll cut this guy's fucking throat from ear to ear,' he said.

'OK, wise guy,' Wilkinson said. 'We ain't had no gripe with you so far. Now you're on our list too. Get it straight. If Jack here shoots off his big mouth to the wrong people, we'll take care of you eventually. It'll be some dark night on some ship a year from now. Or in some bar when you're about to score with a luscious broad. We got a lot of friends in this man's Navy, high and low.'

Arthur McKay picked up the telephone to the bridge. 'This is the Captain. Would you tell the Supply Officer I want to see him?'

An hour later, the supply officer had yet to appear. This time Captain McKay ordered him summoned over the PA system. He arrived within five minutes. Lieutenant Leroy Tompkins was a small balding man with mournful brown eyes and a smile that was closer to a grimace. He looked as if he had never won a bet or a woman in his life. His shoulders slumped, a potbelly bulged, the sole witness to some modest success in the pursuit of pleasure. Like most officers in his line, he was not an Annapolis man. McKay gestured him to a chair beside his desk.

'Mr Tompkins, I told Commander Parker to speak to you about improving the crew's food. He tells me he did speak to you. But the food hasn't improved. Why not?'

'We're using up a lot of second-rate stuff we took aboard in Manila.'

'Manila? That was nine months ago.'

'We got more of the same when we went to Bombay to get our hull repaired.'

'That was four months ago. Why didn't you get rid of it and completely reprovision the ship when we were in Long Beach?'

'No one gave me an order to that effect, Captain. You

signed for what we had aboard without a word.'

Checkmate. Captain McKay could only sit there. Ordinarily, a relieving captain made a thorough inspection of the ship before he signed his approval of the readiness reports from the various departments. After the highly unpleasant conversation he had had with Win the day he took command, McKay had signed all the reports without reading them. It had been a feeble, feckless gesture of reconciliation. He had been trying to show Win how much he trusted him.

Sometimes Arthur McKay wished he had never met Win Kemble. But that kind of thinking led to a whole list of nevers. Never went to Annapolis. Never met Rita and Lucy Semmes. Never was born in Kansas.

'I've been looking over your service record, Lieutenant. It's remarkable how often you and Commander Parker have served together. The only place you didn't go with him in the last ten years was to the US Embassy in London.'

'Yes,' Lieutenant Tompkins said, showing a gold incisor in his nervous smile. 'We been workin' together a long time. He always sends for me whenever he gets a command.'

'You're both from Missouri.'

'That's right. I'm from Jefferson City, in fact.'

'Fascinating. I want to see the crew's food get a lot better, Lieutenant. From now on, submit all your menus to me a week in advance.'

'Captain – I haven't got the staff to handle that sort of paperwork.'

'Then write them up yourself when you're off duty. While you're at it, give me a complete audit of your books for the past year.'

At a pace reserved for the unlikely moment when Abandon Ship was sounded, Supply Officer Tompkins rushed from Arthur McKay's cabin to the office of the Executive Officer. The elongated yeoman first class pounding the typewriter outside the door waved him into the inner sanctum without even an inquiry. A breathless Tompkins told Commander Daniel Boone Parker the orders he had just received from the captain.

'He's out to get us, Dan. Any way and every way he can.'

Parker poured his colleague a drink of twelve-year-old Scotch to steady his nerves. 'Calm down. I've got people in Washington checking him out. If half of what I've heard is true, we'll get him first.'

After another day of firing the *Jefferson City*'s guns at targets towed by the destroyers and at sleeves towed by the scout planes, Captain McKay sat down to supper with his gunnery officer, Lieutenant Commander Edwin Moss; the ship's first lieutenant and damage control officer, Commander George Tombs; and the chief engineer, Commander Oswald Bradley. They were first among equals, under the executive officer. If they did not get along, a ship was perpetually threatened with chaos. The problem was as old as the Navy. They all wanted to use the same men.

The Gunnery Officer wanted to keep the men drilling at the guns from dawn to dusk. The First Lieutenant was responsible for the ship's cleanliness and good appearance (which won him the title of ship's bitch) as well as her seaworthiness when damaged. He wanted the deck divisions to spend their time painting, polishing, scrubbing. He also wanted them to learn the location of every pipe, fire main, wire, hose and watertight hatch in the part of the ship to which they were assigned to fight fires and flooding. For damage control the first luff also drew men from the engineering department, which often got him into arguments with the Chief Engineer, who had his own agenda for the black gang.

Each of these senior officers of the *Jefferson City* gave Captain McKay something to worry about. A string of glittering fitness reports for his skill as a staff officer had won Gunnery Officer Edwin Moss rapid promotion. Although he knew the technical side of the job, McKay feared he was not temperamentally suited for it. He wanted a gunnery officer who emanated aggression and confidence in his men and his weapons. Moss emanated a fussy egotism more than anything else. At Annapolis, where he had graduated third in his class, his nickname had been 'Eaglebeak'. He continued to look condescendingly down on those who lacked his intellectual and moral qualifications. If there was one officer whose transfer McKay would have welcomed, it was Moss.

Stumpy snub-nosed George Washington Tombs, the first lieutenant, was new to the ship. He had been lateralled to the *Jefferson City* when he screwed up a tour as commander of a fleet of destroyer escorts in the Atlantic. Several of his inexperienced naval reserve captains had run aground, and Cominch King had landed on George with both feet. Tombs was particularly vulnerable to a man with King's unrelenting eye. He had graduated 182nd in the 182-man class of 1917.

Arthur McKay still winced, remembering George's agony as he struggled to make sense out of hydromechanics, steam turbines, electrical engineering and other mysteries of the Academy's science courses. As the class's anchorman, forever on the brink of expulsion, he had won everyone's admiration and sympathy. Arthur McKay had spent more than one night tutoring George before a march down Devil's Highway to Satan's Palace, the Academic Building where examinations were held.

George was no genius, but he tackled every assignment with the same energy and earnestness that had got him through the Academy. Captain McKay had no doubt that he would try to be the most thorough first luff that the *Jefferson City* had ever seen. Tombs was appalled by the mess the Terminal Island yardbirds had made of the ship and had submitted a work schedule which would give him control of the deck sailors and the black gang half of each day. George obviously expected his classmate from good old 1917 to back him up.

The chief engineer, Oswald Bradley, growled defiance at this idea. A lantern-jawed laconic man, Oz had accumulated a lot of resentments in his twenty-three years in Navy engine rooms. He considered most deck officers ignoramuses who made impossible demands on a ship's equipment. One of the reasons for McKay's visit to the engine room had been a desire to diminish some of this resentment.

Oz's disposition had never been sunny. At Annapolis, he was always getting into fistfights with people who sneered at his native state, New Jersey. Fate had compounded this problem by marrying him to a virago who used to get drunk and berate him and the Navy in public. He had finally divorced her, and since that time, as far as McKay knew, Oz's only love affair was with his machinery.

Bradley had a programme of his own that he wanted to pursue in the engine and fire rooms. He was particularly worried about the parlous condition of the *Jefferson City*'s eight-year-old boilers. He was also alarmed by the high percentage of good petty officers he had lost in transfers – and the secondraters and screwups he had got in exchange. 'I'm working with guys who barely know a pliers from a monkey wrench – and they're boiler tenders third class,' he said. 'Somebody with a lousy sense of humour gave me Calvin Clark for a chief machinist's mate. I've recommended that psycho for a general court-martial three times. If we can do any swapping at Pearl Harbor, Art, I've got a list as long as the anchor chain.'

'I suspect the only thing we'll do at Pearl is take the gunnery tests,' McKay said. 'Which brings me to the main point of this get-together. We're going to have to shoot a lot better than we have so far to pass those tests – and get this ship back in one piece when we go up against Yamamoto's boys.'

'I know, sir,' Lieutenant Commander Moss said. He was in torment for several reasons. He felt outranked and inexperienced confronting these men from the previous generation at Annapolis. Simultaneously he felt humiliated because so many things had gone wrong during the gunnery drills. Moss wanted to defend himself, but he wondered whether to tell the truth. Could he get away with putting the blame where it really lay? Where did McKay stand as far as his Annapolis roommate Captain Winfield Scott Schley Kemble was concerned?

'What's wrong? I can't believe you didn't drill and drill hard under Captain Kemple.'

'Not after Savo Island, sir. All the way back to California we didn't have a single drill. This ship just . . . slid out of his control, sir.'

Captain McKay glowered at a saltcellar. 'We'll change that as soon as we leave Pearl. We're going to spend nine hours a day firing those guns.'

'What about Commander Tombs's work schedule?'

'The brightwork and rust spots will have to wait,' McKay said, avoiding the disappointment in Tombs's eyes. 'But he can have everyone he wants from the black gang to work on damage control problems.'

That produced a glare but no protest from Oz Bradley. He was used to losing arguments with deck officers. Edwin Moss took a deep breath. He felt a need to say something positive, something idealistic to Arthur McKay. 'I – I want you to know I'm on your side, Captain.'

Moss recoiled from the astonishment on Tombs's face. The First Lieutenant did not know what the Gunnery Officer was talking about. Oz Bradley knew, and he was scowling, his eyes full of contempt. But Moss was even more dismayed by the ferocity in Captain McKay's eyes.

'Is there another side to be on?' he said.

'I hope not, sir. I hope it doesn't come to that. But if you want someone to testify, I'd have a good deal to say. I'd take the risk. For the Navy's sake.'

'I don't want you or anyone else to testify, Commander. I want you to fight!'

Pearl

At first, Hawaii was only a blur on the horizon. Then something took shape, a huge chocolate-coloured mountain shattered and gashed by explosions more stupendous than anything mere humans could foment. 'Koko Head Crater,' Jack Peterson said, in a bored old-salt style. 'Extinct volcano.'

The Pacific rapidly turned a cobalt blue. Soon convoluted green hills were visible above pink beaches crowded by groves of palm trees. A lazy white surf lapped at the sand.

'Hey, I think I just saw Dorothy Lamour in her sarong,' Frank Flanagan said.

'There's Diamond Head,' Peterson said.

Flanagan had seen pictures of this huge chunk of volcanic rock overlooking Waikiki. But the real thing had an aura no camera could capture, especially when Peterson let him study its serrated ugliness through the range finder. There was something malevolent about the way it crouched there like an immense prehistoric beast thrusting its scarred ancient snout into the sea. It summoned thoughts of savage gods and blood sacrifices in its shadow.

Flanagan wondered if his reaction to Hawaii's favourite symbol was influenced by the mood of the *Jefferson City*. The ship was practically vibrating with tension about what might or might not happen in Pearl Harbor. The scuttlebutt admirals were sure they were going to be spectators at the court-martial of the century. Rumours of this officer and that chief petty officer confessing or accusing everyone from the Exec to the Gunnery Officer to the Engineering Officer of cowardice and incompetence at Savo Island swept through the crew's mess at every meal.

The boatswain's pipe shrilled. 'Now hear this. All hands to quarters,' boomed the PA system.

'Here comes Pearl,' Peterson said.

Wearing dress whites, they assembled by divisions in their assigned places on the main deck.

They passed a stubby little ship that Peterson identified as the net tender; she opened and closed the anti-submarine net stretched across the channel. Another ninety-degree turn and they saw the whole inner harbour, the four estuaries or lochs as they were called, crowded with ships of all shapes and sizes. The channel divided around a low flat chunk of land in the centre of the harbour, Ford Island, the Naval Air Station. Most of the havoc wrought by Japanese bombs on hangars and planes and runways had long since been repaired. But two of the biggest victims of the murderous attack still lay in grisly postures of death off the southeast side of the island – the USS *Oklahoma*, which had capsized after being struck by Japanese torpedoes, and the shattered hulk of the USS *Arizona*, which had exploded when a bomb detonated her forward powder magazine.

The upturned hull of the *Oklahoma* looked like an immense whale that had died in some obscure agony. The huge flame-blackened tripod mainmast of the *Arizona*, tilted at a forty-five-degree angle to the dark oily water, reminded Flanagan of a photograph he had seen in one of his fathers books about World War I – an infantryman shot dead, slumped against the barbed wire in no-man's-land. 'That used to be Battleship Row,' Peterson whispered out of the corner of his mouth. 'Now it's Battleship Graveyard.'

'Silence in the ranks,' snapped Ensign Kruger.

On the bridge, Captain McKay listened to his executive officer cursing under his breath as the *Oklahoma* and *Arizona* appeared ahead of them off the port bow. 'Fucking sons of bitches, goddamn bastards,' Parker muttered. Was he trying to demonstrate his fighting spirit? McKay wondered. He doubted it. The Commander's rage seemed involuntary.

'I guess we all lost some good friends on those ships,' he said.

'You can say that again,' Parker growled. 'We know why too.'

'What do you mean?'

'From everything I hear, Roosevelt knew the Japs were coming. He kept the information in Washington because he wanted something like this to happen.'

'I somehow doubt that story,' McKay said.

'Where were you on December seventh, Captain?' Commander Parker said.

'I was preparing a lecture on the battle of Trafalgar that I was supposed to give the next day at the Naval War College,' McKay said. 'I never gave it. My class evaporated and in a couple of days so did I.'

Daniel Parker's lip curled. He had never been invited to attend the Naval War College at Newport. There was no doubt that men like him, who had entered the officer corps, without an Annapolis ring, had some reason to cry discrimination. Since Annapolis began turning out graduates in 1847, no man without a ring had become an admiral.

'A hell of a lot of good the battle of Trafalgar did us here on December seventh,' Parker said.

'I don't know. No one ever surprised Nelson's fleet anywhere, anytime. He did the surprising. "Incessant vigilance" was one of his favourite phrases.'

Commander Parker's lip only curled more derisively. McKay saw he had supplied him with a new way to talk down the Captain. He wasn't a real sailor. He was a bookworm.

'You're slotted for Berth Seventeen,' the pilot said. 'Either one of you fellows want to take her in?'

'I'll do it,' McKay said.

Five years ago, spurred by his wife, McKay had won a reputation as a destroyer captain who handled his ship with the savoir faire of a New York cabbie in these tricky waters. But a cruiser was five times bigger than the old four-stacker he had commanded in 1937. He stayed well below the eight-knot speed limit as they turned to starboard and eased the *Jefferson City* into the Southeast Loch, a narrow passage where the channel dwindled to thirty-seven feet.

'Port engine back one third,' Captain McKay said as they approached Berth Seventeen.

The engine telegrapher repeated the command and shoved the annunciator handle into position.

'Starboard engine ahead two thirds,' McKay said.

The big ship slowly turned on her heel until her bow was pointed toward Berth Seventeen. 'All engines ahead one third,' McKay said. 'Steady as you go.'

'Captain, she's not answering!' the helmsman cried.

'They've lost power in the engine room,' the telegrapher said.

At low speeds, when a ship was docking or getting under way, this could easily happen in a badly trained or badly maintained engine room. But a veteran ship like the *Jefferson City* was not supposed to have such deficiencies. Was this Oz Bradley's way of saying he was unhappy with his reduced share of the crew's time?

The ship began drifting toward the berth, broadside. 'Let go the starboard anchor,' McKay said.

With an enormous rattle, the anchor dropped. McKay got on the telephone to the engine room. 'What the hell's going on, Oz?' he asked.

'We lost steam pressure,' Bradley said. 'That number one boiler isn't worth what they'd get for it in a junkyard.'

'Why the hell are we using it at a time like this?'

'Because number two isn't all that much better.'

Did Bradley think he was the sort of jerk deck officer who did not know the ship had four boilers? 'What about the other two?'

'We shut them down to do some maintenance work on them.'

'Get me some power fast, Oz.'

'We're ready now on number two.'

It took another ten minutes of backing and alternating between port and starboard engines to enter Berth Seventeen. It had to be the worst docking performance in the history of Pearl Harbor. Arthur McKay's brain was a muddle of rage and humiliation. He glanced at his executive officer and saw a sneer in his eyes. Had he arranged this fiasco?

McKay turned his back on Parker and went out on the wing of the bridge to look down on the dock, where scurrying sailors were making the lines fast. A figure in a rumpled khaki uniform stood with his hands on his hips watching the operation. He was alone, and there were no insignia visible anywhere on his uniform except for a thick layer of gold braid on the visor of his hat. He waved to Arthur McKay. The Captain of the *Jefferson City* waved back, although his arm felt detached from his body.

It was Admiral Chester Nimitz, Cincpac himself.

Mail Call

Dear Jacko:
    Here I am back in Seattle, pushing the baked ham special on Monday and the corned beef and cabbage on Tuesday.

The customers aren't any nicer and the tips are still lousy. The pay is a lot better out at the Navy Yard. So I'm taking lessons in how to use an acetylene torch. At the very least it'll be a great defence against sailors.

You'll get this in Pearl and read it while you're heading for Honolulu and one of your favourite ladies, no doubt. One of those marvellous females who, in the words of the great Peterson, 'know what to expect from a sailor and they're glad to get it.'

Your old friend Vinnie St Clair from the *Pennsylvania* took me out the other night. They've towed the old tub to Bremerton and are putting her back together there. Vinnie's such a gentleman, he wouldn't even hold my hand because he thought you and I were engaged. He was delighted to hear that for you, that word is synonymous with cholera.

He's going East to drill boots at the Great Lakes Training Camp. He's a CPO and couldn't believe you weren't one. He had plenty of money to spend and he didn't win it at craps. In case you missed it, that's what's known as a dig.

I had a terrific time in California, even if it was only for two weeks. Let's do it again one of these years.

Love (unfortunately)
Martha

Dearest Frank:

How are you? I think about you all the time. I keep remembering those awful arguments we had the last times we went out but now I'm not angry, my heart is full of sorrow and regret that I didn't just kiss you and tell you to be quiet. We would have a beautiful memory between us instead of this awful sense of failure.

I can't explain myself to you because your head is all full of arguments put there by Satan to stop you from enjoying love as Jesus intended us to enjoy it. All those people who think it is a sin have lost touch with Jesus. I am so much luckier than almost everyone because I'm in touch with Him almost every night in Daddy's church. Even if he can't get a single person to respond, I do. That's why my heart is so full of love. It overflows from the love he brings down from heaven.

But he's failing, Frank. He's failing day by day. The church is failing and he's failing too. There were some sailors the other night who were from New York, like you. But they were cruel. They were drunk and they laughed at him. It was terrible. I didn't find Jesus that night. No one did.

But the next night, one of my old friends from Oklahoma, who was on the battleship *Oklahoma* and was saved from the Japanese bombs at Pearl Harbor came by to see us. He told us he gave Daddy all the credit for being alive. He took me to a hotel in Los Angeles and we made the most beautiful love that night.

It proved to me you were wrong, Frank, in your argument that I shouldn't let anyone else touch me. Should I have sent away that old friend loveless? Don't you see how cruel that would have been? Would Jesus have wanted me to do a thing like that?

But I don't want to argue with you anymore. I refuse to do it! I'm just going to love you and I hope I can prove it to you when you come back to San Pedro.

With all my heart,
Teresa

Dear Husband:

I'm back in the Capital of the Universe and full of the usual rumours, unverified facts and absolutely straight scoop, all of which will no doubt prove erroneous about two hours after I mail this.

First the bad news. As far as reinforcements for the Marines or for you fine fellows afloat are concerned, forget it. Everything that isn't absolutely essential to the defence of the realm is getting shipped to North Africa for the big invasion they're cooking up there. What's left over is going to the Russians via Murmansk, which is like inviting the Germans to a night in a shooting gallery. About one out of every five ships gets through. So far the U-boats are winning the battle of the Atlantic. They practically wiped out an entire convoy off Iceland the other day, Cominch told me.

I've never seen him gloomier. Some nights, lying awake, I wonder if my diabolical brother-in-law hasn't played a winning card with that letter to SECNAV. I told the Admiral about it and he just grunted and said he was sure there were a lot of other letters on the President's desk saying the same thing. If Guadalcanal got any worse, he added, he might write one himself, with his resignation enclosed.

As for Savo, no one's getting the gallows for the time being. You could change that overnight if you pry the right kind of information out of your crew. The more I think about it, the more I'm convinced that old W.S.S. Kemble is guilty of *something* – be it panic, gutlessness, dereliction of duty or stupidity I will wait breathlessly to find out from you, husband dear.

Thinking even harder about it, I begin to suspect your career depends on coming up with something that would enable Cominch to order a court-martial. He's not going to do this unless the evidence guarantees a guilty verdict. An acquittal would make him look even worse that he does already. Win and Mother would have their favourite congressmen demanding an investigation the next day. Another parade of Navy officers appearing before Congress to explain what went wrong in another débâcle would finish Cominch. Roosevelt would throw him to the sharks and find himself another admiral.

I hope by now you've brought the tightest, smartest ship in the fleet into Pearl and parked it at the Ten Ten dock like the hottest destroyer jockey this side of Rabaul, with Cincpac himself standing there watching.

I was down to see our son the other day. He's fuming to get into action, which is only natural, I suppose. But he's threatening to join the Marines! Write him a letter and tell him he absolutely has to apply for flight training. That will keep him out of harm's way for another year, at least.

Ever yours,
Rita

Dearest Joey:
How do I love thee? Let me count the ways. . .

Do you see what you've done to me? I sit around reciting Elizabeth Barrett Browning instead of learning my lines.

Actually, when I can get a slight grip on myself, I prefer John Donne

If yet I have not all thy love
Deare, I shall never have it all,
I cannot breathe one other sigh, to move,
Nor can intreat one other teare to fall.

Since I don't have a grip on myself most of the time, and I can't really stand Browning, I stare mutely into space for hours. Several friends have suggested I see a psychiatrist. I just laugh and then burst into tears, thereby convincing them that I *have* to see one.

Oh, those ten days, my love, my love, those ten days we had together were a world nothing can ever change. I know that isn't true, I know you may find some brawny Australian maiden in knickers with a voice that can be heard across a thousand miles of Outback, drilling a regiment of the home guard. She may awe you into submission with her hockey stick and blot out all recollection of your puny English mistress, with her smoker's cough and tubercular torso.

Or some dark-skinned Samoan beauty may reveal to you the magic of love without inhibitions and a tendency to get violently chilled with no clothes on. You may decide that going native with a native is a lot more fun than going crazy over me.

If you expect me to forgive you – you're out of your mind. I will punt across the Pacific, if necessary, to demolish that Australian with a barrage of sarcasm that will leave her small colonial brain in a permanent state of shock. I will finish off the Samoan with a withering glance *en passant*.

Does being in love make you write drivel like this too? If so, just send me envelopes with nothing in them but kisses. I'll understand.

Madly,
Gwen

Dear Edwin:

I almost hate to write this to you. I know it will upset you. But I'm pregnant again!

It could be from that time we lost our heads in Los Angeles, after that wild party. But the doctor says it could have happened even if we stuck to the damn chart. I'm absolutely miserable. I don't know what to think or do or say. I try to pray about it but nothing comes. I just feel dead inside. I honestly don't know how I can cope with another child and worry about you out there in the Pacific.

But I will. I'll cope, somehow. I'm not asking you to worry about me. I just have to tell someone the bad news. I'm afraid to tell your parents. I know they think I'm crazy already. My devout Catholic mother isn't much better. I think she just kicked my father out of bed one day and that's how she stopped having them. She keeps hinting in the most awful way that I have to 'put my foot down'. I never thought becoming an adult would turn you against your own mother. But it has. I think mine's a monster.

I hope the *Jefferson City* is wowing them in the Gunnery Department. The champion of the Pacific Fleet! I can say a prayer for that, with no trouble. It was so wonderful to see you in Los Angeles. If you can keep on loving me – in spite of the burden I've put on you – you're a saint. You really are, in a way. But don't let the Navy give you any ideas about martyrdom! I want you back in one piece. Make that very clear to Captain McKay.

I've been asking around Norfolk about him. A lot of people say he never had an idea in his life that he didn't get from Captain Kemble. So be careful what you say to him about his wonderful roommate.

Love
Eleanor

Memories

The telephone buzzed in Arthur McKay's cabin. 'Captain! Admiral Nimitz's car is on the pier!'

The voice belonged to Ensign Richard Meade, who was the junior officer of the deck. Dick Meade was on the ball. He would go far in the US Navy.

Yesterday morning, the Commander in Chief of the US Navy in the Pacific had greeted Captain McKay with the cordiality he always displayed to any officer who had served under him aboard the cruiser *Augusta* in 1935. Nimitz regarded that tour as a turning point in his career. He had been a success not only as a captain but as a diplomat in a China on the brink of war. Cincpac's offices were only a few hundred yards from Berth Seventeen. When he saw the *Jefferson City* standing in, he decided to give her new captain a personal welcome.

The Admiral had dismissed the fiasco at the dock with 'It could happen to anyone.' After some pleasantries, Nimitz gave McKay a quizzical look. 'Why don't we go for a little hike tomorrow afternoon? We'll have a chance to talk.'

Even in Shanghai, Nimitz had been famous for his walks.

In Hawaii, although he was seven years older, the walks had got longer. According to rumour, the less vigorous members of his staff hid under desks and in closets to avoid an invitation. As a farm boy, Arthur McKay had thought nothing of walking five miles to visit a friend. He had no problem accepting the Admiral's invitation. He descended the gangplank and found Nimitz's flag lieutenant waiting for him at the wheel of the nondescript Ford that Meade had had the wits to recognize. They drove to CINCPAC, and the Admiral gave him a brief tour of his headquarters.

Above the outer door was the maxim 'Nations, like men, should grasp time by the forelock instead of the fetlock.' Anyone who grew up on a Kansas farm knew what that meant. The Admiral noticed McKay's interest in the quote as they shook hands in the doorway and remarked that he had had to explain to at least half his staff what a fetlock was.

On the desk, McKay was amazed to see a framed photograph of General MacArthur. When Nimitz noticed him staring at it, he grinned and said, 'I keep that there to remind myself not to make Jovian pronouncements complete with thunderbolts.'

That was typical Nimitz, and a good example of why he and Arthur McKay had hit it off on the *Augusta*. The Admiral preferred understatement to overstatement anytime. If Arthur McKay had a hero, it was this quiet Texan with the furrowed brow.

With the flag lieutenant at the wheel and no insignia to indicate Cincpac's rank, they drove to the windward coast of Oahu and started hiking along the beach. 'I can't tell you how pleased I was to see the *Jefferson City* in Pearl, Arthur.' Nimitz said. 'We're in desperate need of cruisers in the Solomons. Instead, Washington sends us battleships! You can't keep those oil hogs at sea long enough to do anything with them.'

'How do you see the situation out there now, Admiral?' McKay asked.

'Grim,' Nimitz said, planting one foot after the other in the loose sand. 'One more Savo Island and we'll have to get out of there the best – or the worst – way we can. The Japs are pouring men on to Guadalcanal. We don't seem able to stop them.'

'Did we learn anything from Savo, Admiral?'

'A few things. I'll lend you a top-secret memorandum on it to read at sea. It will give you and your crew a lot of sleepless nights. That inside paint job you got in Long Beach has to come off. All that comfortable furniture in the wardroom has to go. You've got to get rid of anything that burns. We lost at least one of the cruisers at Savo because they couldn't douse the fires. But that's all trivial stuff. We still don't really know what went wrong. Have you found out anything from talking to your officers and crew?'

Now Arthur McKay knew why he had been taken on this solitary stroll. His first lieutenant, George Tombs, his steward, Horace Aquino; and others had confirmed what Chaplain Bushnell had told him – a lot of officers and enlisted men believed a board of inquiry would greet them at the dock in Pearl Harbor. The expectation explained Parker's defiant manner and the veiled threats made to men such as the fire controlman Peterson.

'I've learned a few things, Admiral. But it's been mostly by accident. I haven't tried to conduct an investigation. I don't think I can be the captain of that ship and a prosecuting attorney at the same time.'

They walked in silence for a good five minutes while Nimitz digested that answer. Arthur McKay was telling Cincpac and Cincpac would soon tell Cominch, scowling Fleet Admiral Ernest J. King, that they could not expect any inside information from Captain McKay that would enable King to hang Win Kemble. That was how King would hear it. This very different man probably heard it too. But he was not a hangman by instinct. He also heard the other side of what Arthur McKay had just said. He heard a captain telling him that he wanted to lead his men out of the shadow of disgrace by appealing to their courage, their pride. Slowly, sombrely, Admiral Nimitz nodded. 'I think you're right,' he said.

It was their second and last night in Hawaii. They were sailing tomorrow for the Solomon Islands. Overhead, the

Pacific sky was an incredible splendour of stars. Across the inky waters of Pearl Harbor, boats moved cautiously, displaying only small riding lights. On highways in the hills, tiny slits of moving light revealed cars. The rest of Oahu was a blacked out mass of darkness.

Flanagan's section did not have liberty. He had no desire for more liberty in Honolulu anyway. Disgusted by the way sailors were confined to a few honkytonk streets downtown, he had got drunk and gone to one of Jack Peterson's favourite prostitutes. He had reeled back to the ship and written a letter to Teresa Brownlow, telling her he could see no difference between the whore and her. It was a lie of course. He was trying to shock Teresa into realizing how violently he disapproved of her sexual theology.

Sprawled on the platform outside main forward, he and Peterson listened to Camutti's usual tale of conquest, this time with an authentic Hawaiian maiden, who had showed him sexual positions hitherto unrevealed to white men. 'She made me promise not to tell anyone else,' Camutti chortled. 'She said it would make Pele, the volcano god, angry.'

'Camutti, you're full of shit, but at least it's entertainin' shit,' Peterson said.

There was a commotion on the dock. The Hawaiian Area Shore Patrol known as HASPs were trying to get a sailor out of one of their cars; he was resisting them. A basso voice drifted up to them: 'Go fuck yourselves!'

'Good Christ, it's Homewood,' Peterson said. 'Come on.'

As they raced down the ladders, the commotion on the dock grew more violent. They found Lieutenant Robert Mullenoe in charge of the quarterdeck. 'Lieutenant,' Peterson said, 'don't call the Marines. Let us go down and get him. We can handle it.'

'OK. But make it fast.'

They ran down the gangplank and along the darkened dock to the Shore Patrol car. Four HASPs were trying to drag Homewood out of the car. 'I want to go back for a blow job,' he roared. 'You fuckers don't have the balls to stop me.'

'Boats, Jesus Christ, you're gonna to have the whole

Marine division down here with drawn bayonets,' Jack Peterson said.

'Bring 'em on. I'll put half of them in the water before they get me,' Homewood bellowed.

'Flanagan's here. What a hell of an example you're settin' him.'

'You should talk, you raunchy son of a bitch. What the fuck's wrong with it anyway? Jesus Christ, you know where we're goin' tomorrow. Goin' up against a bunch of fuckin' slant-eyed killers without doin' nothin' to straighten out this ship. What the fuck else should a man do but get drunk and laid?'

'I know, I know. Let's get aboard and talk it over in the compartment. Mullenoe's the OOD. He says the Exec'll be along any minute.'

'Great! I'll wipe up the fuckin' dock with that cowardly son of a bitch.'

While Homewood ranted, Peterson had somehow eased him out of the patrol car. 'Any charges?' he asked the white-belted HASPs.

'Nah. He busted up one of the Chink joints. They shouldna let him in in the first place. He done the same thing when you guys came through here last year.'

'Grab his other arm,' Peterson told Flanagan. Together they walked Homewood down the dock and struggled up the gangplank with him. Several times his legs crumpled and Flanagan had to support the man's massive bulk. At the top of the gangplank, Peterson said, 'Boatswain's Mate First Class Homewood, F Division, reporting from liberty, sir.'

To Flanagan's amazement, Homewood stood erect, saluted the flag on the stern and the OOD. But he needed serious help getting down the ladders to F Division's compartment. They sat him on his rack out in the passageway and Peterson began untying his shoes.

'You never seen anything like it,' Homewood said. 'Nothin' touched that woman but the head of my cock. It was absolutely the most elegant fuckin' I've had since Shanghai.'

'I hope you put a boot on it,' Peterson said.

'Sure I did. You can't fool around with that kind of pussy

'thout one. But she loved it. She was ready to do anythin' for another ride on old Peter. Then it just went sour. I started thinkin' about Mei-ling. How I treated that woman. Left her with our kid and nothin' but a month's pay. Started thinkin' what a bum I was. Thinkin' maybe I deserved to be on this fuckin' messed-up ship.'

'Oh, bullshit. If you're a bum I'm a fuckin' Western desperado and Flanagan here's the original Bronx punk.'

'S'truth,' Homewood said as Flanagan helped Peterson pull off his pants and jumper. 'I'm a fuckin' bum. If it wasn't for the Navy I'd be a goddamn hobo livin' out of garbage cans. No fuckin' good, Jack. Never treated any woman right in my life. Specially Mei. She was sweetest, smallest thing y' ever seen. I met 'er in Chungking and took her back down the river in my bunk. Old gunboat *Panay*. Captain knew it, but he had one in his bunk too. Way it went in those days. But somethin' 'bout her, so goddamn *tender*. Set 'er up in Shanghai in lil hole in wall and got myself transferred to the *Helena*. Jesus I couldn't wait to see her every liberty. I never went nowhere else. Shore Patrol couldn't figure out why the fuckin' city was so peaceful all of a sudden.

'Then wham, ship's goin' back. I just lef' her the money and goodbye. Couldn't even kiss her, I was so goddamn 'shamed of myself.'

'We've all done that to a dame at least once,' Peterson said. 'You should stay away from Chinese pussy. It stirs up all these morbid thoughts.'

'On'y kind I like any more. Can't even get it up sometimes for these white whores,' Homewood muttered.

'Listen,' Peterson said. 'In two weeks we'll be in the Solomons. We'll be so goddamn busy shootin' Japs you won't have time to think about pussy. Maybe the Captain knows what the fuck he's doin'. Wouldn't that be a novelty? Now roll in there and sleep it off.'

'Yeah. Thanks boys.'

The big body fell back on the mattress. Peterson and Flanagan retreated to the compartment. 'That happens every time he goes to a Chink whorehouse,' Peterson said. 'That little slant-eyed dame really got to him.'

'What happened to her?'

'Who knows? When he got back to Shanghai the Japs had bombed the shit out of it. He never found her or the kid again.'

Flanagan suddenly felt very young. He found himself wondering about the savage letter he had written Teresa Brownlow. He compared it to Homewood's treatment of his Chinese mistress, Peterson's dismissal of that crime and his cool response to Martha Johnson's love. Was learning to hurt women and not worry about it part of becoming a sailor? Maybe they all deserved to be on a messed-up ship.

Captain McKay stood on the brow of one of the hills overlooking Pearl Harbor. Below him, the locks, the ships, the narrow channel to the sea were reduced to the size of an aerial photograph. He was seeing it as the Japanese pilots had seen it as they roared over this hill on the morning of 7 December to change everyone's lives for ever.

If Franklin D. Roosevelt had not badly underestimated Japan's readiness to start a war with the United States, McKay would still be on the faculty of the Naval War College in Newport, perhaps putting the finishing touches to his history of the Union Navy in the Civil War. He also might be divorced from his wife. That was one of the many threats Rita had hurled at him when he told her he wanted to spend the rest of his naval career as a scholar.

But Captain McKay was not up here to ruminate about what might have been. He was visiting a kind of shrine to happiness. Behind him was a sprawling house in the old-fashioned colonial style of the late nineteenth century, with French windows and whirring fans high in the dim ceilings. It was where he and Rita had lived for two years when he was captain of the destroyer *Stacy Wright*.

Like the house in which Lucy Kemble was staying in the Hollywood hills, Kalakaua House (named for a long dead Hawaiian king) belonged to their Annapolis classmate Clinch Meade. Over Clinch's protests, Arthur McKay had insisted on paying a token rent. Win Kemble and Rita had told him he was crazy but McKay did not like owing favours to people like Clinch Meade. He had inherited a suspicion of Eastern capitalists from his farmer forebears.

These niceties of her husband's conscience were irrelevant to Rita. She loved the house and loved him for agreeing to rent it. She had given lavish parties on its porches and in this garden, parties that had undoubtedly had a lot to do with Arthur McKay being promoted to captain and sent to the Naval War College. Not many relatively junior officers had such a show-place to lure staff officers and even an occasional admiral to discover that laconic Arthur McKay had quite a brain hiding behind his modest manner.

McKay shook his head. It was dismaying, the way Rita's voracity invaded even this memory. Happiness was what he wanted to remember here. He was reaching across the years, not to the promotion parties (as Rita called them) in this garden, but to the nights when they would sneak out here and make love in the lush grass, with the trade wind sighing around them.

At first, Rita had been like a wild woman, clawing and biting him, babbling all the vile words she had learned in Shanghai. Then came nights of unbelievable tenderness, when she whispered, 'I love you', and it rang true in his deepest self. For some odd reason, that made him feel he could master anything. At the conn of the USS *Stacy Wright* he had made some of the boldest two-bell landings in the fleet. He had won Navy E's for gunnery and ship-handling on fleet manoeuvres. Old salts in the deck force had uttered the word captain with genuine respect.

They had been the best years with Barbara and Sammy too. They had been old enough to enjoy Hawaii's social life. They had had their own parties in this splendid house. But they were young enough to remain reasonably obedient and worshipful of both mother and father. When they went to Newport and he and Rita began quarrelling about his inclination to accept an appointment to the War College faculty, the disillusionment had begun. Now Sammy was determined to defy both parents when he graduated from Annapolis. Barbara had turned into a Navy hater with a list of grudges the length of a battleship. She and Rita could not spend five minutes in the same room without shouting at each other. It was a replay of Rita's war with her father.

Happiness. Did it only reside in memory? Was he aware then of how precious the two years in this house would become? Arthur McKay's eyes filled with tears. Probably not. That line about 'Getting and spending, we lay waste our powers' had a Navy version. Drilling and swilling? Fussing and cussing? Worrying and currying?

Oh, well. Perhaps the best thing about memory was its independence of time. The days were there, in sunshine and starlight, a shrine to visit whenever the spirit faltered.

'Captain McKay? Arthur?'

It was Mildred Meade, a woman whose company he always enjoyed. He had not even known she was in Hawaii. The house had looked closed.

A willowy blond, Mildred would have made an ideal Navy wife. She was smart but never showed it – one of Rita's flaws. She was charming without being flirtatious – another of Rita's flaws. Unlike Lucy Kemble, Mildred had no scores to settle with SOB-type admirals. She seldom found fault with anyone in a Navy uniform. Serving the country appealed to the deep vein of idealism in her New England soul. She was perfectly willing to devote the several million dollars she had inherited to making Clinch an admiral. But he had had other ideas about what he could do with that money.

'What a pleasant surprise,' McKay said, kissing her on the cheek.

'I'm giving the house to the Navy to use as a rest home for wounded men who are well enough to get along outside a hospital,' Mildred said.

'A lovely idea.'

'I'm going to run it, if the Navy lets me. I think they will. I don't want any special thanks for it. I have this absolutely awful need to do something in this war besides sit home and worry.'

'Of course.'

'I tried to get you on the phone. But Dick said they didn't even hook you up at the dock, you're going to be here such a little while.'

'We're sailing tonight. I came up here for some auld lang syne. Even captains have to keep up their morale. Rita and I had two wonderful years in this house.'

'I envy you that,' Mildred said.

In recent years she had not tried very hard to conceal her unhappiness with Clinch.

'How's Dick doing?' Mildred asked.

'On the basis of three weeks' observation, I'd say he's the perfect ensign. He knows his job and does it without blowing his horn.'

Mildred beamed. 'Win Kemble gave him high marks too.' Her smile faded. 'I gather something awful went wrong aboard the ship at Savo Island. Dick won't talk to me about it.'

'I think everyone will forget it as soon as the shooting starts again,' McKay said.

He regretted the words the moment he saw their impact on Mildred. Her lips trembled. She was obviously thinking of what had happened off Savo Island. 'Will you be going into action right away? Dick says with so many new men aboard you might do convoy duty to Australia or something like that – until you shake things down.'

Ensign Meade was obviously trying to help his mother sleep nights. 'There's a good chance we might do something like that,' Arthur McKay lied.

'Good. Here's Clinch. He'll be as glad to hear that as I am.'

Clinch Meade came toward them with a pleased smile on his wide puffy face. Most people thought Clinch had got his nickname at Annapolis as captain of the wrestling team. But the class of 1917 had given it to him for his boast, 'Once I get a dame in a clinch, she's finished.' She was too, as Mildred Rogers Meade could mournfully attest.

A slab of a man, Clinch had been one of the leaders of the class of 1917. His decision to leave the Navy had shocked everyone. The reason was visible now on his face. Each year brought more egotism and venality to the surface. Arthur McKay believed that after the age of forty almost everybody was responsible for his face.

'You son of a gun I was just about ready to recruit a

boarding party and storm that tin tub you're commanding. I wasn't going to let you get out of that harbour without at least shaking hands.'

Mildred told him what McKay had said about convoy duty. 'Great,' Clinch said. 'You better go through the house and decide what furniture you want to leave. The movers'll be here tomorrow morning.'

Mildred kissed McKay and left him with Clinch, whose jolliness vanished almost instantly. 'Art,' he said, 'there's something I want you to do. You don't understand why Dick asked to become a gunnery officer. He's never got over the bullshit stories I told him when he was a kid about my heroic exploits in turret one and aboard the old *Marblehead*. I want him back in Damage Control, under the armoured deck, where Win had him. I'll get him off your hands on to somebody's staff, MacArthur's, I hope, in two months or less.'

McKay said nothing, his usual tactic when he was angry. He was more than angry, he was outraged by Clinch's assumption that he had the right to arrange for his son's safety. He was also dismayed that Win Kemble had gone along with it.

Clinch, in a hurry as usual, assumed McKay's silence was assent. 'What have you found out about this Savo Island screwup? Is Win in the clear?'

'What's he told you?'

'Not a damn thing. What's he told you?'

McKay described Win's letter to Secretary of the Navy Frank Kncx.

Clinch was appalled. 'Jesus Christ, Art, he's taking on Roosevelt, King, the whole fucking works. I'll lay you ten to one they try to pin Savo on him.'

'How can they do that it he isn't guilty?'

'Come on, Art. You know how the fucking system works. They almost hung your ass in China in 1928.'

'That's Win's version of it. I never had the slightest doubt I'd be vindicated.'

'Win stuck by you in China. Even when he didn't agree with you. He might ask you to stick by him this time.'

'I don't think the two things are comparable, Clinch.'

Arthur McKay was troubled by the bitterness in his voice. But he meant what he had just said. If anything, the incident on the Yangtze had been blown out of proportion by Win's oratorical letter in defence of McKay's decision to ignore a trigger-happy Chinese warlord's shore battery.

McKay suddenly wondered if Clinch was here to find out where he stood in regard to Win. This sudden exhumation of the Yangtze furore made him suspect the letter to Secretary Knox had already backfired.

It was time to take charge of the conversation. McKay dealt first with Meade's weakest demand. 'Clinch, if I put Dick back in Damage Control, he'll know you did it and he'll lose all respect for you, me and himself.'

He was speaking as the Captain of the *Jefferson City* now. He was telling Clinch Meade what he had learned about leading men in the years since Clinch had quit the Navy.

'Maybe you're right, Art. But I can't stand the thought of losing him. I can't do anything with the younger boy. He's a fucking ethical philosopher like his mother. Since Savo, I haven't been able to sleep two hours a night.'

Arthur McKay's detestation was softened by the anguish in Clinch's eyes. Clinch was afraid that God or Destiny or whatever presided over this life was about to exact his favourite son as a penalty for his sins. Arthur McKay, with a son about to graduate from Annapolis, sympathized. Clinch's love for his son was the first honest emotion McKay had seen him display in a decade.

'I'll switch Dick to an eight-inch turret. That's got more armour on it than anything else aboard the ship. He'll think it's a promotion for the good job he's done in mount one.'

'OK,' Clinch said. 'I really appreciate –'

'Tell Win I'll do what I can, if he needs help. I'll be in a better position to judge how much I can do after we've been in action.'

Battle would either heal the wound Savo Island had inflicted on the *Jefferson City*'s soul or reveal its brutal origin. Which did her captain want? At the moment, Arthur McKay would have had to flip a coin to decide. Either way, his opinion was irrelevant. The spinning coin was in the hands of the god of war.

History Spoken Here

Day after day, the *Jefferson City* steamed into the immense blank of the western Pacific on the curving sea trail blazed by broad-beamed Yankee whalers and long lean clipper ships with their clouds of sails. 'Forever advancing we seemed forever in the same place,' whaleman Herman Melville had written, almost exactly a hundred years before. That was how it seemed to the *Jefferson City*'s sailors.

'Every day was the former lived over again,' complained whaleman Melville. The *Jefferson City*'s sailors had a similar complaint. But their days were boring in a drastically different way from the monotony Melville disliked. Every day the men of the *Jefferson City* prepared for battle.

From an hour after sunrise until dark, the cruiser's eight-inch and five-inch and forty- and twenty-millimetre guns blasted at targets on the water and in the air. Standing in the open at his gun director, at the end of each day, Frank Flanagan felt as if his head and body had been pounded by a maniacal heavyweight boxer.

When they were not firing, the men in the turrets and mounts and handling rooms rehearsed the exhausting ritual of passing the shells and powder bags and ramming them home in the guns. The goal was creation of bodies that performed even if their brains were a muddle of terror and confusion.

Over and over, lookouts were drilled in giving ranges and bearings using the escorting destroyers and the *Jefferson City*'s scout planes. Bearings were trickiest for the new men. They came in two varieties, true and relative. True bearings were computed clockwise from the North Pole and were seldom used, except on the navigating bridge. Relative bearings were the important ones. They were computed clockwise from the bow to the stern and around to the bow again. To get the bearing you multiplied the hour hand of the clock by thirty degrees. A ship or plane off the starboard beam, at three o'clock, was reported as bearing nine zero. Something off the port bow, at ten o'clock, was at three zero zero. After the four- or five- hundredth time, the computation became as automatic as telling time, even for mathematical morons like Flanagan.

Overlapping and intertwined with this training were the watches – four hours on, four hours off, night and day. This was Condition Two, the standard schedule of a ship at sea in a war zone. By night, the sections not on watch studied outlines of Japanese ships and planes flashed on screens in the crew's mess compartment. They spent more hours on watch understanding and acquiring night vision. Human eyes use cones to see by day and rods by night. It took a half hour for the rods to begin seeing in the darkness. Thereafter, a man's eyes could not come in contact with any light, even the flare of a match, without losing his night vision for another half hour.

In the wardroom, Captain McKay sat with the deck and engineering officers, throwing situations at them, asking them what they would do.

'Lieutenant Mullenoe, you get reports of torpedo wakes to both port and starboard, bearing zero four five to starboard, two one five to port. What do you do?'

Mullenoe thought for a moment, imagining these two killer fish racing toward his bow and stern and decided he would alter course twenty degrees to port, getting both ends of the ship out of harm's way. Montgomery West said he would call for flank speed and outrun them.

That brought on an intense discussion with the engineers about the ship's limitations. The deck men heard what a year of wartime steaming had done to her eight-year-old boilers, and how little the yardbirds had done at Terminal Island to refit them. Flank speed, the thirty-two knots a cruiser could hit, could not be achieved without giving the engine room a chance to get ready for it. 'Otherwise,' Oz Bradley said, 'you're going to see pieces of the boiler going up the goddamn stack and coming down on the main deck.'

When they were not on watch or training for battle or sleeping, the crew chipped paint. In the interior of the superstructure and below decks, the sound of chippers filled the ship. With it came the almost lethal odour of paint remover. Several men collapsed and were carried to sick bay, dizzy and vomiting. Commander Parker thought the whole idea was idiotic and tried to keep the chippers out of Officer's Country. Captain McKay countermanded his order. He had them do his cabin first. Parker enlisted Dr Cadwallader, who warned McKay the fumes might be affecting the health – and were certainly affecting the morale – of the crew. The chaplain chimed in with an even more lugubrious monody on the fragility of their morale.

'It'll be a lot more fragile if we get hit and the ship turns into a funeral pyre,' McKay said.

Captain McKay dined alone most of the time. The only guests who broke his solitude were the navigator, Commander Robert E. 'Marse' (his inevitable Annapolis nickname) Lee, and the first lieutenant, George Washington Tombs. Neither had been aboard the ship at Savo Island. McKay did not want to hear any more confidential confessions, clues to the *Jefferson City*'s disgrace.

Four years behind McKay and Tombs at Annapolis, Marse Lee (who happened to be from Gettysburg, Pennsylvania) had spent a year on the China Station. Inevitably, their conversation veered in that direction. The captain was relieved to discover Lee was a matter-of-fact man. He had not acquired what they used to call the Asiatic stare. He remained unaffected by the sheer scope and density of the Orient's masses, their appalling misery, their awful disregard for liberty, equality and the pursuit of happiness as Americans understood them.

George Tombs had never got to China. Throughout his career George had endured a steady diet of junk assignments – naval attaché in Peru, commander of the *Reina Mercedes*, the prison ship at Annapolis. He listened to McKay and Lee reminiscing about their Shanghai days with a patina of sadness in his eyes.

Lee began talking about his adventures as executive officer of the gunboat *Monocacy* in 1927. Win Kemble had been captain that year.

'Didn't you have a problem out there, when you were captain of the *Monocacy*, Art?' Tombs asked.

For a moment, McKay wondered if Tombs was involved in the rumours and fears swirling around the ship. The question spun him back to the conversation with Clinch Meade in Hawaii. But honest George Tombs was incapable of duplicity.

'All the captains of the *Monocacy* had problems, George,' McKay said.

'What happened?'

'Off Wu-Han, the local warlord decided to use us for target practice. I ignored him. Some American businessmen wrote a letter home accusing me of letting bandits fire on the flag. The Hearst newspapers raised a stink and the Navy decided to hold a court of inquiry to shut them up. I was exonerated – which didn't exactly surprise me. We had orders to ignore that sort of gunfire unless it endangered the ship or the crew.'

Marse Lee's eyes were opaque during this dry summation. He made no attempt to recall for Tombs the incredible tangle of frustration and insubordination that had raged among the officers and men on the China Station during the years 1925–28. American missionaries had used their influence in Washington to muzzle the Navy's gunboats. Most of the junior officers and the crews had despised the policy and violated it every time the Chinese gave them a chance. In 1927, off Hankow, when Win Kemble had commanded the *Monocacy*, a Chinese machine gun in a pagoda had opened fire on the ship. Win had blown the pagoda apart with a four-inch shell.

Did Lee know the rest of the story? Probably not. The details of courts of inquiry were secret. McKay was even more certain he did not know the deeper background – the violent disagreement between Art McKay and Win Kemble about the role America was playing in China. To Win's astonishment and outrage, McKay agreed with the missionaries, that the United States should stop playing stooge to British colonialism and get its gunboats and Marines out of China. He agreed with the policy of not firing back at provocative shells and bullets along the Yangtze and proved it by refusing to steam the *Monocacy* into a gunnery duel off Wu-Han.

Captain McKay did not sleep well that night. At 3 a.m. he was pacing his cabin, hearing Clinch Meade say, *Win stuck by you in China*. He was back on the Yangtze in the fog and rain of that November day in 1928 with shells bursting off his port and starboard beams, manoeuvring the ancient *Monocacy* to make it a difficult target, while his executive officer angrily demanded permission to fire back. He sat before the court of inquiry while the presiding officer read into the record a letter from Win Kemble defending Lieutenant McKay's decision.

The friend of his life. The letter was an extravagant eulogy of Arthur McKay as a man incapable of dishonour or cowardice and a passionate defence of captain's prerogatives. McKay could still remember patches of Win's grandiloquence. *No one, least of all a civilian, had the right to challenge Lieutenant McKay's command of the USS* Monocacy. *Neither his executive officer* (who had testified he thought the ship was in danger and the artillery fire should have been returned) *nor, at the risk of seeming presumptuous, the admiral in command of the Yangtze Patrol, can or should question a captain's ultimate authority. He and he alone can decide what is best for his ship.*

The friend of his life. Even when disagreement was as profound, as acrimonious as their difference about China, friendship remained paramount. Even when Win despised what his friend had done, he had been ready to defend unto insubordination his right to do it.

Captain McKay got out Rita's letter and reread it. He had not answered it. Once more, he told himself his decision to ignore it was rooted in reality. Nimitz had warned him the *Jefferson City* might be slugging it out with a Japanese fleet within a day of arriving in the Solomons. As dawn began streaking the blank grey face of the Pacific with livid red,

Captain McKay had to admit to himself that he was also using that reality for his own intricate purpose.

What would the epigrammist say about him? *The man who had to choose between his wife and his friend had better be brave as well as wise.*

Not bad. But Arthur McKay wondered if he was either.

'Hey, Flan, you got an education. Write me a letter,' Jack Peterson said as they left the crew's mess after staring for an hour at an awesome array of Japanese ships and planes.

'Who to?'

Flanagan's head ached, his ears were ringing from another day of firing. He was still wrestling with remorse over the sneering letter he had mailed to Teresa Brownlow from Pearl Harbor.

'Martha Johnson. I want to teach that broad a lesson. She just wrote me another snotty letter, tellin' me all about how she made out with one of my best friends from the *Pennsylvania.*'

Two of a kind, Flanagan thought. He and Martha Johnson. That seemed to legitimize teaching her a lesson.

'What do you want to do?'

'Make her feel guilty as hell. Write me a letter tellin' her how I can't sleep, I can't eat, thinkin' about her. How I didn't even take a liberty at Pearl and I've given up cards and dice. Then I get this rotten letter from her. Pull out all the emotional stops, you know? She's ruined my life. I'm goin' back to all my old vices with no hope now.'

'I got you. Give me an hour.'

While Flanagan toiled as a hypocritical ghostwriter, another sailor mailed a totally sincere letter at the ship's post office.

Dear Mother:

I got your letter. I don't want anything for Christmas but a discharge. I hate the Navy! This ship is the most awful place I've ever been in my life. I have a boatswain's mate who beats me up and makes me commit sins that are worse than anything you ever read about in a book. He wants me to sin with him now, but I won't let him touch me.

The ship has a captain who's the best friend of the captain who's just left and he was a coward who let a lot of men drown on it before we got here. We're going out to the Solomon Islands to fight the Japs and I know we're going to get sunk out there. We deserve it. This ship is full of evil men who laugh at God and Jesus. I went to see the chaplain and told him all this and he said I shouldn't say things like that unless I could prove them. How can I prove them when everyone else is almost as bad as the boatswain? They all laugh at me and punch me and kick me whenever they feel like it. If you don't help me I'm going to do something awful.

Love,
Harold

'"There are times when a sailor has to look deep in his heart and ask himself if anything matters. He has to face the fact that he has wasted his affectionate feelings, which don't come easy for him, considering the miserable life he lives, on a woman who simply doesn't care about him, unless he agrees to grovel and beg for her love."'

Expressions of awe and admiration circled main forward.

'How's that for classy bullshit?' Jack Peterson said. 'She'll use up four handkerchiefs readin' this.'

They were sprawled on the deck waiting for gunnery practice to begin. Peterson was reading aloud portions of Flanagan's love letter to Martha Johnson. Everybody agreed it was a masterpiece and Flanagan had malarkey coming out of his ears. Camutti begged him to write similar epistles to three different girls he planned to seduce when he got back to Philadelphia.

Flanagan accepted the praise but he did not find it very satisfactory. He already had one rotten letter to a woman on his conscience. Maybe that was why he was having second thoughts about this one. If Martha Johnson fooled around with other men, Jack Peterson had it coming to him. In the week they had double-dated, Flanagan had never heard Jack say anything even faintly romantic to her after the first date. But Flanagan had concluded Teresa was right, Martha was in love with Jack in some strange deep way that left Flanagan baffled. It did not seem to go with her independence, her tough, cool honesty.

Whatever the reason, it was none of his business. Martha had never hurt him. In fact, she had talked to him as if he were Jack's equal – a real sailor and not a green kid who was in the Navy only because Uncle Sam said join up or else. As the call to General Quarters blasted over the PA system and they headed for their battle stations, Flanagan caught Peterson's arm. 'Jack,' he said, 'I don't think you ought to send that letter.'

'Hey, it's my business. Concentrate on savin' Daley's soul. Or some other twerp's if you gotta be a seagoin' Jesuit.'

WHAM WHAM WHAM. The five-inch guns began knocking compassion out of Flanagan's head. The hell with it, he thought. Maybe it didn't matter. Maybe nothing mattered.

'Lieutenant MacComber, would you mind taking a look at this?'

Ensign Richard Meade stood just inside the door and handed Harold Semple's letter to Lieutenant Wilson Selvage MacComber. Wearing a maroon silk bathrobe and little else, MacComber was reading a book of poems with a weird title, *The Wasteland*, by someone named T. S. Eliot. Meade had made the mistake of passing an obvious Navy joke about the initials the last time he visited the stateroom. MacComber had frozen him with a look that made him feel as if he was back in plebe year at the Naval Academy.

As second in command of Deck Division One, Dick Meade had the unwelcome task of censoring the men's mail. Weary from ten hours in the tiny officer's communal booth at the back of turret one, Meade skimmed most of the letters, making sure no place names, particularly the words Solomon Islands, appeared in them. But Semple's letter involved something more important than a breach of security. He felt MacComber, the division officer, should see it.

'Oh, dear, it sounds like Wilkinson's on the *prowl* again,' MacComber said. Mullenoe, who had been in his class at Annapolis, called him Pussy. To confuse Meade completely, MacComber had a wife and child, about whom he often talked in sentimental terms.

'What do you mean?'

'Oh, he has a weakness for pretty little boys. Is this fellow one?'

'Shouldn't we do something about it?'

'Ensign Meade, this has been going on in the Navy since the Phoenicians. Let nature take its course.'

'Nature?'

'Do you want to confront the Executive Officer with the misbehaviour of his favourite bosun? If so, you have my permission.'

MacComber handed the letter back to Meade and resumed reading *The Wasteland*.

'Isn't it dangerous to the men's . . . morale?'

'*Au contraire*,' MacComber said. 'The rest of them can relax now. They know Wilkinson won't be after them. They will have a scapegoat on whom they can discharge their peasant rage and frustration.'

Meade was appalled by Lieutenant MacComber's attitude toward the enlisted men. He regarded them as appurtenances to the ship's machinery. His opinion of ensigns was almost as snide. In fact, there were few officers in the Navy who won MacComber's admiration. He was fond of saying that the average Annapolis man was a robot with a brain containing only a handful of standard phrases, such as 'Yes, sir' and 'Right away, sir'.

Mullenoe claimed MacComber's contempt for anyone he considered beneath him proved that the Civil War had been a necessity. Meade had enjoyed his first seven months on the *Jefferson City*, when he had been assistant officer of Mullenoe's Deck Division Two. Since he had been transferred to MacComber's domain, he had begun to wonder if his father was right when he predicted that in five years he would change his mind about making the Navy a career.

Mead had grown more and more dismayed watching MacComber in action. Or, to put it more exactly, in inaction. He let Wilkinson run the division. MacComber spent most of his time playing bridge with Dr Cadwallader, Chaplain Bushnell and anyone they could inviegle into making a fourth.

'Lieutenant, I really think we should investigate this.'

'Dear Babyface, will you please get something through your head? The Navy doesn't like people who investigate things. You and your fellow robot Mullenoe thought Captain McKay was going to investigate the daylights out of this ship. You imagined him scourging the evildoers and creating virtue with the crack of a court-martial gavel. Has he done any such thing? Of course not. Captain McKay is a realist.'

'All hell could break loose when this kid's mother reads this letter. She'll be writing her congressman and both senators and the President.'

'Tear it up.'

'Tear it up?'

Lieutenant MacComber yanked Semple's letter out of Ensign Meade's hand and ripped it to pieces. He dropped the shreds into an ashtray and rang for a steward. Almost immediately, Willard Otis, also from Georgia, arrived with a wide smile on his round black face. Meade was always amazed by the servility MacComber inspired in the mess stewards.

'Yes, Lieutenant MacComber?'

'Take this garbage away. And bring me some ice.'

'Right away, Mr MacComber.'

'Care to join me for a nightcap? I shipped some marvellous bourbon in Long Beach. My Kentucky cousin's private stock.'

'I've got another twenty letters to read,' Ensign Meade said. He plodded back to the stateroom he shared with two other ensigns. The hell with it, he thought. Maybe his father was right about the Navy. Maybe it was just as full of cynics and hustlers as Wall Street. They just didn't get paid as much money. Maybe the trick was to rack up a good record and get out as fast as possible.

Somehow that conclusion did not jibe with the pride he had felt when Gunnery Officer Moss switched him to turret one in the main battery. Moss did not tell him why, but

Johnny Chase said it had to be for the good job he had done in five-inch mount one. Meade had made damn sure there were no more dented powder cans or loose shells in the handling room. They had checked 1,600 cans of powder in their magazine and stayed up half the night passing dummy shells.

Maybe pride had nothing to do with the problem in Semple's letter. Maybe the Captain and everybody else did not give a damn about that kind of right and wrong. They were not in the idealism business; they were in the killing business. Maybe that was why his father had not objected to his going to Annapolis.

Where did honour fit into it? That was what his mother said she wanted him to learn at Annapolis. Honour meant a lot of things: courage, honesty, responsibility. An officer was responsible for his men. That was what had sent Ensign Babyface to MacComber. Now he no longer felt proud of himself or the Navy.

Maybe there would be other times, other chances, to live honour to the hilt. To feel completely proud. Meanwhile, Semple was on his own.

'She's got all kinds of quotes from the Bible to back her up. I was hoping you could give me some to refute her.'

Frank Flanagan sat in the chaplain's office talking to him about Teresa Brownlow. It sounded ridiculous by the time he finished trying to explain it. But Flanagan did not care. He wanted someone with a knowledge of the Bible to help him rescue Teresa from her bizarre creed. He would do it considerately. He would try to make amends for the rotten letter he had sent her.

Chaplain Bushnell leaned back in his chair and sighed. 'You say you're a Catholic?'

'Yes.'

'You have encountered what your priests would call a heresy. It's one of the oldest tendencies in the history of Christianity – antinomianism.'

'What does that mean?'

'The literal meaning is from the Greek, *anti*, "against", *nomos*, "law". The antinomians maintain that Jesus's

215

resurrection abolished the rule of law. There is no such thing as sin. Faith is all you need to be saved. It's an idea that has always had great appeal to Americans. It broke loose before the Revolution in what was called the Great Awakening. There were churches in Connecticut where every imaginable passion ran wild. My great-grandfather had a church in Redding where a veritable sexual explosion took place. I have his diary of the whole affair. Fascinating reading. The next outbreak occurred in the Southern back country after the Revolution. Nancy Hanks, Lincoln's mother, was a devotee, according to one of my historian friends. She and her sisters were much sought after for revivals. If the Hanks girls were going to be there, men came from all parts of Kentucky.'

Flanagan listened openmouthed. Lincoln's mother!

'They had a hymn they used to sing. It went something like this.

'Come to Jesus, come to Jesus,
Sinful woman, sinful man.
His love's as sweet as wild honey,
As fine as sugared ham.

'Isn't that marvellous?' Chaplain Bushnell said.

Flanagan nodded numbly. 'How would you refute someone who has this . . . belief?'

'I don't believe in refuting anyone's faith. That's where I differ with your Jesuits. Experience is the only way someone finds their way into – or out of – a faith.'

'You mean – you approve of this kind of thing?' Flanagan said. 'Would you want your wife or daughter to practise antinomianism?'

The chaplain smiled wanly. 'I don't have a daughter. My ex-wife, I regret to admit, embraced the twentieth-century version of antinomianism some time ago – the doctrine of free love. The practitioners of that creed are antinomians without theology. Instead of the grace of Jesus in their souls, they look for sincerity. I can't say I approved of her conduct. It caused me a good deal of embarrassment. But I couldn't in conscience object to her free choice – or choices, to be more exact. So we arranged an amicable divorce.'

Totally bewildered now, Flanagan could only murmur, 'I see.' He took a deep breath. 'What exactly *is* your faith, Chaplain?'

'It would be difficult to sum up in a few words. I've found a great many articles of the Christian creed difficult to accept. The divinity of Jesus, for instance. But I still believe in the power of faith, in the seeking spirit. We're all embarked on a spiritual voyage to eternity.'

'You don't think Jesus was God?' Flanagan said, totally astonished now.

'Neither did George Washington, Thomas Jefferson or Benjamin Franklin. Or my grandfather's good friend, after whom I'm named, Ralph Waldo Emerson. In its founding traditions, America is no more Christian than ancient Rome. Let me assure you I did not give up such a fundamental opinion without a struggle. But when I read Schleiermacher, and this more recent German, Albert Schweitzer, I had no choice. Schweitzer's book *The Quest of the Historical Jesus* proves rather conclusively, I fear, that the most we can accept is a kind of Platonic noumenon, consecrated by history.'

Consecrated by history. The phrase burned through Flanagan's eighteen-year-old brain. This conversation with Chaplain Bushnell was his first encounter with the modern American mind. He had grown up in New York City inside an Irish-Catholic ghetto. The world he had inherited from that ghetto was essentially no different from the one his Irish ancestors had acquired from St Patrick in the fifth century.

'Do you have a copy of that book on Jesus?' he said.

'I'd be delighted to loan it to you.'

Flanagan stumbled out onto the main deck of the USS *Jefferson City* with *The Quest of the Historical Jesus* in his hand. He stared up at the immense canopy of stars in the Pacific sky. *Consecrated by history.* Was that enough to live by? What did it really mean?

History. Flanagan had never thought of it as something people lived on his modest level of life. History was grandiose thoughts and ambitions pursued by kings and prime ministers and presidents. In these oddly named islands they were approaching, the Solomons, would they consecrate this history?

The words of the Mass spoke in Flanagan's mind. *For this is the chalice of my blood of the new and eternal testament . . . which shall be shed for you, and for many . . .* Was that how history was consecrated?

War Zone

In the headquarters of Squadron One, in reality the stateroom of Lieutenant Junior Grade Andrew Jackson, Montgomery West was having drinks with the lieutenant and his partner in crime, Ensign Donald Schnable. The ensign's round freckled face was flushed; his thick-lipped mouth wore a consciously reckless grin. Jackson's rawboned hillbilly face retained its usual deadpan. He made a point of never laughing at Schnable's antics, even when they amused him.

West had been spending a lot of his off-duty hours with these two demolishers of his movie career. Part of the reason was a letter he had received from Uncle Mort, denouncing him and the cloddish Navy roughnecks he had chosen for his friends aboard the *Jefferson City*. West had replied that he preferred their company to the snivelling asskissers with whom Louis B. Mayer surrounded himself. Drinking with Schnable and Jackson reinforced that salty declaration of independence. Besides, he admired the bravado with which they casually risked their lives each day, blasting into the sky from the *Jefferson City*'s catapult in their fragile fabric planes. It made his daily descent into main plot a little easier to handle, although his heart still pounded and his breath still came in shallow gulps.

Schnable drained his second bourbon and pointed on the map to the narrow waterways of the cluster of islands called the Solomons. 'God damn,' he said. 'Maybe we can pick off a Jap destroyer in those canals. No room for them to manoeuvre. From now on I'm takin' up our bomb load, Lieutenant.'

'Don't rush things,' Jackson said. 'We're headin' for Nouméa first, to check in with COMSOPAC. That's a thousand miles south of the Solomons. The less we fly off them catapults with an extra eight hundred pounds in them rubber-band specials, the better.'

'God Christ, am I hearing things? Is Lieutenant Jackson afraid of getting killed?' Schnable said, refilling his glass.

'No, just gettin' killed unnecessarily,' Jackson said. 'By the time you finish that third drink, you're goin' to be shitfaced, Ensign. Anybody flies them planes armed, he's gotta be sober. I'm not thrilled with the liftoff we're gettin' from that catapult. It ain't as good as it was before them Long Beach yardbirds worked it over.'

'Aw, Lieutenant,' Schnable said. 'Just because a flying fish jumped into the cockpit yesterday, that's nothing to worry about.'

'It's an order, Ensign.'

Jackson left them to get some fresh air on deck. Schnable fumed and poured himself a fourth drink. 'West,' he said, 'what would you do if you were the hero of the picture and someone impugned your reputation that way?'

'Calm down, Schnable. Jackson's right. You better make that your last drink or you won't get your plane in the air with or without bombs in her.'

'I'm gonna be the first SOC pilot to get himself a sub,' Schnable said. 'My radioman's got a buddy in Radio Central who'll give him the word if the cans pick up another contact. I'll come down right after they drop their depth charges and get him as he surfaces.'

'I've got the watch,' West said. 'Drink plenty of coffee at lunch, Schnable.'

'Glom my stuff on your radar screen, West. First a blip, then a blop. Sighted sub, sank same.'

'Just make sure it isn't one of our destroyers.'

'You're as bad as Jackson. No confidence in me,' Schnable said, pouring himself another drink.

Schnable made West wonder if having liquor available on

board ship was such a hot idea. The ensign did not handle booze well, and when he drank, his macho rivalry with Jackson became less than amusing. West had been attracted to these flyboys because he thought their courage was authentic. Now he was beginning to think, in Schnable's case at least, it was as manufactured as his own.

On the bridge, West relieved Lieutenant Wilson Selvage MacComber in the usual routine. The OOD's messenger brought up the crew's dinner – soggy pork chops and mashed potatoes. West ate it to eliminate the slight dizziness he felt from the liquor in his bloodstream.

A half hour later, Captain McKay came on the bridge and ordered him to head into the wind while they launched a plane. They were about to begin the afternoon's drills.

'Pilot requests permission to arm the plane,' the telephone talker said.

'Is that all right, Captain?' West said.

'Why not? They better get some practice flying with a full load,' Captain McKay said.

West knew the pilot was Schnable. He knew he had probably had another drink before lunch. He knew Jackson was serious about the danger of catapulting with a bomb load. Yet it was not exactly his responsibility to tell that to the Captain. The chain of command between McKay and Schnable did not run through Montgomery West. Schnable would call him an asskissing creep. Mullenoe's inclination to treat West like a human being might vanish. The Captain himself, having tolerated liquor aboard, probably did not want to be told officially on the bridge that one of his officers was drinking too much. As far as West could see, McKay did not seem to give much of a damn for the *Jefferson City*'s problems. The court-martials Mullenoe and others had predicted at Pearl Harbor had never taken place.

West decided to say nothing about Schnable. 'Affirmative. Arm the plane.'

'Ready to launch,' the telephone talker said about two minutes later.

'Launch,' West said.

He had given the order a dozen times since they had left

Long Beach and nothing bad had happened. Why should anything go wrong now? Schnable regularly flew after several drinks. West waited for the distant bang of the gunpowder in the catapult, almost five hundred feet astern. *Bok*. The ship jolted slightly. A moment, no – less than a moment – a millimoment later there was an explosion. It sounded like two five-inch mounts had gone off at once.

'Oh my God,' Captain McKay said.

'Left full rudder,' West said.

The ship swung sharply into the Williamson turn. 'The plane is in the water burning,' the telephone talker said. 'No sign of survivors.'

In a few minutes the wreckage was visible ahead of them. Bits and pieces of the plane and flickers of flame on the surface of the sea. West's heart pounded, his stomach churned. Was it his fault? Who or what could help him control his fear in main plot now?

'God damn it,' the helmsman muttered. 'We really are jinxed.'

'OK, wise guy,' growled the convict with a face like a graveyard skull. 'We're gonna teach you a lesson in who runs this place.'

Everybody on the hanger deck howled with laughter at the flickering figures on the screen. It was not supposed to be funny. The movie was about a prison and what happens to a young man who gets railroaded into it. Everybody was laughing because the young man was Lieutenant Montgomery West.

'You'll never break me. You know why?' West said. 'Because I'm innocent!'

'Tell it to the Marines,' the snarling older convict said as he advanced on West with a carving knife. That drew another howl.

The warden's wife rescued West just in time. She helped him prove his innocence. The ending left everyone feeling that justice had triumphed.

Harold Semple trudged wearily back to the First Division's compartment. He was exhausted from the endless gunnery drills, the constant working parties to bring up more ammunition from the magazines, more food from the holds. Plus the perpetual insistence on cleaning, scrubbing, shining every square inch of this metal monster. Semple planned to grab his blanket and sleep topside. That was what everybody was doing while the vile smell of paint remover filled the ship. Semple decided he would do it all the time from now on. It would help him avoid Wilkinson.

As Semple picked up his blanket, Wilkinson's hulking follower, Kraus, emerged from the shadows. 'Where the hell have you been?' he snarled. 'Wilkinson wants to see you. He says that handling room looks like a fucking pen in the Chicago stockyards.'

'I swabbed it down before supper.'

'Well you're gonna swab it down again. Get your ass up there.'

His blanket under his arm, Semple trudged forward to mount one's handling room. Wilkinson stood in the centre of the oval steel capsule, glaring at him. 'Look at this fucking mess,' he shouted, pointing at long black streaks and a half dozen heelprints on the deck.

'It wasn't there when I left,' Semple protested.

'Yeah? And these weren't either?' He pointed to a half dozen greasy smears on the bulkheads.

'No.'

'Well they sure as hell ain't gonna be here when you leave this time. Get yourself a bucket and brush and scrub every fuckin' inch of this place. Then shine it with a dry rag. I wanta be able to see my face in that fuckin' deck.'

'Can't I do it tomorrow? I'm tired. We were in here all day. It was so hot.'

It seemed even hotter now. Sweat streamed down Semple's neck and chest. The air was thick with paint remover. Wilkinson loomed over him. He was so big he seemed to fill the handling room. There was a new expression on his face. The disgust, the anger seemed to dissolve.

'Sure you could do it tomorrow, Prettyboy. You could do a lot of things tomorrow. You could be out of this fuckin' sweatbox tomorrow if you did something else first.'

'What?' Semple said. He knew what Wilkinson meant. His soul still revolted but his exhausted body whispered *surrender*. The boatswain's mate was too big, too powerful to resist. For some reason the blanket under his arm made it inevitable.

'Take off your pants.'

His dungarees slid slowly down his legs. Had he unbuckled the belt? He could not remember. Wilkinson pulled down his shorts and his hands moved slowly, relentlessly over his rump, his penis. 'Lie down,' he said.

There was no air now, only the factory smell of paint and grease. Once his father had taken Semple to the factory, to the roaring clanging assembly line, and there was the same smell. Then Semple's face was against the hot metal deck and he was smelling the harsh soap the Navy used, an ammonia smell like the kitchen at home after his mother scrubbed it on her hands and knees. Now he was on his hands and knees and Wilkinson enveloped him, grunting, growling. He was so big he was like the great ape in the movie *King Kong*. Semple was a doll, a puppy, in his ravenous grasp.

Somewhere below them the engines throbbed. The sea sloshed against the bulkhead. Then there was nothing but pain – pain and a kind of oblivion – as Wilkinson entered him. Oblivion in the sea's sound and Wilkinson's guttural groan of pleasure. The shred of manhood to which Semple had been clinging slid into the blank depths of another life. He was lost forever in this life now.

Semple lay flat on the deck, sobbing. The boatswain's mate knelt beside him. Imagining himself as Fay Wray in *King Kong*, Semple rolled over and looked up at Wilkinson with pleading eyes. 'It's OK, Prettyboy, it's OK,' Wilkinson said. 'Once I get that release, everything's OK. I'm your friend now. We'll have good times together. You'll have swell stuff to eat. Sweet jobs. No more workin' parties. No more decks to swab.'

'Oh, thank you, thank you,' Semple said, from the far shore of oblivion.

*

'Flan, come on, you gotta loan me another ten. I can get back in the game with ten. I feel it. Them dice gotta turn.'

'Jack, I don't have another ten. So help me. You owe me forty bucks already.'

Ever since they left Pearl, Peterson spent most of every night in turret three's handling room playing craps. The game was getting wilder and wilder. Five and six hundred dollars changed hands on a single roll. Flanagan went down and watched it one night but he did not bet. That was one thing his cop father had hammered into his brain. Heavy betting was for suckers or crazies. Flanagan was beginning to think Jack Peterson was a crazy.

Peterson went through the compartment wheedling money out of other members of the division. Boats Homewood watched him, scowling. 'It's gonna ruin him,' he said. 'I told him that when he came aboard the *Pennsylvania* ten years ago. He was the skinniest, meanest kid you ever seen. I tried to stop him then and almost talked him into it. But the minute he gets heavy with a dame, he goes back to it. I don't understand it.'

Flanagan was beginning to get some idea of the complicated emotions that linked Homewood and Peterson. Jack was a kind of son to the boatswain's mate, a troubled, rebellious son. At least Boats had stopped worrying about Jack getting thrown overboard. Flanagan had been relieved from bodyguard duty. But Homewood remained intensely disappointed by the Captain's failure to investigate what had happened at Savo Island. To Homewood this meant the dead were unsatisfied; their honour – the ship's honour – remained impugned.

'You coming up to our hotel in the sky tonight, Boats?'

'Yeah, I think I will,' Homewood said.

They had been sleeping in their work station, main forward. With the fore and aft hatches open, it was the coolest place on the ship. A lot of people had begun sleeping topside since they entered the tropics. Below decks the ship's engines seemed to multiply the ninety-degree temperatures outside.

'You can have Peterson's spot,' Flanagan said.

Homewood got his blanket and they climbed the ladders to

the station, forty feet above the main deck. A spectacular full moon bathed the ship and the sea with golden light. The blowers blended with the rush of the water against the hull and the throb of the engines to create a unique sound. The ship was like a living creature in the night.

Behind him, as they reached the platform outside main forward, Flanagan heard Homewood exclaim, 'Holy jumpin' Jesus.' He turned to find the boatswain's mate staring up at the main yardarm, the crossbar high on the mainmast. There was something large and white there. Flanagan could not make it out at first.

'It's an albatross,' Homewood said.

Now Flanagan could see it. The bird was huge, with a hunched neck and gull-like beak and sinister-looking black brows. He just sat there staring down on the ship, utterly silent.

'Don't make a goddamn sound. The longer he stays the more luck he brings,' Homewood said.

He rushed down the ladder to spread the word below decks. Soon practically every man on the ship except the engine-room watch was on deck, staring up at the magical bird. Even Captain McKay joined them. He climbed all the way up to main forward with Homewood. 'What kind do you think it is?' he asked.

'It's a Wanderer, I'm pretty sure, Captain,' Homewood said. 'The biggest kind. Wait'll you see his wingspan. I've seen'm eleven feet tip to tip. They nest all the way down to Antarctica. He's been flyin' a long way.'

'And we've been sailing a long way,' the Captain said.

'He's gonna change our luck, Captain, I guarantee it.'

'I hope you're right,' Captain McKay said. He gazed up at the bird. 'Some people think that's where the souls of the dead sailors go.'

Flanagan was astounded. Did the Captain believe in Homewood's dark fate-ridden universe?

'Maybe it's one of our shipmates, tellin' us it's OK. Now that we've come back to fight.'

'Maybe,' Captain McKay said. 'Let me know how long he stays.'

The Captain went below. For another half hour they steamed across the moonlit sea with the silent bird above them. Then, without a sound, the albatross stretched his immense black-fringed wings and flew into the night. Flanagan heard a long sigh escape from his shipmates' throats and from his own throat. Was it a sailor's prayer?

'That's not much of a stay,' Homewood said. 'I've seen'm roost for a couple of days on some ships. But we'll be OK for a while. As long as we don't do nothin' to spoil that luck.'

'Captain,' Montgomery West said, 'I've got a confession to make. You may decide to kick me the hell off this ship, but that's OK, I deserve it. If it saves a life, it'll be worth it.'

'Calm down, Mr West,' McKay said. 'I don't believe in kicking people off ships. What's on your mind?'

West told him why Schnable had crashed. 'Now his buddy Jackson is into the sauce day and night, blaming himself for it. Neither of them ever should have been assigned to a cruiser, Captain. They were fighter pilots. If you don't transfer Jackson to a carrier, the same thing's going to happen to him.'

'The same thing may happen to him anyway,' McKay said. 'On a carrier, the pilots drink any time they feel like it.'

'If he shoots down a few Japs, he may start feeling better about Schnable.'

'Maybe he should feel bad about Schnable,' McKay said. 'It sounds like he gave him some pretty lousy leadership.'

West was startled by McKay's momentary transformation. Darkness gathered in his eyes. He looked capable of hanging Jackson – or West – from the main yardarm. Then the mild grey colour, the slightly bemused expression returned.

'You're probably right. He belongs on a carrier. The wise guy at flight school who tried to punish them by assignment is really to blame.' He sighed and ran a hand through his thinning hair. 'If you look at anything long enough, West, you can usually find a way to blame the system. It's the easy way out.'

West did not know what to say. Was he about to hear a

denunciation of that sacred entity, the US Navy?

'But most of the time it comes down to a man or a few men screwing up, as we've been screwing up since the Garden of Eden.'

West had nothing to add to that observation, either.

'I'll see what I can do about getting Jackson on a carrier. Try not to feel too bad about Schnable. I would have done the same thing at your age.'

'I think the uniform of the day should be dress whites,' Commander Parker said. 'I was on Admiral Ghormley's staff for a while in thirty-nine. He's a regulations man all the way.'

McKay was dubious. The crew was weary from the weeks of drilling and paint chipping. For the last five days they had wilted under tropic temperatures. Sailors hated dress whites more than any other uniform. It was hard to do anything on a warship without getting them dirty. On the other hand he had not let Parker win any arguments lately. 'OK,' he said.

When the word was passed to the destroyers, the TBS (Talk Between Ships) radio became a series of agitated squawks from the two captains. One intimated his men might mutiny. The other said it would make them the laughingstock of the South Pacific. McKay decided it would look worse to back down, and as the OTC (Officer in Tactical Command) reiterated the order.

So the *Jefferson City* and her escorts stood into Nouméa, capital of French-owned New Caledonia and headquarters of COMSOPAC, with all three crews at quarters in their whites. The harbour was a messy clutter of merchant ships with seamen lazing on their decks. The harbour pilot, a weather-beaten chief boatswain's mate, said, 'Good thing you got the word on the uniforms, Captain. The Admiral's chewed the ass off the last two captains who came in here in dungarees.'

Commander Parker gave him a triumphant look. 'I'm glad you didn't listen to those tin-can loudmouths,' he said. 'I'd report them to the Admiral if I were you, Captain.'

'I don't see much point in that,' McKay said. 'Send them over some ice cream instead. They got us here in one piece.'

A breathless radioman appeared on bridge. 'Urgent message from Admiral Ghormley.'

The message read: WE WELCOME THE JEFFERSON CITY BACK TO THE SOUTH PACIFIC COMMAND. REPORT TO ME IMMEDIATELY.

In fifteen minutes, Arthur McKay was in his gig heading across the harbour to a stubby grey supply ship, the *Argonne*, where Vice Admiral Robert Ghormley lived and worked. Sweat streamed down McKay's face and neck. His armpits were soaked. It was at least a hundred degrees in the crowded harbour, with the tropic sun beating down on the still black water. His high-necked white uniform was almost suffocating him.

Aboard the *Argonne*, he was welcomed by a classmate, lanky Commander Vince Casey, who described himself as the personnel man on Ghormley's staff. Casey was in pressed khakis, with a tie and coat – clothing almost as incongruous in the heat as McKay's dress whites.

'How's it going, Vince?' McKay said.

Casey sighed. 'He'll tell you.'

McKay did not know Ghormley well, but Win Kemble had worked for him when Ghormley was head of the War Plans Division in Washington in 1938. Win had wryly, perhaps enviously, pronounced Ghormley the supreme politician. He had spent most of his career on staffs of influential admirals. A tour at the White House as naval liaison officer with President Roosevelt had been even more helpful. When the war broke out, Ghormley was serving as a special naval observer in London, a job Roosevelt had created to help him run his undeclared naval war against Germany.

As McKay remembered him, the Admiral had been a handsome square-jawed, strong-browed man, with a marvellously self-assured, ingratiating manner. He was the sort of senior officer who was seldom impressed by Arthur McKay's laconic, self-deprecating style, and McKay was prepared to feel several inches shorter before the interview was over.

The Admiral he saw behind a desk piled with papers bore no resemblance to the one McKay had met in Washington. The sixty-year-old Ghormley looked at least seventy. His face was grey with fatigue; the corners of his once-confident mouth drooped. He shook hands and gestured McKay to a seat in front of his desk. 'How is Win?' he asked.

'All right, as far as I know.'

'If you hear anything from him, I hope you'll let him know I had nothing to do with relieving him. That emanated entirely from Washington – from which nothing but bad tidings seem to come these days.'

'I'll tell him that if I get a chance, Admiral.'

'I thought his conduct at Savo Island, in the light of the situation as it developed, and has developed since, was eminently sensible. Nothing would have been gained by sacrificing the *Jefferson City* the way we sacrificed the Asiatic Fleet – to utterly no avail.'

McKay nodded. He was beginning to see where Win had got some of his defeatism.

'Is the *Jefferson City* ready to fight?'

'I think so, Admiral.'

'We'll soon find out. You and the destroyers should get under way as soon as you refuel. You'll have orders to our forward base in the New Hebrides, where Norm Scott is trying to put together a semblance of a task force. The Japs have been bombarding the airfield on Guadalcanal night after night. They're pouring troops ashore. I frankly think the best we can hope for is an evacuation.'

'It's that bad, Admiral?'

'It's worse,' Ghormley said.

He began reciting a catalogue of his woes. Everything was wrong, from the way they were failing to battleload the supply ships in California to a longshoremen's strike in New Zealand which made it impossible to reload them there. Nouméa lacked the port facilities to offload a rowboat. As a result the Marines on Guadalcanal were being threatened with starvation as well as annihilation by the Japanese. Washington refused to commit more men or planes or ships. MacArthur's land-based B-17s were worse than useless. Bombing from 20,000 feet, they had yet to sink a single Jap warship and frequently had trouble telling foe from friend. The other day they had attacked two American destroyers.

'We're losing the war out here, and no one will listen to us,' Ghormley said.

It was worse than defeatism. It was despair. McKay could hear Win Kemble snarling, *I'm going to let you find out for yourself the travesty of war we're fighting out there.*

Vince Casey rushed in with an urgent message. 'Oh, my God,' Ghormley said, mopping his streaming neck and face. The temperature below decks aboard the *Argonne* was at least twenty degrees hotter than the harbour.

McKay said goodbye to Ghormley and chased Casey down the passageway to ask him to transfer Lieutenant Andrew Jackson to a carrier and find him two replacement pilots for the *Jefferson City*. Casey wiped his forehead and said it would take a few days. 'We're all close to collapse, trying to work and sleep in this goddamn hotbox. Those French fuckers won't give us any quarters on the beach.'

Casey launched into an incredibly complicated explanation of why the French governor of New Caledonia was being backed by Charles de Gaulle, leader of the Free French in London, in his refusal to cooperate with the Americans. De Gaulle apparently thought they were planning to steal the miserable island from la belle France. 'I'd like to sink the fucking place,' he said.

'Why don't we just take what we need and let them squawk until doomsday?' McKay said.

'They're afraid that will upset the applecart in North Africa. They need de Gaulle's cooperation there.'

While McKay shook his head in bewilderment, Casey asked the inevitable question. 'What's old W.S.S. Kemble doing? Going on Cominch's staff to win the war for him, after practically losing it for us out here?'

'I don't know.'

'Did you find out what the fuck he was doing at Savo? Or thought he was doing?'

'No. Has anybody found out what Kelly Turner thought he was doing?'

Casey stared over McKay's shoulder, his eyes blank with apprehension. McKay turned to find himself face to face with Admiral Turner in person. His black brows bristled; his usually sallow hollow-cheeked face was livid. 'McKay,' he said, 'I hear you've been bad-mouthing me all over the Pacific.'

'That's an exaggeration, Admiral.'

'You better make damn sure your ship performs at the four point oh level, Captain. Otherwise you're in a lot of trouble.'

'As far as I can see, everybody's in a lot of trouble where we're going,' McKay said.

Admiral Ghormley appeared in the doorway of his office with the emergency cable in his hand. 'Commander Casey. What are we going to do about this?' He looked as if he was about to burst into tears.

Back aboard the *Jefferson City*, McKay was greeted by Commander Parker on the quarterdeck. 'Are they as fucked up as ever?' he asked, within earshot of Ensign Meade, the junior OOD, and a half dozen enlisted men.

'Hell no,' Captain McKay said. 'They're bright-eyed and bushy-tailed. They wished us good luck and good shooting.'

Warm-Up

'Enemy aircraft, bearin' zero zero zero,' drawled the telephone talker on the bridge.

'Sound General Quarters,' Captain McKay said.

The Marine bugler stepped to the PA microphone and sent his brassy notes pealing through the ship. Ernest Homewood, the boatswain's mate of the watch, followed him with a shrill call on his pipe. 'Now hear this. General Quarters. General Quarters. All hands man your battle stations,' he roared, endangering the crew's eardrums. When Homewood got excited, he did not need a PA system.

McKay stepped out on the port wing – the open part of the bridge. Dead ahead in the cloudless blue sky, twelve Mitsubishi Zero-1 medium bombers flying in two V formations seemed to be barely moving. They looked like lazy harmless insects. Their engines were not more than a buzz. The rush of the sea past the cruiser's hull was a louder sound.

'Bettys,' McKay said, using the planes' American nickname. 'Tell the engine room to get up all the steam they can find.'

McKay stepped to the PA microphone. 'Men. This is your captain. I told you last night we'd probably meet this reception committee. It's the Japs' way of saying welcome to the Solomon Islands. Just stay calm, shoot straight and we'll do fine.'

A nice performance, Captain, he thought. But the play is only beginning. How would he handle himself under fire? That was the crucial question. He knew it was in the mind of every man on the ship. Only once before had Arthur McKay experienced the sensation of people firing bullets and shells at him – aboard the *Monocacy* on the Yangtze River, when he was twenty-five years old. His reaction had almost ruined his naval career.

The navigator, Marse Lee, relieved Air Defence Officer Mullenoe as officer of the deck. Commander Parker reported that Batt II, his armoured canning tower aft, was manned and ready. Damage Control informed the bridge that Condition Zed was set throughout the ship. That meant all hatches and watertight doors were sealed.

'Torpedo planes to starboard, bearing one three five,' said the talker.

McKay rushed to the starboard wing of the bridge. Again the Japanese Nakajimi 97-2's, called Kates, looked like insects on the horizon. But there was menace in their narrow green fuselages and their headlong approach, only a few dozen feet off the water. These were a more serious threat than the Bettys overhead.

'Moss,' McKay said to his gunnery officer at his post in main forward. 'Concentrate on the torpedo planes. I think those Bettys are too high to do us any damage, unless they get very lucky.'

Over the telephone circuit came Parker's voice, urgent and shrill. 'Captain, I disagree! You've got to put a few shells up there to rattle those guys. We can't let them make a practice run on us.'

McKay took a deep breath. Don't lose your temper, he told

himself. The man who loses his temper is only a step away from losing his nerve.

'Commander Moss, this is the captain. Acknowledge my order. Concentrate on the torpedo planes.'

'Roger, Captain,' Moss said.

Down in main plot, Montgomery West listened to his thumping heart. 'Now it's a torpedo attack,' the telephone talker said. His jutting underlip trembled. He looked as if he might burst into tears.

Panic flickered across a half dozen other faces. 'Why in hell are they keeping us down here?' Fire Controlman First Class Bourne asked. 'We got nothing to shoot at.'

'Would you rather be topside with shrapnel all over the place?' Bob Edison asked.

'Yeah,' muttered Bob Finch half-heartedly. For once the Bobbsey Twins did not seem to agree.

'I'd rather be anywhere than on this fucking ship!' Bourne cried. 'You assholes can afford not to give a shit. I got a wife and three kids.'

'Bourne, shut up. That's an order,' Montgomery West said.

Bourne leered at him. 'You look like you feel the same way, Lieutenant.'

West struggled for courage, calm. 'I haven't got a wife and three kids, if that's what you mean. But I've got a few people who might be a little upset if I got killed. We all do. There's no point in thinking that way. This is our job. Let's do it and hope for the best.'

In the forward fire room, they were too busy to think about what was happening in the sky far above them. Watertender First Class Cartwright warned Marty Roth to feed that hot oil to the boilers 'like you're puttin' a nipple into a baby's mouth'. Amos abjured the firemen watching the boiler gauges to keep them balanced precisely in the middle of the range. 'We get water in turbine now, and we gonna be up to our necks in water about two minutes later. Glug glug glug,' he bellowed. The men on the air gauges got similar lectures about the importance of keeping smoke to a minimum. 'Them guys at the range-finders gotta see what the fuck they're shootin' at!'

With all the hatches shut and ventilators off, the heat in the engine room rose exponentially. 'God damn it,' Roth gasped. 'It's gotta be a hundred fifty degrees down here.'

'Hell's a lot hotter,' Cartwright said. 'Watch that damn valve.'

In sky forward, another armoured hut aft of main forward, Air Defence Officer Robert Mullenoe asked for ranges and bearings from his range-finder operator and from his radar operator. They disagreed by several hundred yards. Lieutenant Commander Edwin Moss, monitoring the conversation from his post in main forward, went wild. 'Get together, you stupid bastards,' he screamed.

'Three thousand yards and closing,' insisted the range-finder operator. 'Twenty-five hundred,' said the radar man.

'Take the range-finder,' shouted Lieutenant Commander Moss. 'No one knows whether that goddamn radar works.'

Commander Parker's voice came over the line. 'Mullenoe, you son of a bitch, start shooting or I'll come up there and take charge!'

'Mullenoe, take your time. Get it right,' Captain McKay said.

'Mount one, take the leader, bearing one zero five, range two thousand yards,' Mullenoe said. He asssigned planes to the other five-inch turrets in the same smooth reassuring way.

On the bridge, the talker drawled, 'Cap'n bombs comin' down.'

'Right full rudder,' McKay said. 'Flank speed.'

The *Jefferson City* tilted wildly to starboard as she went into the turn at thirty-two knots. In the distance, the two destroyers were taking similar evasive action. One of them had heeled over almost forty degrees, so sharp was her turn.

The first bombs hit a good five hundred yards astern. Huge fountains of water leaped from the sea, remarkably beautiful for a fleeting moment, like giant flowers rising from the dark blue depths. The stunning crash was followed almost instantly by the equally numbing blast of the *Jefferson City*'s five-inch guns hurling metal at the torpedo planes. There were six Kates, and the cruiser was definitely their target. They were paying no attention to the destroyers, who were banging away at them too.

'Forty-millimetre mount one, concentrate on the lead plane, bearing one zero five,' Mullenoe said.

Frank Flanagan hunched against his range-finder. His mouth, his tongue felt as if someone had stuffed a turkish towel down his throat. There was a man in that plane, hurtling toward him with a big tin fish that would kill him and everyone else aboard his ship. He had to kill him first.

The five-inch guns were all firing too high. The bursts were exploding far above the Japs. Flanagan waited for the lead plane to steady in the small circle in the middle of his director's sight. From the corner of his eye he could see his gun crew with the snub-nosed shells piled high in the loaders. He pressed the trigger and a stream of shells spewed across the water. Preferring to fire low rather than high, he was short with the first rounds. The Jap kept coming, even though five-inch shells seemed to be bursting all around him now. The yellow bastard had nerve!

Get him this time. Get him before he lets the fish go. Now!

Another miss. The Kate had begun weaving and dipping. Jinking, they called it. Flanagan almost despaired. He could hear Lieutenant Mullenoe telling the five-inch guns to shorten their fuses. If they stopped to do it, there was no noticeable decrease in the slamming blasts from their muzzles. How could anyone keep a steady hand or eye in the chaos erupting around him?

'*Get him, Flan, you can do it!*' It was Jack Peterson on the platform outside main forward. The main battery had nothing to do in air attack. He had left his GQ station, a court-martial offence, to help him out – and incidentally see the show.

How were the other guns doing? A glance told Flanagan no one had scored a hit yet. The Japs were still coming. An enormous crash to port informed him the bombers overhead were getting closer too. Pieces of shrapnel clanged off metal all around him. The blasts of the *Jefferson City*'s eight five-inch guns threatened to split his head and cave in his chest. Now! He had the Kate again. He really had him!

A stream of two-pound forty-millimetre shells struck the Japanese plane. The pilot veered drunkenly to the left and right as if he had run into a huge invisible spider web out there. Flanagan kept the trigger down and poured shells into him. '*Yeah, yeah, yeah,*' Peterson was yelling. Suddenly the Jap was no longer a plane; he was a hurtling fireball. A moment later plane and torpedo exploded. The deck apes on the forty-millimetre mount burst into cheers and gave Flanagan a V-for-victory salute. Jack Peterson vaulted to the catwalk to pound him on the back.

'Good shooting, Forty-Mill One,' Lieutenant Mullenoe said. 'Take the next one down the line.'

Before Flanagan could obey the order, a five-inch shell hit that Kate on the nose and blew it into a million pieces. A third, hit by forty-millimetre shells from another mount, nosed into the water, cartwheeled and exploded. But the others kept coming. He saw one, two, three of them release their torpedoes and pull up. Was it going to end so soon? he thought, fear sinking into his stomach like a gulp of cold oatmeal.

'Torpedoes bearing two one five, two zero, two two five,' Flanagan shouted into the mouthpiece strapped to his chest.

On the bridge, the talker reported what Flanagan and a half dozen lookouts and gun captains had told him.

'Left full rudder,' Captain McKay said.

The *Jefferson City* swung to port like an overloaded truck on a high-speed curve. Now the churning torpedoes no longer had the length of her long slim hull to hit. Only her trim fantail was exposed to their murderous noses.

'More bombs comin' down,' the talker said.

'Say a prayer,' McKay muttered.

'Sorry, Captain, I didn't hear you,' the talker said. He was a tall serious kid with loving-cup ears.

'Never mind. I was talking to myself,' McKay said.

Uncanny. It was so much like that moment on the

Monocacy seventeen years ago. He had made a decision on the Yangtze that risked his ship then, and he remained convinced it was the right decision. He was doing the same thing now.

He had to concentrate on evading those torpedoes and hope the Mitsubishis' aim was as bad as MacArthur's B-17's. He stepped out on the starboard wing of the bridge in time to see the torpedoes churning past, the closest one a good hundred yards away. Simultaneously, a stack of bombs began exploding off the port bow. One after another, they walked toward the ship, each one heaving up its deadly fountain of water, like the footsteps of an invisible giant.

'Captain, for Christ's sake do something. The next one's gonna hit,' Parker shouted over the telephone circuit.

'Right rudder fifteen degrees,' McKay said.

They sheared drunkenly to starboard as a near miss flung shrapnel and water all over the forward part of the ship. McKay saw a Marine manning a twin twenty-millimetre mount above turret two clutch his chest and topple to the deck. In the same moment one of the Kates came roaring down the length of the ship from the stern, machine guns blazing. Bullets struck sparks off metal everywhere. McKay's Marine orderly leaped out on the wing yelling, 'Watch it, Captain!' He flung McKay up against the bulkhead and covered him with his body. A bullet clanged off the metal shield where he had been standing and dropped to the deck.

'Thanks, son,' McKay said.

It was over. The *Jefferson City* was still afloat, cutting through the greenish-blue water. The Japanese planes dwindled to dots in the sky. Arthur McKay walked to the PA microphone, wondering if he looked as dazed as he felt. 'This is your captain speaking. Well done,' he said.

'I think we got ourselves a real skipper,' Boats Homewood said as they waited in the chow line.

'Shit. He was just lucky. That last stack of bombs fell short by about ten feet,' Jack Peterson said.

'We got that ten feet by the Captain's order,' Homewood

said. 'I was on the bridge. I heard him give the order to put the rudder over.'

'Some guys say he only did it because the Exec told him to.'

'That's bullshit,' Homewood said.

'Wilkinson says he damn near got court-martialed once in China for freezin' under fire. His wife's pull saved his ass.'

Flanagan said nothing. He was just beginning to return to some semblance of normal thinking and feeling. He was also beginning to realize he had killed a man. What was the Jap like? he wondered. Was he one of those grinning buck-toothed sadists in the Hollywood movies who screamed, 'Die, American!' Or did he resemble the Japanese who used to vacation at a big house on the beach near Asbury Park. None of them had buck teeth. They were small, serious men, who nodded and smiled shyly if you met them fishing in the surf early in the morning.

'Did we have any casualties?' he asked.

'A Marine took some shrapnel in his chest. That strafer didn't hit nobody,' Homewood said. 'I told you our luck's changed.'

'I'm gonna try and prove that in the crap game tonight,' Peterson said.

'Where'n hell did you get any more money?' Homewood said.

'I got friends besides you,' Peterson said.

'Jack,' Homewood said, 'one of these days I'm gonna give up on you.'

'*Now hear this. Seaman Second Class Flanagan report to the bridge.*'

'They're gonna court-martial you for shootin' down that Jap without gettin' permission from Kruger,' Peterson said.

'They are like hell,' Homewood said.

Flanagan abandoned his tin chow tray and hurried to the bridge, straightening his hat and hastily trying to increase the shine on his shoes en route. Ensign Kruger, on duty as the junior officer of the deck, greeted him with his usual scowl. 'Flanagan? The Captain wants to see you.'

Captain McKay stepped into the pilothouse from the wing. Flanagan came to attention. 'At ease,' the Captain said.

'I just wanted to let you know how much I liked your shooting this morning.' He studied Flanagan for a moment. 'Haven't I seen you before?'

'At Mast, Captain.'

'Oh, yes. And looking for your Abandon Ship station. Did you forget it again and decide you had to get that guy or else?'

'No, Captain. I remembered it,' Flanagan said. 'After today I'll never forget it.'

'Good. How long have you been in the Navy?'

'Four and a half months, Captain.'

'Well, it's a little early, but you deserve it. From now on you're a seaman first class.'

'Thank you, Captain.'

The Captain nodded to the senior officer of the deck, Lieutenant MacComber. 'Call me if you see anything that looks alarming.'

'Aye, aye, Captain,' MacComber said.

Kruger waited until the Captain left the bridge. He glared at Flanagan. 'You know how long it took me to make seaman first class?'

'No sir.'

'Five years!'

'I don't get your point, Mr Kruger,' MacComber said.

'My point is, we're spoiling these brats. They're never gonna make real sailors.'

'Mr Kruger, that's the best news I've heard since I made the mistake of going to Annapolis,' MacComber said.

'Captain,' Montgomery West said, 'I think – for the good of the ship – I should be relieved of command of the Fire Control Division.'

'Give me a better reason than that, Mr West,' Arthur McKay said. 'From everything I've seen and heard, you've got one of the best divisions on the ship.'

'Captain, I just can't handle the situation down in main plot.'

McKay studied him for a moment. West braced himself for the return of the grim-eyed man he had glimpsed when he told him about Schnable and Jackson.

'You mean you're scared shitless down there. And so is everybody else. You don't know how to handle that.'

'I'm afraid there'll be a panic when we need the main battery guns, Captain.'

'I understand. I remember the first time I crawled into a turret, back in 1919. I felt the same way. A lot of people can't handle a turret – or a main plotting room. Some people need a handy exit. Then they're as brave as the next man. They won't use the exit. They just like knowing it's there.'

'I guess I'm one of those people.'

'Maybe. Maybe not. The fact that you can walk in here and tell me about the problem makes me think not. Who's the most jittery guy down there?'

'Fire Controlman First Class Bourne.'

'Have a talk with him. Tell him you're depending on him to set an example to the younger men. Lay it on thick. How much you need his help. Have the talk *in* the plotting room. Start spending time down there with him. Work on some of the equipment with him. Get some of the other men down there too when they're off watch. Maybe bring some ice cream down from the wardroom after supper. Get them used to the damn place.'

West nodded. Would it work? He had no idea. But it was a lot more appealing than the humiliation he had chosen as a first alternative.

'In the end we may have to get tough. If necessary I'll put a Marine down there with instructions to shoot the first man who doesn't obey an order.'

West could only nod dazedly. Arthur McKay had mentioned this last resort in the same calm almost offhand voice he had used to give him advice laced with kindness and guile. West began to wonder if he – or anyone else aboard USS *Jefferson City* – understood their captain.

Main Event

The equatorial sun beat down on the *Jefferson City*, turning the ship into a giant oven. She was anchored in Segund Channel, off the island of Espiritu Santo in the New Hebrides. Four other cruisers and five destroyers swung on their hooks a few hundred yards away. Nothing moved on the flat glassy water or on the shore, where two stores, a Catholic hospital and a few tin-roofed houses constituted a town, crowded on all sides by dense green jungle. The steel ships seemed absurdly misplaced in this primitive world. They should have been tallmasted square-riggers from the previous century. Time itself seemed immobilized, prostrate in the hot humid air.

'You're late for the party, McKay. But we won't hold that against you. We're going to need every gun we can find tomorrow night.'

Rear Admiral Norman Scott sat at attention in his broiling stateroom aboard the heavy cruiser *San Francisco*. There were no personal mementos on the bulkheads. The room was as sparsely furnished as decency permitted. Comfort and ease were not big in Scott's vocabulary. He wore a permanent scowl on his handsome face. People who had served under him during the previous year, when he was on the staff of the Chief of Naval operations in Washington, still went pale at the mention of his name.

Scott told McKay they were expecting a convoy with major American reinforcements for Guadalcanal to arrive from Nouméa tomorrow night. There was every reason to suppose the Japs would try to intercept it. For the past three weeks, Scott had been in these waters with the four cruisers and five destroyers, rehearsing tactics. 'We're not going to repeat Savo Island and steam around in circles like a lot of ducks while they come and get us. We're going to get them first.'

He handed McKay a diagram of his battle plan. Three destroyers would lead the column, two would bring up the rear. The cruisers would be in the centre. 'We're going to manoeuvre as a group, fight as a group, under my orders. That's what we've been rehearsing. We'll go out tonight and give you a chance to dance with us at least once. Tell your crew to expect to be at General Quarters until dawn. If they complain, tell them the other ships have been doing it every night for the past three weeks. We're never going to beat these guys until we get a lot tougher. Did you read those after-action reports of Savo Island, where everyone bleated about staying at General Quarters for thirty-six hours? They disgusted me.'

McKay decided he liked Admiral Scott. Not that Scott gave a damn. He was here to win a war, not a popularity contest. Maybe there was something to be said for the admiral-as-son-of-a-bitch after all.

Back aboard the *Jefferson City*, McKay summoned Parker to his cabin. 'Get copies of this battle plan to all the department heads,' he said. 'Pass the word for the crew to get some sleep, if they can manage it below decks. We'll be at General Quarters all night.'

'Jesus Christ. What does he expect to accomplish by wearing us out before we fight? It's exactly the same sort of idiocy that left us punch-drunk at Savo Island.'

'Commander, I'm getting a little tired of listening to you snipe at the Navy's admirals. I'm even less inclined to get advice from you over the telephone in the middle of a battle. I think from now on you had better change your battle station to the bridge. If you want to suggest anything to me, you can do it there face to face without the whole ship wondering who's in command.'

'The whole ship is still wondering why you let those Bettys bomb us without firing a shot at them, I can tell you that. They're wondering if you would have thrown that rudder over if I hadn't told you.'

'I was about to give the order,' McKay said.

'I've got five kids, Captain. I want to get out of this thing in one piece. So I reserve the right to make sure you don't repeat a performance you once gave in China. When you froze on the bridge and let the Chinese shell the shit out of your gunboat without firing back.'

'I did *not* freeze on the bridge. I made a decision – a decision I've never regretted,' McKay said. 'A decision that was eventually upheld by the highest authorities.'

'You can get the highest authorities to uphold a lot of things when you've got that ring on your finger and an admiral's daughter in your bed. But I know what the men on the ship – the men in the fleet – thought of it.'

Parker leaned toward McKay, chin outthrust, his whole body emanating aggression, dislike. He had apparently learned nothing from the Captain's decision not to conduct an investigation of Savo Island. He was still determined to rule or ruin the commander of the *Jefferson City*.

Should he put him in hack? No, that was out of the question on the eve of a battle. Parker had a following among the men. They liked his Uncle Dan act, his habit of dismissing minor offences at the exec's mast.

What was Parker trying to hide behind this farrago of bluster and accusation? That was another reason to pay out some more rope and watch what he did with it.

'I see no point in continuing this conversation,' McKay said. 'When General Quarters sounds, Commander, I'll expect you on the bridge.'

'I'll be there,' Daniel Boone Parker said.

'There it is,' Boats Homewood said, squinting into the sea wind on the deck outside main forward.

'Guadalcanal?' Flanagan said, joining him and Jack Peterson.

'No. Savo,' Homewood said.

'Do you see what I see?' Peterson asked.

Twilight was falling on the Coral Sea. Flanagan peered at the island on the horizon ahead of them. A clump of cumulus clouds hovered over it. Gradually, the shape penetrated Flanagan's weary brain. Like everyone else, he was groggy from lack of sleep.

'It looks like a man lying on his back,' he said.

'Yeah,' Jack Peterson said. 'A fuckin' corpse on a bier.'

'Jesus, Mary and Joseph,' Leo Daley said, crossing himself.

'You're all seein' things,' Homewood said. 'It's an island. Nothin' but a fuckin' island.'

A boatswain's pipe shrilled. 'Now hear this,' boomed the PA system. 'General Quarters. General Quarters. All hands man your battle stations.'

On the bridge, Captain McKay stared in fascination at the shrouded bulk of Savo Island. Everything he had read about the August battle stormed through his mind. It was uncanny – and somehow marvellous – that he had brought the *Jefferson City* back to the same waters where she had failed two months ago. Would they redeem themselves tonight? Or fail again? Could Arthur McKay, the follower, succeed where Win Kemble, the leader, had faltered?

'Bridge! Gunnery manned and ready.'

'Bridge! Engineering manned and ready. Boilers, one, two, three, four on line.'

'Bridge! Damage Control manned and ready. Condition Zed set throughout the ship.'

A half hour later, the *Jefferson City* charged through the tropical darkness at twenty-five knots. Sailors who had spent the previous night at General Quarters peered blearily at dials and gauges in the engine rooms and fire rooms, stared numbly at the dark sea on the open mounts and gun directors.

Less than six hundred yards ahead loomed the light cruiser *Boise*, commanded by Captain 'Iron Mike' Moran, a professional Irishman famed for his pugnacity. Ahead of the *Boise* was the light cruiser *Helena* and the heavy cruisers *Salt Lake City* and *San Francisco* and three destroyers. Behind the *Jefferson City* two more destroyers brought up the rear. A dozen miles away in the darkness was the night-shrouded coast of Guadalcanal, where men were frantically unloading the transports that had arrived earlier in the day.

Admiral Scott's tense voice came over the TBS. 'All ships, launch scout planes.'

The *Jefferson City* ignored this order. Lieutenant Jackson had left the ship two days ago for carrier duty. No replacements had as yet arrived for him or Schnable.

'Captain! What the hell is that?' cried Commander Daniel Parker. Ahead of them, one of the cruisers was afire! Flames leaped on her stern, then fell into the sea. 'I think it's their scout plane,' McKay said. 'I bet one of her flares went off ahead of schedule.'

'Jesus Christ. We might as well send Yamamoto an announcement of where we are.'

A minute later the burning plane drifted past them. Then, a strange sight, another scout plane, apparently undamaged, bobbed past. 'What the hell is going on?' Parker asked.

'Someone didn't get the message to launch and decided to get rid of their plane,' McKay said. 'After Savo, Cincpac issued a warning they were fire hazards.'

'I bet he graduated first in his class at Annapolis,' Parker said.

Beside Parker stood his scowling expert on ship-handling, Jerome Wilkinson, as boatswain's mate of the watch. He had given the Executive Officer advice as he coped with two changes of course, a nerve-twisting task while travelling at high speed in the darkness.

At 2228, Navigator Marse Lee rushed to the bridge to warn McKay they were getting dangerously close to the shore of Guadalcanal. According to his antiquated charts, a ship had run aground on a reef here in 1873.

'We'll have to let the Admiral worry about that,' McKay said.

'Captain!' said the talker. 'Radar reports at least three ships bearing three one five degrees, range two seven zero zereo zero yards.'

Over the TBS came Admiral Scott's voice: 'Left to course two three zero degrees.'

'Jesus Christ,' Commander Parker said. 'Doesn't he see them too?'

'They don't have our new search radar in the *San Francisco*,' McKay said.

If the radar was in fact picking up an enemy fleet, this was the worst possible time to reverse course, a complicated manoeuvre even in daylight. Each ship had to swing left in the wake of the one behind it while the lead destroyers made a separate turn that dropped them back to a parallel course with the rest of the column. It would put the destroyers between the Japanese and the rest of the American squadron.

There was no time to inform Scott of the radar sighting and try to change his mind. His flagship, the *San Francisco*, was already executing the wide left turn to begin the manoeuvre. They could only hold their breath and follow the *Boise*'s phosphorescent track as she turned behind the *Salt Lake City*.

The radar reports grew more and more hair-raising.

'Range now one five zero zero zero yards.'

'They're coming straight at us!' Parker said.

'Tell main plot to work on them,' McKay said.

He pondered the vectored radar screen in the corner of the bridge, with the sword of green light sweeping around and around it. Each time it passed bearing 65 degrees relative, 285 true, a cluster of green blips appeared. Did they mean what the Radar Officers said they meant? Or were the electromagnetic waves spewing from the antenna on the *Jefferson City*'s mainmast bouncing off low clouds or the coast of Guadalcanal?

Above the bridge in main forward, Gunnery Officer Moss and the fire control officer, Ensign Kruger, saw the same blips on their radar screen. Moss had no doubt of their meaning 'Captain! Why don't we get permission to open fire?' Moss cried.

'I'll try to find out,' McKay said, wishing his gunnery officer would show a little more grace under pressure.

While he was talking to Moss, the TBS was squawking. Parker told him what it had said. '*Boise* just reported five bogeys at bearing zero six five!'

Bogeys were enemy planes. Were the Japs about to do their flare-dropping routine to light them up like dummies in a department-store window? Or did the *Boise* mean they had spotted ships? The TBS cleared its throat. 'This is *Helena*. Enemy confirmed bearing two eight five true.'

'What the hell's going on?' Parker said. 'They can't be off the port quarter and the starboard bow at the same time.'

Poor Scott, McKay thought. Did Nelson have to deal with

this kind of confusion at Trafalgar? He listened to the Admiral as he tried to locate his destroyers. He obviously thought they were the blips on the radar. Why in God's name hadn't Scott transferred his flag to the *Jefferson City* or the *Helena*, where he would have been able to see the radar sightings with his own eyes? Obviously he did not trust this newfangled gadget. Like many men who relied on iron discipline to lead, Scott was not only tough, he was rigid.

'Captain, target is visible with the naked eye,' reported the talker. 'Main battery range-finder reports range as four zero zero zero yards, bearing the same as radar.'

It was Fire Controlman Peterson with his cat's eyes. Captain McKay decided to get an answer to Gunnery Officer Moss's question. He pressed the button of the TBS and said, 'Interrogatory Roger!'

That was code for permission to open fire. 'Roger,' replied Admiral Scott.

'Moss, pick out a target and commence firing,' Captain McKay said.

Down in main plot, Montgomery West and his team had been feeding ranges, bearings, ship speed and wind speed into the Mark VII computer. He had barely had time to have the talk with Fire Controlman Bourne that Captain McKay recommended, but it had produced a remarkable change.

Bourne had become the leader of the team, making sure everyone had the right data on his dials while for a harrowing ten minutes they had watched the green blips advancing toward them on their radar screen. Instead of cursing the Admiral and the Captain, the fire controlman talked confidently about waiting until they were close enough to guarantee their hits. West did not have to say a word. Was this leadership Arthur McKay style?

At his forty-millimetre gun director, Frank Flanagan and the men on the mount below him were mostly ignorant spectators at this drama. He picked up a few exchanges between the Gunnery Officer and the Captain on his earphones, but for most of the night – it was now approaching 2400 hours – he stood there watching the dark water slide past. His mind wandered through his life. He thought about

Teresa Brownlow and Martha Johnson reading the letters he had written them. He went over his interminable conferences with Father Callow about his vocation. He grappled with the stunning conclusions in Albert Schweitzer's *The Quest of the Historical Jesus*.

Suddenly the five-inch guns just forward of his forty-millimetre mount crashed. Two star shells exploded in the night sky. Simultaneously the main battery's three turrets fired all nine of their eight-inch guns to starboard. The ship heeled to port under the impact. The star shells revealed the latticework foremast and white-banded smokestack of a Japanese destroyer and two bigger ships, long sleek creatures with low freeboard and two fat smokestacks. *Furataka*-class heavy cruisers, Flanagan's photographic memory informed him, from the recognition drills in the crew's mess.

A moment later, one of the cruisers staggered under the impact of a half dozen direct hits from American guns. Flames leaped as high as her mainmast. Up and down the American battle line guns belched orange flame, illuminating the ships as vividly as a star shell. Rapid fire poured armour-piercing explosives at the Japanese.

'Incredible,' Captain McKay said on the bridge. 'We're crossing their T.'

His executive officer seemed unimpressed by this unique naval achievement, which enabled the crossing ships to pound an enemy with broadsides while only his forward guns could fire back. No admiral had managed it since Admiral Togo annihilated the Russian Fleet in the Tsushima Strait in 1905 and catapulted Japan into world power.

'Cease firing!' shouted Admiral Scott over the TBS. 'Repeat – cease firing! I did not give the order to fire.'

'Is he out of his goddamn mind?' Commander Parker shouted.

'Ignore the order. Keep firing,' McKay said.

When Admiral Scott had replied, 'Roger,' to McKay's question he had only meant he had received the message. Everyone thought he was giving them permission to fire. Roger unfortunately meant both things. Americans had a lot to learn about battle communications.

The confusion silenced at least half the American guns. Ahead of them the *Boise* had ceased firing and so had the *San Francisco*. Over the TBS Scott was asking the captain of the destroyer squadron if they were firing on them. 'I don't know who you're firing at,' was the enigmatic answer. In desperation, the confused Scott ordered the destroyers to turn on their running lights. When he saw these green and white lights flicker to starboard, he ordered, 'Resume firing'.

Just ahead of them, the *Boise* snapped on her searchlights to search for a new target. She was not equipped with radar. 'Look what that crazy Irish bastard Moran is doing,' Parker said.

Boise's searchlights picked up a Japanese cruiser and opened fire on her. But the break in the American bombardment had given the surprised Japanese a chance to regain their balance. Their fire controlman and gunners were thirsting for a target, and *Boise* gave it to them.

In three terrifying minutes, the light cruiser was straddled by a half dozen salvos. A tremendous explosion sent flames boiling through the ripped decks around her two forward turrets.

'Christ,' gasped Jerome Wilkinson. 'Nobody in them turrets will get out alive.'

The *Boise* zigzagged, desperately trying to evade the rain of Japanese shells. It did not work. Explosion after explosion gashed her superstructure. Flames gushed from her ravaged bow. 'She's finished,' Parker said.

'Lay us between her and those Japs,' Captain McKay said.

'Are you crazy? Let her take her punishment. She asked for it,' Parker said.

'That's an order!' Captain McKay shouted. He whirled to the telephone talker. 'Tell the main battery to take those ships under fire as we come up.'

'We're supposed to stay in formation!' Parker screamed.

'Engine telegrapher, signal for flank speed. Helmsman, change course to one two zero,' Captain McKay ordered.

'Course one two zero,' the helmsman repeated.

The thunder of the *Jefferson City*'s guns shook the bridge. The muzzle flashes illuminated the faces of the terrified young sailors, the aghast Wilkinson and the frantic Executive Officer. Arthur McKay wondered if he was finding out what had happened at the first battle of Savo Island. There was no time to ask questions now. The *Jefferson City*'s turbines drove every erg of power in their systems into her four propellers and she surged between the battered, burning *Boise* and the Japanese.

Shells screamed overhead. A half dozen raised huge multi-coloured fountains off the bow and stern. 'I hope to hell Homewood was right about that albatross,' McKay shouted.

He knew that an eight-inch shell was liable to launch them all into eternity at any moment. He was delighted to discover he did not find that a terrifying idea. This was battle at its wildest, what he had thought and read about for twenty-five years. This was what he had apparently been born to do, in spite of the unlikelihood of a sailor emerging from land-locked Kansas.

'On target,' crowed the talker. 'We're layin' it into them!'

To port, the *Boise* reeled into the darkness, flames leaping high above her number-two turret. To starboard, a salvo from the *Jefferson City* scored a direct hit on one of the Japanese cruisers. Gushing flames, she staggered in the opposite direction. The other cruiser followed her, guns still booming but most of the shots going wild. Behind her a Japanese destroyer was hit by fire from another American ship.

'Moss, shift to that tin can,' McKay said.

Within sixty seconds, a salvo bracketed the destroyer. Other ships hit her with a waterfall of six- and eight-inch shells. Flaming oil leaped a hundred feet into the air. She rolled over and vanished with a series of explosions under the water as her depth charges went off.

Other American ships continued to fire at the fleeing Japanese cruisers. But Admiral Scott decided the battle was over. 'Cease firing, regain formation, course two two five,' Scott ordered.

Arthur McKay looked at his watch. Could it be right? It was 0020. No more than twenty-five minutes had elapsed since they sighted the Japanese. He felt as if he had spent twenty-four hours in the ring with heavyweight champion Joe Louis. He thought of the carnage aboard the *Boise* and shuddered, knowing the same punishment could have befallen the *Jefferson City*.

For a moment he pondered the dilemma of how to deal with Commander Parker and decided there was no hurry about it. Maybe it was an opportunity to convince Parker, once and for all, that he was not Admiral King's prosecuting attorney. Maybe encouragement, example, could make a decent officer out of this man.

Captain McKay was exultant. He saw himself writing the story of the battle to Rita and to Win Kemble. He thought he was echoing the feelings of everyone aboard when he said, 'I think we evened the score for Savo Island tonight.'

Morale Questions

The men of the *Jefferson City* studied the *Boise*'s torn, smashed superstructure and ripped bow. All morning, landing craft had been taking off her dead for burial ashore. 'I was down in sick bay,' Leo Daley told Flanagan. 'I heard the pharmacist's mates saying they had three hundred and sixty dead. Three hundred and sixty!'

Sprawled on the deck of main forward, Flanagan nodded listlessly. He had watched those six- and eight-inch shells tear the *Boise* apart last night. He had seen men blown overboard by the explosions. He had seen others writhing in the orange flames. For the first time Flanagan began to believe in the possibility of his own death. Terror had engulfed him as he stood behind his waist-high shield and Japanese guns had hurled shells at him. They had roared over his head like subway trains and exploded in the water around the *Jefferson City*. It was helplessness that overwhelmed Flanagan. What could an individual do to protect himself against that rain of steel? There was no way to fight back, no place to hide. Prayer was his only hope, and he was losing that with every page he read of *The Quest of the Historical Jesus*.

Flanagan was at least fit for duty. In almost every division compartment other men lay in their bunks staring into space. A few were sobbing. Sick call had produced a long line of complainers such as Daley searching for a pill to soothe anxious stomachs, agitated bowels.

'I'm glad I can't see anything in the director,' Daley said. 'I couldn't stand it out in the open where you are, Frank.'

'Shut the fuck up,' Flanagan said.

'I'm sorry, Frank,' Daley whined.

Flanagan could see that he was not sorry at all. Daley was sure God had persuaded Flanagan to abandon his relative safety in the main battery gun director to play forty-millimetre hotshot and get himself killed. It would be his punishment for committing mortal sins with Teresa Brownlow and with Honolulu prostitutes and reading heretical books by Protestants with unpronounceable German names. Unfortunately Flanagan was afraid Daley might be right.

Into main forward strutted Jack Peterson. 'Hey,' he said, 'what the hell's the matter with you guys? You look like you just came back from your own funerals.'

'We did, almost,' Flanagan said.

'Are you kiddin'?' Peterson said. 'You see the way we blasted them Nips last night? They thought we was all patsies like the *Boise*. We sunk that destroyer, and I bet one of them cruisers didn't make it home either.'

'You think so?' Flanagan said.

'I know so. I was handin' out those ranges, kid. Right on the nose every time. I don't think we wasted a shell.'

Flanagan started to feel better. 'How many did we sink, all told?'

'Eight, from what I hear in Radio Central. They're listenin' to the flagship's stuff to Nouméa. You won't see them Japs comin' back for more of what we handed them last night for a long time.'

'I'm still glad I couldn't see anything,' Daley said.

'It was one hell of a show,' Flanagan said, almost meaning it.

'That's the spirit kid. We ain't the joke of the fleet any more. This joker is wild,' Jack said. 'We got a captain with balls.

From now on you're gonna find out how it feels to be on a fightin' ship.'

Something indefinable, a blend of electricity and pride, stirred in Flanagan's body. Maybe Jack was right. Maybe this was part of being a sailor too.

'In my opinion,' said Commander Parker as the mess stewards refilled coffee cups after dinner, 'Captain McKay disobeyed Admiral's Scott's orders by leaving the formation. He endangered all our lives by steaming into the line of fire of those two Japanese cruisers. Putting us into the same ranges Captain Moran had attracted to the *Boise* with his idiotic searchlights.'

'In my opinion,' Robert Mullenoe said, 'Captain McKay exhibited seamanship and courage of a very high order.'

'I agree,' said Edwin Moss, although his stomach churned at the thought of what Parker could do to him when he wrote his fitness report.

'Annapolis has been heard from, as expected,' Parker sneered. 'What do you think, Mr West?'

'I'm too far below decks to think,' West said. 'I was too busy obeying orders.'

He was startled by the glares he received from Mullenoe, Moss and several other Annapolis men.

'It's the truth,' he said. 'I don't know enough about seamanship or naval tactics to comment.'

'Hear, hear,' said several other reserve officers.

'At least you don't buy the argument that our heroic captain deserves a medal,' Parker said.

Montgomery West heard Ina Severn saying, *Your Commander Parker is a baddy*.

'Does it matter what any of us think?' West said. 'He's the captain.'

'If he pulls one more stunt like last night's, I may have to appeal to higher authority for all our sakes,' Parker said.

'It seems to me we ought to be talking about the crew's morale,' West said. 'My boatswain tells me he's never seen it lower. That battle last night scared the shit out of most of the new men. And some of the old ones too.'

'What do you expect when we've got a captain who has yet to put a man in the brig?' Ensign Kruger said.

'If you want my opinion,' snapped Lieutenant Buzz Jamieson, their short, peppery communications officer, 'we're all acting like a bunch of assholes who think the war is over because we sank a couple of Jap ships last night. I just picked up an intercept from Guadalcanal to Admiral Ghormley at Nouméa. The Marines are being bombarded by at least two Jap battleships right now. They've destroyed every plane on the damn island and killed God knows how many men.'

The clang of the general alarm, used only in moments of extreme emergency, resounded through the ship. 'Air raid, air raid,' yelled the boatswain's mate of the watch. 'All hands man your battle stations.'

'See what I mean?' Lieutenant Jamieson said as the officers of the *Jefferson City* stampeded from the wardroom.

Mail Call

Dear Husband:

I got your letter about the battle. Your pretensions to being a hero are not visible in Norman Scott's report. The *Jefferson City* isn't even mentioned and the *Boise* gets showered with praise for her gallant fight. You obviously blew any hope of getting mentioned when you declined to agree with Scott's scorecard of the battle. If you think you are making white points in Washington by criticizing Scott's tactics and insisting that we only sank two ships while Scott claims eight, you must be out of your mind. I showed your letter to Cominch and all he did was growl.

As for the rest of that epistle, about your noble decision not to interrogate your crew and find out the truth about Savo, I was – and still am – speechless. How could you let an opportunity like this slip through our fingers over such a ridiculous scruple? If you found out the truth about the débâcle, even if it included revealing the imperfections of your boyhood hero Win, you might have also discovered a lot of bad apples in your crew and gotten rid of them. I don't buy your arguments about hurting morale. Not for one minute. You just didn't have the guts to do it!

Notice I'm writing in the past tense. The opportunity is gone beyond recall now. On the basis of Scott's report, Cominch feels we evened the score for Savo and he no longer has to keep it under the rug. He's appointing old Admiral Hepburn to head an inquiry into the débâcle. At the rate he moves, it will take a year at least to finish – which is fine with Cominch. He's betting by that time he won't have to worry about it, no matter what Heppy concludes.

Cominch sent copies of Scott's report to the President and the Naval Affairs Committee. He's pretty sure it cancels out Win Kemble's letter and any others that may be lurking in Republican pigeonholes. I don't know what he's going to do about Win, who's reporting from his thirty-day leave tomorrow. I suspect it won't be pretty – but it'll be exactly what he deserves. As for you, all you can do now is fight your ship while I try to repair the damage. I have a dreadful feeling you won't stay as lucky as you did in the last battle. If you get shot up the way Mike Moran did, we're finished.

> Your devoted disappointed almost disgusted wife,
> Rita

Dearest Jack:

I read your letter over and over instead of sleeping for about three nights. It made me feel rotten at first. I cried, I swear I did. Imagine shedding tears for you – something I swore I'd never do again, about two years ago. Now I'm starting to feel better. In fact, I feel great. I'm not sure I can make much of a difference in your life over the long haul. I don't rate myself that high. But if I can make any difference at all, even for a while, that's fantastic.

I'm inclined to give a lot of credit to the war. For the first time I begin to think something good may come out of it. If it's changed you that much, maybe it will change a lot of other people too. By the end of the third day (or night) I was almost ready to go to church! I wanted to thank somebody, and he had to be big and important, because that was the way I felt. I was practically exploding! I felt like hiring a blimp and sending it over the Navy Yard at Bremerton trailing one of those ads that said: JACK PETERSON LOVES MARTHA JOHNSON.

I do love you. Hasn't that been obvious all along? But there has to be a limit to how far a woman can throw herself at a guy. I thought all you wanted to find out was my limit. Oh, Jack, you make me so happy when I'm with you. Now you've made me happy when we're apart.

Yours,
Martha

Dear Joey:

I got your empty envelope and I almost died. Then I got the real letter with all those wildly unrealistic tributes to me in it and I recovered sufficiently to go to work that day. Of course I was terrible. I blew at least twenty lines in a row in this dreadful thing we're perpetrating about the fall of Singapore, and Haroosh the Mad Hungarian said he was going to commit suicide definitely, that night, without any ifs or buts. Unfortunately he was back the next day trying to turn me into one of his Budapest schmaltz queens.

Now for the bad news. My contract is not being renewed. My writer friend Rosamund, the one who has all those informants in the front office (actually I think she taps their phones), tells me your dear Uncle Mort is behind it. I have talked about you continuously to numerous friends, and he seems to think I am responsible for your staying in the Navy. That may be my fault. I am terribly proud of what you're doing and I don't try to conceal it. I did not realize I was falling afoul of the local Gestapo.

What to do? I can go back to London and try to convince them I haven't betrayed my art by selling out to Hollywood or I can try Broadway or I can buck the system here. My friends tell me that's a lost cause, once someone as big as Uncle Mort alias Louis B. Mayer passes the word against you. Nevertheless I'm inclined to stand my ground (British grit and all that sort of thing, you know) because I don't want to put several thousand miles between you and me if by some miracle you should come home for Christmas or New Year's or Twelfth Night or St Swithin's Day. Any day will do!

Don't worry about me, darling. I have a fair amount of money saved, which I can make go quite a long way now that I no longer have to live like a would-be star in that oversized cheesebox in the hills. I am really feeling quite wonderful. I have you and I don't have to take any more direction from Haroosh!

Love, my love,
Gwen

Dear Edwin:

How I treasured that letter you sent about the new baby. There aren't many husbands who would write that kind of letter to their wives. It made me feel our marriage had reached a new level of meaning for both of us. For a whole week I didn't scream at the kids once.

I do feel profoundly that we have to accept God's decrees for us. I'm glad you feel the same way. There are times (I know your mother feels this way) when we don't seem meant for each other, but most of the time we are. I can't imagine being married to a man without your ideals. I always thought he'd be a Catholic but I have learned so much about faith as you understand it from being your wife.

I wish you could translate some of your ideals into reality on the ship. But as long as Parker stays as Executive Officer, I think this will be impossible. As for Captain McKay, the more I hear about him, the less I like him. He seems to be one of those Navy politicians who's gotten ahead thanks to a pushy wife and never rocking the boat. I still think you should transfer to another ship as soon as possible.

Love,
Eleanor

Dear Frank:

How are you? I saw your mother last week at a benefit to raise a scholarship fund for the school.

She said you were a fire controlman, whatever that is, and you were on your way to the Pacific. If you get to Espiritu Santo, be sure to look up the Marine chaplain there. He's a Jesuit named O'Brien, an old friend of mine. I wish I was young enough to get out there with you fellows. I hope you're getting to Mass regularly. I heard ships don't have chaplains on them. That's a disgrace.

Let me hear from you, Frank. I hope you've been able to deal with the numerous temptations of the military life and have made some good Catholic friends. That's the best way to handle your situation. Stay with those who share your own moral principles, your own faith in the Church that is built on a rock. I'm remembering you in my Mass every morning.

Your old friend,
Francis Callow, S.J.

Dear Frank:

I felt so awful when I read your letter. I still feel awful. To think that I made you do a thing like going to that terrible place in Pearl Harbor and sinning with a prostitute. I cried when you claimed there was no difference between doing it with her and with me. I simply don't believe you, Frank. We weren't sinning. You can never sin when you have Jesus in your heart. But you can sin, I believe you can sin terribly, when you act without Him within you. You've done that, Frank, and I can only conclude it is evidence of how deep Satan's grip on you still is. You found Jesus for a little while with me but you lost him again. I should have seen that all those arguments you hurled at me – that 'spirit of contradiction', as Daddy calls it – was Satan speaking. I should have prayed over you, for you, as I am now. We will meet again, Frank, of that I am certain, and resolve these painful differences. I have awakened your spirit to a quest that will end in happiness. But Satan may put many obstacles in your path. Trust in the love that's in your heart, Frank. Trust in Jesus, who put it there.

Love,
Teresa

Losses

In his cabin, Arthur McKay read and reread the most recent letter from his wife. Again and again his eyes strayed to the desk drawer where the bottle of Ballantine's Scotch awaited his summons.

No, that was all Parker needed to ruin him. In addition to his other shortcomings, Captain McKay is a drunk.

Why hadn't he banned whisky the day Parker handed him that bottle? Was he toying with the idea of using it as evidence against Win? A wet ship. That would have been all Admiral King needed to hang Captain Kemble from the Washington Monument. Now it was too late to speak, either to Cominch or to the officers of the *Jefferson City*. Captain McKay had accepted a wet ship when he accepted that bottle.

Unspeakable, the thought of betraying Win to Cominch on such a charge. Rita was corrupting his spirit again. *Women who both love and hate their fathers tend to love and hate their husbands too.*

True but not worthy of inclusion in the Duc's select ranks. Try again. *An ambitious wife makes for a discouraged husband.* A little better, and also true.

In defence of said wife, she was not the only reason for the husband's state of mind. Captain McKay's latest confrontation with his executive officer had gone badly. When he asked Parker for an explanation of his conduct on the bridge on the night of the second battle of Savo Island, the Commander had curtly replied that he had only been protesting an order that seemed to him more foolhardy than brave. He practically dared the captain to bring him up on charges.

Then there was the matter of Admiral Scott's claim of four cruisers and four destroyers sunk at the second battle of Savo Island. It was a dismaying glimpse of careerism in the upper echelons of the American Navy. No one had contradicted the Admiral, although every captain in the task force knew there had never been more than five Japanese ships in the battle! Neither had anyone said a word – nor had Scott sought a comment – about American tactics in the battle. They were, to put it mildly, primitive. They had got nothing out of their destroyers, with their high speed and deadly torpedo tubes. By throwing them into the middle of the slugfest between the cruisers, several of them had been horribly mauled.

So far, Win had been right about the kind of war they were fighting out here. Admiral Ghormley sat in Nouméa wringing his hands and Admiral Scott scored fantasy victories over an inferior Japanese battle force that had obviously been taken by surprise on their way to bombard Henderson Field. McKay shudderd to think of what would have happened to them if they had encountered the Japanese battleships that had flattened half of Guadalcanal the following night.

As for Cominch, Rita's letter annihilated one of Arthur McKay's pleasanter fantasies – the thought that through his wife he had access to the Navy's leader and could make constructive criticisms that would speed the day of victory. Cominch did not even want to hear the truth about the Japs' losses! Fundamental information for fighting the war, it seemed to Arthur McKay. But Cominch was fighting many wars – one in the Atlantic, another in the Pacific, another in the White House and another in Congress. A final one against his numerous enemies among his fellow admirals.

A knock on his door. The messenger from the bridge stood there. 'Captain, it's twelve o'clock. The chronometers have all been wound.'

'Ring the bell.'

Somehow this ancient tradition comforted him. He was still captain of this ship. He was still in command. Aboard the *Jefferson City*, it was not twelve o'clock until he said so.

As the bell bonged through the ship, a voice whispered to Arthur McKay: *Now. Take that bottle and pour it down the toilet. Do it now.*

A harsher voice whispered: *No. You might need it. You might need it very soon.*

Dark Victory

'This is it. This is the big one,' Jack Peterson said as they watched Douglas Dauntless dive bombers take off from the USS *Hornet*. In his capacity as scuttlebutt admiral, Jack had been predicting a battle that would settle the war. A few days later Captain McKay had made him a prophet by telling the crew they were going to operate with Task Force 17, built around the *Hornet*, while another task force of about the same size surrounded the carrier *Enterprise*. Most of the cruisers and destroyers were new to the war zone. The Japanese were certain to accept the challenge of these reinforcements.

Moreover, the Americans had a new South Pacific commander. Admiral Bill Halsey had replaced Ghormley, and that too meant action. 'Halsey only knows how to do one thing – fight,' Peterson said. 'You watch us go after these Nips now.'

Flanagan and most of the other members of F Division found it hard to share Jack's cockiness. All they had seen or heard in the anchorage at Espiritu Santo were losses. More destroyers joining the graveyard fleet in Ironbottom Sound – the name some mordant joker had coined for the narrow passage between Guadalcanal and Florida Island. Other destroyers staggered back with bridges smashed, engine rooms flooded, to disgorge another load of burned, maimed men into landing craft. Radio Central, which listened to everything on the air waves, reported growing desperation among the Marines, who faced massive assaults of screaming Japanese by day and murderous bombardments from Japanese cruisers and destroyers by night.

The all too familiar boatswain's whine lanced their eardrums. 'All hands man your battle stations,' boomed the PA. Flanagan watched his deck apes swarm on to the mount below him. Were they also wondering if it was the *Jefferson City*'s turn this time?

On the bridge, Captain McKay was also watching the *Hornet*'s planes take off. She and the *Enterprise* were the only two American carriers left in the Pacific. That Nimitz was risking them was proof, if any was needed, that the situation on Guadalcanal was desperate. COMINCH had ordered CINCPAC to throw everything in their pockets on to the table.

A breathless messenger from Radio Central handed him a flimsy: FROM COMSOPAC TO COMFORS 16 AND 17. ATTACK – REPEAT ATTACK.

Down in Nouméa, they had another aggressive gambler, Admiral Bill Halsey, in command. COMINCH had replaced the discouraged boxer Ghormley with a slugger.

From Lieutenant Mullenoe in Air Defence: 'Captain, radar reports fifty, maybe sixty bogeys approaching bearing one three zero true.'

McKay looked to port at the *Hornet*, with her huge flight deck protruding over her delicate cruiser's bow. There was no armour worth mentioning between the flight deck and the keel. Inside were thousands of gallons of inflammable aviation gasoline and tons of explodable bombs. It was the job of the *Jefferson City* and the other cruisers and destroyers steaming in close formation around her to keep that fragile, ungainly lady afloat. The hooligan navy was running the show.

For Old Navy men, there was a personal dimension to their task. Dozens of the J.C.'s crew had classmates or friends aboard the *Hornet*. Robert Mullenoe's brother was the carrier's engineering officer. Navigator Marse Lee's Annapolis roommate was the first lieutenant.

'Jesus Christ. Here they come,' Parker said. 'There must be a hundred of them.'

McKay had decided to keep his executive officer with him on the bridge. If one of those Jap bombs had McKay written on it, he wanted Parker in parenthesis. He would have far more confidence in his classmate George Tombs, the ship's first lieutenant, as the *Jefferson City*'s commander. He was not the brightest officer on the Navy, but he was steady.

The Japanese planes were visible now, darting silver specks high in the sky to the northwest. 'Where's the goddamn Combat Air Patrol?' Parker asked.

'Just hold your position, Commander,' McKay said. 'Remember that carrier is going to start zigzagging. She can do us a lot more damage than the whole Jap Air Force if she hits us.'

He stepped out on the port wing of the bridge and watched the Japanese attack shaping up. It was beautifully coordinated. High above them, the dive bombers were playing hide and seek in some fat cumulus clouds. Low on the horizon the torpedo planes were forming a wide semicircle to begin their runs. On the outer rim of the task force, the destroyers were already banging away. Now, as both groups of planes came within range, every gun on every ship opened up.

At his forty-millimetre director, Frank Flanagan reeled in the blasts of the five-inch guns and began tracking a dark green Kate as it came towards them, jinking from side to side. Now! He poured shells across two miles of water at him. But it was impossible to tell if he connected. His vision was confused by a half hundred shell bursts between him and his target. Even worse were the violent changes of course being executed by the *Jefferson City*. Again and again, these zigzags left Flanagan and other fire controlmen staring at chunks of open sea or sky.

'All mounts select targets at random,' said their air defence commander, Lieutenant Mullenoe. He was acknowledging the situation was totally fouled up.

Flanagan spun his mount so violently he almost threw the loaders off it into the sea. Finally he got another plane in his director on the opposite quarter.

He had that one! He could see the tracers in the stream of shells he was pouring at the Jap, a burning line that was connected to the centre of the weaving green plane. Flames leaped from Kate's fuselage. The wings tilted radically to the right. But the dying Japanese pilot had a reply to Flanagan's deadly aim. As his plane swerved off course and the flames gushed around him, he plunged toward an American destroyer. He hit the ship head on just below the bridge and his torpedo exploded, engulfing everything from the forward turret to the stack in orange flames. Insanity!

On the bridge, Captain McKay watched the Aichi 99-1 dive bombers come down through hundreds of black bursts of five-inch shells, each spewing deadly fragments around them. Plane after plane disintegrated into shreds of orange and yellow flame, but others kept coming, miraculously penetrating the showers of steel. Soon the air was thick with the roar of motors as the Aichis pulled out of their dives. Moments later, huge crashes split the sky, immense fountains of water leaped between the *Jefferson City* and the *Hornet*.

The *Hornet* zigged and zagged while signal flags raced up her halyards to announce her changes in course. The signals usually arrived after the fact. There was no time to follow standard task force routines. From the signal bridge, just aft the navigating bridge, the *Jefferson City*'s signalmen shouted the changes and Commander Parker translated them into orders to the helmsman. 'Right rudder twenty degrees. Left fifteen degrees,' he roared, sweat streaming down his porcine cheeks. The *Jefferson City* careened to port and starboard like a wingman flying in formation with a fighter plane, maintaining the six hundred yards between her and the swerving forty-thousand-ton carrier.

A wild mixture of pride and tension surged through Captain McKay as his ship performed this deadly dance. One message misheard, one wrong pull on the wheel by the helmsman, one failure of the rudder to respond down in the steering room deep in the stern of the ship, where a half dozen black-gang sailors were feverishly checking the complex gears and shafts that connected the rudder to the wheel five hundred feet away, and that carrier would smash them into a sinking tangle of twisted steel and exploding oil tanks. This was a battle that tested everything – men, machinery, training.

'*Hornet* is hit!' shouted the lookout on the port wing of the bridge.

For a moment McKay could not believe it. He had been so absorbed by their magnificent performance, he had forgotten there was an enemy above them, ready to match them, courage for courage, skill for skill.

A five-hundred-pound bomb had struck the starboard side of the carrier's flight deck, aft. Smoke and debris leaped high in the air. A moment later, two near misses almost obscured her with cascades of green water. Both would wreak havoc on her unarmoured hull. Almost simultaneously, a flaming Japanese plane hit the stack and burst through the flight deck, exploding in the heart of the ship. Then came four more bombs, terrific smashes that annihilated what was left of the flight deck.

Arthur McKay felt those bombs as if they were tearing

apart his own body. They had allowed the Japs to maul their ungainly lady.

'Captain, torpedoes –' the talker said.

He did not have time to finish the sentence. Two tremendous explosions erupted below the *Hornet*'s waterline amidships. With a sickening lurch to starboard, she slewed to a stop, dead in the water. A moment later, a burning torpedo plane headed for the bow. 'Get that Kate, Bob,' McKay said to Mullenoe.

Every gun that could be brought to bear blasted at the dying Jap. Frank Flanagan had him in the centre of his sight and could have sworn he hit him with a dozen shells. But the Jap flew through the blizzard of metal and smashed into the *Hornet*'s bow, causing another fiery explosion. Flanagan saw men in the forward gun gallery leap into the sea, their clothes on fire. The stricken carrier listed even more radically to starboard. She was engulfed by thick black smoke through which tongues of flame darted. Her cruiser and destroyer protectors circled mournfully around her. In his earphones, Flanagan could hear Peterson cursing. 'Jesus Christ. Can't we do anything right?'

'Round two,' Captain McKay said as the *Jefferson City* steamed into the task force around the USS *Enterprise*, the last American carrier still afloat in the Pacific. A signal from the admiral in command of Task Force 17, glimpsed through the smoke shrouding the *Hornet*, had sent them pounding across the ten miles of sea that separated the two task forces. They lined up behind the battleship *South Dakota* and the anti-aircraft cruiser *San Juan* as a Combat Air Patrol leaped from the Big E's deck.

The J.C.'s communications officer, Buzz Jamieson, reported that the American pilots claimed to have sunk or badly damaged two Japanese carriers. But patrol planes earlier in the day had sighted four enemy carriers. That meant two were still in business and they would throw every plane on their decks at them to knock out the *Enterprise*. If they succeeded, it would be Midway in reverse. The American Navy would have to flee the Solomons, leaving the Marines to their fate.

The signal bridge reported a blinker message from the *Enterprise*: WHO ORDERED YOU TO JOIN THIS TASK FORCE?

'Reply, "Signal from *Hornet*",' McKay said.

There was no more time to talk. Out of the clouds whirled another snaking silver line of Japanese dive bombers. The black bursts of the five-inch guns filled the sky, and their blasts shook the deck and bulkheads of the bridge on the *Jefferson City*.

'My God, is the *San Juan* blowing up?' Commander Parker cried.

Ahead of them the anti-aircraft cruiser looked as if it was wreathed in flames. 'I think it's just her guns on rapid fire,' McKay said. It was the first time they had seen one of these ships, with fifteen five-inch guns, in action.

'Bombs coming down,' the talker said.

A hit exploded on the bow of the *Enterprise*. Pieces of the flight deck flew high in the air. 'Jesus, can't we stop these bastards?' Parker cried.

Another bomb exploded only a few feet off the stern of the *San Juan*. The cruiser lurched to starboard and went lunging through the rest of the task force. Her siren whooped and a black breakdown flag leaped to her masthead. 'Her rudder's jammed,' McKay said. 'I hope to God everybody gets out of her way.'

Two bombs exploded in the water that the *San Juan* has just vacated. 'Close up. Take her position,' McKay said.

'Who gave us the order to do that?' Parker said.

'I did,' McKay said. 'If you question one more order I give on this bridge, I'm going to put you under arrest.'

Parker ordered flank speed and they were soon abeam of the *Enterprise*. Above them, the dive bombers were still coming down through the steel canopy of the five-inch shells bursts, pressing home their attack with the same ferocity that had smashed the *Hornet*. Another bomb exploded forward of the Big E's island where the captain and the admiral operated. Smoke and flames from both hits leaped into the air. It looked more and more like a replay of the *Hornet*.

But the guns fell silent as the last of the dive bombers fled into the nearest cumulus clouds. Something had gone wrong with the Japs' timing. Almost twenty minutes elapsed before the talker said: 'Captain, torpedo planes bearing one five five, one five five, one two five, one one six . . .' Before he finished he had practically boxed the compass.

On came the green planes through hundreds of shell bursts and livid streams of forty- and twenty-millimetre shells. 'My God, they've got guts,' McKay said.

The shooting looked marvellous, but the hits were few. At least seven Kates launched torpedoes. '*Enterprise* signals right full rudder,' the talker said.

'Right full rudder,' Parker shouted.

'Three torpedoes to starboard bearing one five zero, range a thousand yards and closing,' the talker said.

Out on the port wing, Captain McKay could see what the *Enterprise* was trying to avoid. Three more torpedoes were slashing toward her starboard bow. At the angle at which they were sailing beside her, if the *Jefferson City* executed the same turn, it would expose the thin middle skin of the carrier to these other torpedoes, approaching at the opposite angle. These computations of speed and course flashed through Arthur McKay's mind like an intuition. Twenty-five years of fleet manoeuvres and drills had given him a seaman's eye.

'Belay that. Steady as you go,' he said. 'We'll have to take those torpedoes.'

'You're out of your fucking mind!' Parker screamed.

'Orderly,' McKay said, 'I'm placing Commander Parker under arrest. Escort him to his cabin.'

'There isn't going to *be* a fucking cabin in another sixty seconds,' Parker shouted. 'Helmsman, right full rudder if you want to stay alive.'

'Steady as you go,' McKay said. 'That's an order from your captain.'

He carefully avoided raising his voice. 'Aye, aye, Captain,' the helmsman said, holding the wheel steady.

'You fuckin' –'

Parker tried to shove the helmsman aside and seize the wheel. The sailor resisted him. With a tremendous thud the three torpedoes hit the *Jefferson City*.

Out on deck, above his forty-millimetre mount, Frank Flanagan had watched the torpedoes racing toward them. One was going to hit the ship just below his mount. 'Get off it,' he shouted to his gun crew. 'Get the hell out of here.'

They had seen the torpedoes too and scrambled for the other side of the ship. Flanagan was too frightened – or too fascinated – to move. He was seeing his own death. In exactly ten seconds he would be blown through the air to land in the water, his body shredded by flying steel, his legs, perhaps his arms gone. *I'm sorry*, he prayed. *I'm sorry I hurt Teresa*.

The three torpedoes hit the ship simultaneously. By all the laws of science and probability, those fuses in their ugly snouts should have instantly ignited a half ton of TNT that would have broken the *Jefferson City* in two. Their impact alone was enough to send a shudder through the entire ship.

But there was no explosion. All three torpedoes were duds. Their murderous charges drifted down into the three-mile deep to which their fellows had sent the *Hornet*.

He was still alive. Frank Flanagan did not know why or how, but he was still alive. Should he thank God or that wandering albatross?

Down in the forward fire room, the thud of the torpedoes had spun Marty Roth around to stare openmouthed at death. All morning he had been tuning his valves to Cartwright's orders in the 130-degree heat, while the fire room talker gave them terrifying glimpses of the chaos raging above them. Now Roth listened, frozen with horror, as one of the torpedoes, caught in the current the ship created as it cut through the sea at flank speed, bumped against the hull. One two three four five six bump-bump-bumps, any one of which could mean death in a cascade of water from the Pacific's blue-black depths.

'Was that what I thought it was?' Roth said, his voice trembling.

'The Lord has been watchin' over us,' Cartwright said in his deep calm voice.

'I asked you a goddamn question. Was that a torpedo?'

'It wasn't no porpoise,' Cartwright said. 'I ain't never heard a porpoise or even a whale make that kind of noise against a ship.' Slowly, carefully, like a doctor examining a wound, he ran his hand over the hull where the torpedoes had hit. 'I knew we had a good captain,' he said. 'But I didn't know he was this good.'

On the bridge, Commander Daniel Boone Parker stared numbly at Captain McKay. The Executive Officer was literally trembling from head to foot. Saliva trickled from the corner of his mouth. He wiped it away with the back of his hand. In his eyes McKay saw a raw animal fear that revealed the essence of the man more nakedly than any imaginable words.

In a shaky voice McKay's Marine orderly asked, 'Captain, do you still want me to put Commander Parker under arrest?'

A sickening mixture of pity and disgust suffused Arthur McKay's soul. 'No,' he said.

In the harbour of Espiritu Santo, Captain McKay boarded the heavy cruiser USS *Pensacola* and was escorted to the Admiral's cabin by the junior officer of the deck, a slim blond ensign who reminded him of his son. 'Did you take any hits, Captain?' he asked.

'Not a scratch.'

'We're about the same. Only a ruptured steam pipe from a near miss.'

The commander of Task Force 17, Rear Admiral Carl Hoffer, had transferred his flag to the *Pensacola* when the *Hornet* went down. Only since they returned to Santo did McKay learn that the task force had struggled most of the day to save the burning carrier. But another wave of torpedo planes and dive bombers had administered the coup de grâce.

Admiral Hoffer fixed Arthur McKay with glaring eyes as he stepped into the cabin. 'Captain,' he said, 'who gave you permission to leave my task force and transfer to the defence of the *Enterprise*?'

'I got a signal from the *Hornet*'s bridge, Admiral, ordering me to go.'

'No such signal was ever sent. I ordered all ships to execute a circular manoeuvre until we could get the *Hornet* under way again. We finally got a tow line on her, but the second Japanese attack was too heavy for us to handle – without your guns. I consider you responsible for the loss of that carrier!'

'That's a pretty strong statement, Admiral.'

'I don't give a goddamn what you think it is. I'm putting it in my after-action report. I'm letting you know it so you can defend yourself. If you can.'

'I'll do my best, Admiral. Thanks for your courtesy.'

Hoffer was furious because he had lost his carrier while Task Force 16 had managed to keep the *Enterprise* afloat. She had limped back to Nouméa, where shipfitters and machinists were repairing her bomb damage. In the King tradition of the admiral-as-son-of-a-bitch, Hoffer believed that when something went seriously wrong, someone had to be blamed. It could never be an admiral, because that would make the Navy look bad. The citizens of the republic could tolerate the idea that the Navy had faulty captains or commanders or lieutenants. A faulty admiral suggested there might be something wrong with the system itself.

Why are you surprised? Arthur McKay asked himself, as his gig approached the *Jefferson City*. You knew this. You have known it for a long time.

Back in his cabin, Captain McKay stared at the desk drawer where the bottle of Ballantine's Scotch lay. *Now you know why you didn't throw me over the side*, it whispered.

Sea Story

As twilight spilled from the jungled ridges of Espiritu Santo, the humid air above the *Jefferson City* pullulated with the heat of thousands of wings. Each evening, great swarms of bats flew across the water to feed on insects and fruit on nearby islands. Used to this grisly local colour by now, Flanagan, Daley and other new sailors sprawled on the deck outside main forward. Boats Homewood had spent the afternoon teaching them how to tie catspaws, bowlines, sheepshanks and other class-one knots. Now Jack Peterson had joined them and they turned to a more mysterious topic: the meaning of the three torpedoes that had failed to go off.

'It's the captain,' Homewood said. 'He makes a ship's luck. McKay's got some kind of special joss goin' for him.'

'Joss?' Flanagan said.

'The Chinks burn it in their monasteries and shrines,' Peterson said. 'It's supposed to keep away evil spirits.'

'What about the albatross?' Flanagan said.

'He was attracted by the Captain's joss,' Homewood said.

'Well I think he's crazy,' Daley said. 'Why the hell should we take the *Enterprise*'s torpedoes? The Japs weren't after us.'

'The kid's got a point,' Peterson said.

'That's the Captain's job, to decide that sort of thing,' Homewood said. 'The minute a ship starts second-guessin' the Captain, it's in trouble.'

'What sort of trouble?' Flanagan said.

'The good spirits don't like it. They won't stick around. I remember the time I was on an old four-stacker back in World War One. I was about Flanagan's age, and I thought I was almost as smart as he thinks he is. We had a Captain who'd have taken her right into the middle of the whole fuckin' German fleet. Nothin' scared him, not even those seventy- and eighty-foot waves that build up in the North Atlantic in winter.

'There was an old bosun on board who'd been with Farragut at Mobile Bay and New Orleans. He said the Captain was tougher than that son of a bitch. But he had a bad habit of ridin' his officers. He'd pick out one of them and spend the month takin' him apart. One day he went after an ensign just out of Annapolis. It was terrible the way he worked this kid over.

'One night the ensign didn't report for duty on the midwatch. The Captain went down personally to drag him out of his bunk. He opened the ensign's door, and there he was, swayin' from an overhead in the battle lights. He'd hung himself.

'That turned the whole ship against the Captain. Nothin'

went right from there on out. We'd drop depth charges that weren't armed. We lost a torpedo and it drifted into a merchant ship in the convoy and blew the shit out of it. We fired on a sub we caught on the surface and hit a British destroyer! Everybody on board knew we was finished. It was just a question of time. The old bosun started makin' friends with guys he'd been workin' to death, because a man like him needed all the help he could get on the other side. He gave away scrimshaw and souvenirs from China and Turkey.

'Sure as hell a week later I was on the graveyard watch and I see the torpedo. It came from nowhere. It was a dead calm sea and I'd been on watch at least an hour. I had my night vision OK and I should've spotted that wake at a thousand yards. But it was practically under the ship when I seen it. The thing took out the engine room and busted the keel. The Captain ordered abandon ship, and everyone still in one piece – that didn't include anybody in the engine room – went over the side. Naturally, the Captain was the last guy off. By that time she was startin' to roll over for the dive.

'We was all swimmin' like hell to get away from her depth charges when they went off underwater. Suddenly we hear a yell. It's the Captain. His manrope's gotten fouled in his life jacket. Don't ask me how or why. The old bosun swims back to help him. It's a sight I'll never forget if I live to be a hundred. The ship is on its side and the bosun is tryin' to get up that bottom with about a million barnacles on it that's cuttin' him to peices and the Captain is fightin' that rope that's like a live thing, a goddamn anaconda, refusin' to let him go.

'"Go back!" he says to the bosun. But the old buzzard don't pay no attention to him. He's climbin' up that slimy bottom somehow with his knife out tryin' to hand it up to the Captain.

'All of a sudden like one of them movie tricks there was a kind of *pop* like a bubble bustin' and they was gone. Ship, Captain, bosun – deep-sixed. It happened as quick as you could blink. Another destroyer picked us up about five minutes later.

'That's what happens when a ship goes sour and the good spirits leave her.'

Ancient Lore

'You know what liberty here reminds me of?' Jack Peterson said. 'A walk from the exercise yard to the cell block at Portsmouth.'

They were strolling along Espiritu Santo's soggy black sand beach. The water was full of jellyfish with murderous stings. The jungle came down to the edge of the little shanty town behind the wharfs. The heat and humidity remained at the equatorial level. They were getting close to the middle of November, but the calendar had ceased to matter. Already, America with its chilly autumn and freezing winter was beginning to seem unreal, a memory from another life.

'You've been in Portsmouth?' Flanagan asked. The grisly naval prison with its sadistic Marine guards was a scare word among sailors, new and old.

'I got friends who were,' Jack said.

'Are we winning or losing this damn war, that's what I'd like to know,' Leo Daley said.

'We ain't winnin',' Peterson said. 'Just glom the Captain's face when he comes back from those conferences on the flagship.'

'Hey, look,' Flanagan said.

Floating up the beach was an empty life jacket. It was not made in America. It had Oriental markings on it. 'What a souvenir,' Flanagan said, splashing into the shallow water to grab it.

At the dock, waiting for the landing craft to take them back to the ship, Boats Homewood gave them the once-over. They were in pretty good shape, because the word had been passed not to bring any liquor ashore. The island's commanding admiral, Kelly Turner, was a ballbreaker who would have everyone's ass if he heard the J.C. was a wet ship. The official drinking limit ashore was two beers to a man. The beer was horse piss brewed in Honolulu. Only a few souses had brought extra bottles from teetotalers or from those who found the swill undrinkable. No one was seriously plastered.

'What the hell is that you've got, Flanagan?' Homewood asked.

'A Jap life jacket.'

'Throw it away.'

'What are you talking about? It's a great souvenir.'

'Throw it away. Don't you know the story? You bring an empty life jacket on to a ship and someone's gonna fill it. I've seen it happen.'

'Boats, give me a break. You expect me to believe that?'

'I saw it happen on the old *Marblehead* when we was in the China Sea. Lot of pirates around in those days, with a civil war goin' full blast in China. This buddy of mine pulled a life jacket aboard. Smart ass like you, he thought it was a find. It was from a Siamese ship the pirates had attacked and sunk. We had this old gunner's mate who'd been with Dewey in Manila Bay. He told him to throw it back. Warned him.

'"Bullshit," my buddy says. "Can't scare me." So he tucks it in the bottom of his seabag figurin' on sellin' it in Shanghai. He was gonna daub a little blood on it to dress it up. Next night, we hit a squall that built up thirty, forty-foot waves. The captain orders our division out on deck to lash down the boats. We're workin' on the number-one boat when this goddamn wave comes over the bow and takes us off our feet. Christ, I bet I was floatin' over turret one, hangin' on to a line and prayin' it wouldn't part. When the water ran off I see my buddy's over the side, still hangin' on his line. "Ernie," he's yellin', "Ernie," I wade over there and start haulin' him in.'

'Just then another wave hit. I wrapped my legs around a stanchion and yelled to him to hang on. But he couldn't do it. I felt the rope go slack in my hands. He was gone. We didn't even try to look for him. That life jacket got filled – in a week.'

Flanagan felt the skin on the back of his neck grow cold. He did not believe in Homewood's good and evil spirits. But he did not want to tangle with them, just in case they existed.

'What am I supposed to do with it? Just throw it away?'

'Oh. I'd love a souvenir like that. Will you buy it for me, Jerry?'

It was Harold Semple. He was talking to Jerome Wilkinson. Semple batted his long eyelashes at the boatswain like one of Andy Hardy's girl friends. Flanagan had heard he was Wilkinson's latest conquest. The boatswain's fondness for prettyboys was a running dirty joke among the crew.

'Sure, I'll buy it. There ain't no fuckin' spirit that can hurt you. I know that much,' Wilkinson said.

'How much?' Flanagan said.

'Five bucks.'

'Sold.'

Homewood glared at Wilkinson. 'If anyone succeeds in fuckin' up this ship permanently, it's goin' to be you.'

Semple gave Flanagan the money and tied the life jacket around himself. 'So solly, Boats. Me not chicken like you,' he said.

'Laugh while you can,' Homewood said.

That night they had an air raid. They went to General Quarters around midnight and blazed away at Japanese planes that seemed more interested in bombing the airfield a few miles away from the harbour. Bombers from Espiritu Santo were giving Jap ships a lot of trouble when they tried to supply their troops on Guadalcanal. The *Jefferson City*'s five-inch guns got at least one Jap plane, which disappeared over the horizon gushing flames.

The next day they went to sea for another round of gunnery manoeuvres with three other cruisers and four destroyers. They were only about an hour out of the harbour when a lookout sighted a raft. As they approached, two Jap airmen became visible, one an officer, the other an enlisted man.

Commander Parker ordered Wikinson's sea detail to haul them aboard. Semple and a half dozen other sailors hurried to the bow while the ship slowed; one whirled a line over his head and threw it down to the Japs. The officer handed the line to the enlisted man and the sailors towed them almost under the bow.

Without a word of warning the officer stood up and emptied his pistol at the sea detail. Semple screamed and fell back against the capstan, blood gushing from his chest.

Calmly, while the astonished sailors watched, the Jap reloaded his pistol and prepared to kill a few more Americans. The OOD ordered full ahead and washed the Jap away from the bow. A Marine on a twenty-millimetre mount opened fire, shredding both Japs and the raft.

Semple died in sick bay about an hour later. That night, beneath the Pacific stars, Homewood sombrely confirmed his dark faith. 'I told you guys. I told you that life jacket would be filled.'

Not for the first time, Flanagan felt bewildered by life aboard the *Jefferson City*, with its strange blend of modern weaponry and primitive taboos and talismans from another time. In this alien sea so far from home, Homewood's voice took on a new authority. The boatswain's mate's superstitions became outriders of that primary force, history, which was whirling them all in its ominous grip.

Loyalty

In his stateroom, Lieutenant Junior Grade Montgomery West was writing a letter to his Uncle Mort, telling him that if he did not get Ina Severn a job with another studio he was going to shell Metro-Goldwyn-Mayer with the main battery when the *Jefferson City* returned to Long Beach Harbor.

Lieutenant Robert Mullenoe stood in the doorway, a saturnine expression on his usually cheerful face. 'Bob,' West said, 'I'm really sorry about your brother.'

'Thanks,' he said.

The word had just got out that Mullenoe's older brother, the engineering officer on the *Hornet*, had been killed by one of the torpedoes that struck the carrier.

'Have you heard what's going on?' Mullenoe said.

West shook his head. He was so tired most of the time, he did not have strength for gossip. When he was not on duty, he slept.

'Parker's trying to get the officers to sign a round-robin

letter to the Admiral, claiming that McKay's unfit to command the ship. He's telling everybody McKay's a madman because he took those three torpedoes fired at the *Enterprise*. They don't plan to mention that, of course. They're going to smear him with all kinds of phoney stuff. Accuse him of being a drunk. Apparently he does have a couple of bad spots in his record where he got in trouble for drinking too much. I'm not signing it, and I hope you won't either. McKay isn't the greatest captain in the world, but he's one thousand percent better than Parker. That man makes me puke.'

At breakfast, dinner and supper in the wardroom, Parker had made no secret of his opinion for the past several days. He even admitted he had refused to obey the Captain's order to stay on course and take the torpedoes.

West did not know what to think about it. 'Would you have taken those torpedoes if you were Captain?' he asked Mullenoe. 'Isn't the Captain's first duty to preserve his ship?'

'His first duty is to win the war,' Mullenoe said. 'We've still got a carrier in the game, thanks to him.'

Perhaps West looked surprised to hear these rah-rah sentiments from Mullenoe. He was even more amazed when Mullenoe's voice thickened, fighting tears. 'I've never been big on this loyalty to the service stuff. I've never taken the Navy very seriously. I let my brother handle that end of it. That happens when you grow up in a Navy family. When I heard Pete was dead, I realized it was up to me now. But you don't know my old man. You don't realize what I'm talking about.'

'Try me.'

'The Admiral ran our family like it was a ship. If you screwed up, you got a captain's mast and if it was serious it could go to a summary court-martial with him and my mother sitting as judges and my brother Pete as the prosecuting attorney. I got a few of those.

'When I went to Annapolis, I figured I'd get thrown out in about six months. I could hardly wait. Then I heard the old man had cancer. For the next three years he hung on, just to see me graduate. I raised some hell, but I stayed in because I couldn't hurt him. He cared about the goddamn Navy. It was a sacred thing to him. He'd been around when his father was fighting to rescue the Navy after the Civil War. The country just forgot about it. Everyone else was building steel ships with steam engines in them and we were still floating around in wooden tubs with sails. They had to educate the public into building a decent Navy, they had to put up with being laughed at by the other navies. Now we've got a Navy. It isn't perfect, but we're going to prove we're the best in the world out here. We can't do it if we start undermining our captains.'

Montgomery West sensed an emotion as real, as meaningful as the one he had felt when Ina Severn told him she loved him. He did not feel this transcendent loyalty to something as abstract and huge as the US Navy. The emotion was almost incomprehensible to him. But he recognized its power, its reality, in Mullenoe's life.

'OK, Bob. McKay's got my vote. I like the guy.'

'Good. Spread that around. You've got a lot of influence with the other reserve officers.'

'I do?'

'Yeah. It's all those movies where you squinted into the sun and waited for the cavalry to show up.'

'I've been hoping that cavalry'd show up around here. In the shape of about six battleships.'

'You'll go blind long before you see them,' Mullenoe said.

'We're not winning this thing, are we?' West said.

Mullenoe shook his head. 'These guys are a lot tougher than I thought they were. That's another reason why we can't let this ship go haywire.'

Lieutenant Commander Edwin Moss ran his finger down the list of the ship's sixty-five officers. He was pretty sure he had a majority behind the Captain. Moss had persuaded the department heads to line up their junior officers. Although all the seniors were Annapolis graduates, only George Tombs, the first lieutenant, was enthusiastic and his motive was loyalty to his classmate. Oz Bradley was particularly dour. He said most of the black gang was in a semi-hysterical state over those three torpedoes. He frankly wondered if the ship's morale might require a change of command. Moss had preached him a veritable sermon about loyalty to the Navy's way and he had capitulated.

A knock on his door. Parker's Marine orderly, a big beefy Texan, drawled, 'Executive officer'd like to see you, sir.'

On the bulkheads of Parker's small office were at least a dozen pictures of him with admirals, congressmen, diplomats. Parker glowed behind his desk. He did not invite Moss to sit down. 'I know exactly what you're doing, Edwin,' he said.

'I beg your pardon, Commander?'

'You're a fucking idiot, Moss. Trying to defend that drunken bum in the captain's cabin and incidentally smearing me with every officer on the ship. I'm going to ruin your goddamn miserable career, Moss. I'm going to arrange it so you never get a ship to command. You'll be supervising cases of defunct five-inch shells at some ammunition depot for the rest of your life.'

'How do you plan to do that, Mr Parker?' Moss said, struggling to control his panic. He could hear his wife telling him, *I still think you should get off that ship as soon as possible.*

'First of all, I'm going to write a fitness report on you that'll make you sound like a cross between a cretin and a coward. If the Captain refuses to approve it I'll go to work on the political side. How do you think I got this job? Do you see any other guys like me, without that ring you've got on your finger, second in command of a cruiser? I'm from Missouri, Moss, and we play politics the hard way. Maybe you've heard of the Dickman-Igoe machine. They run St Louis. My big brother is Bernie Dickman's right testicle. He can make congressmen jump faster and farther than you can make a second class seaman. I'm gonna make them jump, Moss – on you. They're gonna write letters to the personnel boys in the Bureau of Nagivation asking how come they let a queer and a drunk command the gunnery department on a capital ship. We're gonna get affidavits from sailors on this ship about the way you seduced them. Maybe we'll send copies to your wife.'

'Commander Parker,' Edwin Moss said, 'you can do what you – you damn please. I'm not going to alter my support of

Captain McKay. I'm not going to let you blackmail me.'

To Moss's dismay, his voice was trembling. Was it fear or anger? He was terribly afraid Parker could deliver on his threats. He knew how easy it was for a man's career to go sour in the Navy. All he needed was a single scandal, a single bad fitness report – especially if he had no friends in high places, if he simply relied on his determination to do his best.

'You fucking idiot. Can't you see I'm trying to save all our lives?' Parker shouted. 'If we go out there against those Japs again with him at the conn, none of us are coming back.'

Edwin Moss heard the fear in Parker's voice. For the first time he realized Parker was afraid of something that he, Moss, did not fear: death. He was afraid of the violent death they had all agreed to risk when they put on a naval officer's uniform. For a moment Moss felt almost lightheaded – as if he had triumphed over Parker.

'That's a chance I'm willing to take,' Moss said.

'You're a hopeless asshole, Moss.'

Back in his cabin, Moss was assailed by alternating surges of fear and rage. Parker could still ruin him. What could he do to protect himself? He went to see the communications officer, Buzz Jamieson, who was a classmate.

'I think you should report the whole thing to the Captain immediately. No officer should have to put up with that kind of bullshit,' Jamieson said. 'It's up to the Captain to stop this guy in his tracks. It's time someone told him about the other stuff Parker is trying to pull. The round-robin letter. I think we might get the bastard court-martialled if McKay's willing to prefer charges.'

'You're right,' Moss said. 'I'll go see him now.'

He strode to the captain's cabin. His Marine orderly, a beanpole with an Adam's apple that bobbed nervously above his tight collar, said the Captain had left word he did not want to be disturbed.

'Ask him please, if I can see him,' Moss said. 'Tell him it's urgent.'

Moss waited in the humid passageway. Sweat streamed

down his neck. The Marine came out with an odd look on his face – as if he had just seen something that frightened him. 'OK, sir', he said, pushing open the door.

In the cabin, Arthur McKay sat at his desk writing a letter, an almost empty bottle of Ballantine's Scotch only inches from his right hand. There was no glass. The cabin smelled like a barroom – not that Lieutenant Commander Moss had ever been in a barroom. But it smelled like he imagined barrooms smelled – fetid with a sickeningly sweetish odour.

'Wha's wrong, Moss? Captain McKay said.

'It's Commander Parker, Captain,' Moss said. 'I just had a very unpleasant interview with him.'

'Welcome to the club,' McKay said. 'S'unpleasant bastard.'

'Captain, I think he's doing serious harm to the morale – the good order of this ship.'

McKay's head wobbled. Was he nodding agreement? 'Take care of him, Moss. Don't worry. War'll take care of him. Maybe take care of us all.'

'Yes, sir.'

'Don't worry 'bout him. My worry. Jus' do y'job, Moss. Make sure those ranges – right.'

'Yes, sir.'

Moss was so appalled, he did not know where he was going until he found himself on the stern, staring at the night-shrouded jungle of Espiritu Santo. The ghostly grey shapes of the three other cruisers and four destroyers in their task force rode at anchor a few hundred yards away. *Get off this ship as soon as possible*, his wife Eleanor whispered. It was too late to take that good advice.

'What did you say?'

Moss started so violently he almost went overboard. He steadied himself on the lifeline and faced Buzz Jamieson. 'He said not to worry about it for the time being. He was on top of the situation. I think he is. He's still got my support.'

Loyalty. The word blinked wildly in Moss's mind, no longer a beacon guiding him on a safe course. It was an incomprehensible eye in the tropic night, speaking to him in a strange code.

Drunk

Dear Wife,

I'm sitting here in my cabin, blotto, biffed, squiffed, stinko! Do I make myself clear? I'm as gargoyled as a seaman second class on his liberty in Shanghai.

How do you like that? How's that for conduct unbecoming a future admiral? I've got some things to tell you about our miserable country and our fucking Navy and I've got to get drunk to do it. If you want to show this letter to Cominch, go ahead, I don't give a damn.

Don't fail to read Carl Hoffer's after-action report of what we're now calling the battle of Santa Cruz Islands. He blames me for losing the brand new carrier *Hornet*. That's extremely unfair to the pilots of those Japanese dive bombers and torpedo planes that blew the hell out of her in spite of the most intense anti-aircraft fire I've ever seen.

Brave men, Rita! We're fighting brave men out here. Some of the best damn sailors and fliers who ever put to sea. They're ready to die for their Emperor. What are we ready to die for? The goddamn New York Stock Exchange? The Kansas City Board of Trade? General Motors?

I've been reading a book we took off the body of a dead Jap pilot we found floating off Guadalcanal. *Kore dake Yomeba Ware wa Kateru* is the title, *Read This and the War Is Won*. It describes in savage detail how in Malaya, Indo-China, the Dutch East Indies, the Philippines and China a few thousand white men are squeezing profits out of five hundred million Asians. I agree with every word of it!

Just as I predicted fifteen years ago in China, we're reaping the whirlwind we sowed out here over the past century. The goddamn British and French and Dutch did most of the sowing, but we stood by and let our businessmen scramble for the crumbs and said nothing. We joined in the despicable sport of flaunting our flag in the faces of people who didn't have the guns or money to fight back. We deserved to get our asses blown off at Pearl Harbor and Savo Island!

That brings me to what I want to tell you. I've found out what happened at Savo Island. I know exactly what happened to Win because it's also happened to me. Win was paralyzed by disgust. He looked into the greasy, sleazy, soul of America and found himself unable to order men to die for it. He discovered that twenty-five years of apostrophes to God and Country were bullshit!

How do you like that? Ask Cominch how he likes it. Ask him what he really thinks. At the bottom of his black heart I'm sure he believes the same thing.

How did I receive this revelation? Allow me to introduce you to my executive officer, Commander Daniel Boone Parker. He *is* the soul of Twentieth-Century America, in all its repulsive venality.

Do you know what venality means, Rita? It means concentrating on the fast buck first, last and always. Parker gets a cut of every crap game, every card game, every racket on this ship. I can't catch him at it. I'm not sure I want to. I'm convinced, although I can't catch him at it either, that he and the supply officer are selling or trading some of the crew's food. He'd sell the guns of the ship if he could get away with it!

Venality and me-first. That's what America's rugged individualism, survival of the fittest in the competitive jungle comes down to – a slimy readiness to ignore everything that could conceivably be called an ideal to make sure you get yours. Of course, cover your ass at all costs. Even if other men die, so what? Your precious ass is the only thing that counts.

We always knew this about America, of course. How many times did you hear your father denounce the fucking civilians? Now here's the terrible thing, Rita. The Navy's no better. I knew that twenty years ago too, when I watched Win trying to give a bad fitness report to some son of a bitch with the right connections in Washington. I saw the Navy was just another goddamned bureaucracy. I also saw the absurdity of Win's game – the idealist with connections. Determined to get to be CNO thanks to all the wires Mother could pull without violating the code. Making it with honour untarnished!

That's what is called a contradiction. History is full of them. When you try to live them, the result is disaster.

Better to get tanked, boiled, ossified, incandescent, Rita. Why didn't you let me get out of the goddamn Navy twenty years ago? I wouldn't be a drunk. I might have written a couple of decent history books by now. We might even love each other somewhere, somehow. That's the terrifying part of it. I love the idea of loving you, of somehow appeasing that wild rage and hatred in your soul in the name of some impossible ideal, knowing you don't love me, you've never loved me, you never wanted anyone but Win.

The Navy's no better, Rita. That's what Admiral Hoffer is proving. He lost his carrier, but it wasn't his fault Nooooooo. It was Captain McKay's fault. He's using Captain McKay to cover his big German ass. Admiral Scott covers his ass by sinking ships that never existed. Now we've got a new ringmaster, Uncle Dan Callaghan, Ghormley's ex-chief of staff. They just made him admiral of our combined matchbox fleet with orders to stop a couple of Jap battleships coming down from Truk. There are some who maintain Uncle Dan prayed his way to the top. Others see two years of asskissing Roosevelt in the White House as having more to do with it.

Down in Nouméa our new COMSOPAC, 'Fighting Bill' Halsey, has issued a directive which consists of the following: 'Kill Japs. Kill Japs. And keep on killing Japs.' I do not believe this plan has ever been war-gamed at Newport.

Tell Cominch I agree with Win – we're fighting an idiot's war out here, in the name of Navy public relations or the egotism of Ernest J. King, take your fucking pick. We all know the master plan called for a Europe-first strategy. What in Christ are we doing trying to take the offensive without enough ships or men? A lot of Americans have died and more will die soon (probably including me) trying to prove that the Navy and Marines can fight a war without the Army, so please keep those appropriations coming. When we should be saving our ships and men by staying on the defensive around Australia and New Zealand and waiting for the umpteen dozen new destroyers, cruisers and carriers that are under construction to get to sea next year. By that time we might also have Herr Hitler out of the way and add the Atlantic Fleet to the ready list.

But the bulldogs are in control. Brains are the last thing anyone wants a captain to have. So why not get pie-eyed, plastered, polluted, ploshed?

> Your loving husband,
> Arthur McKay
> Captain, USN

Nightmare

'Are you superstitious, Commander Parker?' Arthur McKay asked as they climbed the ladder to the bridge.

'No.'

'Good. We've got thirteen ships in this task force. It's Friday the thirteenth. And we're taking on two Japanese battleships.'

'Battleships! That's insanity. They can blow us apart before we even get within range.'

'The Admiral's plan is to get within range before they find us. Let's hope it works.'

Once more they were plunging through the moonless Pacific night, following the white wake of a cruiser just ahead of them. Once more, Captain McKay would soon stand on the bridge waiting for his Executive Officer to come apart.

After mailing that vituperative letter to his wife, McKay had slept soundly and awakened as calm and fatalistic as a Chinese philosopher. He had let his steward remove the empty Ballantine's bottle with no immediate desire for a refill.

He had remained clear-headed and calm for the rest of the day as the orders arrived from Nouméa to join Admiral Callaghan's hastily assembled task force. McKay had given a talk to the crew about the importance of the battle confronting them and made decisions to prepare the ship for it. He had remained the captain of the USS *Jefferson City*, even if in his heart he had resigned from the Navy in disgust or despair or both.

He had decided to keep Parker on the bridge to display the advantage he had over his executive officer. He was not afraid to die and Parker was violently afraid. It was almost cruel to exploit this weakness. But cruelty was a wasted word when you were dealing with a swine. McKay was convinced Parker's cowardice was the key to the mystery of what had happened aboard the *Jefferson City* at Savo Island. Parker had ruined his best friend. In the name of revenge, in the name of that friendship, which had been at the centre of his life for so long. Arthur McKay vowed he would destroy Parker if the war permitted him.

'Do you know Admiral Callaghan?' he asked as they paused on the platform aft of the bridge.

'I met him when he was the President's naval aide.'

'I wonder if you got the same impression I got. Stupid.'

'No,' Parker said.

'He hasn't even bothered to issue a battle plan. We're just imitating Norm Scott's tactics at Cape Esperance. Except now we've got thirteen ships in line ahead. Nelson would approve. But naval tactics have advanced a little since Trafalgar.'

'Jesus Christ,' Parker said.

McKay found it amusing to watch fear drool down Parker's padded cheeks. What made it doubly amusing was the incongruous fact that he was telling the truth. They were steaming toward a Japanese fleet three times more powerful than they were, using eighteenth-century tactics. Instead of ordering his destroyers to race ahead, discover the enemy and deliver a demoralizing torpedo attack, Admiral Callaghan had leashed his wolfhounds at the head and rear of the column, where they were worse than useless. Thirteen ships in line were twice as unwieldy as Scott's seven at Cape Esperance, where confusion had verged on chaos. They still had not standardized their code words and lookout terminology. For communication they were still relying on the TBS voice radio, which thirteen ships were certain to overload.

He watched Parker relieve Lieutenant Mullenoe, who departed for his GQ station in sky forward. 'That was a great talk you gave the crew, Captain,' Mullenoe said as he left.

'Thank you.'

Acting, was that the key to success as a military leader? McKay wondered. Maybe he could make admiral yet if he took some lessons from Montgomery West. Were the souls of Nelson's captains as full of wormwood as they talked to their crews about honour and duty? He had avoided those abstractions in his talk. Instead he had dwelt on the desperate situation on Guadalcanal. If the Navy lost this battle, America would have the humiliation of seeing her fighting men trapped on another Bataan.

'How are you feeling, son?' Arthur McKay said, putting his hand on the shoulder of the bridge telephone talker.

'A little scared, Captain.'

'That's perfectly all right. I feel the same way. So does Commander Parker, right?'

'Right,' Parker snapped, his eyes on the dark sea ahead of them.

At his gun director above forty-millimetre mount one, Frank Flanagan listened to one of the gun crew, a Kentucky hillbilly nicknamed the Deacon, reciting from the Bible. '"Yea though I walk through the valley of the shadow of death, I will fear no evil,"' the Deacon declared in his chanting singsong, '"for thou art with me; thy rod and thy staff they comfort me."'

Would He? Flanagan wondered. With each battle, he found himself more and more incapable of believing in God's protection. At the same time he found himself curiously aware of Biblical ideas. The idea of being unworthy, for instance. Unworthy of protection or salvation. Frank Flanagan was definitely among the unworthy. He was capable of thinking and feeling and doing all sorts of rotten things. He was still helping Jack Peterson write lying love letters to Martha Johnson. He was still tormented by his visit to the Honolulu whorehouse and what he had done to Teresa Brownlow.

Flanagan had begun to hate his mother for trying to push him into the priesthood and forcing him to join the Navy and come out here to these godforsaken islands to be blown apart by a high explosive shell. He was ready to believe women were the root of all evil – if it weren't for the rottenness that churned in his own soul. He had not written a letter to his mother or father for weeks. She deserved it, but he wished he had a chance to tell his father that he'd shot down a couple of Jap planes before they got him.

He no longer liked the Navy. He hated the endless routine

of watches and musters and drills, he loathed the food, he despised snarling Ensign Kruger and had even grown impatient with Jack Peterson's big talk and Boats Homewood's superstitions. What the hell did any of it mean, when they were probably going to be feeding the sharks before the night was over?

As far as Flanagan was concerned, he was already dead. It was only a question of time before it became official, a fact.

'How you doin', kiddo?' Homewood said, about a foot way from him, giving Flanagan's heart a violent twitch. He was always amazed by the catlike way Homewood moved around the ship in the dark.

'OK,' he said.

'Here,' Boats said. 'Take a slug of this.'

It was whisky. Flanagan took a hefty swallow. 'Where the hell did you get it?'

'Never mind. These night battles are a bitch. Just remember they can't see us neither. We got a hell of a good admiral up ahead. I knew guys who served under Callaghan. He's a fightin' Irishman like you.'

'Is that good or bad?'

'Hey, listen. We come out here to fight, didn't we? Remember what the Captain said about them Marines. They're dependin' on us. We can't let them arrogant fuckin' bastards down. After tonight every goddamn Marine in the world's gonna have to kiss our asses and admit they can't win the fuckin' war without the Navy.'

'Right,' Flanagan said. His heart began to pound. His voice shook. 'Jesus, Boats, I don't know what's the matter with me. I wasn't scared before. I'm not scared in the daylight when I can shoot back.'

'Take another slug. You're gonna do OK. We're all gonna do OK. The Captain's got his joss workin' full blast. I can feel it as sure as I feel them engines down below. Just think of them eight-inch and five-inch guns. Think of how much metal we can throw at them yellow bastards.'

Flanagan took another big gulp of whisky. It burned in his empty belly. He had not eaten any supper. He was afraid he would throw it up. The heads had been full of vomiting sailors all day.

Maybe Homewood was right. Maybe the chaplain was right too. With the help of the powers of darkness, they were about to consecrate some history in the narrow channels of King Solomon's Islands.

'Captain, radar reports two groups of ships, bearing three one two and three one zero true, distance two seven zero zero zero yards and three two zero zero zero yards.'

'My God,' Captain McKay whispered to himself. All Callaghan had to do was alter course to 150 or 145 degrees true and they would cross the Japs' 'T'. One ship after another would be in position to deliver devastating broadsides into the middle of the oncoming enemy squadron. It was Cape Esperance all over again. The Japs were coming down to blast Henderson Field, not to fight a sea battle. Their decks were probably covered with high capacity bombardment shells. A hit from a single salvo would blow them into the stratosphere.

Captain McKay switched on the TBS and reported the sighting to Admiral Callaghan in the *San Francisco*. He had stayed aboard that ship even though she was still not equipped with the latest radar. He was depending on the *Helena* and the *Jefferson City* to give him the ability to see across miles of darkened sea.

Three minutes later, at 0127, McKay was astonished to hear the TBS croak, 'All ships alter course two points to starboard to course three one zero.'

Callaghan was sailing straight into the Japanese fleet! Commander Parker's breath and words mingled in an explosion. 'Is he out of his fucking mind?'

The next several minutes were even more incomprehensible. They pounded through the night toward their approaching foes, closing the gap between them at a combined speed of forty knots. The range fell down, down, with the talker's drone: 'One three zero double zero, one two zero double zero.' Callaghan obviously wanted to get close enough to give his cruisers a chance against the battleships' longer-range guns. But he was in danger of forfeiting the immense advantage of surprise.

'Why don't we open fire?' Parker said hoarsely.

'I don't know,' Captain McKay said. He was beginning to think Callaghan intended to imitate Nelson's maxim, 'No Captain can do very great wrong if he lay his ship alongside the enemy.' But Nelson did not have radar, destroyers capable of thirty-five knots, torpedoes.

Again McKay was at Savo Island with Win, trapped in a vise of command stupidity, in imminent danger of dying, of conning his ship into the jaws of destruction under orders from a man whose ideas were two hundred years out of date.

On the TBS McKay could hear Callaghan asking the *Helena* for ranges, bearings, courses, composition of the enemy force. If the Admiral heard any answers, his ears were better than any aboard the *Jefferson City*. The radio circuit was jammed with requests for information from other ships and questions about when to open fire. Most of the time it was a rasping gargle.

'*San Francisco* changing course! Bearing three one five!' cried the talker.

'Left full rudder,' Parker shouted.

They could hear Admiral Callaghan shouting into his TBS, demanding to know what was happening in the van of the column. Back came a flash from the destroyer squadron commander. 'Enemy destroyers sighted three thousand yards, crossing port to starboard.'

'There goes our surprise,' McKay said.

Now Callaghan *had* to give the order to open fire. The Japs were less than five miles away, in easy range of their six- and eight-inch guns. The *Jefferson City*'s radar had them nailed. 'Range nine five double zero,' the talker said.

No order came. Instead, for another eight minutes the TBS dissolved into a babble of voices getting and giving target bearings without anyone bothering to say whether they were true or relative, visual or radar.

'Stand by to open fire,' Admiral Callaghan roared above the babble.

An instant later, before a single gunnery officer could press his firing button, the lead American cruiser, the *Atlanta*, and behind her the *San Francisco* and *Jefferson City* were bathed in the eerie glow of Japanese searchlights. 'Counterilluminate. Open fire,' cried Commander Edwin Moss in Main Forward.

'Forty millimetres, get those searchlights,' Mullenoe said.

Flanagan could see nothing but glare. He poured a stream of shells at it, while around him the deck leaped, his head ballooned, his chest crumpled with the concussion of the five- and eight-inch guns opening fire.

The Japanese searchlights vanished. He had a wild image of dead and dying sailors in the shattered superstructures of their ships. But that too vanished as an American ship ahead of them was hit by salvo after salvo from the Japanese. It reeled out of the column gushing flames.

'There goes the *Atlanta*,' Commander Parker cried on the bridge.

Captain McKay winced at the vicious things he had said about Admiral Norman Scott in his letter to his wife. He had been maligning a man who was about to die. No one was left alive on the *Atlanta*'s shattered bridge, he was sure of that.

From the *San Francisco* came Admiral Callaghan's thunderous voice. 'Odd ships commence fire to port, even to starboard.'

'Holy shit, are we odd or even?' Parker shouted.

'Odd,' McKay said. 'But it doesn't matter. There are plenty of targets.'

Shells shrieked overhead. Phosphorescent fountains rose on both sides of the ship. They were in the centre of the Japanese fleet. According to plan, the cruisers' five-inch guns fired star shells that burst above them on both sides of the battle line. In their flickering glow, the huge pagodalike superstructures of two Japanese battleships were visible, along with at least ten smaller ships.

It was a mêlée, the sort of sea fight even eighteenth-century admirals considered a violation of the principles of naval tactics and strategy. Only the wild amateurs of the sixteenth and seventeenth centuries had indulged in such slugfests, in which brains and training became irrelevant and not even raw courage guaranteed a ship's survival.

Two tremendous explosions lifted the dying *Atlanta* out of the water for almost half her length. She had been hit by torpedoes from the Japanese destroyers. Another salvo of heavy shells from one of the Jap battleships gouged her superstructure and hull. Ahead of her, an American destroyer twisted and turned like a frantic rabbit in enemy searchlights while salvos churned the sea around her. One hit home, and she exploded and vanished so suddenly it seemed a visual trick.

'On target,' shouted Jack Peterson at the range finders as the *Jefferson City* pumped salvo after eight-inch salvo into one of the Japanese battleships. Flames engulfed her from bow to stern. But her fourteen-inch guns kept booming. 'Jesus Christ, those guys are tough,' Peterson yelled.

'Are we winning, Jack? Camutti yelled from his post an inch or two from Peterson's right knee, inside the spinning range finder. They were all a little drunk from some booze Peterson had liberated from the master at arm's distillery.

'We ain't losin',' Peterson howled, picking out another target, a burning cruiser off the port quarter. The main battery poured a salvo into her. 'It's the goddamnedest fireworks you've ever seen,' Peterson yelled.

On the bridge, it was almost impossible to see anything. They were blinded by the repeated flashes of their own guns. It was equally impossible to think. Blast after blast seemed to tear apart the centre of one's brain. Captain McKay could only hope the men at the radar screens and computers and throttles below him were doing their jobs. All he could do was keep the ship on the chosen course.

The helmsman kept muttering prayers under his breath. 'Shut up for Christ's sake,' Commander Parker barked. He pulled a flask from his pocket and took a quick gulp.

'Cease firing own ships,' shouted Admiral Callaghan over the TBS.

It was incredible. 'Ignore that order,' Captain McKay said. He got on the TBS. 'What the hell's going on,

Admiral? Do you really want us to cease firing?'

'Yes. We're firing on the *Atlanta*! Change course to zero zero zero.'

As they swung due north, the *San Francisco*'s guns fell silent. An instant later, Japanese searchlights gripped her in a glowing vise. A screaming deluge of metal smashed into her bridge – fourteen-inch shells from the other Japanese battleship. Flames engulfed the decks from the bridge to the stern. Arthur McKay realized he would have to regret saying cruel things about another dead admiral. No one on the *San Francisco*'s bridge survived those hits.

'Jesus Christ, it's gotta be our turn next,' shouted Parker. 'One of us better get the hell out of here. I'll go to Batt Two.'

'Commander Parker, you will remain on the bridge. That's an order,' Captain McKay said.

Parker said something that was lost in the thunder of another salvo. McKay could only read the first three words on his lips, *You fucking bastard*.

Parker was shaking so violently, McKay thought he was going to fall to the deck in a convulsion. With each crash of the five-inch and eight-inch guns, he seemed to dwindle, as if he were a human-sized stuffed animal from which the sawdust was being pounded by the concussions.

A ferocious thud shook the forward part of the ship. 'Captain, there's a live shell in turret one,' the telephone talker cried.

Captain McKay grabbed the earphones and heard Ensign Richard Meade speaking to the Gunnery Officer. 'It's an eight-inch. I don't know why it hasn't detonated. I can hear it pulsing like a big heartbeat. I've ordered the men out.'

In turret one, Ensign Meade watched Turret Captain Johnny Chase calmly directing some men out the small hatch on to the main deck and others down the narrow passageway into the handling room below them. When Captain McKay transferred Meade to turret one, he had taken Chase with him. Meade had told the Captain that Johnny deserved equal credit for the good record they had racked up in five-inch mount one. The Captain had warmly approved his request.

He said it was exactly the sort of leadership he wanted his officers to display.

Now there was no one left inside turret one but Meade and Chase. The Japanese shell continued to thud like a heartbeat or a muffled drum. Instinctively, both men knew there was only time for one of them to get out that hatch. Their eyes met and Meade knew exactly what he had to do.

For Ensign Babyface the world had suddenly become very simple. He would not have to worry about deciding between mother and father, between the honour of a Navy career and the profit of the family corporation. Honour was here in this random projectile, his treasure, his price, now and forever. Honour and a kind of pride that Johnny Chase, better than anyone, understood. Their eyes met and Meade said, 'Get going.'

Chase dove out the hatch headfirst and landed in the arms of his men. He knew they would be waiting for him. A second later the shell went off. Chase looked up at the flames gushing from the hatch. 'That's how you win a Congressional Medal of Honour,' he said.

On the bridge, the explosion coruscated over the telephone circuit into the centre of Captain McKay's skull. Ensign Richard Meade would not go far in the Navy after all.

A shaken Commander Moss said, 'Turret one disabled by a direct hit. All other guns continuing to fire.'

'Flood the handling room and forward magazine,' McKay said to the talker. 'Tell Damage Control to get up there and tell me how things look.'

Far down in the ship, the men at the flood control panel board threw switches that sent water surging into these compartments. From the bridge, McKay could see flames roaring from every aperture of turret one. Even the arms of its secondary range finder were spouting fire. In a moment a life raft lashed to the top of the turret was ablaze.

'Tell Damage Control to douse that fire. Change course to three zero zero,' Captain McKay said. 'Give us flank speed.'

'Let me go below. I'll handle it,' Commander Parker begged.

McKay ignored him. He knew the fire was going to attract salvos from every Japanese gunnery officer still afloat. He had to concentrate on saving his ship.

A thunderclap sent tremendous geysers of water leaping hundreds of feet in the air only a few dozen yards off the port bow. Those were fourteen-inch shells. One of the Jap battleships was after them. 'Right full rudder,' McKay said.

The *Jefferson City* heeled to starboard. The Japanese fired at the top of the roll. It would take them another sixty seconds to get off the next salvo. McKay kept his eyes on the second hand of his watch, barely visible in the glow of the binnacle light. 'Left full rudder,' he said, at fifty seconds.

The ship heeled to port. It would take about thirty seconds for the salvo to come in. Right to the second, another thunderclap exploded two hundred yards to starboard, where they would have been if they had stayed on the previous course. Now, count another sixty seconds before the next zag and pray the Japanese gunnery officer was not thinking one step ahead of him.

'Where the hell is Damage Control! That fire is like a goddamn beacon,' Parker shouted.

'Commander Parker,' McKay said, his eyes on his watch, 'I'd appreciate it if you would shut your mouth. Left full rudder!'

Sixty seconds later, an enormous roar filled the bridge. On target? McKay wondered. At least it would be quick. Fourteen-inch shells would obliterate everything and everyone from here to the main deck. *Rr-oooom*, the half-ton messengers of death rumbled over their heads. The thunderclap was off the port beam this time.

'I'm going aft to Batt Two so someone'll be alive to run this ship,' Parker cried.

He fled to the armoured conning tower aft, where six inches of reinforced steel would protect him against everything but a direct hit. Captain McKay let him go. He was confident he could deal with Parker any time he chose now. Never again would he or anyone else be able to accuse Arthur McKay of freezing under fire. But McKay was not thinking about his reputation. The only thing that mattered was the survival of the *Jefferson City*.

'Tell Damage Control to douse that fire,' Captain McKay said, his eyes on his watch. 'Right full rudder!'

'Flanagan! Get your ass down here. You guys on mount one, follow me.' It was Boats Homewood, summoning them to fight the fire inside and outside turret one. The walls of the turret were glowing red. Homewood jammed fire hoses up the ejection slots – the small openings where the shell casings were discharged. 'Get down,' Homewood shouted as another fourteen-inch salvo hurtled toward them with the roar of a dozen runaway locomotives. It exploded off the starboard bow. Shrapnel clanged off the turret.

Flanagan clung to the nozzle of his hose as the ship careened through the darkness, slewing from port to starboard while more salvos of fourteen-inch shells tore the sea around them. In five minutes the fire inside was doused and Homewood ordered Flanagan to join him on top of the turret. He sprayed the ladder with water and foam but it was still so hot Flanagan cried out with pain when he touched it. 'Come on, it's burnin' my hands too,' Homewood bellowed, climbing ahead of him.

They reached the top just as another salvo came roaring in to explode off the port bow. 'Use your knife, cut away them lines,' Homewood shouted, hacking at ropes holding the raft to the turret. The ship lurched to port, and the flames seared Flanagan's face. Another salvo thundered out of the night to land to starboard. 'How do you like the way the old man's chasin' them salvos?' Homewood shouted. 'Didn't I tell you he's a winner?'

Every time the ship heeled to port or starboard, Flanagan had to fall to his knees to stay on the tipping turret. Homewood did not even seem to notice the wild lurches. He stayed on his feet, hacking at the ropes, ignoring the flames swirling around him in the wind. As Flanagan gazed up at him. Homewood became transfigured, mythical. He was Paul Bunyan, John Henry, translated to this nightmare world of sea and fire.

'Now heave,' Homewood roared. An appalled Flanagan followed his example and thrust his hands into a mass of flame. The raft sailed through the air and went sizzling into the sea.

As dawn's grey light seeped across the glassy surface of Ironbottom Sound, the *Jefferson City* was still afloat. Wisps of smoke rose from fire-blackened number one turret. On her bridge, Captain Arthur McKay almost savoured the exhaustion that blended with his disgust. He had saved his ship. He could take some pride in his performance on the bridge. But he no longer gave a damn about pride or courage or glory. He did not even care about his own survival. It was his responsibility to his crew, his concern for them as human beings as well as sailors, that had got him through the night.

In counterpoint to these bitter feelings was the memory of the sacrifice young Dick Meade had made for his men. It did not make sense to have officers like that in the brainless bureaucracy known as the US Navy. Maybe nothing made sense. Swinish Daniel Boone Parker was still alive, cowering in Batt II. Why go on looking for any deeper answer?

The purplish mountains of Guadalcanal slowly took shape. Nine ships were now in sight, five of them afire, crippled or both. The shattered *Atlanta* drifted off the enemy-held shore of Guadalcanal, her decks awash. Another cruiser, the *Portland*, her rudder smashed by a torpedo, steamed slowly in circles. The American destroyer *Aaron Ward* was dead in the water, her fire rooms flooded by torpedoes. Two other American destroyers were aflame and slowly sinking. Ditto for two Japanese destroyers. On the horizon toward Savo Island, a burning Japanese battleship retreated at no more than five knots.

The *Portland* seemed able to take care of herself. As soon as she spotted one of the Japanese destroyers, she sank her with a salvo from her main battery. The Japanese battleship promptly returned the compliment with a salvo that straddled the *Aaron Ward*. Minutes later, a squadron of dive bombers from Henderson Field went after the diving leviathan and those were the last shots she fired.

Captain McKay decided the *Jefferson City* could do the *Atlanta* the most good. She looked as if she might sink at any moment. The J.C.'s guns could hold off the Japanese Army until boats arrived to rescue the survivors. The *Atlanta* welcomed his offer of assistance. 'Have issued small arms to the crew. Could use some big guns,' she replied in answer to McKay's signals.

Around Lunga Point came a Navy tug – a welcome sight to both ships. But the tug, instead of heading toward the *Atlanta*, veered out to sea. Across the water came the chatter of machine guns. 'What in Christ are they doing?' McKay said.

'I think they're firing at Japanese in the water, Captain,' the port bridge lookout said.

'Signal them to stop immediately,' McKay said.

A signalman blinked the message to the tug. The machine guns continued to chatter. Through his field glasses, McKay could see the bullets churning the water, which was dotted with black heads.

'How do they know they're all Japanese?' he said. 'Tell them to stop or I'll fire on them.'

This time the machine guns stopped. A blinker replied. Captain McKay read it. 'Are . . . you . . . in . . . Halsey's . . . Navy?'

'Tell them we're in the American Navy,' McKay said.

They guarded the tug while it towed the *Atlanta* down to an American held part of the shore. Shortly after they got there and the *Atlanta* unloaded her dead and wounded, she settled deeper in the water and sank stern-first.

A flimsy from Radio Central arrived on the *Jefferson City*'s bridge. It was from Gil Hoover, the captain of the *Helena*: WHAT IS YOUR CONDITION? IF SEAWORTHY, RENDEVOUS WITH ME NORTH OF SAVO ISLAND AS SOON AS POSSIBLE.

With Admirals Scott and Callaghan dead, Hoover was the senior officer still afloat, hence the OTC – officer in tactical command. 'Tell him we'll be there,' McKay said.

Off Savo they found the *Helena* shepherding two crippled cruisers, the *Juneau*, which had taken a torpedo that had broken her keel, and the battered *San Francisco*, which looked as if she had been stamped on by a giant wearing steel-soled shoes. The bridge was a mass of crushed, blackened, twisted metal. The rest of the superscructure had gigantic holes torn in it. With three destroyers, two of them also crippled, they formed a column and began limping back to Espiritu Santo at fifteen knots.

Captain McKay set Condition Two, which would permit half the crew to be relieved from General Quarters to get some rest. A sullen Commander Parker rejoined him on the bridge. McKay let icy silence communicate his contempt for his Executive Officer. Last night, in those five wild minutes of outguessing the battleship's salvos, he felt he had established an unchallengeable superiority over this despicable coward. Now he would have to decide what to do with him.

'Captain! *San Francisco* is turning to avoid torpedoes!' cried the lookout on the port wing of the bridge.

McKay got out on the wing in time to see the battered cruiser slewing to starboard. A moment later four white wakes rushed past her stern – straight at the *Juneau*, which was a thousand yards away on her starboard beam. 'Sound the siren,' McKay shouted. The *San Francisco* had no way to warn anyone.

The *Jefferson City*'s klaxon howled, but it was too late. At least two of the torpedoes bored straight into the belly of the *Juneau*. There was an enormous flash, a stupendous explosion – and the *Juneau* vanished. Instead of a cruiser there was only a huge dome of smoke on the sea. Out of this black mass rose an intact five-inch .win gun mount, which hung in the air for a moment and fell back into the blackness.

'Down on the deck,' McKay shouted. Everyone went flat. An instant later, a piece of steel plating the size of a barn door smashed into the bridge and bounced off into the water. Up and down the length of the *Jefferson City* other pieces of the *Juneau* tore through the superstructure. Reports of at least a dozen wounded flowed to the bridge from various parts of the ship.

The column continued to plough toward Espiritu Santo. Were there any *Juneau* survivors? It seemed inconceivable anyone could have got off that ship. Still, if even one man had survived, they owed him some help. McKay waited for Captain Hoover to send a destroyer back for a search. But they continued to plod away from the black pyre.

McKay understood what Gil Hoover was thinking. Two of his destroyers were cripples, easy pickings for the Japanese sub. If he detached his one intact destroyer, he stripped his surviving cruisers of their only protection. McKay suspected he would keep going too if he was in command. But there was something craven, sickening about the way they were fleeing like routed fugitives.

Two days later they stood into Nouméa, and Captain McKay watched while Dick Meade's body was removed from the blackened turret one. 'He never left his seat,' Lieutenant Commander Moss said. 'His finger was still on the firing button.' Moss was looking green, but he had gone into the turret to bring out the charred corpse and estimate the damage to the guns.

McKay went back to his cabin to write a letter to Dick Meade's parents. He was sitting at his desk staring at the blank piece of paper when the officer of the deck informed him that Admiral Richmond Kelly Turner wanted to see him.

In a moment he was facing the dour face, the violent eyes. Turner had been in a command limbo on the COMSOPAC staff since Savo Island. Looking for something to do, he had apparently persuaded Halsey to make him his Lord High Executioner. 'We want a straight answer to one question, Captain,' he said. 'Why didn't you go back and search for survivors of the *Juneau*?'

'Captain Hoover was the OTC and he evidently decided it was too risky.'

'Do you think there were any survivors?'

'I don't know. I doubt it.'

'Why didn't you exercise some judgement on that point? You were closer to the scene than the *Helena*.'

'It wasn't my decision.'

'Admiral Halsey's relieving Hoover of command of his ship. I'm going to recommend the same thing for you.'

'That's the most outrageous goddamn thing I've ever heard in my life! I want to see the Admiral. Now.'

'He doesn't have time to listen to your excuses,' Turner snapped.

'Someone must have listened to yours for Savo Island. Otherwise you'd be on the beach with your friend George Tomlinson.'

'You say one more insubordinate word to me, McKay, and you'll lose more than your ship!' Turner shouted.

'One more?' McKay said. 'I'll say ten thousand more to you, Admiral. I think you fucked up at Savo Island and you know it, and you're trying to cover your ass and Ernie King's ass by crucifying Win Kemble. You're trying to shut me up with the phoniest accusation I ever heard in the history of naval warfare. How's that for insubordination? Want to bring me up on those charges? I'll be delighted to argue them with you before a court-martial board anytime, anyplace.'

'You're backing the wrong horse, McKay,' Turner said.

'I'm not going to waste my breath talking to you. I'm going ashore now and I'm going to sit outside Halsey's goddamn office until he sees me.'

Admiral Halsey had long since moved his staff from the supply ship *Argonna* to comfortable quarters on a windswept hill on the island of Nouméa. He had told the French officials who protested to tell their troubles to General de Gaulle. McKay sat outside Halsey's office for most of the day. Finally his chief of staff, whose disposition was on a par with Kelly Turner's glowed in the doorway. 'You can go in now.'

There sat the Bull with his outsize head and underslung jaw. McKay had been one of his captains when he commanded Destroyer Division 12. He and Rita and everyone else in the division had got drunk with him, celebrating the success of their famous night attack on the Battleship Force during manoeuvres in 1937. Halsey had adored Rita. He shared her blind brainless worship of the US Navy.

'I'm here to tell you what kind of a war you're running, Admiral,' McKay said. 'It would have been magnificent in 1812, but today it's the closest thing to idiocy I've ever encountered. You send cruisers against battleships and you act like destroyer tactics have never been developed and lose eleven out of thirteen ships and when a man like Gil Hoover makes a mistake in judgement after fighting a battle that he knows in his guts was stupidity from beginning to end you disgrace him. I gather you're going to let Kelly Turner give me the business too, so he can start pretending Savo Island never happened. If that's the way we're playing the game, so be it. But I've got a right to tell you how much it disgusts me to see that son of a bitch shit all over men who've been risking their lives and their ships.'

The glaring eyes beneath the bushy eyebrows never blinked. 'Is that all, Captain McKay? Halsey asked.

'In spite of relieving me, I hope you'll take seriously my recommendation of one of my ensigns for the Medal of Order.' He began describing what Dick Meade had done in his turret. In the middle of it, McKay began to weep.

Halsey's face remained expressionless. 'Go back to your ship and get some sleep. If you can't get to sleep try some of this.'

He took a bottle of bourbon out of his desk and handed it to him.

McKay walked to the door. The hard voice spun him around. 'Captain McKay.'

'Yes, Admiral?'

'I read the after-action reports of the battle of Santa-Cruz. The captain of the *Enterprise* says you saved his ship by taking those three torpedoes that didn't explode. Don't worry about Admiral Hoffer's complaints. I'm ignoring them. I'm ignoring Admiral Turner's comments on you in regard to the *Juneau*, too. But I have to relieve Gil Hoover. There were survivors. Left for shark bait. I can't excuse that.'

McKay reached for the doorknob and the commanding voice spun him round again. 'One more thing. If you can tell me how to win a war without losing ships, I'll sign over my salary and pension rights to you tomorrow.'

A half hour later, a dazed Arthur McKay was back in his cabin. He sat down and began the letter he had been unable to write a few hours ago.

Dear Milly and Clinch:
   I want to tell you how Dick died. I think it will make you proud to be his parents. It made me proud to be in the same Navy with him. . . .

Mail Call

Husband Dear:
   I got your letter. I was tempted to show it to Cominch. It would be what you deserve. But I decided to file it with the rest of your explosions of despair about the Navy and the United States of America. It's rather a thick file by now. This one is the worst. If I had to pick one, I'd choose the *cri de coeur* you wrote me from the *Monocacy*. Such a bleating about ethical standards and American foreign policy! Almost as bad was your whine from Shanghai in 1935, after Nimitz left you aboard the *Augusta* without a nice kindly papa to pat you on the head every twenty minutes. And you wonder why I worry that you're not tough enough to make it to the top! I don't know what the hell went wrong with you pioneers out there on the Great Plains. Psychology never did interest me. But something turned you into world champion crybabies. Maybe it was boredom, after you ran out of Indians to kill.
   Anyway, I've got delicious news. Win Kemble returned to duty and promptly got reassigned to the Canal Zone. Can you imagine? I wouldn't be surprised if he spends the war down there watching new ships and captains transit to the Pacific Fleet. You and your pals can take a lot of the credit for it, with those victories you won for old Bulldog Bill Halsey. Cominch is strutting around Washington looking ten feet tall. FDR can't do enough for him.
   I got my hands on Hoffer's after-action report and I can't find a word in it about you. Instead there's a commendation from the Bull for risking your ship to save the *Enterprise*. If I catch Cominch in the right mood, I think I can get you a Navy Cross for it.
   What would you do without me? Don't answer that question. I might not be able to forgive you.

Your loving wife,
Rita

Dear Art:

Win has just suffered the cruellest blow I have ever seen the Navy inflict on anyone. He's been deported – there's no other word for it – to Panama. Can you imagine? Sending the keenest, best-educated mind in the officer corps to that godforsaken place, where he'll command nothing but misfits and drunks no captain will let aboard his ship.

Win's too proud to write you a pleading letter, Art. But you're his only hope now. Clinch Meade has turned into the coward I always suspected he was. This loathsome investigation Ernie King has launched into Savo Island can be turned to Win's advantage with your help. By now I'm sure you've found out what really happened at Savo. How little responsibility Win had for the disaster – and exactly what happened aboard the *Jefferson City*. I don't know myself – Win's never shared his shipboard life with me – but from hints he's dropped I'm sure his crew betrayed him. If you can bring the men responsible to justice, you can clear Win's name.

Ever since I married Win, I've had a terrible premonition something like this would happen. He's always excited so much envy and malicious opposition by refusing 'to hide his light under a bushel', as he put it. I know just how cruel men can be to one another. I remember once, when I was a little girl in Shanghai, one of the sailors on Father's ship fell in love with a Chinese woman and married her. The other men tormented him so unmercifully about his Chink wife, he jumped ship and ran off to the interior with her. He was caught and returned in irons, of course, and sentenced to ten years in Portsmouth Prison.

The officer corps torment each other in more subtle ways. I think there's something about being incarcerated in those awful steel ships that makes men *want* to hurt each other.

Please help Win, Art. I know your loyalty to him remains unchanged, in spite of Rita's awful hatred of him.

Love,
Lucy

Dear Nephew:

I got your intemperate letter about your benighted British bitch. You always had lousy judgement when it came to women, but this time I think you've really rung the bell. Don't you know she's referred to around town as The British Open? She didn't get fired for cockteasing you into the Navy.

She got fired because she has no talent and her lubricity (look that one up) could get us all in a lot of trouble. The last thing we want around here is a scandal. With all the breaks Hollywood and M-G-M in particular are getting from the government (breaks we thoroughly deserve for the movies we're making for them) we can't afford to have some tabloid writing about a certain M-G-M British comedienne who enjoys gangbanging the extras in her dressing room at the end of the day. That's the truth about your beloved, and if you want affidavits from the guys who've been there, I'll be glad to supply them.

If you ever get to Australia, look up an actor named Charles Benbow. He was her lover in London for a couple of years but he couldn't stand the way she two-timed him. She grew up in Plymouth, you know, where her old man was a sailor. Every woman in that town is a part-time whore from birth.

Have you done anything that might with a little nudging get you a decoration? Or has the ship done anything in those big victories the Navy is suddenly announcing? (Presumably they really happened.) Believe it or not, I'm still determined to make you a star for your mother's sake, even though she isn't with us any more. Unless I hear a retraction of certain sentiments in your letter, I'm going to change my mind.

Your ever loving Uncle,
Mort

Dear Edwin:

I don't want to say I told you so, but everything you wrote in your last letter about Captain McKay confirms what I've been hearing about him. When he was in China, he got drunk on a gunboat he was commanding on the Yangtze and sailed the ship right into an artillery barrage without letting the crew fire back. Only his wife's connections saved his neck that time. As for his wife, the stories I hear about her are too embarrassing to spell out in detail. Right now, it's almost certain that she's Admiral King's mistress. He won't be the first admiral to get into bed with her. You better burn this as soon as you read it.

Edwin Jr is getting wonderful marks in school. I hope you can find time to write him a letter telling him how proud you are. Linda and Joanne are doing beautifully too. So we're coping without you. I'm feeling all right, except for the morning sickness and the constant worry.

Love,
Eleanor

Dear Frank:

I had a terrible dream about you last night. You were being burned alive in some fiery furnace. I prayed for an angel to rescue you, the way the Lord rescued Daniel. But nothing happened. My prayers went up into the sky like so much smoke. I hope it was just a dream and not an omen. I hope it doesn't have anything to do with what's been happening to us in San Pedro. Shanghai Red's making so much money he's decided to expand his restaurant. He's bought our building – we only rented the first two floors – and he's throwing us out on the street.

With rents so high everywhere, I don't know where we can relocate. Daddy is terribly discouraged and spends hours at night when he should be sleeping, asking God why He's sent us this latest trial. It's made me wonder if you might be right, if I haven't been the sinner who's been ruining the blessing the Lord wants to send to Daddy as a reward for all his trials. Oh, Frank, maybe now I understand why I've failed to awaken Jesus in your heart. Maybe it was my pride that blinded me to what you were saying about my sinfulness. But I swear to you there was love in my heart for you, Frank, and there still is love there, even if it is speaking in darkness now.

Your friend,
Teresa

Dear Marty:

I have gone through *torments* trying to write this letter. But it has to be written. I have *adored* all the letters I have received from you, telling me about the incredible ordeals you have been undergoing in that ghastly fireroom. My admiration for your courage, your dedication, your moral grasp of this crusade against evil, keeps growing.

But admiration and affection, dearest Marty, are two very different things. I don't think you should allow the memory of our little fling in New York to distort your understanding of this important truth. That was an episode, a momentary overflowing of admiration into the sort of warmth that precedes affection.

For some time I have been seeing a Harvard man named Roland Hathaway. He's a poet of great promise and a political observer of enormous sensitivity. An ear infection, which left him with a perforation and subject to terrible attacks of vertigo, has barred him (to his great distress) from the armed services. Last night, he asked me to marry him and I accepted. Under the circumstances, I think we had better stop corresponding.

Devotedly,
Sylvia

Fire and Brimstone

The torpedoman walked around and around the long gleaming monster on the stern of the *Jefferson City*. 'It's the damndest thing I've ever seen, Captain,' he said.

An alert lookout had spotted the torpedo on a beach on the Japanese-controlled shore of Guadalcanal. Captain McKay had sent the motor whaleboat in under the cover of his guns and towed it out to the *Jefferson City*. Back in Espiritu Santo, he had asked a veteran torpedoman from one of the destroyers to take a look at it.

The thing was almost twice the length of a standard American torpedo. After carefully defusing it, the torpedoman had reported that it also carried twice the explosive punch.

'What would you estimate its range to be?' McKay asked the torpedoman.

'Ten miles, minimum. Look at the fuel capacity.'

McKay told the torpedoman to ferry the weapon ashore and take it apart and write a report on it with the help of the officers on his destroyer. They would forward it to Comsopac and he would forward it to Cincpac, who would forward it to Cominch, who would send it to the Bureau of Ordnance; and maybe, with a little luck, in a year the whole Navy might be alerted to this secret weapon. In the meantime God knows how many ships might go down before its lethal power and range.

At the door of McKay's cabin, Buzz Jamieson, the communications officer, reported there was heavy traffic coming in from Comsopac Halsey in Nouméa. A big Japanese task force had sortied from Rabaul and was heading down the twisting waterway through the Solomons, which everyone called the Slot. 'I think you better make sure we've got steam up,' Jamieson said.

McKay nodded. He found himself welcoming the simplicity of battle, the possibility of an instant solution to his dilemmas with Parker and the women in his life. What better fate for a sailor than to go down with his ship, all guns blazing against a courageous enemy? That was always part of the choice he had made when he put on a Navy uniform. Yet a part of his mind scorned this dolorous solution. The McKays who had fought the slave-owning bushwhackers in Bloody Kansas were not losers.

A telephone call from the signal bridge. 'Captain, Admiral Standish would like you to report to the *Brockton* immediately.'

In the wardroom of the heavy cruiser *Brockton*, McKay found Rear Admiral Theodore E. Standish, the captains of the five cruisers, and the commander of the destroyer flotilla in Task Force 78. Bald, redfaced 'Buddy' Standish was a battleship man by training. He had commanded one of the battleships that Halsey had embarrassed in his famous destroyer attack in 1937.

It was bad enough that Standish had almost no experience commanding destroyers or cruisers. Worse, he had arrived to take over Task Force 78 only yesterday. Whoever was handing out the assignments in Washington was not thinking very long or hard about the South Pacific. All the big brains were obviously absorbed with the invasion of North Africa, which had begun two weeks ago.

Speaking in tense, nervous spurts, Standish confirmed there was a major Japanese battle force coming down the Slot toward Guadalcanal. He said they would follow the battle plan COMSOPAC had worked out for them. The cruisers and destroyers would operate independently. The destroyers would deliver a torpedo attack first and the cruisers would open fire at twelve thousand yards and maintain that distance. Search-lights were banned. Everyone carefully noted the code words for commence firing and cease firing.

Listening, Arthur McKay wondered if his outburst to Halsey had done some good. These were good tactics. For the first time the Americans were trying to learn from their mistakes. But there was a new problem – that Japanese torpedo. 'Admiral,' he said, 'I think we ought to discuss some special evasion tactics.'

He described the torpedo and its probable range. Standish was clearly not interested. He already had too much on his mind. 'Has anyone else seen this thing?' he asked testily. 'Has Buord put out anything on it?'

'If we wait for Buord to do something, we'll all have beards down to our knees or be feeding the fishes,' McKay said.

Too late, he remembered that Standish had been running the Bureau of Ordnance when the war began. 'They do a few things right, for your information, Captain McKay,' he snapped.

'Sorry, Admiral. You get an us-against-them attitude toward Washington when you're out here for a while.'

'The only us-against-them attitude anyone should have out here is us against the enemy,' the Admiral said. He proceeded to elaborate on that point throughout a five-minute pep talk. It was embarrassing – and idiotic. Fifty-year-old cruiser captains did not need pep talks. McKay sometimes thought playing for the Navy football team was the worst possible training for a future admiral. Standish had been a star fullback in 1912.

With a final warning about being ready to sail on five minutes' notice, the meeting broke up. Stuart Payne, the captain of the *Brockton*, put his arm around McKay's shoulder on the way down the passageway. 'Nice try, Art,' he said. 'I'll be watching for those damn things.'

At the Naval Academy, Payne had been known as Sorry because he always had a serious expression on his face. He had been a first classman when McKay had been a plebe. One day, Payne had sent for him and asked if it was true that he was thinking of quitting. When McKay said yes, Payne had urged him to change his mind. 'The Navy needs some guys with brains,' he said.

*

In moonless, starless darkness, the *Jefferson City* threaded the tortuous channel out of the harbour of Espiritu Santo, the Island of the Holy Spirit. Frank Flanagan stood beside his forty millimetre gun director wondering if this time they would run out of luck. Homewood still had faith in the Captain's joss and the good spirits they had lured back to the ship with their victories. Flanagan was not sure if he believed in them – or in anything else.

He had finished *The Quest of the Historical Jesus* and returned it to the chaplain. Bushnell had given him another book by a Danish writer named Kierkegaard, who maintained that every adult found belief in God absurd. What was needed was a 'leap of faith' – a blind embrace of the Incomprehensible in the name of love and trust. Flanagan's dogma-clogged Catholic mind found this hard to grasp, although it appealed to his Irish temperament. He tried to explain it to Jack Peterson, who summed it up in his own inimitable way.

'It's like bettin' you'll draw four aces when you got nothin' in your hand but deuces.'

Down on the mount, the deck apes were arguing with Crockett Smith, a hulking country boy from Tennessee who was convinced Tarzan was real. A week ago they had asked Flanagan if Crockett could possibly be right, and he assured them Tarzan was fiction, make-believe. Crockett just blinked. There was a complete set of Tarzan novels in the ship's library and Crockett had read them all. He declared in his stubborn hillbilly way that he *believed* that somewhere in some jungle, the fabled white ape-man was gambolling with his gorillas.

'Hey, Flanagan,' one of the deck apes asked over the phone. 'How old would Tarzan be if he was real?'

'Older than the captain.'

'Christ, can you imagine the captain swingin' on a fuckin' vine?'

'Mount one, cut the bullshit,' barked Ensign Herman Kruger, who was monitoring their circuit. 'Keep your eyes on the water.'

'*Jawohl, mein Herr,*' Flanagan said.

'One more crack like that, Flanagan, and you're on report!'

'Who me, sir? I didn't say a word,' Flanagan said.

Insubordination was one way of keeping your mind off getting killed.

On the bridge, Captain McKay was silently cursing Admiral Standish. Instead of following the COMSOPAC plan, Standish had leashed his destroyers to the cruisers. They were plodding along in the same stupid column they had maintained in their two previous battles. The Admiral was apparently worried about losing his cruisers. He preferred to let the destroyers draw Japanese fire if it came to a shootout. It was a despicable way to fight a battle.

A few feet away, Commander Daniel Boone Parker paced back and forth lamenting the darkness. The weather report predicted a moonrise about midnight, but the overcast made it unlikely that there would be any increase in visibility. Captain McKay was still treating his executive officer with icy politeness bordering on contempt. Parker returned the feeling with interest. The word captain was covered with slimy sarcasm every time he used it. But he still could not control his fear. He blustered and cursed at the engine room as they changed course rounding Savo Island and increased speed to advance up Ironbottom Sound.

'Radar reports enemy ships,' said the talker. 'Bearing two five zero true. Estimated number ten.'

The enemy was steaming along the darkened shore of Guadalcanal, less than five miles away.

The voice of the commander of the destroyer squadron came over the TBS, asking permission to launch torpedoes.

'Are you in range?' Admiral Standish asked.

'Yes.'

'You're sure of that?'

For another four minutes, Standish debated with him on whether the Japs were in range, while the enemy ships steamed steadily away from the leashed destroyers. It was idiocy! What Standish knew about torpedoes would fit comfortably on the head of a pin. Still dubious, and having clearly established the destroyer commander's responsibility, the Admiral finally gave the order. A moment later, he compounded his idiocy by ordering the cruisers to open fire, instead of waiting until the torpedoes made their long but still potentially murderous run in silence.

Behind them, the *Minneapolis* and the *Brockton* delivered thunderous eight-inch salvos. Ahead, the *Honolulu* and the *Pensacola* waited, groping for a target. They did not have the latest radar. The *Jefferson City* did and should have fired within seconds of the other two heavy cruisers. On the phone circuit, McKay could hear Lieutenant Commander Edwin Moss frantically demanding ranges from the radar operators. They told him the Japs kept disappearing against the land mass that was absorbing most of their signals.

Five miles away across the sound, where the American shells were landing, a ship burst into flames. 'Now you've got a target, Guns,' Commander Parker roared.

Within sixty seconds the *Jefferson City* and every other ship in Task Force 78 was blasting away at the hapless Japanese cripple. She returned the fire sporadically. Watching the splashes fall several hundred yards short of their starboard beam, McKay said, 'That's a destroyer. Let's find some bigger game. Switch targets, Mr Moss. That one's done for.'

They shifted fire and watched the burning red bottoms of their shells arch through the darkness. They did not hit anything. Neither did the salvos from anyone else's guns. Except for a desultory shell from the burning but still game destroyer, there was no return fire from the enemy.

'I think the bastards are running for their lives,' Parker said.

That made no sense. The Japanese had not run away from a fight yet. What was happening? Suddenly Arthur McKay knew the answer. 'It's a destroyer flotilla. They're using torpedoes!'

He lunged for the TBS. 'Admiral, I think you better warn all ships to –'

Just ahead of them, a stupendous explosion tore the *Minneapolis* apart. Flames leaped five hundred feet in the air.

Water mixed with burning oil came cascading down to ignite the ship from bow to stern. An instant later, two similar explosions lifted the *Brockton* out of the water and engulfed her in another inferno.

'Lookouts! Watch for torpedoes!' Captain McKay shouted over the PA system.

'Torpedo off the starboard bow!' cried the talker.

'Right full rudder,' McKay said.

Too late. For five minutes the huge mechanical creature, a twin of the one McKay had removed from the Guadalcanal beach, had been hissing beneath the black waters of Ironbottom Sound, its deadly snout aimed at the *Jefferson City*'s hull. While they had been amusing themselves with gunnery that hit next to nothing, the Japanese had been using destroyers the way they were supposed to be used.

The explosion tore through the *Jefferson City*, flinging men to the deck, in several cases breaking their legs or backs. A geyser of fire and water soared into the dark sky. The blast blew Captain McKay against a bulkhead and sent a small tidal wave crashing through the open windshields on to the bridge. He sat up and found everyone floundering on their backs in a foot of water. All around them was a wall of fire, devouring oxygen from the air. The helmsman crawled through the water and pulled himself erect at the wheel. It was a brave but superfluous gesture. The ship's speed had dwindled almost to zero. Instead of cutting through the water, she seemed to be ploughing into it.

'I can't breathe,' screamed Commander Parker.

'Was that in the forward engine room?' Captain McKay asked.

'Negative,' gasped the engine-room talker, slumped against the bulkhead. 'All engines are ahead full.'

What had happened? McKay wondered. He would probably never know. Another sixty seconds and they would all be asphyxiated by that inferno roaring outside the pilothouse. McKay was swept by an enormous aching wish that somehow, somewhere, he had told Lucy Kemble that he loved her.

'Abandon Ship,' Parker croaked, on his hands and knees. 'Sound Abandon Ship.'

Gone. The flames vanished as if God had snuffed them out

with an omnipotent puff. Captain McKay staggered to his feet. Ships were burning all around them. Every cruiser except the *Honolulu* had been torpedoed. She continued to fling shells into the night on rapid fire, hitting nothing. The five-inch mounts and the after eight-inch turret of the *Jefferson City* were also still booming, but the two forward turrets were silent.

'Captain,' whispered the talker, 'Damage Control wants you to reduce speed as soon as possible. We've lost our bow.'

'How much?'

'To the edge of turret one. And everyone in there is dead.'

'Jesus Christ,' groaned Wilkinson. 'That's half my division.'

Not that it mattered. The torpedo had detonated the forward magazine and the aviation gasoline. In a few minutes, if the fires and flooding below were not quickly controlled, the *Jefferson City* would be on her way to join the other wrecks on the floor of Ironbottom Sound.

'All engines ahead one third,' McKay told the engine-room telegrapher. 'Sound Cease Firing. Sound the fire call.'

The Cease Firing klaxon clanged through the ship, and her guns fell silent. Wilkinson shrilled the fire call on his boatswain's pipe and ordered all hands to join the damage control parties. From the wing of the bridge McKay looked down on the main deck. It was almost level with the surface of the sea. He went back to the navigator's cabin, where Marse Lee and his staff were frantically trying to reassemble charts and papers that had been blown all over the compartment by the explosion. 'We'll never make it back to Espiritu Santo,' McKay said. 'What do you suggest?'

'Tulagi's only twelve miles away. They can't repair anything bigger than a torpedo boat there, but it's safer than drifting around out here.'

'Give Parker a course, pronto. I'll try to keep us afloat.

Dazed from the blast, seared by the flames, Frank Flanagan lay on the deck under his gun director. Rough hands dragged him to his feet. 'Come on, kid,' Jack Peterson said. 'We got some fire-fightin' to do.'

He led Flanagan and the equally dazed crew of the main battery director below decks, where they met a man whom they did not recognize at first. His face was almost black. His shirt was covered with splotches of blood. 'Where the fuck have you been?' Boats Homewood yelled. 'Get to work on the third deck. It's really bad down there.'

Homewood roared additional orders to clumps of sailors who had come below from other gunnery stations. 'Don't stay down there more than five minutes,' he shouted as Peterson led Flanagan and the others down a ladder. 'Them gases'll burn your lungs out.'

On the third deck the heat was unbelievable. It was like standing inside a furnace. A team of fire fighters from another division reeled toward them. Half of them were carrying or dragging sailors who had passed out. 'There's guys trapped in sick bay,' one said.

'Let's go,' Peterson yelled, unreeling a fire hose. 'Take one big breath and try not to take another one. Just little gulps.'

They raced down the passageway. Flames roared out of compartments to port and starboard. Peterson stopped to fling the hose's mixture of water and foam into them. Wilder flames gushed out of sick bay. It was insanity, Flanagan thought. No one could be alive in there. Peterson doused the fire and peered in through the smoke. 'Cover me,' he said, handing the hose to Flanagan. He crawled in, Flanagan behind him, on the nozzle.

'Oh, Jesus!' he heard Camutti scream. Flames had erupted again just inside the hatch. They were roaring around Camutti and Daley. Flanagan sprayed both them and the fire. They crouched there, gooey foam drooling from their faces. Peterson crawled back through the smoke dragging a body.

'There's another guy back there. I think it's the chaplain,' he gasped.

'I'll get him,' Flanagan said, although his lungs seemed to be shrivelling in the inferno.

Peterson ordered Camutti to take the nozzle, Flanagan crawled along the deck, which was hot enough to fry bacon. The pain in his hands was exquisite. He still had raw burns

315

across his palms from following Homewood up turret one's sizzling ladder. He found the chaplain crumpled beside a bunk, curled into a foetal position. 'O Lord, I believe, help thou mine unbelief,' he whispered when Flanagan turned him over.

Flames gushed out of a corner. 'Cover me, for God's sake,' Flanagan yelled.

Camutti was there, his Frankenstein monster's face wild with fear and fury, spraying the murderous fire. Suddenly his eyes rolled into the back of his head and he collapsed.

Flanagan dragged the chaplain back to Peterson in the hatchway. 'Camutti's down.'

'Go get him,' Jack said.

'The five minutes are up,' Daley yelled, scared shitless as usual.

'Fuck the five minutes. He just saved my life,' Flanagan shouted.

Back through the smoke along the livid deck he crawled. Somehow he got to Camutti, hooked one arm under his shoulder and wrapped the hose around his own arm. 'Pull,' he yelled. Peterson, Daley and the Radical hauled them back to the hatch.

They staggered up on deck with their burdens. 'To whom do I owe my life?' the chaplain murmured.

'Seaman First Class Flanagan,' Peterson said, pumping air into Camutti's lungs.

'Ah, yes. I remember you now.'

'Who's the other guy?' Flanagan asked.

'A fuckin' yeoman,' Peterson said. 'We risked our asses to save the fuckin' chaplain and a yeoman.'

Water slopped over the deck. 'Are we going down?' Flanagan asked.

'They'll tell us before it happens. Let's get back to work,' Jack said.

On the second deck Homewood was still directing fire fighters forward. 'We're lickin' it. They got the pumps goin'. All we got to do now is pray them bulkheads hold, where the bow blew off. They're only three quarters of an inch steel.'

'Maybe we ought to use some of the Captain's joss,' Flanagan said.

'Hey, don't be a wise guy,' Homewood said. 'There ain't many ships that stay afloat when the forward magazine blows. Losin' the bow was what saved us. If it'd stayed on, we'd have had most of that blast and fire inside the ship. It would have hit the engine rooms, and that would have been the end of this old lady.'

Commander George Tombs, the damage control officer, appeared out of the smoke, as blackened and bloody as Homewood. Under his direction, they lugged wooden beams and bedding and steel plates forward to the danger zone. There, shipfitters and machinists were frantically welding the plates against the menaced bulkheads to reinforce them. Flanagan could see the steel bulge as the sea surged against it. Water spurted through jagged holes to starboard and port. They used bedding, rags, to plug these leaks, then smeared them with caulking. For one aggressive rivulet, Homewood stripped off his pants and shirt and demanded Flanagan's. 'If we're gonna feed the fishes, we might as well go bare-assed,' he said.

On the bridge, the big worry was whether the *Jefferson City* might capsize at any moment. Her bottom compartments were flooded up to the forward engine room. The drifting bow had gashed a big hole on the starboard beam below the waterline and ripped off a propeller as it spun past, carrying as least forty men to their deaths. Captain McKay spent the night conferring with George Tombs and Oz Bradley shifting fuel oil and water from the centre of the ship aft to stabilize her. Meanwhile, navigator Marse Lee managed to plot a course on the scorched bridge.

Dawn found them off the mouth of Tulagi Harbour. They eased up the narrow channel before the astonished gaze of Marine sentries and the crews of a half dozen motor torpedo boats. McKay walked out on the wing of the bridge as a Marine called to someone on the deck below him. 'Hey, what happened to your bow?'

'Termites,' bellowed a voice that had to belong to

Boatswain's Mate First Class Ernest Homewood.

It was the rough tough bravado of the Old Navy. Suddenly Arthur McKay loved it. He turned to smile at his haggard executive office. Even Daniel Boone Parker became almost tolerable. 'You know,' he said, 'I think we're going to win this goddamn war.'

Two days later he was not so sure. In his cabin, he stared into the haughty astonished face of Captain George Bass, Admiral Standish's chief of staff. 'You mean to say you don't agree with this report? Every captain in the task force has endorsed it. Your own executive officer supports it.'

'I don't give a goddamn if you've got the Archangel Michael for an eyewitness. We did not sink four ships and damage four others. We hit one ship, and I'm not even sure if we sank her.'

'Captain, your conduct in this battle is open to a certain amount of criticism. Your failure to open fire when ordered, for instance.'

'I don't believe in firing until my gunnery officer has a target. I see no point in lighting up the sky like those idiots on the *Honolulu*. All they did was illuminate us for another spread of torpedoes.'

'I'll note your exception to the report, Captain. Good day.'

Good riddance. Arthur McKay thought. For a brief, beautiful moment, the ferocity of his contempt for Admiral Standish and Captain Bass united him with Win Kemble in his exile in Panama. He sat down at his desk and wrote a letter to Ernest J. King, Commander in Chief, US Fleet, and Chief of Naval Operations.

Dear Admiral King:

I am sitting in Tulagi Harbour with the bow of my ship blown off. The *Minneapolis* and the *New Orleans* followed me in here a few hours later in similar condition. The *Brockton* has gone down with all hands and the *Pensacola* is limping for home with most of her guns missing because we were paraded like a procession of targets in a fleet exercise for a Japanese destroyer flotilla. For God's sake, will you find an admiral who knows something about how to handle destroyers and cruisers? I have never seen anything like the collection of bunglers you have sent out here. If I didn't know you better, I'd swear you were trying to lose this war. We're winning it, but the price is a lot higher than it should be. On behalf of my men and what's left of my ship, I feel compelled to tell you that I consider this a disgrace.

It was amazing, how much good a man could do – or at least try to do – once he abandoned all hope or desire for promotion.

Survivors

Frank Flanagan stood on the platform outside main forward watching the wall of water surge toward them. It smashed into the *Jefferson City*'s prowless jaw with a cannonlike boom. The ship shuddered like a used-up boxer who could do nothing but absorb punches. 'Jesus,' Jack Peterson said, 'a couple more like that will finish us.'

There was nothing in sight but miles of foaming, heaving grey-blue water and slate-grey sky. The Coral Sea had given up all pretence of living up to its name. Occasionally the destroyer escorting them would bob to the top of one of these killer waves and slide into the gulf behind it. Flanagan re-examined the knots on his life jacket. Everyone wore one constantly. Some sailors even wore them while trying to sleep.

For the first three days of their voyage to Australia, Flanagan had lain in his rocking bunk shivering and shaking with a fever of 103. Every ten minutes, so it seemed, he had to dash to a head which was crowded with fellow sufferers of dysentery. They had caught it on the vile island of Tulagi while they toiled in that stinking jungle, cutting down trees that the ship's carpenters carved into a stubby wooden bow for the *Jefferson City*.

The sick bay had been wrecked by the explosion and fire. There was no place to put sick men – and besides, there were too many of them. The pharmacist's mates roamed the ship dispensing some sort of sulfa drug which made many men sicker. Boats Homewood finally banned the medics from F Division and undertook his own cure, which combined bourbon, hot soup and tea.

The illness had left Flanagan drained and depressed. He did not respond to his shipmates' gallows humour or attempts at optimism.

'It's funny,' Jack Peterson said, as another wave churned toward them. 'I don't feature drownin'. I never worried about gettin' blown up, but I don't feature drownin'.'

'We're gonna make it,' Homewood said. 'This kinda weather's the best break we could get. We don't have to worry about submarines. Believe me, this old baby's got a lot of life in her yet.'

Life? Flanagan wondered. He had begun to associate the *Jefferson City* with death and more death. On Tulagi, they had buried forty men they had pried out of the blasted interior of turret one and the handling rooms beneath it. The chaplain had urged them to remember the other forty shipmates who had vanished in the amputated bow. For those who had friends among them, he offered the consolation that they had not suffered, nor had the men in turret one. They had all been killed instantly by the concussion when the forward magazine exploded.

Rigor mortis had set in by the time they took the men out of turret one. They were all frozen in the positions assigned to them at General Quarters. The range finder had his hands spread out, adjusting his lenses. The rammer-men leaned forward, arms outstretched to slam shut the breeches. Many had odd smiles on their faces, as if they welcomed death when it came so swiftly, so painlessly.

'I'd give a million bucks to get off this goddamn thing,' Flanagan said.

'What the hell are you talkin' about?' Homewood said. 'You saved this old lady from goin' under. You got a stake in her now. You're part of her, she's part of your life.'

'You'll feel better when we get to Sydney, kid. That's one of the great liberty towns,' Jack Peterson said.

Boats Homewood grinned. 'Yeah. I was there in 'twenty-five. Them Aussies were the only guys I ever met who could outdrink me in them days.'

'I hear the dames are just as wild as the guys. And horny as hell,' Peterson said. 'All the guys've been fightin' in Egypt for the last two years.'

'Good Christ, look what's coming now,' Flanagan said.

They stared at the biggest moving mountain of water yet.

In his cabin, Chaplain Emerson Bushnell shuddered as the sound and shock of the wave surged through the ship. He was going through the personal effects of the men who had died in the turret and in the lost bow. He had almost a hundred letters to write to grieving parents, wives, sisters or brothers. He picked up the wallet of a gunner's mate who had been in the Navy over ten years. Inside it was a worn envelope on which was scrawled 'To be sent to my wife.'

Bushnell opened the envelope and read: 'Beloved, if anything should happen to me, I want you to know you have always been my sweetheart. There has never been any one else. I thank God every night for you and the children. Kiss Bobby and Jennie for me and remember I love you. Not even death can us part.'

In the wallet of another veteran of the Old Navy, a boatswain's mate second class, was a frayed clipping of a poem entitled 'Mother' pasted to the back of a snapshot of a grey-haired woman standing on the steps of a small farmhouse. Other wallets had more predictable material. Snapshots of sailors on liberty raising glasses of beer, or posing with an ersatz Hawaiian beauty in a photography parlour on River Street in Honolulu.

Remnants of lives he had never touched, lives he had allowed to vanish into the void without achieving a sacred moment, or even a comradely one. As a chaplain, he was a walking fraud. Did the men know it? Few even tried to approach him. The Catholic boy from the Bronx, Flanagan, was the only one with whom he had achieved a shred of intimacy.

Chaplain Bushnell struggled against an overwhelming

despair. It was the simplicity of these lives that stupefied him. Was the gunner's mate's devotion to his wife what it seemed – a wholehearted love? Or had he left this letter as an act of repentance? Was the letter a lie? What about the boatswain's mate who loved his mother? Did that love have any impact on his life? Was he just another drunken brawler when he went on liberty?

Opaque, their lives were all opaque to Chaplain Bushnell. Where he hungered for clarity, the visible details told him nothing. Yet he yearned to bless this crew, this ship. In his deepest self, at the core of his doubt-racked soul, he was a priest. He was the carrier of American faith, generation after generation, since the first believers stepped ashore on New England's inhospitable coast to pledge their covenants with the warrior God Jehovah.

Emerson Bushnell no longer believed in that tribal god. But he could testify to an awareness of an incomprehensible, superhuman presence beyond and within this stupendous universe. He wanted to ask this unknown God to banish the evil that was haunting the *Jefferson City*. But he could not do it; he could not summon any priestly power within himself, much less from heaven, without that moral clarity, that perception of mutual anguish and hope, which he still dreamt of achieving.

Perhaps the Captain was his only chance. If he could achieve genuine communication with him, he might discover in himself the power to bless the ship. He thought he had achieved that communion with Captain Winfield Scott Schley Kemble. But something had been fatally flawed in their encounter. Perhaps Arthur McKay could tell him what had gone wrong. Perhaps he was the man who could restore hope to his soul, meaning to his priesthood.

On the bridge, Captain McKay braced himself for the shock of another wave. It struck them hard and high, sending foam up over the useless guns of turret one. 'Captain,' said the talker, 'Damage Control says that one busted a bulkhead.'

The storm had hit them on their second day out of

Tulagi, and its unrelenting fury had begun to acquire a malevolent cast – as if there really was a curse on them.

McKay studied the ugly sea. 'What do you think of backing into it, Mr West?'

'Why not? It can't be any worse than the beating we're taking now,' Officer of the Deck Montgomery West said.

West's admiration for this shy laconic man kept growing. The way the Captain had dealt with West's spasm of cowardice was not the only reason. Since they sailed from Tulagi five nights ago, the Captain had not left the bridge. Several people urged him to get some sleep in his sea cabin, but he preferred to doze in his bridge chair.

Like the other officers of the deck, West was almost as exhausted by the strain of trying to keep the *Jefferson City* on course with only three propellers. She kept falling off to the starboard and required a correction every five minutes. Navigator Marse Lee had not yet recovered from their going 250 miles off course on the night of their departure from Tulagi. It had not been his fault. Lieutenant MacComber had had the deck and had allowed it to happen.

As far as West was concerned, there was no longer any doubt where he stood in the brawl between the Exec and the Captain. McKay's competence, his ability as a ship-handler and a leader were winning his allegiance. He watched now as the Captain gave the helmsman and the engine room orders that brought the *Jefferson City* about in the tumultuous sea, and they began backing their way to Australia.

'Maybe that will confuse the evil spirits,' McKay said when they had completed the manoeuvre.

'You don't really believe in them, do you Captain?'

'One night when my friend Win Kemble was navigator on the *Saratoga*, he had to bring Bill Halsey back from a party and park him in his stateroom. Win helped the Admiral empty his pockets before he collapsed in his bunk. The number of good luck charms Halsey carried around with him was amazing. They ranged from a four leaf clover to a miraculous medal.'

'I just don't buy the idea that you can change what's going to happen by some ritual or charm, Captain.'

'Maybe it's just a sailor's way of admitting we can't control something as huge as an ocean, as unpredictable as the wind. We're really reciting the Navy Hymn.'

'I hate to admit it, Captain, but I don't know the words.'

A foaming mountain of water crashed over the fantail of the *Jefferson City*, sending another cannonlike boom through the ship. The Captain steadied himself on a stanchion and recited in his quiet casual voice.

> 'Eternal Father, strong to save,
> Whose arm doth bind the restless wave,
> Who bid'st the mighty ocean deep
> Its own appointed limits keep,
> O hear us when we cry to thee
> For those in peril on the sea.'

For a moment Montgomery West could barely breathe. He sensed he was in the presence of something authentic. The Captain was not praying for the *Jefferson City*. They were not yet in the sort of peril that warranted prayer. But McKay took the words seriously. They were part of a tradition, a past, to which he belonged. He was confessing their weakness, their frailty in the face of this ferocious sea, this immensity smashing so savagely at them. But it was a confession tinged with pride, with a kind of confidence.

'That makes me almost glad I joined the Navy,' West said.

'Every so often I feel the same way. Almost glad,' Captain McKay said.

Around midnight, the wind died away and the sea subsided. Captain McKay turned the *Jefferson City* around and resumed the journey to Australia bow-first. He decided he could risk a retreat to his sea cabin. He had barely put his head on the pillow when the Marine sentry tapped on the door. 'Captain, Chaplain Bushnell would like to see you.'

'Come in,' he said.

In a moment Bushnell was sitting beside his bed. He looked spectral in the glow of the dim lamp. 'Captain,' he said, 'I don't know what to do with the effects of those dead men. I can't bear to read another letter, to look at another picture. I'm – I'm overwhelmed.'

'We all get overwhelmed occasionally, Chaplain. Maybe it was a mistake to go through so many of them. Write the condolence letters in small batches, a few each day.'

'Could you help me? I don't know what to say.'

Sometimes exhaustion diffuses the ego, letting the mind's eye see things with extraordinary objectivity. Arthur McKay saw that Emerson Bushnell was trying to draw him into the anguish of grieving, of mourning these men and their meaningless deaths. No one could remain a commander in a war if he yielded to that temptation.

'I wish I could help, Chaplain. I told you – I don't envy you your job.'

Bushnell seemed to crumple in the chair. He began to sob. 'My whole life, my whole life, has been a failure.'

'I'm sure that isn't true either. Pour yourself a stiff drink from someone's bottle, if you haven't got your own, and try to get some sleep.'

With almost miraculous swiftness, Chaplain Bushnell stopped crying. He stalked out of the cabin, his face as blank as a corpse.

Captain McKay's head fell back on the pillow. For a moment he wondered if he had just made an enemy. He was too tired to care.

In the Executive Officer's cabin, Supply Officer Leroy Tompkins gazed in dismay at Daniel Boone Parker. 'Dan, for Christ's sake, get a grip on yourself.'

'No good, Tommy. No good. I'm gone. We're gone. Bastard's got us.'

They had killed most of a bottle of Scotch. Tompkins's bulbous nose was turning red, he was sure of it. It always turned red when he drank too much. He could not understand what was wrong with his old friend. Gone was his swagger, his fuck-'em-all-we'll-get-ours style that had made him the only hero in Leroy Tompkins's forlorn life. Dan Parker had got him into the Navy back in the early 1930s, when the Depression had washed away every job in sight. He had sent him into Supply, and they had been a great team for most of the past ten years. They had been able to laugh up quite a few profitable sleeves at the Annapolis bastards with their fat gold rings on their arrogant fingers.

'What're you talkin' about? How's he got us? He'll never figure out those books. You got to be a CPA to figure out those books the way I got them cooked. We got nothin' to worry about, Dan. For Christ's sake, he's the one who got the fuckin' bow blown off his ship. They ain't gonna like that in Washington.'

Commander Parker was not listening. He stared past Tompkins at a picture of himself on the wall escorting some admiral around London. He started to sob. It was unbelievable. Dan Parker on a crying jag. 'Got us,' he said. 'He knows it. He can make his move anytime. Knows it.'

Panic lapped around Supply Officer Tompkins's ears. It was almost as bad as the night they were torpedoed. 'I don't get it, Dan. I just don't get it. What the fuck's been happenin' on that bridge?'

Toward dawn, a damp cold fog engulfed the *Jefferson City*. For another day they groped through murk.

'I feel as if I've died and I'm on my way to heaven,' Flanagan said.

'Or hell,' Daley said, reminding Flanagan of the mortal sins he had on his soul.

'We couldn't get a better break,' Homewood said. 'The Japs've got subs all around the Australian coast. We'd be an easy shot for any one of them. Christ, we can't even zigzag.'

All through the following night the fog persisted. It was uncanny. Were they really in God's sheltering hand? Flanagan wondered. Why? Why did the *Jefferson City* deserve His protection while the *Atlanta* sank, riddled by two dozen direct hits, the *Juneau* vanished in one stupendous explosion? Why was F Division spared and half of Deck Division One, the men who managed the guns in turret one, dead?

On the bridge, Navigator Marse Lee confidently informed Captain McKay they would be in Sydney Harbour the following morning. At dawn, a summer sun burned away the fog. In an hour they saw huge grey and white cliffs with a spume of waves breaking rhythmically against them. The cliffs ended in a majestic headland. Beyond it, the water frothed and foamed and swirled. A candy-striped lighthouse stood on another headland, beyond this turbulent gap.

On the bridge, Marse Lee pointed triumphantly. 'There it is,' he said. 'That's where we go in.'

'Anything to worry about?' Captain McKay asked.

Lee shook his head. 'It's sixteen hundred yards wide and eighty feet deep. Our worries are over for a while.'

Barely making five knots, the *Jefferson City* steamed slowly between the headlands. A moment later Captain and crew stared, dazed by a city and a harbour that spoke silently but eloquently to their battered spirits.

Safe, said the great rock-sheltered expanse of peaceful water, safe from all your enemies, safe from the treacherous sea, safe from fourteen-inch armour-piercing shells by night and thousand-pound bombs by day. Safe from exploding torpedoes and magazines. Safe from fire and shrapnel and dysentery and fear. Safe and at peace, here in my watery arms.

The city was even more unbelievable than the harbour. Its red-roofed tree-shaded houses crowded the bays and coves in all directions. In the distance a magnificent steel bridge and the dignified buildings of the business centre bespoke power, protection. But it was the houses that whispered something even more wonderful than safety, after three months of almost continuous danger. They spoke of home and women and pleasures the *Jefferson City*'s sailors had almost forgotten.

Turning to port, the battered cruiser limped toward a long line of pilings sunk across the harbour. 'There's a gate at the west end,' Marse Lee said, flourishing his charts.

They headed toward a man-made island to which an antique tug, with a stack at least fifteen feet high, was moored. Hooting a welcome, she briskly went to work pulling aside a submarine net tied to several dozen floating barrels. As they passed the tug, whose deck was littered with an incredible assortment of junk, from empty tin cans to piles of uncoiled line, her five-man crew rushed to the bow to whoop and wave. 'Merry Christmas,' one of them yelled.

'Did I hear him right?' Flanagan said. 'What day is it?'

No one knew. They had lost touch with the calendar. Peterson sent Daley below to Radio Central, where they kept track of such things. He came panting back, wide-eyed. 'It's December twenty-fifth!'

Even Flanagan, who thought nothing could surpass New York, and Jack Peterson, who was loyal to the glories of Seattle's Puget Sound, could not stop gaping at Sydney Harbour. On and on went the coves and inlets and bays and the red-roofed houses on the hillsides around them. On almost every cove was a sandy beach. From several of these, young women in bathing suits waved enthusiastic welcomes.

'Swimming on Christmas Day,' Flanagan whooped. 'I'm going to like this crazy country.'

A ferry waddled past them, its decks filled with cheering, waving people. 'They act like we've won the fucking war,' Camutti said. He clasped his hands over his head like a boxer who had just scored a knockout. 'No point in changing their minds.'

'Let's check out some of those broads with the range finder,' Peterson said.

They jammed into the main battery gun director, and Jack spun them left and right until he found a target. 'Oh, Jesus,' he said. 'Take a look at this, Flan.'

There were five of them, four blondes and a brunette, all in white two-piece bathing suits. The range finder's power brought them inside Flanagan's head, larger than life size. The sun created haloes out of their glowing hair. It glistened on their tanned wet skin. Flanagan could almost hear their excited laughter as they pointed and waved at the heroic Americans and their ravaged ship.

Every time they moved, Flanagan's mouth went dry with desire. He had forgotten the soft curve of a woman's arm, the fullness of her thighs, the supple beauty of her neck. He had forgotten almost everything for the last three months but death. Maybe he was ready for a resurrection.

'Get ready to start livin', kid,' Jack Peterson said.

BOOK THREE

Waltzing Matilda

'Whoo Whoo, Woolloomooloo!'

It was the *Jefferson City*'s new war cry. The first two sections reeled back from liberty to report that Woolloomooloo, the dockside part of Sydney opposite Cockatoo Island, the Australian Navy Yard, had more bars and whorehouses per block than any place they had ever seen.

'It's San Pedro, Frisco's Barbary Coast and River Street in Honolulu rolled into one,' said Boats Homewood. 'It even makes Shanghai look like a goddamn Baptist seminary. And they're givin' Americans the first one free!'

'After that, you just head downtown to Macquarie Place. They've got sixteen-year-olds ready to give you the next two for the same price,' Camutti said, a smile of ecstasy on his pockmarked face. 'I didn't even have to show my scars.'

'You got to be careful,' George Jablonsky said, prone on his rack, his voice a croak. 'These broads don't know the word stop. They must have Polish blood somewhere.'

'They're athletes,' crooned Bob Edison, 'Marvellous athletes. I haven't seen anything like it since I left Minnesota.'

'I didn't see anything like it *in* Minnesota,' groaned his Bobbsey Twin, Bob Finch.

'You mean those people on the ferry weren't kiddin'? They really think we're winnin' this war?' Jack Peterson asked.

'I don't know about that,' Camutti said. 'But they're awful glad to see us. Wait'll you get a look at downtown. All the storefront windows are boarded up like they expect a hundred fifty Jap planes overhead tomorrow morning.'

'I hope you assholes told them how single-handed we beat back the Oriental hordes', Jack said. 'One fuckin' cruiser against all the battleships in the Combined Fleet.'

'They know we're one fuckin' cruiser, I can tell you that much,' Homewood said, stealing Jablonsky's favourite joke.

Later, up in main forward, Jack reminded Flanagan of his

disdain for this kind of carousing. 'That ain't the way to operate, Flan. The same thing goes here as in Long Beach. The only way we can have a time to remember is to find some respectable dames with a house – someplace where we can settle in and get to know them. You gotta operate like the officers. You don't see any of them blowin' their cash and riskin' the clap in Woolloomooloo.'

'How the hell do we manage that in a foreign country?'

'I don't know. Let's see what turns up.'

'I'll settle for a good time in Woolloomooloo,' Flanagan said.

He was not sure he wanted to get to know another woman, although the brunette in the white bathing suit he had seen in the range finder aroused him every time he thought about her. Teresa Brownlow was giving him enough trouble to absorb most of his emotions. He had received another letter from her reporting her father's continuing decline and her mounting fear that his sorrows were her fault.

The next day was Sunday. They hit Woolloomooloo at 9 a.m. planning to have a drink to improve their morale before launching their search for respectable women. Flanagan's experience in Honolulu inclined him to rate their chance of success near zero. Daley and Jim Booth tagged along, the Radical proclaiming his eagerness to meet some of the more extreme members of the Australian labour movement, which had supposedly all but defeated capitalism when the Great Depression struck.

They gazed in astonishment up Bourke Street, touted by their shipmates as the heart of Woolloomooloo. There was scarcely a human being in sight. The bars were shuttered and silent. Not a trace of a gaudy lady gazing from the window of a palace of pleasure. Jack strolled over to some bored-looking Shore Patrol. 'What the hell's goin' on? Has a poison gas attack wiped out the city and nobody told us?'

'It's Sunday, pal,' said the weather-beaten boatswain's mate first class in charge of the patrol. 'In Sydney, that's a day of rest. As in rest in peace.'

'You want the address of the nearest cemetery?' asked a grinning gunner's mate. 'It's the hottest spot in town.'

'Whoo whoo, Woolloomooloo,' Flanagan said.

'This could be the best thing that ever happened to us,' Jack Peterson said. 'Now we gotta find some decent dames. There ain't any other kind available.'

'How?' Flanagan said.

'We gonna go where they are,' Jack said. 'We're goin' to church.'

A half hour later, they were sitting in the front pew of a Catholic church in the middle class part of Sydney known as Paddington. A cabbie with a thick Irish brogue had suggested it, and refused to accept any money for the trip. Flanagan found himself growing more and more uneasy. Memories of his encounter with Teresa Brownlow floated through his mind. Was God trying to correct that mistake by sending him back to the one true apostolic church? If so, how did He let a character whose intentions were as dishonourable as Jack Peterson's in the door?

A pudgy pug-nosed priest with a brogue as thick as the cabbie's smiled down at them from the pulpit and welcomed them to Australia. He threw in a eulogy to their courage and said he hoped the parishioners would make sure these brave lads enjoyed themselves in Sydney on Sunday in spite of the wowsers. The Americans did not know what he was talking about, but they soon learned. The Catholics, mostly Irish, detested Sydney's Protestant version of Sunday. A wowser was a frozen-faced Protestant aristocrat, usually pictured in a high black hat carrying a Neville Chamberlain umbrella, who perpetually campaigned against drunkenness, lewd behaviour and similar vices most Australians had taken to their roistering hearts.

Outside the church, people swarmed around them, hurling invitations to dinner. Jack Peterson accepted one from stout Mrs Lundin, who had a blond bosomy daughter named Sally smiling beside her. He nudged Flanagan into the house of broad-beamed Mrs Flood, whose tall dark-haired daughter Annie smiled beside her. The smile was somewhat contradicted by the cool appraisal in her green eyes. Daley and the Radical were swept off by two other families.

Mrs Flood served up a six-pound steak for four people.

Her longshoreman husband, whose girth matched his wife's, dug in and Flanagan followed his example. They washed it down with about a gallon of beer and numerous denunciations of the wowsers. Flanagan regaled them with stories of the *Jefferson City*'s exploits, which did not require much embellishment. He had barely said a word to Annie when Mrs Lundin arrived with Jack and Sally. 'It's such a beautiful day, and Mr Peterson here says he's yet to put his toe in our saltwater,' Mrs Lundin said. 'They could all have a lovely time at our place on Maroubra Beach, don't you think?'

'Are you game, Annie?' Mrs Flood asked.

'Sure,' Annie said.

'Lovely, we'll get the others,' Sally said. She took Jack's hand with a look that practically guaranteed amour. Old Poppa Jack had obviously turned all engines in his charm machine ahead full.

Annie found a bathing suit for Flanagan, and Mrs Flood filled a picnic basket with beer and goodies for supper. Outside, a horn began to blow. They found Jack behind the wheel of a 1936 Ford that looked as decrepit as Martha Johnson's Chevrolet. As they went down the steps, Annie said, 'Let's get one thing straight, Yank. I'm not yours for the asking.'

'Oh, yes. Gwen and I were quite good friends for a year or so in London. Do you know her well?'

'I've worked with her in a picture or two.'

'Ah. She can be a bit standoffish. But if she changes her mind, she can be . . . quite something. I must say I was almost glad the war started. She was wearing me out.'

Charles Benbow had one of those double faces. The right side was noble, valiant, serene. The left side was crafty, crass, petty. Montgomery West cursed himself for going anywhere near the man. They were sitting at a table on the veranda of the Officer's Club on Cockatoo Island in Sydney Harbour. A few hundred yards away, swarms of workers were putting a new bow on the *Jefferson City*.

Benbow had some vague liaison role with the Australian Navy which left him free to spend an inordinate amount of time in the club bar. West had inevitably been introduced to him as a fellow actor. In that first encounter, he had resisted his Uncle Mort's suggestion that he ask Benbow about Ina Severn. But his resistance had slowly crumbled in the ensuing week, as Benbow greeted him every time he walked into the bar.

They talked shop for a while. Benbow was obviously hoping that meeting Americans would improve his chances of getting an offer from Hollywood. He seemed to be in charge of making sure visiting actors and actresses from England and America entertained Australian as well as American troops. The Home Army, which the Aussies had frantically scratched together when the Japanese threatened to invade, seemed to be a major worry. Benbow referred to them as bloody slackers because they had not volunteered to fight Hitler. Australia had no conscription.

'Oh, by the way. Friend of yours is in town with Bob Hope and his gang. Claire Carraway. She asked me to give you her number. She'll be at the Wentworth until next Wednesday.'

Claire Carraway: Red hair, a figure that made even jaded casting directors sit up straight, a theatrical temperament – without the talent to match any of it. But a woman. Memories of several weekends on Catalina Island momentarily made Montgomery West clutch the arm of his chair like a man afraid of falling from a great height.

'You will call her, won't you, old sock?' Benbow said. 'I've got to spend two weeks in Queensland with her and I got the distinct sensation she would make my life miserable if I didn't deliver you to her door.'

'Sure. Sure I'll call her,' West said, simultaneously vowing to do no such thing. After three months of celibacy in the bowels of the *Jefferson City*, one look at Claire Carraway would be fatal.

West found himself wondering how to describe meeting Charles Benbow. Not fatal. Maybe just traumatic. Maybe the difference between getting run over by a small English car and a seven-passenger Packard. He would be limping for a few days, but he would recover. If he managed to avoid Claire.

The thought of Gwen in that two-faced bastard's arms, kissing that spoiled mouth.

Maybe he had been run over by a small English car travelling at very high speed. Maybe it would not make much difference what happened if he strolled into the path of the Packard.

On his first liberty, Marty Roth had joined the rest of the black gang in Woolloomooloo. They had taken over a small hotel and recruited females of all ages and sizes to join them there for an ongoing orgy. Roth had used booze and a half dozen women whose names he barely remembered to obliterate Sylvia Morison from his memory. Except that she refused to disappear. Even while he was balling away, he imagined Sylvia wide-eyed beside the bed begging, *Oh Marty, do that to me, please.* He heard himself using a famous Navy phrase for the first time with scientific exactness: *Go fuck yourself.*

Amos Cartwright had been in the middle of the madness, downing gallons of Aussie beer, cheerfully entertaining as many as three women in his bed at the same time. The next morning, reveille, complete with the bugle which was blown only in port, was an agonizing experience. Everyone had a head the size of a dirigible. Roth, who had never had a hangover before, felt particularly miserable. Noxious gases rose from his bowels into his brain. Dying in superheated steam could not be any worse. It was Sylvia's revenge. She stood beside his rack in her pink silk panties, whispering, *Better you than me, sucker.*

Roth noticed the old salts liked their hangovers. They discussed them with pride, almost with affection. The hangover proved you were a real sailor. Even Amos Cartwright chimed in with picturesque descriptions of his torments. It was the first time Roth saw Cartwright achieve some camaraderie with his fellow petty officers. Roth felt too exquisitely horrible to buy it. There had to be a better way to escape Sylvia.

The following day, sections one and three returned with drunken assurances that the steam was still up at the Hardon Hotel. 'You want to do that again, or look for somethin' interestin'?' Cartwright asked.

'What've you got in mind?' Roth asked.

'I hear they got some original niggers in this country.

Aborigines, they call 'em. I got a mind to locate a few. Always wanted to meet me some original niggers. Never been on a ship that got to Africa.'

'Why not?' Roth said.

Several hours later, with the help of directions from an assistant curator at the Museum of Natural History and a hitch on a US Army truck, they found themselves on the bank of a river about a dozen miles from Sydney. Ahead of them in the twilight loomed a collection of shanties with slanted tin roofs perched precariously on walls ripped from packing cases.

A half dozen small black men with woolly hair were crouched around a fire cooking a fish. They wore cheap dungarees and shirts. Their feet were bare. Cartwright held up his hand, palm out, the way white scouts greeted Indians in the movies, and said, 'Howdy, brothers.'

No one even bothered to look up. A half dozen tiny brown kids were playing in front of the shacks, naked. Roth could not figure out why they were a different colour from the men, whose skin was sooty black. Then a woman came to the door of the hut carrying a baby. She was sooty black too. But the baby was white.

Without looking up, one of the men around the fire said, 'Go away. Our women are not for sale.'

'We didn't come here for that. I'm interested in how black people live around the world. I'm a black American. This fellow here's a Jew. He's a friend of black people.'

'A woman Jew brings us food sometimes. Do you have anything for us?'

'Not me,' Roth said. 'I'm broke.'

'How come you live out here this way?' Cartwright asked.

'Our people die in the city. They can't breathe in those houses. When the white men get drunk they beat us up and take our women.'

A car stopped on the highway above them. A young woman in a tan suit came down the hill toward them. She had a sharply defined nose and prim pursed lips. Nervously adjusting a pair of steel-rimmed glasses, she said, 'What are you seamen doing here?' Her accent was strange, definitely not Australian.

Cartwright tried to explain. She did not believe him. Meanwhile, the men around the fire and a dozen women and children from the shacks streamed up the hill to the car. They lugged cartons from the back seat down to the shacks. They talked excitedly in their own language, looking and sounding like pleased children at a birthday party.

'Are you the Jew lady that brings them food?' Cartwright asked.

'I bring them food, yes. What does being Jewish have to do with it?'

'Not a thing. 'Cept this sailor's Jewish. Meet Fireman First Class Marty Roth from the Bronx, New York.'

'How do you do,' she said, holding out her hand. 'My name is Anna Elias. I am from Vienna.'

'That's a long way from here. Why'd you come to Australia?' Cartwright asked.

She gave him a puzzled, somewhat angry look. 'To stay alive. Don't you know Hitler is killing the Jews in Europe?'

'We don't get newspapers on a ship. I heard he was givin' them a lot of grief, sort of like whites give blacks in the US. Now he's killin' them?' Cartwright said.

'Yes. Soon they'll be like these people. A pathetic remnant everyone despises. Don't you in America see this?' She aimed the question at Roth.

'I don't know. I mean – I guess so,' Roth said. 'But we're pretty busy trying to earn a living. I don't know what we can do about it. Except join the Army and Navy and try to win the war.'

'Yes,' Anna Elias said, in the saddest voice he had ever heard. 'Yes of course you're right. I can't understand why the world doesn't cry out. But who has wept over these people?'

'Are they really being exterminated?' Roth asked.

'They have been exterminated. They exist now in little groups like this one. Their life force, their sense of existing as a people, even a tribe, is gone. Once this whole continent was their country. Now it belongs to another race. They are ghosts in their own country. They live mostly in the dreamtime.'

'What's that?' Cartwright asked.

'It's where they believe we all come from. The eternal soul of the world. It's amazingly similar to the insights of Jung.'

Marty Roth could only look blank. He had never heard of Carl Jung. He had also never met a woman with the kind of fierce intelligence Anna Elias emanated. Amos Cartwright had convinced him that he had a brain. Maybe this woman could help him put something in it besides the thermodynamics of the *Jefferson City*'s fire room.

'The dreamtime,' Amos Cartwright said. 'Now I know I want to get acquainted with these dudes.'

Immaculate in their dress whites, the officers of the *Jefferson City* swarmed on the quarterdeck on their way to a dinner dance in their honour at the Vaucluse Yacht Club. Vaucluse was one of the most elegant suburbs of Sydney, and they got a lecture from Captain McKay, warning them to conduct themselves like gentlemen. 'These are not the sort of women you'll meet in Woolloomooloo,' he said.

The junior officers exchanged furtive grins. The Captain was practically in his dotage. He had no idea what supposedly upper class women were willing to do for a man in a uniform, fresh from risking mutilation and death on the high seas. They had made that marvellous discovery in California. With Lieutenant Robert Mullenoe, the fabled swordsman of the class of '31 at their head, these connoisseurs of female frailty headed for Vaucluse aboard a chartered harbour ferry, all but panting in anticipation.

For the first hour, nothing seemed to suggest they were wrong. The women were spectacular in white muslin or silk. The punch was swiftly spiked to lethal proportions with brandy and champagne. They danced beneath a ceiling festooned with Australian and American flags and made relentless progress in their pursuit of happiness. Still depressed by his brother's death aboard the *Hornet*, Mullenoe was determined to enjoy himself. He was fox-trotting with a pert stacked redhead named Ellen McKinley, who seemed incredibly interested in his analysis of American dance bands. As the number ended, he suggested a stroll on the beach. She cheerfully agreed, but as they emerged on the terrace she stopped and murmured an exclamation of concern.

'Christine?' she said, and walked toward a woman who was standing alone looking out at the water.

'Oh – Ellen.'

'You promised me you'd dance.'

'Oh, I will. It was just . . . rather warm in there. I needed a breath of air.'

'Leftenant Mullenoe, I'd like you to meet my sister, Mrs Wallace.'

She was taller and older than Ellen – closer to his own age, Mullenoe guessed. Her pageboy-cut hair was a deep russet. Her delicate features, particularly her sensitive mouth, suggested a refinement her sister lacked. It was the sort of woman Mullenoe usually fled. He was dismayed when Ellen McKinley said, 'Why don't you two chat while I go get us some punch?'

An old hand at avoiding such traps, Mullenoe protested that he would get the punch. But Ellen McKinley tossed her red head and said, 'You're in Australia, Leftenant. The men don't wait on the women like Americans. We're used to doing for ourselves, thank you.'

Catastrophe. He was certain Ellen McKinley would never return with the punch. At least four of his wolfish shipmates had been eyeing her. He was stuck with conversing with her married sister while the crux of the evening escaped him. Unquestionably, he was born under a dark star. First an assignment to the *Jefferson City*, with Edwin Moss for a gunnery officer, now this.

'Is your husband in the service?' he said, deciding to be as brutal as possible about the main point.

'Yes. I mean . . . he was.'

'Wounded in action?'

'He was killed at Savo Island.'

'I'm . . . I'm sorry,' he floundered. 'What was his rank?'

'Leftenant. He was air defence officer on the *Canberra*.'

Mullenoe had the distinct sensation of being struck on the back of the head by a heavy instrument. 'I'm air defence officer of the *Jefferson City*.'

'How remarkable. You were in the battle, I take it.'

'Yes, we . . . were very lucky.'

He was back six months, back in that black murderous night, hearing the boom of guns, seeing the *Canberra* reel under a rain of six- and eight-inch shells, watching the flames engulf her.

'Thank God someone was lucky. I gather it was an almost total defeat.'

'About as total as defeats can get. Was your husband a career officer?'

'Yes. His father was an admiral in World War One.'

'So was mine.'

Mullenoe heard a hollow bewilderment in his voice. The band struck up 'The White Cliffs of Dover'. 'Would you like to dance?' he said.

Beneath the ballroom's chandeliers, he found a mysterious woman in his arms. The mystery was in her voice, a soft contralto with an extraordinary number of tones. It suggested a spiritual world Mullenoe had never explored. So did her dark blue eyes, full of sadness and something else, a word, an idea at which Mullenoe would have scoffed ten minutes ago: nobility. Christine Wallace reminded him of a poem that Selvage MacComber used to quote by the yard, 'The Blessed Damozel'. Something about a woman of impossible purity reaching down to bestow her blessing from the bar of heaven.

On the bandstand a tenor sang:

'There'll be bluebirds over
The white cliffs of Dover
Tomorrow, when the world is free.'

Air defence officer of the Canberra. The words resounded in Mullenoe's mind. He began telling Christine Wallace about his brother's death aboard the *Hornet*, trying to explain how it had changed his feelings not only about the Navy but about himself.

'It may sound crazy to you, but before I didn't care whether I got killed or not. Now I'd like to live. I'd like to see how far I can go in the service. It probably won't be very far, considering my unvarying mediocrity—'

'I refuse to believe in your mediocrity, Leftenant.'

'I'll send you a few of my fitness reports. They usually begin with something like this: "Lieutenant Mullenoe has the ability to do a better job. But he seems lacking in motivation, indeed there are times when he positively seems to take pleasure in failing to measure up to his superiors' expectations."'

'Do you?'

'Absolutely.'

'But they all know what's wrong – your superiors, I mean. Nap – my husband Napier – was exactly the same way. They have much more patience than you ever suspect.'

'Who's they?'

'Your superiors. I'm sure you've heard all this from your wife.'

'I don't have a wife.'

A shadow of grief, of pain, descended on her face.

'I'm sorry,' he said.

'It's entirely my fault. I shouldn't have come. I am – what do you call it in America? – a wet blanket at any party these days. Ellen insisted I should pretend that I'm perfectly fine. She and my mother maintain that if you pretend hard enough you can actually convince yourself –'

'Sounds like some of the advice I used to get from my father.'

'I fear you're incorrigible, Leftenant.'

'I hope so.'

She threatened something fundamental in his mind, a basic part of his idea of himself. Yet he could not stop dancing and talking with her. He did not even glance at another woman for the rest of the evening. By midnight, the punch had taken its toll. Christine said she was incapable of driving home, and he volunteered to pilot her Aston Martin, even though it was the first time he had driven on the English side of the road since he had visited Jamaica as a midshipman.

Following her directions, they soon left Sydney for the countryside. He let the roadster out, and they raced down narrow roads past orchards and fields redolent with fresh grass and blossoming fruit. 'I could swear I'm back in Maryland,' Mullenoe said. He could not understand why he felt so cheerful.

'With your favourite girl?'

'Never had one.'

Large gates loomed on the left. 'That's it,' she said. In second gear they purred up a winding gravel road to a grey stone house that looked as big as Bancroft Hall. It straddled the top of the ridge, huge wings vanishing into the darkness on both sides of the porticoed entrance.

'Welcome to Fairy Hill,' she said.

'You live here – alone?' Mullenoe said.

'Oh, no. There are servants. Too many, I'm afraid.'

Now was the moment, in the unwritten but nonetheless classic textbook on seduction by Mullenoe the swordsman of '31. With any other woman, he would have invited himself for a drink, then suggested at a strategic moment there might be a better way to say good night. Instead, for reasons incomprehensible to him, he said, 'I'd like to see you again.'

'You'll have to bring back the car. Stay for dinner.'

'The car? Right. I can't walk back to Cockatoo Island, can I?'

They both found this uproarious, even though in the back of Mullenoe's head a voice was growling, *Idiot*. He was acting like a plebe at his first hop.

'I have the duty tomorrow.' His voice was so mournful, it sounded as if it was a suicide mission.

'The day after?'

'Great.'

He wanted to kiss her, but he was paralyzed by something. It was not fear. It was more complicated than fear. She solved it by kissing him softly, firmly on the lips. 'Thank you very much for a lovely evening, Leftenant,' she said.

It was a good thing he was in Australia, where the women did for themselves.

Desire under the Coolabahs

Marty Roth strolled through the Taronga Zoo, enjoying the sunshine, the view of Sydney across the harbour – and Anna Elias's company. He had spent every liberty with her for the past two weeks.

Anna pointed to a small striped-tail kangaroo sitting on a fence, eating a piece of fruit. 'The tree kangaroo is a fascinating example of the reversal of an evolutionary trend,' she said. 'The whole design of the kangaroo's body is for hopping over the ground. But this branch of the species began climbing trees and in a million years or so reduced the size of their hind legs and increased their forelegs. Australia is really a marvellous country. I'm glad I came here. It stimulates the mind.'

'Are you going to live here after the war?'

'Of course not. We'll go back to Vienna.'

'Why not try New York?'

'I cannot imagine living happily anywhere but Vienna.'

'Bunk.'

'Martin. We've discussed very seriously the many grave differences between us.'

'So what. I'm still nuts about you.'

'I can't stand American slang! It's so undignified!'

'The feeling isn't undignified.'

'You live too much in your feelings.'

'I'm an example of reverse evolution. You live too much in your head.'

'I thought you appreciated my head.'

'I do. Haven't I read every book you've given me? Now I want to appreciate all of you.'

'You make me glad I'm from Austria, which doesn't have a navy.'

'If what you think is happening over there is true, if they're murdering Jews on a mass scale, you'll never be able to go back. You'll have to settle for some brainless ocker, or an American schmuck like me.'

'You're not a schmuck. You have a fine intelligence. But it will take time to develop it. I wonder if it can be done in America, where piling up money is all anyone cares about.'

'Come out to the cottage my buddy Flanagan's got on Maroubra Beach. Get to know some Americans. Some Australians.'

'No. You just want to seduce me.'

'I just want you to practise a little reverse evolution. I want you to evolve back from one hundred and three to nineteen.'

Anna was attending the University of New South Wales in Sydney. But she had made very few friends. She regarded the Australians as frivolous children. She spent most of her time in the small circle of refugees her parents' age. After a night of listening to them discuss Freud and Jung and Heidegger, Roth had decided he was never going to be an intellectual.

'OK. Let's go home. I'll call you for another lecture appointment next week.'

'Where will you go for the rest of your liberty?'

'Woolloomooloo.'

'Martin! You'll catch a social disease.'

'Better that than an intellectual hernia.'

'You Americans have no manners! No tact, no nobility of soul! You don't know how to address a woman's feelings!'

'You Viennese are so busy lecturing you won't give us a chance!'

'Oh, look.'

Anna pointed to the koala cage. One of the toy-sized bears was climbing the tree inside the cage, with a baby clinging to her back. Another koala, perhaps the father, watched anxiously from a nearby branch.

'You may think it's foolish,' Anna said, 'but I've made a vow not to rejoice, not to enjoy my life, while so many of our people are dying.'

'I know that,' Roth said, taking her hand. 'I admire you for it. If it would help, I'd do the same. But we can't change what's happening six thousand miles away.'

'I know,' Anna said, staring at the koalas. 'I know it makes no sense, but I can't stop it.'

'Anna, you've made me proud to be Jewish. Just knowing

there are people like you and your parents makes me proud. You've changed me, Anna. Now I want to change you. Doesn't the Bible have something about there being a time to weep and a time to laugh, a time to mourn and a time to dance?'

'Ecclesiastes.'

'This is my time – this couple of weeks here – to try to laugh, to dance. When we go back to the Solomons, there'll be plenty of time to weep – maybe to mourn.'

'Where is this cottage?'

'Maroubra Beach.'

'That's only half an hour away.'

'All 'round my hat, I will wear the green willow,
All 'round my hat, for a twelve month and a day.
If anyone should ask me the reason why I'm wearin' it –
It's all for my true love, who's far away.'

Dark-haired, green-eyed Annie Flood thrummed her guitar and sang these words to Frank Flanagan with a deliciously defiant smile on her freckled face. Flanagan sprawled on the sand meditating on the madness of his life. Four weeks ago, he had been crawling down a smoke-filled passageway with flames roaring out hatches to port and starboard. Three weeks ago, he had been clutching his life preserver while fifty-foot waves tried to smash the *Jefferson City* to pieces. Two weeks ago, he had stood on the empty sidewalk in Woolloomooloo bemoaning Sunday in Sydney. Now he was lying on a beach with Pacific combers breaking behind him, listening to a passionate young woman tell him that she loved him and yet could never love him and nevertheless loved him in spite of – or perhaps because of – sin and war and death.

Jack Peterson lay a few feet away, his arm round curvacious Sally Lundin. Nearby was Leo Daley, the pious prude himself, holding hands with a creature who looked like Betty Grable's kid sister. The Radical, the man who worshipped revolution, was gazing into the eyes of a redhead who had convinced him even Communists could fall in love.

Jack rolled over and whispered in Flanagan's ear. 'Go for it, kid. All you got to do is ask.'

Flanagan shook his head. He wanted and did not want to fuck Annie Flood in almost exactly the same intense proportions as she wanted and did not want to fuck him.

At first these amorous women seemed to have been conjured out of the thinnest imaginable air by Jack Peterson. For a while, Flanagan's admiration for Jack rose to hero worship. Now Flanagan was not sure Jack deserved accolades. He was still glad Peterson had got them out of the dives and brothels of Woolloomooloo with his magnificent church manoeuvre. It was amazing the way Jack's goddess, Lady Luck, had matched them up. Each seemed to have found a woman that perfectly suited his idiosyncrasies.

Daley had dined with towering Mrs Monaghan, whose luscious daughter Stella was the most devout girl in Paddington. She was supposed to be going in the convent next month. They spent their time discussing whether she could become a nun if she was no longer a virgin. No one was sure whether this discussion was based on theory or fact. Daley turned the colour of a ketchup bottle every time Flanagan asked him about it.

The Radical landed in the house of the most militant labour leader in Australia. His red-haired daughter Hilary told him harrowing stories of Sydney during the Depression, when the city was ringed with soup kitchens and grown men begged money on the street. The Radical's lonely crusade aboard the *Jefferson City* was heroism to her. A sexual conflagration was inevitable.

Jack accepted the whole thing as a gift from his deity. 'Enjoy it while it lasts, Flan,' he said.

Jack was still enjoying it. But Sally Lundin wept every time she thought of him sailing away. She was lending him money, begging him to promise her that he would come back to Sydney after the war. As usual, Jack was promising nothing. He was advertising himself as the original sailor, doomed to wander the world like that mythical Jew. Jack simply refused to think about the heartbreak he was adding to Sally's already burdened life. Her father was a crippled veteran of World War I. Two months ago her fiancé had been killed flying a bomber over Germany.

That was the trouble with Jack's approach to women. He kept insisting you could keep everything simple. But it was impossible. Women were not just bundles of curving flesh and kissable mouths that said yes Jack, yes Frank. They were individuals with stories to tell, and you had to listen to them. You had to start caring about them. Flanagan wondered if he would ever master Jack's ability to care and not to care simultaneously. To want a woman as honest and loving as Martha Johnson or Sally Lundin and say no to their love the moment they confessed it, without giving a damn how much you were hurting them.

On sang Annie Flood, telling them how her true love had brought her a diamond ring. Then he had promptly tried to deprive her of 'a far finer thing'.

'Very Australian, that,' sighed Sally, snuggling up to Jack.

Flanagan knew that for Annie the song had a personal meaning. She really had a true love far, far away. She was engaged to an Australian soldier named Frank Clancy, who was fighting in Egypt. He was her older brother's best friend. She was not sure she loved Clancy any more. She was not sure she even wanted to see him again, since her brother had been killed at Tobruk.

It was staggering, the way the war in Europe reached halfway around the world to inflict wounds on the Australians. It was even more unnerving to see people so much like Americans riven by the fear of being overrun by the Japanese Army that had raped Nanking and Singapore. For the first time Flanagan appreciated the American strategy of fighting the Japanese in the western Pacific instead of waiting for them to attack closer to home. He would not want his mother or his sisters to feel the fear rampaging through Australia. Maybe the admirals and generals knew what they were doing after all.

Once more Annie struck the defiant chord of the refrain and reiterated her determination to wear the green willow around her hat.

'And if anyone should ask me,
The reason why I'm wearin' it —
It's my own damned hat!'

'Is that an Irish song?' Flanagan asked.

'You wouldn't recognize an Irish song or an Irish poem if it bit you, poor Americanized clod that you are,' Annie said.

'Hey, what's wrong with being Americanized?' Jack Peterson demanded.

'There's nothing wrong with it for most people. Except for making them awfully self-satisfied. But for the Irish it's a crime. They have a heritage of song and story the British have spent four hundred years trying to destroy.'

'We got song and story in America too,' Jack said. 'My old man sang real good in the shower. He was always tellin' my mother stories. But she never believed him.'

Jack and Annie were constantly crossing swords. Unlike plaintive, clinging Sally, Annie resisted the presumption that every woman in Australia wanted to leap into bed with an American soldier, sailor or airman. She took her Catholicism seriously. She was also the granddaughter of an Irish rebel who had fled to Australia in the 1890s, and she still had a large streak of his defiance in her makeup.

'Don't waste your breath arguing with the lug,' Flanagan said. 'Let's go for a walk.' He took Annie's hand and they strolled down the curving beach together.

'Supper's at eight,' Sally called.

'Yeah. You can't live on love, Flanagan,' Jack said. 'Not that you've had a chance to try. Too bad you drew the frigid one. But I guess you're used to takin' orders from the Pope.'

'Bastard,' Annie said.

Jack insisted he knew what he was doing. He guaranteed Flanagan satisfaction before they sailed.

'Imelda?'

The name leaped from Captain Arthur McKay's lips as he strode up posh Macquarie Street in downtown Sydney. The woman walked toward the silver Rolls-Royce with the Chinese chauffeur at the door stopped. A smile blending disbelief, joy and desire played across her delicate, foxy face. McKay instantly regretted opening his mouth. The last thing he wanted or needed in his life at the moment was Imelda Cruz.

351

'Arthur. Arthur McKay.'

A kiss, expensive perfume, a huge diamond glittering on the third finger of her left hand. 'What in the world are you doing in Sydney?' she asked.

'I'm fighting a war. What are you doing?'

'Fleeing one,' she said, the smile slipping from her red lips, to be replaced by a tremor of sadness.

'It looks like you're doing it in style.'

'Of course. As my husband says, wars are never catastrophes to those who look ahead.'

The smile flickered for a moment and vanished again. 'How is Win? What glorious deeds has he performed?'

'Oh – we'd be here all day if I started reciting them.'

'And you, Arthur?'

'I'm commanding a cruiser. The *Jefferson City*.'

She looked bewildered. 'Isn't that Win's ship? I saw him in Manila just before the war started. It was talking with him that made up my husband's mind to get out.'

'Is your husband here in Australia with you?'

'I suppose you could say that, in the most literal sense.'

Arthur McKay knew what was coming next. He did not want to hear it. He did not want to know the story of Imelda's unhappy marriage. Twenty years ago, walking the beach at Cavite, he had listened to Imelda lament her fate. She had been auctioned off by her family to Manuel Ortiz, one of the slimier specimens in the sewers of Philippines politics. McKay had declined to divorce his wife and rescue her, although he knew Imelda offered him a blind, absolute devotion he would never receive from Rita.

Imelda had not really expected him to say yes. Like most Filipino women, she was resigned to the infidelity of American lovers, which was a prelude to the infidelity of a Filipino husband. McKay had sensed the strange Spanish-inherited fondness for suffering that the Philippines' Catholicism bred in its women, the secret willingness with which they let men abuse them, thereby enabling them to identify with the sorrowful Virgin Mother and ultimately with the sad fate of Mater Filipinas herself, their unfortunate country.

Arthur McKay did not want to hear Imelda's story. He was

not sure he could cope with any more problems in his life at the moment. His executive officer had been drunk since they arrived in Sydney. His chaplain had taken to his bed in a funk that Dr Cadwallader called a depression. McKay had been forced to ask First Lieutenant George Tombs to take over the responsibility for writing letters to the fiancées, parents, wives of the dead. George accepted the chore without a murmur. Maybe he was glad to have an excuse to stay on the ship and avoid the temptations of Sydney. He was happily married to a cheerful redhead whose admiration for him seemed impervious to the lousy way the Navy treated him.

In spite of – or perhaps because of – these doleful thoughts, Imelda tempted Captain McKay. She was an escape from the dismal present. She was part of his sailor's youth, before it ebbed into responsibility and ambition. McKay could hear Win Kemble whispering at the dance in the residence of the High Commissioner to the Philippines. 'That's the one. Imelda Cruz. Incredibly willing. She'd do anything you suggest. Just don't listen to the complaints afterwards.'

Win had already broken her heart, of course. But that was not necessarily a defect, as McKay had discovered in other ports. Broken hearts made women more willing, often more passionate, if you arrived on the scene immediately after the fracture. The consoler could become more beloved than the heartless villain, as long as he did not mind an occasional sigh of longing for the lost predecessor. That was how things had gone with Imelda.

'Come to me tonight. For dinner. My husband is in Melbourne bribing American politicians, as usual.'

'Imelda, I have a shot-up ship to worry about. A thousand sailors running wild.'

'It's only one night, Arthur. Are you afraid to remember?'

Was he? Women were uncanny in their ability to penetrate a man's defences. Maybe they should be the admirals.

'Of course not. What's the address?'

'The car will pick you up at seven. Oh, Arthur, I knew you were here. I saw your name in the paper. I wanted to call you, but –'

'Tonight,' he said and fled to the relative safety of a

conference with Australian police and Navy officers. They were trying to head off the riot that was about to erupt between American soldiers and sailors and local males enraged by the mass seduction of their women.

Frank Flanagan trudged along Maroubra Beach, his arm around Annie Flood's waist. Jack Peterson could not understand why Flanagan had yet to score with Annie. From his lofty years of experience as a seducer, he had pronounced her ready and secretly willing. The guerrilla attacks he had made against her virtue had done their job. All Flanagan needed now was a little aggression. 'One hot kiss,' Jack had told him last night. 'She'll be on her back groaning for it. She's nuts about you.'

Unfortunately, Flanagan did not want Annie that way. He understood all too well her complicated feelings about sin and desire. The knowledge immobilized him.

The sun was sinking somewhere in the vast empty interior of Australia. Flanagan stared out at the twilit Pacific. There was nothing in sight – not an island, a ship. The emptiness seemed to underscore Australia's isolation here at the bottom of the world. The ocean's utter blankness was somehow menacing, almost a synonym for death. Flanagan suddenly remembered the grisly outline of Savo island – the giant corpse floating on its back at the entrance to Ironbottom Sound.

'What's wrong?' Annie said, sensing his mood change.

'I heard today that we'll be sailing in two weeks. Your yard guys have been working overtime.'

'Why don't you throw me down and take me here and now? Isn't that why you told me? So my heart would break and I'd say yes at last?'

'I don't know why I told you.'

'Yes you do.'

'I'm not asking you to feel sorry for me. I'll make it without you. I've made it this far.'

'I've told you. You're too American for me. I grew up hearing my grandfather and his friends damn the Americans. You hung back in the last war until everyone was bled to extinction and then rushed in to claim the victory. You were doing the same thing in this war until the Japs kicked you in the teeth.'

'Annie,' Flanagan said, 'you've given me a lot. If you don't want to give me this last thing, I'll try to understand.'

Oh, you bastard, he thought. He only meant about fifty percent of that noble sentiment. The other fifty percent was designed to break down this passionate woman's resistance. Maybe he was fifty percent true-blue Frank Flanagan but the other fifty percent was mostly Jack Peterson.

He was grateful for the honesty with which they had talked about themselves, love, the war, the Catholic Church. He was even more grateful for the poems she had chanted to him, the way she had awakened him to the special nature of his Irish heritage, the Celtic fascination with the power of the word. She had made him realize his American Catholic education had traduced him in more ways than one. The only poets he knew were second-rate Americans like Longfellow and third-rate English Catholics such as G. K. Chesterton and Alice Meynell. No wonder he thought poetry was strictly for girls and four-eyed limp-wristed grinds.

He had taken one of Annie's books, *In the Seven Woods* by William Butler Yeats, back to the ship and read it five times, ignoring acid comments from Jack Peterson about joining the *Jefferson City*'s daisy chain.

'Maybe Yeats has the answer for us,' he said. While the surf crashed behind them in the twilight, he recited:

'Never give all the heart, for love
Will hardly seem worth thinking of
To passionate women if it seem
Certain and they never dream
That it fades out from kiss to kiss.'

'You really are the devil, damn you. Quoting poetry instead of scripture.'

'Maybe he's right. Maybe you can only love someone for a little while.'

Did he believe that? Or was he a hundred percent Jack Peterson now? Was he seducing this woman just to prove his manhood to Jack? No. It was deeper than his ego. It was need, a need deeper than sex, although sex, desire, had never been more acute. It was a kind of love. It was also a kind of defiance to the death that might be awaiting him in Iron-bottom Sound. Death both created the deeper need and permitted its fulfilment.

'Oh, Frank, don't die on me. I know you're never coming back to Australia. But I want to believe in your life, in its going on to happiness. I love you. I love your American wish to free your mind and soul of all restraints, I even love your defiance of the Church, maybe of God, though I can't follow it.'

Flanagan kissed her gently. Her hair against his cheek made him remember Teresa, the fiery touch of an angel's wing. 'I told you how I started thinking of myself as dead. You've stopped that, Annie. Just being with you stopped it.'

That was better. He was back to fifty percent Frank Flanagan again.

'Will you promise me not to die, Frank?'

'I'll try not to.'

'I'm serious. In a better world I think we could love each other. I think we could love each other for ever. Take me now, take me with love or without love. I'm too Irish not to want to seal this thing between us in the deepest, truest way.'

'It's with love, Annie. So help me. Real love.'

Fifty percent or less for that one. His kiss was at least eighty percent apprentice seducer. Sincerity was impossible with this need, this hunger roaring in his body.

The Pacific's surf crashed in the twilight. The vast ocean's emptiness lapped at their bodies as they caressed each other. Trapped between desire and honesty, Flanagan struggled to care. He admitted to himself that he did not know much about love. He only knew the depth of his longing to cup his hands over Annie Ford's young breasts, to let his lips rove up and down her trembling body. He only knew that this made the death toward which he might be sailing in two weeks more bearable. It almost made it unimaginable.

Temporary lovers, they lay between two emptinesses – between the Pacific's silence and the parched stillness of deserted interior of this strange, accidental continent. He saw how her Irish blood and its sense of exile redoubled her already profound, exposed Australian loneliness, a killing loneliness only women could transcend with the mystery, the power of their bodies, their caring hearts. Loneliness that a sailor who has known the loneliness of the sea could meet with his own longing.

Women, woman, Flangan thought. Was there any creed, any doctrine, any priest, bishop or pope, any god who could deny him this consolation, this hope, this fulfilment? He flung his defiance into the emptiness around them. A defiance infused with an incongruous gratitude that was almost a prayer.

Song of the Kookaburra

Fairy Hill. If anyone aboard the *Jefferson City* found out that was his destination, it would finish his Navy career.

Lieutenant Robert Mullenoe guided his borrowed car up the wrong side of the winding road to the sprawling mansion on the crest of the ridge. A white-haired butler who looked imperious enough to command a battleship emerged through huge double doors. 'Leftenant Mullenoe, I assume,' he said, with what seemed like a glare of disapproval.

He led Mullenoe into the house and down a hall lined with portraits of men and women who stared down on the common herd with regal disdain. Mullenoe's sense of unreality approached hallucination.

The final portrait was a younger man in a naval officer's uniform. His expression struck Mullenoe as devious. There was a subtly mocking smile on his lips, more mockery in his clever eyes. The painting had a black silk ribbon around its frame.

The butler opened French doors at the end of the hall. Mullenoe found himself looking down on a formal garden. Rich summer sunshine played over sculpted hedges and thorny bushes and shiny-leafed trees. Big black birds flitted through the trees, calling to each other with a sound that was a pretty good imitation of a laughing hyena. Were they trying to tell him something? On a bench at the head of the garden, wearing a blue silk dress, Christine Wallace sat with three Airedales at her feet. The dogs rose simultaneously, their hair bristling, growls rumbling in their formidable chests. 'Baldur, Undine, Siren,' their mistress said. 'Stop being silly beasts.'

She smiled at Robert Mullenoe. 'How delightful to see you again, Leftenant.'

The formal words, spoken in her soft contralto, struck Mullenoe in the centre of his body with the impact of an eight-inch shell. For a moment his solar plexus ceased to exist. What was happening to him? Mullenoe – the swordsman of the class of '31, the man who vowed he would never marry until someone pressed a shotgun to his head – in this condition? It was unthinkable. But it was happening, whether he thought about it or not.

They drank champagne in the garden, and he got to know Baldur, Undine, and Siren. They were all thoroughbreds. Christine Wallace bred dogs and horses at Fairy Hill. It was her grandfather's house, she explained. She was trying to keep up a tradition she had inherited from him. But the war made it difficult. 'I think traditions are important, don't you? Australians tend to laugh at them.'

Mullenoe confessed to a grudging acceptance of the value of tradition. He kept expecting a half dozen other guests to arrive at any moment. Not until the butler announced dinner did he realize they were dining alone. They sat down in a wood-panelled room beneath a big old-fashioned brass chandelier. The table could have easily seated fourteen. Unlike the Hollywood version of such dinners, they did not sit at opposite ends. There were two places set on opposite sides in the centre. The butler and a maid served them.

She talked about her family. She had barely known her father. He had been killed in France in World War I, when she was five. Her mother had never married again.

'I'm surprised you married a military man.'

'At least half my friends had lost fathers or older brothers in France in the last war. Almost two thirds of our expeditionary force became casualties.'

He was staggered by her calm acceptance of this horrendous statistic. He had never encountered the kind of courage she displayed. She did more than endure pain and defeat. She purified it, exalted it.

What was he doing here? Mullenoe wondered. Did he really think he could replace that lost aristocrat in the black-ribboned portrait in the hall?

'How did you meet your husband?'

'Oh, he arranged it, I imagine. I was part of his plan, you see.'

'What sort of plan?'

'His father had become an admiral through force of character and courage. Napier proposed to do it the easy way – with a rich wife.'

'You weren't in love with him?'

'I loved him a great deal. But I gradually discovered he didn't love me. I don't know what he loved exactly. An idea of himself, I think. I'd as soon not try to put it into words.'

'But you're still mourning him?'

'I tried to take the same approach as the Navy. Patience. Eventually, Napier was going to come round. He'd be a superb officer like his father. If I persisted in loving him he'd –'

She stared down at her soup plate. 'Lately I've wondered if we both may have been wrong. Love doesn't change much, I'm afraid. We shall never know now.'

'I disagree – about love not changing much.'

She knew exactly what he meant. He watched her weighing in her soul the possibility of believing again, hoping again. She raised the crystal wineglass to her lips. A crest of some sort was engraved on the rounded side.

'It is rather extraordinary. Our meeting this way.'

'I think you should know something else. We didn't fight our ship at Savo Island. We ran out on the *Canberra*. And on the *Quincy* and *Astoria* and *Vincennes*. I had nothing to do with the decision. But I think you should know what happened.'

She looked dazed, disbelieving. 'Should I?' she murmured.

'I want you to know it.'

For a moment she was as still as the aristocrats hanging in the hall. Mullenoe heard the clink of a distant dish in the pantry, the muted mocking call of the kookaburras outside.

'I'm glad you told me,' she said.

His brain barely functioning, Montgomery West danced with Claire Carraway in the faded ballroom of the Wentworth Hotel. It was a farewell party for Bob Hope's troupers before they took off for the Army camps and naval bases in Queensland, Australia's far north. West's nemesis, Charles Benbow, had twisted his arm to show up and mollify Claire. He had not had to twist terribly hard.

At the moment, West's mollification program was getting nowhere. Claire was pouting. That red kissable mouth became babyish, petulant, which somehow only made it more kissable. The rest of Claire was equally enticing. A lot of it was showing in the cleavage of her Dior gown.

'You'd only be gone two weeks,' Claire said. 'Don't they ever give you time off?'

'In two weeks we'll be ready to sail. We may leave even earlier. We may be back in the Solomons in two weeks.'

'Monty, aren't you carrying this hero stuff a little too far? I saw pictures of this ship. What would have happened to you if you were in that bow?'

'I'd be dead.'

'It doesn't make sense to risk that – unnecessarily.'

Like most people in Hollywood, Claire was incapable of saying the word death.

The band was playing 'Sentimental Journey'. Claire moved a little closer to him. West struggled to control the explosions she set off in various parts of his body. He was like a ship being straddled by enemy guns. Nothing was going to save him but an all-out effort at damage control.

A photographer suddenly skittered around them. 'Hey, Lieutenant West, Miss Carraway, give us one for the home folks,' he said.

Claire beamed, West forced a smile. 'What paper are you with?' he asked.

'Paper? I work for M-G-M. On loan to the war effort.'

'Where are you going to publish that picture?'

'Who knows? We give it to the wire services. I'd figure maybe five hundred papers.'

West began composing a letter to Ina Severn, trying to explain why he was dancing with Claire Carraway. *She's an old friend. I wanted to see if I could resist the temptation.* Oh, yeah.

Bob Hope twirled past them with busty singer Frances Langford. 'Hey, Lieutenant,' he said, 'is it true that powdered eggs ruin your virility?'

'I wouldn't know,' West said.

'Neither would I,' Claire said.

'Wow. We've got to work that into the act. Are you coming to Queensland with us?'

'Sorry. The captain says I've got a war to fight.'

'Didn't the Japs just shoot off the most important part of your ship?'

'I'm beginning to think that's not the only thing they shot off,' Claire said.

'Isn't she something?' Hope said. 'I heard she wore out four Australian lifeguards and a kangaroo last night. If you ignore the signals she's sending, Monty, I'm never going to touch powdered eggs again.'

An hour and several drinks later, West sat at the table watching Charles Benbow dance with Claire. The band was playing 'Thanks for the Memory'. West was beginning to think the music had been selected with diabolic intent. He had to remind himself that Hope was identified with the song since he warbled it to Shirley Ross in the *Big Broadcast of 1938*.

Benbow danced Claire over to the table and sat down with them. 'Can't talk him into it, eh?' he said.

'He's too busy being a hero,' Claire said. 'He doesn't even 'preciate my travelling twelve thousand miles to see him.'

She was getting drunk. That ought to be a good thing, but it was actually bad, because it made West remember nights when he and Claire had both been drunk and liquor reduced love to several delicious varieties of lust. He did not want to remember lust, he wanted to banish it from his body, from the globe. He tried to remember tender moments with Claire, moments when they almost regarded each other as lovers. But he was afraid to look at her. Instead he kept staring at the shallow, shifty side of Charles Benbow's face. How could Ina Severn have such deplorable taste in men?

Under the table, a hand began moving across his thigh. Claire smiled at him. On the bandstand, they had persuaded Bob Hope to sing 'Don't Get Around Much Anymore'. The ironic words slithered around the room. Perspiration oozed down West's forehead. 'Is it that hot in here?' Claire said, giving him her Barbara Stanwyck smile, while her hand continued to wander.

'Let's not put up with it for another moment,' Charles Benbow said. 'I've got a lovely little house on the cliff overlooking Manly Beach. We can be there in twenty minutes.'

'Why not?' Claire said, standing up. 'One thing I know about the lieutenant here. He loves to watch the dawn creep across the ocean. He gets positively mystical about it.'

'Surely they can spare you until morning, West old man?' Benbow said.

Montgomery West knew exactly what was going to happen. Benbow would disappear. He and Claire would be alone listening to the song of the islands. Why not? West thought. Why not act like a heel? Considering his past record with women, he unquestionably qualified as one. Where did he get the absurd idea that falling in love would change him? Did he really think he would stop wanting other women? Did he expect love to persist at a distance of six thousand miles? He was not only a heel, he was a naïve heel. But before the night was over, he would not be a frustrated one.

'Let's go,' he said.

'Hey, you wanna be my sheila?' Mess Steward Willard Otis said, slipping his hand under the blonde's sweater. He had forgotten her name. They had been drinking shandy, which was lemonade with ale in it, for a couple of hours in Hyde Park, listening to some digger military band. Now it was getting dark. It was time for the action to begin. In a couple of hours the park would be crawling with sailors and sheilas, which was digger for chippie.

'Sheila's my name, you bloody aboriginal.' She giggled.

'What the fuck's an aboriginal?'

'They live in the never never. The outback. They're black like you. They were here before we came.'

'Hey that ain't our gig. We ain't Indians. We're Negroes. N-e-g-r-o-e-s. From Africa by way of the USA. There ain't nobody in the United States who don't come from some-where else 'cept the Indians, and them dudes got wiped out by the US Cavalry a hundred years ago. But Negroes are special, baby. We the only Americans who really know how to give a girl a good time.'

'Yeah,' said Mess Steward Cash Johnson, who let Willard do the talking. So far they had scored on every liberty. Aboard ship everyone called Willard Motormouth. But the digger chippies lapped up the line of shit he put out. There were times when Cash was sure he was dreaming. White pussy free of charge!

'I want a drink of something stronger than this bloody shandy,' Sheila said. 'Right, Rosie?'

'Yeah.'

'Where you want to go? We got plenty of do-re-mi,' Willard said. 'You like Lennon's? That's where our buddies hang out.'

'Piss on that blood ocker,' said Rosie. 'He stopped giving my old man credit last month.'

'You pick it out. We don't care,' Willard said.

They wandered out of the park down into Woolloomoolo. 'Let's go in there,' Sheila said, pointing to a bar with blackout curtains down. It was named Dunne's Den. The minute they stepped in the door, Cash Johnson smelled trouble. There were no sailors in sight. Only digger shipyard workers. The biggest motherfuckers he had ever seen.

Cash had heard on the grapevine that the diggers were starting to growl about the way the Americans were grabbing all the women in sight. It figured they would be twice as surly about Negroes getting their piece of the action. The stuff about aboriginals had a bad sound to it.

But Willard Otis had drunk a lot of shandy and he was not going to let anyone push him around. He spent too much time on the ship eating dogshit from Chief Steward's Mate Davis and shovelling horseshit up to officers like Lieutenant Wilson Selvage MacComber. Willard bellied up to the bar and threw five dollars on it. 'Hey, man, give us four gin fizzes,' he said.

The bartender served the drinks and Willard handed them out to Cash and Sheila and her friend Rosie. 'What do you do on your ship?' Sheila asked.

'Hey, we fire the guns,' Willard said. 'We the best shots on the old Jaybird. Cash here's got him three Jap destroyers and a battleship. I got about six cruisers.'

'Yeah,' Cash said, noticing and not liking the way the Australians were listening to them.

'How many battleships did you say you got, mate?' asked a digger with a jaw about a foot wide. He was around forty years old, with a mouth full of big yellow teeth. Cash thought he looked as mean as any redneck he had ever seen in South Carolina.

'Hey, we don't keep track, actually. They sink so fast,' Willard said.

'I think you're full of dingo shit. I've been putting your fucking ship back together. It looks to me like the Japs did all the shooting.'

The whole barroom was listening now. Cash Johnson grabbed Otis's arm, trying to stop him. But shandy plus gin meant Motormouth was out of control.

'What the hell do you know about it, man? You're punchin' rivets at double overtime while we're up Ironbottom Sound maybe gettin' our asses blown off.'

'You fucking woolly-headed bastard! I lost a brother on the *Canberra*.'

'We know all about them guys. They forgot to shoot back at Savo Island.'

'What did you say?'

'Hey, don't listen to him,' Cash said. 'He's drunk, you know?'

'I ain't too drunk to recognize a guy whose mamma musta

made it with a fuckin' elephant,' Willard said.

In South Carolina no black man in his right mind ever played the dozens with a white man. It could lead to murder. These diggers were no different. Why couldn't Willard see that? Willard could not see anything while his mouth was moving.

The digger came at Willard with a roar that reminded Cash of fourteen-inch Japanese shells going over the *Jefferson City*. Willard was an asshole, but he was his shipmate and Cash had to stand by him. As the digger grabbed Willard by the neckerchief and started slinging him through the front window, Cash whipped his shiv out of his back pocket and slipped it into the digger's big belly. He sliced him from the side, not too deep. He didn't want to kill him, just make him let go of Willard.

'Come on,' Cash yelled and they got out the door and down the street with the whole barful of diggers after them, screaming they were going to cut off the most valuable parts of their anatomy. They barrelled into the heart of Woolloomooloo yelling, *'Jefferson City*. General Quarters. Man the fuckin' battle stations!'

Sailors poured out of bars and cathouses and saw Willard and Cash about to get taken apart by forty beserk diggers. Boats Homewood led a wave of defenders into the middle of the street. It did not matter to Homewood that the sailors were niggers he would probably be helping to lynch if he was home in Alabama. They were shipmates, and no one kicked the *Jefferson City* around any more. Not after three months in the Solomons. Who the fuck did these ungrateful digger bastards think they were?

It was beautiful, Cash Johnson thought as bottles and rocks flew around his head and the biggest riot he had ever seen exploded in Woolloomooloo. It made him almost proud to be an American.

In the moonlit darkness, the wrinkled Chinese butler and his shuffling wife served the duck à l'orange with silent dignity. When you were rich in the Philippines, you proved it by hiring Chinese servants. There were subtle pleasures no

American could appreciate in employing the Orient's once master race.

Arthur McKay and Imelda Cruz Ortiz sat on a balcony overlooking Vaucluse Bay. Beyond this chaste oval, moonlight splashed across the rippling water of Sydney Harbour. More moonlight gleamed on Imelda's blue and white silk gown, on the tiara of emeralds in her lustrous black hair.

For a while the semidarkness permitted them both to imagine themselves in another time. Imelda's voice had the same tremolo of sadness he had heard in 1923. McKay heard his own voice softening, reaching for the gentleness, the warmth, the sympathy he once thought was all a man had to offer a woman to win her love.

But the present soon became a wilful guest at their dinner party. Imelda could not resist pouring out her resentment – her people's resentment – at the way the Americans had failed so dismally to protect the Philippines against the Japanese. Arthur McKay could only agree with her.

'I thank God for Win every night. Without him we might still be in Manila. He showed Manuel and me the report your Captain Rooks of the *Houston* sent to Washington about the overwhelming strength of the Japanese fleet,' Imelda said. 'Manuel immediately began transferring our funds overseas.'

Arthur McKay could only wonder why Win would reveal such a document – which the doomed Rooks no doubt shared with him confidentially – to corrupt vermin like Manuel Ortiz. He was a paradigm of everything the United States had done wrong in the Philippines. For forty years, American officials had timidly looked the other way while American businessmen and their Filipino political henchmen mulcted millions from the islands. Once more McKay was troubled by Win's readiness to accept what he called 'the mammon of iniquity'.

Still, would anything significant have been achieved by leaving Manuel and Imelda to the mercy of the Japanese? Win was acting as a friend, on the assumption that there were times in life when sentiment was more important than a top-secret stamp on a document. It was also an example of another assumption – that a special few were permitted to ignore the regulations when it suited them.

Over coffee, Imelda's tremolo returned. Manuel had had the effrontery to take his Chinese mistress with them to Australia. He had since discarded her for a twenty-year-old Australian. 'He disgusts me so much I no longer allow him to touch me,' she said.

'Why don't you take a lover?' he said.

'My conscience will no longer permit it. Or perhaps it is my loathing for men. I do not know a single wife in our social class who does not have the same kind of husband. They collect women like they collect houses and cars.'

'Does anyone in Manila marry for love?'

'The rich don't love. They acquire, they amass, they devour.'

The butler poured brandy in huge snifters. Imelda put both hands around hers and raised it to her lips, like a priest raising the chalice in the Mass.

'What I told you twenty years ago remains true, Arthur. I have only loved one man with my soul. He was Win. I have only loved one other man with my heart. You. In some ways I've come to treasure your love more. Win consumed me. I vanished into his spiritual depths. You didn't demand such a sacrifice. You were tender in a way that was beyond Win.'

'I loved you too, Imelda.'

'Are you still married to Rita?'

'Yes.'

'Win told me she has become a monster.'

'That's not quite true.'

'But not quite untrue?'

'Truth is a very dangerous word. It's like a torpedo plane flown by a good pilot. It jinks all over the horizon. It's very hard to get a bead on it.'

'Win always said your kindness would undo you.'

'I've grown somewhat less kind with the passing years.'

'I find that hard to believe.'

'Take my word for it.'

Imelda sipped her brandy. 'Could you love me again, Arthur, for a little while?'

'Won't Manuel object?'

'He doesn't need to know. My servants are loyal to me.'

Desire stirred in Arthur McKay's body. It had been four months since he thought about a woman in this way. Even in middle age the body had its own voice, its own agenda.

Maybe Imelda was a good idea. Maybe she was a way of escaping the dream he kept having in which Lucy Kemble and Rita cheerfully sawed him in half.

A rustle of silk. Imelda vanished into the living room. A moment later she returned and the strangled horns, the syncopated beat of a 1920s dance band whispered through the blackout curtains. The words returned with the long-fogotten music.

> Who stole my heart away
> Who makes me dream all day?
> No one but you!

He took Imelda in his arms, and they began dancing to the lost rhythm. He was the American conqueror once more, she was the violated native girl, still yearning to believe in the heroism, the virtue of these arrogant white giants who had sailed across the immense ocean in their steel ships to seize her islands. Conqueror and consoler, yearning to believe in the virtue of his countrymen yet unable to deny their possibly fatal flaws.

Deep in Arthur McKay's soul, a voice whispered, *Beware*. This was all illusion, and illusions break hearts. In the real world he was the captain of a battered ship that was being haphazardly patched up to be sent back to the war. That was the only reality, the war, a juggernaut abolishing the past as it rumbled into the future.

But hands, voices, reached out from the past. It was easier to believe in them for a little while.

Slumped in the back of Charles Benbow's Jaguar sedan, Montgomery West felt like an inmate being transferred to a new maximum security prison. In front, Claire Carraway chattered about how spectacular the moonlight would look on the Pacific.

'It might look pretty to you,' West said, 'but it won't to me. Moonlight makes a cruiser a sitting duck for a Jap submarine.'

'Please, Monty, you're among friends,' Benbow said. 'No heroics are necessary, thank you.'

West was annoyed. Was he playing hero? He was drunk enough to say exactly what he thought. The goddamn moonlight would never look pretty to him again, he was sure of it.

'Where's this place called Woolloomooloo?' Claire said.

'You don't want to go there,' Benbow said.

'Why not? I hear it's the wildest part of town. I'm in a wild mood tonight. I'd like to see it, at least.'

'We'll drive through,' Benbow said. 'You'll get the idea in ten seconds. I hope I don't run over a drunken American sailor.'

Benbow launched into a lecture on the atrocious behaviour of the American sailor ashore. The British Navy simply did not have the problem, he maintained. He blamed it on the puritanical American policy of banning liquor aboard ships. As a result, American sailors hit the beach, immediately got plastered and ran wild.

West debated whether to tell Benbow how much liquor was consumed aboard the *Jefferson City*, which did not seem to prevent wildness ashore. Maybe it had more to do with the way the average British sailor was a beaten-down, obedient robot who wouldn't know how to get in trouble if he was ordered to.

Jesus, what a vile mood he was in. He was going to fuck Claire Carraway's brains out, if that was possible. Instead of a brain, he suspected she had an extra gland up there.

'What's all that noise?' Claire asked.

They rounded a corner into Bourke Street, the heart of Woolloomooloo. A rock hit the hood of Benbow's Jaguar with a thump like a dud torpedo. Another splintered the windshield. Ahead through the striated glass West saw a blur of shapes, many in Navy whites, fighting in the middle of the street. Shouts, curses and the shrill whistles of the Shore Patrol mingled with the howl of police sirens.

'Look what your bloody animals have done to my car,' Benbow howled.

He flung open the door to protest. He was instantly seized by two huge Australians. 'I'm British,' he screamed.

'Here's one for Gallipoli', one of the Aussies roared and punched him in the stomach.

'Here's another for Singapore,' the other one said and clouted him in the jaw as he went down.

They pulled open the back door to get at West. He dove out the other side and found himself face to face with Boats Homewood and a dozen other members of F Division. 'Hey, Lieutenant, come to join the fun?' Homewood bellowed.

'No,' West snapped. 'I want you to knock it off immediately.'

'OK, but we better take care of these guys first,' Homewood said.

He was referring to the two oversized Australians who had rounded the rear of the car and were lumbering drunkenly toward them. Homewood and company swarmed around the two giants and stretched them both on the cobblestones in about ten seconds.

A squad of shore patrolmen rushed up, clubs in hand and ready to use them. 'Hold it,' West said. 'These men are under my command and are trying to stop this riot.'

'They sure as hell haven't acted that way,' shouted the chief gunner's mate who was in charge of the SP's. 'Especially this son of bitch.' he pointed his club at Homewood, who grinned and thumbed his nose.

An Australian policeman grabbed West's arm. 'There's a man bleeding badly in Dunne's place,' he shouted. 'Someone's going to jail for this. We don't use knives in our fights.'

'Yeah, just bricks and broken beer bottles,' someone from F Division hooted.

'We got orders not to bust any civilian heads,' the chief gunner's mate said. 'How do we stop these diggers?'

'That's your job,' West said to the policeman. 'You concentrate on your people and we'll get the sailors out of the way. Then we'll try to find who stabbed whom.'

Fifteen minutes of furious clubbing on the part of the

Shore Patrol and the Aussie police produced results. The two mobs were separated, although insults and bottles continued to be flung across the dividing line. West waded into the mêlée, shouting orders, ducking missiles. Only after semi-peace had been restored did he remember Claire Carraway and Charles Benbow.

He found Claire beside the car with Benbow's head in her lap. 'You better get him to a doctor,' West said. 'I think he's OK, but it won't hurt to check things out.'

'Where are you going?' Claire cried.

'I'm the only officer around,' he said. 'I've sort of put myself in charge of this situation. The police are mad as hell. I want to make sure they don't throw the wrong people in jail.'

'That's where they all belong!'

'Not really,' West said.

He lugged the groaning Benbow around to the passenger side of the car and told Claire to get behind the wheel. 'I'll see you around,' he said.

'Not if I can help it,' she said. 'Have fun with your men.'

He watched her back slowly up Bourke Street and swing north toward the hotel. 'Holy shit, Lieutenant, that's some dame,' Homewood said. 'I hope we didn't spoil your evening.'

'As a matter of fact you did, Boats. I can't tell you how glad I am.'

For a moment Homewood looked baffled. Then he figured it out on his terms. 'Afraid she's got the clap?'

Love in Exile

'Are you as tired as you look?' Imelda said as Arthur McKay slumped in a chair on the terrace.

'Almost. I spent the day in court persuading an Australian judge to dismiss charges against half my crew, including a mess steward who knifed a man in a barroom brawl. I promised to give them all court-martials.'

'Will you?'

'Of course not. The judge knows it too. But he had to sound off for the newspapers. The Aussies don't really like us very much. I remember when I was here in 1925 on that fleet visit, they had a left-wing parade full of Communists shouting "Americans, go home."'

'They're a strange people. So happy at first glance. But I think they still wonder if they belong in this part of the world. They're so few and we Asians are so many.'

'Any news from Manila?'

Imelda's lips trembled. 'Some of our closest friends have joined the puppet government. What else can they do? I can't sleep, thinking of my father, my brothers. If I did not have you to . . . to comfort me, Arthur, I don't know what I would do. Manuel doesn't care what happens to anyone or anything, as long as he can drink champagne with his whores.'

McKay sighed. Imelda's lamentations for her country and her family were genuine. She had married Manuel Ortiz to enrich her family. It was part of the sacrificial code drummed into the head of every Filipino woman by the Catholic Church. But he found it harder to sympathize with Imelda's complaints about her husband. She had made her bed with Manuel, and if it was not a very loving arrangement it was a damned comfortable one. Her Rolls-Royce, her servants, her silk dresses and her diamonds and emeralds were a consolation, no matter how she professed to disdain them. There was too much Midwest populism in Arthur McKay's blood to feel terribly sorry for the rich.

But he was grateful to Imelda for seducing him into the past – out of the depressing present. She had carried him back to those marvellous days when he and Win had discovered the liquid dark eyes, the creamy brown skin, the luxuriant black hair of Filipino women. Imelda was one of the loveliest examples. She still had her graceful neck, her softly rounded arms, with intriguing dimples in the elbows. In bed she forgot the Virgin Mary, the Pope and all the other frowning gods that haunted her. She reached into her native past, before Europe and its guilts descended on her people, and became as passionate as the primitive maidens of Melville's Samoa.

Was he in love with her? No – his feelings were the same mixture of sympathy and sensuality that had attracted him to her in the first place. Now the sympathy had a broader range. In 1923, he had been consoling her because Win Kemble had stolen her virginity and broken her heart.

They often talked about Win. McKay had told her about Savo Island, Win's reckless letter to Secretary of the Navy Knox, his exile to Panama. Imelda had wept. For a moment McKay almost joined her.

Tonight, they talked about the *Jefferson City*. Imelda showed a surprising interest in his problems with his cowardly executive officer, his crooked supply officer, his eccentric chaplain, his wayward crew.

'Will you be returning to combat soon?'

'In about two weeks. They've almost replaced the bow. But we're going to need at least a week to overhaul the engines and boilers.'

'And Win? You never even give him a thought? All you care about is the glory, the power of your ship? You won't try to help him?'

Arthur McKay slowly set his coffee cup back in the saucer.

'You've heard from Win?'

'I . . . I wrote to him. He . . . wrote back.'

'What did he say'

'He . . . he said he was glad we were together again. This time he hoped you might get rid of Rita and marry me.'

'What else?'

'Oh, Arthur, believe me, my affection for you is genuine. But –'

But Win Kemble was still the dark captain of her soul.

Imelda was weeping, trying to explain between sobs. 'If he asked me to come to him anywhere, anytime, I would leave all this in an instant. For a day, a week, a month with him.'

'What else did he say?'

'He said to give you his love, of course. And to remind you of a passage in a Chinese poem.'

'Recite it,' Arthur McKay said. He was shocked at the cold

empty clang of his own voice. 'I'm sure he told you exactly how and when to do it.'

Imelda's eyes were dark pools of sorrow. Asia's voice spoke the ancient words.

> 'This year there is war in An-hui,
> In every place soldiers are rushing to arms.
> Men of learning have been summoned to the Council Board;
> Men of action are marching to the battle-line.
> Only I, who have no talents at all,
> Am left in the mountains to play with the pebbles of the stream.'

The lines were from the poem 'Visiting the Hsi-Lin Temple'. They had been written by Po Chu-i when he was sent into exile for falling afoul of China's imperial bureaucracy.

There was nothing surprising about it, Arthur McKay told himself. Win had never stopped watching him. Allies aboard the *Jefferson City* may have been writing him regularly. The chaplain, perhaps. Win watched and waited. He learned that Arthur McKay had not got rid of his crooked, cowardly executive officer the day he arrived in Australia, as any captain in command of his own soul, not to mention his ship, would have done. Captain McKay was still undecided. Still a man divided between his duty to his ship and his love for his friend and his disillusion with the US Navy.

'Tell Win I'll do it. I'll take a chance on messing up my ship for his sake.'

He stood up. The Chinese butler materialized through the blackout curtains with his hat. 'Arthur, forgive me, please,' Imelda sobbed.

He kissed her on the forehead. 'I do,' he said.

But he was beginning to wonder if he could forgive Win Kemble.

Moonlight filled the master bedroom at Fairy Hill. Lieutenant Robert Mullenoe lay beside Christine Wallace. He had just finished telling her the *Jefferson City*'s departure date had been changed without warning. They were sailing in two days. His next words had no rational connection with this dismaying news. 'I want to marry you,' he said. 'I want you with me for the rest of my life.'

Insanity, whispered the voice that had been mocking him ever since he met this woman. The voice spoke for all the ghosts and goblins of the past. It warned him that she was bad luck, she had already killed one sailor-husband. She was upper-class Australian, which made her practically English, incapable of understanding earthy, classless Americans. She was refined, she appreciated painting, she quoted poetry; he was an uneducated lug, a gunnery officer who had graduated near the bottom of his class.

All this was undoubtedly true. She knew it; she could see the gulf between them as clearly as he saw it. Yet she put her arms around him and murmured, 'Then let's get married tomorrow.'

'We're sailing the next day.'

'I know that.'

'Would it make any difference if we waited?'

'It would to me.'

'Why?'

'I don't know exactly. Maybe I just want to stop feeling grandfather's disapproving eyes on me for allowing this hulking American to desecrate me – and Fairy Hill.'

'Do you really feel desecrated?'

'You know how I really feel.'

'If I get through the war – which I doubt – I've told you that – could you leave Fairy Hill and live in America?'

'We'll build a house just like it in one of your Southern states – Virginia or Maryland.'

Still he could not say yes. It was the last stand of Robert Mullenoe, bachelor. He was ready to become engaged, to pledge on his honour his love for all time. But he wanted the war to stand between him and ultimate surrender.

Sapping this resistance was the desire his brother's death had awakened in his soul, a desire to which this woman gave flesh and substance – to become a husband, a father, to raise sons.

Her voice came out of the darkness again, seriously trying to explain why she wanted to marry him.

'I suppose I would also like to feel absolutely certain.'

'You don't now?'

'You're a handsome man, Leftenant. Remember, I've already married one sailor.'

And look where he is, whispered the warning voice.

'But if you choose to wait, I'll try to understand.'

Her sadness decimated his resistance. It threatened the most amazing part of Mullenoe's love for this woman – the astonishing pride he took in the thought that he was going to the Solomons, back to night battles and jinking torpedo planes – to protect her.

Mullenoe had always been disdainful of the Navy's supposed role as protector of homes and hearths. Protector of the goddamn civilians' right to guzzle and gorge and drive expensive cars and haul down high salaries while the underpaid soldiers sweated or froze on the uncaring ocean. That was what Mullenoe had concluded was the real story, from some of his father's diatribes in retirement.

But Christine Wallace, Fairy Hill, this whole magnificent country, prostrate before the oncoming Japanese. This justified a man's devotion, his courage, if necessary, his death.

Now he was denying or at least implying there was a limit to that devotion – when there was no limit, when this woman had made the word supremely meaningful in his warrior's soul.

'We'll get married tomorrow. Assuming such things can be done in Australia.'

She kissed him. He was shocked to discover her face was wet with tears. 'It seems to me you've already discovered how much can be done in Australia, Leftenant,' she said.

Dawn was breaking across the immense swath of the Pacific visible from Maroubra Beach. Annie Flood strummed her guitar one last time and sang the eerie final verse of 'Waltzing Matilda.'

Up jumped the swagman, sprang into the billabong,
'You'll never catch me alive,' said he.
And his ghost may be heard as you pass by that billabong,
'You'll come a-waltzing Matilda with me.'

'That really isn't a very happy song, is it?' Frank Flanagan said.

'It's a tale of mystery, imagination and horror,' Annie said. 'The sort of things that make life worth living if you're Irish.'

'A swagman – he's a sort of sailor, ain't he?' Jack Peterson said. 'Except he does his wanderin' on dry land.'

'Yeah. He's got his matilda. We've got our seabags,' the Radical said.

Annie Flood had explained the slang. A matilda was the pack the swagman carried on his back. In the song, the swagman kills a sheep who wanders down to the waterhole. The owner tries to arrest him and the swagman drowns himself rather than go to jail.

'Hey, listen. I'd rather go waltzin' in Ironbottom Sound than go to jail,' Jack Peterson said.

Annie rubbed tears from her eyes. 'You're a heartless bastard, Peterson.'

'Whatya mean? You gotta have a heart to get in the US Navy. You can't pass the physical without one.'

'Yours is made of rock salt.'

They stared out at the Pacific. 'It's a big ocean,' Jack said.

'Hey, we're gonna come back,' Marty Roth said. 'I can't wait to come back to Australia.'

Anna Elias put her head on Marty's shoulder and started to sob. Anna gave them all a bad case of the creeps. She had told them what the Germans were doing to the Jews. It made them feel the world had gone berserk. The worst could happen to anyone. Even Daley, who was convinced that prayer would get him through, somehow, was shaken.

Sally Lundin was sobbing now. She clung to Jack Peterson. Hilary, the Radical's girl, was trying not to imitate her. Good revolutionists never cried. Daley's girl, Stella, wept tears by the gallon. She and the pious prude had decided her vocation was more important than consummation. She was still a virgin.

'Jesus Christ, I knew this was a lousy idea,' Jack said.

He had wanted to dump the girls and spend their last night with Homewood in Woolloomooloo, but Flanagan and Roth had insisted on this farewell party. Annie had been close to tears all night. She had always vowed she would never become a sheila. She regretted her lost virtue. Her love for Flanagan remained entangled with a sense of sin.

'You keep this up,' Jack said as the chorus of sobs grew violent, 'and we're gonna come back here and marry you and ruin your lives. I'd be the lousiest husband in the universe. I'd always have my eye peeled for some sixteen-year-old. Flanagan here would come in second, because he's got an opinion on everything from Jesus Christ to naval strategy and he's convinced he's always right. He and Annie would be so busy arguin' they'd never go to bed. Roth here would stick Anna in an apartment in the Bronx with five kids, and she'd never rewrite Freud and those other birds who specialize in tellin' us what we already know, that guys like girls and vice versa. Instead of cryin' you should be celebratin'. You're gettin' rid of us before we do any real damage.'

'By God,' Annie Flood said, 'you've convinced me.'

She threw her arms around Frank Flanagan and gave him one last angry kiss.

Back in Paddington, Flanagan helped Annie carry blankets and suitcases into her house. The small fieldstone Catholic Church was visible at the end of the block. Upstairs in Annie's tiny bedroom, she suddenly began crying again. 'Frank,' she said, 'come down to the church with me now. We can both go to confession. I'll feel so much better.'

Flanagan thought of the love this woman had given him on the edge of the empty ocean. He thought of Chaplain Bushnell telling him that American faith was not a set of rules or dogmas but a voyage of exploration. He thought of Teresa Brownlow and her father, daring God to fail them. 'I can't do it,' he said. 'I wish I could, for your sake. But I don't believe it any more.'

Mail Call

Dear Frank:

It's wonderful to hear that you have come through all those battles safely and are in Australia. It makes me feel better to know some of my prayers have been answered.

But so many prayers haven't been answered, Frank. Daddy died two weeks ago. He had a stroke while he was preaching on a street corner in San Pedro. We couldn't find the money for another church. It was so awful, the way drunken sailors used to laugh at him and heckle him, I was almost glad when it happened.

That makes me feel terrible now. It makes me wonder if that's why he died so broken and lost. I could see his faith dwindling away day by day. I only hope there was enough left to raise him to the glory he deserved and would have surely have had, if it weren't for his sinful daughter.

Pray for me Frank. There are times when I fear I'll wind up like Momma, seeing people who aren't there.

Your friend,
Teresa

Dearest Jack:

I'm so glad to hear you're in Australia, which means no one is shooting at you for a while. You can't believe how scared I am to turn on the radio or pick up a newpaper for fear of reading something about the Japs claiming they just sank six cruisers and four battleships. I know they make those claims all the time and we don't even bother to deny them any more. But I also know we never admit our real losses either.

I find it hard to believe you and your friend Flanagan are spending so much time at the beach, surfing until you're too tired to even look at the girls. But I'm willing to swallow it from the detailed descriptions you wrote of those waves. I never knew you were that much of a swimmer – or so good with a pen. I've never gotten more than a postcard from you on previous cruises – and when we've gone to the beach, we didn't spend much time in the water. I guess – hope – it's all proof of how much you've changed.

I've gotten a job as an arc-welder at the Bremerton Yards.

The pay is fantastic – I'm making over $200 a week. I'm saving most of it for a trousseau. That's something a woman buys when she's beginning to think she might get married. Look it up, darling, or ask your brainy friend Flanagan what it means.

Just between us, it means I'm seriously crazy about you.

Love,
Martha

Dear Edwin,

I'm sorry to hear you had such a dismal time in Australia. The conduct of the sailors as you describe it is just appalling. The Australian women don't sound much better. I'm sure that Presbyterian minister you met had the right explanation – that they're mostly descended from convicts and their moral standards have never been very high.

Captain McKay's conduct, on the other hand is pretty close to unforgivable. Parading around Sydney with his ex-mistress from Manila on his arm! The man has no moral standards, obviously. He's as bad as his wife. It's dismaying to think someone like that can rise to his rank in the US Navy.

Maybe now you'll agree I'm right – you should get off that ship as soon as possible. There's plenty of new construction coming off the ways that you can apply for. Gunnery offices are high on the list of candidates for destroyer commands, I've been told. If I were you I'd get your request for a transfer off to BuNav today.

I'm feeling much better. The doctor says I'm the biggest he's ever seen in the sixth month. That's a sign it's a boy. The other kids are fine. I'll send you more details in my next letter. I want to mail this tonight.

Love,
Eleanor

Husband dear:

From certain hints in a recent letter from Lucy, I gather she thinks you will come to her heroic husband Winfield Scott Schley Kemble's rescue, somehow. Where she gets this faith in you I have no idea and don't really want to find out. If it wasn't absolutely certain she was incapable of infidelity I would suspect the worst.

Failing that, I will try to head it off by abjuring you to do nothing. Do I make myself clear? NOTHING. From comments by Cominch I gather Admiral Hepburn is telling him Savo is the worst goddamn mess ever perpetrated by so-called commanders in any uniform, let alone US khakis. At least two admirals, one British, the other American, should be court-martialled for gross carelessness and criminal incompetence.

Fortunately, the victories you heroes are racking up will soon make the whole catastrophe more or less irrelevant, except for a chance to settle a few personal scores. For the family's sake, I will try to protect Win in this final stage of the proceedings. I can't guarantee that I'll succeed. I'm only a bystander, after all, of the wrong gender. But I *will* try, I promise you.

Any games you might try to play now, especially with your executive officer and his circle of crooks, will only complicate a lot of things. Parker's friend on the Naval Affairs Committee is trying to gut the Navy's battleship programme. Cominch and company are fighting for the big wagons with all the guile and grease they can find. I'll send you a copy of a recent article in the *Saturday Evening Post* which gives the *South Dakota* credit for shooting down half the Jap air force and saving the *Enterprise* off Santa Cruz Islands in November. Absolute bullshit of course, but it shows how desperate they are.

I know how loath you are to take advice from me these days. But this is *vital*. Don't try to outsmart Cominch for Win's sake. It can't be done. Write the old bastard insulting letters – that one from Tulagi was a beaut – call him a thick-skulled hard-hearted son of a bitch if it makes you feel better – he actually likes that sort of thing. He was just as insubordinate when he was your age. But don't mess him up with those pinheads in Congress. That would be disloyal to the Navy, and *that* – I should not have to remind you – is the sin against the Holy Ghost.

Have you written to Sammy? The last I heard from him, he was about an inch from joining the Marines.

> Your loving wife,
> Rita

Port Admiral Be Damned!

When the *Jefferson City*'s chief engineer learned they were sailing in two days, he went roaring up to see Arthur McKay, clutching the work orders issued by the Cockatoo Island Navy Yard in his fist. Oz Bradley's burly frame almost vibrated as he informed the captain that departure was out of the question. 'We're supposed to spend the next week getting a complete overhaul of our boilers and turbines. The Admiral himself told me he never saw –'

At this point Bradley realized there was another officer in the Captain's cabin. He was a young dark-haired commander with a cocky smile on his handsome face. 'I'm afraid the overhaul will have to wait, Oz,' McKay said. 'Commander Pearce here will tell you why.'

Commander Duke Pearce was from the Naval Ordnance Bureau. Bradley disliked him instantly. His arrogant manner was a kind of summary of the lifetime of deck-officer condescension Bradley had endured. 'My orders supersede all others, Commander. We have a new weapon that the Bureau wants tested with all possible speed. It's been routed to Australia because we didn't want to risk losing it by bringing it into the Solomons on a freighter. I have the authority to commandeer the first available cruiser and this boat is it.'

Boat. That was typical of how these SOB's talked to engineering officers. The word implied they did not even know the Navy's basic terminology. Bradley turned to the Captain to see if he had a glimmer of support. But McKay seemed to be thinking about something else.

'Art, this is serious. We're risking lives, maybe even the ship,' Bradley said.

'You'll have to figure something out, Oz,' McKay said.

He wasn't interested, Bradley thought. He welcomed this opportunity to get himself and the ship mentioned in a report that would go to the top of the Navy. He was going to spend his time kissing the ass of this young hotshot Pearce to make sure the mention was as favourable as possible.

Bradley discarded his tentative opinion that McKay was not just another butt-sucking, eye gouging climber up the deck promotion ladder. He trudged back to the land of Oz and told his chief boiler tender to give him a two-day emergency patchwork programme for number one and number two boilers. His chief machinist's mate was ordered to do the same thing for the engine rooms. That meant their last liberty in Australia was cancelled. They both looked as if they might take out their frustrations on the machinery with sledgehammers.

When Amos Cartwright returned from liberty and heard the news, he shook his head. He was as worried about the condition of their ageing boilers as everyone else. He could not understand Captain McKay's indifference. 'That ain't his style,' he said. 'You heard him when he come down and give us that talk. He wouldn't let no orders from Washington maybe get us parboiled down here.'

'Maybe it's time you stopped thinkin' of this guy as a fuckin' hero,' said the thick-necked machinist's mate Amos called Throttleman. He and his cohorts in the forward engine room never missed a chance to needle Amos – and sneer at his Jewboy striker. 'Maybe it's gonna turn out he didn't do you no favour, promotin' you up from mess steward. Maybe it's gonna take a low-water casualty to change your mind.'

'He didn't promote nobody. I promoted myself,' Cartwright said. 'He must have somethin' real heavy on his mind. Maybe he got his own reasons for wantin' to get us back to the war. Maybe the goddamn diggers is threatenin' to put the whole fuckin' crew in jail.'

Cartwright's opinion of the Australians had declined steadily since he began visiting the aborigines. He shared Anna Elias's indignation and dismay at their treatment.

Marty Roth found it hard to concentrate on the argument. Since he had persuaded Anne to join Flanagan and his friends in their cottage on Maroubra Beach, he had stopped thinking about the *Jefferson City*. Even when he was aboard, he was living mentally and spiritually in Anna's arms. He found it hard to believe that orders from Washington could end his time to laugh and dance and love.

When they were alone, Cartwright got his attention. 'Jewboy,' he said, clapping both his hands on Roth's shoulders, 'one of these days there could be more superheated steam comin' out of that firebox than's goin' up the main line. If that happens, there's only one way to get out of here.'

He led him up to the top plates and pointed through the tangle of pipes to the mouth of a ventilator shaft. 'There's a ladder in there that leads to the main deck. I'm gonna loosen the hatch up there just enough to let us get out only slightly cooked. Just remember to move your ass faster than it's ever travelled since you were born. Cause this big nigger's gonna be right behind you.'

'I haven't changed my mind about my career track. But the goddamned Navy hasn't changed its mind, either. At the rate things are going, I'm likely to be a commander for the rest of my life.'

Arthur McKay tried to listen politely to the troubles Duke Pearce was having with the Navy's encrusted prejudices. He could have said, I told you so, but Pearce would have been hurt by the dismissal. Without any special encouragement McKay could recall, Pearce seemed to have adopted him as a semi-father in matters naval.

Pearce had been one of McKay's students at the Naval War College in 1940. A Californian who regarded Easterners as fuddy-duddies living in the last century, he had exhibited a cheerful disdain for the school and the ideas McKay and his fellow faculty members were dispensing about naval history and strategy. His attendance at McKay's lectures on the great sea battles of history was virtually nil. When McKay asked him why, Pearce had told him he saw no point in finding out what other generations had done with the weapons of their time. 'Weapons are what shape tactics and strategy,' he said. 'We should be developing tactics for the weapons of the future, not mulling over past mistakes.'

At dinner at their house one evening, Pearce had outraged Rita and astonished everyone else at the table, including several War College professors and fellow students, by declaiming against the standard route to promotion, which was based on how an officer performed in various commands aboard ships. Instead, the Navy should be rewarding those who had the imagination to create and produce new weapons and the new tactics and strategies that went with them. When he graduated from the War College, Pearce had applied for the Bureau of Ordnance, claiming his ambition was to be a 'weapons technology manager', a term he invented for the occasion.

Now here he sat in Arthur McKay's cabin with a shiny new weapon – something called a proximity fuse – to introduce to the war. Would he get promoted for it? The traditionalists at the Bureau of Navigation, who were reluctantly entering the twentieth century by permitting themselves to be called the Bureau of Personnel, were not impressed. Commander Pearce lacked sea duty, command experience. He could invent new weapons until doomsday. Until he got some sea duty under his belt, he was 'unpromotable'.

Pearce fumed over the term. 'Isn't that the damnedest thing you've ever heard, Art?'

'No question about it.'

'When you see what this weapon we're giving you sea dogs can do, maybe you'll write a letter to Personnel, telling them what a contribution it's going to make to the fleet. It might help.'

'Sure.'

The request was pathetic evidence of how out of touch Pearce was with the real Navy. No one with good promotion antennae would ask Arthur McKay to write a letter for him. The word was undoubtedly out that he was on Cominch's shitlist.

McKay did not have the heart to tell Pearce the truth. He reminded the captain too much of Win Kemble, with his furious haste to get to the top by using brain power and guile to outwit the Navy's slow, wary promotion system.

Pearce seemed to sense the futility of his request in McKay's offhand acquiescence. His face darkened. 'I'm thinking of getting out of the goddamned Navy,' he said.

'Really make an end run on those bastards in Personnel.'

'What do you mean?' McKay said. In time of war, the Navy did not accept resignations.

'There's something big cooking down at Los Alamos. They're pulling in guys from all the services. If this proximity fuse works the way I think it will, I'm pretty sure I can get myself an offer.'

'Why not?' McKay said.

Duke Pearce's world of weapons technology was too remote for serious thought. His appearance on the quarterdeck of the *Jefferson City* with orders to commandeer the ship to test his new weapon without delay had won Captain McKay's acquiescence for a reason Pearce could never comprehend. There was no time to waste, if the help Captain McKay had promised Win Kemble was to be effective. It had to arrive before Admiral Hepburn's report on Savo Island was on Cominch King's desk.

That was why McKay had welcomed Pearce's orders, why he had ignored his engineering officer's warning that he was risking his ship. He was already preparing to risk his ship in a way that was at least as dangerous as the threat of her ageing boilers. For a moment he was tempted to try to explain it to Duke Pearce. He felt a terrible need to explain it to someone. Would a semi-son understand? Would he be pleased to know that his wonderful new weapon would help his semi-father fight a spiritual battle as well as a real one?

A glance told the captain how little sympathy he could expect. Pearce was much too preoccupied with his own future to worry about the moral problems of unimportant cruiser captains.

'I'm going to do it,' he said. 'I'm going to get into that Los Alamos deal. I don't know what the hell they're cooking up down there, but it's big.'

Montgomery West had the wardroom in stitches, kidding Mullenoe about his collapse into husbandhood. Last night at the wedding, West had wowed the party with his reading of a heroic poem, 'The Fall of Mullenoe'. A joint production of a half dozen wardrobe poetasters, it owed a great deal to

Robert Service's 'The Shooting of Dan McGrew'.

Mullenoe just grinned at him. He was still breathing pure champagne.

Steward's Mate Willard Otis tapped West on the shoulder. 'Telephone call for you, Lieutenant.'

'She's pregnant. You can't sail until you marry her,' Mullenoe said.

Who in hell was calling him at 0700? West wondered. As he picked up the telephone on the bulkhead outside the wardrobe, a boatswain's pipe whined over the PA system. 'Now hear this. Special sea detail report to the fo'c'sle.' They were getting under way within the hour.

'Joey?' said a woman's voice.

'Gwen?' he said, his knees almost buckling. She had seen the picture of him and Claire Carraway. She was calling to tell him he was a heel. 'Where are you?'

'I'm at an airport somewhere in Australia. I think it's near Sydney. I'm on a USO tour. I volunteered when I heard they were going to Australia.'

'We're sailing in an hour.'

'Oh, no. If I was a little less exhausted, I'd cry. But I don't have the strength.'

'I don't know what I can do.'

'Well, I'm glad I at least had this chance to tell you I still love you.'

'Likewise,' he groaned. 'I'm sorry I can't talk. They're casting off the lines. Goodbye, darling.'

He hung up and slumped against the bulkhead like the victim of a firing squad. He did not know how long he sagged there. A voice returned him to reality. 'Lieutenant West, are you all right?'

It was the Captain. He had just emerged from the Exec's office. McKay looked grim. They were probably on their way to take on Yamamoto's Combined Fleet single-handed. That was the way West's luck was running.

'I just heard from my fiancée. She just landed in Australia.' He fumbled out the rest of the explanation.

The Captain shook his head. 'That's lousy timing.'

A half hour later, the sea detail hauled in the last lines and the USS *Jefferson City* edged away from the dock. The crew was at quarters in dress whites. Montgomery West stood beside a restored number one turret, staring forlornly at the stiff office façades of downtown Sydney. Cheers from passing ferries, a salute from an incoming Australian destroyer drifted past him. He was numb.

As they slowed to pass through the submarine net, the PA system coughed and growled. 'Now hear this. Lieutenant Montgomery West, report to the bridge on the double.'

He obeyed, wondering if he had committed some gaffe while in his daze. Were they supposed to man the rails and he had never given his division the order? That bastard Kruger would never bother to tell him. He loved to see the movie star screw up.

'Lieutenant West,' said Captain McKay, 'step into my sea cabin, will you?'

Now he was sure he had screwed up. McKay always issued his reprimands in private. He followed the Captain into the bare tiny cabin aft of the bridge.

'Lieutenant,' the Captain said, 'through an oversight, I've neglected to deliver a signed copy of my orders to the admiral of the port. You haven't been in the Navy long enough to know what admirals of the port are like. If you ever come across a poem on the subject by Frederick Marryat, it will give you a good idea.'

Still frowning sternly, as if it was all West's fault, the Captain handed him a sealed brown envelope. 'I'm afraid I'm going to have to ask you to deliver this to the old bastard. The net tender will get you back to Sydney. You can jump a PBY in two or three days and catch up to us at Nouméa. Can you throw some clothes in a suitcase in about two minutes flat?'

'Captain,' Montgomery West said. 'Sir, I . . . I –'

'Get going,' McKay said. 'You now have one minute forty seconds.'

An hour later, Lieutenant West dialed Ina Severn's room from the lobby of the Wentworth Hotel. Imitating an Australian accent, he said, 'Excuse me, Miss Severn. Do you happen to know a poem about a port admiral by someone named Marryat?'

'Of course I do,' Gwen said, her voice thick with tears. 'I grew up reciting it at parties. It was my father's favourite poem. But I doubt if any American would appreciate it. It's about three British sailors' wives damning a port admiral for sending their men to sea on Christmas Day in a snowstorm.'

'There's a bloke down here in a Yank sailor's suit who says he's got a case of champagne for you if you promise to recite it for him without a stitch on. I know I shouldn't even ask an English lady such a thing, but you're in Australia now.'

'Joey?' she whispered. 'Did you jump ship?'

'No,' he said. 'I just happen to have a captain with a heart.'

BOOK FOUR

The Deadly Fuse

The first bomb hit about two hundred yards off the *Jefferson City*'s starboard bow. The familiar fountain of white and blue water blossomed into the sky. The Japanese pilot pulled out of his dive and streaked for the horizon.

It was Tuesday 26 January 1943. They were about three hundred miles north of the New Hebrides, halfway to the Solomons. Ahead of them the new light cruiser *Montpelier* was blasting streams of twenty- and forty-millimetre shells and five-inch rounds into the sky. The *Jefferson City*'s forties and twenties were also hammering away at the Rabaul Reception Committee, as the sailors called this welcome that the enemy sent down from New Britain every time a convoy headed for Guadalcanal.

But the *Jefferson City*'s five-inch guns were strangely silent. On the port wing of the bridge, Commander Duke Pearce pointed to the retreating dive bomber. 'Go for that one,' he said.

Ordinarily, planes flying away from a ship were almost impossible to hit with a five inch gun. It was too difficult to estimate the rapidly widening range and set the shells' fuses for the right distance.

'Mullenoe,' Captain McKay said. 'Take the bogey at one three five.'

'Mounts one and two, execute,' Air Defence Officer Mullenoe said.

The squarish box-like mounts swivelled, their four guns crashed. The concussion knocked the helmet off Duke Pearce's head. McKay watched the retreating Jap through his glasses. Suddenly the plane disintegrated in a burst of smoke and flame.

'How do you like that?' Duke Pearce said.

It was hard not to like it. It was a little harder to like Duke Pearce. From the sarcastic remarks of the junior officers,

McKay gathered he was so pleased with himself and his weapon, he had set a new standard for condescension in the wardroom. Not even Lieutenant MacComber could match him.

'I think you can stop worrying about air attacks from now on, Art,' Pearce said.

Inside the pilothouse, McKay heard the talker say, 'More bombs coming down.'

McKay stepped into the pilothouse. For ten seconds he said nothing. With a sardonic smile, he contemplated the panic flickering in Executive Officer Daniel Boone Parker's eyes. 'What are you going to do, Mr Parker?'

'Right full rudder,' Parker said. The sweat poured down his thick red neck.

The *Jefferson City* careened to port at thirty-two knots.

'You fucking idiot,' McKay said. 'You didn't even look to see if the *Montpelier* was turning. You're in line of battle, Commander. You have cruisers ahead and astern.'

'Yes Captain,' Parker said.

'Quartermaster, note in the log that Commander Parker made an unauthorized manoeuvre with the captain on the bridge. A manoeuvre that endangered the safety of the ship.'

'Aye, aye, Captain.'

Out on the port wing of the bridge, the supply officer, Leroy Tompkins, squinted skyward from beneath an unaccustomed steel helmet. Sweat poured down his palpitating cheeks. He was out in the open, a target for every strafing Kate or Zero, a likely candidate for acquiring a piece of shrapnel somewhere in his pudgy torso from a near miss.

Tompkins shouted hysterically into the mouthpiece strapped to his chest. 'We got one. The five-inch mounts just blew that dive bomber away. There's two more coming down. We're making evasive manoeuvres. So are the other ships. The *Montpelier* is putting on a hell of a show for a new ship.'

'Try not to sound so scared, Lieutenant,' Captain McKay said. 'You're supposed to make them think we're winning this war.'

'Yes, Captain,' Tompkins said, mopping his brow. He

trembled violently as two more thousand-pound bombs exploded to port.

'Those last two bombs didn't even come close,' he said.

'Six, seven, eight torpedo planes to starboard,' said the talker, who began reciting ranges and bearings.

'Mullenoe, commence firing as soon as you select targets,' McKay said.

'Aye, aye, Captain.'

Mullenoe distributed targets to his mounts in his usual calm authoritative fashion. The five-inch emitted their horrendous blasts of noise and flame. One, two, three, four of the torpedo planes disintegrated when they were at least three thousand yards away. The other three, appalled at such gunnery, veered off to attack the *Montpelier*. The *Jefferson City*'s forty-millimetre mounts tracked one beautifully, and he cartwheeled into the sea, a mass of flames.

'We got five out of the seven torpedo planes,' crowed Supply Officer Tompkins.

'Strafer bearing zero zero zero,' shouted the talker.

It was a Jap fighter plane, coming at them dead ahead.

'Everybody down,' McKay said.

They dove for the deck as a hail of machine-gun bullets and twenty-millimetre shells swept down the ship. Flying lead clanged off bulkheads and the armoured conning tower. Quite a lot came through the open windows of the bridge.

Flat on the deck, Captain McKay heard Commander Parker's breath coming in rasping gulps. Lieutenant Tompkins got to his knees on the wing of the bridge. 'A Zero just strafed us. Maybe the after batteries will get him,' he said.

Tompkins peered over the splinter shield like a frightened chicken. The five-inch guns crashed. 'Yeah. We got him! We got him! We're using a new shell with a proximity fuse. That means it detonates whenever it gets near a target. You don't have to worry about setting ranges. It's a fantastic weapon. It means we don't have to worry about air attacks any more.'

A stupendous blast less than fifty yards off their starboard bow belied this claim. The bomb showered the *Jefferson City* with water and shrapnel. 'Talker, you asshole, why the fuck didn't you report bombs coming down?' screamed Parker.

The talker was on his knees, his head against the forward bulkhead. The quartermaster pointed to blood oozing down his neck. 'He's been hit, sir.'

The young sailor was dead. A fragment from one of the Jap's twenty-millimetre cannon shells had pierced his brain.

'So this is combat,' Duke Pearce said. 'I like it.'

Pearce watched, apparently indifferent, while the quartermaster and the boatswain's mate of the watch carried the talker's body below. Captain McKay's dislike of Pearce redoubled. He saw the world as a series of abstract events. Combat, weapons, tactics. Human beings scarcely existed for him. Perhaps he was necessary to win a modern war. But that did not require Arthur McKay to like him.

Was he being unfair to Pearce? Was his dislike rooted in the way Pearce reminded him of Win Kemble's flaws? Perhaps.

The Captain contemplated the fear-splotched face of his executive officer, the trembling lips of his supply officer. He had converted Tompkins into a 'battlecaster' to keep the men below decks informed of what was happening. But he was only a minor target, a mouse to torture for his own amusement. The major target was not amusing.

'That was an absolutely atrocious performance, Mr Parker. Without the proximity fuse, I'm sure this ship would have suffered serious damage with you as officer of the deck. Quartermaster, record in the log that Mr Parker used obscene and reprehensible language to rebuke a sailor who had been mortally wounded.'

'Aye, aye, Captain.'

Duke Pearce watched, a small smile on his handsome face. He was not even slightly bothered by the way the Captain abused his executive officer. Pearce seemed to like it. He probably thought he was learning something about command.

Captain McKay struggled to control his careening emotions. He wanted to get Pearce off his ship. He even wanted to get him out of the Navy. 'I would say you could start working on that transfer to Los Alamos tomorrow,

Duke,' he said. 'If you think a letter from me will do you any good, just let me know.'

'Thanks, Art,' Pearce said, oblivious to what was happening aboard the *Jefferson City*.

Madhouse Blues

I think Art's coming unglued, I really do,' said the *Jefferson City*'s first lieutenant, Commander George Tombs.

In the privacy of his stateroom, Tombs was expressing the general shock and consternation among the ship's officers at the way the Captain was crucifying the executive officer. Tombs was not an admirer of Commander Parker, but he was not his enemy. As the man at the bottom of the class of 1917, the first luff instinctively sympathized with strugglers against adversity. He had been hoping that a month in Sydney would enable Parker to get a grip on his nerves and make a fresh beginning with the Captain. He was inclined to dismiss as rumours the stories of Parker's previous misconduct on the bridge. Tombs was a strong believer in hoping for the best from people and events.

Arthur McKay seemed determined to prevent any possibility of Parker's reform. He had declared war on his executive officer. It was certain to cause turmoil throughout the ship. When the two top officers began feuding, the men were inclined to think no one was in command. Discipline collapsed, and the ship was on its way to becoming the most dreaded word in the Navy's lexicon, a madhouse.

'I gather the Captain's had a history of . . . shall we say instability?' Moss said. 'Did he show signs of it at Annapolis?'

'Hell no. He was third or fourth in the class. Right behind Kemble. A lot of people say he should have been ahead of him, but he didn't want to embarrass that arrogant bastard by beating him. I never have figured out what Art saw in that son of a bitch. But you get that way about your roommate. At least some guys do.'

'That makes him something of an enigma,' Moss said. 'When did the trouble begin?'

'What do you mean – trouble?'

Moss told him about visiting the Captain's cabin when McKay was too drunk to talk. The First Lieutenant's blue eyes darkened. 'I hope you haven't told this to anyone else.'

'No.'

'I would say that comes under the category of vicious gossip.'

Moss had collided with George Tombs's loyalty to his classmate.

Throughout this dialogue, Oz Bradley sat chewing his stump of a cigar. 'You guys are missing the point,' he said. 'He let that snotty bastard Pearce put us to sea with two boilers that could fall apart any minute. I don't know what the hell's going on. But I'll tell you this much, George. You and I have got some damage control problems to discuss.'

A naked woman was lying against Frank Flanagan, her mouth open, her tongue pushing against his lips. He could feel every part of her body but he could not see her face.

They were lying in a back pew in Fordham's Gothic chapel, where Flanagan had knelt in prayer a hundred times. His spiritual mentor, Father Francis Callow, was at the altar saying Mass.

No, it's a sin. Can't you see we're in a church? When Flanagan tried to say this, the woman's tongue moved deep into his mouth.

Bells rang. *Hic est enim Calix Sanguinis mei*, droned Father Callow. This is the Chalice of my Blood . . . *qui pro vobis et pro multis effundetur in remissionem peccatorum* . . . which shall be shed for you and for many unto the remission of sins.

The words terrified Flanagan. The woman only laughed and moved against him. What would they do if Father Callow saw them? The priest on the altar whirled to meet Flanagan's eyes as he peered over the top of the pew. Wearing the black chasuble of a funeral Mass, Lieutenant Herman Kruger glared at him.

Don't be afraid, the woman said. He could see her face now. It was Martha Johnson.

Flanagan awoke. He was lying in his rack in F Division's almost airless compartment. Sweat oozed from every pore. Around him sixty other sailors breathed the same fetid air. He had a hard-on the size of an eight inch gun barrel.

He lay there in the darkness listening to the *Jefferson City*'s engines thrumming, the sea rushing past them outside the hull. He had been having these bad dreams ever since they left Australia. Annie Flood's tears, her fears for Flanagan's soul and her complicity in his damnation were ruining his sleep.

Lying there in the clammy dark, Flanagan realized Martha Johnson was part of it too. Maybe the most important part. Jack had showed him the loving letters she wrote in response to Flanagan's lying ones. It made him feel guilty. It also made him wish he had a woman like Martha – a woman who wanted a man's love and wasn't afraid to admit it.

Maybe it was just the letters. All those personal details Jack told him to put in. How they liked to do it twice in a row. The second time around, Jack called it. *Sweet seconds*, Flanagan had written *I keep thinking of your sweet seconds, baby*. Maybe he just wanted some of those seconds.

Wanting. Flanagan lay there, desire throbbing in his body, in syncopation with the *Jefferson City*'s turbines. The same desire was beating in the bodies of the sixty men around him. In Jack Peterson's body across the aisle. In Camutti's, even in Daley's.

At night, when they were not at General Quarters, Flanagan lay in his rack and thought of the ship as a giant bomb, six hundred feet long throbbing with desire. Sometimes Flanagan wondered why the crew did not go berserk, assault the officers, smash the engines, turn the guns on other American ships. It was amazing that they kept any kind of order aboard her.

'Let's go kiddo.'

Boats Homewood's big hand shook his shoulder. A moment later, eight bells rang. It was 0400. Time for the messcooks to hit the deck. A different emotion consumed

Flanagan. Desire was replaced by resentment.

A new order reigned in F Division. Their movie star leader, Montgomery West, had been promoted to full lieutenant and put in charge of the ship's Combat Information Centre. Herman Kruger had been promoted to lieutenant junior grade and given command of F Division. He immediately recommended that F Division should be subject to calls for routine working parties, just like other deck divisions – and should also contribute messcooks for three-month stints – like the other deck divisions. Naturally, both ideas were welcomed by the officers of the other deck divisions.

Kruger had also decreed that no one in F Division could sleep topside. It took the men in main plot too long to get to General Quarters. Although almost everyone else had GQ stations topside, it was unfair to penalize the main plot men. Besides, the ship was an unmilitary mess, with sleeping bodies sprawled all over the decks.

For the first draft of messcooks, Kruger selected everyone who was even slightly friendly with Jack Peterson. This included Flanagan, although seamen first class were not supposed to be subject to messcook duty.

When Boats Homewood had pointed this out, Kruger had snapped, 'He may be a seaman first on the books, but he's still second class to me.'

Flanagan stumbled to the head, where he was joined by a dozen other unfortunates, including Daley and the Radical, who cursed steadily while he shaved. 'Fuckin' fuckin' fuckin'.' When Flanagan suggested he shut up, the Radical called him a capitalist pimp. Flanagan threw Booth against a bulkhead. The Radical whipped the blade out of his razor and dared him to do that again. Homewood calmed them down and they trudged sullen to the galley to begin their labours.

In F Division's sleeping compartment, the temperature had been around ninety degrees. In the galley it was a hundred and would soon be a hundred and twenty. The cook of the watch greeted them with a sardonic smile. He was a tall lean Swede with tattoos up both arms and a voice that resembled a bow drawn across an untuned violin. 'Awright, get y'selves some coffee and wake up. We got six hundred pounds of powdered eggs to cook and two hundred pounds of bacon. You two big guys' – he pointed to Flanagan and Camutti – 'get the bacon out of the freezer, and you two little guys start mixin' the eggshit with water.'

Flanagan's appetite had declined fifty percent since he began his tour of duty as a messcook. He saw the vile dehydrated eggs in their primitive state, before water made them semi-edible. He observed the pale grey meat as it came out of the freezers, before the cooks added the artificial colouring and flavours to make the stuff palatable. He cleaned the slop from the trays and lugged the garbage topside to dump it overboard for the sharks, the only enthusiasts for the *Jefferson City*'s menus. When he stood at the hot table shovelling the stuff on to the passing trays, he meditated obscure, inchoate schemes of revenge of his persecutor, Lieutenant Kruger. He did not realise he was in a mutinous frame of mind.

The depression into which Chaplain Emerson Bushnell had plunged on the way to Australia was beginning to lift. He emerged from his cabin to renew his contacts with the crew. He held divine services on the fantail while they were anchored in Espiritu Santo. He resumed his bridge games with Dr Cadwallader and Lieutenant MacComber. Sailors came to see him, seeking his counsel about women with whom they had become heavily involved in Sydney. He gave them advice full of sonorous uplift that made them feel better, at least.

In theological terms, Bushnell remained in a state of despair. But he decided there still might be some useful work for him to do aboard the ship. He reminded himself that his uncle, Bronson Bushnell, had confided to his diary when he was forty that he had lost all semblance of faith in God. But he remained in the ministry, pursuing a career in the social gospel, fighting racial inequality, anti-Semitism and unemployment, until he died in the odour of secular sanctity at the age of eighty.

Bushnell soon sensed a different atmosphere aboard the

Jefferson City. Dark emotions seemed to be swirling through the ship – the very opposite of what one would expect after three weeks of orgiastic pleasure in Sydney. Over a rubber of bridge, Dr Cadwallader and Lieutenant MacComber filled him in on the Captain's declaration of war on Executive Officer Parker and his crony, Supply Officer Tompkins. 'It's absolutely hilarious,' MacComber said as he bid three no trump.

'I think it's shocking,' Dr Cadwallader rumbled.

The chaplain did not need any prompting from the doctor to sympathize with these victims of military tyranny. The Captain soon displeased the chaplain in other ways. He held a series of masts at which he handed out extremely stiff sentences – reductions in rank, heavy fines, in several cases brig time for offences committed ashore. Each sentence was accompanied by a ferocious attack on the executive officer's leniency in such matters, in effect blaming him for the crew's misconduct in Australia.

The Captain also began making surprise inspections. Accompanied by the Executive Officer, he marched grimly through the ship, running a white-gloved finger across tops of lockers, breeches of guns, the stoves in the galley. Whenever a speck of dust or grease appeared on the glove, he excoriated Parker publicly for failing to run a clean ship. The real losers, of course, were the weary sailors, who had to spend hours when they were not on duty scrubbing and polishing everything in sight.

The situation produced a surprising rapport between the chaplain and Lieutenant Commander Edwin Moss. As the son of a Presbyterian minister, Moss had taken an instant dislike to Bushnell's eclectic theology. Now Moss appeared in the chaplain's cabin to confess he too was beset by doubts.

God, the Navy and the Captain were entangled in Moss's mind. All had disappointed him in one way or another. God and the Navy had failed to elevate him on the latest promotion list. Since he was within range, most of Moss's wrath was directed at the Captain. 'He started out saying he was going to forget the past, all he wanted us to do was fight. Now he's persecuting Parker and Tompkins. God knows who or what he'll attack next. I find myself wondering about the Navy as a career. It makes me feel like a traitor, as if I'm betraying something or someone.'

'Now, now,' Chaplain Bushnell said. 'You're the one who's been betrayed. Organizations like the Navy, based on violence and death, have betrayal built into them. Their adherents war on each other as much as they do on some putative enemy.'

Lieutenant Commander Moss gazed into Chaplain Bushnell's myopic eyes. 'There's some truth to what you're saying. But not much consolation.'

'Think about it. The consolation will come, I promise you.'

Toward 2300 hours Mess Stewards Willard Otis and Clifford Johnson finished the last of the dishes in the wardroom scullery and peeled off their sweat-soaked clothes in their compartment. Chief Steward's Mate Walter Davis had told Johnson he was in the scullery 'permanently' for stabbing the Australian, and Otis, his partner in crime, had a similar sentence. 'I'd rather do brig time,' Otis had said, which prompted Chief Davis to bang his head against the bulkhead several times.

Otis and Johnson trudged to the head for a shower. Who should be in there, cooling off, but Chief Davis. He took two or three showers a day and always used a lot more water than regulations permitted. The two stewards ignored him and he ignored them. Otis, unable to shut his mouth as usual, could not resist mentioning that he had heard Commander Bradley complaining about the amount of fresh water the crew was using. Chief Davis glowered at them, but he began soaping up.

Suddenly, as they all reached the point where white suds were gleaming all over their bodies, the water stopped running. 'Son of a bitch!' roared Chief Davis.

He raced out of the head just in time to see a dungareed figure disappearing down a ladder to the lower decks. It was the third time this had happened in the past two weeks – but the first time it had happened to Chief Davis. On the two previous occasions, the chief had received a phone call from someone in the black gang informing him the water was going to be turned off at inconvenient times until the chief agreed to supply them with the kind of well-cooked chickens and tender hams and succulent steaks on which the officers dined.

'This ship is turnin' into a fuckin' madhouse,' the chief said as he tried to get the dried soap off his large torso. 'I told Commander Bradley what those engineerin' assholes are tryin' to pull, and he says, "Tell it to the Captain."'

The telephone in the compartment rang. 'For you, Chief,' said the steward who answered it.

'OK,' the chief said, after listening to the caller for several minutes. 'OK. You got it.'

Chief Davis awoke Wilbur Jones, the head cook in the wardroom galley. 'Startin' tomorrow, you cook a dozen extra of everything.'

'I can't believe it,' Willard Otis said. 'You're not goin' to charge the fuckers anything for it?'

The chief banged Willard against the bulkhead for a while and told him he was going to get his wish about brig time. The Captain had decided to give him and Cash Johnson a month each for stabbing that Australian, and the chief was not going to say a word in their defence.

Captain Jekyll, Meet Captain Hyde

It was a South Pacific sunset to remember. Thick bands of clouds in the south and west were tinted red and gold and purple as twilight gathered on the almost glassy sea, ninety miles south of Guadalcanal. In the *Jefferson City*'s Combat Information Centre, just below the bridge, Lieutenant Montgomery West was not in a mood to admire the spectacle. All afternoon he had been getting reports from his radar operator and from lookouts that there were unidentified planes snooping along the horizon. Sightings of hostile submarines added to his tensions. As CIC officer he was supposed to evaluate this information and pass it along to the Captain.

These days he was never sure whether he was going to get a thank you or a curt grunt from Arthur McKay. Something strange had happened to him in the week West had spent away from the ship. Gone were the kindness, the wry sense of humour, the inner serenity he had admired. The Captain seemed aloof, arbitrary. No one knew what he was going to do next. The wardroom swirled with rumours and theories to explain his change of style. No one could explain why the Captain kept Daniel Boone Parker around if all he planned to do was torment him. That seemed to everyone an unnecessary exercise in sadism. A lot of people, especially among the reservists, were starting to feel sorry for the Exec.

'I'm getting eight, nine, ten bogeys out there,' insisted his radarman, Whizzer Wylie. When he wasn't spotting bogeys, Wylie jived. He hummed nonsense swing tunes like 'Hut Sut Rawson on the Rilla Rah' and executed lindy steps while he sat there. He personified the word jitterbug.

'They could be our Combat Air Patrol withdrawing for the night. Check with the radio boys,' West said.

The talker contacted Radio Central. Affirmative. The Combat Air Patrol was withdrawing to Guadalcanal as twilight came down. But no one had a clue where they were. The Admiral had ordered strict radio silence. The blips on the radar screen might be the CAP – or they might be Japanese snoopers.

'They're not going anywhere,' the radarman said. 'They're just hanging out there. I think we ought to go to General Quarters.'

'Wylie, how many times do I have to remind you that you're not the captain of this goddamn ship.'

'Sorry, sir,' Wylie said, blinking through his thick glasses. He was only nineteen, but he thought that he knew more about radar than anyone in the Navy.

West telephoned the Captain, who was in his sea cabin. He told Arthur McKay about the unidentified planes lurking behind the clouds. 'Maybe we should go to General Quarters, Captain.'

'We'll be going to sunset GQ in fifteen minutes. Just keep your eye on them,' McKay snapped.

Ho-hum. No doubt aboard the other five cruisers in Task Force 18, equally conscientious CIC officers had just been told that they were idiots by their captains. At first, West had been delighted by his new job. It had a lot more responsibility than he had had in main plot, where he was mostly a nursemaid to that Mark VII computer. He had looked forward to working closely with the Captain. Now he was beginning to wish he was back in plot, with nothing to worry about but controlling his claustrophobia and getting the ranges straight.

His basic loyalty to Arthur McKay remained unimpaired. How could he be disloyal to a man who had given him five days of rapture with Ina Severn in Sydney? His mind drifted to one of those afternoons. They had gone to Bondi Beach, just across the harbour. Gwen was wearing a two piece bathing suit –

'Hey, Lieutenant. What the hell's going on?' asked the lookout on the compartment's port wing.

A plane had emerged from the clouds and was flying parallel to the task force about a mile away. Through his binoculars, West could see black objects tumbling from its belly into the water. The lookout on the starboard wing summoned him to watch a similar performance on that side of the formation. The black objects turned out to be flares. Suddenly the task force was steaming between two rows of burning lights, like a parade of trucks along a brilliantly lighted highway.

'The bridge wants to know what you make of those planes and flares, sir,' the talker said.

Lieutenant MacComber was the officer of the deck. Like other OOD's, he found the CIC a wonderful way to cover his ass. If CIC said all was well, and it all turned out to be unwell, it was not the OOD's fault.

'Tell him to notify the Captain,' West said. Let MacComber get his head snapped off this time.

Ten seconds later, the General Quarters bugle blasted through the ship. 'Air raid, air raid,' boomed the PA system. 'All hands man your battle stations.'

'Radar, where are the planes? What are you getting?' West shouted.

'They're all over the place,' the talker gasped. 'Lookouts report planes on every goddamn bearing on the chart.'

'They must have come in under our radar,' Wylie cried, glaring at his screen as if it were a woman who had two-timed him.

West dashed out on the port wing again. The talker was right. Japanese torpedo planes, big two-engined Bettys, were roaring through those burning flares on both sides of the task force.

'Combat,' barked Captain McKay, 'don't you have even a rudimentary grasp of Japanese night-fighting tactics? Don't you remember they used flares at Savo Island?'

'Engine room, stand by to give us flank speed,' cried Daniel Boone Parker, as the five-inch guns crashed and the forty- and twenty-millimetres hammered away at the weaving torpedo planes.

'Belay that order,' snarled Captain McKay. 'Don't you remember what I told you about the condition of number one and two boilers, Commander? We will only go to flank speed when I give permission.'

'Aye, aye, Captain,' Parker said.

It would only take a few more thrusts of the knife, perhaps one or two more air attacks or a night battle to finish this man, McKay told himself. Then he could return to being the kind of captain the *Jefferson City* deserved. It was almost terrifying, the effect of what he was doing on the men – and on himself. He was becoming a martinet who snapped and snarled at everyone.

McKay found himself wishing Parker was more defiant. He would have enjoyed a struggle with the truculent man he had met when he came aboard the *Jefferson City*. That would have been a contest of strength against strength. But this man already knew he was beaten. He was merely waiting for the coup de grâce. It made tormenting him repulsive, almost reprehensible.

Over the gunnery circuit he heard Lieutenant Robert Mullenoe tell Lieutenant Commander Moss, 'We can't see a goddamn thing up here against those flares. I'm going down on deck to find some targets.'

'You will do no such thing,' Moss said.

'You have my permission, Mullenoe. Get moving,' McKay said.

'We're going to take one!' shouted Parker. 'Right full rudder!'

A burning Betty was coming straight at them, its torpedo still glistening beneath its big belly. If they did not turn, it was going to crash into the bridge. But a hard right turn would give the dying pilot six hundred feet of ship to aim at. It only proved that Parker would invariably choose any kind of dishonour to save his despicable carcass.

'Left rudder twenty degrees, you fool,' McKay said. 'Mullenoe, get that plane!'

A twenty-degree turn gave the five-inch and forty-millimetre guns on the starboard side a chance to fire at the flaming death machine. For a split second the two Japanese pilots were visible in the cockpit, their faces twisted into grimaces of pain or horror or both as the flames swirled around them. Then two five-inch shells smashed them and the plane to pieces. Burning fragments drifted past them on the water.

'Good shooting, Mullenoe,' McKay said.

'Thank you, Captain.'

'Thank God we have someone on this ship with some guts and brains.'

'Dive bombers coming down, Captain,' said the new bridge telephone talker.

The son of a bitch, Frank Flanagan thought as fragments of the exploding Betty flew around him and the Captain's sneering remark came over the gunnery circuit. What does he know about guts and brains? What good does either one of them do you in this floating bedlam?

As usual, the five-inch guns were tearing his head apart, caving in his chest. A tremendous crash and a shrapnel-filled geyser to starboard signalled the arrival of dive bombers whose aim was likely to get better at any moment. Exhausted from sixteen hours a day in the broiling galley and sleepless nights in F Division's airless compartment, Flanagan could barely focus his eyes on a target.

All the courage, the caring, the love he had accumulated from Annie Flood in Sydney was disappearing. The good feelings were being obliterated by the heat, his rage against Kruger, and now the old familiar fear of extinction. He found himself wondering why he had not jumped ship in Sydney. Ten or fifteen members of the crew reportedly had vanished.

The smart ones. Even if they got caught and died before a firing squad, it was better than dancing in flaming gasoline or being shredded by shards of a thousand-pound bomb.

'Flan, Flan. Get that son of a bitch.'

It was Jack Peterson, pointing to another Betty streaking past them in a run on the *Chicago*, off their port beam. Where did Jack get that unquenchable love of combat? He was born to fight. He and Homewood. His Navy big brother and his Navy father. Fuck them both. He hated the Navy. He hated Kruger. Maybe he even hated the Captain.

But he locked the Betty in the centre of his sight and pressed the trigger. The four Bofors barrels under his control spat shells. Out of the corners of his eyes he could see the deck apes on the mount cramming packs of shells into the loaders. Work your brainless arms off! He even hated them, stupid automatons, idiotic extensions of the guns.

He had the yellow son of a bitch. His shells ravaged the Betty's guts. But the Japanese pilot was a brave bastard. He kept his plane on course even while Flanagan was hammering him to pieces. The torpedo splashed and the Betty exploded simultaneously.

Jack vaulted over the rail of the main forward platform and landed beside Flanagan. He pounded him on the back. 'Great shootin'! That's the best you've done yet, kid.'

Maybe it did not matter what you thought or felt. Maybe he was just an extension of the guns too. A finger on a trigger, a pair of eyes in a director.

A sickening thunk came across the water, beneath the crash of the five-inch guns. They looked to port and saw the torpedo had hit the *Chicago* amidships. A moment later another torpedo buried its murderous nose in *Chicago*'s hull a hundred feet aft.

'Jesus,' Flanagan said. It always hurt to see another ship get it.

'Peterson! What the hell are you doing down there? That's not your GQ station.'

It was Lieuteant Kruger. He had come out of main forward. He was practically foaming at the mouth.

'Somebody told me Flanagan'd been wounded. I came down to see if he needed a tourniquet or maybe a transfusion.' Peterson drawled, grinning up at their beloved Division Officer. 'The main battery ain't shootin't at nothin'. You know that better'n me.'

The battle was still raging all around them in the last of the twilight. Dive bombers corkscrewed down on them, bombs exploded to port and starboard. Flanagan could not believe Kruger was pursuing him even here, on the brink of extinction. Before he got shredded or drowned, he would tell this bastard what he thought of him.

'Did you shoot down any of these planes, you fucking excuse for a human being? Go back in there and suck Moss's ass and mind your own fucking business. We're getting killed out here while you're inside that armoured fucking tower, you fucking Nazi freak.'

'You're on report for insubordination,' Kruger screamed.

'Make it mutiny,' Flanagan shouted. 'I wish I could turn these fucking guns around and blow you off that platform.'

Kruger wheeled and vanished into main forward. 'Jesus Christ, are you out of your mind?' Jack Peterson said. 'That's brig time, kid.'

'I don't give a goddamn. We're all going to get killed anyway.'

'Not if I can help it,' Jack said. He pushed Flanagan aside

and started blasting at a dive bomber that was making a strafing run on the crippled *Chicago*.

Kruger emerged on the platform with Lieutenant Commander Moss. 'Flanagan, you're under arrest,' Moss shouted. 'Report to the master at arms as soon as we secure from General Quarters. Peterson, get back to your battle station.'

The dive bomber exploded into a fireball that scattered flame across a quarter mile of sea. 'Aye, aye, sir,' Jack said.

It was almost dawn. Captain McKay was in his cabin writing a letter to his wife.

The *Jefferson City* had spent most of the night trying to tow the crippled *Chicago*. It had been a harrowing twelve hours. Snoopers droned overhead, submarines prowled the depths. The Japs knew they had hit a big ship and they wanted to make sure she went down.

Now the Admiral had decided to cut his losses, as admirals were wont to do. He had left the *Chicago* with a Navy tug and a screen of destroyers and headed south with the rest of the task force, out of range of the Japs' land-based planes. Everyone knew the Japs would be back at sunrise and the *Chicago*'s chances were not good. She had taken a horrible beating already. Both engine rooms flooded, almost everyone in the black gang drowned.

Captain McKay had had no sleep for twenty-two hours. Yet he felt incredibly fresh.

Dear Wife:
   I've decided not to take your advice. I have to do something to prevent a terrible injustice from being perpetrated. Do you really want a completely spineless slob for a husband, albeit wearing admiral's stripes? Are we so completely *exteriorized*? I don't believe you are. I know I am not. There are values that transcend promotion – maybe even transcend winning this idiotic war.

'Captain,' his Marine orderly said. 'Commander Parker would like to see you.'

'Let him in.'

Parker trudged into the cabin. His belly bulged, his

shoulders slumped. His eyes darted back and forth. 'Can I sit down, Captain?'

'You may.'

He sat on the edge of the chair. 'Captain, I want to get off this ship. I'll make a deal. I've got five kids. I just want a deal that will let me hang on until I get in my thirty years. You can say anything you want about me in my fitness report. I'll tell you everything that's wrong with the ship. Where the gamblers, the loan sharks are. The way Tompkins and the chief steward have cooked the books. The deal is, you won't mention any of that in the fitness report. You can say I'm a lousy leader, I was an unsatisfactory exec, but leave out the court-martial stuff. You can clean up the ship after I'm gone. What do you say?'

'You know that's not what I want, Parker.'

'What do you want?'

'I want you to confess what you did August ninth last. I want you to admit in writing that you betrayed Captain Kemble and this ship at Savo Island.'

A frantic shake of the head. As if he had reached out and punched Parker in the face. 'No. I didn't. That's a bum rap, Captain. I swear it is. I knew Kemble would tell you that. But I didn't do it.'

'Then who did?'

'Kemble. He was on the bridge. He made the decision. So help me God, Captain. I was out of it. I can't handle myself under fire. I don't know why. I want to, but I can't. My nerves can't take it.'

'You're a fucking coward and you conned the ship *away* from the enemy that night. Admit it!'

'I didn't. Jesus, Captain, you've got to believe me. That's a general court-martial. That's the kind of disgrace I don't want my kids to have on their head for the rest of their lives. I'm trying to get out of this with a few shreds of . . . of honour.'

Parker began to sob. Arthur McKay sat there watching him, feeling not a shred, not a quiver of pity. Cold, he was utterly cold, the way Win Kemble had always maintained an officer should command men. With the cold clear vision of a superior being.

'You're a talented actor. Commander. But until you admit the truth, you're going to stay on this ship. You're going to be on that bridge every time we go to General Quarters.'

As Frank Flanagan slung hash on the trays, he discovered he was a celebrity. Everyone on the ship had apparently heard about him threatening to blow Lieutenant Kruger away with his forty-millimetre guns. A lot of people congratulated him. They told him they wished they had his nerve. By the end of the meal, Flanagan was almost ebullient.

Back in F Division's compartment, Boats Homewood and Jack Peterson sent his bravado crashing to the deck. 'You are in *deep shit*,' Homewood said.

Flanagan struggled to regain his defiance. 'I don't give a damn,' he said.

He was dismayed to discover Jack Peterson also took it very seriously. 'It's my fault. I should have stayed in my fuckin' director,' he said.

'That's exactly right,' Homewood said. 'You're going to have to risk your fuckin' rating to tell that to the Captain.'

'Don't worry. I'll do it. I'll tell him exactly what I think of that bastard Kruger.'

'No you won't,' Homewood said. 'when you get a ship-mate in this kind of trouble, you got to eat shit, Jack.'

The boatswain's mate glowered at Flanagan. 'We can get the chaplain lined up. And Lieutenant West and maybe Lieutenant Mullenoe. They'll say a good word for you. But you're still in deep shit. You threatened to kill an officer. That's mutiny. In the mood the Captain's in, it'll be a miracle if you beat brig time.'

'I can take it,' Flanagan said.

'It ain't that bad,' Jack Peterson said.

'Shut up!' Homewood said, jamming his index finger into Jack's chest. 'You ain't here to give this kid advice. You ain't in a position to give anyone advice about anything. You've fucked up your own career so bad I get drunk every time I think about it.'

He returned to lecturing Flanagan. 'Brig time goes on your record. It follows you everywhere. What if you decide maybe the Navy ain't a bad deal and you want to go to Annapolis? You won't get there with brig time in your file unless you win the fuckin' Navy Cross or the Medal of Honour.'

'If I ever go to Annapolis it'll be to blow up the fucking place,' Flanagan said.

'Hey, wait a minute, you hot headed mick asshole. You don't know what the fuck you're talking about. Annapolis puts out good men. I wouldn't be in this Navy if I didn't believe that. Kruger ain't Annapolis. He's fuckin' eightball who couldn't get to be an officer in a million years if we wasn't fightin' a war. But he's got the stripes and you got to treat him as if he's the real thing. That's the way the system works. You can't run a ship on the idea that an eighteen-year-old wise guy can decide who he's gonna respect and obey and who he isn't. When you get down to the bottom of it, you got to buy the system, even when it don't work perfect. Otherwise we're all in deep shit.'

What the hell was happening? There were tears in Home-wood's eyes. Flanagan suddenly remembered an argument he had had with his father when he was sixteen. He had sided with his mother, who had remarked in her artless irritating way that most cops were crooks. His father had choked up the same way and roared that they did not know what they were talking about.

Flanagan looked at Jack and saw mockery, cynicism in his blue eyes. Jack did not believe a word of what Home-wood was saying. Jack did not believe in much of anything. He refused to take anything seriously except getting laid. But Jack did not have the nerve to talk back to Homewood. Was it because he was afraid of getting broken in half? Or was it because Homewood had been trying for ten years to be his father?

And Flanagan's father? His Navy father?

'I'm sorry, Boats. I'm sorry I messed up.'

Homewood took a deep breath, part exasperation, part relief. 'We'll get you off. We'll talk up them Jap planes you bozos blew away. That'll go down good with the old man. He'll give you a lot worse hell than I just did, but we'll get you off.'

'Seaman Flanagan,' Captain McKay said. 'I find you guilty of one of the most serious offences a man can commit aboard a US Navy ship. You defied a commissioned officer and threatened him with bodily harm. You are hereby reduced to seaman second class and sentenced to ten days in the brig on bread and water, sentence to be executed immediately.'

Montgomery West could not believe his ears or his eyes. The dismay on Boats Homewood's face was painful to behold. Even Robert Mullenoe looked shocked. Homewood, West and Mullenoe had testified that Flanagan, except for this one outburst, was a good sailor, a kid who had proved his courage – and incidentally his skill – on the forty-millimetre guns. Chaplain Bushnell, who looked even more upset than Homewood, told how Flanagan had rescued him from the blazing sick bay after they had been torpedoed in Ironbottom Sound.

None of this had made the slightest impression on the Captain. He had seemed bored by their recital of Flanagan's virtues. He had listened far more attentively to Lieutenant Kruger's absurd claim that Flanagan had threatened to kill him by swivelling his mount around and firing on main forward. Lieutenant Commander Moss, proving himself once more an asshole of unique proportions, had insisted this was a serious threat to his life and limbs too.

As the Captain went on about the need for discipline and respect for authority aboard the *Jefferson City*, Montgomery West suddenly felt a shock of recognition. Those voice tones, rising to the top of the Captain's throat, the way he was clipping off the ends of his sentences. It did not sound like Arthur McKay's slow, deliberate style of speech. Yet it was familiar. Why?

Captain Arthur McKay was turning into Captain Winfield Scott Schley Kemble.

Night Work

'Coco will light his pipe.'

There was not the glimmer of a star, not a trace of light on the silent waters of Kula Gulf. In the inky blackness, the voice of Admiral A. Stanton Merrill came over the TBS like a message from outer space.

'What the hell does that mean?' quavered Commander Daniel Boone Parker.

'Your head grows more sievelike by the hour, Mr Parker,' Captain McKay said. 'It means we will fire star shells the moment we get to the mouth of Blackett Strait.'

'Are we close?'

'We'll be there in five minutes if we don't rip out our bottom on a reef that isn't on the charts,' said Navigator Marse Lee.

Blackett Strait was a body of water whose reefs and shoals were unknown to civilized nations, except the Japanese.

The *Jefferson City* was steaming at eighteen knots. Ahead of her and behind her two more cruisers maintained the same modest pace. At that speed they left no wakes for patrolling Japanese airmen to see. Out on their flanks four destroyers probed for danger below and above them, their sonars pinging, their radars whirling.

On Kula Gulf's northwest shore loomed Kolombangara, a circular island bristling with Japanese shore batteries. On the southeast was the island of New Georgia, with a lofty shoulder called Visuvisu Point. That too was thick with Jap guns. On both islands, dive bombers and torpedo planes squatted in camouflaged hangars, their nearby pilots dreaming of American warships under their wings at dawn.

Guadalcanal had finally fallen to the foot soldiers of the US Army. To the men afloat, the victory had only added a new dimension of risk and fear to their lives. Now the rest of the Solomon Islands had to be conquered. While the Japanese

416

fought for Guadalcanal, they had built a network of bases and airfields on the other islands along the four hundred miles of narrow waters known to sailors as the Slot. It was the Navy's job to soften up these bases for invasion. Night after night, cruisers and destroyers raced up the Slot to bombard one of them.

Every officer and man aboard every ship knew survival depended on speed and darkness. If they were caught in these waters in daylight, they would be pounded to flotsam by enemy guns and planes. Always there was the possibility that the Japanese would risk their still formidable fleet in a night battle, hoping to give the Americans the sort of unpleasant surprise they had encountered when they came down the Slot to bombard Guadalcanal.

'How many Japs do you think we'll find sitting under that star shell, Mr Parker?' Captain McKay asked.

'I don't know, Captain.'

'It could be half the Combined Fleet.'

Two hours ago, CIC Officer Montgomery West had reported a radio message from Guadalcanal warning that patrol planes had spotted at least two heavy Japanese warships heading in their direction. Swirling around the ship, the news had swiftly grown into twenty-two destroyers, cruisers and battleships, all crowding into Blackett Strait to welcome them with salvos of shells and swarms of torpedoes.

A captain should not lend credence to such a rumour on his bridge. Arthur McKay knew this. But he was no longer speaking or acting solely as the captain of the *Jefferson City*. McKay welcomed the tension, he savoured the danger of these night missions, because each one sapped Commander Daniel Boone Parker's resistance a little more. Each one moved them closer to the moment when Parker would confess his act of cowardice. Then Win Kemble would be safe from disgrace. Arthur McKay could regain control of himself; he would resume command of his ship.

The Captain knew and yet did not know the damage he was doing to the *Jefferson City*. He willed not to know it. He was like the ship itself, plunging down a tunnel of darkness, hoping he could navigate his way to safety again through uncharted waters.

In the Combat Information Centre, Montgomery West was getting a stream of reports from the four destroyers attached to Cruiser Division 12. He did not relay most of them to the Captain. As usual the radarmen were going bananas trying to figure out what they were seeing on their screens. In mountain-ringed waters such as Kula Gulf, the electromagnetic waves bounced off all sorts of natural obstacles and turned into weird blips that might be anything – or nothing.

His radarman, Whizzer Wylie, started jumping up and down in his seat. 'We got something this time, Lieutenant. Two ships. I'm sure it's two ships.' Simultaneously, Radio Central reported identical sightings from the lead destroyers.

'That sounds like the real thing,' West said.

He spoke over the voice tube to the bridge. 'Captain, West in Combat. We've got two targets on our radar, bearing one one zero, range nine thousand yards. We've got to presume they're enemy.'

'Are you sure they're not our destroyers?'

'Our destroyers are reporting the same thing on their radars.'

'Tell main plot to start putting together a solution.'

At General Quarters, the Captain was still the same calm, steady presence. For a moment Montgomery West tried to tell himself nothing had changed – that the *Jefferson City* was still the same proud if battered ship that had stood into Sydney Harbour last December.

'What the hell is eating your captain, anyway?'

'What? Nothing. As far as I know.'

The questioner was a new face aboard the *Jefferson City*. Desmond O'Reilly was a reporter, one of three the Navy had decided to allow aboard ships in the Solomons now that the Americans looked like winners. A short florid-faced man who had been covering the war on various fronts since it began. O'Reilly was instantly popular with the officers and crew. He brought them news – good news – of what was happening in Europe and North Africa and Russia. He even seemed to have some straight dope on General MacArthur's inch-by-inch progress in New Guinea.

Naturally, O'Reilly had asked the Captain if he could be on the bridge when they went into action. McKay had abruptly refused and banished him to the CIC. That only made O'Reilly suspicious and not a little surly.

'Why the hell won't he let me on the bridge? I know how to stay out of the way.'

'Maybe he thought you'd get a better idea of what's happening here. The CIC's a new idea. All the action comes through here.'

It sounded lame and West knew it.

'Why's he on the Exec's ass all the time?'

'I have no idea.'

'The Exec's not Annapolis, is he?'

'No.'

'Is that it? How do you get along with the Annapolis types? From what I hear, they specialize in making the reserves feel like shitheels.' O'Reilly lit a cigarette. 'I'm a Democrat myself.'

'I get along with them.'

'They probably kiss your ass. You're a celebrity.'

'They didn't at first.'

'Oh?'

He found himself telling O'Reilly the way Mullenoe and others had treated him. 'West!' snapped the Captain over the voice tube. 'Plot says they haven't heard a word from you. What the hell are you doing down there? This isn't a movie script with a guaranteed happy ending, you know.'

'Sorry, Captain.'

'He's a real winner,' O'Reilly said.

Down in the forward fire room, Marty Roth stared at the steam gauge on the number one boiler. The water level kept dipping for no apparent reason, then returning to the middle of the guage. Below him on the deckplates, Amos Cartwright was adjusting the valves and shutters feeding oil and air to the boiler. As he returned to the upper level to check the purity of the water, Roth asked him to look at his erratic gauge. 'I don't like the way this thing is behaving.'

'I don't either,' Cartwright said.

He picked up the telephone and asked Oz Bradley to come over to the fire room from his station in the forward engine room to take a look at the gauge. Number-one boiler was their biggest worry. It had been showing signs of serious deterioration. Cartwright peered through the glass window at the network of pipes. Even a pinhole break in one of these conveyors of steam at six hundred pounds per square inch would cause a disaster.

Bradley arrived on the double. Cartwright told him what was happening to the water gauge. 'I think we ought to shut this mother down, Commander.'

Bradley shook his head. 'We've been told to stand by for flank speed to get the hell out of here after we bombard. I'm afraid number two won't be able to handle the extra load.'

Number two boiler was almost as sick as number one. From his top watch platform Roth looked down at the white sheet-metalled monsters. There was enough steam in there to roast the entire ship's company – or blow the armoured deck off the *Jefferson City*.

'We've got to sweat it out, Amos. That's all we can do,' Bradley said.

'Sweatin's one thing a nigger's good at, Commander. We been doin' it for two hundred years. But I don't know about this Jewboy here. He'd like to have a reason for riskin' his ass down here.'

'So would I.'

'Captain's still haywire, huh?'

'I've told him about these boilers five times. I've warned him one of them could go anytime. I think he flies the reports off the bridge for twenty-millimetre target practice. Or shoves them up Parker's ass. He's shoving everything but the main battery director up there, I hear. Did he ever act this way when you served under him before?'

'No, sir.'

'Typical deck officer bullshit. They probably got into an argument about passing a buoy or forgetting to kiss some admiral's ass with the right salute.'

'He's still a great captain in my book. But even a great captain has troubles, Commander. And the way things is set up, his troubles are our troubles.'

Commander Bradley thought about this gem of wisdom for a moment. 'Watch that goddamn gauge, young fellow. If you see that water drop out of sight, hit the alarm.'

'Aye, aye, sir,' Marty Roth said.

Frank Flanagan stood beside his gun director listening to the deck apes on the mount below him arguing about the Captain. Some of them said he had gone crazy and they ought to lock him up. Others said the Executive Officer was the one who was crazy and he was turning the Captain zooey. 'I heard Wilkinson tellin' a guy last night that someone ought to put one of them over the side.'

'Hey, that's mutiny. Ain't that right, Flanagan? You're our expert on mutiny.'

'Yeah, Flan. Whyn't you and Tarzan here jump ship and head for the jungle. He's lookin' for a pal to go with him.'

'Yeah, but Flan's too tall to play Cheetah.'

'*Mi no save,*' Flanagan said.

'What the hell does that mean?'

'"I don't know," It's pidgin for "I don't know,"' said Crockett Smith, the Tennessean who still believed in Tarzan. He had asked Flanagan to teach him pidgin. So he could talk to the natives on Espiritu Santo.

Flanagan's ten days in the brig had added to his celebrity status, even if his experience had not lived up to the myth. Sadistic Marines had not tortured him. They had made him scrub his narrow cell with soap and water twice a day. But that was regulations. Most of the time his Marine guards had told him their troubles. The Captain was persecuting their captain. Being a Marine on a ship was like being a boxing instructor in a girls' school. To pass the time, a Marine who had been wounded on Guadalcanal and transferred to the *Jefferson City* had taught him pidgin.

'*Jif i no letem,*' Flanagan said. '*Jif i wan pigin is.*'

'The Captain won't let us go. The Captain's a bird,' Crockett Smith translated.

'*Mitufala i sutum ol pijin ia.*'

'Maybe we'll shoot the old bird.'

'Seaman Second Class Flanagan! What the hell kind of gobbledygook are you putting on this line,' roared Lieutenant Kruger in main forward.

Flanagan put his hand over his mouthpiece and said, '*Man ia won kokonas is.*'

'Kruger's got a head like a coconut,' Smith translated. The whole mount guffawed.

'It'll be a month in the brig this time, Flanagan,' Kruger said.

'Just practising my pidgin, sir. In case we get shipwrecked.'

'No one's going to get shipwrecked if you do your job.'

'Wow. I didn't know I was that important, sir.'

'Shut up. I don't want to hear another sound from you.'

'What if he sees a torpedo comin' at us?' Jack Peterson asked. He was on the same gunnery circuit.

'You shut up too, Peterson!'

'All of you shut up,' shouted Lieutenant Commander Moss. 'We've got targets out there. Enemy ships!'

Tomorrow Boats Homewood would give Flanagan hell. He spent ten hours a week trying to straighten him out. But Flanagan refused to realign any part of himself. He had decided Jack Peterson was right about everything. The Navy was organized for the benefit of the officers, and any sailor who did not talk back to them whenever he got a chance would wind up a sad sack like Daley. You had to be tough to survive as a sailor, and that was not a bad thing, because if you made it into the ranks of the tough you stopped being afraid of getting killed. You still might get killed, but you would go down fighting. You would die like a man, not like a scared altar boy.

Jack was right about women too. Getting laid regularly was the most important thing a tough sailor could do, and it was a waste of time to feel sorry for the women whose hearts you broke. He had stopped writing to Teresa Brownlow and

Annie Flood and cheerfully composed letter after letter to Martha Johnson for Jack, each dripping with romantic bullshit.

'*I no gat wan samting long ples ia,*' Flanagan said.

'Two bits there's nothing out there,' Crockett Smith translated.

The five-inch gun boomed. Up up up mounted the star shell. It exploded over the mouth of Blackett Strait, spraying the inky waters with unreal phosphorescent light. Beneath its glare, along the shore of Vila Stanmore, the Japanese base on Kolombangara, steamed two enemy warships. Jack Peterson trained the main battery range finder on them.

Radar had already targeted them. 'Range five zero zero zero, bearing one one five confirmed,' Jack shouted. 'Looks like a cruiser and a destroyer.'

'Commence firing,' said Commander Moss.

The *Jefferson City*'s main battery boomed. As usual, the concussion flung the ship sideways. Again and again and again the guns thundered and the ship slewed under the thrust of their recoils.

'Check your course, Mr Parker. What is it?' McKay said.

'Zero five zero,' Parker said, his voice trembling. Lately, every time a gun went off, he started to shake.

'What's your bearing, helmsman?' McKay shouted as the main battery continued to pour salvo after salvo at the Japs.

'Zero four eight, Captain,' the helmsman said.

'You're off two degrees, Parker. What the hell kind of a sailor are you? Do you want to pile us on to a reef? Quartermaster, note in the log Mr Parker's criminal negligence in allowing the ship to go off course while we are engaging the enemy.'

'Aye, aye, Captain.'

'Look at that bastard burn,' crowed Boats Homewood, whom McKay had made boatswain's mate of the watch at General Quarters, severing Parker from Wilkinson. American radar fire control was getting better and better. Shells from all three cruisers had turned the bigger of the two Japanese ships into an exploding pyre.

'Torpedo off the starboard bow bearing zero four five,' cried the newest telephone talker.

'Left full rudder,' gasped Parker.

'Torpedo off the port beam bearing two seven zero,' cried the talker.

Torpedoes were coming from both directions.

'There must be a sub out there!' Parker cried. 'What should I do, Captain?'

'Left full rudder and pray,' McKay said.

'*Helena* is hit,' the port bridge lookout shouted.

Ahead of them, flaming oil leaped into the dark sky as the light cruiser *Helena* took a torpedo amidships. Another one tore into her bow. She lurched drunkenly to port and went dead in the water, flames roaring up her mainmast

'Shift targets, Moss. Get that Japanese destroyer,' McKay said. 'You should have had him before he got off a single torpedo.'

'Did you give me such an order, Captain?' Moss said.

'Get him before he gets us, you punctilious fool,' McKay snarled.

'Torpedo amidships!' the talker cried.

Everyone braced himself for the impact. Nothing happened. 'It went right under us,' the talker said.

'I had a feeling it might run deep,' McKay said.

'We still got some good joss left, Captain,' Homewood said.

'On target,' Peterson shouted over the gunnery circuit. The main battery had found the second Japanese ship. She was zigzagging desperately under a hail of shells, flames spouting as high as her funnels. There was a tremendous explosion and she vanished.

'*Helena*'s going down,' Supply Officer Tompkins said. He was on the port wing of the bridge, still giving the black gang and the damage control parties below decks a running account of the action.

'Oh, my God!' Parker cried.

The water ahead of them leaped into spectacular phosphorescent fountains. Those were five-inch shells. Pinpoints of light speckled the coast of Kolombangara.

'Shore batteries. I was afraid we'd wake them up,' McKay said.

Admiral Merrill ordered the two remaining cruisers and four destroyers to form a bombardment column, with the *Jefferson City* in the lead. A shell came hissing out of the night and passed less than three feet in front of the bridge to explode off the port bow. 'Can't we zigzag?' Parker cried.

'Quartermaster,' McKay said, 'record in the log that the Executive Officer attempted to make an unauthorized manoeuvre that can only be attributed to cowardice.'

Explosions hurled water skyward on both sides of the *Jefferson City*. They were bracketed. The next salvo could be on target.

'Gunnery Officer, can't you silence those batteries?' McKay snapped.

'*I can't stand it. I can't stand it,*' Parker screamed. '*I told you I can't stand it. Why are you doing this to me?*'

'Quartermaster, record Commander Parker's cowardly behaviour in the log.'

'*You son of a bitch,*' Parker screamed. He lunged past Homewood and tore the telephone headset off the talker.

'*Do you hear me, men? We've got a captain who's a son of a bitch. An Annapolis son of a bitch who's trying to kill me, kill all of us.*'

'Boatswain, get that telephone away from him. Call two Marines and put Commander Parker under arrest,' McKay said.

He was amazed by how utterly calm he felt. Was it disdain? Or despair? Parker was reducing his ship to a shambles. Homewood had to wrestle the talker's headset away from him. Parker backed out on the port wing of the bridge, shouting incoherently for the Admiral, the chaplain. Lieutenant Tompkins stood there goggle-eyed while the Executive Officer's ravings went below decks over his telephone circuit.

Ashore on Vila Stanmore, an explosion sent flames leaping five hundred feet into the night. Their shells had found an ammunition dump. Dazed by the blast, the Japanese gunners' next rounds were wide. Parker continued to rave, most of his words obliterated by the relentless thunder of the guns. It was almost as if this madness on the bridge was irrelevant. Like a huge impersonal machine, the *Jefferson City* continued to fling destruction at the enemy. West in CIC reported that the black cats, the PBY observation planes flying above them said their shooting was 'perfection'.

Two Marines appeared and dragged Parker off the bridge. '*Help me, help me,*' he screamed. '*They're gonna put me over the side.*'

Admiral Merrill ordered his squadron to countermarch and give the Japanese another dose. Captain McKay asked Navigator Marse Lee to act as officer of the deck. He quietly gave the orders to the helmsman, and the *Jefferson City* came about and resumed bombarding on the new course.

'Captain,' Boats Homewood said, 'I been in the Navy twenty-nine years and I never seen nothin' like that before.'

McKay heard the reproach in his words. It was not insubordination. It was closer to a plea for an explanation. But Captain McKay could not explain himself to Boatswain's Mate First Class Homewood or to anyone else.

'It's almost over, Boats. Almost over,' he said.

'Bridge is ordering flank speed,' shouted the talker in the forward fire room.

Checkman Marty Roth watched his bobbing water gauge as the chief boiler tender began lighting off all the burners beneath number-one boiler. Amos Cartwright was down on the deckplates beside him checking the purity of the oil. It was essential no water was mixed with the oil that was fed into the burners.

Roth felt the vibration as the *Jefferson City*'s engines surged to flank speed. It sent a shiver of pleasure through his body. He could visualize in his mind's eye the high-pressure steam whirling the blades of the turbines to produce the horsepower needed to turn the eight-foot-wide reduction gears and the gigantic propeller shafts. It was beautiful. He felt a part of this magnificent ship in a way no deck-division sailor would ever know. They were mere passengers. He was one of the few who understood the inner secrets of her speed and power.

Still he depended on those idiots above deck to conn and fight the ship through the night. Neither he nor anyone else in the black gang could believe the obscenities and accusations that had poured over the phone circuit from the bridge a half hour ago when the executive officer went berserk. It was unnerving, demoralizing, especially with those near misses from Japanese shore batteries pounding against the hull and the main battery blasting away, straining valves and gaskets with each salvo.

But they had survived again. Now if they could hold these boilers together for the return trip down the Slot, they could look forward to a day on the beach at that garden spot of the Solomon Islands, Purvis Bay, where the temperature never went below ninety and the humidity below a hundred.

Sweat drenched Roth's body. He took a salt pill and gulped warmish water from a nearby fountain. Under his arms and between his legs, a fiery itch began to torment him. Almost everyone in the black gang had some kind of crud. The deck apes had it too, but it was harder to endure in the fire room's 120-degree heat.

Next week, he would take an examination for watertender third class. Amos Cartwright had been tutoring him for the past two months. If he passed, he would be the first man from his boot camp draft to win a rate. That would shake up the high IQ's like Flanagan and his friends in F Division. Roth wondered if his weary brain could retain the complexities of boiler technology. Terms such as waterside corrosion, acronyms like BTU's for British Thermal Units and DFM for Diesel Fuel Marine wandered through his head. These runs up the Slot, with everyone at General Quarters all night, made it impossible to get more than four hours sleep a day.

The talker, an Italian kid from Brooklyn, handed Roth a leg of fried chicken. It was delicious. The deal they had worked out with the mess stewards gave the black gang a steady supply of such goodies. The chow was some consolation for the constant fear of having a boiler explode in your face. The chief boiler tender, who liked seconds on everything, had summed up their philosophy. 'Why shouldn't we eat as good as those bastards in the wardroom? We know ten times as much as they do about the inside of this ship.' Even Amos Cartwright, although he had fussed a little about harassing the mess stewards, had gone along.

A piece of chicken stuck in Roth's dry throat. 'Hey,' he said, 'any cranberry?'

The talker brought over the toolbox in which the chicken was hidden. One of the scoop compartments in the top was full of cranberry. Roth spooned some into his mouth. The chicken went down. He gulped down the rest of the meat on the leg and looked at the water gauge.

Blank. It was empty. There was no water in the gauge. No water! The goddamn water was not just dropping. It had disappeared. 'Water out of sight,' he shouted.

Amos Cartwright whirled. The chief boiler tender backed away from the firebox. Roth flinched before the glare on Cartwright's black face. He had fucked up. How could that water have disappeared so fast?

Cartwright was coming up the ladder towards him. The chief was back at the firebox frantically turning the burner handles. In a low-water casualty, they had about sixty seconds to shut down the boiler before the steam melted the pipes.

'Cross connect number-two boiler,' Cartwright shouted.

Cartwright had painted candy stripes on the valves to be turned when this emergency operation was required. It would enable the pounding turbines to continue to receive steam from this reserve boiler – if the surge in demand did not pull one apart too.

As Roth and the telephone talker raced to the valves, a sound they had never heard before erupted below them. It was like the roar of a hundred subway trains coming straight at them. With it came a scream of agony from the chief boiler tender.

Roth looked down and saw the chief whirling in a cloud of superheated steam, his arms above his head like a dancer in a nightmare ballet. It was a flareback. The superheated steam was boiling out of the firebox into the fire room.

'Run,' Cartwright yelled. 'Get your asses out of here!'

As Roth stared in disbelief, Cartwright plunged into that cloud of deadly steam to seize the chief. Flinging him over his shoulder, he staggered toward the ladder. But he could not get his foot above the first rung. The steam was destroying all the oxygen in the air. Roth ran to the ladder and started down to help him.

'Run. I told you run!' Cartwright roared.

Roth ran. They all ran for the ventilation trunk the only way out at General Quarters, when all the hatches were secured. Frantically they clawed their way up to the hatch on the main deck that Amos Cartwright had prepared for such an exit. In the lead, Roth shoved his palms against it and it popped open. They scrambled out on to the deck. 'Casualty in the forward fire room Boiler out of control,' he yelled.

Then it hit him. Amos Cartwright was dying down there. He had lost his best friend aboard the *Jefferson City*. 'Amos,' he screamed down the dark ventilation shaft. '*Amos.*'

Only the pounding engines and the roar of escaping steam answered him.

'Two good men. I've lost two good men. Because you wouldn't listen to me, Art. Because you turned into a typical fucking deck officer in front of my eyes. What the hell is happening to you? Why is reaming Parker's ass more important than the safety of this ship?'

Oz Bradley raged up and down the Captain's sea cabin. Arthur McKay stared at his painting of a Chinese sage coming down a mountain. He had moved it to the sea cabin because he spent almost all his time in this cubicle now. 'We had orders, Oz. That Buord scientist.'

'I'm not talking about him. That was three months ago. I've been sending you reports about those fucking boilers ever since we started these high-speed runs up the Slot. Why in Christ didn't you send them to the Admiral? He might have detached us for a week in Nouméa. That's all we needed. A week alongside a repair ship with the right equipment, a couple of good boiler specialists.'

'I don't think he would have spared us. We're the only cruiser division left in this game.'

'I thought you'd take losing Cartwright a lot harder. The guy practically worshipped you, Art.'

'He was a good man. But I've got other things on my mind, Oz. Good night.'

Bradley stamped out muttering, Captain McKay poured himself a half glass of Bull Halsey's bourbon. He drank it in one continuous swallow, and stepped on to the bridge. They were out of Kula Gulf, heading down the Slot toward Guadalcanal and safety. The *Jefferson City* was able to maintain twenty knots, which satisfied Admiral Merrill. McKay did not report Oz Bradley's anxiety about the strain on the three remaining boilers. It was not the Admiral's job to worry about the internal problems, mechanical or personal, aboard individual ships.

'I'm going below to see Parker,' he told Officer of the Deck Marse Lee.

Preceded by his Marine orderly, he descended to Officers' Country. At the door of Parker's cabin, two Marines came to attention. 'How is he?' McKay asked.

'Chaplain's with him, sir. Seems to have quieted him down.'

'I want to see him.'

The door opened and Emerson Bushnell stepped into the passageway. His reaction to McKay was a glare. 'What do you want, Captain?' he said.

'I want to see Commander Parker.'

'I don't think that's advisable.'

'That's for me to decide, not you.'

'It is for me to decide, Captain. In my official capacity as the man responsible for the spiritual condition of this ship.'

'It's about time you've taken some responsibility for it. But your authority doesn't supersede mine, Chaplain, and it never will.'

'You put yourself above charity, above compassion, Captain?'

'I put myself above you, Chaplain. It's very clear in the chain of command. Get out of my way.'

He pushed the chaplain aside and stepped into the room.

Daniel Boone Parker was lying in his bunk. It occurred to McKay that he had never visited this man in his cabin before. On the bulkhead above the bed was a portrait of his wife and five children. The wife was a plump square-jawed woman who looked into the camera with a faintly puzzled expression on her face. She was familiar. McKay had seen her at a hundred church picnics in Kansas. A good-hearted, forthright woman, baffled by what life had done to her. The children, three girls and two boys were dressed in Sunday clothes. All wore formal expressions imposed on them by the photographer.

Parker said nothing. He just stared at McKay.

'I'm here to tell you that you can get off this ship tomorrow, Commander. If you'll sign the statement I've drawn up for you.'

Parker shook his head. 'I'll be off this ship tomorrow anyway, Captain. I've had a nervous breakdown, thanks to you. That's Dr Cadwallader's diagnosis.'

He spoke slowly, thickly. McKay realized Cadwallader had probably given him a sedative. 'I'll decide whether you've had a breakdown or are simply trying to escape combat.'

Parker began to weep. Fat babyish tears trickled down his cheeks. 'You fucking bastard. You fucking Annapolis bastard.'

Captain McKay returned to the bridge and asked for a report from the engine room. The runaway boiler had been secured. Feed pumps and turbines were functioning satisfactorily. In the sea cabin, McKay poured himself another half glass of bourbon and telephoned sick bay. 'Do you have Cartwright's body?' he asked Dr Cadwallader.

'Yes.'

'I want to see him.'

He descended to the second deck and the dim silent sick bay. 'It isn't pretty,' Cadwallader said.

'He was an old friend,' McKay said. 'Let me sit with him for a while.'

Cadwallader untied the shroud in which Cartwright was lying. They had had to sew two of them together to fit him.

McKay looked down at the black face. The skin hung in loose folds where the steam had scalded it. What had he accomplished by giving Amos Cartwright a chance to prove he could learn as much about a fire room as a white man?

Amos, Captain McKay whispered inside his head. Amos. I'm sorry. If you can hear me, let me explain. I had to do it for my friend. The best friend a man ever had in this lousy world. He's more than a shipmate. You died trying to rescue a shipmate. Can you understand loving another man that much? I hope you can. Otherwise, there's no hope for me.

Sick Call

'The whole goddamn ship is going haywire,' Dr Cadwallader said, as his fingers probed Gunnery Officer Moss's tender stomach.

'What do you think is wrong, Doctor?'

Moss was talking about his stomach, not the *Jefferson City*. He knew what was wrong with the ship.

'I don't know. There's a locus of infection somewhere, Commander.'

Moss had been assailed by agonizing stomach pains on their return from bombarding Vila Stanmore. A large crab seemed to be moving around his midsection, trying to claw its way out. Was he developing an ulcer? He was in a panic at the thought of such a disability. An ulcer was a physical weakness. It suggested a man could not handle the stress of combat. He had decided to apply for a transfer, but now he wondered if he should drop the idea. He could not have an ulcer. He willed it away. But the pain persisted. He writhed as Dr Cadwallader pressed hard on his upper abdomen.

'What do you suggest, Doctor?'

'How are your teeth? Any trouble with them?'

'No.'

'Let's have the dentist look you over. Bad teeth can wreck the system. We may have to pull a few.'

'What's happening to Commander Parker?'

'He's still aboard. The chaplain's threatening to go to the Admiral. I don't think the Captain can stall much longer. The man's deteriorating by the hour. I can't keep him sedated indefinitely. He'll turn into a dope addict – or a raving maniac.'

'Do you understand what's going on?'

'I think the Captain ought to be court-martialed. What do you think?'

The claws in Edwin Moss's stomach pinched again. He was trapped aboard a madhouse – the nightmare of every career officer.

'Doc, I can't sleep. I go up on deck and try it there. I go back down to the compartment. My head's killin' me. I don't know what's wrong. I'm on the bum.'

Dr Cadwallader peered down Jerome Wilkinson's throat. 'Maybe you've got cat fever. Your tongue's a little inflamed.'

'My head keeps killin' me, Doc. It's like there's pressure buildin' up there all the time.'

'Take these aspirins. Four a day.'

'Doc, how's the Exec?'

Dr Cadwallader shook his head. 'He's through.'

'I saw it comin'. The Captain hated him from the day he come aboard. It's the Annapolis thing. They never wanted him to command a ship. They sent this guy out here to get him.'

'Maybe.'

'It makes me wonder about the whole fuckin' system, Doc. I mean, what are we fightin' for? To let these guys destroy a good Joe like the Exec? I been with him a long time. I seen the kind of shit he's had to swallow. I could give that reporter an earful, let me tell you.'

'Why don't you talk to him?'

'I don't wanta get my ass in a sling.'

'He won't use your name if you tell him not to.'

'No kiddin'?'

'I'll tell him to look you up.'

The End of Spring

At your quiet gate only birds spoke;
In your distant street few drums were heard.
Opposite each other all day we talked,
And never once spoke of profit or fame.

Captain McKay sat in his cabin reading Arthur Waley's 1919 translation of the poems of Po Chu-i. The *Jefferson City* was back in Nouméa, capital of New Caledonia, headquarters of COMSOPAC. Boiler technicians and shipfitters and welders were swarming through her fire rooms and engine rooms, giving her the overhaul she should have received in Australia.

A knock on the door. 'The chaplain wants to speak to you, Captain.'

'Let him in.'

Emerson Bushnell strode into the cabin. McKay had never seen him looking so determined. Instead of his usual cloud of doubt, a battle light shone in his eyes. 'Captain, if you don't let Commander Parker go ashore at once to receive medical treatment, I intend to speak to Admiral Halsey.'

'What are you going to say?'

'I'm going to accuse you of being responsible for his breakdown and then maliciously preventing him from receiving adequate care.'

'As usual, Chaplain, you don't know what you're talking about.'

'Captain, I am defending a beaten man against the tyranny, the sadism of the military mind.'

'No you're not, Chaplain. I can't explain what I'm doing. But I can assure you it's for a good cause.'

'You mean your promotion to admiral? That will be your reward, won't it? For crucifying this man in your search for a scapegoat for Savo Island?'

'I'm not searching for a scapegoat. I'm searching for a guilty party.'

'What if there *is* no guilty party? What if guilt only exists in your rigid mind?'

'You sound so certain of that, Chaplain. Is there something you know about what happened that night that ought to be on the record?'

'My task is to console, to heal the wounds war inflicts on men. I will have nothing to do with prosecuting or accusing anyone.'

For a moment, Captain McKay was tempted to snarl some Old Navy epithets at Chaplain Bushnell. But he restrained himself. Bushnell was another warning sign. The situation was almost out of control. Earlier today, Lieutenant Mullenoe had told him some of the men were talking about a round-robin petition on Parker's behalf – a gambit only a half step short of mutiny. He could not let his ship collapse into total chaos. He had done everything in his power for Win Kemble. The record of Parker's cowardice, his incompetence, was in the *Jefferson City*'s log. His breakdown could be cited as further evidence of his probable guilt. He would have to let him go without the signed confession.

'Commander Parker will go ashore today,' he said.

'Thank you,' Chaplain Bushnell said and hurried out to report his victory over the powers of darkness. Captain McKay turned to another favourite poem, 'At the End of Spring'.

If the Fleeting World is but a long dream,
It does not matter whether one is young or old,
But ever since the day that my friend left my side
And has lived an exile in the city of Chiang-ling
There is one wish I cannot quite destroy:
That from time to time we may chance to meet again.

Captain McKay threw the book on his bunk. Enough brooding on Tao and the fleeting world. Life was not a dream. The ageing machinery in the belly of the *Jefferson City* was real. So were the guns she fired and the men who manned them. There was a war to fight, a ship to restore. He had to start healing the wounds he had inflicted on her.

Another knock on the door. 'Captain, a message from Radio Central for you.'

The Marine handed him the flimsy. Captain McKay read it once, twice, three times. WIN KEMBLE DIED YESTERDAY OF A SELF INFLICTED GUNSHOT WOUND IN THE HEAD. RITA.

The Joker Is Wild

Ninety miles south of Guadalcanal, near Rennell Island, where the *Chicago* had gone down a few months ago, the *Jefferson City* steamed in column behind the *Columbia*. She had also spent a week in Nouméa, getting a turbine replaced. Captain Arthur McKay sat in his bridge chair, looking wan. According to the rumour around the ship, he had not eaten anything for three days. Horace Aquino, his Filipino steward, was tearing his hair out.

Edwin Moss was the officer of the deck. He kept stealing sidelong glances at the Captain, trying to decide if he was hung over or, worse, drunk. With some reluctance, Moss decided he was neither. With the same reluctance to abandon his worst opinions, Moss was impressed that a man could grieve so intensely at the death of a friend. As someone who had made no close friends at Annapolis, Moss envied McKay this emotion. It was noble, it was approved by those who studied human nature.

On the other hand, the Captain might be mourning the ruin of his career. According to recent letters from Mrs Moss, who seemed to be compiling a veritable dossier on McKay, he had tied his future to Kemble's perpetually rising star.

The thought of a ruined career sent pain knifing through Edwin Moss's belly. The crab's claws had been replaced by a pair of pruning shears. He had had three teeth removed two days ago, and his jaw ached in dubious syncopation with his stomach. Obviously, Dr Cadwallader had not yet located the locus of the infection. Yesterday he had given Moss a purgative which had kept him running to the head for most of the night. The infection was not in his bowels either.

A man's career depended on so many things beyond his control. His own body. His temperament. The commanding officers he got. Would the Captain call him a 'punctilious fool' in his fitness report? To Moss's surprise, McKay had apologized for saying that to him. He had invited him to his cabin and had a long talk with him about the gunnery department. He urged him to be calmer, more deliberate when he gave orders under fire. Moss had not found the talk reassuring as far as his career was concerned.

'Tell the lookouts to keep their eyes on those clouds,' Captain McKay said. 'There's too damn many of them for comfort.'

'Aye, aye, Captain.'

As usual, thick cumuli were piling up on the horizon to the northwest and drifting toward them on the trade wind. It was the rainy season in the Solomons.

Ahead of them, the *Columbia* was at General Quarters. Her captain was taking no chances on getting surprised by the Rabaul Reception Committee. Moss had suggested *Jefferson City* imitate her example, but McKay said the men would be at GQ all night. They were making another run up the Slot with Crudiv 12 to paste the Jap airfield at Munda. He was inclined to let the crew get as much rest as possible. Three destroyers did their usual wolfhound act on their flanks, alert for submarines. One of them, the *Casey*, was commanded by a Moss classmate. That piece of news did not soothe his stomach, either.

Would the Rabaul Reception Committee let them get by this time without a slash at their jugular? Maybe there was nothing to worry about, with a full supply of promixity fuse shells on board.

Moss got part of his answer ten sceonds later. 'Bogeys bearing three one five,' gasped the talker. 'More bogeys bearing zero nine zero.'

'They may be ours,' Captain McKay said. 'The Admiral promised us some air cover from the Canal. Sound General Quarters.'

The Marine bugler stepped to the PA system and blasted General Quarters. 'All hands man your battle stations,' roared the boatswain's mate of the watch.

The new executive officer, George Tombs, raced on to the bridge to take command as officer of the deck. Moss dashed to main forward to take charge of the gunnery. The twenty or so American planes looked like Douglas Avengers and Wildcats. They were high in the sky, roaring across the bows of the ships. Toward them growled a veritable cloud of Zeros, at least forty of them. Behind them came at least fifteen Aichi dive bombers and an equal number of torpedo-carrying Kates. How in God's name were they going to tell friend from foe when they started tangling overhead?

Mullenoe was in sky forward, checking the readiness of the men on the five-inch and forty-millimetre guns. Moss's stomach throbbed. He always felt superfluous in an air attack. These days he felt even more so. Mullenoe had been promoted to lieutenant commander. Moss no longer outranked him.

That only made Moss more determined to assert his authority. 'What's your situation, Mr Mullenoe?' he asked.

'Oh, I think everything's copacetic, Commander,' Mullenoe said. 'We've shit, showered and shaved and are all ready for the party.'

'Could you give me a more exact report, Commander?'

'All guns manned. Enemy aircraft at three one five, range three miles and closing.'

'You may commence firing.'

'Thank you, Commander.'

Did he hear guffaws on the circuit? Moss's face burned, his stomach twinged, his jaw ached.

'All right, boys and girls,' Mullenoe said. 'Let's concentrate on the torpedo planes and let the hotshot pilots take care of the dive bombers. If they get us we can say it wasn't our fault, glug glug. On the other hand, they can't claim we splashed the wrong guys.'

'Does the CAP know about this arrangement?' Moss asked.

'CIC says they do. Us dumb gunnery types never argue with CIC. Right, Lieutenant West?'

'Right,' West said. 'It's a court-martial offence.'

'Enough chatter. Why aren't you firing?' Moss said, his voice rising into that upper register the Captain had urged him to avoid.

'The Kates are playing hidey-seekey in those clouds, waiting for the dive bombers to get in position. We're dealing with pros, Commander.'

Ahead of them, the *Columbia* began firing. '*Columbia* has a target,' Moss said.

'Mount one,' Mullenoe said, 'take the leader. Mount two –'

The five-inch guns crashed, sending waves of pain through Moss's head. Overhead, the air was saturated with the roar and whine of diving planes, the chatter of machine guns as the Zeros and the Combat Air patrol tangled in a mêlée. Moss went out on the wing behind main forward and watched as the situation degenerated into total confusion. Zeros and Wildcats dove to sea level and zoomed skyward again in wild evasion tactics. The *Jefferson City*'s forty- and twenty-millimetre guns blasted at the enemy pursuit planes while the five-inch guns concentrated on the torpedo planes. The promixity fuse worked its magic on a half dozen in the first sixty seconds, but then the clouds of drifting gunsmoke, the dozens of black bursts dotting the horizon, the darting pursuit planes destroyed everyone's concentration.

Moss watched an Aichi dive bomber coming down with a Wildcat on his tail and a Zero on the tail of the Wildcat. The machine guns of the two pursuit planes breathed speckles of flame along their wings. The Aichi spiralled away in visible agony, his bomb falling far away from the *Jefferson City*. The American never pulled out of his dive. He kept coming straight down and crashed into the sea only a few hundred feet off their port beam.

More Kates exploded and burned. Lookouts shouted bearings of torpedoes. The *Jefferson City* sheared to port to comb their wakes. A Zero snaked away from a pursuing Wildcat and raced towards the ship, his machine guns blazing. Flanagan shot him down. But not before the Zero had decimated mount one's gun crew. It was chaos. Another Aichi coming down and no one trying to stop him. 'Mullenoe, get that dive bomber,' Moss shouted.

'Are you sure he's a Jap?' Mullenoe said.

'Of course I'm sure. I can see the bomb.'

Actually he could see very few details through the smoke. But why else would anyone be diving on them? The five-inch mounts elevated abruptly and fired. The concussion almost knocked Moss down. The dive bomber exploded into a ball of flame. He had showed Lieutenant Commander Wiseguy Mullenoe!

Off the port beam, another plane levelled off from a dive and came roaring at them. 'Mullenoe, get that Zero bearing two seven five,' Moss cried.

'Negative, that's American!' someone shouted over the phone circuit. It sounded like Flanagan.

But Mullenoe had lost control of his air defence team. They were obeying Lieutenant Commander Moss. As the silver plane streaked toward them in the twilight, the five-inch guns boomed. A proximity fuse shell exploded dead ahead of it. The plane pulled up abruptly like a wounded bird, and they saw the blue and white stars on the bottom of its wings. An instant later it tilted to the right and skidded into the sea.

While Moss watched in horror, the plane began to sink. The pilot shoved back the canopy and struggled to get out. He finally managed to topple into the water, where he floated faced down. 'Away the motor whaleboat,' shouted Captain McKay over the PA system. 'Is there a strong swimmer who can rescue that man?'

Frank Flanagan raced down ladders to the main deck, kicked off his shoes and dove into the sea. The motor whaleboat was lowered while Flanagan swam through a heavy swell toward the drifting body of the pilot. The air battle was over. The surviving Japanese planes were fleeing toward the horizon.

Lieutenant Commander Edwin Moss went down the ladders like a man descending into hell, condemned by his pride, his envy, his ambition. He did not stop until he reached the safety of his cabin. He sat there looking at his .45 revolver, wondering if Captain Winfield Scott Schley Kemble had chosen the best solution to a ruined career.

Arthur McKay was down on the main deck when they lifted the pilot aboard from the motor whaleboat. He smiled feebly at the Captain and whispered, 'Looks like the J.C. had my number after all.'

It was their old shipmate Lieutenant Andrew Jackson. A moment later he was dead.

'Jesus,' Boats Homewood said. 'Where in Christ are we ever gonna find enough joss to get *this* off our backs?'

'Commander Moss,' said a voice on the telephone, 'the Captain would like to see you in his cabin.'

To put him under arrest? Court-martial him? McKay could take his pick. He would endure it somehow. By this time Edwin Moss had decided not to kill himself. He had other responsibilities besides his miserable career. He had Eleanor and four children to think about. Above all, Eleanor. It was her love, the knowledge that she at least would forgive him for this blunder, that had sustained him.

He plodded to the Captain's cabin. 'Sit down, Commander,' McKay said.

'It was my fault. I take complete responsibility,' he said. 'I want to make that clear. Lieutenant Commander Mullenoe is not at fault in any way.'

'I know that. I want you to know that the accident has not been mentioned in the ship's log. That won't prevent it from getting talked about in the Navy. But I don't intend to give it any official standing. There will be no action taken. I regard it as a mistake anyone could have made in the heat of battle.'

'Captain, I . . . I don't know what to say.'

'Don't say anything then.'

'I want to say something. I want to admit I've been less than loyal to you lately. I've been critical. I don't deserve this generosity.'

'Maybe I've deserved some criticism. There's something

else I want to suggest. Since I made George Tombs executive officer, I don't have a first lieutenant aboard. I'd like to move you over to that job. I think you'd make a very good damage control officer. I want to make Mullenoe the gunnery officer.'

Moss could only nod. Drink the cup, he told himself. Drink the cup of humiliation as Jesus did. His career was still in ruins.

'Commander,' the Captain said, 'as a rule I don't lecture people. I've always dreaded turning into one of those pontificating old sea dogs I met when I was your age. But let me give you a little sermon about ambition. It's a good thing. You have to have it, in the Navy, in just about every walk of life. But whether you possess it – or it possesses you – makes all the difference.'

Suddenly the Captain's voice was choked with emotion. 'I've seen – I've seen what happens when it possesses a man. I don't want to see it happen to you.'

Mail Call

Dear Arthur:

I can't stop crying I hated him and I can't stop crying I know you'll say that's because I've always loved him and I only hated him because he wouldn't marry me but that's only partly true. Isn't it crazy the way things get partly true and mostly untrue as you go on living? I don't want you to think that I don't love you because I keep crying for Win, it's the guilt, something I've never felt before in my life. Guilt for what I've done to Lucy and that's stirred up the most awful thoughts about the way I treated my father and mother. Oh Arthur how in God's name have you stood me all these years?

But I never dreamt, never once did I dream that such a thing could happen. I thought I was dealing with a man. I thought it was a fair contest – actually unfair considering the grip Win has had on you all our lives – the struggle I've gone through to make you act and think like an independent man with a good brain of your own. I loved the contest and I cordially detested him, Arthur. If I ever loved him it was an adolescent emotion. As an adult I detested him and his arrogant self-assurance. I detested him even more for the way he reduced Lucy to a cipher.

He was not a decent human being, Arthur. You are probably going to hate me for saying this, but I know you are going to hate me anyway, so why not say everything? Win Kemble was not a decent human being. He used you, he used everyone for his own detestable ambitious purposes. Even in China, when he wrote that arrogant letter to the court of inquiry defending you, he was really trying to promote his right to shoot back at every drunken Chinese soldier who fired a bullet at him between Canton and Chungking. He didn't love anybody, not even Lucy. I'm sure of it, even though she'll probably deny it. She'll go on propagating the myth of her tragic hero. Otherwise her life will have no meaning.

That's why my mother stayed with my father. She heard all the stories about his mistresses, about his Chinese and Filipino children. But she had to consider the alternative. She had given her life to the monster, and was there anything to be gained by leaving him? That's why ninety percent of the women stay with the miserable husbands they've married. They want to give their lives some meaning.

With you and me it's been different. That's why I'm so terrified by what's happened. We've grown to love each other more and more. I know that's true, Arthur, though I frequently pretend otherwise. I'm not sure if you do. At this moment I'm sure you don't. You loathe me. All right, loathe me for a while. But don't stop believing in our love.

I can't stop seeing the whole thing exactly as it happened. Win flew to New Orleans to see Admiral Hepburn about Savo Island. I promised you I'd try to talk Cominch into calling off that pompous old porpoise. If Win hadn't written that letter to Knox I think I might have succeeded. Hepburn's questions made it pretty clear he was going to blame the whole disaster on Win. He asked him bluntly why he had sailed west into the night when all the transports and the Marines he was supposed to be protecting were in the other direction. Win went back to Panama and wrote him a letter trying to prove he was only following instructions. He mailed it, but he must have known it wouldn't wash. That night after not saying a word to Lucy at supper (not an unusual performance, I gather) he went upstairs and shot himself. He left a note asking Lucy to cremate his body and sprinkle his ashes over the Pacific off Pearl Harbor.

Oh Arthur, try to forgive me. Start now. Maybe by the time this war is over we can face each other again.

Your wife,
Rita

Friend of all my life:

By the time you receive this letter my spirit shall have joined those of my ancestors who spent their days in the service of our imperial majesty, treading the round world in a service we always knew was thankless, whose only justification was honour. I shall be part of the Pacific billows on which you and your strong ship ride, still in pursuit of that elusive dream.

All choices are hard, we always knew that, but choices for those who serve an ideal are hardest. The choice I have made is in behalf of honour, even though I no longer believe in its possibility. Can you understand that? You are the only person I want to understand what I am about to do. Perhaps you are the only person who can understand. It actually began many years ago, when I visited the great seat of empire, our beloved Peking. You were not with me. Perhaps if you were I would not have had this terrible vision, which has haunted me ever since.

I climbed to the top of Jingshan, Coal Hill, where the last of the Ming emperors hanged himself from a locust tree and looked down upon the string of pleasure lakes below me. From the top of Jingshan I saw a line of power running from south to north through the centre of the Forbidden City, I saw in my mind's eye the matchless assembly of palaces, temples, gardens and gazebos created for the Son of Heaven. I walked past the grimacing lions of golden bronze, the huge sculpted tortoises, the incense burners, the ancient crinkled rocks. I passed the Palace of Heavenly Purity and the Hall of Supreme Harmony, where thousands grovelled before the Emperor on his gold and vermillion throne.

I followed the line of power through these wonders to the Meridian Gate and the Quianmen Gate to the Outer City and finally reached the Temple of Heaven in the south. Three times a year, the Emperor journeyed to this holy place to communicate with the gods. All windows were shuttered for his passing. The city was plunged into silence. At the temple, after suitable sacrifices, he ascended the circular mound. In his divine footsteps I mounted the terraces one by one and stood where the Son of Heaven had once stood and gazed down on his empire. Suddenly for no reason I can explain, my voice cried, 'All power is illusion!' The echo instantly surrounded me. *Power, Power, Power, Illusion, Illusion!*

Oh, my friend, if you had been with me, I know you would have laughed in your steady farmer's way, you would have stood with your feet firmly planted in the centre of our American continent and laughed at the idea – and at me. But without you, those words planted a foreboding in my soul which I have never escaped.

Now the bitter fruit of that moment is ripe. I must taste it. I can only hope that you will not let it poison the memory of our friendship. Farewell.

Win

Dearest Robert:

Undine and Baldur sit watching me as I write this letter in the garden. They are patently jealous because they both know I am not thinking about them – not even the tiniest part of my heart is in their possession at the moment. The sun is beating down on the gum trees, the kookaburras are fluttering from branch to branch. All this peace at Fairy Hill while you dodge bullets and bombs for my sake, for all our sakes.

I wonder if, in years to come, Australians will remember how grateful they feel for you Americans (or should I say we Americans) at this awful time. To think that in a year you have entirely dissipated the terror we felt at the news of the Japanese armada ploughing towards us across the Coral Sea. I wonder if anyone in the world will remember how and why you came 6,000 miles to fight the Japanese?

Probably not. My father wrote my mother a memorable letter on this point only a few days before he was killed in France in the last war. He told her that if he died, she was not to go on demanding tributes from anyone for his sacrifice, or hers. He said it was too much to expect of human nature and would only make her miserable. It was enough for 'we precious few' to know and remember. That's rather good philosophy, don't you think?

However, if you think I shall apply it to my own life, if anything happens to you, I assure you that you're wrong.

When I lost Napier, I lost (I told myself) a hope for happiness. If I lose you, I lose happiness itself. Do you love me as unashamedly as I hope you do? I know men hate to admit such things. But I hope you still do.

> Your devoted war bride,
> Christine

Dear Frank:

I have written you four letters without an answer. I hope it's because your ship is in some remote place in the Pacific, where mail seldom arrives. I don't like to think you have stopped writing to me, Frank. Although we knew each other only a little while we exchanged a part of our souls. We had a meaning for each other that went beyond the time in which we met.

Oh, Frank, it grows harder and harder to feel Jesus's love in my soul. I go to other churches, but none of their preachers can awaken the smallest stirring. I have tried to find it in the gift of myself to sailors like you, but that has turned out to be as barren as any road through the Oklahoma dust bowl. None of them understand or care about what I am trying to do. They treat me like a whore, Frank. They offer me money. Sometimes I take it because I need it. I haven't been able to hold a steady job. I keep looking for someone I can respect, who has proof of the Lord's grace in his soul. But they are not very visible in Los Angeles.

Do you ever pray any more, Frank? I still pray for you. It's the only sincere prayer I can make, these days. I can't pray for my worthless sinful self.

> Teresa

Dear Frank:

What a bastard you are. Five letters and not a word from you. I thought I meant a little something to you while we were together. You've made me feel as cheap as a tart in Woolloomooloo. I won't even wear a green willow around my hat for you, Flanagan!

I think all you Americans are going to have to pay a price for the way you've debauched half the girls in Australia. See what a little neglect can do to someone with a strong dose of Irish puritanism in her blood? I mean it, tho. It's gotten so any girl who's even seen with an American serviceman is presumed to be a tart or a sheila, at best.

Still I'm too Irish not to admire a fighting man. I hope you've gotten that book of Yeats's last poems I sent you. There's a good motto in it that he wrote for his tombstone. 'Cast a cold eye on life, on death. Horseman, pass by!'

Love (in spite of your neglect),
Annie

Dearest Joey:

I'm still in the colonies fending off advances from countless slavering American officers. If I went into business I could match my Hollywood salary here! But I've been excruciatingly true to you, darling.

The news about your executive officer seems to have swirled around Sydney. That newspaperman who was on the ship for a while has been telling everyone about it. I don't understand why your captain didn't just sack the bastard. But take it from a sailor's daughter, the Navy is a very complicated world. There are feuds and alliances that stretch across oceans and continents. I think it has something to do with feeling so lonely at sea. The people you sail around with become almost too meaningful. Maybe when you get down to it, you're all mentally unbalanced!

But then, how does that explain your falling in love with someone as rational as me?

To get serious for a moment, I am thinking of going back to England. I am just a little discouraged by the chill that's descended on my career in your country. Charlie Benbow thinks I should go back and regroup. I know you detest Charlie and I almost think you don't quite believe me when I tell you he's as queer as Chinese currency and that story about us having an affair was the brainstorm of his publicity agent. But he is an old friend and awfully shrewd about show business. What do you think?

As ever,
Gwen

Dearest Jacko:

One more letter like the one I just got and I will swim out to wherever you are with a gold wedding band in my teeth. I've got to strike while your heart and head are in this state of romantic mush! It can't last, although of course I hope it will.

Forgive me for sounding cynical, but I have known you for a while. Everyone at Navy yard in Seattle (the navy officers, I

447

mean) is talking about how your ex-Captain Kemble blew out his brains. (I haven't been dating officers, I've been listening at nearby tables in the cafeteria.) Nobody seems to be shedding any tears for him. But I suppose his wife loved the guy. That's an awful thing to do to a woman. Deep down I think he must have hated her.

I bought myself an Easter hat. The first money I've splurged since I started saving for my trousseau. Tell me I'm not being unrealistic. I need to hear it as often as possible.

Love
Martha

A Hell of a Way to Fight a War

Captain Arthur McKay sensed something was wrong as he mounted the steps of the tin-roofed Officer's Club on the shore of Purvis Bay to confer with Rear Admiral A. Stanton 'Tip' Merrill and the three other captains of Cruiser Division 12. Bill Heard, the big jovial Texan who commanded the *Columbia*, barely said hello. Leighton Wood, the shy, introspective captain of the *Montpelier*, avoided his eyes. The captain of the *Akron*, erect, always correct Ed Bowers, an ex-submariner who had acquired that service's tradition of silence, seemed to be glaring at him.

But Admiral Merrill's expression was the real storm warning. Normally, Tip greeted his senior officers with a broad Georgia smile and a glass in his hand. Admiral Merrill preferred this somewhat unorthodox site for a council of war because it guaranteed them a steady supply of bourbon. He was one of the club's better customers. If you made the mistake of meeting him in the bar after supper, you might not get back to your ship until dawn. Like Bull Halsey, Tip believed a man should drink as hard as he fought and vice versa.

What could be wrong? McKay wondered. Last night they had had a successful run up the Slot, even though they had lost the destroyer *Casey* to Jap batteries concealed around

Munda Airfield. The *Jefferson City* had done a nice job of silencing the batteries after they had surprised the *Casey*. The admiral had flashed them a Well Done, which considerably expanded the confidence of their new gunnery officer, Robert Mullenoe.

McKay thought he had found the answer to the mystery when Admiral Richmond Kelly Turner emerged from the head to join them at the table. Turner would destroy the conviviality of any meeting. He had the same intense glower on his beetle-browed face he had worn the last time McKay had seen him in Nouméa. There was something else in his expression that made McKay uneasy. The hint of an unpleasant smile played across Turner's lips. From his pocket he took a newspaper clipping and spread it on the table in front of them, like a poker player throwing down an ace.

McKay could read the headline on the story without his glasses: A HELL OF A WAY TO FIGHT A WAR.

'As I've explained to the other fellows, Admiral Turner's here to discuss the landing on Munda scheduled for the end of next month.'

Triumph glittered in Turner's eyes. He had apparently done sufficient penance for Savo to win a second chance from Cominch King.

'But before we get to that,' Merrill continued, 'we've got somethin' a lot less pleasant to discuss. Have you seen this, Art?' He pointed to the newspaper clipping.

McKay shook his head. It was a wire story by Desmond O'Reilly for the International News Service. That probably meant it had appeared in a lot of newspapers.

'Admiral Turner brought it up from Nouméa this morning.'

McKay put on his glasses to read the text.

As I have reported earlier in this series, thanks to my tours aboard a half dozen American ships, I can tell the American people that the US Navy has the situation very well in hand in the Pacific. We are beating the pants off the treacherous little yellow monkeys, sinking their ships, shooting down their planes, blowing their airfields apart with bombs from the air and salvos from the sea.

But that does not mean all is perfect in the US Navy. There is a tradition of snobbery, of privilege that runs deep into the Navy's system and is in sharp contradiction to the goals of universal democracy and equality enunciated by America's leaders in this global war. Sometimes it manifests itself in the most pernicious way.

I saw an example of it aboard one of our cruisers in the Solomons. The Captain, an Annopolis graduate, decided to get rid of his Executive Officer, who was not an Annapolis graduate. The man had apparently risen too high for the Navy, who has never had an admiral who was not an Academy graduate, to tolerate. The Captain began a campaign of harassment, of insult and humiliation, to destroy this officer. . .

The story went on for another six paragraphs, depicting in largely imaginary detail how the sadistic Captain drove the brave, loyal Executive Officer over the edge of sanity.

'Is any of that true?' Admiral Merrill asked.

'No,' Captain McKay said.

'But the reporter was on your ship?'

'Yes.'

'How do you explain it?'

'I don't think I have to explain it, Admiral. It's an internal matter – a matter that concerned the discipline and good order of my ship. It's a captain's responsibility.'

'The hell you say,' Merrill snapped. 'This happened under my command. In Cruiser Division Twelve. It's my responsibility as much as yours.'

Kelly Turner sat there, his arms crossed on his chest, saying nothing. But his eyes were full of savage delight.

Merrill was right, of course. In the Navy, responsibility always travelled up on a curve that eventually landed on the desk of the Chief of Naval Operations. That was why everyone wanted and needed to find out who was at fault when something went wrong. If someone could not be found, the responsibility kept rising like the temperature in a runaway boiler until the explosion threatened everyone.

'The story is wrong. The guy doesn't know what he's talking about.'

'But Parker – your executive officer – did have a

breakdown. He was transferred off last month?'

'Yes.'

'Did any of the harassment he described take place?'

'If by harassment you mean correcting his gross mistakes as officer of the deck and noting in the ship's log what I considered cowardly conduct, the answer is yes. I had decided to get rid of the man.'

'Why didn't you? Why didn't you just tell me you wanted a replacement? I would have found one for you in twenty-four hours.'

'The man threatened me – he threatened all of us – with political retaliation. He has powerful friends in Congress. I felt we needed evidence to make a case for his incompetence.'

'Why the fuck didn't you talk to me about *that*?' Merrill said. 'Maybe I would have gone along. Maybe I would have advised you to get rid of him and let the whole fucking Congress scream their heads off. As long as we keep winning this war, they can't touch us.'

McKay faced Kelly Turner's mocking eyes. Oblivion, he thought. That was the only answer to this mess. Why hadn't one of those Japanese shore batteries planted a five-inch shell on the bridge last night? Why didn't his body revolt against days and nights of sleeplessness, words from Rita's letter and Win's letter marching and countermarching through his mind? Why did he still have a ship, a reputation to defend?

McKay looked into the stony faces of his fellow captains. They could not help him. They had all dealt with delicate problems on their ships. Ed Bowers, in a moment of candour late one night at the bar, had admitted he was tolerating rampant homosexuality aboard the *Akron*. The ship was a giant daisy chain. 'As long as they fight, I don't give a damn what they do off watch,' he said. But the moment a problem got off their ships, it became the admiral's, the Navy's headache.

'Maybe I should have done that, Admiral. But you've been captain of a ship. You know how a captain wants to solve his problems on board.'

'Sure. And I made damn sure they didn't get off my ship and turn into a fucking Frankenstein's monster that smears the whole US Navy.'

Arthur McKay saw Win Kemble turning his back on Lucy, on new ships transiting the Panama Canal to come out to the war, turning his back on the Pacific and the Atlantic, and mounting the stairs to his study. He saw him placing the black barrel of the .45 service revolver in his mouth. Why did he know he placed the barrel in his mouth? No one had told him that. Across the table he could see Kelly Turner smiling, even though his face remained contemptuously sombre.

Maybe the Navy deserves to get smeared. Maybe I'm glad I did it, even if the smear is a lie. Maybe I'm glad I've made Cominch squirm.

Say it, whispered a voice in McKay's head. Say it and end your career here and now. Say it and you will be off that ship and on your way to a kind of oblivion tomorrow.

But he did not say it. That ship out there in the harbour and the men aboard her were still his responsibility. He belonged to them now. Not to the Navy, to his career, to Rita. Only to them. He had wounded them in the name of a false ideal. He had allowed his personal life, his loyalty to a friend, to interfere with his loyalty to them. He would try to atone for that sin by becoming their captain, nothing but their captain.

'I'm sorry if that's happened, Admiral. I didn't foresee it – any more than you foresaw those Jap shore batteries that sank the *Casey* last night. War, life, is unpredictable as hell.'

That did it. He was telling the Admiral he might have made the same mistake. McKay could see pain in Leighton Wood's eyes; he was trying to say, *No, no, Art. Eat a little shit. They'll take your ship away from you.* McKay felt closest to Wood among the captains in Crudiv 12. He was another shy bitch, a reader and a thinker.

'Well I want to make a prediction now that I think will be on target,' Admiral Merrill said. 'You and your goddamned ship will no longer be under my command, one week from today.'

'I concur wholeheartedly with Admiral Merrill's decision,' Kelly Turner said. 'I hope I never see the *Jefferson City* in any operation I command.'

BOOK FIVE

Siberia Patrol

The coldest wind Frank Flanagan had ever felt in his life whirled across the Bering Sea, flinging great splinters of ice from the foaming tops of the waves. In the distance, some small humps known as the Komandorski Islands, the property of Soviet Russia, appeared and disappeared in the freezing rain and fog. Occasionally he glimpsed the other ships in their task force, the light cruiser *Richmond* and four destroyers.

They had arrived at Dutch Harbor, the American outpost in the Aleutian Islands, a month ago, after a harrowing voyage from the South Pacific. COMSOPAC had had no winter gear to give them when they were ordered to join the North Pacific Fleet. They had had to sail through these arctic seas in their dungarees. Sick bay had been jammed with cases of the grippe. Hands froze to guns when they went to General Quarters passing Attu and Kiska, the two Aleutian islands the Japanese had seized last year.

Now at least they had fur-lined oilskin zoot suits, gloves, hats with earflaps. But these improvements did not make life on the Siberia Patrol much more appealing. The desolate rock-strewn shore around Dutch Harbor made the very idea of liberty laughable. Day after day they prowled the sea between Attu and Kiska and the Japanese northernmost islands, the Kuriles, looking for enemy attempts to reinforce its only garrisons on American soil.

Most of the time they ploughed through fog so thick not even the navigator knew where they were. Officers of the deck awoke pouring sweat; even in their dreams the dread of a collision with a wandering iceberg or one of their own ships pursued them. At Abandon Ship drills, the Captain urged everyone not to go over the side unless ordered. The temperature of the water around them was twenty-eight degrees. A man would only live about twenty minutes if he had to swim in it.

A hand tapped Flanagan on the shoulder. It was Camutti in his white messcook's apron. He stuck a mug of steaming coffee in his hand. 'Hey, thanks, Mutt,' Flanagan said.

Strange, what was happening aboard the *Jefferson City*. Flanagan had discussed it with Marty Roth, who had noticed it in the black gang. The crew seemed to be drawing together in a new way. People did favours for friends and even for enemies. They offered to stand a watch for someone who was running a fever; the unfortunates with messcook duty risked pneumonia to bring coffee to those freezing topside. Guys actually offered people cigarettes after chow instead of threatening to punch a mooch in the mouth for bumming one too many. Even the cooks seemed to be trying harder. The food was almost edible.

'Where the hell are the Japs?' Camutti yelled into the wind.

'Home in bed drinking hot sake,' Flanagan said.

'Fucking US Navy. We got maniacs in charge,' Camutti said.

'Certified loonies,' Flanagan agreed.

That night at supper in the crews' mess, the conversation was mostly oaths against the Navy for sending them to the North Pole and obscene prayers that Admirals Turner and Merrill would fail miserably in the Solomons without the *Jefferson City*. Several members of the crew had received copies of O'Reilly's newspaper story from home and soon the whole ship figured it out: They had been sent into exile. This conclusion had a peculiar effect on most sailors. It inclined them to back the Captain against the Navy.

They took it as a personal insult that the admirals could let something so trivial as a newspaper story incline them to think they could do without a ship with the *Jefferson City*'s fighting experience. Two days before they left the Solomons, the best artist aboard had carefully painted on the splinter shield of the bridge the nine Japanese ships the *Jefferson City* had sunk and the twenty-two planes she had shot down. On their last night in Purvis Bay, an unknown culprit had turned one of their searchlights on this art work, so everyone could get a look at the kind of ship they losing. Admiral Merrill had cholerically demanded an explanation for this breach of blackout regulations. Lieutenant Montgomery West, who had the misfortune to be OOD, struggled in vain to supply it.

Now, on their thirtieth day of the Siberia Patrol, even Boats Homewood joined the chorus of resentment. His mighty brow furrowed, he struggled to reconcile his faith in the US Navy and his loyalty to the Captain. 'The old man got us through the Solomons in one piece. Now he's in hot water with the brass and we got to help him out. We got to prove all over again that we're a fightin' ship second to none.'

Only to Flanagan and Peterson did Homewood later confide his grave doubts about the future of the *Jefferson City*. Something was horribly wrong with the Captain's joss. Shooting down Lieutenant Jackson, their former shipmate, was grisly proof of it. There was an evil spirit haunting the ship, and Homewood did not know how to exorcise it. He thought they had got rid of it in the Solomons. Now it was back, more ominous than ever.

'Send out an emergency call for an albatross,' Flanagan said.

'There ain't no albatrosses flyin' this far north, and I don't think one of them would do us any good anyway,' Homewood said.

'What's the answer?' Flanagan asked.

'We got to win a big one,' Homewood said. 'We got to bring the good spirits back by winnin' a big one.'

'You and me and Jack. We'll attack Attu in the motor whaleboat,' Flanagan said.

'I'm serious, wiseguy.'

Flanagan still enjoyed talking back to Homewood, even though his disillusion with the US Navy was no longer so intense. The Captain had repromoted him to seaman first class for rescuing Lieutenant Jackson. He shared the general feeling that this exile was an insult to his fighting prowess. Jack Peterson was even more incensed because there was no liberty at Dutch Harbor. He had always wanted to make it with an Eskimo woman. Flanagan told him they rinsed their hair in urine, but Jack said that would not bother him in the least.

Jack had gone ashore a few days ago to get some spare parts for the main battery director. He ran into an officer on the pier talking to a representative of the USO. The officer was a grizzled old bird with a Swedish accent, a local fisherman who had been drafted into the Navy because he knew the location of every reef in the Aleutians. The USO guy was asking him in a high-pitched voice about the kind of recreation the men would like. The Swede called Jack over and asked his opinion. Jack said he could not tell him without getting court-martialed.

'See?' the Swede said to the USO type. 'Dat's vat I'm telling you. Vat dese men need are vimmin – t'ousands of dem.'

In the wardroom, the conversation at the dinner table was sombre. Closer to the Captain and to the Navy's hierarchy, they knew Arthur McKay had become a pariah – and there was a good chance they would meet the same fate. 'We may end up like the Flying Dutchman,' Lieutenant MacComber said. 'Sailing from one war zone to another as fast as the local admiral can get rid of us.'

MacComber had a classmate on the staff of balding Admiral Charles H. McMorris, known as 'Soc' (for his Socratic wisdom) to his classmates of 1912. He reported that the Admiral had filled the airwaves with protests when he discovered the *Jefferson City* was being sent to his cruiser-destroyer squadron to replace the *Indianapolis*.

Adding to the gloom was the sense of timelessness and futility that permeated operations in the northern Pacific. The weather and the enemy were equally frustrating. The Japs did not attack. They hunched in their holes on Attu and Kiska and ignored air raids and naval bombardments.

Executive Officer George Washington Tombs did his best to combat the prevailing pessimism without telling a lie. He stubbornly supported his classmate Captain McKay, proving the truth of the old Annapolis adage: A man put his roommate above a classmate, a classmate above a shipmate, a shipmate above a wife. Tombs was too true blue to add the final line of this old saw – and a dog above a sailor. He convinced no one when he said their transfer made sense. But Tombs went on arguing that they needed a cruiser up here with the *Jefferson City*'s experience and punch. The only other cruiser around was the twenty-two-year-old six-thousand-ton *Richmond* – little more than an oversized destroyer.

Lieutenant Commander Moss did not agree with Tombs. He was even more pessimistic than MacComber, although he refused to blame the Captain for their troubles. Moss excoriated the Navy. He said their exile was dolorous proof that politics permeated the service from the top to the bottom. There was no room in it for an honest man. He had changed his mind about making the Navy a career. When the war ended, he was getting out. He was going to study for the ministry.

Emerson Bushnell sat beside Moss, smiling like Alice's Cheshire cat. Moss spent a great deal of time talking to the chaplain. Mullenoe told Montgomery West he had begun to think Bushnell was an enemy agent.

Nevertheless, Moss had tackled his new job of damage control officer and first lieutenant with his usual passion for perfection. Division officers were bombarded with letters about dirty quarters and work spaces. Damage control crews were dragged out of their racks at all hours of the night to perform drills with hoses and fire mains and pumps. Moss issued an order that everyone in Damage Control should take his gas mask to General Quarters. This created consternation for several days. Most people, including officers, had discarded their masks a year ago. Moss had found out they could be used while fighting smoky fires.

The Captain let Moss have his way on everything. A strange bond seemed to be forming between them. MacComber thought it consisted of mutual despair. Both knew their careers had been ruined. 'They are two lost souls,' he declared.

Fascinated by what was happening, Montgomery West violated a regulation and began keeping a diary, which he sent in instalments to Ina Severn. He had originally thought his motive was purely personal. He was trying to keep her interested in his naval days and nights. He was not thrilled by her inclination to take Charlie Benbow's advice and go home to England. But West soon saw his diary's theme was his growing emotional involvement in this incredibly complicated system of reward and punishment, honour and glory called the US Navy.

'I started out looking for a story with a moral,' he wrote. 'But it goes on and on without anything that obvious emerging. Maybe in the real world, as opposed to the movies, morality flickers in and out of life like radio messages from CINCPAC or COMINCH. In between, things like sea battles and air raids, victories and defeats, deaths and narrow escapes just happen without any reference to our ideas of right and wrong.'

Cops and Robbers

As the second month of the Siberia Patrol began, Boats Homewood found himself in the Captain's cabin confronting the challenge of his life. 'Homewood,' McKay said, 'I want you to be my new master at arms.'

'Captain,' Homewood gasped, 'have you looked at my service record? I got more court-martials on there than the whole rest of the crew combined.'

'Those were in your salad days,' McKay said. 'You haven't got in serious trouble since the war started. I need someone like you, an old hand, to clean up this ship. I don't mean turn it upside down. But I want to put a stop to stealing food from the ship's stores by taking it directly or terrorizing the mess stewards into giving it away. I want to get rid of the heavy gambling among the chiefs and higher rates, the loansharking and the thievery. They're all connected, don't you think?'

Homewood's jaw sagged. The Captain had the *Jefferson City* cased. How did he learn so much, sleeping alone in his cabin and spending ninety percent of his waking hours on the bridge?

Still the boatswain's mate resisted. 'I'm no good as a cop, Captain. I did a lousy job whenever I drew Shore Patrol in China or the Philippines.'

'You won't have to arrest many people. You know what's going on and where. The minute I announce your appointment, sixty percent of it will stop. If we have to get tough with some of them, I know you can do it.'

'I hate to leave the kids in F Division. Maybe I'm wrong, Captain. But I sort of keep up their morale. They got the most important job on the ship – aimin' them guns.'

'You can stay in F Division. Pick four fire controlmen for your assistants. They'll be perfect for the job. They're supposed to be smart, and they don't identify with the black gang or the deck apes. You should be able to clean things up in a month. If you want to quit then, it's OK with me. Have we got a deal?'

Homewood nodded forlornly. He knew an order when he heard one, even if it was accompanied by a handshake and a pat on the back.

'A cop! Get lost. My old man's a cop. I swore I'd never be one. They'll put us over the side,' Flanagan said.

Homewood ignored him. 'Jablonsky, you're number two on the list. Fillmore, you're number three, and Bradford, you're number four.'

He had chosen four of the biggest men in the division. Jablonsky had added several inches to his girth in Australia. Harry Fillmore was from New Hampshire and was known as The Hulk. Danny Bradford was from New Jersey, where he boxed, he claimed, as The Irish Tornado. They all beefed as vociferously as Flanagan about the new assignment. 'Stow it,' Boats said. 'This is a direct order from the Captain.'

Homewood was equally immune to Jack Peterson's mockery. He needled the boatswain's mate day and night about turning cop. Jack called him Sherlock and asked him if he had arrested anyone lately. 'Keep your nose clean or it'll be you,' Homewood said.

Biff Nolan, the deposed master at arms, was put ashore at Dutch Harbor Bay and told to find his way back to civilization by dog sled, if necessary. Homewood convened a meeting of fellow Old Navy types in the crews' mess and told them to pass the word that the lid was on until further notice. Those who did not get the message would soon find themselves at captain's mast.

Lieutenant Tompkins suddenly became the most parsimonious supply officer in the Navy. His yeoman was even worse. Locks were changed so often, not even the best machinist's mate on the ship could come up with duplicate keys. Marty Roth told Flanagan how the watertenders extorted goodies from the mess stewards, and that racket too was ended by a warning. The black gang was forced to return to the crews' mess for their chow. Without the guarantee of the Exective Officer's protection, the big crap games in the handling rooms faded away. Jerome Wilkinson's private dining circle, the Muscle Inn, also collapsed. Without his patron, Wilkinson was just another petty officer.

Only one man resisted the cleanup – Tony Bucks, the loanshark. He saw no reason to stop collecting his weekly payments, which had swollen threefold on money borrowed for liberties in Australia. As storekeeper, he controlled the gedunk stand and ship's stores; he could make life miserable for a lot of younger sailors, who could not even buy an ice cream sundae without paying him first. Others were reduced to shaving with bar soap and wearing ripped shirts and dungarees so thin from washing they were practically see-throughs.

Flanagan wanted to arrest Tony Bucks. Homewood was in a quandary. He owed him money. He was a shipmate from the *California*. Loansharking was such a Navy tradition, Boats found it hard to condemn it. The shark was the closest thing the sailor had to a bank. Bradford, Fillmore, and Jablonsky, all of whom also owed Tony Bucks money, were equally dubious. Jack Peterson, who joined the conference without an invitation, was violently opposed. Flanagan pounded on the desk in the Master at Arms' office and made a speech worthy of William Jennings Bryan. Tony Bucks was crucifying his fellow sailors on the cross of five for four. 'You arrest that guy and the thief will disappear,' he prophesied.

'Bullshit,' Jack Peterson said.

'Maybe the kid's right,' Homewood said.

Under Inspector Flanagan's direction, they compiled a dossier from a dozen sailors who admitted they paid Tony Bucks twenty percent interest on loans. On the basis of their testimony and other evidence, Flanagan estimated he had the *Jefferson City* in thrall for at least $15,000. Homewood sent the shark a final warning. Tony Bucks told him to perform the usual impossible anatomical feat. They put on their badges and marched to Tony Bucks' office. He was in the middle of a transaction, his doomsday book open on the desk.

'I'll take that,' Homewood said, reaching for the evidence.

'It's all yours,' Tony Bucks said, his gold tooth glittering in the corner of his wise guy's smile.

'You're under arrest for loansharking,' Homewood said.

'You got to prove it,' Tony Bucks said.

'We got the proof right here,' Homewood said, flourishing the book.

'Take a look at it before you say that.'

They paged through the book. It was full of symbols that looked left over from the era of hieroglyphics. 'What do these say?' Homewood demanded.

Tony Bucks's gold tooth gleamed. 'It's a diary, where I record my intimate thoughts,' he said. 'That's why it's in code.'

Homewood pointed to page ten. 'What's that say?'

'It's a copy of a letter I wrote to my mother. "Dear Mom: How I miss you and your cooking out here in the Pacific –"'

'Arrest him anyway,' Flanagan said. 'We've got the testimony to convict him.'

They arrested him and the gears of Navy justice began to grind, punching holes in the prosecution's case. Lieutenant Leroy Tompkins, his division officer, appeared at captain's mast to vouch for Tony Bucks's efficiency and honesty. His account books were models of neatness and integrity. Flanagan's dozen witnesses also appeared with their division officers, who had advised them not to incriminate themselves by testifying they had paid the shark illegal interest. Under questioning from Captain McKay, they admitted they gave him 'a little extra' above their loan. But it was out of gratitude, not duress.

The *Jefferson City* rolled and pitched through the swells of the Bering Sea. Homewood produced the book of hieroglyphics and placed it in evidence. The Captain studied it for a moment. 'You say there's nothing here but love letters to your mother?' he asked Tony Bucks.

'That sort of thing,' Tony Bucks said.

'You don't even list a next of kin in your service record.'

'I don't want the poor old lady to get one of them telegrams, Captain. If I get killed, I'd rather she heard it from my friends.'

'How touching. Does your mother save your letters?'

'Oh yes, Captain. She reads them over and over.'

'Good. Then you don't need this.'

Captain McKay opened the porthole behind him and flipped the doomsday book into the Bering Sea. 'Case dismissed for lack of evidence,' he said.

Tony Bucks looked as if he had been impaled. Without the book there was no way to prove who owed him what. He was out of business.

That night there were celebrations all over the *Jefferson City* when the word got out that Tony Bucks had been deep-sixed. The loanshark lay in his rack flinging Sicilian curses on the Captain. Flanagan became an instant hero in F

Division and among the deck apes on his mount. Marty Roth spread his fame among the black gang. He was showered with congratulations on the chow line.

When he got back from supper, Flanagan noticed the door to his locker was ajar. He peered inside and roared with frustration. There was nothing left. His tailor-made uniform, his extra shoes, everything including his underwear had been stolen. The thief was sending him a message about human nature.

'As usual, you had to learn it the hard way,' Boats Homewood said.

Admiral for a Day

On the bridge at dawn, Captain McKay sat in his tilted chair staring out at the Bering Sea. The wind had died overnight, leaving the icy black water looking like a gigantic version of the Kansas ponds on which he had skated as a boy. He was glad Cincpac had sent him to the northern Pacific. Did Nimitz, with his sensitivity to the personal dimensions of command, know Arthur McKay was looking for a wasteland of cold and desolation in which to bury himself?

Rita pursued him with desperate letters. He took the latest from his pocket and read it again.

Why don't you answer me? Don't I at least deserve that much?

If you had listened to me, if you had taken my advice on Parker, the whole thing wouldn't be so unbearable. Can't you at least make a start on seeing what Win did to you? What he's done to you all your life? He used you, he lured you into making a last desperate gesture on his behalf. (Lucy's told me about the letter she wrote you.) Then when he saw how hopeless the situation was, how much of a case they had against him, did he stand up like a man and say it was his fault? (I still think Savo was his fault, although I can't prove it.) Did he even thank you for your attempt to save him? No, he leaves you, Lucy, me with the terrible burden of his death. Isn't that the act of a complete egotist? A totally selfish human being? Face it, Arthur. Face how this man has exploited you, ruined you. Ruined all of us.

Jesus, if he could believe that, he would be free. But it was not true. It was the Navy, it was the relentless, heartless bastard who personified the system, Fleet Admiral Ernest J. King, who had destroyed Win. Fleet Admiral Ernest J. King and his collaborator, his probable mistress, Rita Semmes McKay. As usual Rita was trying to have it both ways. She wanted him to go on loving her, she wanted him to forgive her. When she had made an irrevocable choice. She had fomented Win's destruction and that meant she was banished from his heart for ever.

Win's farewell letter created a different kind of torment. It enabled Arthur McKay to see how much damage their experience in China had wreaked on Win's soul – and the part he had played in it. Win's outrage at the policy the Navy allowed the civilians to inflict on them in China had been fuelled by intensely personal feelings on the subject. Win not only prophesied war with Japan for control of the Orient, he looked forward to it as a Navy officer's supreme opportunity to win fame for himself and imperial power for his country. When he saw how little enthusiasm Americans had for imperial adventures, his vision of himself, of the future, was profoundly shaken.

After China, they had both understood they were no longer in agreement on fundamentals. They had used the fiction of writing as Po Chu-i and his shy friend and fellow poet Yuan Chen to conceal this fact and avoid quarrels as much as they used it to commemorate their friendship. The letters had been Win's idea. They were also a kind of witness to the impact China had had on him. Its long history as an imperial power, its aristocratic traditions, had had enormous appeal to Win's own strong sense of being a member of an elite.

And more, Arthur McKay saw how much more the letters meant now. They were a kind of yearning for a world of power and privilege that was passing into oblivion everywhere, in Depression-racked England and America, in chaotic Spain, in totalitarian Germany and Italy. They were a dream of nobility, a fantasy of pride, a way of escaping the petty envies and demeaning politics of the peacetime Navy. Ultimately they were the stifled cry of a tormented soul, of a man who had lost faith in his destiny, even as he struggled to perform the role he had assigned himself.

O friend of my life, why didn't you give me a chance to help you?

'Captain, Combat reports five ships twelve miles due north,' the telephone talker said.

A moment later the TBS crackled. The voice of Admiral Charles H. McMorris growled, 'All ships, execute Plan Baker.'

The Admiral was concentrating Task Force 16.6, which was spread over twelve miles of water, cruising at fifteen knots. Captain McKay called Oz Bradley in the engine room. 'Can you give me another ten knots? We've got to catch the *Richmond* and a flock of Japs.'

'Sure. I've got all our boilers on line.'

The engine-room telegrapher shoved the handle of the annunciator forward. The *Jefferson City*'s turbines thrummed as she cut through the dark water at twenty-five knots. Soon they were within three miles of the *Richmond* and closing. Two of their four destroyers were in position off the flagship's port beam, two others were in line to starboard.

For the Bering Sea, visibility was surprisingly good – about twenty miles. The grey clouds were holding at about 2,500 feet. In another ten minutes the Japanese should be close enough to get a good look at them. McKay ordered the bugler to sound General Quarters.

Soon lookouts were straining their eyes towards the brightening horizon in search of enemy masts. In the CIC, Radarman Wylie was already revising his count. 'I'm getting six, seven, eight targets. What do you make of it, Lieutenant?'

'Probably a Jap convoy trying to resupply Attu and Kiska.'

'Merchant ships? Easy pickings for the boys in Main Plot.'

'We hope,' Montgomery West said.

On the bridge, Captain McKay was studying a black blur on the horizon through his binoculars. 'That doesn't look like a merchantman to me,' he said. 'What are we getting from our top lookouts? What does the range finder see?'

The talker passed the query about the range finder to Gunnery Officer Mullenoe. In sixty seconds Mullenoe had an answer. 'That's a heavy cruiser and there's another one right behind it. *Nachi* class.'

All by itself that was bad news. *Nachi* heavies could hit thirty-five knots, three more than the *Jefferson City*. In about sixty seconds Mullenoe was reporting that Peterson could see two more cruisers, at least two destroyers and two other larger ships with plenty of guns on them. 'Probably converted merchant cruisers,' Mullenoe said.

He was being nonchalant for the benefit of the men on the guns. But Mullenoe undoubtedly knew they would soon be within range of enough firepower to scatter pieces of Task Force 16.6 all over the Bering Sea.

McKay matched his casual tone. 'It looks like we're going to have some target practice, Bob,' he said.

'We're ready when you are.'

Both CIC's radar and the lookouts reported that the Japanese force was splitting up. The warships were heading for the Americans, the merchantmen were fleeing in the other direction with all the steam they could muster.

'*Richmond* is signalling course two three zero,' the talker reported.

That was west, a course that would bring them within range of the retreating merchantmen. Admiral McMorris was gambling that the Japanese admiral would take some time to get his ships organized to attack. There was a possibly fatal flaw in this strategy. McMorris was letting the Japanese warships get between him and his home base, to the east. He was risking annihilation to fulfil Task Force 16.6's mission, to block enemy reinforcements.

'Would you take this kind of gamble, George?' Arthur McKay asked his executive officer.

'Nope,' George Washington Tombs said. 'I'd get the hell out of here as fast as possible.'

'Think of how that would look in the Admiral's after-action report.'

In another ten minutes, Admiral McMorris found out the hard way that the Japanese admiral knew something about courses and tactics. He swung his ships between the Americans and the fleeing merchantmen. At a range of twenty thousand yards – almost twelve miles – his guns spoke. The *Richmond* vanished in cascades of icy water as four salvos straddled her.

'Signal bridge reports *Richmond*'s changing course forty degrees to port,' the talker said.

McMorris was putting open water between himself and those guns. Swinging to port in the *Richmond*'s wake, the *Jefferson City* was now the rear guard in the American flotilla.

'Captain McKay,' said McMorris over the TBS. 'I'm afraid we will have to fight a retiring action. I will adapt our manoeuvres to yours. I'm afraid the outcome of this encounter will depend on the *Jefferson City*'s gunnery.'

The Admiral was admitting that only a heavy cruiser could fight a heavy cruiser. Only eight-inch guns could duel with other eight-inch guns. It was obvious this admission almost made McMorris choke. Captain McKay smiled at George Tombs. They knew how the Admiral felt about having the *Jefferson City* in his task force.

It would be amusing, if it wasn't so serious. This could well be the *Jefferson City*'s last fight. Those Japanese heavies were going to concentrate on her as soon as they realized she was their only opposition. With the J.C. out of the way, they could pulverize the rest of Task Force 16.6 at leisure, without even getting in range of their lighter guns.

Arthur McKay felt incredibly calm, almost cheerful. Death would solve the mess he had made of his life, his career. But he had no intention of committing suicide. He was at one with his crew in a ferocious desire to show the

Navy that the *Jefferson City* was not a madhouse, it was a fighting ship. Nevertheless, his utter indifference to living or dying added clarity to his mind. He began thinking about strategy and tactics for a running battle.

The Japanese lead cruiser fired first. The salvo was hasty and wide. A moment later two spotter planes leaped from her catapults. With them overhead it would be a different story. Maybe the *Jefferson City* should try to score first.

'Bob,' McKay said to Gunnery Officer Mullenoe, 'take the leader under fire.'

In the main battery range finder, Jack Peterson focussed his lenses on the big cruiser. They were still twelve miles apart, tough shooting, but it could be done. In seconds, Peterson was barking the range and bearing to CIC. In that busy compartment, Radarman Wylie confirmed Jack's estimates from the blips on his glowing screen. Montgomery West hurried the numbers to main plot to match against their radar. In the turrets, shells slammed into breeches, officers pressed the ready buttons. Robert Mullenoe had shaped the gunnery department into a smooth confident team.

'Fire,' Mullenoe said. Four salvos slammed from the big guns in rapid succession.

'We got him,' George Tombs shouted on the bridge.

A gush of yellow flame rose around the lead cruiser's bridge. It was followed by the thick black smoke of an oil fire. Another fire began burning on her stern. But her guns spoke in return. This time booming fountains full of yellow dye leaped toward the sky only a hundred yards off the *Jefferson City*'s port quarter. Like the Americans, the Japanese dyed their gunpowder so they could decide who made the hits in target practice.

The Japanese leader, undoubtedly their flagship, kept coming in spite of their hits. The oil smoke soon vanished. 'Good damage control,' George Tombs said.

'Too damn good,' McKay said.

The enemy flagship began firing again. The salvos walked toward the *Jefferson City* as if an invisible giant in yellow seven league boots was stomping towards them. This laddering was one of the basic techniques of long-range naval gunnery. Captain McKay did nothing until a fifth salvo landed less than a hundred yards off their port quarter. 'Ten degrees right rudder, George,' McKay said.

The helmsman spun the wheel, the *Jefferson City* swung to starboard – and thirty seconds later another salvo tore up the water where she had been a half minute before.

'Fifteen degrees left rudder,' McKay said.

The *Jefferson City* zigged in the other direction. This time the Japanese salvo screamed overhead to crash off the starboard beam.

'By God, George, I haven't had this much fun since I learned to fence at Annapolis,' McKay said.

That had been Win Kemble's idea. He had been in love with the military traditions of the eighteenth century, when every officer and gentleman knew how to handle a blade. Arthur McKay had thought fencing was ridiculous and said so. But he had changed his mind when he analysed it as a military exercise. The thrusts, the parries, the feints were remarkably similar to what a commander was supposed to do fighting ship-to-ship or fleet-to-fleet.

Now, twenty-five years later, facing the real thing, Arthur McKay decided the comparison still rang true. Separated by a dozen miles, there was a ritual quality to the movements of the antagonists. He watched as the Japanese captain swung to port to unmask his stern batteries. His guns bloomed fire. Thrust. Once more the shells walked up the murderous ladder toward the *Jefferson City*.

'Ten degrees to port,' Arthur McKay said.

Again the yellow fountains rose where the *Jefferson City* had been thirty seconds before. Parry.

In this sport, however, a touch was not something recorded by a judge; the match was not a contest between gentlemen playing games with blunted foils. A touch from this enemy was deadly.

Moreover, in this particular match, it was one against two. Poor odds for even the most devious fencer.

Thrust. This time both Japanese heavy cruisers swung to port to fire broadsides. Parry, the *Jefferson City* zagged to starboard as Captain McKay anticipated the angle and deflection of the salvos. Feint, the *Jefferson City* swung to port as if she was about to unmask her forward batteries and return a broadside of her own. The Japanese captains did some hasty zigzagging, which considerably confused their fire controllers. The next salvos were a thousand yards off target.

To Frank Flanagan and the men of his forty-millimetre gun crew, in the open on the *Jefferson City*'s deck and superstructure, the Jap ships were grey silhouettes against the grey horizon, cardboard cutouts from which clusters of yellow flame bloomed and vanished every thirty seconds. In some ways it was worse than a night battle. You could see your death hurtling at you across the black water, exploding ever closer with each salvo.

In CIC, Montgomery West reported a message from Radio Central. 'The Army Air Force says they'll have planes here in five hours. Ain't that sweet?'

'Good,' McKay said. 'We won't have to worry about them bombing us by mistake.'

Out of the clouds overhead droned the two Japanese spotter planes. 'Get rid of them, Bob,' Captain McKay said to Mullenoe.

All of the *Jefferson City*'s five-inch and forty-millimetre guns opened up on the two hapless targets. They skittered back into the clouds, one gushing smoke.

Out on the port wing of the bridge, Lieutenant Leroy Tompkins, looking more than ever like a Walt Disney rabbit wearing a helmet six sizes too big for him, shouted, 'We got him! You should see that bastard run for cover!'

McKay had offered to relieve Tompkins from his post of danger. The Supply Officer had become indignant. He insisted the crew depended on him for information. He was essential to their morale. He begged McKay to let him keep the job. 'For the first time I feel like a fighting sailor, Captain,' he said.

He also promised to keep an honest set of books. Did the discovery of courage produce this miraculous moral regeneration? Arthur McKay had no idea.

'We're gonna win this one, boys. They got more guns but we got more brains,' Tompkins yelled.

'Left rudder twenty degrees,' Captain McKay said, for the tenth or fifteenth time.

Again the huge yellow fountains leaped from the icy sea a hundred yards from the *Jefferson City*'s slewing bow.

The deadly fencing match had now lasted three exhausting hours, with McKay miraculously staying one step ahead of the Japanese salvos. 'Come on, George,' he said after an especially close call. 'You make the next guess.'

'I never took fencing, Art,' Tombs said. 'You better stay in charge.'

'They've got to get lucky eventually.'

Thirty seconds later, the cruiser shuddered as the nearest miss yet glanced off her hull amidships and exploded a few feet from her bottom. Five minutes later, a shell or a fragment of a shell set the scout plane on their after catapult afire. Within five minutes Damage Control Officer Moss reported the fire was out. The plane drifted astern, still burning.

'We've got good damage control too, George,' McKay said.

'I trained those guys,' George Tombs said.

'That's life, George. Someone else always gets the credit.'

'Look at that light cruiser, Captain,' Bob Mullenoe said. 'I think they're using her as a flank spotter.'

Sure enough, an old British Navy trick. One of the Japanese light cruisers had crept up on them to starboard and was probably guiding the fire controllers aboard the two heavies.

'Admiral,' Arthur McKay said over the TBS, 'I'm going to sheer out and take that light cruiser under fire.'

The *Jefferson City* swung north, and in five minutes her main batteries had the light cruiser within range. Eight salvos boomed in swift succession and the Japanese captain took off like a frightened hare, zigzagging in a wild 360-degree circle.

'That got the shit running down their legs, Captain,' Boats Homewood shouted.

'Their Admiral is playing it safe,' Arthur McKay said. 'If he had real nerve, he'd press an attack with his light cruisers and destroyers from that angle and clean us up. He might lose a ship or two, but he'd win this thing. He wants to win without risking very much.'

'Heavy cruisers are cutting across our track bearing one eight zero,' West reported from CIC.

The thunder of exploding shells to port revealed the Japanese were firing full broadsides. The splashes walked towards them up the usual deadly ladder. As the last salvo exploded only fifty yards away, McKay ordered twenty degrees right rudder.

'She's not responding sir!' the helmsman cried.

Over the telephone from the engine room a frantic Oz Bradley told the Captain what was wrong. 'The concussion of our guns carried away the hydraulic unit on the steering gear. Without that on the line we won't be able to get more than a ten percent response.'

Once more the *Jefferson City* was showing her age.

'Give me ten degrees when I want it and we'll hope for the best,' McKay said.

Horace Aquino arrived on the bridge with a bowl of beef broth. 'You must keep up your strength, Captain,' he said.

'Bring some for everybody.'

'The men too?' Aquino said. He did not approve of McKay's democratic tendencies.

'Everybody.'

McKay sipped the soup. He did not realize how hungry he was until he tasted it. The Japanese had begun this fight before breakfast. He wiped sweat from his brow. With the *Jefferson City* able to turn only ten degrees, the odds were dangerously uneven. He continued to read the minds of the Japanese fire controllers with a skill everyone on the bridge now regarded as supernatural. But the enemy salvos were coming closer now. Ten-degree turns were not enough.

The thunder of another salvo landing. This time it included a tremendous clang, as if a gigantic metal punching machine was operating nearby. The ship shuddered like a living creature. 'Where did that get us?' McKay asked.

'Amidships, I think,' George Tombs said, getting on the phone to Damage Control.

In sixty seconds he had the information. An eight-inch shell had torn through the hull amidships and exited below the waterline without exploding.

Damage control parties rushed to stop the flooding, but the *Jefferson City* began to develop a ten-degree list. Gunnery Officer Mullenoe reported an even more serious problem. The after turret was running out of ammunition. They had carried the brunt of the battle. 'Resupply them,' McKay said. 'Make sure some are high capacity shells. Don't use them until I give you an order.'

Down on the main deck, Frank Flanagan obeyed Lieutenant Herman Kruger's summons. 'Let's go. Move your lazy asses. We're shifting ammunition,' he shouted. He commandeered the men on Flanagan's mount and every other mount forward of them. The 260-pound eight-inch shells were raised from the handling rooms below the forward turrets and placed on dollies. They ran out of these rolling wire baskets as Flanagan got to the head of the line. Kruger and another man swung a shell into the hands of Flanagan and the man beside him. Their knees buckled under the weight. 'Get these to turret three,' Kruger said. 'We'll fix your hernias later.'

Salvos continued to throw up huge yellow geysers as they staggered down the deck. Behind him Flanagan heard the Deacon, the mainstay of his forty-millimetre mount, cry out as a piece of shrapnel tore into his body. 'Keep going, keep going,' Kruger snapped. He was behind them helping to carry another shell. They stumbled through the cascades of icy water to the after turret, where eager gunners relieved them of their burdens.

The Deacon lay on the deck sobbing in agony. Flanagan knelt to help him. Kruger dragged him to his feet by his collar. 'Go back and get another one,' he said.

*

On the bridge, Arthur McKay was telling George Tombs a curious story about the bombardment of Kiska that he had heard from a destroyer captain. When the Americans used high capacity shells, the Japanese had put up a curtain of anti-aircraft fire, thinking they were bombs. On the receiving end, it was hard to tell the difference between HC's and bombs. HC's were shore bombardment weapons, designed for maximum blast and shrapnel – the opposite of the armour-piercing shells used when fighting ship-to-ship.

Still the Japanese salvos rained down while the *Jefferson City* twisted right and left to avoid them. With the list further reducing her mobility, it was only a matter of time before one of them caught her again.

Once more, it was a single shell, causing the ship to shudder like a wounded animal. Again, they waited on the bridge for word from Damage Control. 'That one exploded in the after engine room,' George Tombs said. 'It killed a lot of people.'

'Admiral,' Captain McKay said on the TBS, 'I'd like the destroyers to lay smoke.'

Boats Homewood looked at the Executive Officer and shook his head, a big grin on his face. Tombs knew what he was thinking. Arthur McKay was the real commander of this battle. He was showing Soc McMorris – and the rest of the brass, all the way up to Cominch King – that he could manoeuvre a fleet as boldly as he conned a ship.

Two of the destroyers swung astern of the *Jefferson City* and got the chemical smoke pots on their sterns going. In five minutes a curtain of thick grey smoke, mineral oil atomized by steam, lay between them and the enemy.

Down in the dimly lit bilges below the engine rooms and fire rooms, Edwin Moss was up to his waist in freezing water, directing a team of men who were frantically trying to stop the rising flood. Fuel oil tanks had been ruptured by the last Japanese shell and their contents coagulated in the cold, forming heavy shreds and sheets of tarry stuff that clung like black glue.

'Use your shirts, your pants, men,' Moss shouted, and stripped to his undershorts to set an example. They hammered their clothes into the leaks and smeared caulking over them. Still the water rose. Moss dove down into the gummy freezing mixture of oil and water and found more leaks beneath the surface. One after another, the men grimaced and followed his example, shoving rags and undershirts and socks into the spurting crevices, then caulking them.

'Hey, Commander,' shouted a squat shipfitter, rising from the goo with oil coating his face and chest. 'Do they give you the Navy Cross for this sort of work?'

'Only if you die of pneumonia,' Moss said, trying to stop his teeth from chattering.

In spite of his violent chills, Moss realized he was enjoying himself. He was leading men. He was saving the *Jefferson City*. Damage control could not compare to gunnery in glamour, but it was a tremendously satisfying job. How did Arthur McKay know he would like it? The man was uncanny.

'It's goin' down!' shouted a carpenter who was in charge of measuring the water's depth.

Then everyone noticed a strange silence. The *Jefferson City*'s engines had stopped! 'What the hell's going on?' the shipfitter asked.

Edwin Moss clambered out of the bilge. He was vaguely aware he was a ridiculous sight in his shorts with all of his bony six feet four inches dripping oil. But he did not give a damn. In the forward fire room he encountered frantic Oz Bradley.

'We got water in the fuel lines. It's put out the boilers.'

On the port wing of the bridge, Arthur McKay had already got this bad news. He stared at the feeble curl of white smoke coming out of the *Jefferson City*'s stacks. 'Hoist "My Speed Is Zero,"' he told his signal officer.

He walked to the TBS. 'Admiral,' he said, 'I recommend a torpedo attack by our destroyers.'

'I'll give them the order.'

With his hand still holding the TBS circuit open, McKay turned to the PA system and spoke to his crew. 'Men,' he said, 'I urge you not to panic. I just received word from Admiral McMorris that Army planes are overhead and should begin attacking the enemy within minutes.'

He closed both circuits and spoke to Gunnery Officer Mullenoe. 'Start firing those HC shells.'

As the stern turret began firing the HC shells, George Tombs looked at Captain McKay with baffled eyes. He knew from the CIC message that the Army planes were still three hours away. 'It's a long shot, George, but it's the only one we've got left,' McKay said. 'I'm betting those Japs are listening to our TBS.'

Three of the four destroyers swung to port and raced through the smoke screen toward the enemy. The fourth remained behind to keep making smoke. The *Jefferson City* lay motionless on the almost glassy sea, blinded as well as shielded by the smoke. No one could see the gallant charge of the destroyers. But everyone knew it was a suicide mission. The Japanese fire controlmen in those heavy cruisers would blow them apart five miles before they got close enough to use their guns. They might not even get off their torpedoes.

Arthur McKay shook hands with George Tombs. 'If it doesn't work, George, at least we'll know we tried everything.'

In the forward fire room, Watertender Third Class Marty Roth was frantically cross-connecting fuel lines to reserve tanks not contaminated with seawater. He added a personal passion to his task. Amos Cartwright's ghost would haunt him forever if the *Jefferson City* went down because of contaminated fuel. He would not regard the intrusion of a few Japanese eight-inch shells as an adequate excuse.

'Now try lighting off number one,' he shouted to the men on the deckplates beside Oz Bradley.

'It's catching. It's burning,' they yelled.

Bradley picked up a phone and called the forward engine room. 'Stand by for steam,' he said.

*

On deck, Frank Flanagan checked his rubber life belt to make sure it was ready for inflation as soon as he hit the water. He took off his foul-weather jacket and his bulky windproof overalls. He kicked off his shoes. He stood there in the freezing wind looking at the black icy water. 'The hell with it,' he said. He put his winter clothes back on. He would rather die quickly from an exploding shell than endure slow death in the Bering Sea.

Through the smoke, those above decks heard the distant boom of the Japanese heavy cruisers' guns firing at the destroyers. The *Jefferson City*'s stern batteries replied with more HC shells. Then they fell silent. So did the Japanese guns. On the bridge, Arthur McKay winced at the thought of the shattered little ships sinking in this desolate sea, only 125 miles from the Japanese Kuriles.

He was distracted by an amazing sensation. The *Jefferson City* was moving again! The engine room was telephoning him. 'We've got two boilers back on line,' Oz Bradley said. 'I estimate we can make twenty-five knots in ten minutes.'

Over the TBS came an even more startling sound, the voice of Captain Ralph S. Riggs, commander of the destroyers squadron. 'The enemy is retiring westward. He seems to think he's under air attack. He's firing every anti-aircraft gun he's got.'

The HC shells had worked.

Beautiful light brown smoke was pouring from the *Jefferson City*'s stacks. 'What speed can you make?' asked Admiral McMorris over the TBS.

'Any speed you suggest, Admiral,' Captain McKay said.

From sick bay came a call from Lieutenant Commander Edwin Moss. 'Captain, my men have just spent an hour up to their chins in freezing oil and water. I believe they could all use an allowance of medicinal alcohol. Does the doctor have your permission?'

'Have an extra snort on me.'

George Tombs held out his hand. 'This time it's not goodbye, Art. It's congratulations.'

★

They were back in Dutch Harbor by supper time. In the crew's mess the universal opinion was voiced by Boats Homewood. 'I don't give a fuck what the admirals think of him. We've got the best goddam captain in the US Navy. I don't care if they send us to the fuckin' North Pole for the duration, anyone who transfers off this old baby is nuts.'

'I got a hunch you won't have to transfer to get warm,' Jack Peterson said. 'The dope from the black gang says we're headin' for Long Beach to get them holes plugged and the turbines in the after engine room put back together.

He turned to Flanagan. 'Get out your bullshit machine, kid.' That was Jack's name for Flanagan's fountain pen. 'I want you to write the best letter yet to old Martha. We got to start warmin' her up.'

Long Beach made Flanagan think about Teresa Brownlow. Would he see her? What would he say to her? Would he play Jack's game, lay on a nice smooth line and cheerfully fuck her brains out?

Sure. Why not? He was a sailor.

In his cabin, Arthur McKay was writing a letter.

Dearest Lucy:
   I haven't had the heart to write to you since Win's death. But now we're coming back to Long Beach for repairs. I hope we can meet. I hope I can offer you something – whether you chose to call it consolation or love is up to you. . .

The Good Old USA

Escorted by one of the destroyers who had defended her so valiantly when she lay crippled on the icy waters of the Bering Sea, the *Jefferson City* limped into Long Beach Harbor. In the bilges, her pumps worked wearily against the leaks inflicted by the Japanese shells. Captain McKay conned her to a buoy and went ashore to discuss the repairs she needed. Admiral Tomlinson was still presiding over the Terminal Island Navy Yard. He listened, frowning, to McKay's description of the ageing cruiser's wounds and her need for a thorough overhaul. Then the Admiral demanded a narrative of the running fight with the Japanese heavies. McKay made it brief and stressed his luck. The Admiral snorted. He had obviously heard a more detailed version of the encounter from others.

'You ought to get an extra stripe for the way you handled that thing. From what I hear, Old Soc just sailed along in the *Richmond* waiting for you to tell him what to do next.' Tomlinson's frown grew fiercer. 'But you're never going to get noticed for anything short of shelling Hirohito out of his palace after that story about your executive officer. What the hell was going on in your head, Art, to let a thing like that get out?'

'I got too involved in trying to win the war, Admiral. I forgot to cover my ass,' he lied.

'I don't believe a word of that. Some day when you feel like it, I'll buy you a drink and you can tell me what really happened.'

McKay said nothing. The Admiral got the message. 'Well, here's a little bit of good news, anyway. Your wife's flying in tomorrow. One p.m.'

'Great,' Arthur McKay said. Another lie.

In the crew compartments of the *Jefferson City*, the talk was not just of liberty but of leaves. If the ship was in dry dock for thirty days, that would give everyone time for fifteen days off. Swordsmen like Camutti were ecstatic. He figured he could manage seven days in Philadelphia and was plotting a different seduction each night. Jack Peterson was equally optimistic. 'We'll get us a bungalow somewheres, Flan, maybe go up to Seattle where you can get one cheap.'

'Yeah.'

'What's eatin' you?'

'If I get fifteen days, maybe I ought to go home.'

'Come on. What the hell are you doing'? Turnin' into a mamma's boy in front of my eyes?'

'I don't know anybody out here except Teresa Brownlow.'

'Is that dame still bugging' you? Never let a woman get to you, kid. There's always another one around the bend. I got a list of addresses in Seattle that'll wear out your schwanz in a week.'

'What are you going to do with fifteen days' leave, Boats?' Flanagan asked Homewood.

'Hell, I don't know. I ain't got nobody to go home to 'cept a sister in Mobile. She don't want to see an old bum like me. I'll probably hole up in a hotel with a couple of other guys and get drunk. Maybe bring in a little pussy once in a while, you know.'

'Why don't you come up to Seattle with us and let Jack fix you up with his mother?'

'I wouldn't wish that bitch on my worst enemy, let alone my best friend,' Jack said.

'She sounds like what Boats needs. Someone to reform him.'

Peterson threw a shoe at him. 'You're still a fuckin' civilian,' he said.

'Say, West,' Robert Mullenoe said as they finished dinner in the wardroom. 'What are you doing tonight?'

'Not a goddamn thing,' West said. 'My girl is in Australia. I might just possibly murder the son of a bitch who sent her there. Otherwise I have no ideas.'

'I'm in the same boat. It's the first time I've had liberty as a married man. What the hell do they do?'

'They send telegrams to their wives telling them to get on the first plane.'

'That won't do me much good.'

'I can arrange dates for both of us.'

They looked at each other. 'No,' Mullenoe said. 'Neither one of us is very good at resisting temptation.'

'I've got another idea,' West said.

Two hours later, in civilian clothes, Mullenoe and West sat in a borrowed car near Uncle Mort's white-pillared house in Beverly Hills. West knew that Mort, who imitated everything Louis B. Mayer did, down to wearing the same colour socks, was an avid collector of starlets. The chances were fairly good that West would recognize the one who tripped up to Mort's door to entertain him for the evening.

Sure enough, she turned out to be an ex-girlfriend, a redhead named Diane Morris. The thought of her yielding to Mort's graceless advances redoubled his determination. At a nod from him, Mullenoe strode up the gravel path and pounded on the front door.

'You've got the woman I love in there. I'm going to kill you for taking her away from me,' he roared.'

At the Los Angeles airport, Arthur McKay stood at the gate awaiting the arrival of Flight 78 from Washington, DC. He should have known Rita would be following the *Jefferson City* around the Pacific, mile by mile.

She was wasting her time and his money with this dramatic rush to welcome him home. He no longer had a home. He was not even sure he had a country. He read a story in the Los Angeles *Times* about the scandalous way racetracks were refusing to close their parking lots. Each day they were jammed with cars – an obvious violation of the government ban on pleasure driving. Another story told how war workers were spending their money on eighteen-year-old bourbon and expensive jewellery for their wives and girlfriends. In New York the nightclubs were making astronomical sums of money.

'Hello, husband.'

Rita stood about six feet away, waiting for him to make the first move. She had lost thirty, perhaps forty pounds. She was wearing a simple beige suit with natural shoulders that made her look even slimmer. The padded shoulders of the 1930s had never looked good on her chunky body. Physically, she was the wife who had greeted him after other tours of sea duty. But the old ebullience had been replaced by an anxiety that gave her a waiflike aura.

When he did nothing, she kissed him boldly on the

mouth. He did not return it. 'I can't wait to hear about the battle in the Aleutians,' she said. 'Everyone in Washington's talking about it.'

'How nice,' he said.

They picked up her suitcase at the luggage terminal and walked to the car. 'I've reserved a room in the Beverly Wilshire,' he said.

'Good.'

'For one night,' he said as she got into the taxi.

'Whoo Whoo – Woolloomooloo!'

The *Jefferson City*'s war cry echoed through the streets of San Pedro. Boats Homewood swore it was the wildest liberty he had ever seen. 'Why the hell shouldn't it be?' Flanagan said. 'How often do you get back from fighting seven or eight major sea battles to receive the plaudits of your countrymen?'

'What the hell is this plaudits shit?' Boats said.

'Yeah. What the hell is it? A new word for blow job?' Jack Peterson said.

'It means praise, you ignoramuses,' Flanagan said.

'Hey,' Boats said, jabbing a finger an inch or two into Flanagan's chest. 'We didn't fight for that. We fought to prove we had the stuff. Fought to prove we didn't have no yellow stripe down our stack.'

'OK, forget it,' Flanagan said. 'We're not getting any fucking plaudits anyway.' He was thoroughly plastered. 'I don't think anyone in this fucking country gives a damn what happens to us out there.'

In the recesses of his numb brain Flanagan realized that San Pedro was not exactly the place to search for grateful citizenry. They had already spent a lot of their back pay at one of the more expensive brothels and four or five of the bars. With them were Camutti, the Bobbsey Twins, the Radical, Jablonsky and a half dozen other F Division stalwarts. Camutti had tried to get it for nothing, using his battle scars routine and had been told by his whore that she ought to charge him double, he was so repulsive to look at with his clothes off. This had prompted them to consider dismantling the brothel, but Homewood had ordered them to desist. He said they owed it to the captain not to add any additional blots to the *Jefferson City*'s reputation.

'Hey, look at that!' yelled Camutti.

A large, crudely lettered sign read: COME SEE SAM SLADE AND HIS NUDE ALL GIRL ORCHESTRA AT SHANGHAI RED'S.

'I hate to put a dollar in that bastard's pocket,' Homewood said. But even he had to admit the invitation was irresistible. They staggered into Red's foul-smelling saloon. If the orchestra was playing, it was being drowned out by the drunken conversations of the patrons. Shanghai Red drifted by, crook written all over his piggish face. 'Hey, Red, where's your fuckin' orchestra?' Homewood demanded.

'Over there behind the bar,' Red said with a leer that should have made them suspicious.

They fought their way through swarms of sailors to the bar – and stared at a painting of a nude all girl orchestra. 'It's not even good art,' Flanagan said.

Everyone was giving them the horse laugh. They had to admit it was not a bad gag, considering some of the other ways Red took a sailor's money. They decided to pay him the compliment of buying some of his rotgut booze.

They sat down at a table and Flanagan was prevailed upon to give them his imitation of Chaplain Bushnell trying to persuade the customers to repent. 'Friends, boys, darlings,' he lisped. 'Such rowdy behaviour can't possibly be acceptable to the unknown unfathomable being who presides over our destinies. You are behaving like sailors! What will your mothers think?'

A woman's face drifted through his alcoholic haze. It had the saddest eyes, the loveliest russet hair, the most mournful mouth he had ever seen. It was Teresa Brownlow.

'What the hell are you doing here?' Flanagan said.

'I work here,' she said.

'Yeah. And she's with me, big shot,' said a squat pugnacious gunner's mate first class who looked like Al Capone's first cousin.

'The hell you say. She's my girl.'

'I work here, Frank. You'll get me fired.'

'You should be fired. You should be arrested. You should be – Christ what are you doing in this goddamn joint?'

'Pal, didn't you hear her? She *works* here,' the gunner's mate said.

'Not any more,' Flanagan said, grabbing Teresa's arm and starting for the door.

The gunner's mate spun him around and knocked him over the next table. It happened to be occupied by six Marines from the *Jefferson City*. 'Are you gonna let him do that to a shipmate?' Flanagan asked.

They rose as one man. By that time, Homewood had demolished the gunner's mate. Unfortunately he was from an aircraft carrier and there were a lot of his shipmates in Shanghai Red's. Teresa screamed and dove under a table. Flanagan crawled through the carnage to find her.

'How could you do it?' Flanagan shouted as bodies crashed and glassware smashed all around them.

Tears streamed down her cheeks. 'I'm a whore. I might as well get paid for it.'

'No, No. Never.'

'Why didn't you answer my letters?'

'Because I'm a bastard. But I love you. I won't let you do this to yourself.'

The angry whistles of the Shore Patrol filled the night. 'Come on, kiddo, let's get the hell out of here,' Jack Peterson said.

'I'll see you the day after tomorrow. At the Pico Avenue landing,' Flanagan said.

'No you won't. Forget me, Frank.'

'I'll find you!'

'Come on,' Homewood roared, dragging Flanagan out from under the table by his neckerchief as the Shore Patrol waded into the brawl, clubbing in their usual indiscriminate fashion.

'Arthur, for God's sake, listen to me.'

Rita had started weeping in the restaurant while they

were arguing about his failure to stop their son, Sammy, from joining the Marines when he graduated from Annapolis next month. Now the tears were ravaging her face, washing away make-up, revealing wrinkles and pores that too much alcohol had opened years ago.

'I *have* listened to you,' he said. 'The answer is no.'

He stood by the tall window staring down at Wilshire Boulevard, where svelte women shoppers strolled in the California sunshine. Rita sat on the bed on the opposite side of the room. If the window had been a door that opened on to a terrace, he would have gone out on it. He wanted to get as far away from her as possible.

'If you come back to Washington with me, I can arrange for you to see Cominch privately. You can explain the Parker mess to him. He wants to believe there's an explanation for what you did. You have one. A good one. He has no real interest in defending a slob like Parker.'

'I'm not going to kiss the ass of the man who destroyed my best friend. I told you already, I can barely look at you without loathing for the part you played in it.'

'I didn't play a part. I was a spectator. Maybe I rejoiced at first. I was glad that for once it was Winfield the Great who was on the griddle and not you. But I never dreamt it would lead to this sort of horror. Anyway, Win brought the worst of it on himself with that letter to Knox. Do you think Cominch could just sit there and let someone get away with that? Would you, if you were in his place?'

'I'll never be in his place, so the question is irrelevant.'

'It isn't. If you're going to judge him, condemn him – and me.'

'Is he screwing you?'

'No! Jesus Christ, he thinks of me as a . . . a daughter. A daughter he can talk to. So help me God.'

McKay returned to watching the strollers on Wilshire Boulevard. Two of them happened to be Montgomery West and Bob Mullenoe in civilian clothes. They were with a pretty redhead. They were all laughing heartily about something. So much for fidelity.

'You don't know how lonely that man is.'

'So, I understand, is Stalin. And Hitler.

'Arthur, please. It's not too late. You're a brilliant officer. You've got twice as many brains as Winfield Scott Schley Kemble ever had. Everybody knows it. King would love to have you back on his staff. If the war lasts long enough, you'll go out to the Pacific in six months an admiral. I guarantee it. You proved you've got the stuff, in the Solomons, in the Aleutians. Everyone knows it.'

'I'm not interested in being an admiral in this despicable Navy. Get that through your head – now and for ever.

'How can you turn your back on something we've spent our whole lives working for?'

'You worked for it. And you browbeat me into it.'

'What's wrong with that? I saw you had the talent. But somebody – I blame your mother, your father and Win Kemble in that order – gave you this idiotic inferiority complex. Now you tell me I have nothing to say about your career? I've invested as much blood, sweat and tears into it as you have. I've got a right to be heard.'

Her face was twisted, red, unlovely, pitiful. But he was beyond pity. 'No you haven't,' he said.

'You son of a bitch. I've fucked for you!'

'I don't recall asking you to perform such a task. I don't believe it's included in the duties of Navy wives. Who was it? Or should I ask Who were they?'

'Never mind. It was a long time ago. I hated myself for it. I almost hated the Navy for it. I never did it again.'

'And now you consider it an act of nobility? You present it to me as the ultimate sacrifice?'

'I don't. Anyway, are you in a position to lecture me? I've heard my share of rumours about your women in China, the Philippines.'

'I've had a few. They gave me something I never got from you – tenderness. What a marvellous marriage this has been. All we've ever had going for us was my career and your Shanghai fuck book. Love never had anything to do with the whole business, did it?'

'That's not true. I loved you. I still love you. I know I'm not easy to love, but I thought you loved me.'

'I loved to screw you. That's all.'

Was that true? In his rage he was committing a kind of murder. He was aware of it, but he was out of control. He was like the *Jefferson City* without her rudder stops. A slewing weapon of destruction, still capable of spitting death.

To his surpise, Rita crumpled under this final retort. 'Oh, Arthur, Arthur,' she said. She fell sideways on the bed, drawing up her legs until she was almost in a foetal position. 'Please take that back. I don't think I can live with that.'

'You better learn.' He walked past her to the door. 'Do you have enough money to get to the airport tomorrow?'

There was no answer. Rita lay with her back to him. She had stopped crying. She was as inert as a corpse. Had he gone too far?

He did not care. If she went out the window later tonight, he did not care. It would even the score for Win.

No, wait. This was the mother of his children. This was the woman he had once yearned to comfort, console. He threw a hundred dollars on the bed beside her and considered touching her shoulder, at least saying he was sorry it had ended this way.

The hell with it. He was through trying to comfort Rita Semmes McKay. There was another woman in his life who needed a deeper comforting – and could comfort him in return. He knew exactly where to find her.

His heart pounding, Arthur McKay drove up the curving driveway to the white house in the hills above Los Angeles. The Spanish maid, Juanita, greeted him with a knowing smile. 'Oh, Captain McKay,' she said, 'Mrs Kemble said you might call. She said to tell you she was in Hawaii and she would see you there.'

Hawaii. Of course. Win's last wish – to have his ashes scattered in the sea outside Pearl Harbor.

Hawaii. It was perfect. Where his love for Rita had been strongest – that now dead, discarded, despised love. Hawaii was the perfect place to create a new love, a new life with Rita's opposite, with a woman who had compassion, tenderness, understanding as basic components of her soul.

'How is she?'

'She's just fine,' Juanita said. 'Just fine considering –'

'It must have been terrible.'

'It was, Captain. But she's a brave woman. I don't think she shed a tear.'

'She's staying in Hawaii?'

'Yes, with Mrs Meade. Working in a rest home for wounded officers.'

'I'll be there in a month,' Arthur McKay said.

Love for Sale

On his next liberty, Flanagan prowled the streets of San Pedro searching for Teresa Brownlow. Jack Peterson went with him, although he insisted that Flanagan was as crazy as Teresa. Shanghai Red confirmed this diagnosis. He said Teresa gave away the money he paid her to bums and derelicts squatting in nearby doorways begging handouts.

They finally found her on the Long Beach Poke, cruising for sailors. She was wearing a cheap red dress and too much lipstick. She refused to let Flanagan touch her. She pulled her arm away and her fingers became claws. 'You want it, you've got to pay for it,' she said.

'I'll pay for it,' Flanagan said. 'I've got six months' back pay in my pocket. Come up to Seattle with us. Jack's girl, Martha – remember her? – has a house on Puget Sound. It'll be like old times.'

'No,' she said. 'I told you to forget me, Frank.'

While Jack watched, appalled, Flanagan slowly changed her mind. In another hour they were on the coast highway, hitching a ride to Seattle. They got picked up by a travelling salesman who felt guilty because he was driving on black market gas. Teresa told him he should be ashamed of himself but Flanagan and Peterson gave him absolution.

Martha Johnson looked as dubious as Jack when she saw

Teresa. They stopped to buy her a couple of less colourful dresses and drove to Martha's house. She was living on a peninsula a few miles from Seattle, a lovely woodsy place overlooking Puget Sound.

Everything went beautifully the first night. They drank California wine and Martha cooked them a superb chicken dinner. Martha and Jack retired to reminisce and Flanagan and Teresa went down to the shore of the Sound, where they made nostalgic love in the darkness, with the water lapping, the wind sighing around them. Flanagan felt triumphant as Teresa wept in his arms.

'Oh, Frank, Frank,' she sobbed. 'If only you'd written.'

'It's all right now. It's all right,' he said.

But it was not all right. Teresa insisted on telling them all the vile and despicable things her customers had required her to do. She had turned into a monologist with a pathological obsession with sin. This did not make for pleasant conversation.

When they were alone, Flanagan tried to tell her about Australia, about the enthusiasm for Irish poetry he had acquired from Annie Flood. She barely listened. The more time they spent together, the more silent she became. She stared out at Puget Sound, brooding.

At dinner on their third night, Martha insisted on hearing a description of their night battles in the Solomons, the long-range duel in the Bering Sea. Jack did most of the bragging about their gunnery, although he did not stint in his praise of Flanagan's work with his forty-millimetres.

'How many Japs do you think you killed?' Teresa asked.

'I don't know. A couple of thousand,' Jack said.

'You think you can escape punishment for that? For killing and maiming your fellow human creatures?' Teresa asked.

Jack went pale. He thought Teresa was putting a curse on him.

'You're like all sailors. Arrogant killers, torturers. You don't give a damn for anything but your filthy appetites. God doesn't tolerate such people for long.'

'I think you're full of shit, Teresa,' Martha Johnson said.

'You despise me because I've taken money for doing it,' Teresa screamed. 'But there's no real difference between you and me. Is there a wedding ring on your finger? Do you think he's faithful to you for more than five minutes after you're out of sight?'

That night Teresa refused to let Flanagan make love to her unless he paid ten dollars in advance. When they finished and went out on the porch to join Martha and Jack for a nightcap, she displayed the money to Martha and asked, 'How much did you get?'

'Teresa,' Martha said, 'I want you the hell out of my house by noon tomorrow.'

Teresa screamed an obscenity at Martha and fled into the bedroom.

'I hope you don't go with her, Frank,' Martha said in an amazingly calm voice.

Teresa locked herself in the bedroom. Flanagan sat out on the porch wondering what he should do. Hours later he heard footsteps. It was Martha Johnson. She sat down, lit a cigarette and offered him one. 'They say good sex makes you sleep like a baby. But not tonight. What are you going to do, Frank?'

'I don't know. I feel she's my responsibility.'

'She isn't. She's been sliding this way for a long time. Let her go, Frank. You've got enough on your mind, trying to survive a war.'

'What's going to happen to her?'

'She's going to go completely nuts one of these nights. She'll stab someone or pour boiling water on him. If you hang around with her, it could be you.'

He told Martha why he felt responsible. He told her about the letter he had written Teresa from Pearl Harbor. 'Jesus,' she said. 'You don't look that mean.'

'I'm going with her,' Flanagan said.

'You're the last person in the world who can help her,' Martha said. 'Can't you see that every time she looks at you she remembers when she only did it for love? When she wasn't a whore?'

'I'm still going with her.'

'As my father used to say, never argue with a mick.'

The bedroom door was still locked. When Flanagan knocked, Teresa said, 'Go away.'

'There's a daybed out on the back porch,' Martha said.

Flanagan awoke the next morning to find thick white beams of sunshine filling the woods. He looked at his watch. It was ten-thirty. He walked into the kitchen feeling as forlorn as the day he was sentenced to the brig. Martha Johnson was cooking ham and eggs for Jack.

'Where's Teresa? Is she packing?'

'She's gone. I drove her to the bus station in town and gave her a hundred bucks to get her back to San Pedro,' Martha said.

'Who the hell authorized you to do that?'

'Nobody. Think of me as your big sister. Maybe then you'll let me get away with it.'

'I'm going after her.'

'I don't think you can afford it. You owe me that hundred bucks.'

'I don't need anybody to mind me,' Flanagan raged.

'The hell you don't,' Martha said, flipping the eggs.

'Why didn't you stop her?' Flanagan demanded of Jack.

'It was all over when I got out of bed,' Jack said. 'But I can't say I wasn't glad to find out she was gone. That dame is bad news, kid. She was givin' me the creeps.'

'I've got a girl I want you to meet. She works with me on the swing shift at the Navy Yard,' Martha said. 'Give her a chance. If it doesn't jell, you can go get stabbed by Teresa tomorrow.'

Two nights later, Frank Flanagan sat on the shrouded shore of Puget Sound beside a plump, soft-voiced blonde named Andrea Hollins, while she told him how religious she felt when she was surrounded by the green sweet-smelling forest, the vast expanse of glistening starlit water. There were nights when she could not sleep. She would walk the shore naked in the darkness, letting the wind touch all of her body. She felt as if she was being caressed by divine hands. She would go back to her cottage and sleep like an innocent child.

Andrea was not very innocent in other ways. She had already demonstrated an almost atonishing readiness to go to bed with Flanagan. Sex was part of nature, and she saw nothing whatsoever wrong with it. On the green fringe of westernmost, northernmost USA, Andrea had become something new – and something very old. She was a pagan. Flanagan decided he would be a pagan too for a while. He was enjoying Andrea in the bedroom and on the beach and in the woods, where she was really wild. He told her she was a maenad. She liked that, especially when he explained it. There were times when Flanagan wondered if he was right.

But he could not stop thinking about Teresa Brownlow. Maybe that was why his lovemaking with Andrea became more and more perfunctory. He did not refuse her. He was nineteen and acutely aware he might never reach twenty. But there was no afterglow, no sense of having reached a level of feeling that could not be explained by Andrea's ripe breasts and inviting thighs.

He talked about it to Martha a few nights later, after Andrea had gone home to her cottage and he was sitting on the porch unable to sleep. She had joined him, complaining of the same problem. 'Now what are you worried about?' he said.

'Love for sale. What every woman worries about when she's trying to hang on to a guy.'

'Why bother to hang on?'

'I'm talking about a special guy. One who gives you that certain feeling, like the song says.'

'I wouldn't know,' Flanagan said.

'Yeah. I can see that – with Andrea, I mean.'

'I don't get this whole love thing. As far as I can see, it means getting stuck with someone you may learn to hate in a year or two.'

'If you have the feeling, you're ready to risk it.'

'I don't rate feelings that high.'

'Yeah, I know. That's why you're Jack's friend. A real sailor, he calls you. But I think everybody rates feelings pretty high. Some of us just don't admit it. That can mess up your life.'

'It seems to me it can get messed up the other way too.'

'Sure. But that way, you go down fighting. It's the woman's version of the Navy's code.'

'I never met a woman like you before. On your own – not married.'

'And not a slut? There's a lot more of us around than you'd think. But we're all looking for the right guy. I wasn't sure about Jack until he wrote me some letters from the Pacific. I was crazy about him physically, and that's damn important. But those letters – they really saved my life. I was starting to sleep around – trying to forget him. Those letters changed everything.'

A clammy hand was grabbing the back of Flanagan's neck. 'That's . . . great,' he muttered.

'I know what you mean – about marrying the wrong guy. I watched my mother and father drink their way into a divorce court. My mother was a Catholic, and that really screwed her up.'

'She's dead?'

'The booze got her. I blamed my father. Now I'm not so sure. Maybe he did the best he could. Why the hell am I telling you all this?'

'Maybe because I'm your little brother?'

Martha laughed. 'Let's drink to that.'

She poured them generous jolts of bourbon. Contradictory feeling stormed through Flanagan's mind. Admiration for this woman's courage and honesty. Guilt for helping Jack deceive her.

'You were raised a Catholic?'

'My mother's maiden name was Burke.'

'You quit?'

'I don't like being told what to think and feel about so many things. I'm no good at taking orders.'

'I'm coming to the same conclusion. It's what I don't like about the Navy too. But they don't mess around with your head as much.'

'Maybe it's why I've always fancied sailors. They play the game aboard ship. On the beach they're independent as hell. I like that in a man.'

Suddenly, incredibly, Martha Johnson was sitting beside Flanagan on the daybed, her mouth against his mouth. His hands were moving up and down her lean lithe body. It was happening in his head. She had not moved out of her chair. Flanagan was stunned by the intensity of the wish. It had something to do with the sound of her voice in the darkness, the throaty knowing way she said 'man'.

It was unthinkable, of course. She was Jack's woman. She adored the lying bastard. Flanagan gulped half his drink. 'I appreciate Andrea. But I've got to make another try with Teresa.'

'I knew you would. You're a typical mick. Anybody can make you feel guilty.'

Footsteps. Jack loomed up in the darkness. 'What the hell's goin' on?'

'I'm having a drink with my kid brother.'

'Hey, that brother-sister stuff's OK in daylight. After dark I'm not so sure.'

Flanagan felt too guilty to think of a comeback. He let Martha pour Jack a drink and welcome him as big brother.

Three days later, Jack and Frank hitchhiked back to San Pedro. All the way down they argued about Teresa. Jack got jumpier and jumpier. 'I don't wanta see that dame again,' he exploded. 'She gives out really bad signals.'

'So go back to the ship. You don't have to mind me either,' Flanagan said in his most obnoxious style.

Alone, he headed for Shanghai Red's. The proprietor greeted his inquiry with a curse. 'You wanna see her, call the prosecutor's office! That fuckin' bitch maybe put me out of business.'

'What the hell are you talking about?'

Red picked up yesterday's Los Angeles *Herald*. In true Hearstian style, a headline screamed: PROSTITUTE STABS SAILOR. Beneath it in smaller type ran: 'Raving Bar Girl Claims Victim Was Beelzebub.'

'Did she kill him?'

'She stuck it in his heart. Standin' right here at my fuckin' bar.'

'What ship was he from?'

'The *Jefferson City*.'

Only the Brave

'That was a stupid thing to do,' Ina Severn said. 'It was stupid in essence, and it was even more stupid to let him catch you at it. What have you – or I – to gain by making an enemy of this man?'

'He's already an enemy,' Montgomery West said. With the help of friends who eagerly repeated the gossip to him, West was now convinced that Charles Benbow and Claire Carraway had both been acting as Uncle Mort's agents in Australia, with orders to break up his affair with Ina.

'I don't believe that gossip. His nose was out of joint because you showed some independence. But a little diplomacy could have brought him around.'

'Hey, listen. That's about all the lecturing I'm going to take.'

'Well it isn't all you're going to get,' Ina said.

There she stood, 110 pounds of woman, clad only in a towel, telling off a man who had guided the *Jefferson City* (with some help from the Captain) through the darkness of Kula Gulf and across the shell-ravaged waters of the Bering Sea. It was outrageous.

West had been ecstatically surprised to discover Ina knocking on his door two nights ago, after three days of flying across the Pacific in Army Air Force planes. He had thrown out Mullenoe and two or three other married bachelors who were standing a precarious 'celibacy watch' with him. He and Ina had retired upstairs to re-enact the delights of their first night together.

When they awoke in the morning, instead of repeating the performance he had told her about his escapade with

Mullenoe and Uncle Mort. How Mullenoe had burst into the house to find Mort, not in flagrante delicto, but in the process of taking lewd pictures of Diane Morris with the help of several burly assistants. Mullenoe had had to fight his way back to the car, which Uncle Mort had easily traced to the friend who had loaned it to West.

Ina had exploded and the fireworks were still continuing. 'I love you but does that mean I have to let you ruin both our careers?' she cried. 'You forbid me to go to London where I could get some work and when I come back here you tell me this.'

'It sounds to me as if your feelings for me and for your career are very delicately balanced, and my side of the scale is about to take a steep drop.'

'I almost wish that were true, but it isn't,' she said, her voice thick with tears.

West saw how much he had hurt her. He was talking to her as if she was a foe at the wardroom table. 'I'm sorry,' he said, putting his arms around her. 'Now I know what it feels like to be a louse.'

He lit a cigarette and gave her one. 'Let's calm down and think about this thing. Diane Morris walked out in the mêlée and we met her later and found out Mort has been shooting these pictures for years. He's into some sort of pornography, whether for his own amusement or for cash. Maybe we can blackmail him.'

'Nobody would believe you without some very convincing evidence.'

'That leaves us with only two choices. Either you go back to London or we get a divorce.'

'We're not even married, darling.'

'You know what I mean. You'll start dating other men. I'll date other women. I'll go crawling to Mort, beg his forgiveness and get you back on the payroll.'

'I don't believe I could live with that.'

'Then it's London.'

'Oh, darling. Can't you go on loving me even though we're twice as far apart? Is there any chance of the ship coming to Europe?'

Montgomery West shook his head. 'I was talking to the Captain the other day. He expects to get orders for Pearl Harbor next week.'

West was suddenly swept by an extraordinary premonition. He was going to die aboard the *Jefferson City* and leave this woman defenceless, friendless, her career wrecked, her heart broken. If he really loved her, the decent thing to do was to end this affair now.

'I'm not kidding about the divorce. Contrary to the story-books, serious romance and war don't really mix. It might be better for both of us if we called this off. You could go back to London without anything on your conscience. I could do my job aboard ship a lot better. The ideal CIC officer should have nothing on his mind but his radar screens.'

Disbelief mingled with pain on Gwen's face. 'You're serious?' she asked.

'Yes,' he said.

'Do you know what I think you're doing? Using the Navy as an excuse to go back to the old Monty West. You were a sailor before you became one. You had a sailor's attitude toward life. Do you know what that involves? It's not only the freedom to screw any woman who's willing to lie down for you. It also requires a secret belief that you aren't really worth much, anyway. You don't want to go on loving me, because I tell you what you don't want to hear. You've real talent. You could become something more than your Uncle Mort's errand boy. Or the stupid opposite of that role – his ungrateful, obnoxious pseudo-son.'

'None of that's true,' he shouted.

'Prove it by letting me go to London without making rotten threats to stop loving me.'

'I'll never stop loving you,' he said, shocked at the bitterness (or was it loss?) in his voice. 'But I think it would be better for you if you stopped loving me. You've got a life ahead of you. I'm not sure if I do.'

She kissed him wildly, tearfully. They made the most exquisite love yet, full of regret and forgiveness. When it was over, Gwen nestled against him. 'That settles it,' she murmured. 'I'm staying here if I have to sell apples on the corner of Hollywood and Vine.'

'I'd feel better if you went to London.'

'Shut up, Lieutenant,' she said. 'When it comes to understanding women, you're a combat misinformation officer.'

Lieutenant Commander Edwin Moss gazed in astonishment at his wife, Eleanor. As if to make sure he had not missed her message, she said it again. 'You will do no such thing!'

They were in the bedroom of their leaky-roofed two-story house on the outskirts of Norfolk. He had just finished telling her he had decided to quit the Navy when the war ended and study for the ministry. There was no point in returning to the Pacific aboard the *Jefferson City* in search of further glory. He was going to see if he could exchange his eighteen months of sea duty under fire for a comfortable slot in Washington, DC for the duration.

'You want me to go out there and risk my neck again? With four kids to worry about, don't you think it makes more sense to try to get through this war in one piece?'

'I'm talking about your plan to quit the Navy and study for the ministry. I find that totally unacceptable. I'm not going to become a Presbyterian. How are you ever going to find a church that will swallow a Roman Catholic wife? But that's not the main point. I'm proud of being a Navy wife. I'm proud of the years I've put into it. I'm not going to let you walk away from it because you turned out to be less than a great gunnery officer.'

Moss reeled as this salvo of claims and accusations straddled him. 'I thought you hated being a Navy wife. You've never stopped complaining about everything from the moves to the housing to the low pay.'

'I'm like the crew. Griping is one of my prerogatives. But I'm still proud to be aboard.'

Moss grew more and more flabbergasted. This once docile, adoring creature was turning into an amazon in front of his eyes. He saw she was telling him, even though she could not quite put it into words, that she found the idea of him transferring to a safe job in Washington equally unacceptable. She wanted a warrior husband.

'The best, the happiest letter you wrote to me,' Eleanor continued, 'was the one after the battle in the Aleutians. Where you told me about splashing around in those bilges full of freezing water. You were proud of yourself and I was so proud of you. Who put this crazy idea in your head?'

'Nobody put it in my head. I put it in my own head after talking things over with Chaplain Bushnell.'

'I don't like that little man. He reminds me of a cat that my aunt used to have – a black Angora. She'd run her paw along your arm and then with no warning she'd sink in her claws.'

'He's a sympathetic listener. There aren't many of those in the Navy.'

'I thought I was the one who supplied the sympathy. Edwin, I couldn't be saying all this if you hadn't taught me a new kind of faith – a willingness to take risks with the trust – or at least the hope – that God will protect us. I got it from you. I hate to see you letting one disappointment change that. Even if we fail, I'd like to fail at what we started out to do.'

Quietly, with a smile in his eyes, Edwin Moss began to recite. '"Who can find a virtuous woman? For her price is far above rubies. The heart of her husband doth safely trust her, so he shall have no need of spoil. She will do him good and not evil all the days of her life."'

'You won't die. I know you won't. I have faith!'

'I do too,' he lied.

Portents

'God damn it,' Jack Peterson said as they watched the coastline of California recede to a blur on the horizon. 'I shoulda jumped ship.'

'What the hell are you talking about?' asked an astonished Flanagan.

'That fuckin' broad you brought up to Seattle put a whammy on me.'

'If she put it on anybody, it'd be on me.'

'No. She knew I was the guy who broke you in. Who made a real sailor out of you.'

Jack kept staring at the now almost vanished coast.

'I had a feelin' when I said goodbye to Martha that I was seein' her for the last time. I was seein' the whole thing for the last time. They're gonna get me this trip, Flan.'

Boats Homewood climbed the ladder to join them. Flanagan told him what Jack was saying.

'Oh, bullshit,' Boats said. 'We're winnin' the goddamn war. We've got those yellow bastards on the run.'

There was a lot of truth to that statement. The Japs had been kicked out of the Solomons two months ago. Now the scuttlebutt had them going up against the Japanese islands in the central Pacific. All the strategists in F Division – there were at least a dozen who talked like admirals without shoulder boards – said that was basic to Plan Orange, the Navy's prewar scenario for fighting the Japanese.

'Look at them big babies,' Homewood said. 'That's only a sample of what we've got on our way to finish off the treacherous bastards.'

He pointed to starboard and port. Wallowing through the heavy swell were two of the battleships that had been smashed up at Pearl Harbor, the *California* and the *West Virginia*. There was menace in their massive superstructures, their jutting batteries of sixteen-inch guns. Beyond them on both flanks steamed a screen of new destroyers, fast powerful-looking creatures.

'You think the Nips are gonna roll over and play dead when they see a couple of battleships?' Jack said. 'We're gonna to have to blast our way to Tokyo foot by foot. A lot of us are gonna get it in the process.'

'Jesus Christ,' Boats fumed. 'It's enough to make a man wonder if they oughta let guys like you have liberty. Here you got fifteen straight days of all the nooky you could possibly want with a dame who's twice as good as a bum like you could expect. And what happens to your morale? It's down in the fuckin' bilges.'

'OK, OK. I should be dancin' on the mainmast. But I aint',' Jack said. 'I just got this bad feelin'. I get it whenever things start goin' too good. I don't know why. This time it's really bad.'

'Hey, you want me to write a letter to Martha?' Flanagan said.

It was the first time he had ever volunteered for this duty. Jack gave him a funny look. 'No,' he said.

Mail Call

Dear McKay:
    You've written me a couple of obnoxious letters. Now I'll write you one.
    I don't know what the hell's going on between you and your wife. No one can ever figure out exactly what two people do to each other inside a marriage. I gather it has something to do with Kemble's suicide and Hepburn's report on Savo Island.
    I've known Rita since she was a chubby little kid running along the banks of the Whangpoo River in Shanghai. She sat on my shoulders to watch the horses run during Race Week and I never lost a bet with her up there. I thought her mother was the finest Navy wife I ever met. She taught Rita to love the Navy. She even helped me figure out that I loved it too.
    Whatever the hell you've done to Rita should make you so ashamed of yourself you ought to resign command of the *Jefferson City* and apply for duty in the Madison, Kentucky, Ammunition Depot. That's where I ought to send you, as far away from the sea as possible. I only hope you aren't treating your crew the way you're treating your wife. If I hear anything like the number you did on your executive officer, I'll yank you back here and put you in charge of filing toilet paper for the duration. I'm giving you more rope

for her sake, understand? No other reason.

Your friend Kemble blew out his brains because he was guilty as hell. How or why you think this is my fault or Rita's fault is beyond me. I don't give a damn what you think of me. But to mess up your wife this way is unforgivable.

Do you know what it means to have a wife like Rita? A woman who really loves the Navy? There are a hundred men I could name who've had their careers ruined because their wives hated the Navy. They took to drink or screwed around or both. You've got one wife in a million and what do you do? You kick her in the teeth.

I just want to tell you, one man to another, that you're a crumb. You may be as smart as a lot of people say you are, but you're still a crumb.

Sincerely,
Ernie King

Dear Frank:

We were sorry you couldn't get home on that short leave you had. But I guess you would have spent most of your time travelling, like you said.

I'm afraid I've got to tell you some real bad news. Your father's had to retire. He got caught in some investigation Mayor LaGuardia decided to launch into gambling in the Bronx. It's all politics, of course. He didn't do anything wrong. But he had to retire to protect his pension. He's awfully blue about it. Write him a letter if you can and try to cheer him up.

Your sisters are both fine. Beth is a sophisticated college girl now. She loves Mount St Vincent. Meg is thinking of going to nursing school instead of college. A good idea, I think. We're all well. Father Callow sends his regards. We had him to dinner last Sunday.

Love
Mother

Dear Jack:

Two whole weeks and no letter. That's the sort of time warp that makes a girl nervous. I was sort of hoping there might be a ring at the end of our fling in Seattle. But I begin to think the only way I'll ever get one is on the merry-go-ground. I just hope it's brass and not tin. See how you've worn me down? I used to swear I'd settle for nothing but a gold one.

Try to be a little more fatherly to Frank Flanagan. He's a pretty mixed-up kid, after the job Teresa did on him. He's trying to figure out a lot of things about life, and he could use a little more of the positive and less of your cynical side. This may be too much for you to manage. But give it a whirl.

I saw your mother downtown the other day and she was awfully hurt when she found out you were in town and never went near her. Write her a postcard, at least.

Oh, God. Now I'll never get a letter. I'm still trying to reform you! It's because I love you, you lug.

Ever yours,
Martha

Dear Dad:

Well I got through Marine Officers Training School! If you think that's just an offhand remark, I'll fill you in on the details when we get together on a beachhead some one of these days. I have now learned to regard all sailors as inert forms of life, only one level above a soldier. I did my best to conceal the fact that I had a Navy background, but when it finally got out I had to do the obstacle course wearing handcuffs and jump from the parachute tower without a chute.

Seriously, I'm loving every minute of it. Mother is distraught over losing the next generation of Semmes-McKays to the Marines, but my kid will probably tell me to go to hell and start singing 'Anchors Aweigh' in the cradle. It's the way of the world, I guess, and I want to tell you how grateful I am that you let me make up my own mind. If you had lined up with Mother I don't think I could have done it. It's really a great feeling, to make your own choice and then break your butt to live up to it.

Don't win the war out there before I get a chance to potshot a Jap or two!

Love
Sam

Romance

Pearl!

Arthur McKay allowed the pilot to conn the *Jefferson City* past the submarine net tender into the inner harbour. Only the rusting superstructure of the USS *Arizona* remained as a reminder of 7 December 1941. Elsewhere there was vivid evidence of a revived America, preparing to flex her global muscles in the war's second year. There was scarcely a berth or a buoy without a ship. Bulky attack transports, huge aircraft carriers, new *Cleveland*-class light cruisers bristling with anti-aircraft guns jammed the narrow waters.

'Maybe we just ought to take a picture of all this and send it to Hirohito,' George Tombs said. 'If he had any brains he'd surrender on the spot.'

'He'd probably send us a shot of the Combined Fleet at Truk,' Navigator Marse Lee said. 'They've got a hell of a lot of fighting ships left, George.'

Captain McKay stood on the bridge barely listening to his officers. On the voyage from Long Beach he had let his department heads run the ship. Bob Mullenoe had scheduled hours of gunnery practice; Edwin Moss had had damage control drills at all hours of the day and night. Now he let Tombs, who was a superb ship-handler, tie up at the Ten Ten Dock and went ashore to pay his courtesy call on Admiral Nimitz. He knew it was going to be more than a courtesy call. Nimitz waved him into his inner sanctum and sat there studying him for a full minute.

'Art,' he said. 'Art.' He was silent for another full minute. 'Do you want to tell me what happened out there in the Solomons? With your executive officer?'

'No.'

'I didn't think you would. OK, you've got to live with it.'

'I'll try, Admiral.'

For a moment he wanted to show him Ernie King's obnoxious letter. He wanted to tell him that if Chester Nimitz were Cominch, it would be a different Navy and he might be a different man. But those were idiotic thoughts. He had made his choice and he was going to live with it.

They talked about the next phase of the war. It was Plan Orange, the drive across the central Pacific, and a climactic battle with the Combined Fleet. Except for one very large difference named Douglas MacArthur.

'Roosevelt's scared to death of MacArthur.' Nimitz sighed. 'He keeps giving him more and more ships and men. He's got a full-fledged fleet down there with a four-star admiral in command of it. We're rapidly acquiring that two-headed monster known as a divided command out here, and there's nothing we can do about it.'

Captain McKay did not care. He listened and nodded but he did not care. His mind was in the hills above Pearl, where Lucy Kemble was waiting for him.

The motor torpedo boat swung west as they emerged from Pearl Harbor and ran at moderate speed along the Hawaiian coast. Arthur McKay stood on the stern, beside the racks of depth charges, with his arm around Lucy. She smiled sadly at him. It was a glowing glorious Pacific day. The sun glistened on the gently swelling blue-black surface of the sea. In her hands Lucy carried a small metal urn. She gazed down at it and whispered, '"Home is the sailor, home from the sea. And the hunter home from the hill."'

'How far do you want to go, sir?' asked the rangy young lieutenant in command of the boat. He did not look as old as Sammy.

'I think this is far enough. Don't you, Lucy?'

'Yes. As long as we're beyond the scummy waters of Pearl Harbor and its environs,' she said.

Something about her choice of words scraped at Arthur McKay's nerves. So far, this rendezvous with the woman who had always personified romance for him had not gone the way he had envisioned it.

To begin with, he discovered Lucy wanted him to join her in scattering Win's ashes on the ocean. He had hoped this task would have been long since accomplished when he arrived. He had hoped Lucy would be thinking of a new life, not still completing the grisly tasks of warrior widowhood.

He had sought her at Kalakaua House and instead found Mildred Meade supervising the convalescence of some thirty wounded officers. Sad but serene, Mildred had thanked him for recommending her son Dick for the Medal of Honour. She was going to Washington next month to receive it from the President. The tribute had failed to console Clinch; he had become a virtual alcoholic. They were close to divorce. When McKay asked for Lucy, Mildred's wistful smile hinted she understood why. She said Lucy was living in a beach house in Kailua on Oahu's windward coast and seldom came to Kalakaua House.

He had found Lucy there surrounded by the Chinese paintings and sculptures, the Buddhas and ivory elephants and glaring dragons Win had collected over the years. On one wall the centrepiece was the painting of the Chinese traveller descending the mountain in the mist. For a moment Arthur McKay had almost wept.

Now he held Lucy's arm as she leaned over the stern of the torpedo boat and the young captain headed her into the wind. She opened the urn and the earthly remains of Winfield Scott Schley Kemble became a grey film on the shimmering sea. In less than sixty seconds it was gone.

'Oh, Arthur,' Lucy whispered. 'I couldn't have done it without you to help me.'

That was much closer to what he was hoping to hear. But back on the enclosed porch of the beach house, looking down on the surf Win had loved to ride, she began talking about him again. McKay reproached himself for his impatience. He would listen. He was here to comfort as well as be comforted.

'I was always afraid it would end this way – or some worse way. A court-martial would have been worse. To see the envy and hypocrisy that Win had to face all his life tormenting him. It would have been unbearable.'

'Perhaps,' McKay said. 'But I wish – I have to tell you what I honestly feel, Lucy – I wish he had fought it out with them. I think he would have been acquitted.'

'How loyal of you, Arthur. You were the true friend, always the true friend.'

'You were the true wife.'

'I did my best, Arthur.'

Her delicate lips trembled. She made a spasmodic attempt to deal with her windblown hair.

'Oh, Arthur. My heart breaks for you – as much as for Win. It was so diabolical of Rita to involve you in this mess.'

'Rita specializes in the diabolical.'

'I know. She was always that way. She was exactly like my father. The same wilful temperament. The same rages. I can remember when you married her – I asked Win why he was encouraging you.'

'He was trying to help me – help my career.'

'He was wrong. It was wrong.'

She picked up a wedding photograph of her and Win in the garden of the house at Patapsco. For a moment Arthur McKay could have sworn she was going to say something angry.

'Win wasn't quite as perfect as you always thought he was.'

'I never considered him perfect, Lucy. Just . . . admirable.'

She gave him a wary look this time. He could not understand why she did not simply agree with him.

'There are some things that may be impossible to forget. I wonder if what we've gone through is in that category.'

'I don't know. I only know – I've always loved you, Lucy. I've broken with Rita. I've told her I never want to see her again.'

'Arthur! What about Sammy and Barbara?'

'They'll understand. Barbara will, anyway. Sammy –'

He was not so sure about Sammy. He worshipped his mother. He had always been Rita's favourite. McKay sometimes wondered if Sammy covered Rita's bet on her husband. If father fell on his face – as, it turned out, he had – Sammy would still be available for another run for the gold.

It did not matter now. Nothing mattered except Lucy Semmes Kemble's delicate, careworn face, so exquisitely beautiful, like a Chinese jade carving. Nothing mattered but his desire to love this woman and let the past and the future vanish for a few hours.

He drew her out of her chair into his arms. 'Let's try to pretend nothing matters except you and me. For a little while, at least.'

'No! No, Arthur.'

She broke away from him and stepped back, almost falling over the arm of the chair. 'It's too soon. Too soon for anything like that.'

'Lucy, I'm leaving in two days. We're part of a fleet that's going to advance across the central Pacific. I don't know when I'll be back.'

'Arthur, I never thought you felt that way about me. I never saw us as more than the deepest, closest friends.'

'I'm not talking about friendship. I'm talking about love.'

'You loved Win, didn't you?'

'Of course I did. As my best friend. But that's not the way a man loves a woman.'

'Why not? Isn't it more important – for souls to touch – isn't that more important than bodies?'

'They're both important. That's why I love you. For the first time in my life I think I may be able to unite both kinds of love.'

'Sammy and Barbara will hate me. They're the only children I have.'

'Lucy, can't we begin living for ourselves – instead of for other people?'

'You'll have to give me time –'

'There isn't any time. There never is in a war.'

'I didn't start this despicable war. Don't expect me to alter myself on its behalf. Win didn't . . .'

McKay struggled like a man overboard in a heavy sea. What was happening?

It *was* too soon. He was acting like a greedy swine. Or a romantic fool. Or both.

He could not expect her to open her body to him on request. She had belonged to Win for twenty-five years. He reminded himself of how thoroughly Win had dominated her. Lucy never expressed an opinion without asking Win if he agreed. At times McKay had considered her almost oppressed by her husband. It had sharpened his sympathy for her.

'I'm sorry,' he said, 'Can you forgive me?'

'Of course I can,' Lucy said.

She kissed him on the cheek, and Captain McKay went back to preparing the *Jefferson City* for war.

It was another beautiful day on the Kahoolawe Firing Range off Oahu; visibility was at least ten miles. The ship cut through the light swell at twenty-five knots. Jack Peterson fed the ranges to main plot. Radar supplemented Jack's visuals. No one felt any sweat. In main plot, the Mark VII computer crackled and burped; people joked about submarines. In the turrets, the officers grinned and confidently gave the ready signals.

'Commence firing,' Robert Mullenoe said, and the big guns thundered. Captain McKay watched the shells explode precisely in the centre of the target on the scarred side of the tiny island that Navy ships had been bombarding for decades.

Beside him, Captain Miles Pollock, in charge of handing out the passing marks for ships joining the Pacific Fleet, grunted and lowered his binoculars. 'That's pretty damn good,' he said.

'You've got a bunch of pros here, Miles,' George Tombs said. They had been shipmates in their ensign days.

'How come we're not getting paid professional wages?' Navigator Marse Lee said.

The main battery scored the equivalent of 4.0. The five-inch guns got a 3.9. One had fired a wild round. It was probably a defective shell. The forty-millimetre and twenty-millimetre guns had blasted a half dozen small drone planes out of the sky sixty seconds after they were launched.

As Pollock left the *Jefferson City* at Ten Ten Dock, he shook hands with McKay. 'Everybody says you've got a madhouse on your hands, Art. But I don't see any sign of it. The old scow looks like a happy ship to me.'

'We're only mad at the Japs, Miles,' McKay said.

He stood on the bridge watching the first and third sections go ashore for liberty. A couple of men saw him and waved cheerfully. He waved back. George Tombs told him his popularity with the crew was at an amazing zenith. They were convinced he had saved their lives in the Aleutians.

His men. He belonged to them. It made him feel guilty about the loathing for the Navy still seething inside him every time he thought of Win Kemble and his persecutors. If it got any worse, he really would have to take acting lessons from Montgomery West.

Yes, the men had claims on him. He would continue to do his best for them. But there were other claims which his soul refused to relinquish. Claims to some share of happiness, consolation, that could only come from the enigmatic dark-haired woman in the house on the hill above Kailua Beach.

Arthur McKay was startled when Lucy Kemble took out the poems of Po Chu-i and began to read 'Going Alone to Spend a Night at the Hsien-Yu Temple'. It told of the poet's discovery of the joy of solitude.

'I've been reading that over and over again,' Lucy said.

MaKay had never shared Po Chu-i's poems with Rita. He was not entirely sure he was pleased to discover that Win had done so with Lucy. He was also less than pleased with her fondness for this particular poem.

'I didn't know you were in on those secret communications,' he said.

She smiled in a strange, proud way. 'Win told me everything.'

He smiled too. The words were a touching illusion, of course, proof of Win's spell. 'With Rita, that policy would have been fatal long ago.'

Lucy laughed harshly. 'Of course.'

For a bizarre moment, McKay could hear Ernie King snarling. *You're a crumb*. He knew Lucy and Rita were not close. But he had never heard from Rita the contempt with which Lucy obviously regarded her younger sister. It almost made his loathing of Rita seem excessive.

This uneasiness made Lucy even more desirable. Tonight she seemed to have gone out of the way to increase his longing. She was wearing a black dress with a bare neck and shoulders and a pearl necklace Win had bought for her on Bubbling Well Road in Shanghai in 1927. McKay had been with him when he bought it. The pearls against her white skin, the delicate swan's neck and the bare shoulders were overwhelming.

She broiled mai mai for them, and they drank white wine. 'That poem worries me,' he said. 'Do you see yourself in a temple worshipping the changes of the moon for the rest of your life?'

'I'm afraid I do.'

'Win sent me a letter about an experience he had in a temple in Peking. It made me realize how deeply he'd been wounded by our experience in China.'

For a moment Lucy looked angry. 'I know nothing about it,' she said.

'Did you ever discuss China with him?'

'Quite often, as the years passed. We agreed, I think, that the ancient Chinese were right. Trying to change the world is a fairly futile exercise. Trying to change something as rigid, as vicious as the US Navy is even more futile.'

'He never said anything like that to me.'

'I know. To you he could never bear to admit any kind of defeat.'

'I'm amazed.'

'Oh, Arthur. I want to console you the way I consoled him. I knew he was going to fail from the very beginning. I saw how much he needed me.'

McKay struggled to conceal his astonishment. He had never thought of Win needing Lucy Semmes that way. She was a decoration on his escutcheon, no more. He had never thought of Win needing any woman – or any man, except, perhaps, him. Even that was more a suppressed wish than an acknowledged fact.

'I suppose you can't get out of the Navy until the war's over. But you can resign your command of that loathsome ship. Persuade Nimitz to put you on his staff. Why should you take any more risks to help them win their despicable war?'

Again McKay was staggered by the ferocity, the clarity of Lucy's convictions. He had always thought of her as a being without opinions, except those she acquired from Win. A creature of pure feeling.

'I . . . I couldn't do that, Lucy. It would be almost an act of betrayal to my men. We're going back into action tomorrow. I owe it to them to stay aboard.'

Lucy sighed. 'You don't know how that complicates my feelings for you, Arthur. But it will give me more time – time I need – alone.' She smiled bitterly. 'That was the only part of being a Navy wife that I enjoyed. Being alone.'

In Dubious Battle

With beaverish haste, like a puppy obeying a formidable mother, the destroyer laid a smoke screen off the port beam of the USS *Maryland*. Precisely at 0505, a flash of exploding gunpowder leaped from the stern of the squat battleship. Her scout plane struggled skywards in the pale predawn light. Almost instantly, guns boomed behind the smoke screen which had been supposed to conceal the flash from the Japanese defenders of a two-mile-long sandspit called Betio. Shells splashed around the American battleship, which responded with two thunderous salvos from her sixteen-inch guns.

The invasion of Tarawa had begun.

The foot-thick operations plan lay on a shelf beside Captain McKay's bridge chair. For the previous nine days, he and every other captain in the task force had been studying it. So had his executive officer George Tombs, and his other senior officers. Their forty-ship armada had sailed from Pearl Harbor under the command of the *Jefferson City*'s nemesis, Admiral Richmond Kelly Turner.

Throughout their voyage from Pearl, Turner had maintained an incessant schedule of manoeuvres against imaginary submarines, dummy air attacks staged by planes from their five escort carriers, gunnery against targets towed by destroyers and planes. Operating under radio silence, the orders came via blinkers and signal flags snapping from the halyards of the Admiral's flagship, all of which had to be acknowledged within seconds or a followup message asked, 'Is anyone awake on your bridge, Ragtag?'

Ragtag was the J.C.'s code name. Every ship in the task force had one to conceal her identity if the Japs picked up their radio communications. With an admiral like Turner, a code name was an opportunity to express his opinion of the ship. As far as Turner was concerned, Ragtag never did anything right. Even when they had the best gunnery score of the day, they were faulted for firing late or too slowly. When the whole task force executed emergency turns, Ragtag was asked if she had a rudder problem, because she had fallen a fraction of a point off the bearing. When a rattled signalman aboard the *Jefferson City* flew an Affirm pennant upside down, the whole task force heard about it.

For the ship's crew it was only more evidence of the Navy's determination to persecute their captain. For their captain, it was evidence that Lucy Kemble might be right. Maybe he should get off the *Jefferson City* as soon as possible. Resign from the Navy in everything but fact. He might be doing his men a favour if he departed to some obscure berth ashore.

Admiral Turner did not give Captain McKay much time to think seriously about this or about the unnerving conversations he had had with Lucy. He was too busy responding to demands to PREP or POSIT from Turner's flagship. Now the most important of those flags flew there, ordering the four battleships to form a bombardment line. Behind them came the *Jefferson City* and four other heavy cruisers. Closer inshore a string of destroyers began flinging shells from their lighter guns.

For two and a half hours, salvo after salvo blasted Betio's 261 square acres. It seemed inconceivable to sailors topside

515

that anything could still be alive on the sandspit. A dozen fires blazed through the haze of smoke and dust created by the cascade of high explosives. Navigator Marse Lee estimated they had hurled three thousand tons of steel and gunpowder at the Japanese.

Next, under Admiral Turner's stern orchestration, ninety-six planes from carriers just over the horizon dumped several hundred tons of bombs on the island. The battleships and cruisers added a few additional salvos, and the amphtracs and Higgins boats of the first three assault waves swirled away from the transports. The mottled green cloth-covered steel helmets of the Marines could be glimpsed above their gunwales. Captain McKay found himself taking a more than ordinary interest in their progress. In a few months his son might be in one of these rectangular steel boxes, assaulting a similar sandspit. Beyond this island chain, known as the Gilberts, there were the Marshalls, the Marianas, Ulithi, Truk – all scheduled for conquest in Plan Orange's advance to Tokyo.

A strong westerly breeze had sprung up, slowing the landing crafts' progress through the heavy swell. Their blunt bows were not designed to deal with ocean surfaces. McKay could see cascades of saltwater hurtling down on their passengers. The assault was almost an hour behind schedule when they finally formed a line at the designated point offshore and began their advance toward the still dust-shrouded island. Past two destroyers that continued to shell the beaches they ploughed with a precision learned in a dozen rehearsals.

But no rehearsals prepared anyone for what began to happen when the first line of amphtracs crawled across the reef on their alligator treads and approached the beaches. Machine guns blazed from slits in bunkers. Mortar shells flung up spumes of water. Marines sprang from the landing craft to be decimated by bullets and shrapnel. The Navy's three thousand tons of high explosives had not liquidated the 4,500 Japanese defenders of Betio.

The next hours were a nightmare. Amphtracs blew up crawling across the reef. The bodies of Marines littered the beach and floated in the shallow waters of the inner lagoon. Worse, the tide began running out, and none of the Higgins boats carrying the later waves could cross the reef. Only the amphtracs, steadily dwindling in number, could get the Marines ashore. Others had to wade across the seven hundred yards of water. Most of them died long before they got close to the beach.

'It's a goddamn slaughterhouse,' gasped George Tombs.

'Kelly Turner knew that tide was liable to run out too fast. It happens all the time on these islands,' McKay said. 'But he decided to gamble on it not happening today. If you or I made a mistake like that, George, we'd be cashiered. But he'll get a medal.'

Tombs looked uneasy. He did not approve of talking down an admiral on the bridge with so many enlisted men listening. He did not understand what was happening to his classmate.

'I'm afraid the Japs know more about naval gunfire than we do,' McKay continued. 'When you bombard an island as flat as this one at point-blank range, you can't do much damage to underground bunkers. Those battleships should have been ten miles away, so the shells came down like bombs from a plane.'

'Did you tell Turner that?'

'I didn't think of it until this minute, George. But even if I had, would it have done any good? You know nobody can tell Kelly Turner anything. He knows more than God.'

He was pure bile now. Nothing but bilious rage and contempt for the system that protected admirals and crucified those below them. If he had the authority, he ought to arrest himself for mutiny. But he was a captain. He could say what he pleased on his own ship. In his bitter heart, Arthur McKay consoled himself by thinking that Lucy Kemble would be proud of him.

'We let them gyrenes down, sure as hell,' Homewood said. 'We're gonna pay for it, you watch. Them guys were our responsibility. We brought'm out here and told'm we'd make dogfood outa them Japs before they went in. We told'm we was finally gonna make it up for leavin' them on the beach on Guadalcanal after Savo. Instead, what do we do? We don't kill more'n ten Japs with all them shells and then we don't even give'm the right kinda boats to get over that goddamn reef! Somebody fucked up, that's all I know.'

The boatswain's mate was voicing an almost universal sentiment aboard the *Jefferson City*. Everyone was quoting what the Captain had said on the bridge about Admiral Turner. The slaughter on Betio had made sailors embarrassed to look a Marine in the face if they met him in a passageway or sat opposite him in the mess.

'What do you mean, we're gonna pay for it?' Flanagan asked.

'I mean the same thing that happened in the Solomons. When a ship runs away, the good spirits go sour on it. When a fleet runs away, the same thing happens. All them ships and men we lost down there, that was the price we had to pay for gettin' them back on our side.'

'Nice guys, your good spirits. They want a pound of flesh and a gallon of blood for every mistake we make,' Flanagan said.

'I'm not talkin' mistakes. I'm talkin' fuckin' up for the wrong reason. For being an arrogant son of a bitch like Kelly Turner. Or a fuckin' coward like Captain Kemble. You watch what happens. We're gonna lose a big one before we get back to Pearl,' Homewood said.

Flanagan was more vulnerable to Homewood's dark superstitions on this voyage. So was Jack Peterson, who had yet to recover from the intimation of death he had had as they left California. The news of his father being forced to resign from the police force had been a shock to Flanagan. Somehow he had come to accept the idea that he and his friends might die violent deaths out here in the Pacific. That was part of the deal, as Jack Peterson would say, part of being a sailor. But the civilian world back home was timeless, it existed in a kind of bell jar in his mind, cut off from decay and loss.

That night the *Jefferson City* and another cruiser received orders to join the carrier task force manoeuvring off the

Gilberts. They steamed toward the southernmost island in the chain, Makin, which another task force had captured a few days earlier against only token resistance. They joined the three carriers shortly before dawn. There were only four destroyers guarding them. It was obvious they needed some additional ships in their screen.

As they went to General Quarters at dawn, CIC reported bogeys were turning up on the radar screens. Then a float light came drifting down from the sky a few miles to port. This was a familiar warning sign to all veterans of the Solomons that a torpedo-plane attack might be coming at any moment. Everyone began scanning the grey horizon.

They were running close to the carrier *Liscome Bay*, no more than a thousand yards off her starboard beam. Suddenly an incredible blast sent a column of bright orange flame leaping a thousand feet in the air. The carrier exploded like a giant bomb, sending fragments of planes, steel hull and human bodies cascading down on the *Jefferson City*. Flanagan and his men on the forty-millimetre mount were knocked flat by the explosion.

The entire after third of the carrier had vanished. The rest of it was a monstrous pyre on the dark silent sea. Within minutes it sank hissing into the depths. The *Jefferson City* and other ships lowered boats, hurled lines and dropped life rafts to rescue the survivors. Flanagan and his gun crew helped carry some of them down to sick bay. All of them were covered with viscous fuel oil which left them blind and vomiting. Many of them were obviously dying.

Boats Homewood hefted man after man in his arms and carried them without help from anyone else. Soon his dungarees and shirt were smeared with oil and blood. Flanagan glared at him, almost weeping. 'Are your lousy fucking good spirits satisfied now?' he asked.

'Let's hope so,' Homewood said. 'Incidentally, when the fuck are you gonna grow up?'

Chaplain Emerson Bushnell sat beside the retching survivor of the *Liscome Bay*, thinking of what he had seen and heard off the beaches of Tarawa yesterday. Dr Levy said there was a strong possibility this boy would be blind for life. Flame and shrapnel from exploding bombs had struck him in the face.

Bushnell's detestation of war had been reawakened by Tarawa. It was 1917 all over again. Another generation of young men was being ordered to make frontal assaults against machine guns, the way his brother had died in France. Someone had to speak out against it.

Who was better qualified than Captain McKay?

Since their quarrel over Commander Parker, the Captain had said little to the chaplain. But Bushnell had been watching him closely. He had wondered how he would react to the suicide of Captain Kemble. From everything Bushnell had seen and heard, the tragedy had awakened McKay's flickering disillusion with the military system to which he had given his life. Perhaps now was the time to see if he could be redeemed – and used to redeem thousands of others from slaughter.

Bushnell found McKay in his cabin reading a book of Chinese poems.

'Captain, I wonder if I might share with you my feelings about the awful fiasco the Navy and Marines perpetrated yesterday at Tarawa. All those dead young men to get our hands on a piece of sand with an airfield on it. Isn't there a better way to win this war?'

'I don't know, Chaplain. I'm trying not to think about it.'

'I suspect you do know, Captain. Why not speak out? Why not try to save the lives of tens of thousands of young men who are going to die assaulting other islands?'

'Are you trying to get me court-martialled, Chaplain?'

'Of course not. I could arrange for you to speak off the record to a reporter.'

'The same one you told about Parker?'

'Captain, I've wondered if you suspected me of that. I *did* talk to the man, but he had the whole story before he came to me. I only corroborated a few facts. I certainly didn't accuse you of misconduct.'

'I'm sure you didn't,' McKay said wryly.

'Is there some other strategy you could suggest? Couldn't

you – at the very least – say what you think about the way the operation against Tarawa was conducted? I gather from certain remarks you've made on the bridge that your opinion of it is low.'

'It's easy to criticize from hindsight,' McKay said. He stared at the book of Chinese poems for a moment.

'Sometimes the criticism is justified.' Chaplain Bushnell paused, strategically. 'If your friend Captain Kemble were alive, he'd speak out.'

A shadow passed over McKay's face. He glanced up at the painting of the Chinese traveller on the bulkhead.

'I'll think about it. I'll talk to you again when we get back to Pearl Harbor.'

The Truth Shall Make You Free

With saturnine eyes, Captain McKay stood on the bridge watching the white hospital ship *Solace* pass the anti-submarine tender and enter Pearl Harbor. The sinking sun ignited the great red cross on her hull. Aboard her were some of the 2,391 Marines wounded on Tarawa.

The Japanese strategy was now obvious. They were going to invoke the fanatic streak in their national character. The garrison of each island outpost would fight to the death, killing as many Americans as possible in the hope the slaughter would become so appalling that the United States would abandon the struggle and negotiate peace.

Was there an alternative to this kind of gruesome warfare?

According to the doctrine taught at the Naval War College, in a conflict with an island empire whose strength depends on sea power, the enemy's fleet should be the main objective. Once that was destroyed, the island nation had no way to defend itself. With the revival of America's naval strength, why not seek out the Japanese Fleet and smash it? Their supply lines severed, the defenders of the isolated outposts would either starve or surrender. The home islands would face the same fate.

Could the Japanese Fleet be brought to battle without unacceptable risks? Would the Japanese, their fanaticism fanned to frenzy, admit defeat without invasion and virtual annihilation?

The pilot came aboard and conned the *Jefferson City* toward the entrance to Pearl. Maybe strategy had nothing to do with it. Maybe he was just looking for a chance to get even with Kelly Turner, with Ernie King, with all the self-satisfied bastards with stars on their collars.

The trouble was, the chaplain revolted him too, with his mindless hatred of war, his vision of himself as a crusader for peace and brotherhood.

He would say nothing, do nothing for a day or two. His mind and heart were absorbed by other hopes, other visions now.

If Lucy said yes, if Lucy was ready to open her arms to him, he would speak out. He would not hide behind an off-the-record interview. He would use his name. Captain Arthur McKay, USN, would tell America what he thought of the nation's brutal, brainless Pacific strategy, its competing divided commands.

'We've got our old berth at Ten Ten Dock, Art. Want to take her in?' George Tombs asked.

'You do it, George. You're better at it than I am.'

'That sort of flattery will only win my undying loyalty Captain.'

As the lines snaked out and the sea detail performed its hectic tasks, McKay strolled to the starboard side and looked down on the dock. He was remembering what he had thought and felt when the *Jefferson City* had tied up here and he had found Chester Nimitz standing beside his battered staff car.

Now there was another car on the dock, a blue-four-door Buick with no military markings. It was parked well back from the scrambling sailors flinging hawsers around bollards.

Who was it? Maybe that English actress who followed Montgomery West around the world?

The driver's door opened and a petite dark-haired woman in a white suit got out. She peered up at the *Jefferson City*'s superstructure and a smile transformed her delicate face. Captain McKay's battered heart leaped.

Lucy Semmes Kemble was saying yes.

Thick with sea warmth, with the scent and feel of the Pacific's distance, the trade wind filled the car as they drove down the twilit coast highway to the beach house in Kailua. They barely spoke. That suited Arthur McKay, who had never had much faith in words. At his insistence, they stopped in a liquor store in Kailua to buy champagne. Lucy almost objected. 'Arthur, really,' she said. 'It isn't . . . necessary.'

He loved the delicacy, the shyness of her reluctance. 'Don't worry,' he said. 'We'll drink it slowly.'

He struggled to put himself in Lucy's place, to imagine her feelings. She had every right to assume that Rita's husband expected a drunken orgy. He vowed he would show her how wrong she was, how little of his soul Rita had touched.

They kissed in the doorway – and in the kitchen as they put the champagne in the refrigerator. In the living room McKay expected more kisses, a gentle, lovely progress to the bedroom. There was one more kiss before a fifth-century Chinese painting of the Buddha beneath his famous tree. Then Lucy stepped back, her eyes aglow, and said, 'First, Arthur, we have to tell each other everything.'

'About what?'

'About Rita, to start. Then I'll tell you about Win. I want to hear all the ordeals Rita's put you through. Including her affairs. Did she make you perform any of those obscene acts from that awful book she found in Shanghai? She used to read some of them to me at night and swear she was going to make her husband do every one of them.'

'I'm not sure if there's any point in discussing Rita. I told you I'm through with her.'

'I don't want to discuss her. Not now, anyway. I just

want to hear everything. Then I'll tell you about Win.'

'Lucy, it isn't necessary. I've thrown Rita out of my life. I'd prefer to leave it that way.'

'It *is* necessary. If we're going to love each other, we have to know everything. We have to open our minds and hearts to each other, absolutely, without any hesitation or conceal-ment. That was the rule – the one unbreakable rule – between Win and me.'

'Win – really told you everything?'

She laughed softly. 'Yes. That shocks you, doesn't it? I know every woman he ever . . . screwed – as you sailors put it. I insisted on it. I made it a condition of my marrying him. But he didn't object. He said that without my for-giveness he could never survive the role he was playing.'

'Role?'

'From the moment he walked into Annapolis, he was playing a part. He knew he had to be a leader, a man among men, no matter how much he loathed the crudities that involved. Visiting brothels on your midshipman cruises, drinking oafs under the table. He knew there was no other way to win their respect.'

'You know about Imelda Cruz?'

'Of course. And Doris Chang in Shanghai. And that White Russian girl in Canton. The Czar's Pig he called her. And that sugar heiress here in Hawaii. He despised them all. It was part of the role. And of course, they satisfied certain . . . needs. I made it clear I could never completely satisfy them.'

'He told you everything?' Arthur McKay said dazedly.

'Yes. Even those visits you made to that place in Shanghai, the House of a Thousand Pleasures. Where you watched them perform every obscenity imaginable.'

'Did he tell you how sickening it was? They had ten-and twelve-year-old girls doing some of those things.'

'I'm not surprised you found it sickening. Win enjoyed it. He enjoyed what he called the degradation of the species.'

'I never heard him say that.'

'He didn't tell you everything. He used to say there were certain ideas that didn't travel as far as Kansas.'

'He said that?'

'Yes.'

'Why did you insist on knowing everything?'

'I vowed I would never let my husband lie to me the way Father lied to Mother. That was the awful part of my parents' marriage. The way he kept her in total ignorance. About his women, about the horrible things he did to junior officers. He was a monster. She worshipped him blindly. He made such a fool of her.'

'But –'

'Oh, I know what you would have done. You would have promised me everything and told me nothing. You're one of those people, Art, who hate to cause pain. Someone said that's the true definition of a gentleman. Win wasn't that kind of gentleman. He liked to cause pain. He thought being able to cause it without flinching, without feeling, was the essence of being an officer.'

Was she deliberately destroying Win? Was she trying to obliterate him as totally as the sea had swallowed those ashes? No. The whole thing was being revealed to him with reverence, with the deepest delight. Lucy's eyes were aglow with profound excitement, an almost ecstatic joy.

'I can see you don't believe me. But your marriage to Rita is a perfect example. It was Win's idea. He knew she was a monster. But he also knew that made her ideally suited to be a Navy wife. She didn't love you. She didn't love her children. She didn't love anything but the Navy. By now even you know how monstrous that can become.'

'I'm afraid I do.'

'Win knew she'd make you miserable. She would cause you terrible pain. But he never had the slightest qualm. You'd be there to help him when he needed you. That's what being a leader is all about.'

'Lucy, you're going too far. This has got to be an exaggeration. A wild exaggeration!'

'Oh, Art, I can never go too far on your behalf. I know you've loved me. I've loved you too, more and more over the years. I lay awake at night thinking of what Rita was inflicting on you. The rages, the drinking. She's exactly like my father. The same temperament. The same cold, uncaring voracity.'

The word made Arthur McKay tremble. He had thought of Rita that way. He might have even used the word if he had begun describing her to Lucy. But it was terrifically unnerving, demoralizing, to have Lucy use it first.

It was her pity. He never expected this much, this kind of pity. His self, his manhood, was dissolving in this torrent of pity.

Lucy sank down beside him and rested her dark head on his knee. 'You don't know how I hated to write that letter asking you to help Win. He forced me to do it. It was part of his cruelty. The part of him I was never able to love, even though I know he cultivated it out of necessity.'

She said nothing for almost thirty seconds. Then she spoke in a more sombre, strangely timorous voice. 'He sent a copy of that letter to Imelda Cruz.'

'What are you trying to say?'

His hand gripped her arm hard enough to inflict a bruise. Lucy winced and turned her head away, so that she spoke into the wind, into the emptiness of the night-shrouded Pacific.

'At Savo Island, Win rushed to the bridge when the opening guns were fired. He found Parker there in a hopeless panic, the *Jefferson City* hurtling west, away from the battle at twenty-seven knots. When the *Canberra* was smashed to pieces a few thousand yards away, Win realized what was happening. He knew what he should do. Turn east instantly and put his ship between the Japanese and the transports on the beachhead and come to the support of the other three cruisers.

'But he couldn't do it. The stupidity of the operation, of the whole war, ovewhelmed him. He thought of Al Rooks going down with the *Houston* and realized he did not want to become that sort of sacrifice to the ambitions of Franklin D. Roosevelt and Ernest J. King.'

Lucy Semmes Kemble looked up at Arthur McKay, her eyes ablaze with pride and anger now. 'I think he did the right thing. I hope you think so too – in spite of the pain it's caused you.'

Voiceless, mindless, bodiless, Arthur McKay sat there while Lucy Kemble exulted in Win's decision at Savo Island. No victim of a direct hit was ever more instantaneously annihilated. McKay was sure there were tiny pieces of him all over Oahu. Oblivious, Lucy declared Win's defiance the finest act of his noble soul, his ultimate indictment of a Navy that had failed to live up to his ideals of honour and service and selfless devotion to country. For a half hour she told him why rampant hypocrisy, stupidity, venality, careerism disqualified the US Navy from claiming any man's or woman's loyalty.

As he listened, some combination of mind and feeling, perhaps an instinct for survival, continued to operate in Arthur McKay's soul. He was thinking, even though what he was hearing demoralized him. He saw that Lucy had lied to him about the letter he received in the Solomons. She had written it willingly. She had been Win's collaborator from the start. She had loved the idea of helping a man who had defied Cominch Ernest J. King, the supreme example of the admiral as SOB, the replica of the father she had secretly hated all her life.

Finally Lucy subsided. McKay said nothing. His hand stroked her dark hair, but it was an automatic gesture. This woman was not the Lucy Kemble he had loved. She had been a myth he had created out of wish and dream. This woman, the real woman, had destroyed her.

'Now you know the whole truth, Arthur,' Lucy said. 'I hope it makes you free.'

'Free to do what?'

Lucy's voice dwindled. It was barely audible above the surf's rumble. 'To love me. Oh, Arthur, Win didn't. He tried. But the kind of love you and I could have was beyond him. He was always on a height beside his mother, looking down on mere mortals – including me.'

Silence, except for the surf and the sigh of the trade wind.

'Now I've told you everything. Do you understand why it's necessary?'

Captain McKay stood up. He was trembling from head to foot. The ghost of the woman he had loved was whispering those words. With uncanny skill, Lucy was still playing the part Win had assigned her. In the wreckage of her life, she wanted Arthur McKay as her consolation, her opportunity to inflict at least a minor wound on the Navy and a major wound on the sister she hated. That she also yearned for his love was almost irrelevant.

'Lucy,' he said, 'I'll always love you. I'll always love Win. But I wish you'd never told me. I wish you had lied to me. I wish you had kept on lying to me for the rest of our lives! Now – now I don't know what I'm going to do.'

Time and tide, time and tide. The words coruscated through Arthur McKay's mind as he trudged the dark beach. He had left Lucy weeping on the porch and plunged down the slope to the soft sand. He felt as if he was sinking up to his knees in it with every step. It suited his mood. He was sinking into his life with every step.

Not Win Kemble's life, but Arthur McKay's life.

Beside him in memory walked Admiral Chester Nimitz, the patient Texan with the furrowed brow, the quizzical eyes. They had trudged this beach together last year. *I think you're right*, Nimitz had said, when Captain McKay told him he was going to defy the great god Cominch, that he was going to fight his ship and let the past be past. But the past was never really past. It was always there in the present, always ready to rend and wound, thanks to memory.

McKay saw it all. He saw Win's rage and disgust; he had felt the same emotions. It was the special pain of those born too soon or too late in history's blind, blundering voyage. He and Win and other men their age lacked those crucial five or ten years of seniority that gave the Annapolis graduates of the first decade of the century the power to command fleets, to plan the strategy and tactics that won them fame, while younger men died obeying them. The graduates of the following decade were old enough to see the horrendous mistakes that were being made and powerless to do anything about them.

Time and tide. Time and tide. They wait for no man, and no man can alter their pace. Vice Admiral Richmond Kelly Turner, egotism personified, had killed and maimed three thousand Marines at Tarawa thinking he could outwit the tide.

But Win! What had Win done? Now McKay understood why it had been impossible for him to accuse Parker of cowardice at Savo Island. Win had been guilty of something far worse than cowardice. He had betrayed the tradition they had sworn to uphold when they took their oaths as midshipmen in 1913. They had promised to abide by the Navy's code, to obey the orders of their lawful superiors. Over the next four years they had looked a thousand times at the plaques and monuments to Somers, Caldwell, Decatur and other men who had died obeying hard orders. Almost as often they had been told the meaning of John Paul Jones's words: *I wish to have no connection with any ship that does not sail fast, for I intend to go in harm's way.*

At the battle of the Santa Cruz Islands, Captain McKay had taken those three torpedoes intended for the *Enterprise* without hesitation, not because he was a hero, but because he had accepted that commitment to harm's way in some deep part of his soul by the time he graduated from Annapolis. It had survived his disillusionment with the Navy, with the American economic system.

In the battle off the Aleutians, when he had been admiral for a day, he had calmly ordered those destroyers to attack in a last desperate gamble to save the crippled *Jefferson City*. Their captains had obeyed without a word of protest, although each man knew he was conning his ship to almost certain destruction.

Win had violated that commitment to harm's way. He had placed his intellect, his ambition above the promise he had voluntarily made in 1913. That was the most terrible truth. Almost as terrible was the truth that stood beside it. Win had confessed his failure, his sin, by his suicide. All Arthur McKay could do now was weep for the friend of his life.

*

Dawn was beginning to streak the sky when Captain McKay reached the Pearl Harbor gate. The young Marine on guard was more than a little suspicious of this dishevelled character in a captain's uniform who murmured something about a car breaking down. But a call to the USS *Jefferson City* quickly confirmed that she did indeed have a commanding officer named Arthur McKay. He was allowed to enter the base.

He walked past the motor pools and the Quonset huts, past the cranes and dockyards where workmen swarmed over the hull of a carrier that had been gouged by a torpedo off Rabaul. Behind CINCPAC's blackout-curtained windows, duty officers were no doubt working on the next operation in Plan Orange. Soon he was striding along the dock, gazing out at the shadowy shapes of a hundred warships. He thought of the years when he walked beside these dark waters as an ensign aboard the battleship *California*, as a lieutenant commander with a destroyer waiting for him to conn.

The years of his life flowed around him. Had they been ruined by what he had just heard? Or was he freed by this truth in a different, more profound way than Lucy Kemble imagined? Was Arthur McKay free, finally, to be the man, the officer, he might become, on his own terms?

Never mind that his career was ruined. Never mind that he had stripped himself of the consolation of a woman's love. The answer must be yes. What else explained the hope that stubbornly asserted itself in the wreckage of his life?

As he reached Ten Ten Dock, the bugler sounded reveille aboard the *Jefferson City*. The flag rose on her stern. A moment later, bugles blew on a dozen other ships nearby. Boatswain's pipes skirled. Ernest Homewood's basso voice rumbled, 'Reveille. Turn to. The smoking lamp is lit. All sweepers man your brooms. Clean sweepdown fore and aft. Empty all trash cans and spitkits.'

Another day was beginning. Another day in the life of his ship, in the history of the US Navy. He was still a part of this day. He still belonged to this ship, to his men, to this world of steel and oil and high explosives to which he had given his life.

He had made that choice. No one else had made it for him. Now he would make it again.

Captain McKay walked up the gangplank of the *Jefferson City* and saluted the flag.

Chaplain Bushnell was understandably excited when Captain McKay invited him to breakfast in his cabin. He sat down before steaming cups of coffee and plates of scrambled eggs and ham. The chaplain thought McKay looked haggard. But that was to be expected when a man was making a decision to repudiate his whole way of life.

'I've been doing a good deal of thinking about things, Chaplain. The war, the experience of this ship. There's one thing we've never really discussed. What happened on the bridge at Savo Island. Were you up there?'

'No. But I discussed it with Captain Kemble the next morning. He was going through – a good deal of anguish about it. He turned to me as a friend. There was no one else on the ship he could talk to. No one who could understand what he faced that night.'

'What do you mean?'

'The meaningless sacrifice of this ship and its crew. We'd been discussing the situation in the Far East for some time. He made no secret of his disagreement with the government's insane policy of starting this war with Japan –'

'How fascinating.'

'Captain Kemble was a remarkable man. He had a luminous intellect. He analysed the Navy, its policies, its problems, with amazing clarity. But, I'm sorry to say, I couldn't resolve his anxiety. It's all too clear that his decision continued to torment him.'

For a haggard man, Captain McKay was eating his breakfast with considerable gusto. He seemed more interested in the food than in Bushnell's remarks. Suddenly he looked up. There was a new expression on his face, one Bushnell had never seen before. There was only one word for it: ferocity.

'Why didn't you just say, "Go in peace, your sins are forgiven"?'

'How could I do that? I agreed with his position.'

'Chaplain,' McKay said, 'remember when we talked about the difference between faith and belief?'

'Yes.'

'You still don't know the difference.'

'You think Captain Kemble was wrong?'

'I think Captain Kemble had sinned, Chaplain. He was coming to you, the only priest around, in search of forgiveness. Instead, you discussed politics with him. Jesus Christ, Chaplain! When are you going to start doing your job?'

Captain McKay sat there frowning at the bewildered chaplain for a silent minute.

'You're not going to talk to the reporter?' Bushnell said.

'No. And if you talk to him, I'll have you court-martialled in twenty-four hours. We have no business talking to reporters, Chaplain. We each have a job to do. Mine is to fight. Yours is to pray for me. For all of us.'

A terrible hollowness seemed to swell inside the chaplain's body. 'But I'm no good at it. Praying.'

'I know that. Cadwallader isn't the greatest doctor in the world, either. But I haven't thrown him off the ship. I can't throw you off because you say second- or third-rate prayers.'

The captain was smiling. He was sounding incredibly cheerful. Was he going crazy? Suddenly he was serious again. 'I thought about throwing you off, Chaplain. But that's the easy way to do it. I could get someone a lot worse. Let's work together. Maybe we'll both learn something about leadership – and faith.'

BOOK SIX

Gambles and Gambols

Hands on his hips, Jack Peterson squinted disgustedly down tawdry River Street in Honolulu. With thousands of additional sailors swelling the uniformed population, the place had become impossible. Long lines snaked along the sidewalk outside the government whorehouses. The bars were so crowded you had to fight to get a drink.

'This is for the birds, Flan. We got to get ourselves an apartment,' Jack said.

'Apartments are going for about three hundred bucks a week. Are you planning to rob a bank?'

'How much dough you got?'

'Fifty bucks.'

'I got a hundred. Homewood's good for another hundred, if we get him before he goes on liberty again. So we need maybe another three hundred to have a good time.'

Flanagan was unimpressed. To someone getting paid seventy-eight dollars a month, three hundred dollars was as remote as three million. Unless Jack got lucky with the dice – lately his luck had been terrible – they were not likely to get their hands on more money.

'What do you think of my chances of gettin' to see Admiral Nimitz?' Jack said.

'About as good as your chances of getting his job.'

'I wouldn't be surprised if a lot of guys would lay ten to one against me gettin' in to see him.'

'I'd lay a hundred to one.'

'It's a good thing you're a buddy. I'd own you for life.'

Back aboard ship the next day, Jack strolled up to Jerome Wilkinson while he supervised a scrubdown of the main deck. 'Hey, Wilkie,' he said. 'Tomorrow I'm goin' over to CINCPAC to pay my respects to Admiral Nimitz. Anything you want me to tell him?'

Wilkinson's ugly face broke into a leer. 'What the fuck are you talkin' about?'

'The Navy's always puttin' out this jive about how we're all a band of brothers, and officers and crew are one big team. I thought he might like to hear how the guys in the white hats think he's doin'.'

'You've finally popped your cork. I always knew sittin' in that fuckin' range finder with them fuckin' radar waves all around you was goin' to affect your fuckin' brain.'

'You don't think I can do it? If you're so goddamn sure of that, what kinda odds will you give me?'

'Ten to one. What are you bettin'?'

'I'll lay you twenty bucks. My buddy Flanagan here's holdin' the money.'

Wilkinson grabbed his hand. 'That's the easiest twenty I ever made,' he chortled.

The word swept the ship like a gasoline fire. At dinner a half dozen of Jack's dice-playing foes stopped to place bets at varying odds. By this time several people began to wonder if he had some sort of inside track that he was concealing. But no one, try as he might, could figure out what it was. They were reassured by Boats Homewood, who insisted Jack had definitely slipped his cable.

After supper, Homewood dragged Jack and Flanagan up to the fantail and threatened them with dismemberment if they did not let him in on the game. 'What's the angle?' he asked. 'I smell a fuckin' general court-martial in this thing. You plannin' to crawl in a window at CINCPAC and claim you seen the Admiral? Then ten Marines drag you off to the base brig and we sail without you?'

'What the fuck do you mean by that?' Jack demanded.

'I mean I think I smell shit runnin' down your legs,' Homewood said. 'That bull you've been throwin' about never seein' home again. As if you had any fuckin' use for home or mother. Are you just tryin' to get off this ship before we sail again?'

'Jesus Christ,' Jack said. 'If you weren't an old man, I'd kick you in the nuts and never speak to you again. Who the fuck are you to tell me what I should feel? If you wanta know the fuckin' truth, I don't have a clue to how I'm gonna get in to see Nimitz. What I'm tryin' to find out is just how good my luck still is. So I dreamt this up to put it to the test.'

'You gonna take this kid with you? If you wanta act like a goddamn screwball, that's your business. But don't mess this kid up too.'

'He's holdin' the money, that's all,' Jack said.

'OK, go ahead. I never could figure out what the fuck went on in your head.'

'I never *asked* you to figure it out! If you'd stop screamin' for ten seconds, you might see I got a better chance than you think. When Nimitz hears I'm from the *Jefferson City*, he might want to ask me a few questions about what the hell's been happenin' aboard this tub.'

Homewood seized Jack by the throat. 'You mean you're gonna talk down the Captain?'

'Hell no. I'll tell him everything's great. I just want to win the fuckin' bet. Can't you get that much straight?'

'You're the one who'd better be straight on this thing,' Homewood said. 'If you ain't on this ship when we sail for the next operation, I'll find you when we come back and beat the shit out of you, if I got to bribe twenty-two Marines to let me into your cell to do it!'

'Come on,' Jack said the minute they set foot on the Ten Ten Dock.

'Come on where?' Flanagan asked.

'You're comin' with me.'

'You told Boats –'

'Forget what I told that gasbag. I just been thinkin'. One guy shows up, he could be a nut. They'll be more inclined to throw him out. Two guys are less likely to be crazy.'

They walked through the base to CINCPAC's low-slung headquarters building. Two tough-looking Marines with white helmets and white holsters for their .45 revolvers glared at them. 'Whatta you swabbies want?' one of them growled.

'We're from the *Jefferson City*. We'd like to pay our respects to Admiral Nimitz,' Jack said.

'Your *what*?' the Marine said.

'Our respects. We been fightin' under his command from Guadalcanal to Tarawa. We'd like to tell him how much we enjoyed it.'

The Marines looked at each other, trying to decide what to do. Arrest these nuts? Tell them to shove off? Inform the Admiral?

'Flanagan here's from New York. I'm from Seattle. Different ends of the continent, you know. But in the same Navy.'

'Is this for some sort of news story?'

'No. This is our idea.'

One Marine disappeared into the building. He came back in five minutes looking bewildered. 'Lieutenant Lamar says to send them in.'

They sat in an outer office for about fifteen minutes while Lamar, Nimitz's aide, looked them over. His questions were similar to the Marines' and so were Jack's answers. At any moment, Flanagan was sure ten Marines were going to arrive and take them away. They had to be breaching some supreme article of the Navy's regulations.

The phone on Lamar's desk buzzed. 'Yes, Admiral,' he said, 'they're still here.'

He gestured towards a set of double doors and in ten seconds they were shaking hands with Admiral Chester Nimitz, Cincpac himself. Flanagan was barely able to talk, but Jack retained his composure. 'Admiral,' he said, 'we really did want to pay our respects. But to tell you the whole truth, we also got about a thousand dollars in bets ridin' on this thing.'

'I figured it was something like that,' the Admiral said. 'You're a couple of lucky sailors. You got me on the one morning when Lamar here decided I needed some comic relief. How are you going to prove you got in to see me?'

'I don't know, Admiral,' Jack said, momentarily panicked.

'Lamar, get the staff photographer in here.'

The photographer arrived on the double and took several shots of the Admiral standing between them, smiling broadly. 'How are things aboard the *Jefferson City* these days?' Nimitz asked.

'Couldn't be better, Admiral. It's a happy ship,' Peterson said. 'We think we got the best captain in the fleet.'

'I'm glad to hear that,' Nimitz said.

That night Flanagan sat in the mess compartment, the photographs on the table, and collected their money. Boats Homewood watched, an uncertain expression on his face. He could not decide whether to be proud of Jack or angry with him. He had pulled off a stunt Homewood would never have dreamt of trying. Jack fondled the cash – which came to $1,980 – and announced they were going to have the revolving party to end them all in their rented apartment.

Unfortunately, they were in Hawaii, not Australia, and the only women Jack or any other sailor ever met in Honolulu were the whores along River Street.

They paid the hundred dollars to a Chinese landlord who looked like Charlie Chan's twin's brother and lugged a case of booze and mixers up the narrow smelly stairs to the four tiny rooms. Jack went off to negotiate with a couple of madams and returned with three girls, one of them his old friend Sally. Camutti, Homewood, Jablonsky and other members of their F Division circle were invited to drop in, and Jack said other girls would be along for the free booze.

'The word's out that Gentleman Jack's in town with a pocket full of dough,' Sally said, throwing her arms around him. 'What the hell did you do? Hit the ship's safe?'

Jack handed her a bourbon and soda and gave a splendid rendition of their Nimitz gambit. This catapulted the girls' admiration of Jack – and by association, Flanagan – to stratospheric heights. The other two girls were named Terry and Genevieve. Terry was from Brooklyn. She was short and dark, with thick wiry hair and olive skin. Her nose was wide and her jaw was heavy. Put a helmet on her and blow her up to twice her size and she would have looked like one of the seven blocks of granite who played in Fordham's line. Genevieve was from Chicago. She was lanky, lean, with a face that reminded Flanagan of Olive Oyl, except that the cartoon was somehow smudged.

Sally was from Seattle, which turned out to be one of the reasons why she and Jack were friends. After a drink or two, Jack grew less friendly. 'Jesus Christ, Sal, your ass is gettin' as wide as a battleship,' he said. 'You shoulda seen her when she first came out here. If she turned sideways she disappeared.'

Sally looked hurt. Terry defended her. 'You don't get no exercise in this business,' she said. 'I mean, you woik all night and you sleep all day. So y'gain weight.'

'I eat like a fuckin' truck horse,' Genevieve said. 'I never gain nothin'. Not an ounce.'

'Hey, I remember you in them days, Jack. You looked like you was a candidate for TB,' Sally said. 'You're puttin' it on too. In a coupla years your neck'll be as thick as Boat's here.'

'I wouldn't be surprised,' Homewood said.

'Bullshit,' Jack said. 'I'm gonna get out of the fuckin' Navy the minute the war ends. I'm gonna go into pictures. Act, you know?'

'Come on. The only fuckin' actin' you ever done is at captain's mast,' Homewood said.

'Hey, Flan's seen me perform. You think I can make it in pictures, Flan?'

'Sure,' Flanagan said. He was ready to believe Jack could do anything, at this point.

'See?' Jack said. 'This kid's got a brain. He's gonna be a hell of a writer some day. Maybe he'll write a story with a part in it for me. They'll buy it for the movies and I'll act in it.'

'What the fuck kind of a story would that be?' Homewood asked. 'From the drunk tank to the brig and back?'

'Hey, I don't mean the story of my crummy life. Somethin' that comes out of his head. That's how stories get written. Right, Flan? A guy dreams them up. A guy with the gift of gorgeous bullshit. I got it, but I don't know how to write it down.'

Jack started telling the whores about the letters Flanagan had written to Martha Johnson. To his surprise, they were outraged.

'If I ever found out a guy did that to me, I'd kill him,' Terry said.

'Me too,' Sally said, glaring at Jack and Flanagan.

'Christ almighty, you never know what the fuck a dame's gonna think about anything,' Jack said.

A furious argument erupted over the letters. Boats sided with the whores, which further enraged Jack. The quarrel made Flanagan feel guilty. He remembered the joy in Martha Johnson's voice that night on her porch in Seattle as she talked to him about the letters. Now here was Jack, up to his eyeballs in whores in Honolulu and Flanagan beside him.

Other F Division stalwarts joined the party. The liquor continued to flow in prodigious quantities and Flanagan's perception of what was happening grew hazy. More whores arrived and Jablonsky offered to service them all to prove the Poles, not the Germans, were the master race. Bets were placed on his endurance. The ladies lost, even though there were at least six in the lineup.

At another point, Flanagan was in bed with Terry and she was telling him that she was going home to Brooklyn after the war to open a beauty shop and maybe they could meet in Manhattan and who knows they might fall in love and she could support him while he wrote his stories. At still another point Camutti and Genevieve demonstrated the finer points of fucking while a drunken circle applauded.

The hilarity was abrupt demolished by a scream. People in various stages of undress or no dress at all blundered into the living room and then into a bedroom where they found Jack Peterson smashing Sally in the mouth with back and forehand cuffs. 'You always did remind me of my goddamn mother,' he raged.

They dragged Jack off the bed and tried to fix up Sally's face, which was a mess. Charlie Chan rushed in demanding a little peace and quiet. Homewood dangled him out a window by his ankle, and he became more agreeable. But no one could placate the whores, who decided the damage to Sally's face could only be assuaged by a hundred dollars. They got the money and departed with a marvellous imitation of offended virtue.

Other revellers drifted away as the liquor ran out. Finally only Flanagan and Homewood and Jack were left. Jack sat on the side of the bed in his undershorts shaking his head. 'It's no good any more,' he said. 'I don't know what the fuck's the matter, but it's no good any more.'

'Aw, shit,' Homewood said. 'What you need's a couple of months at sea. There's nothin' like sea duty to beat the blues. I always get down when I'm on the beach too long. A good fight'll help too. A coupla big hits with them eight-inchers and you won't have a worry in the world.'

Jack sat there shaking his head. 'I don't know, Boats, I don't know if it'll work. The whole thing's no good any more.'

Love Letters

Dear Rita:

I've spent several weeks trying to begin this letter. Now we're at sea, on the way to invade the Marshalls.

I don't know whether we can begin again after what I've said and done to you. But I would like to try, some day.

During these weeks of indecision, I've thought mostly about love – how hard it is to understand it – how easy it is to misunderstand it.

I think I've always misunderstood it. Maybe it goes back to my mother, the first woman I loved. Maybe it's part of a wider misunderstanding, which afflicts the whole race of males. I don't know.

But I do know this. For the first time I recognize the depth of your love for me. I'm afraid too often I thought of it as nagging, even as a kind of dislike. Maybe I was just too damn stubborn, too determined to be a lonely hero, making it on my own in my own perverse way. Maybe that was why I resented your advice, your concern.

You must be wondering if I've been hit on the head by an eight-inch shell. In a way, I have. I won't tell you what happened, but I've found out you were right and I was wrong about Win at Savo Island.

Not completely wrong, I should add. You could argue that with a different executive officer the thing would never have happened. Parker's cowardice exposed Win to a terrible temptation – and he yielded to it. You could also argue that Win's whole life had been a long tragic progression to that terrible moment.

You can see I still love him. He's still my friend. You'll have to understand that. Some wise man wrote that to know all is to forgive all. I don't know all, but I know enough to forgive him. I also know – as he knew – that the Navy could not forgive him. Can you forgive me? Do you know enough? Do you still care enough? I hope so.

Your husband,
Art

Dear Barbara:

There is no need to keep apologizing to me for not joining the WACS or the WAVES. Somebody in the country ought to be getting an education they can use after this interminable war finally ends. If it lasts much longer we'll have eight or ten million male ignoramuses on our hands who don't know how to do anything but shoot guns. We'll need some educated women around.

Most of the time, Bobbie, I've tried to stay out of the fights you have with your mother. That was probably a mistake. But women have mystified and confused me from birth. It may have something to do with having three older sisters. I sort of instinctively keep my distance from the female world for fear of being overwhelmed. Now I'm issuing an urgent recommendation that you sign a treaty of peace with your mother. She could use some support from a loving daughter. She and I have had a profound disagreement, in which I behaved pretty badly. I won't go into details, but we came close to breaking up. I'm trying to repair the damage, but in the meantime (or if in the long run I fail) I wish you'd let Rita know you want to help. She's very proud and fancies she's as tough as any son of a seacook who ever walked up a gangplank, so it won't be easy. But if you can do the job, you will have made a lot bigger contribution to my personal war effort than you could ever make banging a typewriter in uniform.

With much love,
Dad

Dear Martha:

We're pulling out of Pearl tomorrow. I can't tell you where we're going, naturally, but it's going to be big. I keep thinking about you all the time.

Flanagan was reading a poem to me the other day. The guy's getting queerer by the minute, with this poetry stuff. Anyway, it was about the Lady of the Lake. I said to him, Hey, Martha's my Lady of the Sound. I mean Puget Sound. It's not very poetic. Flanagan, the snob, turned up his nose at it.

Hawaii was a bore as usual. We spent most of our time swimming and drinking beer. I got a sunburn like you can't believe. If only you were around to rub some Unguentine on it. I'd rub some on you and you know what would happen next.

Jesus what a difference you've made in my life! I'm so different, I'm thinking of changing my name. How would you like to be Mrs Roland Effingham. Or Mrs Wilbur St John? Or Mrs Theodore Van Pelt? Seriously, I might want to change my name because I'm beginning to think I'll blow the Navy and try to get into something legit, like the movies. Would you like a little forty-six-room place in Beverly Hills? Stick with Jack.

I'm sticking with you, Baby.

Jack

Dear Gwen:

I've been racking my brain for some way to get you to Honolulu and now it's too late. We're off to see the Wizard again. I was ecstatic to hear you'd got a small part in Preston Sturges's next film. He's the most talented director in Hollywood and you are perfectly suited to his kind of comedy.

If I get out of this thing in one piece, I'm beginning to think I'd like to direct instead of act. Maybe I'm just tired of taking orders and I'd like to give a few. Not to you, though. You're much too hotheaded.

At the moment, the idea of having another life beyond the war is as fanciful as another life beyond the grave. I spent most of my time in Hawaii going to a school for CIC officers. They're giving us more and more responsibility. Too bad some rank doesn't go with it.

Naturally, the rest of the ship takes a dim view of my overweening power. Recently Mullenoe put out the word that CIC stands for Christ I'm confused. I retaliated by announcing plans to take over the navigator's duties. I might throw in a little night work as engineering officer on the side.

The Captain has gone through some sort of a sea change. After being in the most tremendous funk for six months or so after that story about Parker got out, he is now as serene and smiling as he was when he first came aboard. It's put everybody in a good mood. I even saw Kruger smiling the other day.

Thank God you're a Navy brat! Otherwise this ship gossip would be a total bore. Or is it anyway?

Your inveterate sailor,
Sinbad

Dear Dad:

Mom tells me you're really feeling on the bum since you retired. I'm sorry to hear it. Maybe you ought to look at the bright side. You're young enough to start a new career and you don't have to overwork, with your pension coming in regularly.

Still I guess you miss the cops. There are a lot of guys on this ship like my boatswain who'd miss the Navy if they got out of it. So I understand a little of how you feel.

Don't worry about me. We've got a good crew on this ship. We can handle anything the Japs throw at us.

Love,
Frank

Dear Anna:

I keep wishing we'd get close to Australia and then strip a bearing in a turbine and limp to Sydney for repairs. I passed my watertender's second class test last week, so I shouldn't be talking this way. I'm a rated man – with responsibilities.

Now I've got a striker I'm supposed to be teaching, the way Amos Cartwright taught me. He's kind of a dumb goy but willing to learn.

I really like teaching. That must be your influence. I'm struggling with some of those German books you sent me. Ye gods, they're skullbreakers. I don't know what the hell Thomas Mann is talking about most of the time. So write me long letters explaining it all, will you? Consider me your culture-striker.

I'm glad you've made a little progress with the authorities on behalf of your aborigines. What an impression they made on Amos! They really spooked him. He said they made him feel he was in touch with the creation of the world. He loved their idea about everyone living forever in the dreamtime. I hope that's where he is right now.

We're going into action again. Everyone is hoping this is the last time around. I doubt it. We've been looking for one big battle to end it all ever since we came out here. The Japs won't oblige.

Your wandering Jew,
Marty

Onward Christian Sailors

'From now on,' Officer of the Deck Lieutenant Wilson Selvage MacComber said, 'it's going to be a rout.'

'I hope you're right,' Captain McKay said.

Around them steamed an awesome array known as Task Force 58 – six heavy aircraft carriers and six light carriers with over seven hundred planes on their hanger decks, eight battleships, six cruisers and thirty-six destroyers. Just ahead were two of the battleships, the recently launched *Missouri* and *New Jersey*. Long streamlined monsters, without a trace of the old battleships' squat gun-platform look, they were capable of hitting thirty-two knots – as fast as any carrier or cruiser. America's productive might was giving the Navy overwhelming superiority in the sky and on the sea.

Behind them lay another conquest – Kwajalein, the key to the Marshall Islands. It had been captured with amazingly light casualties. Admiral Kelly Turner applied the bitter lessons learned at Tarawa. For three days, instead of for three hours, this awesome fleet had pounded the Japanese with an incessant rain of shells. The task force's seven hundred planes had dropped additional tons of bombs, and land-based planes flying from Tarawa had added still more destruction. The dazed, decimated Japanese defenders had offered little more than token resistance.

At this very moment, planes from the carriers were swarming over the great Japanese naval base of Truk, 660 miles southwest of the Marshalls. The battleships and cruisers and destroyers had their turret hoists and handling rooms loaded with armour-piercing shells for the Combined Fleet if they came out to fight. Among the crew, tension ran high. Jack Peterson spun the main battery director back and forth like a dervish. He was sure the decisive battle he had been predicting ever since they had sailed from Long Beach was looming just over the horizon.

In CIC Montgomery West tried to keep score on what the pilots claimed they hit. If they were even half right, the Japanese fleet had been wiped out. When he reported this news to Captain McKay, he grunted sceptically. 'Everything looks like a hit to those guys. And every ship looks like a battleship. They're not as bad as the Army flyboys, but they're cousins under the skin. Check with the Admiral's staff for the real score.'

From the *Jefferson City*'s mainmast fluttered the four-star flag of Admiral Raymond Spruance. Having an admiral aboard complicated life for everyone. Room had to be found for his staff in Officers' Country. The *Jefferson City*'s CIC was sliced in half to create a flag plotting room, where Spruance and his staff worked. Flag signalmen took over the *Jefferson City*'s halyards, and flag radiomen commandeered a large chunk of the radio room. Spruance occupied a stateroom reserved for such starry visitors, directly behind the flag bridge.

'Admiral Icicle' was the nickname the crew quickly chose

for the lean severe Spruance. Not that Spruance ever said a word to any of them. He regarded himself as strictly a passenger aboard Captain McKay's ship. But the crew had a chance to study him for two hours each afternoon when the forecastle was cleared by the Marine detachment and Spruance walked briskly up and down, accompanied by one or two of his staff officers.

Spruance's choice of the *Jefferson City* for his flagship baffled McKay at first. As Nimitz's chief of staff for the previous year, Spruance obviously knew all about the travails of Captain McKay and the ship. McKay had been one of his students at the Naval War College in 1938, when Spruance was the second-ranking professor on the faculty. But McKay, as shy as Spruance himself, had not become close to this taciturn man. Had Spruance been ordered by Admiral King to get enough evidence against Captain McKay to send him home in disgrace?

McKay soon discovered that Spruance disliked Fleet Admiral Ernest J. King at least as much as he assumed McKay did. Spruance's chief of staff, Captain Byron Masher, was a victim of King's SOB style. A chunky, balding man with the mournful eyes of an abused beagle, Maher had been one of the brighter members of the class of 1917. Given a cruiser when the war broke out, he had run it aground off Hawaii. King had relieved him and vowed he would never get another ship and would never be promoted to admiral. Cominch ignored Spruance's repeated recommendations to make Maher a rear admiral.

Inevitably, this bond of animosity – and Spruance's recollections of McKay as one of his better students at the Naval War College – led to an invitation. 'Art,' Byron Maher said, 'the Admiral wonders if you'd like to join us for a walk this afternoon.'

'I'll be delighted.'

Spruance liked to talk while he strolled. That afternoon he discoursed on the strategy of the war as it was evolving in Washington and Pearl Harbor. He was not happy with it. 'We're spending as much time and energy brawling with each other as we are fighting the Japanese,' the Admiral said.

'MacArthur wants to invade the Philippines, which will take a good year to capture. He wants to rescue the reputation he lost there in 1941. He should have been court-martialled and retired for losing them in the first place. That fiasco was worse than any mistakes made at Pearl Harbor. King is furious with MacArthur for stealing an entire fleet from him. He wants to invade Formosa, but he can't get enough troops out of the Army or the Marines to do it. The Army Air Force says they can bomb Japan to its knees if we get them bases in the Marianas. What do you think, Art?'

'Why take any more islands? Why not sail this fleet into Japan's home waters and force their fleet to come and fight? We win and Japan has no choice but surrender.'

'I've already got that recommendation from a half dozen aviators,' Spruance said, using his term for the carrier admirals. Spruance was still a battleship man, even though carrier planes had won the battle of Midway for him. 'What makes you think the Japanese fleet will come out and fight if they don't think they can win? We don't have the oilers, the ammunition ships, to maintain a fleet this big at sea for a long period of time. And we'd be very vulnerable to their land-based planes.'

McKay sighed. For a moment he was back at the War College, squirming while Captain Spruance urged him to think harder about his estimate of the situation. 'It's going to get tougher and tougher to take these islands. From now on, they'll know exactly where we're going.'

'I know,' Spruance said. 'Kwajalein was a fluke.'

'Maybe we can decide it all at Truk.'

Spruance shook his head. 'The aviators got very few capital ships. Mostly auxiliaries. The main fleet was gone before we got there. Maybe we can do a little hunting tomorrow. Tell your gunnery officer to make sure his boys are ready to shoot.'

That was typical Spruance. He treated his staff the same way, as Byron Maher was wont to complain to his classmate McKay. 'He'll discuss grand strategy by the hour. But if you want to find out what he plans to do tomorrow, you have to be a mind reader.'

The next day, the carriers launched another strike at Truk. Spruance detached the battleships *New Jersey* and *Iowa*, cruisers *Jefferson City* and *Minneapolis*, and four destroyers. The heavies steamed in line of battle column, the destroyers scurrying ahead through the placid seas. Soon they were opposite the northern entrance to Truk Lagoon. Inside they could see dark green cone-shaped islands, rising to a height of fifteen hundred feet. Spruance ordered a countermarch, and the American squadron proceeded to plough past the entrance from the opposite direction.

No one could figure out what the Admiral had in mind. McKay invited Byron Maher up to the bridge and asked his opinion. 'I think he's just enjoying himself. He's thumbing his nose at the Japs,' Maher said. 'Imagine how we would have felt if Yamamoto did this sort of thing off Pearl Harbor on 8 December 1941?'

'Maybe it's more serious than that,' McKay said. 'Maybe he's hoping that by humiliating them this way, the war party in their government will collapse and we can negotiate peace.'

Peace. The word stirred an enormous wish for it, in all its meanings, in Arthur McKay's soul. Peace would mean that Sammy was safe, that he could devote himself to regaining Rita's love. Peace would lift the burden of the *Jefferson City* from his shoulders.

'What's there to negotiate as long as Roosevelt insists on unconditional surrender?' Maher said. 'You should hear what Spruance thinks of that idea.'

As they turned back toward Kwajalein, lookouts sighted smoke just over the horizon. Soon they saw it was coming from two crippled Japanese ships, a destroyer and a cruiser. In between them was a smaller patrol craft, which the destroyers' shells had left burning on the water. Spruance telephoned the *Jefferson City*'s bridge. 'Art,' he said, 'you and the *Minneapolis* will take the cruiser. The battleships will take the destroyer.'

McKay realized Spruance was looking forward for the first time in his life to a sea battle. At Midway he never saw the enemy fleet. All the destruction on both sides had been wrought by planes. He could have left these cripples to be finished off by Task Force 58's planes. But he wanted the thrill of fighting ship to ship.

Neither McKay nor his crew shared the Admiral's enthusiasm. The smoking cruiser reminded them too much of the *Jefferson City* off the Aleutians. The battered destroyer brought back memories of the morning after the Friday-thirteenth night battle off Guadalcanal, when Ironbottom Sound was littered with crippled ships.

As the *New Jersey* passed the sinking patrol boat, she opened fire at point-blank range with ten of her five-inch guns. The Japanese ship disintegrated into flaming debris. 'Jesus Christ,' gasped George Tombs. 'That isn't war.'

'Yes it is,' McKay said.

McKay saw two flashes of light on the destroyer's deck. 'Torpedoes,' he said. 'Alert the lookouts. Notify the other ships.'

Tombs shouted the warning over the TBS. The *New Jersey* turned just in time to escape the deadly fish. A moment later, her main battery and the main battery of the *Iowa* fired salvos. The destroyer, game to the end, replied with her five-inch popguns for another sixty seconds. Then she crumpled into a mass of extruded burning metal as the huge shells struck her.

Simultaneously, the *Jefferson City* and the *Minneapolis* opened fire. The Japanese cruiser's guns flashed in return, and shells straddled the *Minneapolis*. But within five minutes this enemy ship too was a smashed burning hulk. Her forward turret somehow fired one last round which fell a thousand yards short of the *Jefferson City* as she exploded and sank.

Led by the mighty battleships, the American squadron turned away, letting the Japanese on Truk hunt for survivors, if any. From flag pilot came a message. 'Admiral Spruance congratulates the *Jefferson City* on her shooting.'

'I don't know about you,' George Tombs said, 'but I don't think I'll be able to eat much supper tonight.'

A weight heavier than the burden of command pressed

Captain McKay's shoulders. The mixture of dismay and weariness on Tombs's honest face was part of it. Sinking a virtually defenceless ship in broad daylight at point-blank range somehow offended the feelings every sailor shared about their calling. It made them all sick of the war. But the war had its own timetable, its own malevolent life.

Return of the Invisible Man

The thief was back. He slithered through the ship day and night, stealing with incredible effrontery. A man would take his wallet and watch to the head and leave them on the shelf above the sinks while he showered. During the ten or twenty seconds that he had soap in his eyes, they would disappear. Fire Controlman First Class Bourne, who wore a money belt, had $150 extracted from it while he slept. Even a tailor-made uniform, laid lovingly on a rack while its owner shined his shoes a few feet away, was not safe.

Boats Homewood was in despair. He no longer issued fiery pronunciamentos about stopping the thief. Instead he tried to be philosophic. He said there was one on every ship and they should not let him ruin their attitude toward the Navy. Flanagan could not understand his acquiescence.

Others were not as philosophic. Even the Bobbsey Twins, one of whom lost his second gold watch, swore they would put the thief over the side if they caught him. Flanagan, fascinated by the thief's on-again, off-again larceny, speculated on his state of mind or soul.

'He seems to run wild whenever we fuck up in a big way,' he said. 'Tarawa started him again, I'd bet on it.'

'Bullshit. It's Pearl Harbor,' the Radical fumed. He had lost his wallet, with a precious picture of Lenin in it, given to him by his father. 'He's nothing but a fucking capitalist acting out his instincts. Stealing directly, instead of through the wage-price system.'

'He ran wild after we got our asses blown off in the

Solomons,' Flanagan persisted. 'And when we got exiled to the Siberia Patrol. When we do something right as a ship, he's OK. It's the Navy he hates, not the *Jefferson City*.'

'I think he hates the whole fuckin' system,' Jack Peterson said. 'In the Navy and out of it. The system ain't no different outside. Big deals eatin' in expensive restaurants and the rest of us in hash houses.'

'Why does he steal from his shipmates if he doesn't hate the *Jefferson City*?' Daley asked.

'We're the only game in town,' Flanagan said. 'I think he hates to do it. He hates himself for it. But he can't help it.'

'You are really full of shit, you know that?' the Radical said.

'I agree,' Jack said. 'But it's good bullshit. He's gonna make money sellin' it some day.'

'Shit. Nobody's gonna make any money after this war. The fucking capitalist bosses are gonna be in the saddle,' the Radical said. 'We're gonna have a depression twice as big as the last one. Our only hope is the Russians. After they beat the Germans, they may decide to use their army to liberate the workers of the whole world.'

'Hey, I wanta be around for that scrap,' Jack said. 'What kind of a Navy do the Russians have?'

'They don't have one,' the Radical admitted, looking glum.

'Ain't they gonna have some trouble gettin' an army across the Atlantic or the Pacific to liberate the workers of the USA?'

'With the military training we've got, we may be able to liberate ourselves.'

'They got any thieves in Moscow?' Jack asked.

'None. Why should the people steal anything? They own everything already.'

'You mean if we're Russians and you got a watch on your wrist, I own it?'

'No. But you can get a watch from the government free of charge. So why steal it?'

'Hey, that's some system. You mean there ain't no expensive restaurants, no high-priced cars? Everybody eats the same, wears the same, drives the same?'

'Absolutely. That's what Communism is all about.'

'What about the officers in the Russian Army? Do they get paid the same as the privates?'

'Sure.'

'Even the generals?'

'Sure.'

'Flan,' Jack said, 'is any of that true?'

'Nope,' Flanagan said. 'It's all bullshit.'

The Radical practically foamed at the mouth. 'It isn't! It's the truth!'

Flanagan and everyone else knew by this time that it was a waste of breath to argue with Booth about his Russian fantasies.

'Even if you're right,' Flanagan said, 'I think the thief would steal in Moscow. He does it for kicks. I'm convinced of it.'

'Me too,' Jack said. 'The guy's a psycho. You know, he's got kleptopatra or whatever the hell it is.'

'Kleptomania?' Flanagan said. 'I don't think so. They want to get caught. This guy's kick is *not* getting caught. He's smart as hell.'

That night as the boatswain's mate of the watch piped Lights Out and they crawled into their racks for a few hours of sleep, a scream arose from the far corner of F Division's compartment. It was the Radical. He was standing in front of his locker wailing like a blues saxophone.

'It's all gone. Everything. He took everything!' he howled.

The thief had cleaned out his locker. Gone was his copy of *The Communist Manifesto* and Stalin's *Life of Lenin*. Also gone were all his clothes. He had nothing left to wear but what he was standing in. It would cost him a month's salary to refit himself.

'That settles it,' the Radical cried. 'The minute this war's over, I'm, applying for Russian citizenship!'

Newspaper Days

The Dream Life of Leutnant Flugel

Thanks to the codebreaking skills of US Naval Intelligence, this first edition of your ship's paper is privileged to bring you a series of breathtaking reports on the problems of the German Navy. Chief among them is Leutnant Otto von Himmel Flugel, commander of the garbage scow SS *Grossfart*.

Irked that he was the oldest lieutenant in the German Navy (or in any other navy, for that matter) Flugel ceaselessly bombarded the Admiralty and occasionally the Führer himself with plans for winning the war. He fancied himself an expert in fire control, for instance, and proposed converting the *Grossfart* into a secret weapon that would confound Allied radar by emanating odours so strong, antennas would warp at a single whiff.

The only trouble was, the *Grossfart*'s odours were already warping antennas throughout the Reich. The Führer could not even get the Berlin Symphony on the radio at Berchtesgaden! The Admiralty ordered Flugel another fifty miles onto the North Sea and hoped he would be captured by a neutral Irish fishing boat.

Any sane man would have committed suicide at this point, but Flugel was undiscouraged. His secret was his dream life. Each night, after spending another momentous day making sure that there was not a single wormy potato in the spud locker, Flugel retired to his cabin and had another glorious dream.

Last week Flugel dreamt he was in command of the battleship *Scharnhorst*, the pocket battleship *Gneisenau* and the watch pocket battleship *Gesundheit*. Destroyers and U-boats swarmed around them, firing salutes. Down the Rhine they steamed to do battle with the American Fleet. Flugel had a plan to annihilate it, which he radioed to the Führer.

'Dumbkopf!' screamed the Führer. 'It is the British Fleet you are fighting. The Americans are all in the Pacific. Which is where you will soon be heading, in a dinghy. What is your plan for winning the second battle of Jutland?'

'Inwisible ships, mein Führer. We don't have enough ships to win, so we must convince the British we have many more which are inwisible.'

'Brilliant, Flugel. You are hereby awarded the Iron Cross with three sauerkraut strands. How will we produce these inwisible ships?'

'The problem is not inwisible ships, mein Führer. It is inwisible sailors. How do you put wisible sailors aboard inwisible ships?'

'I have news for you, Flugel.'

'Yes mein Führer.'

'You have just been demoted to mess steward.'

'But there are no mess stewards in the German Navy. We consider the term humiliating to a member of the master race. We call them Geheimnitzkartofflenmeisters.'

'Then join the British Navy!'

Even in his dream, Flugel was a jerk.

To improve the crew's morale, the chaplain had started a ship's newspaper, *The Hawthorn* (named after the state flower of Missouri). Captain McKay gave it his reluctant approval, after Bushnell flourished an Alnav from Washington recommending the idea.

Flanagan was one of the first contributors. The chaplain was somewhat hesitant about accepting his story. But Flanagan convinced him the paper needed humour if it was going to be read. He also assured him his effusion contained no references whatsoever to anyone aboard the *Jefferson City*.

The first edition had barely begun circulating on the way back from Truk when Lieutenant Kruger climbed the ladder to Flanagan's watch station beside his forty-millimetre director. He clutched a copy of the paper in his hand.

'Did you write that?' he said, pointing to the Flugel story.

'Sure,' Flanagan said.

'You son of a bitch, when I asked you a question, answer it with sir!'

'Sure, sir,' Flanagan said.

'You want a war with me, you've got it,' Kruger snarled. 'You're going to be on every working party that's called out on this ship from now until the end of the war, got me? You're going to messcook every third month and you're going to need the cleanest uniform, the best-shined pair of shoes in the fucking fleet if you ever hope to make liberty. Do you read me, sailor?'

'Yes, sir. You're going to persecute me for a harmless bit of fun, sir.'

'There's nothing harmless about it. You're trying to undermine my authority. You're a fucking subversive. If you do it to me, you'll do it to the Executive Officer and the Captain and the Admiral! You want to start a revolution on this ship?'

'No, sir. I just want a few laughs, sir. The men are pretty discouraged, sir. We thought this raid on Truk was going to end the war, sir. Now it looks like we'll be out here for the rest of our lives, sir. Anything wrong with trying to cheer people up, sir?'

'Plenty. When you do it this way!' Kruger yelled.

While Kruger was raging, Flanagan slipped the switch on the mouthpiece strapped to his chest. The lieutenant's threats and insults went out over the gunnery circuit to every lookout on the ship and to anyone else who was listening in main plot and sky plot, CIC and other nerve centres.

Mullenoe heard it in main forward and telephoned Montgomery West on the bridge. Captain McKay asked West why he was laughing so hard. When he explained, McKay looked grave.

'I knew something like this was going to happen,' he said. 'Newspapers and the Navy don't mix.'

'As far as I'm concerned, Captain, Kruger's just getting what he deserves.'

McKay shook his head. 'Kruger's a good man. He knows more about fire control than the rest of that division put together. But he doesn't have a sense of humour. Especially about being an officer. You'd have to know the Old Navy, the tremendous gulf between officers and men, to understand it. Becoming a lieutenant is the most important thing that's ever happened to him.'

West accepted the rebuke in silence. He simply did not believe the Captain. That night at supper, the wardroom seemed to share his opinion. Everyone tormented Kruger.

'Say West,' Mullenoe said, 'how come CIC didn't pick up on this hot scoop about the German lieutenant, Flugel? It's no worse than a lot of the other drivel you send us.'

'I didn't have the right code.'

'They ought to change your letters to LTK Last to Know. Do you think anyone as dumb as Flugel could really exist?'

'Sure. I bet he graduated first in his class at Annapolis.'

'What do you think, Lieutenant Kruger?'

'I have no opinion,' Kruger snapped, slicing his steak as if he wished it was Mullenoe's throat.

'What do you make of it, MacComber?' Mullenoe said. 'Is it literature? Is that why I don't understand it?'

'It's a satire, Mr Mullenoe,' MacComber said. 'S-a-t-i-r-e. You may have come across the word in that course in basic English we took at the Academy. Satire pokes nasty fun at someone.'

'But who could that be?' Mullenoe said. 'It couldn't be Kruger here, could it? I mean, I hear him walking up and down in his cabin singing "Deutschland über alles". But I don't take it seriously. He said Heil Hitler to the Captain the other day, but he didn't take it seriously either.'

Kruger slammed down his knife and fork. 'You son of a bitch,' he screamed at Mullenoe. 'That goes for all of you!' He flung down his napkin and stalked out of the wardroom.

Mullenoe looked thoughtful. 'Maybe the war has lasted too long,' he said.

After supper, West received a summons from the Captain. In his cabin, he found McKay with the chaplain, who was wringing his hands. 'Lieutenant Kruger has complained to me about that column in *The Hawthorn*. He says he wants me to ban Flanagan from writing for the paper. But he's the only decent writer I've got. I don't know what to do,' Bushnell said.

'What do you think we should do, West?' McKay asked.

'I have no idea.'

'You better get one fast. I'm putting you in charge of the paper. You'll have to deal with this kind of problem. Do you want a suggestion on Flanagan?'

'I sure do.'

'Make him the editor. I've always found the best way to deal with a rebel is to give him some responsibility.'

'I'll give that serious consideration, sir.'

'In the meantime, I suggest you go see Lieutenant Kruger and tell him you'll make sure he won't be abused in the future.'

'Yes, Captain.'

West went below, wondering if he had been sandbagged. The answer was clearly yes, but he would not quite believe it. He had begun to think of the Captain as that rare human being, a genuine liberal. Instead he was closer to Machiavelli.

You are in the Navy, and you have received an order, West told himself. He rapped on the bulkhead outside Kruger's stateroom.

'Who is it?'

'West.'

He pulled open the folding plastic curtain and found Kruger hunched over something on his bunk. The only light came from a tiny reading lamp. In its feeble glow, West made out a dark blue object on the blanket. He heard the click of metal on metal. 'Is that a gun?' he asked.

'Yes,' Kruger said, spinning around, his service .45 in his hand. 'I'm going to blow his fucking head off.'

'Whose head?'

'Flanagan's. Then I'll get Mullenoe and that asshole of a chaplain. They're all trying to destroy me. But I'm going to get them first.'

West thought he saw Kruger's finger tighten on the trigger. What a hell of a way to die, he thought. 'Wait a second,' he said. 'The Captain sent me down here to apologize.'

'Why didn't he come himself?'

'Maybe he will. Let me go ask him.'

'Too late. I'm going to kill that Irish wiseguy and his

friends Peterson and Homewood. They've been on my back for months. I can't take any more bullshit!'

'Sure, sure,' West said. 'But why don't you give the Captain a chance first?'

'I'll wait five minutes.'

West backed into the passageway and fled to Mullenoe's stateroom to tell him what was going on. 'I'll go see him,' Mullenoe said.

'No!' West cried. 'You're too high on his hit list. Call the Marines. Tell them to guard the passageways, I'll go get the Captain.' West scrambled up the ladders to the Captain's cabin.

'God damn it,' McKay said. 'I had a feeling this might happen. Have you called out the Marines?'

'Yes, sir.'

'I'll go see him.'

'It's too dangerous, Captain! I saw him loading that gun.'

'He won't use it on me.'

McKay said this with such certainty, West was awed into silence.

When they got down to the second deck, they found officers in the passageway, warily watching Kruger's stateroom. Several, including Mullenoe, had guns in their hands. Marines were visible at the door to the wardroom.

'Put those guns away,' McKay said.

He knocked at Kruger's cabin and asked if he could come in. For five minutes he vanished into that dim interior. Any moment, West expected to hear a shot. Murder on the high seas. Maybe Kruger was right, they were in danger of a mutiny. Maybe that kid Flanagan was an *agent provocateur*.

Then the most incredible sound filled the passageway. A kind of a sobbing wail. It reminded West of a recording he had once heard of the death song of an Indian warrior. Someone had proposed it for possible use in a western he was making. Everyone decided it was too eerie.

The Captain emerged from the stateroom with Kruger's gun. 'Send for the doctor. Give him a sedative,' he said.

He handed West the gun. 'If you make Flanagan the editor, tell him about this,' he said.

Absalom! Absalom!

Captain Byron Maher's voice on the bridge telephone was brisk and matter of fact. 'Art, Admiral Spruance would like you to alter course to one five zero and rendezvous with the attack transport *Mountain Valley* at 1800 hours. Get a sea detail ready to transfer an important passenger by breeches buoy.'

What the hell was going on? Captain McKay wondered. Just over the horizon was the island of Saipan. Around them steamed the greatest naval armada ever assembled – two dozen aircraft carriers, almost as many battleships, at least as many cruisers and over a hundred destroyers. They were escorting 127,000 Marines and Army troops to assault this inner fortress of the Japanese Empire, a full thousand miles closer to Tokyo than their previous conquest, Eniwetok.

His was not to ask admirals why. Captain McKay ordered the change of course and Navigator Marse Lee hastily plotted the rendezvous, which was not more than a half hour away. It was exactly 1800 hours when they sighted the big bulky transport, her rails crowded with Marines. The sea was calm as they pulled alongside her and the detail under Boatswain's Mate First Class Wilkinson fired the breeches buoy line to the sailors on the *Mountain Valley*'s bow with the first shot. In five minutes, the other lines were hauled across and the important passenger began his swaying journey in the canvas bosun's chair. He was wearing a life jacket, and the visor of a Marine officer's hat obscured his face.

'He's just a kid,' remarked the venerable officer of the deck, Lieutenant Montgomery West, who was all of thirty-one. 'Wonder what he has to tell Spruance?'

'Maybe he knows something about Saipan from a previous incarnation,' McKay said. He stared gloomily at the two-foot-thick operations plan. 'That's about the only thing they haven't put into this encyclopaedia.'

As the bosun's chair grew closer, the important passenger

tilted his head to look up at the ship. 'My God,' Captain McKay said.

It was his son, Second Lieutenant Semmes McKay, USMC.

In Captain McKay's cabin, after Sammy had met Admiral Spruance, Byron Maher and other members of his grinning staff, the lieutenant's cheerful manner vanished. 'OK, Dad. What the hell's going on?' he demanded. 'Am I being shanghaied? Are you going to park me on this tub while my men hit the beach without me? If that's the plan, I'm not buying it.'

'There is no plan. Spruance just took it into his head that it would be nice if we had dinner together.'

'On the level?'

'Sea scout's honour,' McKay said. 'You'll go back to your men tomorrow morning, when we arrive off Saipan.'

A broad smile – Rita's smile – sprang across Sammy's face. 'It's a deal,' he said, holding out his hand. He was a head shorter than his father, with the same slim, angular build. But he had Rita's features – the determined chin, the bold blue eyes, the combative mouth. He had little of his father's intellectual interests, his wary approach to life. In the perverse way that nature switched genes, it was McKay's daughter, Barbara, who had inherited his temperament.

For supper, Chief Steward's Mate Horace Aquino outdid himself. He mixed two of the coldest most perfectly balanced daiquiris McKay had ever tasted. The meal that followed – shrimp cocktails, steak, chocolate ice cream sundaes – was a masterpiece. Between courses, Horace showed Sammy pictures of his ten children, including a high school graduation picture of his oldest son, who was in the mountains of Luzon fighting the Japanese. Finally, after spiking the coffee liberally with brandy, he withdrew.

Now what? McKay wondered. Since Sammy became a teenager, he had had difficulty talking to him. He seemed to prefer sharing his secrets, if any, with his mother. His attitude toward his father – and the Navy – had been so antagonistic, McKay had been amazed when he decided to go to Annapolis.

'Barbara tells me you and Mom are having a fight about something.'

'That's hardly news, is it?' McKay said.

'I hope it isn't about me.'

'Of course not.'

'I gather she wanted you to talk me into aviation. I'm really glad you let me make up my own mind, Dad. I meant what I said in my letter.'

'I . . . I'm glad you feel that way.'

He sounded tepid. Was he revealing he had been too absorbed in his ship, in Win Kemble's fate, to think about Sammy's choice? Should he lie outrageously, preach an Emersonian sermon on self-reliance? No.

'What's bugging you and Mom – the usual? She's got you a juicy assignment on King's staff or something like that and you don't want it?'

'Something like that,' McKay said.

'Mom's great, unique. But without your example, Dad, I would have wound up the most total yes man in the US of A. You showed me how to stand up to her. How to do it without – you know – losing her affection.'

Captain McKay nodded, too amazed to say anything.

'I can see why you want to stay out here and win this thing. It's great for me – to know we'll be on the same team. When we hit the beach tomorrow and I see those shells taking the Japs apart, I can tell my guys, "That's my old man."'

'We'll be doing our best, you can depend on it,' McKay said. 'The new battleships from Task Force Fifty-eight bombarded today. Seven of them. They fired 2,432 sixteen-inch and 12,544 five-inch. Presuming they obeyed the operations plan.'

'Wow!'

There was no point in telling Sammy the fast battleships had never bombarded before and the chances of their hitting anything significant were minimal.

'The old battleships and other rusty hulks like us go to work tomorrow.'

'Great. We'll have nothing to worry about but where to bury the bodies.'

Dread clutched Arthur McKay's heart. 'Let's hope so,' he said.

A waning moon gleamed feebly through the clouds as the island of Saipan took shape in the greyish green dawn. For fourteen of the previous twenty-four hours, the *Jefferson City*'s guns had pounded Japanese positions. Eight old battleships, seven heavy cruisers, six light cruisers and twenty-six destroyers had joined her. Unfortunately Saipan was not a coral atoll that could be flattened by a three day hurricane of metal, like Kwajalein. It was twelve miles long and fifteen miles wide. It had mountains and valleys, railroads and towns and a civilian population, as well as a 30,000-man garrison. Targets had to be carefully selected, if any impact was to be made on the Japanese defences. The bombardment force had divided the island into six sections. The orders from Admiral Spruance emphasized accurate, deliberate fire. Not a shell was to be wasted. Replenishment ammunition was thousands of miles away.

In turret three, Johnny Chase and his men had fired, by Johnny's count, 3,338 eight-inch shells. No other turret on the ship had been able to maintain fire from all three guns for the entire fourteen hours. Johnny's scarred, mask-like face glared down at the crews as they performed their endless mechanical dance around the insatiable guns. They were not just working for Johnny. There was another presence in the turret, watching them as their backs heaved with the clack and hiss of the breechblocks opening, the roar of compressed air rushing through the hot barrels. It was not the green ensign sitting in the little steel booth at the rear of the turret. It was Richard Meade, Ensign Babyface, the man who had saved their lives off Guadalcanal. They were working for him, and Chase never let them forget it.

'Bores clear!' shouted the gun captains. The turret whistle hooted like a berserk owl, straining arms shoved the 260-pound shells into the open breeches. The rammer men threw their levers, the shells thudded home, more arms and shoulders swung the powder bags after the messengers of death, backs bowed and heaved again, and the breechblocks hissed and crashed. With a whir of gears the big silver breeches sank into their pits as the guns elevated. Back danced the men and the firing buzzer went *dot-dot-dash*. The guns crashed; inside the turret it was more a concussion than a sound, felt more than heard. The guns leaped back, the hungry silver breeches rose, hissing and whining and spat out their empty shell cases. The dance began again.

After fourteen consecutive hours of this labour, the turret crews staggered on to the main deck looking like corpses coming out of a grave. Many of them collapsed and had to be carried to sick bay where Dr Levy and Dr Cadwallader, agreeing for once, said it made no sense to drive men past their breaking point. But neither protested when Johnny Chase and the other turret captains came down at dawn to order the hospital cases to the guns. Even Levy had begun to accept the war as a greater god than science.

As turret three resumed firing at 0430, Johnny Chase made one of his rare utterances. Even off duty, the turret captain seldom spoke. He spent most of his time on deck, staring out at the sea, or in his rack, staring at the overhead. The men were convinced he was communing with the dead. Chase spoke to a little rammer man named Flynn, who drooped beside number two gun.

'I ate chow with the radioman in our scout plane,' Johnny said. 'He told me we didn't hit a goddamn thing worth shooting at yesterday.'

'Did anyone else?'

'Not as far as he could see.'

'Stand by to elevate,' the ensign said.

The turret trained to starboard, the guns lifted their menacing snouts, the shells rose on their hoists and slid into the gleaming breeches.

'Hit something, you no good fucker,' Flynn said. 'Hit one for Babyface.'

The ensign pressed his ready button. 'Commence firing,' growled Gunnery Officer Mullenoe in main forward.

Dot-Dot-Dash went the warning buzzer. The guns crashed, the breeches rose, spat out their empty casings and the dance began again. Johnny Chase's green eyes acquired their otherworldly glow. Little Flynn crouched by his rammer, gazing in awe at their turret captain. Johnny was talking to Ensign Babyface, Flynn was sure of it. Maybe they were not hitting anything, but they were doing their jobs. Maybe that was all Babyface wanted them to do.

For two hours the *Jefferson City* and three other heavy cruisers pounded the Charan Kanoa beaches where the Marines were to land – the same beaches they had bombarded for fourteen hours on the previous day. Finally, as the sun rose in a blaze of red and gold, the transports carrying the first wave of Marines steamed into position. Overhead roared wave after wave of bombers from the carriers to blast the beaches with 500- and 1,000-pound bombs. For another half hour the cruisers bombarded again. Then the signal fluttered from the halyards of Admiral Kelly Turner's flagship: 'Land the Landing Force.'

Lieutenant Semmes McKay was not in the first wave. But Captain McKay watched the small boats churning toward the shore with his mouth dry, his heart pounding. The sandy beach was only a few yards deep. It vanished into scrubby grass, palm trees, an occasional flame tree blooming with vermilion flowers. Then the land rose steeply in a series of steps to a looming green ridge called Mount Tapotchau.

'I feel like we're invading Hawaii,' George Tombs said.

'I wish we were,' McKay said.

As the line of assault boats advanced, the battleships and destroyers joined the cruisers in a final stupefying bombardment of the beaches. While the amphtracs crawled across the barrier reef, another wave of seventy-two planes roared in from the carriers, some firing rockets that echoed across the water like the crack of a giant whip.

The moment the amphtracs began the final rush to the beaches, the impossible began to happen. Sheets of Japanese machine-gun fire poured across the water towards them.

Geysers leaped beside the fragile boats as mortar and artillery shells fell among them. On the beaches, machine guns cut down hundreds of the first Marines out of the boats. Mortar and artillery fire blew up amphtracs and LST's.

'I can't *believe* it!' George Tombs cried, watching the bodies pile up. 'How in Christ could they have survived that bombardment?'

'They did,' McKay said. 'Now the question is what are we going to do about it?'

For the time being, the answer was nothing. They could only watch as the situation on the beaches worsened. Japanese artillery firing from concealed positions inland soon had the coral reef zeroed in. As the forth wave of amphtracs began crawling across it, the whole reef erupted with explosions from heavy shells.

'My God, they must have mined it,' George Tombs said.

'That's artillery,' McKay said. 'Watch. You'll see the rounds coming in.'

'What wave is Sammy in?'

'That one.'

He picked up the telephone and called Byron Maher in flag plot. 'Why can't our spotter planes locate that artillery?' he asked. 'We could blow them away with a couple of salvos.'

'I'll mention it to the Admiral.'

Maher was back on the line in sixty seconds. 'He says he doesn't want to interfere with Admiral Turner's operation.'

By the book. That was how Spruance operated. It was also an admission that he had no desire to tangle with Kelly Turner's violent temper and gigantic ego. At the War College, Spruance had been the senior faculty member, but Turner had overshadowed him with the brilliance of his imagination, the sheer cleverness of his lectures. He had only one flaw. He was incapable of admitting a mistake.

Was his son being sacrificed to the system that had destroyed Win Kemble, the system that said, in essence, Those whom Cominch blessed could do no wrong?

No, no. McKay struggled to control his careening emotions. It was the fog of war – one of Spruance's favourite phrases – that was menacing Sammy. He could hear Spruance's dry voice in the lecture hall describing how they must try to plan every detail of a forthcoming battle – and at the same time be prepared, once the battle began, to deal with confusion, chaos as the fog of war descended.

For the rest of the day, the greatest naval force ever assembled could only watch helplessly, less than a mile offshore, while the Marines fought for their lives against an enemy who resisted with apparently unquenchable confidence. The night brought furious counterattacks, which were repulsed with the help of showers of star shells fired by the fleet. Their phosphorous glow illuminated the Japanese tanks and infantry at point-blank range for Marine field artillery.

Around midnight, an exhausted McKay tried to sleep. It was impossible. He got up and tried to write a letter to Rita, telling her about his dinner with Sammy. No go there, either. It was too unbearable. All the love he had never been able to express, the words he had never been able to say to Sammy wound through his brain, punctuated by the distant explosions on the beach.

On the bridge he found Montgomery West was OOD. 'I don't think we're going to sit here much longer, Captain,' he said.

'Why not?'

'Spruance just got a message from a submarine in the Philippine Sea. The whole Japanese fleet is heading this way.'

The Fog of War

Our air will first knock out enemy carriers, then will attack enemy battleships and cruisers to slow or disable them. Battle line will destroy enemy fleet either by fleet action if the enemy elects to fight or by sinking slowed or crippled ships if enemy retreats. Action against the enemy must be pushed vigorously by all hands to ensure complete destruction of his fleet.

There it was – the battle plan that might end the war, that might get everyone, or almost everyone, home alive. On the bridge of the *Jefferson City*, Captain McKay read and reread the message Admiral Spruance had just sent all the ships of the Fifth Fleet. There was no question that the showdown of the century – the decisive battle between the Japanese and American navies – was about to take place. Somewhere in the blank six hundred miles of ocean to the west, the Combined Fleet was steaming towards them.

He thought of Sammy, under ferocious Japanese machine-gun and mortar fire on Saipan. Keep your head down for a while, kiddo, he begged him. If we can do the job out here, those bozos may realize it's time to surrender.

'Captain,' the talker said, 'Admiral Spruance wonders if you would like to join him on the fo'c'sle.'

In five minutes he was walking up and down beside the man on whom his hope – all their hopes – depended.

'You've done your share of night fighting in the Solomons, Arthur. What do you think of this?'

He handed him an exchange of messages with Rear Admiral Willis Lee, commander of the battleship force, and Admiral Marc Mitscher, commander of the fleet's carriers.

First came a query from Mitscher. 'Do you desire night engagement? It may be we can make air contact late this afternoon and attack tonight. Otherwise we should retire to the eastward tonight.'

Lee replied, 'Do not (repeat *not*) believe we should seek night engagement. Possible advantages of radar more than offset by difficulties of communication and lack of training in fleet tactics at night. Would press pursuit of damaged or fleeing enemy, however, at any time.'

What daring, McKay thought. Was there an admiral in the world who would hesitate to pursue a damaged or fleeing enemy? McKay suddenly remembered Bull Halsey's anguished face in the Solomons. He heard him saying, *You can't win a war without losing ships.*

'I'd ignore Lee if you want a fight to the finish. It may cost us a few ships, but once you sink your teeth in to them, they'll never get away.'

Spruance looked past him into the empty western ocean, his face expressionless as usual.

'Do you remember my lecture on the battle of Tsushima Strait?' Spruance asked.

'Of course.'

'I've always admired the way Admiral Togo waited for the Russian fleet to come to him. Do you think this situation is similar?'

'In some ways. But not in others.'

'You're thinking of the carriers. You were always talking about carriers at the War College, Arthur. Why didn't you become an aviator?'

The irritation in Spruance's usually emotionless voice was unmistakable. It was the old struggle for rank and power between the battleship and carrier men, still being fought out here six hundred miles from the Japanese coast.

'My wife – and my friend Win Kemble – talked me out of it.'

They walked up and down the forecastle for another hour. Spruance maintained an icy silence.

Back on the bridge, Officer of the Deck Montgomery West ventured a cautious question.

'Is there a fight for the heavyweight championship on the card, Captain?'

'I doubt it,' McKay said. 'We're going to play it safe.'

For a moment he saw himself storming into flag plot to berate Spruance, to goad him into becoming Bull Halsey for a day and a night. Ships would sink, men would die – but thousands more could die the other way. The war would stretch over time's horizon, where grinning death waited for Sammy, the crew of the *Jefferson City*.

But he was only a captain. A man who gave orders – and obeyed them.

Again the intimation of death seized him like a spasm of malaria. It simultaneously burned and chilled his flesh. He struggled for calm, for hope. Maybe it was only his own death that he foresaw.

For the first time, Captain McKay hoped so.

★

'What the fuck's goin' on?' Jack Peterson wanted to know.

He and the team of his gun director – Camutti, Daley, the Radical – stood on the wing outside main forward in the dusk watching the fleet swinging east, away from the enemy. From horizon to horizon, the carriers and battleships and cruisers made graceful simultaneous turns like dancers in a gigantic ballet. Their wakes formed huge white loops in the inky water.

Lieutenant Commander Mullenoe emerged from main forward to join them. From his post at the forty-millimetre gun director just below them, Flanagan asked the gunnery boss for an explanation.

'I don't know any more than you do,' he said. But his disgust was evident. The Japs were somewhere in the darkening sea to the west. They were running away from them.

'We can't be afraid of those guys, can we, Commander? With this fleet?' Jack said.

'I hope not,' Mullenoe said.

'All hands man your battle stations!'

The blue sky was full of Japanese and American planes, rolling, diving, climbing, burning, exploding above them.

On the bridge, Captain McKay watched the struggle unfold with bitter satisfaction. Instead of hurling a first strike at an enemy already battered by American radar-controlled gunnery during the night, the Fifth Fleet was fighting on the defensive, allowing the Japanese commander to throw every plane in his air force at them, plus whatever he would scrape from nearby Guam. He was demonstrating to Admiral Spruance and Admiral Lee that war at sea had changed drastically since the battle of Tsushima Strait in 1905.

The *Jefferson City* was part of the inner battle line, close to the carriers. Beyond them stretched a dozen battleships and six times that many destroyers, their guns pointing skyward.

In the first stages of the battle, the flagship did not have to fire a gun. 'Our Combat Air Patrol is doing an incredible job,' Montgomery West reported from CIC. 'They shot down ninety percent of that first attack, and the picket destroyers got the rest.'

But the first attack was only the beginning. Within the hour, the radar screens swarmed with pips of over a hundred more planes. Some of the torpedo bombers, Nakajima B6N's known as Jills, got past the CAP and roared over the battleships toward their primary target, the carriers. Frank Flanagan hunched against his forty-millimetre gun director and poured shells at one of these two-engined craft as it zoomed past them at wave-top height. Ships all around them were firing at it too. Flames burst from its belly and it exploded.

A cry of anguish from the men on the forty-millimetre mount below him jerked Flanagan's eyes away from this satisfying sight. The pointer on the mount, the man who aimed the guns if Flanagan or his director was disabled, was sprawled over the breeches. The other men were screaming and falling off the mount, frantically brushing at some substance that was all over their blue shirts. It took Flanagan a moment to realize it was blood. It took him another moment to realize that the pointer, an easygoing kid from Boston, had no head. His body had spewed blood all over the rest of the gun crew.

'What happened?' Flanagan shouted.

They pointed hysterically across the water at a cruiser that was firing at another Jill up ahead of them. As the plane passed between them and the *Jefferson City*, at least a half dozen forty-millimetre shells whined over Flanagan's head.

'Bridge, this is forty-millimetre mount one,' Flanagan cried. 'Tell those guys to starboard that they're firing into us. They just killed my pointer.'

'Get him off the mount and resume firing,' said the new air defence officer, Lieutenant Salvatore Calabrese.

Flanagan passed on the order. The gun crew refused to obey it. They were totally demoralized, crying, brushing at the blood, staring at the cruiser, ready to duck another round. Flanagan scrambled down the ladder to the mount and dragged the dead pointer off his seat, trying not to look at the ugly mass of ravaged flesh between his shoulders.

'Now get back on those goddamn guns,' he shouted.

They obeyed him and Flanagan scrambled back to his gun director. He had barely put on his earphones again when Calabrese said, 'Mount one, take that plane bearing zero one five.'

It was another Jill that must have been hit by the Combat Air Patrol. It was smoking and burning, and the pilot, visible at the controls, looked dead. His hands were on his wheel but his head lolled to one side. The five-inch guns erupted with their usual ear-splitting concussions, but the Jap was too close for the proximity fuses to work. It happened so fast, Flanagan could not get him in his gun director. His hands, slippery with the pointer's blood, could not seem to grasp the handles firmly. His guns pounded, but the shots went low and his next rounds were high.

The careening green plane tipped to one side. He had no torpedo. He had launched that long ago. His nose dipped and it looked as if he was going to crash either in the water or against the cruiser's hull. But at the last moment the pilot tried to pull up and get over her to the carrier a thousand yards beyond her. The Jap had just enough strength to attempt this last defiant manoeuvre.

He did not manage it. Instead, he smashed into the main battery gun director. The plane cartwheeled to the right and exploded in the water on the port side. The impact tore the gun director off its hydraulic moorings as cleanly and as murderously as the forty-millimetre shell had decapitated the pointer. Over the gunnery circuit Flanagan heard Jack Peterson cry, 'Jesus Christ!'

Before Flanagan's horrified eyes, the director toppled from the superstructure, hit the railing of the flag bridge and bounded out beyond the main deck into the sea. For a second it poised there on the surface beside the burning fragments of the plane and Flanagan thought, It will float. They'll get out. A second later the director vanished. There was only a swirl of blue-green water and the sea resumed its blank expressionless face.

'Jack, Jack,' Flanagan sobbed. 'No. Jesus. No.'

★

The air battle raged for the rest of the day, with amazingly light damage to the American Fleet. Listening to the exultant American pilots as they blasted the enemy from the sky, Captain McKay soon realized that the Japanese were not the skilled airmen who had swirled out of the sun to smash the *Enterprise* and the *Hornet* in the Solomons. They were poorly trained replacements for those lost veterans.

From CIC, the number of reported kills reached astronomical heights. 'We've shot down at least three hundred and fifty of them,' West reported.

By the time the defensive battle ended, it was late in the afternoon. The American carriers turned into the east wind to launch their dive bombers and torpedo planes. When these pilots reached the enemy, three hundred miles to the west, there were only twenty minutes of daylight left. They scored hits on a few carriers but darkness swiftly shrouded their targets. Ninety percent of the Combined Fleet steamed on untouched.

As the American pilots groped back to their carriers, the radio became a chaos of desperate voices reporting imminent disaster.

'Candy? Candy? This is Batman. Come in, please.'

'Can anyone tell me where I am?'

'Give me a vector. Can anyone give me a vector?'

Spruance was finally forced to order the carriers to turn on their landing lights to prevent a catastrophe. The Americans spent the night frantically fishing pilots from the sea – while the beaten Japanese Fleet, shorn of its air defences, fled to safety. The frustration in the wardroom of the *Jefferson City* was intense.

'We should have had them by the balls by now,' Bob Mullenoe yelled, kicking a chair halfway across the room. 'We should be flipping coins to see who was going to sink the cripples.'

Everyone felt the same way. Even Edwin Moss could not think of anything good to say about Admiral Spruance.

'Clean out their lockers. Put all their stuff in their seabags and take them down to the chaplain.'

Boats Homewood's voice was thick with grief. He was in a daze. Flanagan was almost as bad. He went to work on Daley's locker first. In the back was a glossy purple rosary, a packet of holy pictures his mother had sent him, a picture of a dark-haired Italian-looking girl he had never mentioned to anyone.

Camutti's stuff was mostly photos of females in various alluring poses. Some were movie starlets, others were straight porn from girlie magazines. Not one had a personal inscription. There was a packet of letters from his father but none from his supposed squadron of Philadelphia girl-friends.

Jack Peterson's locker was the hardest. Almost everything in it made Flanagan weep. The spitshined black shoes, the carefully folded tailor-made blue uniform. In the back, a lot of pictures of women with undying testaments of love written on them and a packet of Martha Johnson's letters, which triggered a spasm of guilt as well as grief.

What else? His hands touched metal – a lot of it. Almost as much leather. He peered into the dark coffinlike rectangle and saw at least a dozen silver bracelets and as many wallets.

Jack was the thief. For a moment Flanagan was too stunned to think. Then he acted instinctively. He stuffed the loot into the pockets of his dungarees. No one was watching him. Everyone in the division was in a funk over the way Jack and his team had died. They stayed as far away as possible from this ritual removal of the effects of the dead.

Flanagan took the seabags down to the chaplain's office and left them with his yeoman. Then he began a frantic search for Boats Homewood. He did not know what to do with the loot. If he returned it to the rightful owners, Jack's reputation would be ruined forever. If he threw it over the side, was he Jack's accomplice?

He could not find Boats anywhere. Flanagan's bulging, clinking pockets made him more and more frantic. Some-one said he had seen Homewood go up on deck. Flanagan started at the bow and worked his way down the starboard side. The ship was steaming west with the rest of the fleet, in pursuit of the Japs. The grand strategy of the battle of the Philippine Sea was beyond Flanagan. He still thought the shootout that would end the war was imminent.

They might all be drifting down into a thousand fathoms by tomorrow night. Maybe Jack's reputation was irrelevant. But he could not bear the thought of betraying him.

A huge figure loomed up in the darkness at the fantail, outlined against the phosphorescence of their wake. It was unquestionably Homewood. He was talking to someone. Flanagan hesitated, confused. There was no one else in sight.

'What did y'ha have to go and do that to me for?' Homewood said. 'Why? He was all I had. This other kid Flanagan is ten times smarter but he hates the Navy. Jack didn't, no matter how much shit he threw at it. He was a sailor all the way. Why did y'have to take'm away from me? I know I don't deserve nothin' from you. I'm seven kinds of a bum. But I been tryin' to keep my nose clean for a long time now, tryin' to do my job with these kids.'

Was he talking to God? No. Gradually, Flanagan realized Homewood was talking to the sea. To the Pacific's immense blackness. The only god he knew or understood in his sailor's soul.

'Boats?' he said. 'It's Flanagan. I . . . I've got to talk to you.'

'About what?'

'About Jack.'

'You feel it too? How goddamned unfair it is? How fuckin' awful?' The huge hand grabbed Flanagan's shoulder and shook it until he thought his brain would tear lose.

'I wish you remembered him the way I did. He was the skinniest smart-aleck kid you ever seen. Trouble was his middle name. The drinkin' we done together, the dames we had, Jesus, you'd never believe it. But then I saw how fucked up he was, how really fucked up. I mean he was on his way to serious brig time, Portsmouth you know. So I got to work on him. That meant I had to get to work on myself first. I finally had to look myself in the fuckin' mirror and say, "Homewood, you bum, are you goin' through this fuckin' Navy without accomplishin' nothin' but getting busted and goin' up the ladder and gettin' busted again?'

'So I shaped up and I got to work on him the way I tried to get to work on you 'cept you're too fuckin' smart for me. I worked on him and I got somewhere. He was almost straightened out, I swear to God he was. I guess that dame Martha Johnson had a lot to do with it, but I got him started, don't you see? I could remember where he came from, that skinny fuckin' wise guy who wouldn't salute nobody unless they was pointin' a gun at him!'

The mighty hand was mashing Flanagan's shoulder into mush. The sea hissed past them with the stars in its blank face.

'Now he's gone. He's down there, maybe where we're all headin'. I'm glad you feel the same way about it. Ain't that what you wanted to tell me?'

'Yes. That's it. I just . . wanted to let you know. And listen. I don't hate the Navy the way you think I do. I just like to give you a hard time. I like to give everybody a hard time. I've got a big mouth.'

'Aw, shit, I *know* that. You think I'd waste ten seconds on you if you was a fink? Go get yourself some sleep. You got a graveyard watch, don't you?'

Amidships, Flanagan looked carefully around him. There was no one in sight. Over the side went a dozen silver and gold chains and a dozen wallets. It was a rotten thing to do to his shipmates. He would have it on his conscience for the rest of his life – if he had a life. But it was a small price to pay for Boats Homewood's peace of soul.

Mail Call

Dear Frank:

I can barely see this sheet of paper, and it's been a week since I got the news about Jack. Of all the rotten deals life has shuffled my way, this is the worst. I finally met a guy I really loved, who really loved me, and what happens? He said that damn ship had Jonah written all over it since Savo Island, but he wouldn't get off it. That would have been cowardly. God, the way you men think. It isn't with your brains. It's with your gonads. You're all afraid someone's going to impugn your courage. You're ready to get killed to prove how brave you are! When no woman in her right mind really gives a damn about it.

Oh, hell, that isn't true. I'm not making any sense. I'm just drivelling as well as sobbing all over this letter. It was swell of you to write me, Frank, and if you get to Seattle again I'd love to see you. We'll have a drink in memory of Jack.

Fondly,
Martha

Dear Joey:

Miracles do happen! Your friend Preston Sturges made some calls per your desperate request and I've got a part in a film Universal is making, an imitation of *A Yank in the RAF*. Except that this time the Yank (Ronald Reagan) is in the US Army Air Force. I'm the snooty English girl who doesn't like Americans, and when he splashes a gallon of muddy water all over me as he whizzes by in his jeep, my opinion of you beastly barbarians sinks even lower. That soon changes, for no particular reason the script writer has been able to come up with so far, and we go on to the usual mush.

War pictures are definitely on the wane in Hollywood. Escape is in, the war is out. The Crosby picture *Going My Way*, the most sentimental treacle I've ever seen, is the smash of the year. After that comes *The Song of Bernadette*, about the miracles at Lourdes. Not being a believer in that sort of magic, it left me cold. Ditto *National Velvet*, starring a precocious brat named Elizabeth Taylor and a horse, who stole the show. You get the feeling the Home Front doesn't want to think very much about you brave boys bobbing around in the western Pacific. Which leaves me outraged and frustrated. My only consolation is the way the Allies are wiping up the Boche in Europe.

Speaking of frustration, is there any hope of you coming back to California soon? I keep reading about these wonderful task forces, complete with oilers and ammunition ships and supply ships which means you can stay at sea indefinitely. Are they also sending you some floating brothels? That seems to me the only thing the Navy hasn't added into the equation for fighting this war for the rest of the century without letting you off that damn ship.

> Tell me you're as lonely as I am.
>
> Gwen

Dear Robert:

Fairy Hill is blooming, but I hardly look at the place these days. I spend most of the time reading the war news and corresponding with real estate agents in your state of Virginia. There seem to be plenty of places available, if we can get a decent price for Fairy Hill.

Your son is sitting up in his cradle, studying the world with your aggressive American eyes. I'm not sure I want him to be the star of the Annapolis football team in 1964, but we can argue about that some other time. My sister Laura says he is going to be one of those hulking ocker types, who consume immense quantities of beer and talk sports from dusk to dawn.

She's just jealous. She's been misbehaving with a lieutenant colonel in your Air Force, but he's not about to marry her. In fact, she's just found out he has a wife and two children at home. You can imagine what my mother is saying about it all.

You've driven the Japs so far from our shores, I have no hope of seeing you until you get to Tokyo. What fun it would be to have tea with you in the Imperial Hotel there – if it's still standing. I fear you are going to have to reduce the whole country to rubble before they surrender.

> With much love,
>
> Christine

Dear Frank:

I wish you'd write more often. Your father is so down in the dumps since he retired. He just sits in the parlour all day, staring at the window. The only thing he's interested in is the war news from the Pacific.

Father Callow was asking for you. He says he hasn't had a letter from you in a good year. Shame on you, Frank! I'm sure you're still alive only because he remembered you in his daily Mass ever since you enlisted. I told him the other day I thought the war and the suffering and death you've seen might make you realize how badly the world needs spiritual guidance. It might confirm your vocation. Do you think so?

Your loving,
Mother

Boarding Party

Ensign Herbert J. Brownmiller, Columbia V-12 '43, known to the crew as Ensign Brownnose for his obsequious style with his superior officers, paced the quarterdeck of the *Jefferson City* off Saipan. The island had been pronounced secured after four weeks of ferocious resistance by the trapped Japanese defenders.

'Oh, Christ.'

Brownmiller pointed over the side. Another Japanese body was floating towards them. At the close of the battle, hundreds of civilians had committed suicide by leaping into the sea from the island's cliffs. This body was a woman. She floated on her back, a mass of black hair streaming around her face.

'Call the motor whaleboat to tow her away,' Brownmiller said to Homewood, the boatswain's mate of the watch. 'I can't stand looking at her.'

It was not a chore that the motor whaleboat crew relished. It was the fourth time Brownmiller had required them to perform it since he came on watch. A disgusted Homewood blew the signal on his pipe and called the whaleboat to the accommodation ladder. Brownmiller pointed to the woman. The equally disgusted sailors looped a line around her body and towed her out to sea.

Brownmiller retreated to the OOD shack and contemplated the overdone hamburger and mashed potatoes the crew was being served for lunch. 'Christ, I can't eat this slop now,' he said.

A Higgins boat churned towards the ship and began

discharging passengers at the accommodation ladder. 'People coming aboard, sir,' Homewood said.

The first face to appear at deck level was the dour visage of Fleet Admiral Ernest J. King, Cominch himself. After him came Fleet Admiral Chester Nimitz, Cincpac. After him came Admiral Raymond Spruance.

'Bosun,' gasped Brownmiller, 'get me thirty-six sideboys and the ship's band.'

'Too late for that, sir,' Homewood said. 'Just salute your fuckin' arm off.'

'Homewood,' King said, after performing his ritual salutes to the flag and the petrified OOD. 'How the hell are you? I haven't seen you since we were on the *Lexington* together.'

'Got off that flattop a week after you left, Admiral. Never did like them floatin' airports.'

'How many hash marks have you got on that sleeve, Homewood?'

'Not as many as you, Admiral. You just don't have to admit it.'

King turned to Nimitz. 'If we could make carbon copies of this guy, we'd be in Tokyo the day after tomorrow. Then God help the Japs when they all got liberty.'

Ensign Brownmiller goggled at Homewood, whom he had heretofore regarded as an ignorant Alabama cracker. 'What should I do now, Bosun?' he said in a tone he usually reserved for the Executive Officer.

'You might notify the Captain. He'd like to know he's got the three top admirals in the Navy aboard.'

'I've got nothing to say to you professionally, McKay,' Admiral King said. 'But I've got a message from your wife.'

They were in Admiral Spruance's cabin, which King had commandeered for this interview.

'I'm listening, Admiral.'

'She doesn't want to hear from you. Not another snivelling hypocritical line. Is that clear?'

'I suppose so, Admiral. Did she tell you why?'

'You know goddamn well why. Everybody in the Navy

581

knows you spent your last layover in Pearl fucking the brains out of Win Kemble's wife. Your sister-in-law. Jesus Christ! Isn't that forbidden in the Bible or something?'

'I don't know, Admiral. I can only tell you it isn't true.'

'Don't tell me what isn't true. I had it checked out by Naval Intelligence, for Christ's sake!'

'Those same bright lights who warned us of Pearl Harbor?'

Cominch gripped both arms of the chair he was sitting in. 'McKay, I left you on this ship only because you were married to Rita. That's no longer a factor, except in the legal sense. You'd be on the beach tomorrow if you didn't have a son who's probably going to get the DSC for what he did on Saipan. I don't want to burden a kid like that by telling the whole world he's got a crumb for a father.'

'You can do anything you damn please to me, Admiral. I never asked to hide behind my wife – or my son.'

Cominch growled like a frustrated grizzly. 'Nobody wants this fucking ship anyway. It's got Jonah written all over it. I told Spruance he's nuts to use it as a flagship. If he'd been aboard anything else, he'd have deep-sixed the whole goddamn Jap fleet last week and the war'd be over.'

King squirmed in his chair like a man sitting on hot coals. 'I know what you're thinking, wiseguy. He hates my fucking guts so much he'll go on sailing with you until somebody sinks you. I hope it's soon.'

That night, Captain McKay sat alone in his cabin writing a letter.

Dear Lucy,

I keep thinking of you and the awful way we parted. I keep thinking of Win and what you told me about him. My mind keeps revolving around and around him and you and the love we shared. That love, as I tried to tell you that night, Lucy, will never die. It should never be regarded as wasted. Nothing you could ever tell me about Win would alter my friendship with him. You can't tear up those kinds of roots.

But I can't change my mind about what Win did at Savo. It was wrong. It was a betrayal of himself, his men, his ship.

A spiritual betrayal. Physically, he was their saviour. At the risk of sounding very Japanese, the spiritual *is* more important, Lucy.

There is another dimension here that I am only beginning to enter. How and why the spirit fails, the heart breaks, the lifeline unravels and the sea swallows us. When I see how hard, how uncaring some men feel they have to make themselves in order to command, I understand part of it. When I think of a man burdened with an impossible task, I understand a little more. When I encounter real loneliness for the first time in my life, I understand a little more.

Love,
Art

Volunteers

The big crane lifted the new main battery director high above the *Jefferson City* and lowered it into position in the superstructure. Shipfitters and electricians and fire control experts swarmed around it, connecting it to the ship's circuits, restoring eyes to the big guns.

They were back in Pearl Harbor, no longer a flagship. Admiral Spruance had gone ashore, and the command of the fleet had passed to Admiral Halsey. They were to rejoin the armada as soon as the gun director was in place. Every ship afloat in the Pacific was needed for the invasion of the Philippines.

Boats Homewood squinted up at the new director. 'Who the hell are we goin' to get to man it?

'I'll do it,' Flanagan said. 'Jack taught me how to operate the range finder.'

'I was kind of hopin' you'd say that.'

Finding other volunteers was not easy. No one wanted to go anywhere near the rotating coffin. Homewood gave lengthy lectures on the metaphysics of luck. He argued that this was now the safest assignment on the ship. Lightning never struck twice in the same place. Still no takers.

Flanagan finally solved the problem by offering the job to members of his forty-millimetre gun crew. Delighted to get into F Division, where working parties were few and deck swabbing was limited to several small compartments, they were so eager that the winners had to be chosen by pulling high cards from a deck.

The next day they steamed from Pearl, and Flanagan crawled into the director for gunnery practice. The moment he took Jack's seat, sweat oozed from every pore in his body. His heart pounded, his breath was shallow. Was he afraid of dying? Or was he afraid of becoming Jack? He concentrated on explaining the equipment to the new-comers, who were not thrilled to discover they could see nothing but a couple of dials in front of their faces. Flanagan soothed them with tales of his fictitious orgies in Australia. They decided maybe listening to his malarkey was better than staring at the water worrying about tor-pedoes.

Three were from small towns in Texas. Flanagan chris-tened them the three mesquiteers. The gun director became the Alamo, Flanagan claimed he was a direct descendant of Davy Crockett, who had not died in the battle. He had joined the Mexican Army and later became a Jesuit. Bap-tists all, his team did not even know what a Jesuit was. 'They work for the Pope,' Flanagan said. 'I used to be one myself. But I got tired of eating spaghetti.'

When they began firing at targets towed by an escorting destroyer, Flanagan started sweating again. In the range finder the yellow square of canvas bobbing along on floats seemed too small to hit. *What makes you think you can match my stuff, kid?* Jack sneered. Flanagan's hand was all thumbs on the dials; he stuttered and sprayed spit all over the lens as he gave the ranges to main plot. Their first salvo was a straddle that brought congratulations from Lieutenant Commander Mullenoe but did not cheer Flanagan in the least. He hated the thought of firing shells into the sea, Jack's resting place. He could see Jack floating inside the old director, fishes nibbling at his sightless cat's eyes. Daley was there too, clutching his rosary. Camutti and the Radical were drifting languidly around them in the cold dark water.

Jesus! Flanagan was finding out that a vivid imagination was not always an asset. When the gunnery drills ended at 1900 hours, he was a dishrag. He wandered down to the main deck and stared out at the empty ocean. Jack was down there. His best friend. The hiss of the sea against the hull, the darkening water began disconnecting his mind from his body.

The sea seemed to be telling him something. It was sad and terrible. But he did not understand the language. Maybe he was afraid to understand it. Then a voice in his head started to translate the words.

Come, the sea whispered. *Come. Get it over with. You're going to end up in my arms anyway, sailor. Get it over with. Slip quietly over the side. No one will notice.*

Why not? There was something religious about it. Maybe he was offering himself up as a sacrifice for his shipmates. It would be so peaceful down there. No more worries about Teresa Brownlow, Martha Johnson, his father – no more anxieties about being a man, about losing his nerve. Maybe Jack had been glad as the dark water filled his lungs. Flanagan remembered the night Jack went berserk and beat up Sally in Honolulu. *It don't work any more*, he cried. For Jack it had never really worked. Maybe it never really worked for anybody who figures out that the Church, the Navy, the government, including President Roosevelt, were all full of shit.

A huge hand clamped his shoulder. 'What the fuck are you doin'?' Homewood growled.

'Nothing – I was thinking about Jack.'

'You want to do that, go below and lie in your rack. Don't do it here. Not lookin' into that fuckin' ocean.'

'Why not?' Flanagan said, feebly defiant.

'It talks to you. But it don't have nothin' good to say. You got to talk back to it like a man. It's so goddamn big, that ain't easy. But you got to do it. You don't know how.'

'I'm not scared of dying, if that's what you mean.'

'That's not what I mean,' Boats said. 'You were thinkin' of takin' a dive. I've seen it happen before. Especially to guys like you with too much goin' on in their heads. It's awful temptin' when you're feelin' sorry for yourself or your nerves is shot from bein' at sea too long. Don't ever do that again, do you hear me?'

'I hear you,' Flanagan said.

'Come down to main plot. We're thrown' a little party to welcome your boys into the division.'

About a third of the division was jammed into main plot. Their new division officer, Lieutenant Wilson Selvage Mac-Comber, had contributed some of his family bourbon, and somebody else had purloined some medicinal alcohol from the sick bay. The baker had produced a cake in the shape of a gun director.

Several hours and numerous drinks later, Flanagan was giving them a demonstration of Irish clog dancing as prac-tised in Gaelic Park in the Bronx. Boats Homewood beamed at him. 'That kid's gonna be an admiral some day. I'm predictin' it here and now. He's gonna go to Annapolis after the war and go right to the top.'

'Annapolis,' said Lieutenant MacComber with a hiccup, 'is a place to which innocent boys are sentenced for four years and spend the rest of their lives commitin' crimes.'

No one paid any attention to him. 'Is that true, Flan?' asked one of the mesquiteers. 'You goin' to Annapolis?'

'Sure,' Flanagan said.

Why not keep Homewood happy for a while? Flanagan was never going to Annapolis. He was going to die. They were all going to die. That was what the sea had been saying to him.

Jack was dead, but his hoodoo was very much alive.

The Divine Wind

As the moon waned over Surigao Strait, a narrow passage between the islands of Mindanao and Leyte in the Philip-pines, sheet lightning flickered across the water. Thunder rumbled from the nearby hills. The *Jefferson City* was in a column of five cruisers that had been plodding back and forth at the mouth of the strait, using stopwatches and radar to tell them when to turn and countermarch. A few miles behind them a column of six battleships was doing the same thing.

The Japanese were coming through Surigao Strait to try to smash up the beaches and transports where General Douglas MacArthur's soldiers were landing to make good on his famous promise that he would return to the Philippines. The *Jefferson City* was now in the Seventh Fleet, which was known as MacArthur's Navy.

Only a few of the cruisers, such as the *Minneapolis* and the *Columbia*, had been with them in the Solomons. How would the others react to a night battle? The pessimists aboard the *Jefferson City* predicted disaster. The battleships would shell them, not the Japanese. In the main battery director, the three mesquiteers were in a panic. Flanagan calmed them down by telling them the cruisers could handle the Japanese without the battleships. He had no idea whether this was true, of course. But it worked. The Texans stopped whimpering and hunched before their dials while he probed the darkness with his range finder.

On the bridge, Captain McKay and Commander Tombs listened to radio reports of the Japanese approach. Swarms of American PT boats attacked them at the western end of Surigao Strait. Squadrons of destroyers spewed more torpedoes at them. Some hits were reported, but the Japanese kept coming.

'It's Tsushima in reverse,' McKay said to George Tombs, pointing to the plotting board on which he had been sketching the positions of the two fleets. 'They're sailing right into our "T", Admiral Togo must be spinning in his grave.'

The two lines of American heavy ships formed the top of the 'T'. The Japanese column was the vulnerable stem. From CIC and main plot came reports of a perfect fire control setup. Almost every ship in the American fleet was now equipped with Mark VIII radar, a vast improvement over the primitive equipment they had had in the Solomons.

The Japanese column was a clearly defined line of blips on the green scopes.

'*All ships. Commence firing!*'

The order came blasting over the TBS from the flagship *Louisville*. One second later, the night exploded with salvo after salvo of eight-inch and fouteen-inch guns. Flames erupted from a half dozen ships in the Japanese column. In the lenses of his range finder, Flanagan saw the pagoda mast of a burning battleship crumble like a sand castle in the tide.

'On target,' he shouted. Jack Peterson could not have been more exultant.

For the next fourteen minutes the rain of steel continued, the arc of red-hot shells looking like a line of railroad cars going over a hill. The stunned Japanese barely fired a shot in return. The salvos only stopped when another shout came from the flagship: '*Cease fire. Cease fire. We're hitting our own destroyers!*'

At dawn, the flagship ordered the *Columbia* and the *Jefferson City* to proceed up the strait in search of enemy survivors. In the rotating range finder, Flanagan peered wearily into the grey light as the lenses swept back and forth across the narrow funnel of water. They passed an American destroyer under tow, with a twenty-degree list and smoking badly. Suddenly there was a Japanese destroyer at six thousand yards, dead in the water with its bow blown off. The sight stirred memories of the *Jefferson City* in Ironbottom Sound.

Flanagan barked the range and bearing to main plot. With defiant courage, the Japanese captain fired a salvo at the oncoming Americans. It did not even come close. The two cruisers' main batteries boomed. The destroyer writhed in a hail of hits and near misses. Like a dying animal, she rolled over on her side. Flanagan could see tiny figures leaping off her as more shells exploded on the hull and in the water around her. Two more salvos and she sank.

'It's gone,' he said. 'You can cease firing!'

'What did you say, Admiral Flanagan?' Lieutenant Commander Mullenoe asked.

'Sorry, sir. There's a lot of them in the water.'

★

The *Jefferson City* groped through the pre-dawn murk in search of the ammunition ship *SS Free Enterprise*. Captain McKay, in his twenty-sixth consecutive hour on the bridge, read the latest reports of the battle raging a few hundred miles north of them, in San Bernardino Strait, at the northern end of Leyte. Another Japanese squadron had burst through this narrow neck of water and was smashing up American escort carriers and destroyers protecting the Army's landing beaches. The ships of the Seventh Fleet had been ordered to the rescue. But they had shot off most of their armour-piercing ammunition last night in Surigao Strait.

'There she is,' said Navigator Marse Lee, pointing a few degrees off the port bow.

'Turn out the working parties,' Captain McKay said.

'Now hear this. Ammunition working parties stand by,' boomed the boatswain's mate of the watch over the PA system. Obediently, the exhausted deck apes from the turrets and five-inch mounts formed up along the rail. They were joined by drafts from the black gang and F Division. Speed was all important. If the Japanese battleships broke through to bombard the landing beaches, the war could be set back six months.

At 0530 there was just enough light to see the *SS Free Enterprise* in detail as they pulled alongside. There was not a human being in sight. She might have been a ghost ship riding at anchor in Leyte Gulf.

'Ahoy the *Free Enterprise*,' Captain McKay said over the bullhorn.

No answer. He repeated it three times and finally blew the ship's whistle. A fat man in khaki pants and undershirt straggled on to the deck beneath the pilothouse. 'Didn't you get our radio message? We need ammunition and we need it fast,' McKay said.

'Sorry. You can't do a thing until eight o'clock.'

'Why not?'

'Union rules. My crew works by union rules.'

'How much do your men get paid, Captain?'

'Six hundred a month, on the average.'

A growl of outrage swept the deck of the *Jefferson City*.

'And they won't work more than forty hours a week?'

'Union rules. I can't do nothing about it.'

Captain McKay picked up the gunnery circuit telephone. 'Commander Mullenoe,' he said, 'train the main battery on that ship.'

'Aye, aye, Captain.'

Slowly, awesomely, the *Jefferson City*'s nine eight-inch guns revolved to port until their muzzles were aimed straight at the *Free Enterprise*.

'Tell your crew to get up on deck fast. Or there's going to be a very unfortunate accident that will send them someplace where, as far as I know, there aren't any union rules.'

The Captain vanished. In ten minutes the *Free Enterprise* was swinging ammunition from her booms to the deck of the *Jefferson City*.

'It's over. What have they got left?'

This was the considered opinion of the dean of the wardroom's strategy board, Lieutenant MacComber. There was a lot of evidence to support his argument. While the Seventh Fleet had been annihilating the Japanese thrust through Surigao Strait, Halsey's Third Fleet had been wiping out the last of their carriers far to the north. Both fleets had rushed to San Bernardino Strait, and the Japanese squadron there fled without bombarding the beaches. Halsey's planes destroyed most of their ships in the pursuit. As a fighting force, the Japanese Combined Fleet had ceased to exist.

Executive Officer Tombs, at the head of the table, shook his head. 'The Captain doesn't think it's over.'

'Oh?' MacComber's dislike of Captain McKay had only grown more virulent with the passage of time. 'Tell us what Father thinks.'

'He thinks the war will last as long as the Japs have a single plane that will fly or a single ship afloat.'

'That doesn't make sense,' MacComber said.

'Who's talking about making sense?' Tombs said. 'We're fighting a war.'

*

'Greetings, Americans,' cooed Tokyo Rose. 'Especially to my old friends on the *Jefferson City*, who have been demoted from flagship of the Fifth Fleet to a mere ammunition ship in the Seventh Fleet because of your disgraceful performance off Saipan, where your cowardly Captain manoeuvred his ship so badly you received fearsome damage from Japanese planes. You will soon receive another visit from the heroic pilots of the Imperial Air Force to mop up what is left of your ships after the beating you received yesterday from the Imperial Fleet.'

'Ain't she somethin'?' Boats Homewood said, chomping on the steak which the Captain had ordered for the crew's dinner to celebrate the victory in Surigao Strait. 'What do you think she looks like?'

'A hootchy-kootchy dancer I used to fuck in East Chicago,' Jablonsky said.

'The nun who taught me in the eighth grade,' Flanagan said.

'Lieutenant MacComber says the war's over,' one of the Bobbsey Twins said.

'Yeah? Then why did we load all that ammo yesterday?' Homewood asked.

Tokyo Rose continued to chatter. They were waiting for her to get through the propaganda and play some jazz. She still had the best record collection in the Pacific.

'Today you will feel the breath of a new weapon, a divine wind that will scorch your fleet and make you welcome death in the cool depths of the sea.'

'A divine wind,' Flanagan said. 'You think they're going to use poison gas? I lost my gas mask about a year ago.'

'You can't have mine,' Jablonsky said.

The alarm bell rang. The bugle blew. 'General Quarters, General Quarters. All hands man your battle stations,' yelled the boatswain of the watch.

'God damn it,' Homewood said, sticking the rest of his steak in his pocket.

In the gun director, Flanagan's heart pounded. It was his first air attack since he had taken Jack's place. Jablonsky had replaced him on the forty-millimetre director for mount one. It was the mount that would do the most work if a crippled plane came at the forward part of the ship. Keep your mind on the sky, George, he thought. Forget about nooky for the next few hours.

'Give us a rundown, Flan,' one of the mesquiteers begged. 'Tell us what the hell's happening.'

'Air battle,' Flanagan said, watching American planes from their escort carriers roaring down on a flight of Japanese Vals. To his surprise, the Vals scattered in all directions. They had no interest in making a coordinated attack. One after another, they dove to wave-top level and streaked through the task force. The American ships, including the *Jefferson City*, fired everything they had at them. The blasts of the five-inch guns shook the director. The blam-blam of the forty-millimetres mixed with the louder sound.

What was happening? Those Japanese planes were not carrying torpedoes. Ten seconds later Flanagan had his answer. He watched a Val dive straight into the aircraft carrier *Santee*, triggering an enormous explosion. Another plane hit the battleship *New Mexico* on the bridge, turning the whole superstructure into a roaring inferno. A third Val smashed into the cruiser *Louisville*. The ship shuddered under the blow, and smoke and flames leaped high in the air as the bomb the plane was carrying exploded.

'They're crashing into our ships!' Flanagan shouted. 'They're out of their fucking minds!'

The divine wind was scorching the American Fleet.

On the bridge, Captain McKay instantly grasped what was happening. This was a new weapon – suicide attacks by Japanese pilots recruited to die for the Emperor.

'Bob,' he said to Gunnery Officer Mullenoe, 'if any plane attacks this ship, concentrate every gun on it. You're going to have to destroy these things in the air. They're not going to drop any bombs. They're flying them right into us.'

'Roger, Captain.'

'I don't think there's much point in manoeuvring the ship to avoid them. I'm going to hold a course to give your guns the best possible aim.'

'I agree with that idea.'

For the next eight hours, the *Jefferson City* steamed through Leyte Gulf following this battle plan. It required excruciating self-control not to order a turn when one of the suicide bombers hurtled toward them, often with flames gushing from his engines, even his cockpit. Again and again, George Tombs looked to McKay, begging him for a right or left full rudder. Each time, McKay shook his head and watched while their five-inch and forty- and twenty-millimetre guns shredded the attacker and sent him plummeting into the sea.

Other ships that attempted violent evasive manoeuvres were hit with horrendous results. On one destroyer, the captain staggered out of the pilothouse, a human torch. Two more light carriers were torn by explosions and fires from their aviation gasoline. At twilight the attacks subsided. But the fleet was ordered to remain at General Quarters. They stayed at their battle stations until midnight, growing more and more exhausted.

'The war isn't over,' George Tombs said.

'Not for a while,' Arthur McKay said. He looked out at the night-shrouded coast of Leyte. Flashes of artillery fire lit the sky. 'If they're willing to die like this for the Philippines, can you imagine what they'll do when we get to Japan?'

The Visitor

'Secure from General Quarters. Set Condition Two.'

Eight bells bonged, 0400. The seamen, firemen, electricians, ship-fitters, and boatswain's mates in Repair Three, just aft of the wardroom, put away their breathing apparatus and other equipment and shuffled off to seek some sleep in their humid compartments. Among the more weary shufflers was Jerome Wilkinson. The kamikazes were straining his nerves to the snapping point. They seemed to be at General Quarters twenty-four hours a day, slumped against bulkheads at the damage control station, never knowing when a random bomb would hurl fire and steel down the passageway.

In the sleeping compartment of Deck Division One, Wilkinson flung aside his shoes and sweaty dungarees and stripped for a shower. 'Have those fuckin' shoes shined when I get back,' he said to one of the seamen. 'Get these duds to the laundry.'

In the shower, Wilkinson thought of Prettyboy, of sweaty desire in a handling room. He hated the *Jefferson City* without his friend and protector, Commander Parker. Although he eyed the young sailors in his division with wary desire, he was afraid to risk seduction. He could trust no one. Flanagan, the snotty kid who ran the ship's newspaper, had reporters in every division who told him everything that was going on.

Back in the compartment, Wilkinson slapped the usual quantity of cologne on his big body and crawled into his rack. No go. He could barely breathe. He lay there thinking of his days of glory. He began to hate Captain McKay with a new, fierce intensity. He had ruined Parker, ruined Wilkinson's sweet deal, for only one reason: revenge.

His whole life was going wrong. He was sliding down-hill, he was getting fat, sick, crazy in this heat, with madmen flying planes into ships. The more he thought about it, the more convinced he became the *Jefferson City* was doomed. Her past – that night of terror and cowardice off Savo Island – was pursuing her.

He should have said something that night. He should have stopped Parker before Kemble got to the bridge. He should have been a man, a fighting sailor. Instead he had been afraid too. He had never been able to forget that. He had been afraid.

Had Captain Kemble been afraid? Wilkinson had never been able to penetrate his silence. The Captain had said nothing, while Parker babbled. The boatswain's mate hoped Kemble was afraid. But somehow he doubted it.

There was another reason for what he had done, a reason Wilkinson did not understand.

The mystery tormented him. Now it threatened him. It seemed to be part of the madness, part of things happening without a reason, like the kamikazes.

He crawled out of his rack and rolled up his mattress. Maybe he could sleep topside. At the head of the ladder to the second deck, he peered down the dim passageway. There was someone there, standing just behind a red battle lamp.

He seemed to be an officer or a chief petty officer. He could see the gleam of a visor above the shadowed face. 'Is that you, Mr MacComber?' he said hopefully. MacComber was cracking up too. Sometimes he got drunk and came down and talked to Wilkinson about the stupidity and injustice of the Navy, telling him things every enlisted man knew five minutes after he came aboard.

There was no answer from the shadowy figure. Wilkinson repeated the questions. It was probably MacComber, too drunk to talk.

The figure stepped in front of the battle lamp. Blood streamed from his right eye. It was Captain Winfield Scott Schley Kemble.

The next morning, a still terrified Wilkinson told Joe Garraty, the first class boatswain's mate who ran Deck Division Two, what he had seen. Garraty had a big mouth. In four hours the story was all over the ship. The three mesquiteers told Flanagan, who told the chaplain. Flanagan wanted to make it the lead story in the next edition of *The Hawthorn*.

'Out of the question!' Bushnell said. Flanagan was amazed by how agitated the chaplain became.

'Do you believe in ghosts?' Flanagan asked.

'I believe in the soul's survival, Frank . But in what form and whether the dead have any power or influence on us, I can't say.'

'I can,' Flanagan said with the heady confidence of the twenty-year-old sceptic. 'When you're dead you're out of it.'

'I wonder if anything that lives for a while is ever really out of it? Life is a vast continuum, Frank.'

'Sounds like more of your atheistic mysticism to me, Chaplain.'

'Don't mock me, Frank.'

'Why not? Mock me back. I'm a lot more confused than you are.'

Flanagan had begun to like the chaplain, even though he considered his tortuous theological musings ridiculous.

'My brother was killed in World War One. My wife started seeing him in our house. Eventually she confessed she loved him more than she ever loved me. I had known that for a long time. But I was enraged because she could see him and I couldn't. It seemed to imply a lesser love on my part. Which wasn't true. I loved him more than any other human being I ever met. Including my wife. It was the beginning of the end of our marriage.'

Flanagan barely listened. He had no interest in the passions of middle age. 'Wilkinson's probably going bananas without any prettyboys to screw,' he said. He had told the chaplain about Wilkinson's seduction of Semple and other sailors in his divison.

'I find it hard to believe that really went on, Frank.'

The chaplain still had a great reluctance to accept the existence of evil. Flanagan was inclined to see it everywhere he looked. Goodness was what he found hard to accept.

The story soon reached the wardroom. No one took it very seriously except Bushnell and Lieutenant MacComber. 'I grew up in a house haunted by my grandfather, who was killed in 1862 at Malvern Hill,' he said.

'You think Kemble has come back to haunt us? Why?' Montgomery West asked.

'I have no idea. My grandmother thought Grandfather was taking revenge on her for remarrying too soon. He was an imperious bastard.'

'Has anyone talked to Wilkinson?' Dr Cadwallader said. 'He may be cracking up.'

'Wilkinson's not the crack-up type,' MacComber said.

'He isn't the type who sees visions, either.'

'You think he really saw something?'

'Yes! If you want to know the truth, Mr West. Yes.'

MacComber reached for his water glass and knocked it over. He was trembling.

'It's all too possible,' Chaplain Bushnell said.

For the first time, Montgomery West felt a tremor of unease. He looked around the table. Ensign Brownmiller looked vaguely frightened. So did Lieutenant Commander Moss. Were they afraid of seeing Captain Kemble too? Was he afraid?

Oz Bradley grunted. 'Maybe he'll finally pay a visit to the engine room.'

The Other Enemy

As usual, the *Jefferson City*'s aerographer sent her weather balloon aloft from the highest point in the superstructure, the space between the main battery gun director and main forward. Flanagan watched him, predicting, also as usual, that he would be wrong.

'How much will you bet,' Flanagan said. 'Come on. Jack Peterson made a living off you. I've got Jack's job. I'm entitled to the same income.'

From Minnesota, the aerographer fancied himself a direct descendant of the Norse chieftain Eric the Red. He had the name and the red hair, but the rest of his physique was closer to the ninety-seven-pound weakling in the Charles Atlas ads. He used rhetoric to compensate for his lack of muscles.

'Be silent, you elongated Celtic clod. My ancestors were carving yours up in the eighth century. I'm at least a hundred years ahead of you on the evolutionary scale.'

'Give us a chance to get even.'

'Peterson was a reincarnated Norse warrior. One of nature's gentlemen. I was glad to contribute to his well-being.'

'You're as bad at judging character as you are at the weather.'

Down came the balloon, leaving the weatherman up to his knees in fifteen hundred feet of line, which his striker stolidly wound around a spool. The man of science studied the thermometer and other instruments attached to the balloon.

'At this time tomorrow,' he said, 'we'll be in the middle of a typhoon.'

'Hey, give me a piece of that one,' Flanagan begged. The sky was a cerulean blue. The wind was barely caressing the surface of the sea.

'Fifty bucks.'

'You're on,' Flanagan said.

Even if he lost, at least it would take his mind off getting killed by a kamikaze.

'I hear the kamikazes got another carrier yesterday. The *Princeton*. When the *Birmingham* pulled alongside her to fight the fires, the *Princeton* blew up and killed just about everybody topside on both ships.'

'Makes me glad I work in the fire room,' Marty Roth said.

'The guys in the fire rooms on the *Princeton* got roasted alive when burning gasoline came down the ducts.'

Standard conversation at breakfast, dinner and supper aboard the *Jefferson City*.

Nobody laughed at Tokyo Rose any more. Everybody talked about going home, how the J.C. was overdue for leave. No one ever got a full night's sleep. Every time an unidentified plane appeared on the radar screens, every ship in the fleet went to General Quarters. The kamikazes had changed everyone's feeling about the war. Part of it was exhaustion, part of it was the feeling that it was unfair. They had won their slugging match with the Combined Fleet. It was at the bottom of the ocean.

'Why don't these bastards admit they're beaten?' George Jablonsky wanted to know.

To keep from growing crazy, he had shaved himself bald

and planned a career as a professional wrestler. Others had grown beards. Flanagan had not had a haircut in weeks. The Captain seemed to understand. He let them break trivial rules as long as they did their jobs.

'They like dying for a noble cause. I dig that,' Flanagan said. 'It's better than dying for no particular reason.'

That was what the sailors hated about the kamikazes. They destroyed the exultant sense of survival everyone experienced for a day after the battle of Leyte Gulf. Everyone had to resume wondering if he would get killed. But dying no longer seemed noble, sacrificial. There was no danger of losing the war. No one had to worry about mothers and sisters and fiancées being bombarded by Japanese battleships, bombed by Japanese planes, raped by Japanese armies. Dying now would be dumb, meaningless. It would be like getting drunk and falling overboard. Or getting hit by a shell from another American ship. It made the idea of death more intolerable.

Homewood sat down beside Flanagan at the mess table, with double portions of everything on his tray, as usual.

'How's it look topside?' Flanagan asked. He was worried about his bet with the aerographer. The sunny skies had vanished. Thick grey clouds were scudding up from the south.

The ship suddenly rolled thirty degrees to starboard. Trays, food, sailors went sliding across the compartment in a crashing, cursing torrent.

'I think you're gonna lose fifty bucks,' Homewood said. He had hooked his legs around a table leg and continued to eat his ham and beans.

They were about to discover the kamikazes were not the only Pacific wind that could kill.

'Why doesn't Halsey get us the hell out of this?' George Tombs asked.

The Executive Officer gazed uneasily at the forty-foot swells looming around them. A gale-force wind lashed spray against the bridge's windshields. Ahead, two destroyers were trying to refuel from a hulking oiler. They had spent the last two hours at it. Twice the hoses had parted, spilling thousands of gallons of oil into the heaving ocean.

'He wants to get in one last punch at the airfields in the Philippines,' Captain McKay said.

The kamikazes were driving everyone zooey, from the sailors to the admirals. Here was Bull Halsey, trying to refuel the Third Fleet in the path of an oncoming typhoon. He should be running for the open ocean, but he was sure if he could get in one more strike at the airfields of Luzon the kamikazes would disappear. Halsey was allowing his contempt for the Japanese to muddle his judgement. The kamikazes were not going to disappear. You could hide the flimsy planes they were using on obscure dirt airfields in the jungle, in mountain caves, you could move them around on trucks. It was the Japanese answer to American steel and high explosives, to the enormous fleet, the swarms of planes advancing across the Pacific towards them. They would triumph through spiritual supremacy, now that the last of the Combined Fleet, their hope of physical supremacy, lay at the bottom of the ocean.

As daylight faded, the destroyers still had not managed to refuel. A sinister red glow filled the western sky. The sea was deep black, with white spindrift whipping off the tops of the waves. McKay called the aerographer to the bridge. 'Where do you locate this storm, Eric?' he asked.

'I don't have all the reports they're getting on the flagship,' he said. 'I'm using the old seaman's rule of thumb. "Face the wind and the centre lies ten points to your right."' He put his finger on the map. 'Just about here.'

'We're sailing right into it?'

'If I'm right.'

'What do you think, Boats?'

'It's a good rule. I seen a lot of captains use it out here,' Homewood said.

By morning the wind had risen to sixty knots. Saltwater was blowing horizontally at bridge level, making it almost impossible to see anything dead ahead. An unearthly wail emanated from the radar antennas as the wind whipped through them. Conversation on the bridge was possible only in shouts. Waves kept building to awesome heights. The barometer began to fall with meteoric speed, going from twenty-nine to seventeen in the space of an hour.

The wind began whirling counterclockwise, driving waves to new heights and making it impossible to maintain a headway of more than three knots. The ship was rolling thirty and forty degrees to port and starboard. The weight of her five-inch and forty-millimetre guns had never been figured into her original design. There was a serious possibility of capsizing.

Over the radio came frantic reports from captains of destroyers and escort carriers. Destroyers were rolling seventy degrees. One call from the *Monaghan* simply said, 'We're going over.' Then there was silence. On the escort carriers planes ripped loose and caught fire. Aboard the *Jefferson City* there was another worry.

'Captain,' said Edwin Moss on the telephone, 'I don't like the way the bow is working. We're taking water through a half dozen sprung plates. I'm afraid it could snap off if this storm gets any worse.'

It got worse. The wind rose to a hundred knots, with gusts that screamed to a hundred twenty. The sea and sky blended into a blinding wall of flying water. On human skin, it was like a sandblaster. Lookouts, signalmen, anyone who exposed his face to it sought shelter with blood streaming from his forehead and cheeks.

Edwin Moss reported water was pouring into the ship through supposedly watertight hatches. The chief electrician's mate reported some of this water had caused short circuits in the main electrical switchboard, located just above the steering-engine room. They were fighting a half dozen small fires down there. Oz Bradley said that with each roll to starboard the forced draft blower intakes were sucking a thousand gallons of water into the fire rooms.

That was only the beginning of the ordeal in the fire rooms. They turned off the blowers, and the temperature soon rose to 140 degrees. Another wild roll to starboard burst open the hatch on the weather deck that Amos Cartwright had loosened for emergency escape. Water cascaded down on the boilers. Marty Roth clawed his way over blistering steam lines and up the escape ladder inside the ventilator. Hundreds of gallons of water poured down on him while he fought to close the hatch. Twice he got knocked off the ladder and started falling. Clawing frantically, he grabbed a rung after a few feet and returned to the struggle. Half drowned, he finally got the hatch dogged shut and spun the wheel to secure it.

As he returned to the fire room, drenched and seared, he could have sworn he heard Amos Cartwright's voice whisper, *Nice goin', Jewboy.* Nobody on watch said a word to him. They were too busy trying to rig hose pumps to get rid of the three feet of water on the deckplates. With every roll they grabbed the overhead pipes or anything else that offered a grip. Otherwise they were flung from one side of the work space to the other with the sloshing tidal wave of oily water. One watertender first class had blood streaming from a cut over his eyes. A fireman first class had broken his arm. He crouched on the ladder, whimpering, 'We're going' over. I know we're goin' over.'

By now Captain McKay had been on the bridge for twenty-four consecutive hours. So had Executive Officer Tombs. From the after steering room came ominous reports of the loss of lubricating oil suction on the port engine every time they rolled to that side. They had to shut down the engine to prevent a catastrophic burnout. Commander Moss reported the bow was starting to wobble one or two degrees off the keel. There was three feet of water in the mess compartment. Another cascade of water knocked out the main switchboard. Below decks, the only light came from the eerie red battle lamps.

'What do we do, Art?' Tombs shouted.

'Shut down the engines,' McKay said.'

'What?'

'It's an old merchant captain's trick. I heard one of them describe it in a bar in Shanghai fifteen years ago. I can still hear him saying, "You can't fight a typhoon." Now that I've seen one, I'm sure he's right.'

Tombs clearly did not agree with him. 'You're sure you want to do it, Art?'

'Yes.'

'Shut them down,' Tombs said to the engine telegrapher operator.

The sailor shoved the annunciator handle to zero. Almost instantly, Oz Bradley was on the telephone from the engine room.

'Is that signal correct?'

'Yes,' McKay said.

'Captain,' cried a quavering voice over the telephone, 'this is Emerson Bushnell. Have the engines failed?'

'No. I shut them down.'

'Is that a good idea?'

'We'll soon find out.'

'Is there anything I can do?'

'Try prayer, Chaplain.'

In the engine rooms and fire rooms, where faith in the ship's survival was essentially faith in the power plant, fear rampaged. 'Parker was right, the bastard's crazy,' cried the machinist's mate known as the Throttleman. 'He's been waitin' for a chance to kill us.'

'Shut up,' Oz Bradley said. 'He knows what he's doing.'

'Have you ever heard of anybody turnin' off the goddamn engines in a typhoon?' the Throttleman screamed.

'I'm not a fucking sailor and neither are you,' Bradley answered.

The words tormented him, but they were true. He had to admit for the first time that their ultimate survival on the ocean depended on the seamanship of the Captain, on knowledge and skill that pre-dated his beloved engines.

'I'm goin' up. I'm gonna get topside before we roll over,' the Throttleman screamed.

He started scrambling up the ladder to the upper level, where Bradley was standing. Oz blocked him. 'Get back to that goddamn throttle,' he said.

The machinist outweighed Bradley by fifty pounds. But twenty-five years of giving orders were on Bradley's side. The Throttleman retreated to the deckplates. He could not look at anyone in the engine room. He just slumped in front of the throttle mumbling, 'I got nothin' left. I got nothin' left.'

Only in F Division was the panicky rage held to a minimum. Homewood assured them Captain McKay had made the best choice. 'You watch,' he said. 'We'll get knocked around some but we'll ride it out. She'll find her own way now. Them engines were just gettin' us into trouble, tryin' to fight a hundred-knot wind.'

'Are you just bullshitting us, Boats?' Flanagan asked.

Homewood shook his head. 'We're gonna find out this old lady's a ship, not just a hunk of floatin' machinery.'

For the next two hours, the *Jefferson City* lay hove to, while gigantic pyramid-shaped waves whirled and crashed in frenzy around her. Again and again from the bridge they looked up at moving mountains of water on all sides. The cruiser slid up and down these foaming slopes and rolled violently in the troughs between them. But she was no longer fighting the typhoon. She was surrendering to the storm's power like a confident woman yielding to an angry lover. The strain on the engines and bow vanished. Her essential shipness, the bouyancy her designers had created in the complex space of her hull, sustained her in the chaos of wind and water.

Their escape from the typhoon was so sudden it seemed miraculous. It was like emerging from a thundercloud in a plane. One minute they were in a soup of wind and spray, next they were drifting on a sea with a half mile visibility and only a mild swell.

On the bridge, George Tombs ordered the engines ahead one third. He regarded Captain McKay with something close to awe. 'I thought we were finished for a while, Art. Without you, I think we might have been.'

'Just trying to earn my salary, George,' McKay said.

Mail Call

When the *Jefferson City* pulled into Ulithi Atoll, the Navy's forward base in the western Pacific, Admiral Spruance and his staff came aboard. Bull Halsey had gone home for a rest, and the J.C. became a flagship again.

Byron Maher, Spruance's chief of staff, handed Captain McKay a letter. The return address was in Hawaii. Above the street number was written: 'Kemble'. In his cabin, McKay opened it and a piece of blue paper fell out. He picked it up and recognized Win's handwriting.

'It is a long way to go,' said Yuan Chen.
'There are rivers too swift for any boat,
Mountains that no chariot can cross.
What am I do to?'

Humility shall be your boat, said Po Chu-i.
Pliancy shall be your chariot.

'It is a long way to go,' said Yuan Chen.
'The lands are not inhabited.
There are no villages where I can buy provisions.
I should die before I reached my journey's end.'

Lessen your wants, husband your powers
And you will have no need to buy provisions on your way.
You will cross many rivers and come at last to a sea
So wide you cannot see the further shore.
Yet you will go on, without knowing whether it will ever end.
Here all that came with you will turn back.
But you will still have far to go.

He who needs others is forever shackled.
He who is needed by others is forever sad.
I would have you drop these shackles,
Put away your sadness
And wander with me in the kingdom of the Great Void.

In the Middle of the Darkness

'The Marines asked for a ten-day bombardment. Kelly Turner gave them three. As usual, Spruance is letting the son of a bitch do it his way.'

Byron Maher's voice was weary. He had been working eighteen hours a day on the plans for Iwo Jima for two months. He leaned back in his chair, his big round face sagging.

'What do you think?' Arthur McKay said.

'I don't think we should go near the goddamn place. We're only doing it because the Army Air Force tells us they can't hit anything over Japan at thirty thousand feet, and they're afraid to come lower because their fucking B-29s might get shot down. We killed five thousand kids to take Saipan, Guam and Tinian for these wonderful planes. So far as I know, they haven't hit a single target selected for them. Especially the aircraft factories. We put them at the top of the list. The Japs are still turning out thousands of planes for these kamikaze maniacs to fly into our ships.'

The Marine first lieutenant who mounted the accommodation ladder of the *Jefferson City* had the gold braided loop of a general's aide on his shoulder. The junior officer of the deck assumed he had a message for Admiral Spruance and offered to call his flag lieutenant.

The Marine shook his head. 'I want to see Captain McKay. I'm his son.'

In the Captain's cabin, the Lieutenant pointed to his fourragère and said, 'Did you have anything to do with this?'

'I know nothing about it.'

'On the level?'

'On the level.'

'Why the hell would I get derricked into this nothing job? They've handed my men to some guy who's so green he must be part Christmas tree. It doesn't make any sense.'

Arthur McKay suspected Rita was responsible. But he decided it was better to play dumb. 'It may have something to do with getting that DSC. Generals like aides with decorations.'

'That wouldn't surprise me in the Army. But in the Marines? I thought fighting was our business – not running messages.'

'That's how a general fights. With messages. You know that as well as I do. Calm down, Sammy. This is an honour. Don't be so touchy about avoiding favours that you can't accept one you deserve.'

Sam's anger vanished. A mournful light filled his eyes. 'I'm not touchy. It's just that I feel I ought to stick with my men. The ones who are left. I know the score now, Dad. I know what we're likely to be up against.'

'Your men know how to take care of themselves. And your replacement in the bargain, probably.'

The Lieutenant allowed himself to be persuaded to stay for dinner. The mournful light remained in his eyes. He began telling Arthur McKay about Saipan and Tinian and Eniwetok. Especially Saipan. 'We did things that bother me, Dad. They bother me a hell of a lot.'

'For instance.'

'The day after we landed, when we moved inland we found thirteen Catholic nuns stretched out on a hillside with their habits pulled up around their waists. They'd all been raped and their throats cut.

'After that we stopped taking prisoners. Contrary to what you may have heard, a fair number of Japs tried to surrender. We just shot them. Towards the end, we found about fifty Jap soldiers in a cave with a lot of geisha girls. They were smoking marijuana and having a farewell party. They said they'd surrender. We told them to come out and the captain ordered my thirty-cal machine gunner, a kid from North Carolina, to gun them down. I didn't say a word.'

The fog of war? Spruance's phrase was much too antiseptic for the Marines' ordeal. On Sammy talked, the mourning in his eyes seeping into his voice. He told of losing his sergeant, his two corporals, and thirty percent of his men.

Not all of them died from Japanese bullets. A dismaying number were killed when Navy ships and Marine artillery fire fell on their positions.

'We couldn't do anything about the ships except curse them over the radio. But our artillery was within reach. After they shelled us for the fourth night in a row, my captain sent me down there with ten men and some satchel charges. We blew up their fucking guns and killed some of them – I hope.'

Sam McKay, his son, was gone. He had vanished in front of Arthur McKay's eyes. Confronting him was a grey-lipped killer. Even Sammy seemed to sense his loss of self. He struggled to emerge from the nightmare memories of Saipan.

'I hope this doesn't shock you, Dad. You fight like gentlemen, compared to what we do.'

'There's nothing gentlemanly about a kamikaze,' he said. 'We're fighting people with different ideas about life and death. But I don't believe all of them buy this Bushido, the warrior code. That's a lot of hot air cooked up by their militarists.'

Sammy nodded. He was barely listening. 'The General says Iwo's going to be tougher than Tarawa. He's furious with you guys for refusing to bombard it more than three days.'

'I'm only a spear carrier in this thing. Don't blame me.'

'I guess there's a good reason. There's always a good reason, isn't there?'

'If there isn't, we make one up.'

Sammy frowned. 'Listen, Dad. If anything happens, I don't want you or Mom to feel – well – any regrets.'

'I don't think you can tell us what to feel, Sammy.'

'I mean about raising me in a military family. Pointing me towards the Academy. I made the big choice on my own. Including what we did on Saipan.'

Son, son, Arthur McKay wanted to cry. You're not the only American who has failed to be always noble, wise, fair. Instead he squeezed his hand and said, 'I don't give a damn what you did on Saipan. I just wish we could give you that ten-day bombardment.'

Rita's defiant smile curled on Sammy's lips. 'We'll do OK in spite of you fucked-up sailors.'

*

It was the Siberia Patrol all over again, as far as the crew of the *Jefferson City* could see. Snow mixed with rain lashed their faces and chilled their bones as the cruiser ploughed through icy heaving seas only a hundred miles off the coast of Japan. In the distance, planes roared down the rain-soaked decks of the big carriers to disappear into the low-hanging clouds. Task Force 58 was attacking the home islands of the empire.

Byron Maher showed Captain McKay a message they had received from Admiral Marc Mitscher, the carriers' commander, predicting 'the greatest air victory of the war for carrier aviation'. Like his chief, Maher was a battleship man, with minimum enthusiasm for the aviators. 'They shouldn't even be flying and Spruance knows it,' Maher said. 'The weather over Tokyo is worse than we've got here. They're not going to be able to see a damn thing.'

Maher did not have to elaborate. This attack was part of the ongoing war the Navy was fighting with the Army Air Force. Spruance was naturally on the Navy's side. He wanted to prove that carrier planes could accomplish what the vaunted B-29s had failed to do. Having come this far, he could not bring himself to restrain the aviators, even though he knew the chance of hitting their targets was close to zero.

'We should be back there pounding the bejesus out of Iwo Jima,' Maher said, looking eastward across the wind-lashed sea.

A cool dawn breeze riffled the Pacific as the *Jefferson City* took her bombardment position several thousand yards off the landing beaches. A red sun rose in a clear sky. The grey island, covered with volcanic ash, loomed like a medieval fortress in the rosy light. The ugly cone of an extinct volcano, Mount Suribachi, dominated the barren flatlands where the Marines would come ashore.

Once more the big guns spoke. Battleships, cruisers, destroyers poured high explosives on the fortress. Swarms of planes from Task Force 58 added their bombs. For three days, while Task Force 58 was returning from its fruitless raids on Japan, a squadron of ancient battleships had bombarded the island with dismayingly poor results. The admiral in command of the battleships admitted he had hit almost nothing of importance. Nevertheless Kelly Turner decreed that the landings would proceed on schedule.

It was infinitely worse than Tarawa or Saipan. As men from the Fourth and Fifth Marine divisions hit the beach, the Japanese unmasked pillboxes and artillery positions on both flanks, undetected and unharmed by the bombarding ships. Tanks and landing craft exploded, mortar shells poured down on knots of men huddling in the grey sand. Bodies drifted in the backwash of the four-foot surf.

Captain McKay watched from his bridge, numbly grateful that Sammy's Third Division was in reserve. But there was no doubt they would have to be committed to the battle. On the port side of the forecastle of the *Jefferson City*, Admiral Spruance paced up and down, ignoring the thunder of the eight-inch guns booming to starboard only a few feet away from him. His hawkish, raw-boned face was preoccupied. If he had any regrets about refusing the Marines the ten days of bombardment they had pleaded for, he did not reveal them.

Five days later, Task Force 58 sortied for another raid on Japan. It was a repeat performance of the first disaster. The weather was atrocious. Forty-foot waves damaged several of the destroyers. Clouds and murk shrouded the aircraft factories Spruance desperately wanted to hit. Weather reports from Siberia, on which they depended for planning the operation, turned out to be worthless. Byron Maher cursed the Russians and the aviators.

They returned to Iwo Jima to find the battle still raging. The action off the beaches had been almost as bloody. The carrier *Saratoga* had been ravaged by kamikazes and was limping back to Pearl Harbor. The escort carrier *Bismarck Sea* had been sunk. A half dozen other ships left behind to give fire support for the Marines had also been scorched by the suicide bombers. Accidents revealed how badly ships and men were wearing out. The old battleship *New York* lost her propellers to metal fatigue. Other ships had collided or run aground.

The *Jefferson City* was swiftly assigned a bombardment slot. All day beneath lowering grey clouds, ideal for concealing kamikazes, she steamed slowly back and forth responding to requests from Marine and Navy officers on Iwo Jima to hurl shells at a pillbox or cave or trenchline from which the Japanese continued to spew bullets. It required exact aim, a painstaking study of maps and coordinates.

Late in the afternoon, Captain McKay looked over the splinter shield on the open bridge and saw Byron Maher on the flag bridge below him. 'Has the Third Division gone ashore?' he asked. Maher nodded. 'They've had to use everything they've got. The casualties are horrendous.'

Later in the afternoon, kamikazes sent the fleet to General Quarters. But the Combat Air Patrol shot them down before they got close to the *Jefferson City*. The main battery continued to bombard. McKay worried about the men in the turrets. By the time darkness fell, they had been on duty for ten hours. When Admiral Turner informed him that the *Jefferson City* would fire star shells to illuminate Iwo against a possible banzai charge and if necessary bombard throughout the night, McKay ordered Mullenoe to rotate rest periods between the three turrets.

Horace Aquino telephoned to ask the Captain when he would like his supper served. 'Whenever it's ready,' he said.

He stayed on the bridge, watching the star shells turn Iwo Jima into a ghastly glowing spectacle. Bursts of orange gunfire flared in their crepuscular light. The shells of the big guns exploded against the grisly slopes of Mount Suribachi, trying to reach an underground warren of tunnels in which the Japanese had burrowed. Aquino told him supper was ready and he went down to his cabin. They talked about MacArthur's progress in the Philippines, the collapse of Nazi resistance in Germany. Horace worried about the safety of his family in Manila, which the Japanese were defending house to house.

His Marine orderly knocked on the door. 'Admiral Spruance would like to speak to you, Captain.'

McKay knew, instantly. The Admiral's words were superfluous. The hard mouth moved in the grave face. 'I just got some very bad news, Art. Your son was killed by a sniper this afternoon while they were trying to reorganize one of the forward battalions.'

Loneliness, Captain McKay thought as Spruance sat down on the edge of a chair beneath the painting of the solitary Chinese traveller. The picture seemed to speak to him. *Now you will find out what loneliness really means.*

Spruance wrung his slim weathered hands. 'I know how you feel, Art. I've had my only boy on a sub since this thing started. I've braced myself for this kind of news a hundred times.'

What would the Admiral say if he cursed and reviled him for killing his son? Would a ten-day bombardment have made any difference? Would hurling the full weight of the fleet at Iwo instead of a handful of old battleships, have changed anything? Arthur McKay found it impossible to make such a claim. This earnest, silent man was part of a system, a process, that only deserved one name: history. The pain he felt now was history, part of the pain of a million other American fathers in this war and other wars.

The thought did not lessen the pain. But it made it more bearable.

'I'd like to see him.'

'Of course. I'll radio the General to meet you at the beach.'

Horace Aquino was weeping. 'Oh, Captain,' he said, 'he was such a fine boy.'

'Thank you, Horace.'

In ten minutes he was in his gig, riding toward the beach. Around him the war went on. The big guns boomed on the battleships and cruisers, the shells hurtled in burning arcs over his head. Ashore the star shells drifted down in glowing clusters on the living and the dead. As they drew close to the shore, the hammer of distant machine guns, the bark of rifles could be heard.

The Marine General was waiting on the beach. They had met somewhere. At a War College lecture? He gripped McKay's hand. 'I feel like I just lost one of my own kids,' he said.

They rode in silence through the landscape of war – past wrecked tanks and artillery pieces, overturned jeeps. At the hospital, a collection of dilapidated tents, the General's senior aide, a husky major named Price, mashed his hand. McKay said goodbye to the General, and Major Price led him through the rows of Marines waiting for medical treatment, many obviously dying, to a room in the rear, where forty or fifty bodies lay wrapped in ponchos.

The Major turned on an overhead bulb and led him to a table. Uncovering the poncho, he stared down at Sammy's body. 'I only knew him for a couple of months, Captain. But he was . . . the best.'

'Thanks.'

'I'll wait outside.'

'You better go back to work. I'm going to stay here for a while.'

'Sir, I've got orders. I'll wait.'

The bullet had struck Sammy in the heart. His shirt was stained with blood. But his face was unblemished, undistorted. He had had time to compose himself, to face death with a warrior's stoicism. He looked at peace.

Captain McKay thought of the good times. The years in Hawaii, when they had swum and sailed and fished together. The year Sammy had starred at halfback for the high school in Newport. He had been tremendously disappointed to find he was not heavy enough to make the team at Annapolis. But he had turned out to be a good baseball player.

That brought back another memory. Throwing the ball around. Something they did in a casual way, within a day or two of his return from sea duty. *What do you say we throw the ball around, Dad?* Sammy would ask. They would go out on the lawn or into the backyard and throw a baseball back and forth for a half hour. It was a ritual. They never said much. They just threw the ball. As the years passed, and the ball smacked harder and harder in the centre of his glove, Sammy let him know he was becoming a man.

Did he regret the sea duty years, the awful gaps when he came back to face a stranger son? For a reason he did not understand, he no longer felt cut off from Sammy by those inescapable necessities of Navy life, or by the vagrant emotions that floated through a family. They had never had many man-to-man talks, it was true. But he was not sure the young wanted to reveal their souls to the old. He had shunned it when his mother had tried to make herself his confidante.

There was never any doubt they loved each other. That was the only thing that mattered now.

Arthur McKay did not know how long he sat there in the tent of death while the war exploded relentlessly outside. When he emerged, the Major was waiting for him. They rode back to the beach in the star shells' unreal light. The coxswain of his gig was idling offshore, beyond the surf. He gunned the motor and charged through the waves. In five minutes they were on their way back to the *Jefferson City*.

As the Captain came up the accommodation ladder, he noticed clumps of men along the rails from the stern to the forecastle. On the quarterdeck, George Tombs held out his hand. 'Art,' he said, 'on behalf of the officers and crew, I want to extend my deepest sympathy.'

'Thank you.'

'I'd like to give you this message. It's a spontaneous thing. Signed by every member of the crew. They stayed up most of the night putting it together.'

He handed McKay a thick envelope. In his cabin, he opened it. The message, scrawled in ink by a bold hand, read:

Dear Captain McKay:
    The crew of the *Jefferson City* want you to know how bad they feel about your son's death. We will try to help you bear your sorrow the only way we can – by continuing to try to make this the best ship in the fleet. If there is anything else we can do, just ask us.

Beneath this, the signatures began. Over 1,300 of them in long columns. Homewood, Flanagan, Roth, Mazerowski, Bradford, Bourne. Name after name of men who had faced almost three years of danger and death with him.

Arthur McKay pondered the painting of the lonely traveller. He thought of Win Kemble's poem. *He who needs others is forever shackled. He who is needed by others is forever sad.*

He would accept his shackles. He would accept his sadness. Even if the way led nowhere but to the Great Void.

BOOK SEVEN

The Sky Is Falling

'Raid one. Bogeys closing from northwest, fifty miles north of Bolo. This is Delegate. Out.'

On the bridge, Captain McKay listened to the central fighter director in the command ship *Eldorado*. Bolo was the code name for a peninsula on the island of Okinawa, 845 miles south of Tokyo. On Easter Sunday, 1 April 1945, 120,000 Marines and Army troops had landed there to begin another savage struggle against entrenched Japanese.

The war went on. Sammy slept in the Third Marine Division's cemetery at the foot of Mount Suribachi. Rita maintained a dark silence in Washington, DC, ignoring letters. Lucy Kemble was equally silent in Hawaii. His daughter, Barbara, was his only consolation. She had written him a ten-page letter full of grief and pride and devotion. McKay carried it with him like a talisman. Sentences from it floated through his weary mind. *I was afraid I might hate you or Mother if Sammy died. That terrified me almost as much as him dying. But it hasn't happened. It tore me open and suddenly love was there, impossible to deny or fear or be ashamed of, ever again.*

'How many planes did he estimate?' asked George Tombs.

'I think he's given up counting them,' McKay said.

Day and night for a week the Japanese had flung hundreds of kamikazes at the fleet. Over thirty ships had been sunk or damaged. The crew of the *Jefferson City* was groggy with exhaustion. Dr Cadwallader reported a half dozen nervous collapses. Chaplain Bushnell told him four more men had seen the ghost of Win Kemble stalking the passageways.

Where this loathsome fantasy had begun, McKay did not know. He found it infuriating. He did not believe in ghosts. He did not believe Win was haunting his ship. Even if he were, he was not afraid of him. The *Jefferson City* belonged to Arthur McKay now. No one could take it away from him. Not even Admiral King. But the idea still enraged him.

Maybe they were all going as crazy as the Japanese.

Judging from appearances, madness did seem rampant on board. Everyone on the bridge and on any other exposed post, such as the forty-millimetre mounts, had his face and hands covered with blue grease, issued by the Navy to protect them against flash burns from exploding kamikazes. They were also wearing one-piece jump suits which were supposed to protect the wearers against shrapnel wounds. Unfortunately, the inventor had not figured out how to ventilate them. After two hours, the wearer felt as if he were standing inside a boiler.

On most ships, captains had refused to issue these to their men, they were so unpopular. Captain McKay had decided even acute discomfort was a small price to pay for survival. So he zipped himself into his 'shoot suit', as the men called the baggy garments, each day. The crew, bound to him now by sympathy and an almost mystical faith in his judgement, reluctantly followed his example.

'Here they come,' George Tombs said, studying the horizon with his glasses. 'Looks like a hell of a lot of them have got through the CAP.'

'Bogey bearing zero nine zero,' said the bridge talker.

'CIC reports another bogey at one eight zero.'

'Another bogey at two zero five.'

'Flank speed, steady as you go,' George Tombs said.

The five-inch guns blasted, the forties hammered. Would it ever end? Arthur McKay wondered. He was so tired. At night, Horace Aquino had to practically undress him. He was barely able to sit at the table and eat his supper.

The first three kamikazes went after the carriers. One hit the *Franklin* and hurt her badly. The big ship was racked by tremendous explosions. A column of smoke rose a thousand feet in the air. George Tombs was distraught.

His Annapolis roommate was the gunnery officer.

The sky filled with black bursts from the five-inch proximity fuses. Kamikazes flamed and fell like quaint paper birds. The talker droned bearings, his voice full of suppressed terror. Only if a suicide pilot made a run at the ship did everyone's fear become visible.

'Here comes one,' George Tombs said.

The Zero was dead ahead. A tough target for the five-inch guns. He was already smoking. Flames gushed around his engine. A fat five hundred-pound bomb clung to his undercarriage. He knew he had very little time left and was picking the first available target.

'Get him, Guns!' McKay said.

The Jap's machine guns flared. Marines manning the twenty-millimetre mount above turret one toppled to the deck. Others leaped to the guns and kept firing. The plane kept coming. The forty-millimetre mount on the bow was firing wild, missing him by twenty feet. Panic was ungluing their fire controlman. The Jap was going to crash into the bridge. 'Do something, Captain,' the talker screamed.

The two forward five-inch mounts fired simultaneously. The Zero turned into an immense fireball. The left wing fell off and he plunged into the sea a few points off the port bow, hurling a wave of burning gasoline across the men on the forty-millimetre mount. 'Fire, fire on the main deck forward,' roared the boatswain's mate of the watch.

A fire-fighting team burst on to the deck dragging hoses. Water and foam smothered the blaze. They staggered across the slippery deck to drag the scorched bodies off the forty-millimetre mount.

'Nice shooting, Guns,' McKay said to Bob Mullenoe.

'We should have got him at three thousand yards,' George Tombs growled.

'They're doing their best,' McKay said.

'Turn on all lights. Search all compartments. There may be a Jap aboard!'

It was Ensign Brownmiller on the PA system. Had he

gone crazy? They were anchored a mile off the Okinawa coast. In the Marine compartment, their commander ordered everyone to load his rifle. He rushed six Marines to the Captain's cabin; they practically broke down McKay's door, pounding on it. His regular guard was already inside, his .45 pistol drawn. The corporal in charge stationed three men on the wing deck outside his sea hatch. Similar reinforcements surrounded Admiral Spruance.

While the Marines began a frenzied search of the ship, Captain McKay pulled on a pair of trousers and climbed to the bridge to find out the source of the uproar. He discovered Ensign Brownmiller with gun in hand interrogating a machinist's mate with a large bruise on his cheek. Brownmiller ordered him to repeat his story for Captain McKay.

'I woke up and for some reason I decided to go down in the after engine room to check on a couple of things. I got there and found this guy foolin' around with the locks on the main reduction gears. "What the hell are you doin'?" I said.

'He didn't pay no attention to me. I started comin' down the ladder to grab him when whoa, I slip on a wet step and land on my head. When I woke up he was gone.'

'What did he look like?' McKay asked.

'He was tall. Dark hair. He had an officer's uniform on. That's all I can tell you. He didn't look like a Jap. I mean, most of them are runts, ain't they?'

'Most of them.'

Was it possible some survivor of the defeats of the Combined Fleet, inspired by the kamikazes, had swum out to the ship, hauled himself up on the lines dangling from the boat boom and come aboard with a plan to blow up or cripple an American warship?

'Tell the Marines to pay especially close attention to the magazines and the fuel tanks. Any place where someone could cause an explosion,' McKay said.

A frantic hour later, the sweat-soaked Marine captain reported to the bridge. 'Sir, we've searched every inch of the ship. We haven't found a thing. We've got guards on every magazine and in the engine and fire rooms, just in case.'

No one slept for the rest of the night. In the crew's compartments, men sat on bottom racks embellishing the story. 'I heard a Marine caught him on the quarterdeck and tried to bayonet him. It went right through him,' one of the mesquiteers told Flanagan.

'It would go right through you too,' Flanagan said.

'He means it was a spook. Somethin' you couldn't kill,' a second mesquiteer explained.

'Who could it be?' Flanagan said, knowing the answer.

'Captain Kemble,' said the third mesquiteer.

'I'm betting it was some chicken-livered guy in the black gang. My friend Marty Roth tells me if you throw sand in those reduction gears, the ship's out of action for six months. I wish he told me that when we were in Long Beach.'

'That's enough outa you, wiseguy,' Homewood roared.

The mysterious intruder remained unfound, and the spooky explanation swiftly became the prevailing wisdom. Not content with simply haunting them, Captain Kemble was now trying to destroy the *Jefferson City*.

'Raid number thirty-seven. Bogeys closing from the northwest. This is Delegate. Out.'

Only two hours had passed since the first raid of the day and Delegate was hoarse already. In the *Jefferson City*'s CIC, where Montgomery West was responsible for coordinating what he heard from Delegate, from the ship's lookouts and from his radar operators, the problem was more complicated. His radarscopes were a wild confusion of enemy and friendly planes as the Combat Air Patrol tangled with the kamikazes. It was impossible to separate them. That meant they had to wait until a kamikaze got so close, the CAP broke off pursuit. With the plane hurtling towards them at 350 miles per hour, the J.C.'s gunners then had about 120 seconds to shoot him down.

On top of fighting for her life, the ship had regular bombardment assignments, to assist the troops ashore trying to pry the Japanese out of their holes and caves. These requests for artillery support were often as urgent as the kamikaze warnings that flooded the airwaves from Delegate.

After a week of dealing with this murderous chaos, West was glassy-eyed with fatigue. He began to wonder if he had ever been anything but this harried creature in earphones. The memories of his previous life were as hazy as the scenes of the movies in which he had acted. Gwen's letters telling him how Hollywood and everyone else in the country seemed to have forgotten the war infuriated him. He almost wished she would stop writing to him.

'Lookouts report two bogeys, bearing one five zero, two four zero,' the talker said.

'Yeah, yeah. What do you get on radar, Wylie?' West said.

'Confirmed. I've got three others,' Wylie said, and mumbled the ranges and bearings.

'What the fuck did you say, Wylie? We haven't got time to repeat anything. Speak slowly, clearly.'

'Lieutenant, I don't feel good. I need another pill.'

'We all need pills, Wylie. Give me those fucking bearings again.'

Wylie started to blubber. His nerves were shot.

In the director for the five-inch guns, Frank Flanagan rubbed sweat from his raw streaming eyes and waited for the next kamikaze. The fire controlman who usually operated the director had collapsed. The setup was the same as the main battery director, with a high-powered range finder that spotted targets and estimated distance. But the speed at which things happened in the air was so different, it was like going from running the mile to the hundred-yard dash overnight.

'Bogey bearing two seven zero,' said the Air Defence Officer, Lieutenant Calabrese. He was tough and cool. The deck apes had nicknamed him the Enforcer.

Flanagan spun the director to port. It was a Val, with fixed landing gear – an ancient crate. But he had a big black bomb under his belly that could blow them all to pieces. 'Director, this is sky forward. Have you got him?' Calabrese asked.

'Roger. Range six thousand yards, altitude one thousand.'

'OK. We've got a good setup in plot. We'll stay on automatic.'

The five-inch guns boomed. The Val jinked right and left. The proximity fuses exploded all around him. Pieces of the plane flew off. An easy one, Flanagan thought. The next salvo would finish him. But the Val abruptly climbed to two thousand feet and the next salvo whizzed over the horizon. Suddenly Flanagan knew they were not going to stop this one.

'Range three thousand yards.' It was incredible how fast the range dropped. 'Two thousand yards.'

'All mounts, go to local control,' Calabrese said, giving each five-inch mount the freedom to do its own aiming and shooting.

'Range one thousand yards,' Flanagan said.

In his powerful lens, Flanagan could see the pilot's face. He was smiling. The forty-millimetres were firing now. The ship was throwing up a wall of exploding metal. He could not possibly get through it. A forty-millimetre shell smashed the cockpit. The pilot's head vanished. But the plane kept flying, a headless corpse at the controls. It was the stuff of myths, of nightmares.

Down the Val came in a relentless dive at the midships superstructure. The forty-millimetre guns were literally hammering it to pieces. But they could not stop it. Flanagan braced himself for the fire and explosion. It would probably blow the director into the sea. He would die like Jack Peterson.

A final blast from a five-inch gun drove the Val toward the stern. He'll miss by inches, Flanagan thought. Please make him miss. At such moments even sceptics prayed.

He did not miss. There was a snarling, screaming crash as the motor collided with metal. The whole ship shuddered under the impact of a terrific explosion.

'Ah, Jesus, ah, shit,' Flanagan gasped. He was weeping, banging his head against the range finder. They had done everything right. They had hit him with almost every gun on the ship. How did he keep coming? Had their luck finally run out?

'I think that fucker is coming in,' said Mess Steward Cash Johnson in Repair Five, the damage control station for the after part of the ship. It was the last thing he or anyone else in Repair Five said or thought. The plane tore through the main deck and the bomb went through two more decks before exploding only a few feet away from Repair Five, killing all of them instantly. Fire erupted around the magazines and powder rooms for the after turret.

In Damage Control Central Lieutenant Commander Edwin Moss made a swift, vital decision. 'Flood all after magazines,' he said.

His men spun the dials that sent seawater rushing into these spaces. He called Repair Five and got no answer. He tried to call the engine rooms. 'I think the power's gone aft, sir,' his talker said.

Strapping on his inhalator, Moss rushed aft to assess the situation. He found men from Repair Three and Four under the leadership of Boats Homewood fighting the fire with water and foam in the semi-darkness. All power was out in the after part of the ship. Homewood told him there were at least six holes in the hull and nine compartments flooded. A stumpy shipfitter pointed to a hatch that led to the central electricity room. 'Some of my best buddies are down there,' he said. 'What the fuck's wrong with our gunnery department?'

As the fires were extinguished, they were able to approach the slaughterhouse that Repair Five had become. Bodies and parts of bodies lay among the twisted steel and charred hoses and breathing masks, mercifully covered by the foam. Moss picked up the hat that had belonged to the ensign in charge, an easygoing kid from Connecticut. Numbly he wiped the foam off the visor. How long would this go on?

A messenger rushed up to him. 'Sir. Flag wants to know if you've seen Admiral Spruance!'

'I've got other things on my mind.'

'He was walking on deck when the plane hit. No one's seen him since.'

Moss went up on deck, where more fire fighters were dealing with the roaring blaze around turret three. All of them wore dungarees and had their faces painted blue. At the head of one of the hoses was a figure in khaki with no paint on his face.

'Admiral,' Moss said, 'Flag wants to know if you're all right.'

'Tell him I'm fine. If you can scrape together anything that's left of that Jap pilot, see if he was carrying a code book. If we could break the code they're using, we might be able to shoot these maniacs down over Japan.'

The Admiral went back to fighting the fire.

'Captain,' the helmsman said, 'we've lost steering control.'

'Shift to steering aft,' McKay said.

'Captain,' said the signal officer, '*Eldorado* wants to know if we can handle our bombarding assignment.'

'Signal affirmative,' McKay said.

Damage Control had reported all fires extinguished. Turret three was out of action, but the other two were unharmed. Seventeen men were dead, seventy-seven wounded, another twenty missing – trapped and presumed drowned in the flooded compartments. The flooding had caused the cruiser to settle five feet. But Captain McKay wanted to prove to the world – and his crew – that the *Jefferson City* was still a fighting ship.

The bombardment orders flowed in from the *Eldorado*. McKay could see Admiral Kelly Turner in his flag plot, predicting that the Ragtag would quit. She was still a disgraced ship, as far as he and Ernie King were concerned. In their son-of-a-bitch code, mistakes were never erased, sins never forgiven.

'George,' McKay said to Executive Officer Tombs, 'take us in to three thousand yards before we bombard. Marse

Lee will have a conniption, but tell him it's an order. I'm going below to see the wounded.'

In sick bay, he talked to men waiting for the doctors to operate, to others who lay naked, smeared with jelly for their burns. A seaman second class who had been on the forty-millimetre mount on the bow when the kamikaze drenched it with flaming gasoline had burns over sixty percent of his body. He said he was not in any pain and Dr Cadwallader had told him he would be fine. Dr Levy, standing a few feet away, caught the Captain's eye and mournfully shook his head.

'We've been trying to get him to write a letter to his mother,' the chaplain said.

'Why don't you?' McKay said. 'Dictate it to the chaplain. I'll write a postscript, telling her what a great job you've done.'

As the boy began his letter, the *Jefferson City*'s main battery boomed. 'Dear Mom,' he said. 'We've just been hit by a kamikaze and I've been hurt pretty bad. But I think I'm going to be OK. We're still fighting. In sick bay, where the chaplain is helping me write this, I can hear the guns banging away. Believe it or not, they're beautiful music when you're hurt or scared. Lots of love, Andy.'

'We'll get it by the censor, won't we, Captain?' the chaplain said.

'Guaranteed,' McKay said.

'Give them hell for us, Captain,' an older sailor said, as two mess stewards picked up his stretcher and carried him to the operating room. McKay saw his right leg was missing below the knee.

Movie stuff. But the burned sailor had it right. Men said things like that when they were in agony. 'That's what we're doing,' McKay said.

Back on the bridge, Tombs reported the Marine spotters ashore were ecstatic over the hits they were scoring on an array of Japanese bunkers slotted into one of Okinawa's murderous ridges.

'Captain, CIC reports bogeys in large numbers closing from due north.'

'Flank speed. Let's get out of this shoal water,' McKay said.

Would they get hit again? It did not seem fair. But who ever said fairness had anything to do with this business?

Once more the first wave of kamikazes concentrated on the picket destroyers on the fringes of the fleet, pathetically naked to attack. They listened to the desperate calls for help from destroyer captains, the terse announcement that the *Leutze*, the *Rodman*, the *Bush* were abandoning ship. Then the kamikazes were streaking through the sky around the *Jefferson City*. The guns hammered and boomed once more.

'Bogey bearing two one five, range eight thousand,' the talker said.

'Art,' George Tombs said, 'what do you say we try to manoeuvre this time? Give them a tougher target.'

All McKay's instincts said no. It was still wiser to hold the ship steady and give the gunners a chance to get the plane. But it had not worked the last time. The men at the guns and the fire control instruments were no longer functioning at a hundred percent. Maybe nothing was going to work, once one of these death planes got close to the ship of its choice.

Was Win Kemble aboard, laughing at this new war, which neither skill nor courage could win? Madness. 'All right, George, let's try it,' McKay said.

A kamikaze roared past at two thousand yards, heading for the *Enterprise*. Cruisers on both sides, including the *Jefferson City*, blazed away at him. Again they scored hits, there was a burst of flame – but the plane hurtled into the big carrier that the J.C. had stopped three torpedoes to preserve off the Santa Cruz Islands in the Solomons more than two years ago. Fire and smoke towered into the sky.

'God damn it,' George Tombs said.

Another kamikaze made the same run, only a few feet above the water. The guns of the cruiser opposite them spoke. A forty-millimetre shell hurtled into the starboard hatch of the *Jefferson City*'s pilothouse and exploded against the opposite wall. Everyone was knocked flat by the blast. Captain McKay staggered to his feet and found a chunk of smoking metal in the chest of his flak suit. One after the other, the rest of the men on the bridge stood up, amazed that they were still alive. The engine room telegrapher was bleeding from a shell splinter in his cheek. Otherwise, no one was hurt. They had been saved by their shoot suits.

'Bogey at one eight five,' gasped the bridge talker.

'Left full rudder,' George Tombs said, swinging the ship to port to give more guns a shot at him.

A mistake. The kamikaze was already a ball of flame. He might have fallen short or missed the ship if they had stayed on course and let the after guns handle him. Now he had a target even a dead man could not miss. Maybe George was in a daze from the explosion of that shell. Maybe it was the Captain's fault for letting George change his battle plan. Passivity, his old weakness, haunting him one last time?

'Oh, Christ,' George gasped, seeing what he had done.

A passage from Moby Dick flickered through McKay's mind and vanished before he could grasp it. Later he realized it was Starbuck's plea as the whale charged the ship. *Is this the end of all my bursting prayers? all my life-long fidelities? My God stand by me now!*

The burning plane smashed into forty-millimetre mount one just aft of the bridge. Flames leaped as high as the stacks. The ship jerked convulsively as another bomb exploded deep in her midsection.

'I hope that isn't the sick bay,' McKay said.

'Fire on the main deck,' roared the boatswain's mate of the watch.

The bomb exploded in the passageway outside sick bay, where dozens of wounded were waiting for treatment. At least twenty were killed instantly. The blast blew in the bulkheads of sick bay, killing more men in bunks on that side as well as pharmacist's mates and men assigned to sick bay at General Quarters. An inferno roared in the passageway, threatening to incinerate or suffocate the survivors. But the flames were snuffed with almost miraculous speed by men from Repair Two.

'Take the wounded to the wardroom dressing station. We'll work there,' Dr Cadwallader said.

On the bridge, Captain McKay listened to the grim reports from Damage Control. Everyone on forty-millimetre mount one and in the starboard five-inch mount had been killed by the second kamikaze. Those guns were out of action. The bomb had wrecked sick bay and added another set of punctures in the hull amidships. The *Jefferson City* was now down eight feet. Another twenty men were dead, at least sixty wounded.

From flagship *Eldorado* came another message: 'Ragtag, can you resume bombardment at 1330?'

'Reply affirmative,' Captain McKay said.

Once more, while her doctors struggled to save the wounded and her repair parties fought the rising water on the lower decks, Navigator Lee fretted over his charts and helped guide the ship to within a mile of Okinawa's shore. They still had no steering power on the bridge. Orders were sent to men in the after steering station, deep in the stern of the ship as they threaded the shoals and reefs.

Two miles farther out, the battleship *Mississippi* hurled fourteen-inch shells over their heads. Directions for the *Jefferson City* crackled over the radio from Marine spotters ashore. While smoke curled from her charred deck amidships, the main battery's two surviving turrets thundred, and the eight-inch shells crashed into a Japanese strong point the Marines had christened Plasma Ridge.

The spotters shouted their approval of the destruction. Gunnery Officer Mullenoe walked the shells up and down the mile-long ridge. 'If there's anyone left alive up there he's got to be wearing armour plate,' the spotter said.

As dusk fell, the ship withdrew to rejoin the rest of the fleet at sea. From flagship *Eldorado*, a blinker flashed a message. Minutes later, the J.C.'s chief signalman handed it to the Captain. *You've got a lot of sand, Ragtag.*

It was as close as Admiral Turner could get to admitting he was wrong.

From Admiral Spruance in flag plot came another message. *The performance of the* Jefferson City *today is in the highest traditions of the American naval service. My congratulations to you and your men.*

Captain McKay read both messages over the PA system to the crew.

The harbour of Kerama-retto, a mountainous island fifteen miles off the southern tip of Okinawa, was not a place anyone in the fleet wanted to visit.

'You think we got it bad, look at those poor bastards,' Homewood said to Flanagan and other members of F Division.

They stared at grotesquely twisted superstructures and hulls with gaping holes. Most of the kamikazes' victims were destroyers that had been on the radar picket lines. Among them loomed the battleship *Tennessee*, with her signal bridge burned out, and the attack transport *Lauderdale*, which had been shot up by American guns during the last attack.

Small boats buzzed around the harbour carrying wounded to white-hulled hospital ships. On the warships, flags were all at half mast as they buried their dead. The *Jefferson City* soon joined them in this funereal business. Flanagan stood among the mourners on the fantail while Chaplain Bushnell droned through a eulogy to 'our lost heroes'. George Jablonsky lay among the shrouded corpses. If Jack Peterson had lived, Flanagan would have been manning the gun director for forty millimetre mount one. He would have been incinerated by that kamikaze, along with his gun crew. The three mesquiteers snuffled and rubbed their noses beside him. They too would be lying next to their buddies if Jack had not died.

If. If. If. Flanagan was too tired to think beyond the word.

After the ceremony, the bodies were transported to a cemetery on the beach. A Navy repair ship came alongside and divers went down to investigate the damage to the hull. Other experts descended into the darkness around the propeller shafts.

Two hours later, Captain McKay was reporting what they

found to Admiral Spruance. The propeller shafts had been knocked out of line by the blast from the first kamikaze's bomb. The propellers themselves were bent and unstable. The damage to the hull required the attention of a dry dock if the cruiser hoped to survive a major storm.

'I'm afraid we're going to have to part company, Art,' Spruance said. 'You deserve some leave time, anyway. I was tempted to send you back after Sammy died. I'm sure Rita needs you badly.'

'I haven't heard a word from her.'

Spruance stared straight ahead. He could not become entangled with personal lives. War required one man whose brain retained the cold calm of God. 'We'll write up the orders immediately,' he said.

As Spruance and his staff prepared to transfer to the battleship *New Mexico*, the news swirled through the *Jefferson City* like a typhoon. It started with the Marines, who heard it from the orderlies who were guarding the Admiral.

'Maybe the goddamn war will be over by the time they finish the repairs,' Flanagan said to Homewood.

Dusk was falling over the harbour of Kerama-retto. They were topside, looking at the gouged, battered ships around them in the gloom.

'It won't,' Homewood said.

'How the hell do you know?' Flanagan said.

'I don't know how I know some things. I'm just tellin' you. We ain't finished with the war. It ain't finished with us.'

Home Front

Into Long Beach Harbour the *Jefferson City* limped once more, after a slow difficult voyage from Okinawa. The damaged propeller shafts and screws had made it impossible for her to run at over twenty knots. At sea, they had been shocked to hear that President Franklin D. Roosevelt had died. But the new President, Harry S. Truman of Missouri, made it clear that nothing essential had changed. America and her allies were still committed to a fight to the finish – the unconditional surrender of German and Japan.

On the forecastle, the crew mustered by divisions in their long-unused dress whites. On the bridge, George Tombs conned the ship to buoy twenty-two in the outer harbour. As the buoy man began running the anchor chain through the buoy's big metal grommet, every ship in the harbour blew her whistle and siren. Factory whistles and automobile horns and police sirens ashore added to the racket.

'I knew we did a great job out there, Art,' Tombs said. 'But I didn't realize it was this good.'

'Don't let it turn your head, George,' Captain McKay said. 'I think it has something to do with the German surrender.'

Minutes later, a message from the radio room confirmed his guess. Germany had surrendered unconditionally the previous day. Truman had just announced it at the White House.

'Do you think the Japs will fold now?'

'No,' McKay said.

Home. Arthur McKay paced the empty rooms of Clinch Meade's house overlooking the Pacific. It was as good a home as any. He had never lived in any house he had thought of as home except the house in Hawaii. Maybe the whole country was his home.

At Pearl Harbor, he had asked Mildred Meade if he could have the house for a month. She had agreed, of course. When he candidly admitted that Rita had yet to answer one of his letters, Mildred had grown confused. He could see her wondering if he planned to spend the month with Lucy – or some other woman – then wondering why she was so firmly excluded from his feelings. They shared a common wound now. Her eyes had filled with tears as she struggled to tell him how awful she felt about Sammy.

Arthur McKay had wanted to tell her how much he regretted the impossibility. He had always thought he would have been happy with Mildred. But she would have made any

632

sensible Navy man happy. Why was life so often grotesquely out of joint? Was it because history or fate insisted on
people playing multiple roles? Mildred Rogers Meade had
wanted to match her heart to some noble cause. But she was
also the inheritor of a fortune that her grandfather, Henry
Huttleson Rogers, had built on rapacity and amoral cun-
ning. It was fitting that she and most of the fortune should
be captured by a modern version of the same piratical
breed.

The day dwindled into dusk. Still no Rita. No wife. Only
silence on the long distance telephone. Should he get on a
plane and burst into their Washington, DC, house, perhaps
finding her in bed with Ernest J. King? No. He had issued
the best, the most honest invitation he could write. He
could only wait and hope. Meanwhile –

McKay opened the bar. He gazed at the rows of bottles
with familiar names. Old Overholt. Canadian Club, Ballantine's Scotch.

There was a limit to loneliness. He would give Rita
another twelve hours.

'Teresa? It's me. Frank.'

The blank face stared past him at the blank wall of the
California State Mental Hospital in Sonoma.

'I tole you it'd be a waste of time,' the Negro ward
attendant said. 'She don't talk to nobody.'

'I'm back from the Pacific in one piece. In spite of those
bad dreams you had about me. Jack Peterson got killed. So
did a lot of other guys on the ship. But I'm back. I just
wanted you to know I still care about you. I'd like to help
you if I can.'

The eyes remained blank. Her face had shrunk. It
seemed withered, as if she was growing older at an
accelerated pace. Her arms were pipe stems.

'She looks starved. Don't you feed her?'

'She don't eat. You got to cram it down her throat.'

'What are those burns on the side of her head?'

'From the shock treatment. They keep givin'm to her but
they don't do no good.'

'I'm going East to see my parents, Teresa. The first time in almost three years. I'm not looking forward to it. I'd rather stay out here with you – if you were OK.'

Silence. Wherever Teresa had gone, she refused to talk about it. Flanagan told her about the kamikazes, about Kruger going crazy, about editing the ship's paper. Finally he ran out of things to say. He became part of Teresa's silence.

With a sigh he walked to the door. 'Goodbye,' he said.

'Go fuck yourself,' Teresa said.

'Yes, my friends, I think we can safely rejoice in God's blessing on this chosen people. The success He has bestowed on our men in uniform is proof of it. We have triumphed because we have fought the good fight. We have fought for justice and brotherhood and freedom. I am confident that our remaining enemy, Japan, will be swiftly subdued and we will welcome the victors from this battlefield with the same heartfelt thanks for God's blessing that we offer now for our victory over Germany'.

It was wrong, Edwin Moss thought, looking up at his father's exalted face in the pulpit of Morristown's First Presbyterian Church. The Reverend Woodrow Wilson Moss was making the war sound easy. Easy to win, easy to understand. When anyone who fought in it found it incomprehensible.

It had been difficult to understand even before the kamikazes. But the suicide bombers stretched understanding over a horizon the mind could not reach. Wars are inevitably streaked with madness; loss of control lurks at the edges of everyone's soul. But the kamikazes were like a comet in the sky, a blaze of fearsome meaning that eluded thought.

Eleanor and his four children sat beside Moss in the pew. She was raising them as Catholics, something that had troubled him for a long time. Now it seemed of utterly no importance. The war had opened spaces in his mind that organized religion could not touch. There were fundamental experiences more important than opinions on the

Trinity and whether faith or good works were crucial to salvation.

Moss studied his oldest son, Woodrow, fourteen. The boy had just told him he was thinking of going to Annapolis. Moss had had to force a smile, summon words of insincere approval to his lips. He did not want his son to practise the truths he had learned within the narrow world of the Navy. Yet he could not imagine where else he could learn these truths. Commander Moss was confused. Perhaps there was something else he had yet to learn.

Later, at a reception in the garden of the manse, a broad-beamed lady approached him and Eleanor. 'You must be so proud of him,' she said.

'I am,' Eleanor said.

Moss realized that Eleanor had not said a word about his career since he arrived home. That subject too had been transcended by a deeper caring the war had taught her as well as him.

'Where will you be stationed now, Commander?'

'Stationed? I'm going back to my ship. The war isn't over. We still have to invade Japan.'

Eleanor was holding his hand as he said this. He felt a tremor run through her body. He wondered if he had told her too much about the kamikazes.

Later, at the dinner table, his father said, 'You're awfully quiet, Eddy. I guess you're itching to get back into action.'

'What?' Moss said.

'You want to get out there and finish them off. The Japs,' his father said.

Commander Moss looked across the table at his son. His answer was intended for him and no one else.

'No,' he said. 'You're wrong. I wish I didn't have to go. I wish none of us did.'

Montgomery West did not know what to do or say. He read the story in Louella Parsons' column for the third time.

It told how a certain English actress was two-timing a naval hero. Such disloyalty, such dishonour, should for ever bar her from getting a part in Hollywood.

Uncle Mort's welcome-home present. It was a sort of climax or anticlimax. Nothing had gone right since he arrived. Gwen had dragged him to parties at which people asked him inane questions about the war and he gave them curt answers. He got the feeling she was using him to re-establish her standing in Hollywood. It stank. He began to think he hated Hollywood. He could not tolerate another artificial smile. All he wanted was Gwen, her touch, her lips, her body, Gwen and quiet. A place where Delegate could not get at him. Where burning kamikazes did not fill his radar screen.

'I've got the perfect answer,' he finally said, after staring at the paper for five minutes. 'I'll marry you.'

'Is that a serious proposal or a publicity stunt?'

'What the hell do you mean by that?'

'You want to prove to everyone in this filthy place that you haven't been made a fool of. You've satisfied yourself of the relative virtue of your English slut.'

'Jesus Christ. You make me wonder if there might *be* something to the story.'

'What if there were? You don't have your brand on me, Mr West.'

'Do you realize what I said several lines back?'

'You made some offhand reference to marrying me. As if it was something you might do one of these days, after you get a haircut.'

'You've got terribly temperamental.'

'I've always been temperamental. Now I've got something to be temperamental about. I have been starved, ostracized and now slandered on your behalf. And your answer is "I'll marry you". I am not thrilled. I am not moved. I am not impressed. I'm mad as hell.'

'So am I.'

'You don't act it. Or is that what you do when you get mad – get married?'

'I'm sorry. I meant it. I'm not thinking very straight. I came home hoping for a minimum of hassle. The job I've got out there is all hassle. About twenty hours a day.' He started to weep. 'I'm sorry, Gwen.'

'Oh, Joey. What a selfish bitch I am. We'll go away someplace quiet. No more parties. No more Hollywood. We'll rest. I didn't realize how much you needed rest.'

Halfway to the bottom of the bottle. Halfway to the bottom of his life. Arthur McKay poured himself another drink. What would happen when he got to the bottom? He did not know and he did not care. While his ship was being repaired and his crew was pursuing happiness elsewhere, he was voyaging across loneliness. That was a captain's fate. Loneliness. He accepted it.

You will come at last to a sea so wide you cannot see the further shore.

Was he there? Was this the point where all those who came with you turn back? Father, son, friend, gone. Nothing left but his women, and the one who promised to make the journey with him has turned back. His daughter's love was a consolation, but she had her own journey to make. He did not blame Rita for abandoning him. He was a romantic fool. He had driven her out of his life with his fantasy of the perfect woman, his dark lady.

A sound. Was it a cry? A sob? Was it Rita? He blundered around the house calling her name. Suddenly he saw him standing in the centre of the living room. Incongruous place to encounter the dead. It was his house, really. He had sold a part of his soul for it. Sold it to the mammon of inquity, in the person of Clinch Meade, in return for some pieces of silver influence.

Win Kemble stood in the centre of the living room in the moonlight. Blood steamed from his right eye. It was exactly as Lucy had described finding him. He had put the gun in his mouth and pulled the trigger. Blood had gushed from his eye.

Those psychiatrists in Kansas, the Menningers, said the way a man killed himself was very significant. It revealed what was devouring his soul. What did a gun in the mouth signify? A hatred of all the lies the mouth had spoken in all the years of playing a part the soul detested?

Arthur McKay sat down in a chair and regarded the ghost

of his friend. Whether he existed inside or outside his head, he did not know or care. He did not try to find out. He only knew one thing. He was not afraid of him.

'You were wrong, Win,' McKay said. 'It isn't all illusion. It isn't meaningless. A ship is real. A crew is real. Shipmate is a word that means something. War is terrible but real. Courage is real. Honour is real. History is real.'

The ghost's face contorted. McKay could not tell whether it was rage or grief.

'There's something beyond loneliness. Something I believe in even if I can't reach it, thanks to you. It goes by a lot of names – marriage, friendship, fatherhood. It's more important than politics or war, and maybe it's more powerful too.'

Something struck him in the face. The whiskey bottle slipped from his hand. Captain McKay toppled to the rug.

The Army transport plane came down through a fine mist that left Seattle and everything around it looking like a world seen underwater. Frank Flanagan braced himself in his bucket seat while the co-pilot and the pilot argued about the location of the airport. They finally found it and came roaring in, pursuit plane style.

Exhausted from three days of sitting up on such planes or in dusty hangars waiting for them, Flanagan hunched into his blue peacoat and straggled into the rain. His week at home in the Bronx had been dismal. His father stared out the window. His mother chattered about the jobs he could get but wouldn't try for, his sisters mooed over Frank Sinatra and other crooners. Father Callow called three times, but he refused to speak to him.

Flanagan's mother told him he had changed and not for the better. He told her she was responsible for the depressed man in the living room. Her endless demands for new dresses, coats, furniture were the reason why he had looked the other way while hoods ran numbers and set up bookie parlours all over his precinct. She wept with rage and denounced him as a worse than worthless son.

No one seemed to give a damn about the war. Everyone

was already talking about what they were going to do afterwards. As if the Japs had already rolled over and surrendered. He spent his time reading Irish poetry and the newspapers, which told of more ships burning off Okinawa as the kamikazes continued to swarm.

Now he was going to see Martha Johnson. Why, he did not know. He was a glutton for punishment. It had been an impulse thing. He was planning to go back to San Pedro, where Boats Homewood had rented an apartment for the homeless members of F Division. Suddenly there was a plane leaving for Seattle and he got on it.

Martha did not sound thrilled to hear from him. 'Frank? You're here in town? Sure. Come on out.'

The house overlooking Puget Sound was a shock. It was no longer neat or charming. Pieces of clothing and empty glasses and ten-day-old newspapers were strewn all over the living room. Martha greeted him with a faded smile and a big wet kiss. The shrewd cool woman had vanished. She was wearing a wrinkled kimono and she had not combed her hair in a week.

'Oh, Frank. It's so swell to see you.'

'Swell to see you too,' he lied.

She got out a bottle of bourbon and poured him half a glass. 'Let's drink to Jack,' she said. 'That's all I've been doing for the last six months.'

He was appalled, but he did not know what to do or say. He drank to Jack.

'The whole thing's just convinced me I'm born unlucky,' she said, slurring her words. 'I mean, first I draw a son of a bitch for a father and a drunk for a mother, and then I finally get a terrific guy to love me and what happens? He gets killed by a dumb Jap who's busy crashing his plane. How's *that* for luck?'

'Lousy,' Flanagan agreed.

They drank and he listened to an endless eulogy of Jack. His charm, his looks, his wit, his brains. Above all his love. How when he finally discovered love, he surrendered to it. He had the courage to admit it. Martha got out some of Jack's letters and read from them.

Around midnight, Flanagan was drunk enough to say anything. Martha started looking for Jack's first letter, the one in which he admitted his love.

'I wrote that,' Flanagan said.

'What?' Martha said.

'I wrote it. I wrote them all.'

He started reciting passages from the first letter and from others she had not read aloud.

'He read them to the guys in main forward before he mailed them. He called them classy bullshit. He didn't love you. He didn't love anybody.'

'I don't believe you.'

'It's the truth. You told me the truth about Teresa and now I'm telling you the truth about Jack. He was no damn good. He was a liar and a bastard and a thief. Why the fuck are you drinking yourself to death over him?'

'You son of a bitch! You're making this up!'

'I wish I was.'

He told her about the wallets and fountain pens and gold and silver chains and bracelets in Jack's locker. He told her about the women in Australia and in Hawaii. He told her how Jack used to laugh about having her on a string.

Martha smashed him in the face. He saw it coming but he did not try to duck. 'You lying bastard,' she screamed. 'He was your shipmate. You pretended to like him. Now you tell these lies about him when he's dead and can't defend himself. Even if they're true, you're worse than he ever was.'

'I didn't pretend to like him. I loved him. I loved him almost as much as you did. But he was no damn good.'

Tears streamed down his face. 'We're going back out there, and this time the kamikazes will finish us. We've run out of luck. I can feel it in my gut – the way Jack felt it before it happened to him. Boats Homewood feels it too. I want to do one thing right before that happens.'

No longer drunk but utterly bewildered, Martha sat down in a chair on the other side of the littered room. She started crying too.

'Oh, Frank,' she said, 'we're so fucked up.'

He sprang across the room and seized her by the arms and shook her so hard he almost broke her neck. 'You're not fucked up. You're the straightest, bravest, kindest, most intelligent woman I've ever seen. If it wasn't for Jack I'd –'

He was roaring this into her face. She put her hand over his mouth before he could say that he loved her but could never touch her because of Jack. It gave him just enough time to realize Jack was gone. He was gone into the deepest deep, the darkest dark. Frank Flanagan was still alive. So was Martha Johnson.

He kissed her long and hard. She began kissing him back.

Moonlight poured through the palm trees. Arthur McKay was making love to Rita in the lush grass of Kalakaua House. Woman, he thought, this was woman as the gateway, woman as the guardian of the spirit house of the soul.

A hand gripped his shoulder. He sat up in the disordered bed to find a very different woman confronting him in the daylight. It was still Rita, but she looked more inclined to shoot him between the eyes than welcome him into her arms.

'Mildred Meade called me. She said you were here with Lucy. Where is she? I'm going to tear that sanctimonious bitch to pieces. I should have done it long ago.'

'There's no one here but me, Rita. Waiting for you.'

'Waiting for me. The place smells like a cheap saloon. You're doing your usual act. Pathetic Arthur. So is she, telling you how sorry you should feel for yourself. Except now she can go all the way with the consolation.'

'She's still in Hawaii, Rita. Mildred knows that. Lucy's dispensing pity to guys who need it more than me. I can't compete with the amputees, the blind, the brain-damaged. That's what ruined our romance.'

'Don't try to be amusing,' Rita raged.

'I'm not, really.'

'She isn't here?'

'No. Just me. Your husband, Rita.'

Slowly, sadly, Rita sank down on the edge of the bed. She had got fat again. Somehow that made her more endearing.

'I still love you, Rita. I think you still love me.'

She shook her head, fighting tears.

'We haven't lost Sammy, Rita. He belongs only to us now. No one else. The Marines, his friends, his classmates will gradually forget him. But we won't. It's something we can't share with anyone else. All by itself it's a reason for staying together.'

She shook her head again, although she could no longer stop the tears.

'Even if he were still alive, I'd want to be your husband. I know who I am now, Rita. I have no doubts, no reservations. I'm a Navy man. The Captain of the *Jefferson City*. Your husband. I won't be complete until you say yes to the third part of that proposition. I wouldn't be the first two without you.'

Rita was sobbing now. The bed shook with her grief. 'Oh, Arthur, Arthur,' she said. 'How could everything go so wrong?'

'If you mean how is it we didn't get what we thought we wanted – I don't know. I don't think anyone ever gets more than a small part of that. The crazy thing is – when you stop to think about it – you find out how unimportant so much of it was. It's amazing how grateful you become for the things you do get.'

'I won't. I'll never be happy again for the rest of my life.'

'Yes you will. Before the end of this month out here, you'll be happy. And so will I.'

He sat beside her on the bed and kissed her gently on the lips. A comrade's kiss. Passion could wait for happiness to return. It would not be the old violent happiness, shot through with wild hopes and desperate denials. That was the happiness of youth. The happiness of age was different – a blend of memory and acceptance in which love was still the vital force.

'You know what we're going to do first?'

'What?'

'Make love in my cabin.'

For the first time the Captain was in command of his wife, his soul, his life.

*

'This is crazy,' Martha Johnson said, drawing the blinds to let the July sunshine pour into the room. 'I still feel like I'm robbing the cradle.'

'You say that once more,' Frank Flanagan said, 'and you're going to get a fat lip.'

Hands on her hips, not wearing a stitch, she still managed to look defiant. 'Don't threaten me, sailorboy.'

He dragged her back into the bed and kissed her violently. His hand wandered until it found a very important part of her and her breath came faster and faster. 'Christ,' she said. 'I'm going to be late for work again.'

The first morning, when he awoke in bed with Martha, Flanagan had been assailed by guilt. What right did he have to steal the rest of Jack's life? He had stolen his job, his place in Boats Homewood's affections, now he was taking his woman.

Jack, he had whispered, starting a dialogue with the dead like so many other people on the *Jefferson City*, *I'll make it up to you. I'll really try to love her.*

Someone was banging on the door and yelling, 'Western Union.' Martha finally put on a robe and answered him.

'For you,' she said. 'From Uncle Samuel. Why the hell did you give them an address?'

'Because I couldn't get an emergency leave to see my sick sister without it,' he said.

YOU ARE HEREBY ORDERED TO REPORT TO TERMINAL ISLAND NAVY BASE IMMEDIATELY. JEFFERSON CITY WILL SAIL FOR THE WESTERN PACIFIC IN 48 HOURS.

'God damn it,' Flanagan said. 'They told us we wouldn't sail until the end of July. They must have moved up the date of the invasion.'

She heard the sadness in his voice. He had told her about the rumour that the Japanese had six thousand kamikazes waiting on the home islands. Martha reached for the telephone.

'What are you doing?'

'Calling the shipyard. I just got sick.'

She delivered the message and came back to bed. A line from Yeats ran through Flanagan's mind. *Hearts are not had as a gift but hearts are earned! By those who are not entirely beautiful.*

It was incredible, how much he loved her. A lot of it was the freedom, the boldness, with which she gave herself to him. Everything about her body, from her small coned breasts to her full hard thighs, was right. But her absolute honesty, her courage, were equally important.

'They tell us every rivet we drive is an act of patriotism,' Martha said, putting her arms around him. 'But I've got something more patriotic to do for the rest of the day.'

'I don't like the smell of the whole thing,' Arthur McKay said.

'It could be a good sign. King may have changed his mind about you,' Rita said.

His look silenced her. In the last month he thought they had got beyond worrying about Ernest J. King's opinion of him. But Rita would never stop hoping against hope. It was an inescapable part of that combative spirit she had inherited from her sailor ancestors.

'They're turning my ship into a freighter,' McKay said. 'If I'd gone into the merchant marine, we'd be a lot richer.'

'You just can't stand the thought of taking orders from Duke Pearce.'

'That's true. Why do I dislike that arrogant son of a bitch so much?'

They laughed simultaneously. In other years, Rita would have given him a lecture on the importance of charming someone with Duke Pearce's influence and charisma.

The orders that had sent Captain McKay rushing back to the ship were the strangest he had ever received in his thirty-two years in the Navy. Admiral Tomlinson, still cracking the whip over the yardbirds at Terminal Island, said they were the strangest he had seen in his forty-two years of service.

The *Jefferson City* was to be ready to sail in four days. This meant the skeleton crew on board had to spend the next twenty-four hours sending telegrams to men on leave or attending service schools in various specialities. The moment a man returned, he found himself in a working party, lugging stores or ammunition aboard. The Terminal Island yardbirds cursed and tore their hair as they worked nights to complete the repairs and clear the ship of hoses, tools, debris.

Instead of a leisurely shakedown cruise to make sure the repairs had been properly done, McKay was to take his ship to sea and give it the standard tests en route to San Francisco. There, at the Hunters Point Navy Yard, he was to pick up Captain Warren Pearce, USN, known to his friends as Duke, the cocky genius who had brought them the proximity fuse. He would supervise the loading of two objects of crucial importance to the war effort, for transportation to the island of Tinian.

Neither Captain McKay nor his crew would be told what was inside the two objects. They were not to inquire. Both objects would be guarded by the ship's Marines twenty-four hours a day. In case of an emergency at sea, Captain Pearce would assume command and the crew of the *Jefferson City* would join him in doing their utmost to guarantee the survival of these two objects, which was more important than the survival of the ship.

'What the hell have they cooked up in the laboratory now?' McKay said. 'It must have something to do with stopping the kamikazes. Maybe we're transporting a high-speed printing press. They're going to drop copies of Fanny Farmer's cookbook in Japanese on the aircraft factories. Drive the poor starving bastards crazy.'

'Maybe,' Rita said.

He suddenly sensed she knew the nature of his cargo. Or at least suspected. It was not all that surprising. She had spent half the war listening to Ernest J. King talk away his sleepless nights.

'What is it?'

'I promised I'd never mention it to anyone.'

'I'm not anyone.'

'It's a new kind of bomb. They've been working on it for

years. It's made from uranium. It's the most powerful weapon ever invented.'

'I'll be damned,' Arthur McKay said.

Commander Robert Mullenoe raised his champagne glass. 'To eternal happiness,' he said.

His wife, Christine, who had flown to California the moment she heard the *Jefferson City* was going there, joined him. 'I believe in it, for some ridiculous reason,' she said.

Montgomery West and Ina Severn, aka Joey Shuck and Gwen Pugh, accepted the best wishes. They were drinking champagne in a private room at the Brown Derby. It was a small party by Hollywood standards. Only a dozen people. Preston Sturges and a few other personal friends were from the movie colony. The rest were Navy, Captain McKay and his wife. The chaplain, who had performed the wedding service in the wardroom of the *Jefferson City*. Commander Edwin Moss, who drank too much champagne and kept saying he wished his wife were with them. Like several other officers, Moss had rushed back to the West Coast when the *Jefferson City*'s departure date was abruptly revised.

'My only regret is I have a honeymoon to give for my country,' West said. He gazed mournfully at Gwen. They had planned on two weeks at Lake Tahoe.

'It's a good thing you're marrying a sailor's daughter,' she said.

Suddenly she started to cry. It was the damnedest thing. She lost her marvellous English self-control. She cried and cried. 'I guess I'm going to miss the honeymoon more than I thought,' she said.

Nobody believed a word of it.

At the Pico Avenue landing, Captain McKay and Rita got out of the car and walked to the edge of the dock. His gig was waiting. The coxswain grinned up at him. 'Ready to go when you are, Captain.'

He turned to Rita. 'Goodbye, wife.'

'Goodbye, husband.'

They kissed. It was supposed to be a gallant flourish, no more. But it became something much deeper and somehow sad. He did not understand the sadness; it had a new, hard edge.

It was coming from Rita. She clung to him in a fierce almost angry way. Had a glimpse of the future reached her in a daydream or nightmare? Had she seen a kamikaze plunging into the *Jefferson City*'s bridge?

He climbed down to the gig and the coxswain barked the orders to cast off the bow and stern lines. They headed toward the ship, far out in the harbour. Captain McKay turned in his seat. Rita was waving and crying. Behind her the flat suburban roofs of Long Beach spread out toward the brown California hills. In his mind's eye McKay vaulted those hills and the mighty Rockies beyond them to stand for a moment in America's heartland, on the vast plains of Kansas, where his grandfather had fired the first shots in a war to make the United States truly the land of the free. He felt a rush of love and pride and longing. He wondered if he was seeing his wife, seeing his country, for the last time.

They sat in Martha's old rusting Chevrolet at the Pico Avenue dock. She had insisted on driving him from Seattle.

'I don't even want to look at it,' Martha said.

'Why not? It's a handsome ship,' Flanagan said.

'You know why.'

'I don't know why.'

He assumed she was thinking about Jack Peterson. It made him feel forlorn. He had hoped they had got beyond Jack. Now he wondered if they could ever escape him. He never imagined himself matching Jack's magic with a woman.

'Because I love you, you big Irish jerk. And that miserable tin tub is taking you away from me – maybe for good.'

'I'll come back. If I have to swim all the way.'

'Promise.'

'Promise. Then we're getting married.'

'We'll see. You may change your mind about a lot of things once you're out of that monkey suit.'

'He kissed her. 'Nothing's going to change my mind about you.'

'Oh, shit. Oh, Christ,' She wiped the tears from her cheeks and let him kiss her again. 'Go fight your goddamn war.'

He had the salt taste of her tears on his lips all the way out to the ship.

Mission Imponderable

'All hands. Stand by for full backdown,' boomed the boatswain's mate of the watch.

The *Jefferson City* was boiling north from Long Beach at flank speed, thirty-two knots. 'All engines back full,' Executive Officer George Tombs said, grabbing an overhead stanchion.

The engine telegrapher shoved the annunciator to reverse. The big ship shuddered as if she had run into a brick wall. Metal shrieked and groaned. Water boiled up over the fantail. Slowly, steadily, she began to back down. The propellers were still on their shafts.

'All engines ahead one third,' Tombs said. He smiled at Captain McKay, 'Looks like the yardbirds did a good job, Art. I've never seen her running better.'

'It just shows what getting paid triple overtime will do,' McKay said.

Darkness was falling when they stood into San Francisco's magnificent bay. As they steamed under the Golden Gate Bridge, McKay got on the PA system. 'This is your captain. I know it hurts, men, but there will be no liberty in San Francisco. We're sailing at dawn tomorrow, and I don't want anyone getting in trouble by missing the ship. I'm proud of the hundred-percent return you made as we left Long Beach. I don't want to take a chance on spoiling the record.'

Admiral Tomlinson had told him many ships were sailing

with a hundred to a hundred and fifty men missing from their crews. A lot of sailors were having second thoughts about facing the kamikazes. George Tombs said the crew's hundred-percent showing on such short notice was a tribute to Captain McKay and no one else.

'Stop it, George. You're making me feel venerable,' McKay said, 'If that gets back to Rita, she'll divorce me for sure.'

At the Hunters Point Navy Yard, the pier at which they docked seemed strangely deserted. A closer examination revealed at least a dozen husky men in the shadows. Duke Pearce and two men in Army uniforms came aboard. Pearce introduced them as artillerymen. McKay thought they looked uncomfortable with the word.

'When does the cargo come aboard?' McKay said.

'About 0300.'

'This must be important, Duke.'

'It is.'

Pearce seemed strangely subdued. His cocky grin was gone. 'I trust there's no problem about our occupying flag plot,' he said.

'None whatsoever.'

'How's Rita?'

'Good.'

'I heard about Sammy. I was sorry as hell.'

'Thanks.'

The cargo arrived on two trucks at 0400. McKay had ordered reveille sounded at 0300. A working party from Deck Division One was ready. Quickly they threw straps around the first object, a big rectangular crate. A team of shipfitters secured it to the deck amidships. Two other sailors took the second object off another truck. It was a cylinder about eighteen inches in diameter and two feet high. On orders from Pearce, they slipped a crowbar through a ring and tried to pick it up. Grunts of surprise. The thing was very heavy. They finally got it off the truck and followed Pearce up the gangway into Officers' Country.

In the cabin normally used by the admiral's chief of staff, Commander Moss was waiting with another team of shipfitters. They welded pad eyes to the deck and fitted them with steel straps on hinges. The cylinder was placed in the middle and the straps were closed over it. Duke Pearce secured the cage with a padlock and dropped the key in his pocket.

Back on the main deck, Pearce handed McKay a piece of paper. 'Here's what I'd like to tell your crew, Art.'

EVERY DAY THAT WE CAN SAVE GETTING THIS CARGO TO ITS DESTINATION WILL SHORTEN THE WAR BY A DAY.

On the second night of the voyage, Captain McKay invited Captain Pearce to dinner. 'Well, you got the promotion,' McKay said. 'Congratulations.'

'General Groves, the head of the project, got it for me. The Navy fought him every step of the way. The same old story. Not enough sea duty. It's kind of ironic. This weapon will end the war. That will shut down the project and end my chances of making admiral.'

'You're sure about this miracle weapon? The proximity fuse didn't exactly end our worries about air attacks.'

'We're sure about this one. We've tested it. But' – Pearce stared gloomily at the sirloin steak on his plate – 'not everyone agrees on the best way to use it.'

'But you've got orders.'

Peace nodded. 'Very explicit orders.'

'The fog of war's closing in a little?'

Pearce grimaced at the old War College term. 'More than a little.'

'You've got the mechanism of an atomic bomb in that crate. The cylinder's got uranium 235 in it, right?'

'Jesus Christ! Where did you hear that? I could have you taken off this ship and put under arrest in Pearl Harbor. I could have you court-martialled on the spot.'

'There wouldn't be much point to that, would there?'

Pearce subsided. 'I saw the test at Alamogordo. The night before you got to San Francisco. It flattened everything within three square miles. It blinded a man ten miles away. I've got film in my suitcase to show Nimitz and Spruance.'

'What are you going to do with it?'

'Drop it on a Japanese city.'

'You think that will knock them out of the war?'

'If it doesn't, we're going to drop another one.'

Arthur McKay sat there listening to the throb of the *Jefferson City*'s engines, seeing his ship, her guns, her magazines, her engine rooms. Seeing this warship, returning to battle under his command, her prow cleaving the Pacific. 'I don't like it,' he said.

Pearce stared at his half-eaten steak.

'You don't like it either.'

'I'm proud of creating it. We worked eighteen and twenty hours a day for months at a stretch. But I'm not proud of dropping it. Especially when I'm going to arm it. I'm going to be up in the plane arming it.'

Captain McKay leaned back in his chair and gazed up at the overhead. 'Let me tell you what I'm thinking. This thing gives us a chance to save the lives of my men, the lives of thousands of men on the other ships who might die if the Japanese throw six thousand kamikazes at us in an invasion – but it simultaneously deprives them of a victory they've won with their courage, their seamanship, their loyalty. It gives the Japs a chance to claim, some say, that we'd never have beaten them without this weapon. When in fact we've sunk just about every goddamn ship in the Combined Fleet. That's a hell of a choice. I wonder what the men would say about it if they were given a chance.'

'You think they'd vote in favour of an invasion?' Pearce said, an edge of scorn in his voice. He was not enjoying this conversation.

'Probably not. Why don't you drop it in an open field? Blow a three-mile-wide hole in the ground. That might convince them to quit.'

'We've only got enough uranium for two bombs. We won't have any more for six months. The invasion goes in three months. You've seen the kamikazes. Do you really think these fanatics can be scared into surrendering?'

'The kamikazes aren't fanatics. They're kids who've been told they should die for the Emperor. It's *ran* – part of the

651

tradition of gratitude to family, ancestors, country. The Japanese are only spooky if you don't understand them.'

'I'm afraid a lot of people in Washington don't understand them.'

'How many people do you think this bomb will kill?'

'With the blast – about thirty thousand. Radiation will kill a couple of thousand more. The radiation part is messy. We really don't know what the hell it will do.'

'And you're going to arm it.'

'Yes. There's a B-29 all set up for it, the *Enola Gay*. I've helped train the crew.'

'I can see why you're upset, Duke.'

'Orders are orders, aren't they?'

'We've got a tradition in the Navy – of talking back. Trying, at least once, to change the orders.'

'I'm not in the Navy any more.'

'You're still in it. That's why we're having this conversation.'

'I'm working for an Army general. Who's done a lot more for me than anyone in the Navy ever has.'

McKay sighed. 'I can't tell you what to do, Duke. I can only tell you I don't like it.'

Choices. Was he making one by not telling this young man, his former pupil whose arrogant style concealed a grudging respect for him, to refuse to kill thirty thousand civilians? For a moment dread filled Arthur McKay's soul. Did mere knowledge involve him in this stupendous decision? Could he take legitimate refuge in the chain of command, in the comforting fact that he was not supposed to know anything about this weapon? It was obvious Duke Pearce half wished he would tell him to refuse to obey his orders. But he also wished, yes, even visibly hungered for reassurance.

Even if he convinced him, would it change anything? Someone else would arm the bomb. Duke Pearce's career would join Arthur McKay's in the Navy's junk heap of hopes and promises.

There was another even more demoralising thought. Were they all, as members of the armed forces, as

Americans, part of this decision, whether they chose to be or not? Whether their ignorance remained total or their knowledge as complete as Duke Pearce's? Were they a people in the sight of God, like the Israelites of the Old Testament?

The Captain did not know. He was in a moral world beyond his experience, if not beyond his fears. Suddenly the *Jefferson City* was voyaging into history and beyond it, along the horizon of eternity. Softly, sadly, he repeated his last words.

'I can only tell you I don't like it.'

'I don't like it either,' Duke Pearce said. 'But you do a lot of things you don't like in a war.'

Across the Pacific the *Jefferson City* pounded at flank speed. In the engine rooms and fire rooms, Oz Bradley and his men fretted over their turbines and boilers, shifting the burden whenever a gauge warned them of fatigue. On their first day out, the Captain had visited them with his mysterious passenger, Captain Pearce. He had told them how much he was depending on them to set a speed record to Tinian. Pearce had spent the rest of the day with the black gang, discussing ways to improve the engines' performance. Every one decided he was their sort of guy. He loved machinery.

As the *Jefferson City* approached the submarine net at the mouth of Pearl Harbor, Navigator Marse Lee emerged from his sanctum behind the pilothouse. 'We've just set a world's record for a ship sailing between San Francisco and Hawaii,' he said. 'The old record was seventy-nine hours. We've done it in seventy-eight and a half.'

Captain McKay passed the information to the crew. 'Balls,' roared Flanagan, who had bet ten dollars on the anchor pool. Marty Roth, who had the mathematical brain to figure out the probability of an early arrival, won.

At Pearl, they stopped only long enough to refuel. They were back at sea, pounding west again, before the end of the day. Homewood was wistful. 'I was gonna visit one of them little Chinese girls on River Street,' he said. 'Behave myself too.'

'Sure,' Flanagan said, razzing him as usual.

'You gonna marry that girl?' Homewood said. Flanagan had introduced him to Martha when they drove down from Seattle. They had spent the night at Homewood's San Pedro apartment.

'I hope so.'

'You can't go to Annapolis if you're married.'

'I don't want to go to Annapolis, Boats.'

'Jesus Christ, I ain't surprised. You've turned into a fuckin' yeoman in front of my eyes.'

Homewood was referring to the time Flanagan spent editing and writing the ship's paper. It appalled the boatswain to see a sailor he liked pounding a typewriter.

'The hell I have. Give me a knot. Any knot.'

Homewood pulled a piece of line from his pocket. 'Carrick bend.'

Flanagan bent the line into a figure eight.

'Timber and a half hitch.'

He looped the line over the railing outside main forward, snaked it through two loops and flipped it over the rail in one large reinforcing loop.

'You got a great future in the Navy. I know it.'

'Too much regimentation for me, Boats. I'm a free spirit.'

'Aw, bullshit. I got that line from Peterson. What'd he ever do with his fuckin' freedom except get into trouble? You're goin' the same way, I can see it.'

The aerographer joined them with his balloon. Homewood drew him into the argument. 'You're stayin' in, ain't you, Eric?'

'Goddamn right,' Eric said as the balloon soared into the blue sky. 'The minute this war ends, the fucking country is going to nosedive into another depression. You don't have to worry about that in the Navy.'

'That settles it,' Flanagan said. 'I'm going to become a stockbroker. When you predict disaster, I know there's nothing to worry about.'

'What about the typhoon?' the prophet indignantly demanded.

'You've got to get lucky once in your life.'

'What do you think's in that goddamn coffin amidships, Eric?' Homewood asked.

Eric shrugged. 'Maybe it's for the body of Halsey's aerographer,' Flanagan said. 'While we were back in the States, he sailed them into another typhoon.'

Homewood gazed up at Eric's dwindling balloon, then started gloomily at the timber and a half hitch on the rail. 'Wiseguy,' he said.

He left Flanagan there feeling like a crumb.

He still did not like it, Arthur McKay thought, as he watched a half dozen admirals and Army Air Force generals swarming on to his quarterdeck at Tinian. They congratulated him for his swift passage, but they pumped Duke Pearce's hand with far more enthusiasm. McKay did not like the greedy anticipation in their smiles. They were too cocky, too eager to get on with the business of the bomb. The idea of advising Pearce to walk out on the project swiftly became ridiculous.

Over the side, using their seaplane crane, went the coffin. The cylinder was lowered into another boat. Pearce held out his hand. 'Thanks for the transportation, Art.'

'Good luck.'

'I'll need all of that I can find.'

In an hour, the *Jefferson City* was under way for Guam, CINCPAC's new headquarters. Later in the day, they stood into Apra's oval harbour. What now? McKay wondered. Would they ever bother to send them to the war zone? Those grins on the faces of the brass at Tinian made him think the war really was about to end.

McKay went ashore in his gig and reported to CINCPAC. His classmate Byron Maher, still a captain thanks to Ernie King's unrelenting son-of-a-bitch code, invited him to lunch with Admiral Spruance. They sat on an airy veranda and ate Spruance's usual meal – salad and soup. The Admiral looked as spare and fit as ever. He liked the news that the *Jefferson City* had broken the speed record to Pearl Harbor. 'I must mention that to Chester, so he can put it in his next letter to King.'

The admirals were still feuding.

Spruance told him there was no point in having the cruiser sit in Apra Harbor. She might as well join the Fifth Fleet which was operating off captured Okinawa. 'You'll have to go to Leyte for refresher training,' he said. 'The staff and I will be moving to Manila soon. We can pick you up there.'

'What are you planning these days?' McKay asked. 'The invasion or the surrender of Japan?'

'A little of both,' Spruance said warily.

'No one's told me anything,' McKay said. 'But I gather we're going to drop something awfully heavy on them.'

Spruance's normally impassive face convulsed. 'Pearce flew over from Tinian last night to show us the pictures. I think it's monstrous! I'd rather lose four hundred ships than drop it!'

Byron Maher looked appalled. In his old-womanish chief-of-staff way, he perpetually worried about his boss getting into trouble. 'Admiral, those opinions simply can't be . . . stated.'

'I know it. They won't be. Except to people I trust.'

After lunch, Captain McKay strolled down to the Naval Operating Base near the harbour and asked to see the convoy and routing officer. He was a pleasant young lieutenant junior grade, with a desk awash in papers. They discussed what route the *Jefferson City* would take to Leyte and the speed at which she would travel. McKay quickly discovered he did not have much choice. The top speed was fifteen knots, to conserve oil. The route, Course Peddie, was practically a straight line.

'What about escort?' McKay said.

'I don't think there's one available,' the Lieutenant said.

'Could you inquire? We don't have any sonar gear on a cruiser.'

'I *know* that, sir,' the Lieutenant said.

He telephoned the office of the admiral in command of the Marianas. 'Is there an escort available for a cruiser going to Leyte?'

'Not necessary,' said a gravel voice on the other end of the phone.

The Lieutenant glowered at the phone. 'They treat us like shit over there,' he said. 'Excuse my French, sir. The policy is pretty set, Captain. That's MacArthur's Navy in the Philippines, and we don't send any escorts, because the bastards don't send them back. We spend more time fighting them than we do the Japs. Anyway, there haven't been any serious submarine contacts in the waters between here and there for months.'

'OK,' McKay said. Having decided it was not his job to order the President around, he was not about to try to change the way General MacArthur and the Navy had divided up the Pacific.

Twenty-eight hours later, the *Jefferson City* was steaming toward Leyte on Course Peddie. At 2300 hours McKay went up to the bridge to have a last look around before going to sleep. The sky was overcast, with only a slice of a moon showing through the clouds. The day had been uneventful. One or two contacts with submarines had been reported by nearby merchant ships. They were periscope sightings, a not unusual phenomenon. Sailors on merchant ships seemed to specialize in seeing periscopes. So did their captains. In three years of war, the *Jefferson City* had received at least five hundred such reports. No one ever paid any attention to them.

During the day, the ship had been zigzagging, standard procedure in a war zone. When darkness fell, and visibility under the clouds sank to minimum levels, McKay had told the Officer of the Deck he could quit zigzagging, which was a useless manoeuvre in his opinion, anyway. If a submarine was lurking out there, a zigzag course might carry you towards rather than away from it.

The one thing he did not like about their course was the speed. Travelling at fifteen knots, the ship could be overtaken by a submarine. If CINCPAC had let her clip along at close to flank speed, only incredible luck could give a submarine a shot at them. The sub would have to be sitting right on their course, a one in ten thousand chance in an ocean as big as the Pacific.

Commander Moss was the Officer of the Deck. The weather was deteriorating, the barometer falling. The sea was choppy, almost rough. 'Anything happening that I should know, Ed?' McKay asked.

'Not a thing, Captain. I just checked with CIC. They're as bored as we are.'

'In that case, you better needle the lookouts every half hour.'

'Aye, aye, Captain.'

'Where are the night orders?'

The quartermaster of the watch handed him the documents, prepared as usual, by Navigator Marse Lee. McKay signed them without reading a line. It was the kind of routine that made a captain feel good. It demonstrated the mutual trust between him and his men.

'Captain,' Moss said as McKay was leaving the bridge, 'was that stuff we brought out to Tinian bacteriological warfare?'

'No.'

'I'm glad to hear that. Good night, Captain.'

Back in his cabin, McKay wrote a letter to Mildred Meade, thanking her for 'persuading' Rita to come to California. *Only the truest of friends, which you will remain forever in my heart, would have done it.*

He was turning into a sentimental slob.

Horace Aquino came in to ask him if he would like a cup of tea or some broth. The steward talked excitedly about getting to Manila at last. Only one thing troubled him. He did not have the right to wear a chief petty officer's uniform. Chief mess stewards had grey, inferior-looking uniforms. 'I have served in the American Navy for twenty-five years, Captain. Why won't they let me wear the same uniform as other men with such long service?'

'Write to Admiral King about it. I'll give you his address tomorrow.'

Aquino departed. McKay pondered the painting of the Chinese traveller for a moment. He turned out the light and lay down in his bunk. Ten seconds later, a tremendous explosion tore through the *Jefferson City*. McKay knew instantly it was a torpedo in the bow. He sprang out of his bunk. His feet were barely on the deck when a second, more terrible blast ripped into her amidships. The shock of the second explosion seemed to rush like a terrific jolt of electricity up the ship's steel frame into the Captain's body. His head snapped back; he felt bones break in his neck. He was flung to the deck as if a violent hand had gripped him by the throat. Around him bulkheads buckled, beams crashed down, trapping him in a maze of wreckage.

On the bridge, Edwin Moss stared in disbelief at the sheet of red-yellow flame that rose above the bow. My fault, he thought. My responsibility. The shock wave hurled him against the bulkhead. Half the men around him were knocked to the deck.

The second explosion was much more violent and more deadly. For eighteen months Moss had spent much of his waking hours thinking about ways to preserve the *Jefferson City* if a torpedo struck her. He knew exactly where she was most vulnerable – amidships, where the second torpedo had hit. In his mind's eye he saw tons of water rushing into fire rooms and other compartments that would fatally destroy the ship's metacentric balance, already too low from the extra guns on her deck.

For a half minute after the second explosion, there was total silence. The only sounds were the rush of the sea, the throb of the turbines. The talker staggered to his feet and Moss said, 'Get Damage Control.'

'Everything is dead on the sound phones, sir,' the talker said.

'Stop the engines,' Moss said to the engine telegrapher.

The sailor shoved the annunciator handle to stop. 'I don't get a response, sir,' he said.

The *Jefferson City* continued to churn ahead through the moonless, starless darkness. Moss knew tons of water were gushing into the smashed bow. 'Go below and pass the word, "All hands topside,"' he ordered the messenger.

From deep in the ship emanated the most chilling sounds Moss had ever heard. A weird combination of groans and shrieks. 'Where's the Captain?' he asked, amazed that McKay had not yet reached the bridge.

'I'll go get him,' said Ensign Brownmiller, the junior officer of the deck.

He was back in thirty seconds. 'He's trapped in his cabin. The explosion buckled the hatches on both sides. He says he's hurt. He can't move.'

The ship was beginning to list to starboard, the bow plunging deeper and deeper into the dark sea. 'Get some shipfitters up there. We've got to get the Captain out of that cabin,' Moss said.

He sent the boatswain's mate of the watch to the radio room with orders to send out an SOS. He told the engine telegrapher to go below and order everyone out of the fire rooms and engine rooms.

George Tombs appeared on the bridge. 'Where's the Captain?' he said. 'I recommend we abandon ship.'

On the main deck. Flanagan tied the straps of his kapok life jacket with trembling fingers. It could not be happening. Torpedoes, their old enemies from the Solomon Islands. Torpedoes, not kamikazes.

The *Jefferson City* shuddered and groaned again. He had never heard such unearthly sounds. 'She's finished,' Homewood said. 'That's the good spirits givin' up on her. I can't understand it. I was sure the Captain's joss'd get us through somehow. I thought maybe we'd take a couple more kamikazes, but never this.'

'What do we do?' Flanagan asked. He was a raw recruit again. So were the rest of F Division, those who had got out of the compartment after the second torpedo hit.

'Start cuttin' away that life raft,' Homewood said, pointing to the raft on turret two. 'We're gonna need anything that can float pretty soon.'

Montgomery West had been sitting in the wardroom watching' and listening to Lieutenant MacComber, Chaplain

Bushnell, and Dr Cadwallader playing bridge with a new ensign just out of Annapolis. MacComber was giving him his usual line about the Academy being a waste of time. Bob Mullenoe sat nearby making acrid remarks about Southern disloyalty.

The first torpedo knocked everyone out of their chairs and sent flames roaring down the passageway from Officer's Country. The second one hit just beneath them, and the whole room burst into flame, like the inside of a giant firecracker. West rolled under the table to escape the first gush of flame and in one continuous movement worthy of Douglas Fairbanks, Sr, escaped the second flash by coming out the other side and diving headfirst through the pantry window, landing on top of the mess steward of the watch, Willard Otis.

The flash fire died away. West stumbled back into the charred wardroom and found Bob Mullenoe lying on the deck, his hair, his arms, his chest aflame. West tore off his own jacket and beat out the fire. 'Get him up on deck,' he said to Otis.

'There's fire everywhere!' Otis said. Flames were roaring through the hatches fore and aft.'

The chaplain crawled over to them. 'I think Dr Cadwallader's dead,' he said. 'So is Lieutenant Mac-Comber.'

Smoke was rapidly filling the wardroom. West dashed to a porthole and tore it open. He stuck out his head to get a gulp of air and a manrope dangling from the main deck hit him in the face. With the help of the chaplain and Otis, he lifted the semiconscious Mullenoe through the porthole and hoisted him to the main deck. He went down to pull out the chaplain. When he returned for Otis, the steward lifted MacComber up to him. 'I heard him screamin'. He was lyin' in the fire,' he said.

MacComber's face looked like underdone steak. The flames were roaring all around Otis. 'Put your arms around my neck!' West said.

'I'm goin' below to see if I can help my buddies!'

'They're all dead. That second torpedo hit right under

their compartment,' West said. 'Get out here. That's an order!'

Otis climbed out the porthole and grabbed West around the neck. As sailors hauled them up to the main deck, flames leaped out the porthole, searing West's legs.

Marty Roth had been standing the top watch in the after fire room when the torpedoes hit. Looking down on the four men on the deckplates before the boilers, he saw a wall of water and oil from the reserve tanks burst over them. He leaped to the ladder that led to the ventilator shaft. The water was swirling around his feet as he got to it. Behind him, he saw the terrified face of his striker. Roth had calmed his fear of the engine room by showing him how to get out fast, the way Amos Cartwright had showed him almost three years ago. Now Roth grabbed the striker's outstretched arm and hauled him on to the ladder. Together they scrambled up the dark narrow tube to the top, where Roth shoved open the hatch and stumbled on to the main deck.

Where was his Abandon Ship station? Where was a life preserver? 'What's gonna happen? Are we sinking?' the striker asked.

'I think so,' Roth said. He was amazed at how calm he was. Amos, he prayed, if you've got any influence where you are now, help me out.

An officer came by. It was Commander Moss. He was handing out life jackets. He had Marines with him, each carrying a half dozen of the bulky things. 'Is there anyone here from the black gang?' Moss asked.

'Here. Watertender Roth, sir.'

'We can't get them on the telephones. Go down there and make sure everyone knows we're abandoning ship.'

It was a terrifying reversal of the race he had run three years ago, when Amos Cartwright showed him how fast he could escape from the fire room. Down the ladders Roth clattered to the after engine room. For a moment he thought he was hallucinating. Lights blazed, the turbines throbbed. Oz Bradley was on the telephone, urgently calling the bridge.

'Abandon Ship. They told me to pass the word,' he shouted from the top plates.

'Who told you?' Bradley roared.

'Commander Moss.'

'That birdbrain hasn't got the authority to give that order,' Bradley growled. 'We staying here till we get it from the Captain.'

'Everything amidships is gone. Power, light. The forward fire room and engine room are under water.'

Terror blanked the faces of the enlisted men. Bradley was unmoved. 'All the more reason for us to stay on duty.'

The ship listed another ten degrees to port. It was time to stop arguing with Commander Bradley. Roth fled up the ladders to the main deck. As he got there, the list became a lurch. The *Jefferson City* was starting to roll over. Roth decided it was time to get in the water.

Outside the Captain's cabin, shipfitters and machinist's mates directed by George Tombs attacked the crumpled bulkheads and twisted steel beams with sledgehammers and welding torches and metal cutting saws.

'We'll get you out, Captain, don't worry,' one shouted.

Above the crunch of the hammers and the rasp of the saws, Captain McKay heard the shrieks and groans of his ship's death throes. The deck shuddered beneath him.

"Art,' George Tombs shouted, 'are you badly hurt?'

'Yes. I'm pretty sure my neck is broken.'

'I recommend we abandon ship. She's losing seaworthiness fast. Should I pass the word?'

'Yes. Abandon ship. Take those men with you. She's going to roll over any minute, George.'

'Captain, I swear to Christ we can get you out,' the shipfitter roared.

'Abandon ship. That's an order.'

The deck tilted steeply under Captain McKay, sliding him against the crumbled bulkhead. He looked up and saw Win Kemble standing beside the painting of the Chinese traveller. They were in darkness now, the blackest imaginable darkness, but Arthur McKay somehow saw the friend of his life, pointing to the image of the sage descending the mountain in the mists of Asia a thousand years ago.

Blood streamed from Win's eye. He glared triumphantly at Arthur McKay. *Now do you believe me?* he said. *Do you still believe in your ridiculous ideas about loyalty, compassion, brotherhood?*

Win was asking for his soul. He was asking Arthur McKay to join him in eternal loneliness.

No. In this moment of supreme terror and grief there was still a sense, a knowledge, of purpose. They were playing two parts. One was innocence, courage, honour, crucified by meaningless accident. That was the way the world would see the fate of the *Jefferson City*. The way her crew would see it for a long time, perhaps for ever. But the Captain saw they were also playing another part in a larger drama. They were the sacrifice, the bullock laid on the sea's altar to warn men that God still watched over the world. From an immense distance His hand could still reach out to warn, to teach, to chastise.

Would Americans see the meaning? He doubted it. But he saw it. It gave Arthur McKay the strength to repudiate Win Kemble's choice, one last time.

Tears of grief for his friend, for himself, streamed down his face. 'It was still wrong, Win. It's not all illusion. I won't come with you.'

Win's face contorted into a mask of rage more terrible than anything Arthur McKay had ever seen. From his mouth came the wail of a damned soul. Then he was gone and the *Jefferson City* was gone too. The sea thundered up through the compartments to swallow the living and the dead. Captain McKay heard it rumbling towards him. Mingled with it were the screams of men still trapped below decks.

His men, his crew! Would any of them ever understand, accept, the sacrifice they were becoming? All he could offer was a captain's version of the sceptic's prayer. *O Lord, I believe, help thou their unbelief.* Without reproach to God or man, Arthur McKay accepted his sailor's death.

On deck, Homewood seized Flanagan's shoulder. 'Did you hear that?' he shouted.

All Flanagan and everyone else heard was another

unearthly shriek, not so different from previous ones coming from the hull. But it was the signal Homewood seemed to be waiting for. 'She's finished,' he said. 'Let's get in the water. Remember what I told you about stickin' together. We're five hundred miles from land. Stick together and the Navy'll be here by noon tomorrow.'

The deck suddenly turned into a vertical skidway. There was no need to jump into the ocean. The sea rose to meet them. Flanagan got a glimpse of the mainmast crashing down on men already in the water. He went in headfirst and swallowed a nauseating mouthful of oil. Homewood was beside him, shouting to the others to push the raft free. No one paid any attention to him. They were too busy trying to get away from the ship.

The stern of the *Jefferson City* loomed over them for another few seconds, one of the screws still slowly turning. With a sucking sigh she plunged beneath the surface. They were alone on the dark face of the Pacific.

O Hear Us When We Cry to Thee

For Frank Flanagan the first hours in the water were pure nausea. The oil he had swallowed made him violently ill. He puked until his whole body ached. So did almost every other member of F Division. The heavy chop of the sea sloshed more oil in their faces. It burned their eyes and nostrils and puckered their lips. In the moonless darkness, they rapidly became demoralised. Flanagan heard men sobbing and praying.

Homewood spent the night steadying them. He swam around them, urging them, to stay together. 'They'll be out to get us as soon as it's light,' he shouted.

The sun rose to reveal they were part of a pod of perhaps a hundred and twenty men in the middle of a vast heaving slick of oil. About a half mile north was another pod of about three hundred men, also in the oil. Smaller groups were spread out almost to the horizon. In the centre of Flanagan's pod was a life raft. In it were Jerome Wilkinson and a half dozen of his friends.

Some men had no life jackets. They clung to cork-rimmed floater nets which had been attached to the turrets and bulkheads above decks and automatically rose to the surface when the ship went down. Others were depending on rubber belts, inflated by a capsule of CO_2. Others were using crates, empty ammunition cans and other pieces of flotsam to raise themselves a few inches above the surface of the sea.

Homewood circled the pod and swam back to Flanagan. 'I can't figure it out. There ain't no officers worth mentionin'. What happened to them?'

'The two torpedoes bracketed Officers' Country,' Montgomery West said. 'Most of them never got out of their staterooms.'

West was unrecognizable, his handsome face smeared with fuel oil. He was supporting another man, equally smeared. It took Flanagan a moment to realize it was their gunnery officer, Commander Mullenoe. A few feet away, Mess Steward Willard Otis was holding Lieutenant Mac-Comber's head above water. He was babbling a woman's name. It sounded like, 'Melanie'.

'Somebody's got to take charge of these guys, fast, Lieutenant,' Homewood said to West. 'It looks like you're it.'

Dr Levy swam over to them. 'We've got a lot of wounded men,' he said. 'We can't do anything for them in the water. Let's get as many as possible on the life raft.'

They pushed through the ring of men around the raft. 'Make way, make way,' Homewood roared. Flanagan, his strength returning as his stomach settled, helped Otis drag Lieutenant MacComber. Neither had a life jacket.

At the raft, West said, 'If you people aren't hurt, get in the water. We need this raft for the wounded.'

'Go fuck yourself,' Wilkinson said. 'I cut this fuckin' raft away and it's mine. No one's gettin' in it who ain't a pal of mine.'

'That's mutiny, you son of a bitch,' Homewood said.

'Yeah? Put me on report, you butt sucker,' Wilkinson said.

Mullenoe opened his seared eyes. In a voice that was barely a croak, he said, 'Wilkinson, get out of that raft.'

'I'll get out. But I ain't goin' more than a foot away from it. I'm gonna be the first guy back in when the sharks arrive.'

A ripple of fear swept through the men in the water. There were about a dozen manropes on the side of the raft. Wilkinson kicked away six men clinging to them and appropriated them for him and his friends. West and Flanagan got into the raft and started pulling Mullenoe aboard.

'No, no,' he said. They paid no attention to him. They assumed he was crying out from the pain of his burns.

'Put me back in the water,' he said as Homewood towed a half dozen wounded men towards them.

'No, Bob,' West said.

'The men come first,' he said. 'I don't think I'm going to make it anyway.'

'Yes you are!' West said.

'Put me back.'

They lowered him into the water, and someone gave him a manrope. To their amazement, when they tried to haul Lieutenant MacComber aboard, he imitated Mullenoe's example. For the next half hour, Flanagan and Homewood towed other wounded men to the raft. West and Levy hauled them aboard, jamming a half dozen on the oval bottom, sitting them on the sides if they had the strength. At least twenty others drifted nearby in their life jackets, many barely conscious. Levy did what he could for them. But he had no instruments or medicine, except some surettes of morphine which he had grabbed as he fled sick bay.

West wondered if God was mocking Levy and his faith in science. All the doctor could offer these men was a few shreds of information. Levy gave a lecture on how to survive a shark attack. 'Just float as quietly as possible on your back. The chances are good they'll go away.' He spent even more time warning them against drinking salt-water. 'It causes convulsions. It's a horrible way to die,' he said.

By ten o'clock they had discovered another enemy: the sun. It beat on them with tropic ferocity. Flanagan could feel his lips swelling, blistering. The glare on the water was unbearable. Soon there were cries of panic. 'Doctor, I'm going blind.'

'It's photophobia,' Dr Levy said. 'Like snowblindness. Close your eyes. It'll help.'

Flanagan and others obeyed and were horrified to discover that their pupils glowed like two red balls in their heads. Some of them could not handle it.

'We're turning into freaks,' one of the Bobbsey Twins cried.

'Into deep-sea fish,' the other one said.

'No you ain't,' Homewood said. 'Cut the bullshit. The less talkin' the better.'

'Mr West,' asked Fire Controlman Ralph Bourne, West's old nemesis in main plot, 'did we get off an SOS?'

'I'm sure we did,' West lied.

The sun beat down. One of the wounded men sitting on the side of the raft pointed to the edge of the pod. 'Oh, Christ,' he said.

'What is it?' Flanagan asked. It was difficult to see above the heads of the men around him. He boosted himself up on the raft and saw a half dozen black fins moving back and forth through the dark blue water.

'Ahhhh!'

A scream from a man on the fringe of the group. He flailed the water with his hands, and Flanagan saw the froth swiftly turn to blood. Dr Levy stared in dismay as hysteria annihilated his scientific advice. Men beat the water to drive the killers away. At least a dozen abandoned the group and swam off to form a small pod of their own around a crate. Wilkinson climbed back on the raft, flinging wounded men into the water. The sharks struck again and again. Then for no reason anyone could discern, they vanished.

West ordered Wilkinson back in the water. Spewing curses, he obeyed.

'Where's the fuckin' chaplain?' Homewood said. 'We could use some prayers.'

Chaplain Bushnell was with the 300-man pod. Discipline was much better in this group. The Executive Officer, George Tombs, and the Damage Control Officer, Edwin Moss, were with them; Tombs took charge. They too had their quota of badly burned and wounded. There were two rafts in the centre of their pod, and the wounded were placed in them with no arguments. Bushnell did his best to console them. Like Dr Levy he assured everyone they were going to be fine, and rescue was certain to come before the end of the day.

Commander Tombs promptly made a fool out of him. Someone asked him if an SOS had been sent.

'I ordered one, but with all the power knocked out I doubt if they got it off,' he said.

'When'll they start looking for us?' Marty Roth asked. He had swallowed oil when he hit the water and had been sick most of the night, like Flanagan.

'Tomorrow is the soonest we can hope for,' Tombs said. 'That's when we're due at Leyte.'

'Tomorrow?'

The thought of spending another night in the water horrified everyone. Chaplain Bushnell urged them to pray. While they said the Our Father in unison, he asked himself why he had been spared from the flash of flame that had incinerated the wardroom. What was the purpose behind it? His intellect told him there was none. It was all part of the cosmic joke nature had played on man two million years ago, when it allowed him to develop a brain that asked why. But his battered heart persisted in asking the question and in hoping for an answer.

'A plane! Oh, Christ, look, a plane!' someone yelled.

Photophobic eyes were lifted to the glaring sky. It was four o'clock in the afternoon, 1600 hours Navy time. They had been in the water sixteen hours and it already seemed like sixteen thousand.

The murderous sun glinted on a silver fuselage, no larger than a fingertip. It had to be flying at 25,000 feet. They watched it bore into the blue distance.

'They've got to be lookin' for us,' Homewood said. 'Why are the dumb bastards flyin' so high?'

'They're afraid we might shoot them down,' Flanagan said.

'There's a Very pistol in the raft. Should we fire it?' Dr Levy asked.

'What do you think, Boats?' West asked.

'Too high,' Homewood said.

As night fell, the wind rose and the water turned cold. For many it seemed like death was creeping from the deep with icy fingers. For some death was real.

'West,' Mullenoe whispered. 'I can't hang on any longer. I wanted to stay till dark, so the men wouldn't see me go. Take off my life jacket and give it to someone who needs it.'

'Bob, they'll be here tomorrow. We're due at Leyte tomorrow. They've got to start looking for us.'

'Take off the jacket.'

Weeping, West obeyed him.

'The men are your responsibility now.'

'I'll do my best.'

'Tell Christine I still want the boy to go to the Academy.'

'I will.'

Mullenoe let go of the rope and drifted into the darkness. West passed the life jacket to Homewood, who gave it to one of the men clinging to the floater net. Back at the raft, Wilkinson raged at Homewood. 'Where's your fuckin' rescue ships, big shot?'

'They'll be here tomorrow sure,' Homewood said.

It was a bad night. The darkness was ripped by screams and cries and sobs as sharks attacked again and smaller fish, perhaps barracudas, tore chunks of flesh from men's legs and buttocks. Dr Levy swam out to these new wounded and tried to stanch the flow of blood with tourniquets of cloth ripped from shirts.

Other men fell asleep and drifted away from the group. Their cries of terror filled the distance as they struggled to swim back in the clumsy life jackets through the choppy sea. Flanagan and Homewood swam out to some of them and towed them back. 'Don't sleep. If you can't stay awake tie yourself to another guy with your belt,' Homewood shouted.

In the darkness Flanagan actually swam into a shark. He felt the careening bulk of the monster against his chest. Apparently the fish was as frightened as the human. It vanished into the night and Flanagan dragged his sobbing drifter back to the group.

As the sun rose on their second day in the water, it seemed to speak a word: *thirst*. No one had had anything to drink for thirty-six hours. The word expanded in everyone's brain until by noon it was written on the horizon in gigantic letters. What made it terrifying was the omnipresent water in which they floated. The water that was death. The water that yearned to swallow them as much as they yearned to swallow it.

A small sip couldn't hurt you, Flanagan thought as it lapped around him.

'Don't drink it,' Homewood said, raising his big fist in front of Flanagan's face. 'If I see you drinkin' it I'll knock your fuckin' teeth down your throat.'

Dr Levy climbed into the raft and found that four of the burn cases had died. They stripped off their life jackets and shoved the bodies to the edge of the group. They drifted away like flotsam. It was horrible.

Maybe it was seeing the dead, maybe it was simply the thirst. By noon men started coming apart. Bob Hansen, one of the Bobbsey Twins, swam up to Flanagan. 'Drink the water,' he said. 'It doesn't hurt you.'

'No,' Flanagan said. 'Boats. He's drinking the water!'

'It doesn't hurt you,' the twin said and scooped a swallow with his hands. 'It tastes great.'

'On the level, Bob?' asked the other twin, Bob Finch.

'Have I ever lied to you?'

Finch drank it too. 'You're right. It does taste great.'

Homewood reached them in time to knock the next swallow away from Finch's mouth. 'Stop it,' he shouted. 'You're gonna die like a fuckin' blowfish on the beach!'

In this swirling hysteria, there was a small island of calm. A half dozen men from turret three had got off the ship with Johnny Chase. They formed a circle around him, convinced Chase would survive, if anyone did. He talked to them in the same calm emotionless voice he had used in the turret. 'It ain't dyin' you have to worry about. That's the easiest thing in the world. I done it. I know what I'm talkin' about. It's a lot harder to stay alive, anywhere, anyplace. You assholes are gonna do it because you owe it to me and Ensign Babyface.'

A different crisis confronted the northern group. Around noon, George Tombs died. He had exhausted himself swimming around their group during the night, chasing drifters. A barracuda had taken a fearful slash out of his leg during one of these expeditions. His last words were 'You're in command now, Moss.'

Edwin Moss almost laughed in the dying man's face. Moss was grappling with a terrific sense of doom. His naval career, his life, had been one long slide to this final disaster. He was one of the damned, one of those whom God consigned to hell for reasons only He understood. Perhaps he was already there.

Bushnell divined what Moss was thinking. He understood Moss's Presbyterian soul and Flanagan's Catholic soul and Captain Kemble's faithless soul and Homewood's Baptist soul. Now Bushnell suddenly knew his own soul. He was ready to give his first sincere sermon.

He stood on the raft and preached an elegy for George Washington Tombs's honest soul, which transcended sects and churches. 'There's a time to live and a time to die. Commander Tombs died as he wanted to live – as an officer

672

leading his men. Leading them, helping them, caring for them. He did not question God or the Navy or his country for our terrible plight. He didn't waste his time, his strength, in such pointless exercises. Let us imitate his example. Let us pray Job's prayer: "Yea though he destroyeth me, yet will I worship Him." This is our challenge, our fate – to say that prayer and mean it!'

Homewood's authority was eroding. It was noon and there was not a sign of a rescue ship or plane. At various points in the pod, other people began drinking saltwater. Within an hour the convulsions began. Dr Levy could only watch and weep at the futility of science. Others swam away from the thrashing, cursing victims who beat the traitor sea with their fists and howled like dogs at the glaring sun. When they died, they too were stripped of their life jackets and allowed to drift away.

'Bob, Bob,' sobbed the surviving Bobbsey Twin.

'We oughta say some prayers for them,' Homewood said. 'Where's the fuckin' chaplain? Did he go down with the ship?'

'Here I am,' Emerson Bushnell said. He had swum down from the northern group, almost a half mile away. He did not try to explain it. He had just begun swimming in response to a sense that these men needed him. He had always been a good swimmer. But he was fifty-eight years old. He did not think he was capable of swimming a half mile with a life jacket on. Strange things were happening in his body and soul.

From the raft in Flanagan's group, Bushnell preached another sermon on confronting their fate and courage and prayer. Flanagan saw the chaplain was asking them to take a leap of faith – a leap he had finally taken himself. Faced with the absurd, he was the one man on the ship capable of surmounting it. Could he persuade them to follow him?

A shark attack began within seconds after Bushnell finished his sermon. Wilkinson climbed back into the raft and threw the chaplain into the water. 'I always thought you were a fuckin' asshole, and now I know it,' he yelled. He picked up the Very pistol in the raft. 'Fuck God,' he said. 'This is what's gonna save us. If the fuckin' Navy ever gets around to lookin' for us.'

The last of the wounded died as the second day ended. Lieutenant West said they would take turns sitting in the raft during the night. Wilkinson announced that no one was getting into the raft who was not a friend of his. He meant it. When Homewood tried to climb in to throw him out, he kicked him in the face. Homewood tried to turn the raft over, but it was too big. He tried to rally a team of men to join him, but no one responded. His status as a leader was gone.

Instead, some men wheedled and begged Wilkinson to let them come aboard. He exacted tributes from them. A potato, a knife, a flashlight, a shirt to protect his head from the sun.

Homewood grew more and more enraged. He denounced Wilkinson and his sycophants. He swore that he would see them all court-martialled and hanged within a week of their rescue.

'What happens if we're the only ones still alive, Big Shot?' Wilkinson sneered.

'I'll get you before I go, Wilkinson,' Homewood said. 'I'll get you if I got to chew a hole in that fuckin' raft with my teeth.'

'He's going apeshit. He thinks he's a fuckin' shark,' Wilkinson said.

Everyone on the raft thought that was a howler. They laughed and laughed in the darkness. In the sea around them, men wept and cursed.

The chaplain swam back to the other group as darkness fell. He found them in chaos. Men had begun drinking saltwater and were dying in agony. Others were fighting over the water bottles in the two rafts. There had been another shark attack. Moss was doing nothing. He floated in his life jacket like a dead man, staring into the twilight.

'Commander!' Bushnell said. 'You're acting more like a

moonstruck divinity student than a US Navy officer. When are you finally going to abandon your ridiculous egocentricity and become a true member of the human race? Even if you're doomed to hell by your ridiculous theology, wouldn't you rather go as a man?'

'What can I do?'

'Take command of these men. Give them some leadership, some example.'

'What good will it do? We didn't get off that radio message. No one pays much attention if a ship's overdue. All sorts of things could explain the delay. They won't start looking for us for a week. We'll all be dead by then.'

'Even if that's true, let's die like men instead of sheep. Let's start rotating people in the rafts. Let's try to stop them from drinking saltwater. Let's pray.'

He was trying to rip Moss's undeveloped soul out of his body, trying to whelp it into this world of murderous sun and deadly water. Trying to create impossible faith in an invisible improbable god. Exultance rang through the chaplain's being. This was what he was born to do!

Another night of horror – of struggling against sleep, which had become the precursor of death. Of waves slopping oil and cold water in the face. Or realizing that the kapok life jackets were beginning to lose their buoyancy.

On the raft, Wilkinson continued his programme of barter and revenge. No one got on who did not pay some form of obeisance to him. He had a knife and made it clear he was not afraid to use it.

As the third day began, Flanagan's tongue was too swollen to move in his mouth. His chin was only inches from the water. Almost everyone else was in the same condition. He noticed the group had grown smaller during the night, even though there had not been a shark attack. People were just giving up, slipping out of their life jackets and drifting down into the darkness.

Flanagan thought about the chaplain's proposition. He thought about dying. Did it depend on his faith in a god?

No, the answer to not dying lay in his life, not in faith in a god who had condemned him to this agony. He thought about his reasons for living. He had promised Annie Flood he would not die. He was in love with Martha Johnson. She was waiting for him. She needed him. If he died she would take to the sauce and never stop. He thought about Martha's vibrant body, her confident passion. Woman. She was his reason for living.

Bullshit, Jack Peterson whispered from somewhere beneath the sea. *Woman's your reason for not living, kid. She'll drive you nuts just like your mother drove your old man. Just like my mother drove my old man. They want to remake you their way, kid. They want to cut your balls off. Why not come down here with me, where it's cool and quiet and we can sit in main forward and roll the dice and shoot the breeze all day?*

'Flan,' one of the mesquitters said to him, 'she's down there. She didn't sink after all.'

'What's down there?'

'The *Jefferson City.* She's right under us, only about ten feet down. Everything's goin' full blast. The gedunk stand's open. They're servin' six different kinds of ice cream. Coco-Cola. The cooks're makin' gallons of iced tea. Come on down with me.'

He slipped out of his life jacket and dove down. He did not come up. The two other mesquiteers swam over to him. 'We saw it too,' they yelled. 'We're goin' down.'

'No,' Flanagan shouted. 'You're nuts. There's nothing there. So help me. Don't go. Boats!'

Homewood was swimming around shouting at them. So were Lieutenant West and Dr Levy. They couldn't stop the crazies from diving. Almost all of them were young like the mesquiteers. They seemed to be looking for an excuse to swim down into the sea's murderous embrace.

A few came up looking scared. Most of them stayed down.

In the Northern group, madness was the island. They had spent a relatively peaceful night rotating men on and off the rafts, giving them and their kapoks a respite from the water. About ten o'clock Ensign Brownmiller swam over to

Commander Moss. 'Sir,' he said, 'I request permission to take twenty-five men and swim to that island.'

'*What* island? We're five hundred miles from land.'

'That one.' Brownmiller said, pointing toward the horizon. 'We've been drifting toward it since dawn. It's got a big resort hotel on the beach, just waiting for us.'

'I see it too,' shouted the quartermaster who had been on the bridge when the torpedo hit. 'I'll go with you. It looks like an easy swim.'

'Let us take one of the rafts,' Brownmiller said.

'There is no island, Ensign,' Moss said.

'Don't call me Ensign,' Brownmiller screamed. 'My name's Herbert. Herbert Brownmiller. I'm never going to let anybody call me Ensign again. When I get to that island I'm quitting the fucking Navy. I'm going to marry a native girl and spend the rest of my life letting her suck my cock.'

'There's no island there, Herbert,' Moss said.

'Yes there is.' He smiled exultantly at the men in the water. 'Everybody smart enough to see an island out there follow me.'

At least twenty-five men swam after Brownmiller. Moss watched them go, weeping. 'Why did you give me this fucking job?' he screamed at the chaplain.

'I didn't give it to you. It chose you. You chose it.'

'They both can't be true!'

'Yes they can,' Bushnell said.

'Oh, Jesus, Chaplain. Pray for us.'

'I am,' the chaplain said.

Flan, why ain't you listen'? Jack Peterson crooned as the sun went down in a blaze of red and purple. *Still hung up on that dopey dame? Flan, a real man don't depend on a woman. He fucks one here another there. Come on down, Flan. No woman to worry you here. No worries.*

'Boats, I can hear him. Jack. He's talking to me.'

'He's dead. No one's talkin',' Homewood said. His voice whistled in his swollen throat. It seemed to be coming from a terrible distance. Even his strength was dwindling.

'What happened? Why don't they come get us?'

'Somebody's fucked up. Somebody in the goddamn Navy's fucked up.'

The confession was a kind of weight. It seemed to sink Flanagan another inch into the darkening water.

The men are your responsibility now. Bob Mullenoe's last words tolled in Montgomery West's brain as he swam through the darkness after a man who had floated away. Insanely, exultance alternated with fear in West's soul. He was in it now, all the way; he had broken through the last barrier. He was part of this real world he had entered so halfheartedly, this great whale called the US Navy. He was in its belly, accepting the ultimate meaning of the part he had chosen.

Why did he feel exultant, free, instead of trapped, doomed? Maybe Gwen was the difference. Maybe it was Gwen and Mullenoe, wife and friend, both with the sea in their blood. Maybe it was the knowledge that they had accepted him, the B-picture star, the spoiled semi-celebrity, as their equal in this special fraternity.

'Help. Oh, please help,' the drifter screamed.

'It's OK, sailor. I'm here,' West said. 'Hang on to my neck.'

He began swimming back to the men around the raft. 'I'm sorry, sir. I fell asleep. Are they ever comin' to get us?' the sailor sobbed.

'Tomorrow – for sure,' West said, almost sinking under the extra weight. He did not believe it. He was playing the officer's part in this tragedy. Lying, keeping up hope, was part of the job.

Something bumped against his flailing legs in the dark water. At first he thought he had kicked the sailor. It bumped again and this time he felt pain race up his right leg into his belly. He felt the leg and discovered the bottom half of the trouser was gone. In a moment his fingers found a deep gouge in his calf.

By the time West got the sailor back to the group around the raft, he was so weak he could not swim another stroke. 'Where's Levy?' he asked.

'Here,' the doctor said, swimming towards him.

'A shark or some goddamn thing got me in the leg.'

'Let us into that raft, Wilkinson,' Levy said. 'I want to dress Lieutenant West's wound.'

'Fuck you and him,' Wilkinson said.

Flanagan held the leg and Homewood supported West's head and shoulders as the doctor applied a tourniquet. 'It's a bad one,' Levy said.

'Doctor,' West said. 'I'd like to apologize to you for something. I never defended you against MacComber. My mother was Jewish.'

A few feet away, Fire Controlman First Class Bourne burst into tears. 'Oh, Jesus, Lieutenant,' he sobbed. 'I wish you hadn't told us that.'

'You're going to make it, Bourne. I guarantee it,' West said.

The men are your responsibility now.

In the other group as night fell someone screamed, 'A Jap. There's a Jap trying to pull my life jacket off.'

Hysteria annihilated their dwindling sense of fraternity. Men smashed at each other with fists, slashed with knives. Everyone became an enemy. Commander Moss and Chaplain Bushnell swam among them, trying to restore order. Moss assigned everyone a number, and when they got called they were supposed to swim to the raft for fifteen minutes out of the water. Half the numbers did not make the trip. They no longer had the strength to swim even a few feet.

By dawn, many life jackets were in terrible shape. A few feet away from Marty Roth, a Marine began to drown in one. He could not untie the strings. He choked and gurgled and finally died. Moss decided to give those with the most waterlogged jackets more time on the raft. This ignited a terrible quarrel. Men showered him with curses. Someone accused Moss of spending more time on the raft than anyone. He declined to go on the raft at all, even though his jacket was in very bad shape.

Marty Roth was one of those who qualified for extra raft time. His mouth was only an inch from the water. He could feel the jacket dragging him down. When he climbed on to the raft, one of his old enemies from the forward engine room, the Throttleman, shouted, 'You're givin' that fuckin' Jew more time on there than anyone.'

Roth saw hate glaring from a half dozen other seared blackened faces. 'Shut up,' Moss said, in a croak that had only a vestige of authority.

When Roth returned to the water, the Throttleman and his friends went after him. 'Why the fuck should a Jew even have a life jacket?' the machinist snarled.

One had a knife. They cut Roth out of his life jacket. Moss warned them they would be court-martialled. The Throttleman told him to go fuck himself. Moss pulled Roth over to the raft and gave him one of the manropes. 'I'm sorry, son,' he whispered.

As darkness fell without a sign of a plane or ship, Roth decided he was going to die. The hope of marrying Anna Elias, of going to Stevens Tech or maybe even MIT and living up to Amos Cartwright's vision of his future had sustained him. But three days without sleep, and now the loss of his life jacket, made these visions more and more ridiculous. He was the schmuck from the Bronx, son of Izzy Roth, the unlucky halfhearted capitalist. He was about to disappear, like the Jews that Anna had told him about, the ones Hitler deported to camps from which there was no return.

Let go of the rope. It'll be easy. Maybe those anti-Semitic bastards did you a favour. It will be a lot easier than drowning in your life jacket.

A hand grabbed his arm. The chaplain whispered, 'Here's a life jacket.'

'Where did you get it?'

'Never mind. Put it on.'

'Doctor,' Willard Otis said, 'I think Lieutenant MacComber needs help. He don't answer when I talk to him.'

In the twightlight, Levy could see MacComber in his life jacket, his head drooping forward. The doctor swam over to him and took his pulse. He was dead.

'No one can help him now, Willard,' he said. 'Get him out of the jacket and give it to someone else.'

'Oh, Jesus.'

Levy could not believe his eyes. Otis was weeping.

'What the hell's wrong with you? All he ever did was order you around.'

'He was from home,' Otis said.

The chaplain swam into the grey light, fishy, light-bodied, free. He had found the final stone in his private temple. He had given his life for a man who was neither his friend nor a Christian. The purpose of this ordeal was no longer opaque to him. The future into which he swam transcended the past, with his narrow theologies. He swam into a dream of fraternity, a new covenant in which all Americans vowed fealty to each other and to their pilgrim quest.

'Chaplain?' It was Moss, floundering after him in the waterlogged jacket. 'Where are you going? What are you doing?'

'I'm going over to the other men to see if they need me.'

'It's too far. Where's your life jacket?'

'I can swim better without it.'

On he swam until he encountered a lone sailor bobbing on the light swell, his head lolling. Here was another man in need of help. 'Son,' he said, 'come along with me. Join the others.'

He reached out to the boy's scorched, oily face to gently slap him awake. He tipped over, and the chaplain saw he was only half a man. The sharks had devoured everything below the water.

Nooooooooooooooooooooooo. No!' the Chaplain screamed. He rose up in the water and shook his fist at the darkening sky. All his loathing of this incomprehensible god who mingled cruelty and kindness in such discordant demoralizing ways returned. In the name of Captain McKay, in the name of the *Jefferson City*, he shouted defiance. On behalf of the honour they had redeemed, the fraternity they had achieved, the victories they had won, he cursed God. He cursed Him for his brother Alcott and the millions who had died in the barbed wire and trenches of the Western Front in the First World War, for the millions more who had died and were dying in this Second World War.

Moss was floundering towards him again, calling to him. Moss, the personification of duty, responsibility, narrowed to a knife blade on which he impaled himself. He had awakened faith in his squeezed Presbyterian soul. For what? The chaplain swam into the darkness and let Moss find the devoured sailor. He would take his life jacket, practical, tormented man. The perfect Damage Control officer.

The chaplain was through with Damage Control. He swam and swam until he was too tired, too sleepy, to swim any further. He lay on his back on the ocean's bosom like a child in a cradle. Suddenly he was in his grandfather's parsonage in Ohio. He heard his mother laughing on the porch. His brother was reading from Grandfather's book, *The Spiritual Uses of Dark Things*. 'You see,' Alcott said. 'There's absolutely nothing to fear.'

There wasn't now. He had done his ultimate duty as chaplain of the *Jefferson City*. He had rebuked God for His blunders. As he drifted down into the depths, Emerson Bushnell heard another voice, a whisper in the deep. Perhaps it was the Saviour who had cried out on the cross against the Father's uncaring cruelty. Perhaps it was Captain McKay saying, 'Well done.'

As the fourth day dawned, water slopped against Flanagan's mouth. He had spent the night arguing with Jack Peterson. It had grown nasty. Jack had accused him of stealing his life. Didn't that give him the right to steal Flanagan's life? He had stolen Martha from Jack. Now Jack had a right to steal Flanagan, this sodden, scorched, blinded, dehydrated piece of human flotsam, from Martha. He was actually doing her a favour. What was she going to do with him, when the Navy dumped what was left of him at her door?

Jack was a clever son of a bitch. He was offering him booze now, Scotches and soda in the crew's mess. They'd turned it into a restaurant. Camutti was the bartender. Daley washed the dishes. They were all waiting for him down there. The mesquiteers, too. His buddies.

Homewood swam over to him. 'Lieutenant West's in a bad way. We got to get him into that raft.'

'How?'

'Someone's got to kill that son of a bitch Wilkinson. I can't do it. He's watchin' me every second. But if I get his attention, maybe you can get up on the raft and stick this into him.'

He handed Flanagan his knife. 'Boats,' he said. 'I'm so goddamn weak.'

'You can do it! Come on. Pull yourself together. West and a lot of other guys are gonna die if we don't get rid of that bastard.'

We're going to die anyway, Flanagan thought. But he struggled to respond to Homewood's leadership. He was now the boatswain's only follower.

Homewood asked Wilkinson to let Lieutenant West aboard the raft. Wilkinson refused. Flanagan swam around the other side of the raft while Homewood and Wilkinson insulted each other with every obscenity in the Navy's vocabulary. Flanagan slipped out of his life jacket and tried to get into the raft.

Wilkinson whirled when Flanagan only had one leg over the side. He kicked Flanagan in the face, knocking him back into the water. Flanagan clung gamely to the side of the raft. Wilkinson reached down and shoved his head under the surface.

'Stop it, you're drowning him!' Montgomery West shouted. He struggled over to the raft. With his free hand, Wilkinson picked up a paddle and jammed it into the Lieutenant's chest, keeping him two feet away while he went about the business of drowning Flanagan.

On the other side of the raft, West's words gave Homewood a superhuman burst of strength. He flailed past the sycophants and got one arm and one leg into the raft. A half dozen of them fought to shove him back into the water. Groping for a grip on something inside the raft,

Homewood's hand touched metal. It was the Very pistol, with a red flare already attached.

'Let him go, Wilkinson,' Homewood roared.

Wilkinson turned, an obscenity on his lips. Somehow, with two men clinging to his arm, Homewood raised the pistol and pulled the trigger. The flare hit Wilkinson in the face, blowing his head apart, scattering blood and red phosphorus all over the raft.

The sycophants went berserk. They flung Homewood back into the water and clubbed away those still clinging to the raft's man ropes. Screeching and howling and wailing, they paddled away with Wilkinson's corpse, a parody of a funeral ship. No one ever saw them again.

Homewood ordered Flanagan to take charge of Lieutenant West. The struggle with Wilkinson had used up the last of his strength. Around noon he became delirious. He seemed to think Flanagan was his wife. 'What a part I've got, Gwen,' he said. 'It's the best damn part I'll ever play. I only wish you were here to see it. I'm *good* at it, Gwen. I really am. For the first time in my life I'm really good at something.'

Suddenly he looked at Homewood and seemed to know exactly where he was.

'I was pretty good, wasn't I, Boats?'

'I've been proud to be your shipmate, Lieutenant,' Homewood said.

Suddenly there was a plane, a PBY, roaring low over them, waggling its wings. It dropped stuff to the larger group to the north, a raft, some water. The southern group was too weak to swim up to share them. No one tried to swim down. They were all close to death.

Flanagan regained his life jacket. The plane disappeared into the glaring blue sky. Hope flickered in his dehydrated brain. If he could only keep his head above water.

'How long do you think it'll take for a ship, Boats?'

'At flank speed for a destroyer? Maybe twelve hours.'

'Jesus. That means another night in the water. I don't

think I can take another one. Jack keeps talking to me.'

'He's no fuckin' good! He was never any fuckin' good! Do you hear me? He was a fuckin' liar – and a thief!'

Even though he was practically comatose, Flanagan realized the enormous significance of those words. Homewood had known Jack was the thief! He had loved him so much he had allowed him to go on stealing. The truth flashed like a bursting shell in Flanagan's exhausted brain. Stealing had been Jack's way of saying fuck you to Homewood as well as to the Navy, to everyone.

Jack really was no good. He was evil.

Everyone strained his eyes towards the horizon, yearning to see a ship. But night began to fall without a glimpse of a mast. Maybe the PBY had crashed. Maybe his radio was not working. They could not last another day without water.

Flan, you don't believe Homewood's bullshit about me, do you? Did I ever steer you wrong? Didn't you always have the best booze, the best nooky on the beach? Why don't you trust me now, you cowardly son of a bitch? Afraid of the dark, afraid of coming down here with me?

Flanagan's heart pounded in his chest. Who, what, can defend him against this evil voice?

With the last dregs of energy in his soul, Flanagan prayed. He leaped across the chaplain's absurdity, across the void to the Unknown, the Unknowable. To the creator of the shark. To the ruler of the sea. To the lord of the universe.

Suddenly rough arms surrounded him. Someone was putting another life jacket on him. In the darkness he fought against it, wondering if the man was trying to drown him. But he did not have the strength to resist. He hung there while deft hands knotted the other bigger jacket around him.

'You'll make it now,' Homewood whispered. 'Even if they don't get here before dawn. Just promise me this. Amount to somethin'! Don't be a fuckin' wiseguy all your life.'

'Boats – no.'

He had finally grasped what was happening, what Homewood was doing.

'Never mind. Amount to somethin'.

Homewood told Dr Levy he was going to swim to the other group and bring back a keg of water. 'It's too far. You can't make it,' Levy said.

Homewood ignored him and swam into the night. Somewhere in that journey the boatswain's mate discovered there was a limit even to his strength. He was a man not a myth. A man with the burden of an exhausted body and a wounded soul. His beloved Navy, with its perpetual insistence on order, regularity, system, its hierarchy of respect and responsibility, had failed him. They had abandoned him and his shipmates to the sea's cruelty. He had confessed to Flanagan and to himself that he had also failed the Navy by allowing Jack Peterson to go on stealing, unpunished.

Flanagan saw none of this during that night in the water, of course. In that final night of horror he could only concentrate on keeping a tiny fragment of life aglow in his body. Around midnight, Lieutenant West died. Dr Levy was the only officer left. Totally abandoning his scientific objectivity, he cursed them, he exhorted them, he ordered them to stay alive. The mere sound of his rasping voice may have helped some men make it, even though sharks struck again and others vanished without a cry.

Suddenly there were motors, searchlights, glaring through the dawn. Hands dragged them into whaleboats and lifted them to steel decks and then to sick bays where pharmacist's mates bathed their fragile bodies and soothed their ulcerated wounds. Later they were carried aboard the hospital ship *Tranquility*, where smiling nurses reintroduced them to the possibility of a woman's touch.

At Guam, Admiral Spruance visited them. He told them how much he grieved for their lost shipmates, especially his friend Captain McKay. He tried to explain what had gone wrong, why it had taken so long to rescue them. In the middle of it he started to weep. The tears were better than any explanation he could have given them.

The Admiral's chief of staff, Captain Maher, added some good news. He told them the war had ended with the explosion of the atomic bomb which the *Jefferson City* had brought to Tinian.

Their voyage was over.

The *Jefferson City*'s voyage into history had begun.

Ave Atque Vale

On 26 July 1985, the fortieth anniversary of the *Jefferson City*'s torpedoing, Martha Johnson Flanagan finished reading the last page. She put the manuscript aside and paced up and down the room, running her hands through her dark hair. She looked out at another full moon spilling gold on the Pacific's blank face. The high tide rumbled and crashed against the cliff below the house.

Frank Flanagan was writing a letter to Marty Roth, who was chairman of the annual reunion of the surviving members of the *Jefferson City*'s crew. Flanagan was urging Roth to invite as their dinner speaker Captain Robert Wallace Mullenoe, Annapolis '64, currently commander of one of the Navy's new supercarriers. Roth, now associate professor of naval engineering at the Webb Institute, had helped design her.

Flanagan added other bits of gossip he had picked up as corresponding secretary of the Jefferson City Association. Fire Controlman Ralph Bourne was still writing to admirals and congressmen, trying to get a Navy Cross for Lieutenant West. Johnny Chase, the turret captain with the charmed life, had recently died in bed at the age of eighty-two. Dr Aaron Levy was still thriving as professor of surgery at Tel Aviv University. Captain McKay's grandson, Commander Semmes McKay Meade, had just become the executive officer of the nuclear submarine *Kingfish*. He was rising rapidly in the Navy, even though he had not gone to Annapolis. A man no longer needed a class ring on his finger to make admiral.

'Do you think you've been fair to everyone?' Martha asked.

'Of course not,' Flanagan said.

'I'm serious,' Martha said.

'So am I.'

'All right.'

Martha placed the manuscript before a Chinese painting of a solitary traveller descending a mountain. They had found it in a used-furniture store in Honiara, the ramshackle capital of Guadalcanal, thirty years ago. No one could tell them how it got there. The bored Chinese merchant said the store's previous owner, an Australian, might have brought it from a passing freighter. Her crewmen might have stolen it in Hawaii or California or New York. They had bought it for a hundred dollars.

The manuscript would remain there for a week to see if further messages emerged from the mysterious depths in which books were born. Flanagan did not expect any for this book. Long before he reached the last page, she had become a living thing, more and more indifferent to her author.

Beyond memory, beyond the vagaries of time, the moon-tugged tides of circumstance, the *Jefferson City* voyaged towards eternity.

Acknowledgements

The author gratefully acknowledges permission to use material from the following:

'Love for Sale.' By Cole Porter. Copyright © 1930 Warner Bros., Inc. (Renewed). All rights reserved. Used by permission.

'Never Give All the Heart.' Reprinted with permission of Macmillan Publishing Company from *The Poems* by W. B. Yeats, edited by Richard J. Finneran (New York: Macmillan, 1983).

'A Prayer for My Daughter.' Reprinted with permission of Macmillan Publishing Company from *The Poems* by W. B. Yeats, edited by Richard J. Finneran. Copyright © 1924 by Macmillan Publishing Company, renewed 1952 by Bertha Georgie Yeats.

Translations from the Chinese. Translated by Arthur Waley, Copyright © 1919, Alfred A. Knopf, Inc.

'Under Ben Bulben.' Reprinted with permission of Macmillan Publishing Company from *The Poems* by W. B. Yeats, edited by Richard J. Finneran. Copyright © 1940 by Georgie Yeats, renewed 1968 by Bertha Georgie Yeats, Michael Butler Yeats, and Anne Yeats.

Virgil by T. R. Glover, Copyright © 1912 by Methuen & Co. Ltd.

'Waltzing Matilda.' Music by M. Cowan, words by A. P. Paterson. Copyright © 1936, 1941 by Carl Fischer, Inc., New York. Reprinted by permission.

'The White Cliffs of Dover.' By Walter Kent and Nat Burton. Copyright © 1941 renewed by Shapiro, Bernstein & Co., Inc., New York, and Walter Kent Music, Woodland Hills, California.

'Who.' Written by Oscar Hammerstein II, Otto Harbach, and Jerome Kern. For U.S.: Copyright © 1925 T. B. Harms Company (c/o The Welk Music Group, Santa Monica. CA 90401) and Bill/Bob Publishing. Copyright renewed. International copyright secured. All rights reserved. Used by permission. For all other territories: Copyright © 1925 T. B. Harms Company. Copyright renewed (c/o The Welk Music Group, Santa Monica, CA 90401). International copyright secured. All rights reserved. Used by permission.

Colin Forbes
Target Five £2.99

No quarter is asked or given when a top Russian oceanographer defects across the Arctic icefields with plans of their submarine network. The Americans send in dog teams and an unconventional trio under Anglo-Canadian agent Keith Beaumont. The Russians use everything they have in an increasingly bloody life-or-death struggle to win him back . . .

Colin Forbes
The Stone Leopard £3.50

'A real cracker ripping through Europe. The heart of the story is a plot which could destroy the Western world. The action is based on the threat to a President of France from a mysterious and vicious resistance leader from the past. Hard, bitter and compulsive; and the ending . . . Wow!' DAILY MIRROR

Colin Forbes
Cover Story £3.99

'Adam Procane has to be stopped . . .'

It was the last message his wife ever sent. And even as he read it, foreign correspondent Bob Newman knew she was dead. Soviet Intelligence had sent a film of her murder to London with the warning – *tell other people to keep away from Procane . . .*

Procane, a top Washington official, is about to defect, and with the Presidential election two months away, it's the last thing the Americans want. Trouble is, until they know exactly *who* he is, they can do nothing to stop him.

In London, Tweed of SIS watches and waits. Four highly suspect Americans have already passed through en route to Scandinavia – the Deputy Head of the CIA, the National Security Adviser and his wife, and the Chief of Staff of the Armed Forces. Any one of them could be Procane.

Meanwhile Newman has slipped off to Finland, bent on revenge. So it's time for Tweed to act. To get back into the field. To stop Newman and find Procane – before the dreaded GRU do the job for him . . .

C. S. Forester
Brown on Resolution £1.95

VICTORIAN ENGLAND . . .

Lieutenant-Commander R. E. S. Saville-Samarez, RN, travelling from the Royal Naval College, Greenwich, towards London and a not very closely planned week of relaxation, blushes as an attractive young lady in his compartment smiles at him . . .

THE FIRST WORLD WAR . . .

On the rocky, desolate island of Resolution in the Pacific, Leading Seaman Albert Brown defies alone the might of the German battle cruiser *Ziethen* and is eventually responsible for its awesome destruction . . .

A strange destiny links both these events.

In this dramatic novel – a moving story of passion, bravery and a peculiar irony – C. S. Forester reveals his formidable narrative power as he describes men and ships in action, and all his uncanny insight as he probes the wellsprings of human behaviour. It is a story at once thrilling and poignant. And only the creator of the mortal Hornblower could have written it.

C. S. Forester
Death to the French £1.95

1810 . . . THE PENINSULAR WAR . . .

Beset on every side by the invading French, Wellington's outnumbered army retreats towards Lisbon, and the Lines of Torres Vedras . . .

Separated from his regiment by the fortunes of war, rifleman Matthew Dodd of Craufurd's famous 'Ninety-Fifth' flees for his life from a group of pursuing French infantry led by sergeant Godinot. Eventually he stumbles across a band of Portuguese guerrillas and with rough inventiveness dragoons them into harrying the infuriated enemy . . .

The thrilling story follows the adventures of Dodd on one side and Godinot on the other as they march inexorably towards their destinies.

Once again the creator of the immortal Hornblower demonstrates his supreme storytelling ability.

Jack Higgins
Confessional £3.50

Do I presume that you gentlemen believe that the man Kelly, or Cuchulain to give him his codename, is actually active in Ireland . . .?'

Mikhail Kelly's credentials were impeccable. Russian mother, Irish father hanged by the British. He could split an apple – or a head – across a large room with a handgun. And his special talent was acting. The KGB gave him the perfect part . . . assassin.

For more than twenty years Cuchulain has created chaos, fear and disorder in Ireland by hitting counter-productive targets on both sides of the border, making fools of British Intelligence and the IRA. But Cuchulain is a man whose time is nearly up.

The one person who can identify him is the beautiful Tanya Voroninova, daughter of a KGB general. And the one person who can persuade her to defect is Liam Devlin, poet, scholar, IRA gunman retired.

Hunted by the combined forces of British Intelligence, the IRA and the KGB who now regard him as an expendable embarrassment, Cuchulain prepares to hit the most counter-productive target of all time . . . Pope John Paul . . .

Jack Higgins
A Prayer for the Dying £2.99

'What do I have to do? Kill somebody?'

Fallon was the best you could get with a gun in his hand. His track record went back a long and shady way.

This time the bidding came from Dandy Jack Meehan, an underworld baron with a thin varnish of respectability. Not exactly the type you'd want to meet up a dark alley.

The job Dandy Jack wanted doing was up North, but when Fallon got there he soon found himself changing sides. Which put him in opposition to Meehan. A place where life expectancy suddenly gets very short indeed.

Jack Higgins
The Last Place God Made £2.99

World War I ace Sam Hannah was down to pushing ancient planes across the worst jungles in the world.

Mallory was one of the new generation who would rather fly anything than not fly at all. Mallory needed a job and Hannah needed a partner.

Two men in patched-up planes . . . against the savage Huna Indians of Brazil's Rio das Mortes – The River of Death.

Anthony Hyde
The Red Fox £2.95

On the very anniversary of his father's suicide twenty years earlier, Soviet affairs specialist Robert Thorne received a cry for help from the woman he once loved. May Brightman's own father had disappeared, and she feared for his life. So began the hunt – through America, Europe, and Russia – for a missing man, a missing fortune, and the key to a mystery, its roots buried deep in the past . . .

'A first-rate political thriller, full of action, brilliantly descriptive of landscape and characters, informed with a penetrating analysis of the emergent and evolving Soviet state'. THE TIMES

Derek Robinson
Goshawk Squadron £2.50

Wooley was a professional, in business with death – flying with him is like living with a maniac. Brutal, callous and obscene, without manners or morals, he moulds green young pilots into ruthless killers. By 1918 chivalry had been a long time dead.

Derek Robinson
War Story £3.50

'There is going to be the most enormous battle, and the war will be over by Christmas. Which Christmas, God alone knows . . .'

Lieutenant Oliver Paxton was eighteen years old and desperately keen to help win the war, when he was promoted to France in June, 1916.

In the war-streaked skies over the Western Front, his education was hurried and painful. The rest of Hornet Squadron thought him a pompous idiot, but a very available lady behind the lines thought him the loveliest killer she'd danced with all night, while he could hardly wait to get a Hun in his sights when the order came for the Big Push.

And the fearsome first day on the Somme waited gaunt in the wings of history . . .

Derek Robinson
Piece of Cake £4.50

Their flying was breathtaking, they played God in the sky. They lived as they flew – reckless, flamboyant, no time to lose. For Hornet Squadron even dying was a piece of cake. From the early days of the war in France to the Battle of Britain's 'finest hour' the squadron fights on through terrible losses and triumphant victories.

Douglas Reeman
The Iron Pirate £2.95

'Surprise will be total. It will show the world what we can do. You will do it for Germany!'

The crack German heavy cruiser *Prinz Luitpold* had always been lucky in battle. To the beleaguered army on the Baltic coast she was their one remaining symbol of hope. But it is the summer of 1944, and on every front the war is going badly for Germany.

When the order comes to leave the Baltic to attack and destroy enemy shipping in the Atlantic, Kapitan zur See Dieter Hechler knows that once out in this vast killing ground it will only be a matter of time before the hunter becomes the hunted. The *Prinz* will need all of her legendary luck to survive.

As he faces the challenges of his enormous task, Hechler's problems increase when a ruthless, glory-seeking admiral arrives on board with some mysterious boxes, a floatplane and a beautiful girl pilot . . .

Piers Paul Read
The Free Frenchman £3.50

The Free Frenchman is the story of Bertrand de Roujay – first-born son of a land-owning dynasty – from the years that led up to the war and occupation, through the betrayal of the Vichy, to the Liberation and the long healing that came after.

It is also the story of de Roujay's women – Madeleine, his first wife and final ally; Lucia, the refugee from Franco's Spain who was his passionate mistress; and Jenny, the faithless English wife of his second disastrous marriage.

Above all, it is the story of the cause de Roujay made his own – the fierce resistance of freeborn Frenchmen to Nazi oppression as they rallied around the Cross of Lorraine.

Here is an epic canvas of triumphs and disasters, bitter conflict and ultimate reconciliation, through four turbulent decades in the history of the French nation and its people.

All Pan books are available at your local bookshop or newsagent, or can be ordered direct from the publisher. Indicate the number of copies required and fill in the form below.

Send to: **CS Department, Pan Books Ltd., P.O. Box 40, Basingstoke, Hants. RG21 2YT.**

or phone: 0256 469551 (Ansaphone), quoting title, author and Credit Card number.

Please enclose a remittance* to the value of the cover price plus: 60p for the first book plus 30p per copy for each additional book ordered to a maximum charge of £2.40 to cover postage and packing.

*Payment may be made in sterling by UK personal cheque, postal order, sterling draft or international money order, made payable to Pan Books Ltd.

Alternatively by Barclaycard/Access:

Card No.

Signature:

Applicable only in the UK and Republic of Ireland.

While every effort is made to keep prices low, it is sometimes necessary to increase prices at short notice. Pan Books reserve the right to show on covers and charge new retail prices which may differ from those advertised in the text or elsewhere.

NAME AND ADDRESS IN BLOCK LETTERS PLEASE:

....

Name ————————————————————————

Address ————————————————————————

————————————————————————

————————————————————————

————————————————————————

3/87